Order in C

Jack Whyte was born and raised in Scotland, and educated in England and France. He migrated to Canada from the UK in 1967 to teach English, but he only taught for a year before starting to work as a professional singer, musician, actor and entertainer Whyte's interest in the history of Britain springs from his early Classical education in Scotland during the 1950s, and he has pursued his fascination with those times ever since. Whyte is married, with five adult children, and lives in British Columbia, Canada.

ORDER IN
CHAOS

Book Three of the Templar Trilogy

Jack Whyte

This novel is entirely a work of fiction.
The names, characters and incidents portrayed in it are the work
of the author's imagination. Any resemblance to actual persons,
living or dead, events or localities is entirely coincidental.

Harper
An imprint of HarperCollins*Publishers*
77–85 Fulham Palace Road,
Hammersmith, London W6 8JB

www.harpercollins.co.uk

A Paperback Original 2010
1

A catalogue record for this book
is available from the British Library

ISBN: 978 0 00 720749 7

Printed and bound in Great Britain by Clays Ltd, St Ives plc

Mixed Sources
Product group from well-managed
forests and other controlled sources
www.fsc.org Cert no. SW-COC-1806
© 1996 Forest Stewardship Council

FSC is a non-profit international organisation established to promote the
responsible management of the world's forests. Products carrying the FSC
label are independently certified to assure consumers that they come
from forests that are managed to meet the social, economic and
ecological needs of present and future generations.

Find out more about HarperCollins and the environment at
www.harpercollins.co.uk/green

To my wife, Beverley,
mentor and care giver, who knows,
invariably, when to leave me alone and when to
haul me out of my hermitage and back into the light of life . . .
Thank you yet again.

I will give them into the hands of their enemies …
and I will make [them]a desolation.

—Jeremiah 34:19–22

FRANCE

THE WOMAN AT THE GATES

1

Even a man with no eyes could have seen that something was wrong up ahead, and Tam Sinclair's eyes were perfect. His patience, however, was less so. The afternoon light was settling into dusk, and Tam was reduced to immobility after three days of hard traveling and within a half mile of his goal. The reins of his tired team now hung useless in his hands as a growing crowd of people backed up ahead of him, blocking his way and crowding close to his horses, making them snort and stomp and toss their heads nervously. Tam felt himself growing angry at the press around him. He did not like being among large numbers of people at the best of times, but when they were compressed together in a solid crowd, as they were now, the stink of their unwashed bodies deprived him of even the simple pleasure of taking a deep breath.

"Ewan!"

"Aye!" One of the two young men who had been lounging and talking to each other among the covered shapes of the wagon's cargo pulled himself upright to where he could lean easily with braced arms on the high driver's bench. "Whoa! What's happening? Where did all these people come from all of a sudden?"

"If I knew that, I wouldn't have had to interrupt your debate wi' your young friend." Tam glanced sideways at the other man, quirking his mouth, almost concealed by his grizzled beard, into what might have been a grin or a grimace of distaste. "Go up there to the gates and find out what's going on and how long we're to be stuck here. Maybe somebody's had a fit or dropped dead. If that's the case, I'll thank you to find us another gate close enough to reach afore curfew. My arse is sore and full o' splinters from this damned

3

seat and I'm pining to hear the noisy clatter as we tip this load o' rusty rubbish into the smelter's yard. And be quick. I don't want to be sleepin' outside these walls this night. Away wi' ye now."

"Right." Young Ewan placed a hand on the high side of the wagon and vaulted over it, dropping effortlessly to the cobbled roadway and pushing his way quickly into the crowd. La Rochelle was France's greatest and busiest port, and the high, narrow gates of its southern entrance, directly ahead of him, were fronted by this wide approach that narrowed rapidly as it neared the check points manned by the city guards.

Tam watched the boy go and then swung himself down after him, albeit not quite so lithely. The wagon driver was a strong-looking man, still in the prime of life, but the ability to do everything his apprentices could do physically was something he had abandoned gladly years before. Glancing intolerantly now at the people closest to him, he made his way to a small oaken barrel securely fastened with hempen rope to the side of the wagon. He took the hanging dipper and raised the barrel's loose-fitting lid, then brought the brimming ladle of cool water to his lips and held it there as he looked about him, seeing nothing out of place or anything that might explain the blockage ahead. He did notice a heavy presence of guards with crossbows lining the walkways above and on each side of the high gates, but none of them appeared to be particularly interested in anything happening below.

In the meantime, young Ewan had moved forward aggressively, anonymous among the crowd. He was soon aware that he was not the only one trying to find out what was happening, and as he drew closer to the gates he found it increasingly difficult to penetrate the noisy, neck-craning throng. He was eventually forced to use his wide shoulders to clear a passage for himself, elbowing his way single-mindedly towards the front, ignoring the deafening babble of shouting voices all around him. He was almost there—if he stood on his toes he could see the crested helmet of the Corporal of the Guard—when he became aware of louder, shriller voices directly ahead. Three men came charging towards him, plowing through the crowd, pulling at people as they went, pushing and shoving and trying to run, wide eyed with fear. One of them shouldered Ewan aside as he surged by, but the young man regained his balance easily and swung around to watch the three of them scrambling into the throng behind him, dodging and weaving as they sought to lose themselves among the crush.

The crowd, like a living thing sensing the terror of the fleeing men, pulled itself away from them quickly, people pushing and pulling at their neighbors as they fought to keep clear of the fugitives, and in so doing exposing them to the guards in front of and on top of the gate towers.

The Corporal of the Guard's single shout, ordering the fleeing men to halt, went unheeded, and almost before the word had left his lips the first crossbow bolt struck the cobblestones with a clanging impact that stunned the crowd into instant silence. Shot from high above the gates, and too hastily loosed, the steel projectile caromed off the worn cobblestone and was deflected upwards, hammering its point through the wooden water barrel from which Tam Sinclair was drinking, shattering the staves and drenching the man in a deluge of cold water that soaked his breeches and splashed loudly on the cobbles at his feet.

Cursing, Tam dropped down onto the wet stones, landing on all fours and rolling sideways to safety under the wagon's bed as the air filled with the bowel-loosening hiss and sickening thud of crossbow bolts. His other apprentice, Hamish, jumped from the wagon bed and dived behind the protection of a wheel hub, fighting off others who sought the same shelter.

None of the three fleeing men survived for long. The first was brought down by three bolts, all of which hit him at the same time, in the shoulder, the neck, and the right knee. He went flying and whirling like a touring mummer, blood arcing high above him from a jagged rip in his neck and raining back down and around him as he fell sprawling less than ten paces from where he had begun his flight. The second stopped running, almost in mid-stride, teetering for balance with windmilling arms, and turned back to face the city gates, raising his hands high above his head in surrender. For the space of a single heartbeat he stood there, and then a crossbow bolt smashed through his sternum, the meaty impact driving him backwards, his feet clear off the ground, to land hard on his backside before his lifeless body toppled over onto its side.

The third man fell face down at the feet of a tall, stooped-over monk, one outstretched hand clutching in its death throes at the mendicant's sandal beneath the tattered, ankle-high hem of his ragged black robe. The monk stopped moving as soon as he was touched, and stood still as though carved from wood, gazing down in stupefaction at the bloodied metal bolts that had snatched the life so brutally from the running man. No one paid any attention to his shock, however; all their own fascinated interest was focused upon the dead man at his feet. The monk himself barely registered upon their consciousness, merely another of the faceless, wandering thousands of his like who could be found begging for sustenance the length and breadth of Christendom.

So profound was the silence that had fallen in the wake of the shattering violence that the sound of a creaking iron hinge was clear from some distance away as a door swung open, and then came the measured tread of heavily booted feet as someone in authority paced forward from the entrance to the tower on the left of the city gates.

And still no one stirred in the crowded approach to the gates. Travelers and guards alike seemed petrified by the swiftness with which death had come to this pleasant, early evening.

"Have you all lost your wits?"

The voice was harsh, gravelly, and at the sound of it the spell was broken. People began to move again and voices sprang up, halting at first, unsure of how to begin talking about what had happened here. The guards stirred themselves into motion, too, and several made their way towards the three lifeless bodies.

Tam Sinclair had already crawled out from his hiding place and was preparing to mount to his high seat, one foot raised to the front wheel's hub and his hand resting gently on the footboard of the driver's bench, when he heard a hiss from behind him.

"Please, I heard you talking to the young man. You are from Scotland."

Sinclair froze, then turned slowly, keeping his face expressionless. The woman was standing by the tail gate of his wagon, white-knuckled hands grasping the thick strap of a bulky cloth bag suspended from her shoulder. Her shape was muffled in a long garment of dull green wool that was wrapped completely around her, one corner covering her head like a hood, exposing only her mouth and chin. She looked young, but not girlish, Tam thought, judging from the few inches of her face that he could see. The skin on her face was fair and free of obvious dirt. He eyed her again, his gaze traveling slowly and deliberately but with no hint of lechery, from her face down to her feet.

"I am of Scotland. What of it?"

"I am, too. And I need help. I need it greatly. I can reward you."

This woman was no peasant. Her whisper had been replaced by a quiet, low-pitched voice. Her diction was clear and precise, and her words, despite the tremor in her voice, possessed the confidence born of high breeding. Tam pursed his lips, looking about him instinctively, but no one seemed to be paying them any attention; all eyes were directed towards the drama in the nearby open space. He sensed, though he knew not how, that this woman was involved in what had happened here, and he was favorably impressed by her demeanor, in spite of his wariness. She was tight wound with fear, he could see, and yet she had sufficient presence of mind to appear outwardly calm to a casual observer. His response was quiet but courteous.

"What trouble are you in, Lady? What would you have of me, a simple carter?"

"I need to get inside the gates. They are … People are looking for me, and they mean me ill."

Sinclair watched her carefully, his eyes fixed on the wide-lipped mouth that was all he could really see of her. "Is that a fact?" he asked then, his Scots brogue suddenly broad and heavy in the rhetorical question. "And who are these people that harry and frighten well-born women?"

She bit her lip, and he could see her debating whether to say more, but then she drew herself up even straighter. "The King's men. The men of William de Nogaret."

Still Sinclair studied her, his face betraying nothing of his thoughts although her words had startled him. William de Nogaret, chief lawyer to King Philip IV, was the most feared and hated man in all of France, and the woman's admission, clearly born of a desperate decision to trust Tam solely on the grounds of their common birthplace, invited him instantly either to betray her or to become complicit with her in something, and complicity in anything involving the frustration of the King's principal henchman surely led to torture and death. He remained motionless for a moment longer, his thoughts racing, and then his face creased beneath his short, neatly trimmed beard into what might have been the beginnings of a smile.

"You're running from de Nogaret? Sweet Jesus, lass, you could not have named a better reason to be seeking aid. Stay where you are. You are hidden there. I need to see what's going on ahead of us."

Something, some of the tension, seeped visibly out of the woman, and she drew back slightly, concealing herself behind the rear of the wagon. Sinclair began to haul himself up onto the hub of the front wheel. He was still apprehensive and curious about the woman, but felt somehow that he was doing the right thing. He paused with one foot on the hub to look over the heads of the crowd and across the open space to where the monk still stood over the dead man, hunched as though petrified, and after a moment Sinclair gave a small snort and swung himself up and onto his seat.

There, settled on his bench above the crowd, he gathered the reins of his team in his hand, reached for the whip by his feet, and gave a piercing whistle. His two lanky but strong-looking apprentices came running to his summons, swinging themselves lithely up into the vehicle. The one called Ewan took a seat on the bench beside Tam, and the other settled himself comfortably again among the covered shapes of the cargo in the wagon bed. But, whip in hand, Tam Sinclair made no move to start his animals. He had nowhere to go. The crowd was jostling and shuffling, milling at the edges of the space surrounding the slain men, but it was not going forward. The guards were still intent upon discovering whatever it was that had set the trouble afoot, and none of them had thought to marshal the waiting traffic.

The three dead men had apparently been pulling a handcart with them, and from the garbled commentary of the people around him, Tam gathered that it was when the guards, their suspicions aroused for some reason, had set out to search the cart and then attempted to seize one of the men that the trio broke and ran. Now, watching a handful of guards swarming over the high-piled contents of the handcart, Tam wondered idly what could have been in there that was worth dying for. He would never find out, because even as his curiosity stirred, the Corporal of the Guard ordered the cart to be taken into the guardhouse and searched there. Tam eyed the guards as they hauled it out of sight, then shifted his gaze to the swaggering figure of the harsh-voiced knight who had emerged from the tower and was now stalking about the open space where lay the three dead men.

He was not a tall man, this knight, but his burnished half armor, worn over a suit of mail and topped by a domed metal helmet, enhanced his stature in the late-afternoon light, and the scapular-like King's livery he wore, a narrow-fronted, dingy white surcoat edged with royal blue, the embroidered fleur-de-lis emblem of the royal house of Capet centered on the chest, added to the air of authority that set him apart from everyone else within sight.

Gazing stolidly from his perch high on the driver's bench, Tam Sinclair was not impressed by what he saw in the knight. He himself had been a soldier too long, had traveled too far and seen too many men in situations of dire, life-threatening peril, to be influenced by a mere show of outward finery. External trappings, he had learned long years before, too often had little bearing on the substance of what they adorned. The man he was looking at was a King's knight, but in the driver's eyes that in itself was no indicator of manhood or worth. People called the King of France Philip the Fair, because he was pleasant, almost flawless, to behold, but beauty, Tam knew as well as anyone, went only skin deep. No one who knew anything real about the puissant monarch would ever have considered referring to him as Philip the Just, or even the Compassionate. Philip Capet, the fourth of that name and grandson of the sainted King Louis IX, had shown himself, time and again, to be inhumanly self-centered, a cold and ambitious tyrant. And in Tam Sinclair's eyes too many of the knights and familiars with whom the King surrounded himself were cut from the same cloth. This particular example of the breed had drawn his long sword slowly and ostentatiously and walked now with the bared blade bouncing gently against his right shoulder as he made his way towards the tall monk who stood isolated on the edge of the crowd, still stooped over the man who had died clutching his foot.

"Ewan." Tam spoke without raising his voice, his eyes focused on the knight's movements. "There is a woman at the back of the cart. Go you and help her climb up here while everyone is watching the King's captain there. But do it easily, as though she is one of us, and on the far side, where you won't be as easily noticed. Hamish, sit you up here with me and pay no attention to Ewan or the woman." Ewan jumped down from the wagon, and as Hamish moved up to take his place on the bench, Tam tipped his head, drawing the younger man's attention to the tableau on his left. "I think yon monk's in trouble, judging by the scowl on that other fellow's face." Hamish leaned forward to see, and watched closely.

As the knight drew closer, the monk knelt slowly and stretched out a hand to lay his palm on the dead man's skull, after which he remained motionless, his head bent, obviously praying for the soul of the departed. The knight kept walking until he was within two paces of the kneeling monk, and then he spoke again in his harsh, unpleasant voice. "That one is deep in Hell, priest, so you can stop praying for him."

The monk gave no sign of having heard, and the knight frowned, unused to being ignored. He jerked his right hand, flipping the long sword down from his shoulder, and extended his arm until the tip of his blade caught the point of the monk's peaked cowl and pushed it back, exposing the scalp beneath the hood, the crown shaved bald in the square tonsure of the Dominican Order, the sides covered by thick, short-cropped, iron gray hair. As the knight's arm extended farther, the monk's chin was pushed up and tilted back by the pull of his cowl, showing him to be clean-shaven and pallid. The knight bent forward until their faces were level, and his voice was no quieter or gentler than it had been before, ringing harshly in the absolute hush that had fallen at his first words.

"Listen to me, priest, when I speak to you, and answer when I bid you. Do you hear?" He drew back until he was once more standing erect, his sword point resting on the ground. "I know you." The monk shook his head, mute, and the knight lifted his voice louder. "Don't lie to me, priest! I never forget a face and I *know* you. I've seen you somewhere, before now. Where was it? Speak up."

The monk shook his head. "No, sir knight," he brayed. His voice was surprisingly shrill for such a tall man. Shrill enough that Tam Sinclair, who had turned to see how young Ewan was faring with the task he had set him, shifted quickly in his seat to watch the interplay between the knight and the monk.

"You are mistaken," said the monk. "I am new come here and have never been in this part of the world before. My home is in the north, far from here, in Alsace, in the monastery of the blessed Saint Dominic, so unless you have been there recently you could not know me. And besides"—his eyes, blazing in the late-afternoon light, were a pale but lustrous blue that held more than a hint of fanaticism—"I would not forget a man such as you."

The knight frowned, hesitated, then swung the sword blade back up to rest on his shoulder again, his face registering distaste. "Aye, enough. Nor would I forget a voice such as yours. What is your purpose here in La Rochelle?"

"God's business, master knight. I bear messages for the Prior of the monastery of Saint Dominic within the gates."

The knight was already waving the annoying Dominican away, his altered demeanor indicating his reluctance to interfere with anything that concerned the Order of Saint Dominic, the Pope's holy, hungry, and ever zealous Inquisitors. "Aye, well, move on and finish your task. You know where the monastery is?"

"Yes, sir knight, I have instructions written here on how to proceed within the gates. Let me show you."

But as he began to reach into his robe the knight stepped back from him and waved him away again. "Go on with you. I don't need to see. Go on, go on, away with you."

"Thank you, sir knight." The tall monk bowed his head obsequiously and moved away towards the city gates, and his passage seemed to be the signal for a general admission. The crowd surged forward in an orderly manner as Ewan and the mysterious woman climbed in over the right side of the wagon, and the guards casually scanned the passing throng. Sinclair noticed, however, that they were questioning every woman who passed by, while allowing the men to pass unchallenged. He straightened up in his seat and kneaded his kidneys with his free hand.

"Lads," he said, speaking the Scots Gaelic in a normal, conversational voice, "you are now promoted to the nobility. For the next wee while, you will be my sons. Ewan, when you speak to any of these buffoons, make your Scotch voice thicken your French, as though you were more foreign than you are. Hamish, you speak only the Gaelic this day, no French at all. You are new arrived here in France with your mother, to join me and your brother, and have not had time to learn their tongue or their ways. Now shift into the back and let your mother sit here." He turned casually and spoke to the woman behind them. "Mary, come here and sit by me. Throw back the hood from your face, unless you fear being recognized."

She pulled back the hood wordlessly, revealing a handsome, finely chiseled face with wide, startlingly bright, blue-gray eyes and long, well-combed dark hair. Sinclair nodded in approval as she took her place beside him, and he jogged the reins and set the wagon rolling slowly forward. "Now hold on tight and be careful. For the time being, you are my wife, Mary Sinclair, mother of my sons here, Ewan and Hamish. You are comely enough to make me both proud of you and protective of your virtue. And you speak no French. If any question you, and they will, look to me for answers and then speak in Scots. And try to sound like a household servant, not like the lady you are. They are looking for a lady, are they not?"

The woman met his gaze squarely and nodded.

"Hmm. Then try you not to give them one, or we'll all hang. Come around the end of the bench there, but mind your step. Hamish, help her, and then stand behind her, at her shoulder. The two of you have the same eyes, thanks be to God, so be not shy about flashing them, both of you."

Sinclair reined in his team. "Right, then. Here we go. Here comes the popinjay who thinks himself a knight. Just be at ease, all of you, and let me do the talking." He brought the wagon to a halt just short of where the guards stood waiting.

The knight arrived just as the Corporal of the Guard stepped forward to challenge Tam, and he stood watching, making no attempt to interfere as the guardsman questioned Tam.

"Your name?"

"Tam Sinclair," Tam responded truculently. He pronounced it the Scots way, *Singclir*, rather than the French *San-Clerr*.

"What are you?" This with a ferocious frown in response to the alien name and its terse iteration.

Sinclair responded in fluent gutter French that was thick with Scots intonations. "What d'you mean, what am I? I am a Scot, from Scotland. And I am also a carter, as you can see."

The frown grew deeper. "I meant, what are you doing here, fellow, in France?"

Sinclair scratched gently at his jaw with the end of one finger and stared down at the guard for long moments before he shrugged his shoulders and spoke slowly and patiently, with great clarity, as though to a backward child. "I don't know where you've spent your life, Corporal, but where I live, everyone knows that when it comes to the nobility, there's no difference between Scotland and France, or anywhere else. Money and power know no boundaries. There is an alliance in force between the two realms, and it is ancient.

"What am I doing here? I'm doing the same thing in France that hundreds of Frenchmen are doing in Scotland. I'm doing my master's bidding, attending to his affairs. The St. Clair family holds lands and enterprises in both countries, and I am one of their factors. I go wherever I am sent. I do whatever I am told. Today I drive a cart."

The answer seemed to mollify the man, but he cast a sideways glance at his superior standing by. "And what is in your cart?"

"Used iron, for the smelters within the walls. Old, rusty iron chains and broken swords to be melted down."

"Show me."

"Ewan, show the man."

Ewan went to the back of the wagon, where he lowered the tail gate and threw back the old sailcloth sheet that covered their load. The corporal looked, shifted some of the cargo around with a series of heavy, metallic clanks, and then walked back to the front of the cart, wiping his rust-stained fingers on his surcoat. Ewan remained on the ground beside him as the guard pointed up at the woman.

"Who is she?"

"My wife, mother to my two sons here."

"Your wife. How would I know that's true?"

"Why would I lie? Does she look like a harlot? If you have eyes in your head you'll see the eyes in hers, and the eyes in my son beside her."

The guardsman looked as though he might take offense at the surliness of Sinclair's tone, but then he eyed the massive shoulders of the man on the wagon and the set of his features and merely stepped closer so he could see the woman and the young man behind her. He looked carefully from one to the other, comparing their eyes.

"Hmm. And who is this other one?" He indicated Ewan, still standing close by him.

"My other son. Ask him. He speaks your language."

"And if I ask your … wife?"

"Ask away. You'll get nothing but a silly look. She can't understand a word you say."

The corporal looked directly at the woman. "Tell me your name."

The woman turned, wide eyed, to look at Tam, who leaned back on the bench and said in Scots, "He wants to know your name, Wife."

She bent forward to look down at the corporal and the watching knight, glancing back at Tam uncertainly.

"Tell him your name," he repeated.

"Mary. Mary Sinclair." Her voice was high and thin, with the sing-song intonation of the Scots peasantry.

"And where have you come from?" the corporal asked her.

Again the helpless look at Tam, who responded, "This is stupid. The fool wants to know where you're from. I told him you can't speak his language, but it hasn't sunk through his thick skull yet. Just tell him where we're from."

Tam didn't dare look at the watching knight, but he felt sure that the man was listening closely and understanding what they were saying. "*Tell* him, Mary. Where we're from."

She looked back at the corporal and blinked. "Inverness," she intoned. "Inverness in Scotland."

The guardsman stared at her for several more moments, then looked wordlessly at the white-and-blue-coated knight, who finally stepped forward and gazed up at the woman and the young man standing beside her. He pursed his lips, his eyes narrowing as he looked from one to the other of them, and then he stepped back and flicked a hand in dismissal.

"Move on," the corporal said. "On your way."

NOT MANY MINUTES LATER, having passed through the city gates and out of direct sight from them in the rapidly gathering dusk, Tam stopped the wagon and turned to the woman in the back.

"Where do you go from here, Lady?"

"Not far. If your young man there will help me down, I can walk from here with ease. I have family here who will shelter me. What is your real name? I will send a reward, as token of my thanks, to the Templar commandery here, down by the harbor. You may claim it by presenting yourself there and giving them your name."

Sinclair shook his head. "Nay, Lady, I'll take no money from you. The sound of your Scots voice has been reward enough, for I am long away from home. My name is as you heard it, Tam Sinclair, and I have no need of your coin. Go you now in peace, and quickly, for William de Nogaret has spies everywhere. And give thanks to God for having blessed you with those eyes of yours, my lady, for beside young Hamish's here they saved our lives this day. Ewan, go with her. Carry her bag and make sure she comes to no harm, then make your way to where we are going. We'll meet you there."

The woman stepped forward and laid a hand on Tam's forearm. "God bless you then, Tam Sinclair, and keep you well. You have my gratitude and that of my entire family."

It was on the tip of Sinclair's tongue to ask who that family might be, but something warned him not to, and he contented himself with nodding. "God bless you, too, my lady," he murmured.

She was a fine-looking woman, judging only by what he had seen of her face, and now as she made her way down from the cart with Ewan's help, Tam watched her body move against the restrictions of what she was wearing and tried to visualize what she might look like without the bundled blanket that enfolded her. He stopped that, however, as soon as he realized what he was doing. Beauty apart, he told himself, the woman had courage and a quick mind and he was glad he had done what he had.

He watched her go with Ewan until they were out of sight, and then he turned his team laboriously from the main thoroughfare into a darkening, deserted side street. He traveled halfway along the narrow thoroughfare before hauling on his reins again as the stooped Dominican monk from Alsace stepped out from a doorway in front of him. Young Hamish jumped down to the ground, where he was joined by three other men who had witnessed the killings in front of the city gates and had since walked at various distances behind the wagon. They gathered at the tail gate and began to rummage among the cargo there, displacing metal objects with much grunting and puffing. Sinclair thrust his whip into the receptacle by his right foot as the monk spoke to him, keeping his voice low so that the others would not hear him.

"Who was that woman, Tam, and what were you thinking of? I saw Ewan helping her into your cart as I left the yard and could hardly believe my eyes. You know better than that." There was no trace of shrillness in the monk's voice now. It was deep and resonant.

There came a grunt, a startled curse, and the scuffle of feet as a length of heavy chain slithered and clattered to the cobbles from the back of the wagon. Sinclair glanced that way and then turned back, his eyes sparkling and a small grin on his face.

"What woman are you talking about? Oh, *that* woman. She was just someone in need of a wee bit o' assistance. A Scots lass who spoke like me, and a lady, or I miss my guess."

"A lady, traveling alone?" The question was scornful.

"No, I think not. I doubt she was alone at the first of it. I think those three poor whoresons killed out there were supposed to be her guards. She told me she was fleeing from de Nogaret's men, and I believed her."

"From de Nogaret? That's even worse. You put us all at risk, man."

"No, sir, I did not." Tam lowered his shoulders and set his chin. "What would you have had me do, betray her to the popinjay knight and watch her hauled off to jail and who knows what else?"

The other man sighed and straightened up from his hunched stoop, squaring broad shoulders that the stoop had effectively concealed. "No. No, Tam, I suppose not." He fell silent for a short time, then asked, "What was her crime? I wonder. Not that de Nogaret would need one." He looked about him. "Where is she now, then?"

"On her way to join her family, somewhere in the city. I sent Ewan with her. She'll be well enough now."

"Good. Let us hope she will be safe. But that *was* dangerous, aiding her like that, no matter what the cause. Our business here gives us no time for chivalry, Tam, and debate it as you will, you took a foolish risk."

Sinclair shrugged. "Mayhap, but it seemed to me to be the right thing to do at the time. You were already through the gates and safe by the time I took her up, and you are the one charged with our task. The rest of us are but your guard." Sinclair lowered his voice until it was barely louder than a throaty whisper. "Look, Will, the woman needed help. I saw that you were going to be fine, then I weighed everything else and made a decision. The kind you make all the time. What's the word you use? A *discretionary* decision. A battle-field decision. It had to be made, yea or nay, and there was no one else around to tell me what to do."

The monk grunted. "Well, it's done now and we're none the worse for it, by God's grace. So be it. Let's get on. Aha! My sword. Thank you, Hamish."

Hamish and his helpers, working so industriously at the rear of the wagon, had unearthed a cache of carefully wrapped weapons from the bottom of the pile of rusted scrap that filled the bed, and had quickly stripped away the protective wrappings before Hamish himself brought the monk a sword that was clearly his own. The monk instantly grasped the hilt with sure familiarity and he drew the blade smoothly from its belted sheath, holding its shining blade vertically to reflect the last light of the fading day. As he did so, they heard the sound of racing feet, and the last of their number came rushing towards them.

"They're coming, Sir William," he gasped, laboring for breath. "The knight remembered you. It took him a while, but sure enough, he straightened up suddenly, right in front of me, and his face was something to behold. 'Templar!' he shouts, and roused the guard again. Ranted and raved at them, then sent them after you. Ten men at least he turned out, I saw that much before I left, but there may be more. But he thinks you were alone. He sent them to find *you*, nobody else, so they'll not be expecting opposition. They went off in the wrong direction first, along the main road."

"Aye, towards the monastery, because they are looking for a monk, not for me." The man addressed as Sir William was shrugging quickly out of his threadbare black habit. He pulled it forward over his head, then gathered it into a ball and flung it into the bed of the wagon. "Quickly now, Watt," he said, gesturing to the newcomer. "Arm yourself, quick as you like, and let's be away from here. Tam, we'll leave the wagon here. No more need for it, now that we're inside."

He turned away from all of them then, pulling and tugging in frustration at the tunic he had been wearing beneath the monk's habit. He had tucked it up around his waist earlier, to safeguard against its being seen through his rent and ragged habit, and now it was gathered thickly in unyielding layers around his waist and loins. He grimaced and cursed under his breath, squirming and wriggling until he eventually teased the bunched-up garment out of its constricting folds and wrinkles and arranged it to hang comfortably about him.

"My hauberk, Tam," he said then, "but keep the leggings with you. There's no time now to put the damned things on. I'll do that later."

From the bed of the wagon, before he jumped down himself to the cobblestones, Tam heaved him another, longer garment, this one a full coat of calf-length fustian, split to the groin in front and rear and covered in links of heavy mail.

"What about the horses?" he asked, vaulting down to the ground with a helmet and mailed hood in his hand.

"Leave them here. Someone will think himself blessed to find and claim them. Here, help me with this." The knight had immediately donned the mailed coat, but his impatience was frustrating his efforts to fasten the leather straps that would hold it in place beneath his arms, and now one of the other men stepped forward to help him, concentrating closely on feeding the straps through the buckles beneath Sir William's shoulders. The knight felt the last of them being tugged shut and he raised his arms high and flexed his shoulders, checking that they were securely covered yet not too tightly bound for swordplay. He then took the mailed hood from Tam Sinclair and pulled it over his head, spreading the ends of it across his shoulders and tugging at the flaps that he would lace together later, beneath his chin. When he was satisfied with how it felt, he took the flat crowned helm from Tam and settled it on his brows. "My thanks, Tam." He nodded tersely to the other man who had helped him. "And to you, Iain. And now my sword, if you will."

He hefted the long, cross-hilted broadsword and grasped it near the top of the belted leather sheath, then slung the belt aslant across his chest so that the sword hung down along his back, its long hilt projecting above his shoulder. "Now, quickly, lads. We've been here overlong already and they'll be on our heels once they discover I am not ahead of them on the road to the Dominican House. Bring the bag, Thomas, and you, Hamish, bring the coats and hand them out as we go. The rest of you, stay together and make haste, but be quiet and be prepared for anything. Keep your weapons sheathed and your hands free, but if anyone tries to stop us, or to contest our passage, be he guardsman or citizen, I care not, cut him down before he can raise an alarum. Come!"

They moved away immediately, the former monk and his attendant wagon driver striding at the head of the group while their companions positioned themselves protectively around and behind them, and as they went the tall apprentice called Hamish held a large leather bag open in front of him, from which one of the others pulled out and distributed tightly rolled bundles of cloth, all save one of them a pale yellowish brown. As each man received his, he grasped a flap of the cloth and snapped his bundle open, shaking it until it was loosened, and then he shrugged it over his head, transforming himself instantly from a nondescript but strongly armed pedestrian into an instantly recognizable Sergeant of the Order of the Brotherhood of the Temple, his ankle-length brown surcoat emblazoned front and back with the equal-armed red cross of the Templar Crusaders. Their leader's surcoat, the only white one among them, marked him clearly as a Knight of the Order, and he now walked ahead of them once more, his bare ankles and sandaled feet pale and strikingly evident beneath the heavy hem of the armored tunic under his white coat.

Tam Sinclair shifted a bulging sack effortlessly on his shoulder. "So, Sir Willie, are you going to tell me? Who was that popinjay knight? He knew you, plainly, but from where?"

Sir William Sinclair smiled for the first time. "Well, he did and he did not, Tam, but I'm surprised you even have to ask. Of all the people he might have been, he was the one I should least have expected to meet here. Did you really not know him?"

"No, but I knew there was something far from right when you started braying like a donkey. Where did *that* come from?"

"From need, Thomas, from necessity. I find it unbelievable that you didn't recognize the man. How could you forget such a grating, swinish squeal? Less than a year ago you wanted to gut him, and I was hard put to pull you away. That was Geoffrey the Jailer. We crossed paths with him when last we traveled to Paris. He was in Orléans then, in charge of the King's prison."

At the words, the frown vanished from the other man's face. "Of course! Virgin's piss, now I remember him. It was the armor that obscured it. The torturer! He was an unpleasant whoreson even then, without the King's surcoat—too fond by far of causing pain to the people in his power. But never mind *me* wanting to gut him. He made you clutch at your dagger, too, at one point. I thought you were going to fillet him right there in his own jail."

"Aye, that's the man. Geoffrey de something … *Martinsville*, that's the name! I knew I knew it. But it's the worst of chances that I should run into him here. He didn't recognize me because my beard is gone and my head is shaved, but he obviously does have a memory for faces, as he claimed."

"Here they come." The voice came from the rear rank.

"How many, and where are they?" Sir William did not even glance back, and it was Tam Sinclair who answered him, his voice tense.

"Three pair of them. A hundred paces behind, perhaps more. At the far end o' the street."

"Can they see us clearly?"

"No, no more than I can see them, and that's but poorly."

"Good, keep going, then, and don't look back unless you hear them running. They're looking for a monk—a single man. Bear that in mind. They'll take no heed of us as a group, not in our coats and this close to the Commandery."

The seven men kept walking as a loose-knit group and apparently in no particular haste, yet managing nonetheless to cover the ground quickly as they made their way through the twisting streets of the ancient town towards their destination on the waterfront, the fortified group of buildings that made up the regional Templar headquarters known simply as the Commandery. Five of the men were strangers to the city—only Sir William and Tam Sinclair had been there before—and as they walked they looked about them, straining to see the gray stone buildings now in the rapidly falling darkness while keeping their ears cocked for the sounds of running feet or raised voices. No lights had been lit yet in the buildings they passed, and it seemed as though they were the only people alive and stirring in the entire city of La Rochelle.

The white-coated knight did not look about him. He strode along with his head high, gazing straight ahead, the monkish sandals on his bare feet making no sound on the cobblestones, and his mind was filled to distraction with an image of that woman. A woman of astounding beauty, with enormous eyes. She was no one he had ever met, for he had known no women in his adult life, celibate for so long that the condition was as normal to him as breathing. And when he tried to fasten on the image of this woman's face he could not. He saw only those remarkable eyes.

Angry at his own folly in wasting time with such ridiculous meanderings, he shook his head as though to dislodge the treacherous thoughts, and lengthened his stride, forcing himself to concentrate on the task he faced. The Commandery of La Rochelle lay mere minutes ahead of him, and his mind filled now with the things he had to say to the men with whom he would be meeting very shortly. He was struggling to redefine, for perhaps the hundredth time, the arguments he would marshal. He knew that no matter how circumspectly he approached his explanation, and irrespective of the tact and skill he might use in laying out his tidings, his report, by its mere delivery, would inspire anger, disbelief, dismay, and doubts about his sanity.

Sir William Sinclair had spent his life acquiring a reputation for service and dedication to the ideals of the Order of the Temple, traveling so widely and for so long upon Templar affairs that he was now more familiar with France and Italy than he was with his native Scotland. And now, as a man in the earliest years of midlife, prematurely graying and grizzled yet still hale and strong, he took enormous pride in his newly acquired status as a member of the Inner Circle, the Order's Governing Council. The last thing he had any need for now was the slightest hint that he might be delusional. And yet he knew that the information he was carrying would be unbelievable to *him* were it laid baldly in front of him by someone else. His record of service, he knew, would prevent him from being laughed out of countenance as he delivered the unimaginable tidings he bore this day, but the truth was that the story he had to tell defied credence, and his fellow knights, if they were nothing else, were pragmatists, known for neither gullibility nor inane credulity. To their ears his story *must*, and surely would, reek of delusion and outright folly. Their hard-nosed common sense and the fabled integrity of their senior elders were firmly grounded in a two-hundred-year-long tradition of probity and service to the Church and to Christendom.

Sir William's task in the hours ahead was to convince the Knights Commander of the preceptory in La Rochelle that their world—the absolute power and influence enjoyed by the Templars throughout Christendom and beyond—would cease to exist within the week.

He knew, although he found little comfort in the knowledge, that he really had no need to convince them of the truth of his astounding message. He had the authority to enforce his mandate, to demand the full compliance and assistance of the La Rochelle commandery in prosecuting his own official duty, laid upon him personally by the Grand Master of the Order, Jacques de Molay. All he had to do was order them to withdraw all their forces and possessions inside the temporary safety of their gates and remain there, fortified against the deadly and treacherous approaches of the King of France.

Lost in his ponderings, Sinclair was nonetheless aware of his surroundings, and he felt a surge of recognition as he rounded one last bend in the narrow street and saw the spill of light that marked the end of his journey and the broad, cobbled plaza that fronted the main entry to the Templar compound.

The preceptory buildings of the Commandery had been built by the side of the harbor, along the water's edge, to accommodate the comings and goings of the vessels and the teeming personnel of the Order's massive fleet of galleys, the majority of them cargo vessels that plied all the seas of the trading world. But a significantly large contingent of the fleet was composed of ferociously efficient war galleys, manned and commanded by brethren of the Order. This force, the Battle Fleet, existed for the sole purpose of precluding any possibility of theft of the Order's assets at sea.

Sir William Sinclair hitched his shoulders and with both hands loosened his sword blade in its sheath, a habit so ingrained in him that he had lost awareness of doing it. But he expected no trouble now that he could see the lighted square ahead. The guardsmen who had been behind them earlier had vanished to search elsewhere, paying them no attention, plainly having accepted them for what they were. He flexed his fingers and grasped the sheath of his sword more firmly, straightening his shoulders and addressing himself once more to what he would say to the preceptor, and as he did so he became aware of a dark, narrow slash, a lane or alleyway between the high buildings on his left, mere paces ahead of him. He paid it little attention and strode by, followed by his companions, but in passing he heard a clamor of voices spring up from the blackness of the alley's shadowed depths.

"Keep moving," Sir William growled. "Pay no attention."

"Halt!" The shout echoed from deep in the alley's gloom. "You there! Halt in the name of King Philip." They heard the clatter of running footsteps.

William Sinclair kept walking, lengthening his stride as he spoke over his shoulder. "Challenge them, Tam. Stop them, but no fighting if you can avoid it. Just keep them far enough away from me to keep them from seeing what I'm wearing. If they see that I am not wearing leggings and only have on the sandals of a monk, one of them might be clever enough to guess I'm the monk they're looking for and we'll have to spill blood. And they are King's men, so that might not be a wise thing to do under our current circumstances."

He strode on, headed directly for the open end of the street less than thirty paces away, and soon stepped into the empty square that stretched as far as the Commandery's main gates. Once there, he looked back to where his six men had spread themselves in a line across the road with their backs to him, facing the junction with the lane and holding their drawn swords point down on the stones of the street. As they stood there, each with sufficient fighting room to defend himself with ease, a group of unkempt garrison soldiers poured out of the lane and skidded to a halt, their clamorous shouting fading instantly into silence. There were only ten of them, and they had clearly not expected to find a line of six Templars awaiting them with drawn swords.

As he watched the confrontation take shape, Sir William became aware of running footsteps approaching from the direction of the Commandery, but when he glanced over to see who was coming, he recognized the young sergeant, Ewan, who had gone off to escort the lady.

"Sir William!"

Sir William swung back to face the young man, chopping with his hand to quiet him, but Ewan was beside him now, and urgent with tidings.

"Sir William! I—"

"Shush, boy! Be silent."

"But—"

"Silent! And pay attention here." He waved his arm towards the street from which he had just emerged.

Tam Sinclair had given the King's guards no time to rally themselves but had jumped right into confrontation, addressing himself to the lout who seemed to be their leader. The loud, hectoring voice he assumed, speaking flawless street French and betraying no sign of his true nationality, carried clearly down the tunnel of the street to Sir William's ears.

"Well, filth, what would you have of us? Eh? What? By what imagined right do you dare challenge the Brotherhood of the Temple? You accosted us, ordered us to stand, in the name of the King. Why?"

None of the guardsmen made any attempt to answer him, their ignorance of what to do next betrayed by the way they glanced at each other, avoiding looking at any of the Templars.

Tam raised his voice even higher. "Come now, it is a simple question. And it demands a simple answer. Why did you shout at us to halt? Are we criminals? Do you know what you *did*, making demands of any of our Order without due authority? Where did you find the stupidity to attempt to interfere in the affairs of the Temple?"

Still no one answered him, despite the open insult in his words, and he gave them no respite. "Are you all mute? Or are you simply even more stupid than you look? You are King's men—at least you wear the uniform—so you must know who we are. And you must know, too, that you have neither the right nor the capability to call us to account, for anything. We are sergeants of the Temple and we answer solely to our Grand Master, who answers, in his turn, to the Pope. Your king has no power to bid us stay or go in our affairs. No king in Christendom has such a right."

He paused, as though sizing up his now bemused opponents. "So what is it to be? Will you search us and die, or merely question us and die, or fight us and die? Your choice. Speak up."

The leader of the King's men finally found his voice at this. "You can't threaten us," he said, his tone more of a whine than a complaint. "We are King's men. We wear the King's uniform."

Tam Sinclair spoke as though nothing had been said. "On the other hand," he said, "you have a fourth option. You may stand here, as you are, and without argument, and watch us as we walk away leaving your blood unspilled. Then, once we are gone, you will be at liberty to leave, too, and none of us, on either side, will breathe a word of this encounter. Are we agreed?" He addressed the man who had voiced the complaint, and he was impatient with the time it took to gain an answer. "Well, are we? Do we walk away or do we fight?" He raised the point of his sword to waist height, not threateningly but emphatically.

The other man nodded. "We walk."

"Excellent. Stand you there, then, until we be gone."

Sir William's men turned their backs on their hapless challengers and, swords still unsheathed, walked down the now dark street to join him. Only then did he turn to the young man beside him, and Ewan began to speak immediately.

"My lord, I have—"

"Hush you. I know you have something to say, but it will wait until later. I have more pressing matters on my mind. Rejoin the others now, and don your surcoat."

As the sergeant walked away, crestfallen, Sir William turned back towards the Commandery, knowing he had been seen from the gates as soon as he emerged into the open square, and that the senior guardsman on duty would immediately have summoned the Guard Commander. Now, striding towards the main gates, Sir William smiled in recognition as a veteran sergeant walked swiftly from the gatehouse, followed by four men, and then stopped short, frowning as he took in the bare ankles of the beardless man approaching him in the white surcoat of a knight and followed by an escorting group of sergeants. He raised one hand slightly in a restraining gesture to his men, until the man in the knight's surcoat had reached the gateway.

"Tescar, well met. You look distrustful. Do you not know me? Or are you to bar me from the Commandery for a shaven chin?"

The sergeant's wrinkled frown smoothed out in astonishment. "Sinclair? Sir William, is that you? God's holy name, what happened to you?"

"A long tale, old friend, but I have urgent tidings from Paris for the preceptor. Is he within the walls?"

"You, too? Aye, he is, but you might have to wait in line. It's first come, first served tonight, it seems, and you're the third to come seeking him within this half hour."

"Then I must claim priority, Sergeant. As I said, I bring urgent tidings from Paris, from Master de Molay himself. Is the admiral, too, inside?"

Tescar grinned. "Aye, he is, and the Master's tidings are well delivered. Your brother knight arrived not ten minutes past, straight from the South Gate, no doubt with the same message."

"What brother knight? We came in through the South Gate just as it closed, and we had to wait. There was no other Templar knight there. We would have seen him. Are you sure he said the *southern* gate? Who is he?"

The Sergeant of the Guard shrugged his wide shoulders. "That's what he said, the South Gate. As to who he is, he's a new one on me. I've never seen the man before. But he and another are here from Paris, bearing tidings from the Master for the preceptor and the admiral."

Sir William Sinclair's hands had dropped to his sword, one on the hilt, the other on the scabbard, as it occurred to him that this must have been the urgent message that had so agitated the young sergeant Ewan. He drew Tescar away by the sleeve, out of hearing of the others, and spoke in a low voice. "Listen to me, Tescar. There's something wrong here. There is no other messenger. I am de Molay's sole messenger to La Rochelle. What did this fellow look like?"

"Like you but better dressed." Tescar was frowning now, beginning to look angry. "White mantle, white surcoat, full forked beard. Said he came from Paris with urgent tidings from the Grand Master. I passed him inside. Why shouldn't I?"

"Did you ask his name?"

"Aye. It was English. Godwinson or Goodwinson, something like that. But he's a Templar, beyond doubt."

"Nothing is beyond doubt, Tescar. Not nowadays." Sinclair had started for the entrance, his pace lengthening rapidly, and he waved a hand to bring Tam and the other sergeants after. "What did this fellow look like?"

"I told you. Like you, a Templar knight." Tescar was hurrying to keep up with Sinclair, and the others followed them. "Big fellow, long beard, bright red with a pure white blaze on one side."

"What?" Sinclair stopped in his tracks, spinning to face the sergeant and stopping him with a straightened arm. "A full red beard with a white streak? On the left?"

"Aye, that's the one." Sergeant Tescar, a veteran of many years, had learned to recognize urgency when it confronted him, and he wasted no time on useless questions. "I'll take you in directly. Come. Your fellows here can go to the refectory. They'll still have time for dinner."

"No, they'll come with me and I'll make my own way in. You stay here and bar the gates. Seal this place up right now. No one is to leave here or come in until I say so, is that clear?"

"Aye, but—"

"No time for buts, Tescar. Seal this place tight and pray we're not too late already. Tam, quickly, with me, and bring the others."

MEN OF GOODWILL

1

S ir William Sinclair strode through the main gate tower and emerged into the spacious quadrangle of the headquarters complex. It was enclosed by four buildings, each three stories high, and he angled left immediately towards the heavy double doors that fronted the main administrative building containing the offices and living space of the garrison's senior personnel. Tam Sinclair almost had to run to catch up to him, but when he did he grasped his taller cousin by the sleeve and pulled him around.

"Wait, damnation, wait now! Just hold hard for a minute. What are we rushing into here? What's amiss? Why are you running?"

"Because I don't like the smell. Something stinks here, Tam. Didn't you hear what Tescar said?"

"Aye, some, but not all of it. The two o' you were whispering like lovers. Who's this other knight, this Godwinson?"

"I don't know, but whoever he is, he's a liar. There is no brother knight involved in this with tidings from de Molay. You know yourself, de Molay sent no other messenger but us. And there was no other Templar waiting to get in at the South Gate while we were there." They had stopped at the foot of the shallow flight of steps up to the doors. "So who is this Godwinson and where did he come from? Not from the South Gate—you know that. Do you recall seeing de Nogaret in Paris, two weeks ago?" Tam nodded, his face troubled, and Sir William continued, walking up the steps. "Aye, you do, but obviously not as well as I do. D'you recall who was with him at the time? Think hard now. They had just emerged from the King's residence and were waiting for a carriage."

"Aye, I remember seeing the fellow, but I don't know who he was. I was too busy looking at de Nogaret himself, bad luck to him. But the other one was a big, red-bearded— By the Christ!"

"Aye, big and red bearded, with a white streak in his beard. But was he a Templar? I think not. Nor was he dressed like one. No, Tam, the Christ has nothing to do with this one, not if de Nogaret's involved." They had reached the top of the shallow steps fronting the administrative building's entrance, and Sir William swung the doors open wide before striding through, his men behind him fanning out and looking about them, plainly not knowing what they were looking for.

"Keep your wits about you, lads," Sir William said quietly, "and tread softly. I don't know what we may find in here, but this is no time to be clattering around, so move quietly. And be prepared for the worst."

He led them to a passageway that bore away to the right from the far end of the cavernous entranceway, but he suddenly stopped short. Tam Sinclair bumped into him.

"What is it?" Tam's voice was a hoarse whisper.

"No guards." Another pair of closed double doors was set into the wall ahead of them, and Sir William drew his sword with a long, slithering of steel. "I've been here a score of times, Tam, and never have I seen those doors unguarded. Hold! Someone's coming."

Now they could clearly hear the sounds of shod feet coming from farther down the passageway, rapidly growing louder, and then a white-mantled knight stepped into view. He saw them immediately and gasped in alarm at the sight of Sir William's bare blade, but Sinclair was already approaching him, raising his finger to his lips in a signal for silence.

"Admiral," he whispered urgently, "stay there. It's me, William Sinclair."

Admiral Charles de St. Valéry was clearly astonished, but he remained where he was.

"Where's de Thierry?" Sinclair asked him.

St. Valéry looked as though he might answer angrily, but then he merely shrugged. "I have no idea. He was in the Day Room when

I saw him last, but that was half an hour ago. I have been upstairs ever since. What need have you and your men of bared blades here in the Commandery, Sir William?"

Sinclair was looking about him, but the passageway was empty on both sides, save for his own men.

St. Valéry spoke again, his voice still soft, but with an edge to it. "Do you not intend to answer me, sir?"

"Aye, I'll answer you, my lord Admiral." Sinclair threw him a quick glance, but then looked back to the closed doors of the Day Room where the Commandery's business was conducted. "In a few moments I hope to be able to tell you that no, we have no need for bared blades here, but for the present that is not clear. Where are your guards?"

"My—?" St. Valéry looked beyond Sir William to where his two guards should have been. "Where *are* my guards?"

"What of this Godwinson, where is he?"

"What are you talking about? Who is Godwinson?"

"Aye. You've been upstairs for half an hour, you say?"

"I have."

"Then you were gone when Godwinson arrived. And I see you are neither armed nor armored."

"No, I am not. What need have I of arms or armor in my own house?"

"Come with me, Admiral, and do as I say."

He turned on his heel and led the admiral back to where Tam Sinclair and his sergeants stood waiting. "Tam, two of your men to guard the admiral here and keep him safe from harm." As Tam signaled two sergeants forward, Sir William turned back to St. Valéry. "I have reason to believe enemies are waiting for you on the other side of that door, Admiral, and that whoever goes in there first had best be well armored. I hope I am wrong, but I fear I am correct. So you stay here, against the wall, until we find out what's inside. Tam!"

"Aye, Will."

"Four of your men back outside, quickly, to Tescar at the gates. Tell him they need crossbows. Do it quickly, but without attracting attention."

"Aye."

While they waited for the four sergeants to return, Admiral St. Valéry studied Sinclair, who, in turn, stood gazing silently at the closed doors to the Day Room.

"What are you thinking, Sir William?"

"About armor, my lord Admiral. You have armor in your quarters?"

"Of course."

"And have you a metal cuirass?"

"I have."

"Go then, if you will, and don both, as quickly as you can."

The admiral smiled wryly. "Don both? I have an extra tunic, too, of the finest Moslem chain mail, the strongest, lightest armor ever made. Should I put that on, too?" He was being facetious, but Sinclair was not.

"Aye, you should." He saw the widening of the admiral's eyes and held up a hand. "The first man through that door, Sir Charles, might well take a crossbow bolt in the chest, and so a triple layer of protection would be no excess. I would take your mantle myself and play your part, but I have no beard today and am fresh shaven, whereas your appearance is … otherwise distinctive. So you should enter first. I will be beside you, and we will have four crossbows of our own trained on whatever lies inside that room."

"Hmm. Who *is* in there?" No one had ever accused St. Valéry of being excitable or lacking courage, and now his voice revealed only curiosity, with no trace of alarm.

Sir William's headshake was brief. "I know not, but I suspect we will find two dead guards, and the preceptor, Sir Arnold de Thierry, either dead or being held captive. We have been infiltrated, Admiral. Our defenses have been breached, and all I know of our visitor is that I saw him last in the company of the King's chief lawyer, William de Nogaret, less than two weeks ago in Paris. I do not know his name, but he gave the English name of Godwinson to Sergeant Tescar at the gates and was admitted. He is dressed as a knight of the Temple, but he is no Templar and no friend of our Order."

"You recognized him?"

"No, I have not yet set eyes on him, but I recalled him from Sergeant Tescar's description."

St. Valéry was frowning. "Then how can you know this is the same man? Descriptions are vague at best. This man may well be a visiting brother from England."

"Then where are your guards, Admiral? Or did this Godwinson merely see fit to dismiss them? Tescar's description left little room for doubt. A big man, wearing a full, red beard with a bright white streak down the left side of it. Now, there may be two men in France with long red beards so singularly marked, but until I know I am wrong, I'll act as though I'm right. Please, go and put on your armor. We will wait for your return. Whatever has occurred within that room is long since done, and plainly no one is anxious to come out."

Tam Sinclair's four sergeants arrived back moments after St. Valéry left to put on his armor, and Sir William drew them aside and explained what he wanted them to do. Two of them then took up positions on each side of the double doors, their backs to the wall, while the other two lay on their bellies on the floor, their bodies angled away from the entrance, their loaded, drawn weapons trained on the doors. Sir William would enter first with the admiral, he told them, and would thrust the older man aside as they went in, in the hope of saving him from attack. He himself would dive to the other side, leaving the crossbowmen free to shoot from the floor into the open room. To the best of his knowledge there were only two men inside, he told them, but he could not be sure of that. Treachery spread in France like dry rot today, he said, pointing out that William de Nogaret had spies and employees everywhere. In any event, there would likely be only one crossbow inside the room, and once it had been fired, its wielder would have to reload. If the two men on the floor could not finish him, it would be the turn of the two by the doors. They would enter the room immediately, at the run, and switch sides. Among the four of them they should be sure of dealing with one bowman. Sinclair himself would take care of the red-bearded impostor.

Admiral St. Valéry returned, looking distinctly larger and walking with far less ease, his sword slung from his shoulder. Sir William swished his own sword through the air and then concealed it behind his back.

"By me, if you will, Admiral, on my left, and let's find out what lies in wait for us. Those doors *do* open inwards, do they not?"

"They do … Ready?" St. Valéry went quietly forward until they stood facing the doors, side by side. He took hold of the black iron rings of the handles, raising them gently, one in each hand, then drew a deep breath, twisted both handles, threw the doors wide, and stepped inside.

At first Sinclair could see nothing at all. The large room appeared to be empty. But then he saw the broad smear of blood on the floor to his left where someone must have dragged a body aside, and at the same time he saw a flicker of movement to his right.

He reacted instantly, thrusting out his arm, straight and hard, in a blow to the admiral's shoulder. The older man had been tense, and the unexpected push sent him spinning, barely in time as a hard-shot missile smashed into him, jerking him bodily off his feet and hurling him sideways to crash on the floor against the wall. Sinclair had used the strong, straight-armed blow to push himself sideways, in the other direction, and even as his shoulders slammed into the open door he saw another blur of motion from his left, and a second steel bolt, this one intended for him, half buried itself in the solid oak of the door by his head.

From below him he heard the thrum of a crossbow then and looked to see the man who had tried to kill him, his crossbow still at his shoulder, transfixed by a bolt from one of the sergeants on the floor of the passageway. Angled upwards as it was, the bolt passed cleanly through the man's neck, beneath his chin, and shot out through the base of his skull before digging itself into the crevice between two of the stone blocks of the wall.

Sir William thrust himself forward from the door, whirling, sword in hand, as the rest of his men stormed into the room.

The red-bearded man in the knight's mantle stood against the wall, still holding the crossbow that had struck down St. Valéry, and as he looked at Sinclair and the men pouring through the doorway he opened his hands and dropped the useless weapon, then shrugged out of his great Templar mantle and let it fall to the floor behind him as he drew his sword and fell into a crouch. Beneath the beard, his mouth was a snarling rictus.

"Mine," Sinclair said.

The red-bearded man circled away from him, and Sinclair followed, waiting for him to make a move. Then came a whirling blur, a loud, meaty-sounding blow, and the stranger fell to his knees and pitched onto his face as Tam Sinclair's dirk clattered on the stone floor beside him.

Sir William straightened slowly from his crouch. "Was that well done, Tam?"

"Aye, sir, it was. A perfect throw, hilt first. Unless, of course, ye really wanted to give the whoreson a second chance to kill ye."

"He would not have killed me, Tam."

"No, likely not. But you would ha'e killed him, and there would ha'e been an end o' it. But now he's still alive, I think, and we'll ha'e a chance to find out what he came here for."

"I know what he came here for, and he succeeded. He came to kill the admiral and the preceptor."

"Shit, aye, but why?"

"To cause chaos tonight. In preparation for tomorrow."

"Then he's missed his aim. The admiral's alive. The bolt but caught his hauberk and threw him away, but it didna hit him. He'll be fine. Battered about a bit, but he's no' even bleeding."

Sir William turned quickly to look to where a couple of his men were raising the limp form of the admiral from the floor. "Thank God for that. I thought I had been too slow. Send someone to the infirmary to fetch a surgeon or a physician, and have someone else remove the admiral's armor before the fellow comes. Where is the preceptor?"

"Over here, sir." The voice came from the far end of the room, where another sergeant was standing looking down at the floor behind one of the room's long tables. "Him and the two guards. All dead."

"Ah, God!" Sir William slowly walked the length of the great room until he stood looking down on the three corpses that had been dragged out of sight behind the table. Two were sergeants of the Order, their brown surcoats now black with blood. The third man was much older, dressed in the white mantle of the knights, with the Temple cross embroidered on its left breast. He, too, had been killed by a crossbow bolt, shot from a distance short enough to drive the lethal bolt clean through his chest, so that half of its length protruded from his back. There was little blood, apart from the exit wound itself, so the elderly man's death must have been instantaneous.

Sir William knew the old preceptor's story as well as he knew his own. Arnold de Thierry, a childless widower of one-and-twenty, had joined the Order on the island of Cyprus, thirty-one years earlier, on the fourth day of July in 1276, and had become one of the Temple's most honored knights in fifteen years of campaigning in the Holy Land. His career there had ended when he was wounded in the earliest stages of the final siege of Acre in the year 1291 and was shipped out by sea and committed to the care of the Knights Hospitallers at Rhodes. There he was expected to die, but he fought instead for life, earning himself an undying reputation for futile bravery by refusing to allow the surgeons to amputate his wounded arm when it was deemed to be gangrenous. The wound, it transpired, was merely infected, and de Thierry in time regained almost full use of the limb. But while he was undergoing his long, slow recovery, his comrades in Acre were overrun and slaughtered by the Seljuk Sultan's Mamelukes.

Hampered by his crippled arm, which was too gravely disabled for swordplay, de Thierry eventually returned to duty and was rewarded for his years of faithful service with the post of Preceptor of the Commandery of La Rochelle, a posting that he had rightly regarded as the highest honor he could have earned.

Preceptorship of a commandery was a military posting, as opposed to the administrative rank—something of a cross between an abbot and a small-town mayor—held by the preceptor of a Temple. Throughout Christendom the Temples run by the Order were civil institutions,

financial and administrative posts, and their members, all nominally
Templars, were artisans and traders of all stripes. Commanderies, on
the other hand, were garrisoned posts, staffed by the fighting members
of the Order, the knights and sergeants, and their purpose was purely
military—the protection and guardianship of the Order's affairs. The
preceptor of a commandery was the first officer, responsible for all
aspects of the installation, and nowhere was that responsibility more
onerous or honorable than in La Rochelle, the most important location
in France for the Order's trading activities.

The commandery in La Rochelle, fronting the harbor with its extensive and easily defensible anchorage for ships of all sizes and types,
was the primary garrison in the entire country, utterly essential to the
worldwide welfare of the Order and its business. All of the industries
and activities that the Templars pursued throughout Christendom and
beyond—manufactories, plantations, orchards and farms; warehousing
and storage facilities for the trading and sale of goods; distribution
channels for commodities of every kind; real estate holdings and international banking activities—intersected at one time or another in the
Commandery of La Rochelle, on the wharves and piers of the harbor
or in the holding warehouses or the cargo shipping sheds.

Now, staring down at the preceptor's still form, it came to Will
that in merely witnessing this death, he was witnessing the end of an
epoch. De Thierry was gone, and with him had vanished an era of
unshakable integrity, absolute honor, and the purity of an ideal.

No more, Sinclair thought now. *No more honor in the eyes of the
law. No more fearlessness in the faithful performance of duty. And
no more trust in the integrity of kings from men of goodwill.
Farewell, old friend. You will be sorely missed, but you will suffer
nothing by missing what will come tomorrow.*

He turned away with a sigh and looked at Tam Sinclair, standing
across from him on the other side of the three corpses. "Tam, send
someone to bring Tescar. Tell whoever you send to say nothing but
to bring him directly to me."

"What in God's holy name has happened here?" The voice was
loud, and Sir William turned to look at the man in the doorway, then

raised his hand to attract his attention. When the white-robed brother looked at him in outrage, the knight raised one finger, bidding him wait, then turned back to Tam. "Remember now, your man must say no word to Tescar."

"Aye, I'll send Ewan. He knows how to keep his mouth shut."

Sir William made his way then to the newcomer. "What is your name, Brother?"

The other man blinked at him, plainly wondering who he was, pale faced and clean shaven yet wearing the surcoat of a Temple Knight. "I am Brother Thomas," he said. "I run the infirmary. What has happened here?"

"Are you surgeon or physician, Brother Thomas?"

"I am both, but—"

"Excellent. Now listen closely. I am William Sinclair, recently appointed to the Governing Council. I am beardless because I came here tonight in disguise, bearing instructions from our Grand Master in Paris to the preceptor and the admiral here in La Rochelle. And what has happened here is assassination. The preceptor has been killed, and the admiral has had a narrow escape. He is unconscious but unwounded, it appears. Listen carefully, therefore, to what I require of you, and take this under your vow of obedience. There are four dead men in this room. That one over there by the wall was one of the assassins. Behind the table at the back there you will find the bodies of two of your own garrison who were posted here tonight as guards, and the Brother Preceptor himself.

"You will bring your people here immediately, enjoining them to silence and obedience as I have enjoined you, and remove the bodies to the hospital. And then you will set them to cleaning this place up, removing the bloodstains and restoring the room to its former condition. As soon as you have issued your instructions, I need you to bring Admiral St. Valéry back to awareness. I have orders for him from the Grand Master, and their gravity permits no further loss of time. I need him—our Order needs him—awake and alert. Do you understand me, Brother Thomas?"

Brother Thomas nodded, but his eyes were drawn to the red-bearded man slumped unconscious over a table, closely watched by two of Tam Sinclair's sergeants. "Who is that?"

"A prisoner. The second assassin. We will see to him. He will be in no need of your assistance for a while yet."

"Yet?"

"Hurry, Brother Thomas."

Tescar and Brother Thomas passed each other in the doorway, and Tescar stopped, mouth hanging as he gaped at the unconscious Godwinson. Wasting no words, the knight quickly told the sergeant what had happened, and then asked him for the names of the two deputy commanders, naval and garrison based. He remembered both names and sent Tescar to summon the men, again with a warning to say nothing of what he knew.

2

An hour later, having done everything that he could do to repair the ravages caused by the man Godwinson and his murderous associate, Sir William finally found himself back in the Day Room, with nothing to do but wait upon events that he could not control. He crossed his legs, shifting his backside as he sought a comfortable spot in the wooden armchair by the fireplace of the great, freshly scrubbed room that was the center of the Commandery's daily affairs. He no longer wore his mail hauberk and surcoat, having changed them for a plain white monk's habit, covered by the simple but richly textured white mantle of a Templar knight, with the embroidered cross on the left breast. He had not, however, set aside his sword, and now he sat staring into the flames and frowning, one hand supported on the cross-hilt of his upright weapon as though it were a staff. The entire room smelled of lye soap, and his eyes were burning from the stench of it, but he could tell it was fading, if only gradually. Nonetheless his head was aching from the stink, and he had spent much of the past hour outside, conducting the business of the garrison in the fresh air.

Godwinson, whatever his true name might be, was safely locked up in a heavily guarded cell. He had regained consciousness eventually, but had refused to say a word when they interrogated him, and Sinclair, finding himself growing dangerously angry, had ordered him taken away and confined. He had then briefed the two deputy commanders on how to pacify the outraged and humiliated garrison, although he had said nothing to either of them about the purpose of his mission there. They had accepted his credentials and had carried out his wishes obediently, accepting it as their duty.

He could tell them nothing of the truth, however, before he had informed St. Valéry of his reasons for coming to La Rochelle. He had returned from the infirmary a short time earlier, where Brother Thomas had assured him that the admiral was showing signs of returning to consciousness and that he expected no complications as a result of the violent fall. The crossbow bolt had missed the admiral's body by the narrowest of margins, striking his cuirass and glancing off to lodge in the metal mesh of his hauberk, the violence of its delivery throwing the old man to the floor.

It still lacked three hours until midnight, and all the Scots knight could do was wait and try to hold himself in patience until St. Valéry was well enough to talk to him and listen to his tidings. Once those were formally delivered, Sir William could take over the admiral's command, at least until such time as the man was fit to resume his post properly. Sinclair had the authority to do so in an emergency, granted him by the Grand Master in person.

Across from him, Tam stood against the far wall, his eyes downcast and his hands clasped quietly in front of him. They had discussed the evening's events at length, but Sir William had been out of sorts and was well aware that he had abused his friend several times, deflecting much of his own anger and frustration onto his faithful kinsman's uncomplaining shoulders. Now he felt stirrings of guilt and sought to make amends.

"You're very quiet, Thomas. Why?"

Tam raised his head and looked at him, one black eyebrow lifted high, then turned away and stooped to throw three large logs onto the fire, pushing them firmly into place with the sole of his boot until he was satisfied that the new fuel would catch quickly. He stood straight again, wiping the dust from his hands with an edge of his surcoat, and turned at last to Will.

"Are you still fretting about me and that woman this afternoon?"

Will sat straighter in his chair and stared wide eyed at his sergeant cousin, who leaned against the mantel, looking down at him.

"Fretting, about you and a woman? I hope I need have no such concerns, Thomas."

"No, well, you needn't, but that's about the tenth time you've called me Thomas this night, and that usually means you're no' pleased wi' me. And when you say things the way you did just then, all proper and prim, that means the same thing. But I misspoke. I didna mean about me *and* the woman, the way you took it. I meant about me *helpin'* the woman."

"I know what you meant, and I *have* been thinking about it. What you did was wrong."

Tam whipped his head down and away quickly, as though he might spit into the fire, but then, equally quickly, he swung back to face his cousin, and his voice was tight with aggravation. "How was it wrong, in God's name? I told ye before, I only helped a fellow Scot escape from a man we despise. That she was a woman's neither here nor there. She needed help, Will, and I was there to provide it, and all's well. Had it been a man, you would ha'e thought nothing of it."

"Not so. It might have put our mission at risk either way, Tam."

"Och, Will, that's rubbish and you know it. You're bein' pigheaded for the sheer pleasure o' it. Our mission was ne'er in danger. Had it been you there, faced with her plight and her plea, and no' me, you would ha'e done the same thing. You know you would."

"No, I would not. I would have walked away from her."

"You would ha—? You would ha'e *walked away*? *Why*, in the name o' God? Because she was a woman? Sweet Jesus, Will, what if it had been your mother or one of your sisters? Would you not want someone to offer her help?"

"It was not my mother, Tam. Nor was it any of my sisters."

"Well she was *somebody's* mother or sister, or both."

"Not so. She was a single, unescorted woman, traveling alone. An occasion of sin, waiting to avail itself of opportunity."

"Och, for the love o' Christ!" The disgust in Tam Sinclair's voice was rich and undisguised. "How long have we known each other, Will Sinclair?"

Will raised an eyebrow. "Thirty years?"

"Aye, and more than that, and I swear you've become two people in those years."

The knight tilted his head. "I don't know what you mean."

"I know you don't, and that's the shame o' it. The lad I knew back then would ne'er ha'e spewed such canting, canonical rubbish. But since you came back from Outremer and began to grow involved in the Inner Circle, you've changed, my lad, and little for the better."

Will stiffened. "That is insolent."

Tam folded his arms over his chest. "Oh, is that a fact? After thirty years I've grown insolent, have I? Thirty years of encouragement from you to speak up and say what's in my mind, to tell ye the truth where others might not want to, to be comfortable in being your equal when there's just the two o' us around, and all at once I'm insolent?"

Will's ears had reddened and he sagged back into his chair. "You're right," he said. "That was unworthy. Forgive me."

"Happily. But what's eating at you, Will? This isna like you."

Will tensed and then sat forward, tightening his grip on his sword's cross-guard and narrowing his eyes as he stared right into the heart of the fire. "I don't know, Tam. I just don't know. It's this thing tonight, I suppose—the malice of it, the sheer evil. A King's minister—his chief lawyer—arranging murders. It's insanity, unthinkable. And yet it happened … And I've been wondering about God's will this past half hour. Was it God's will, think you, that we should be in that part of Paris that day, at that particular time when de Nogaret and this scum Godwinson were emerging from the residence? Had we not been there and seen them, him with his white-streaked red beard, I would never have reacted when Tescar told us about his arrival, and St. Valéry would now be dead, too."

"Ach, you would have reacted anyway, as soon as you heard that shite about his coming from Paris wi' word from de Molay. You knew that was a fleering lie as soon as you heard it, and you would have behaved the same way, even if you hadn't seen the whoreson in Paris and recognized the description. No God's will there."

"Well then, was it His will that this creature should succeed and take the life of Arnold de Thierry? There was a man who never offended God in all his life."

"Whoa there now." Tam threw up his hands as though conceding defeat. "You're getting into things too deep for my poor head. I canna tell you anything about that, and neither can you. You'll just drive yourself daft. Master de Thierry died an ill death, I'll grant ye, but he died at his post and on duty, and that means he died on God's business, so he'll be wi' all the others now, enjoying his reward."

"All *what* others?"

"What others?" Tam sat blinking at him. "The other thousands like him who died blameless doin' their duty. Ye surely dinna think he's the first man ever to die the way he did? What about your ain family? Sinclairs ha'e been involved wi' the Temple since the start o' it. We canna say how many o' them ha'e died uselessly in the service o' God and His Church, but they died nonetheless. Three o' your ancestors at once, and no' so long ago—blood uncles and cousins—French and Scots, St. Clair and Sinclair, the three o' them in Outremer at the same time, under that whoreson Richard Lionheart, fightin' God's ain Holy War against the Saracen Saladin and his Muslims ... D'ye think God in His wisdom had decreed their deaths for standin' wi' the

Plantagenet, a man weel-kent for his depravity an' foul habits?"
Tam shook his head. "It's no' left to the likes o' us to judge God's
reasons, Will. God knows we ha'e enough o' our ain faults to
live wi' ..."

"Have I really changed that much, Tam? Am I really the prig you
described, spouting cant and nonsense?"

"Aye, you can be, sometimes, a wee bit." Tam grinned suddenly,
his whole face lighting up. "But not often, thanks be to God."

Will stared into the fire again, and just as Tam began to think he
would say nothing more, he spoke.

"I have been thinking about that woman, Tam."

"Aye, well, she was a fine-looking woman. There's nothing
wrong wi' that."

"But there is!" Will whipped his head around to look in his
sergeant's eyes. "I am bound by oath to avoid women."

"Ach, come away, Will, that's not true, and the young Will St.
Clair I knew, knew that as well."

"It *is* true. I undertook a vow of chastity."

"Aye, you did, that's right. A vow of *chastity*. You swore not to
fornicate, with either women or men. Fine and well—a vow's a vow
and I've taken a few mysel'. But tell me this, is fornication wi' a man
more evil than fornicating wi' a woman?"

Will looked shocked. "Lust between men is unnatural, the foulest
of mortal sins."

"Aye, it is, I'll grant ye that. And it's disgusting even to think about,
but it still happens. But is it worse than fornicating wi' a woman?"

"Why are we even talking about this?"

"Because you started it. Is it worse?"

"Of course it's worse."

"Because it's unnatural."

"Yes."

"Aye. So the other way—with a woman—is that then natural?
Don't get angry, I'm only asking you because I wonder why it is that
you never try to avoid men."

"Avoid men? What are you talking about?"

"I thought I was being clear. If fornication between men is unnatural and worse than the other, natural kind, then why do you not avoid consorting with men? A man wi' the will for things like that could corrupt you into sin."

Will reared back in his chair. "That is ridiculous. Not one man in ten thousand would ever dream of thinking such a thing. The very idea is laughable."

Tam nodded. "I agree. It is. But so is the thought of your lumping all women into one mass of sin, as though they threatened your chastity."

"That's different. It's not at all the same thing. I have no attraction to men. But I might find a woman attractive. And that would confound my vow."

"What vow? Oh, aye, your chastity. Right. But tell me, when did you ever swear to deny a woman the right to live—the right to seek freedom or to escape an enemy the likes of de Nogaret and his animals? When did you vow to shun them all as people?"

"I never did any of those things."

Tam's face was somber. "You must have, Will, somewhere deep inside yourself. And you're doing it now. All this muttering and mumbling only started when you saw that woman with us today."

"That's not true. I never even saw her from near enough to be aware of her as a person."

"And yet she has been in your mind ever since?"

A brief silence fell between them, and Tam moved to sit in the armchair next to Sir William's. "Have you ever really known a woman, Will?"

"That's an asinine question. Of course I have known women."

"Who? Name me one."

"My mother. Several aunts. My sisters, Joan and Mary and Peggy."

Tam shook his head. "Those are all relatives, Will. I was asking about women, flesh-and-blood people who are not kinsfolk. Have you?"

Sir William faced his friend again. "No, I have not, and you know that. You have been with me constantly these thirty years."

"Aye, I was afraid you would say that. The sad part is that I believe you. But I was hoping I'd be wrong. As you say, I've been with you these thirty years. But I've had women, now and then, and you knew nothing of it."

Tam watched the younger man stiffen in horror. "What can I say, lad? I'm a sinner. I'm a Templar sergeant, but I'm a man, too, first and foremost. I've been tempted, and I've yielded to it—not often, mind you, I'm no goat—and I've enjoyed it most times. And then I've confessed and been shriven. Forgiven by an all-forgiving God. You remember Him, the All-Merciful?" He leaned forward anxiously. "Say something, man, and breathe, for you look as though you might choke."

Will's eyes were enormous, his lips moving soundlessly, and Tam Sinclair laughed. "What is it, man? Speak up, in God's name."

That was effective, for the knight's mouth snapped shut, and then he found his voice, although it was a mere whisper. "In God's name? You can invoke the name of God in this? You took a sacred vow, Tam."

Tam's mouth twisted. "Aye, I know that. And I broke it a few times. But as I said, I confessed and was shriven and did penance thereafter, as all men do. We *are* men, Will, not gods."

"We are Templar monks."

"Aye, but we're men first and beyond all else. And we have Templar priests and bishops to match God's other priests and bishops everywhere, and nary a one of them that I know of but has a whore hidden somewhere. What kind of world have you built for yourself, Will, in there behind your eyes? Are you deaf and blind to such things? You must be, for they're plain to hear and see."

The knuckles of William Sinclair's hand were white with the pressure he was exerting on the hilt of his sword, and when he spoke again his voice was icy. "We … will … not … speak … of … this."

Nor did they, for at that moment the doors behind them opened and they looked over to see Sir Charles de St. Valéry watching them from the threshold.

3

S ir William was on his feet instantly, crossing towards the older man, but the admiral held up a hand to signal that he required no help. As the others watched him, St. Valéry looked slowly around the room, his eyes coming to rest on the raw scar in the wall where the bolt that killed Godwinson's fellow assassin had chipped out a large splinter.

"It stinks of lye in here."

"Aye, Admiral, I was thinking the same thing myself. But it is getting better. An hour ago, you could hardly breathe in here without choking."

St. Valéry nodded absently and made his way towards the fireplace, and Sir William stepped aside to let him pass, but instead of sitting, the admiral leaned against the high back of one of the armchairs fronting the fire. He looked as though he had aged greatly in the few hours since they had last met. His face was pallid, his eyes sunk deep into his head, and the skin beneath them appeared liverish purple. But he held himself erect, and his posture was defiant.

"I have seen Arnold," he said in a calm, flat voice. "The surgeons tell me there was little blood and that his death was instantaneous, which means he felt no pain. In truth, it means he might not even have seen death approaching. I would like to think he died that way, without feeling himself betrayed, for if he saw his murderers, he must have thought them Brethren of the Order. Such a betrayal, even the semblance of one, would have pained Arnold greatly. I shall regret his passing. He and I were friends for many years ... more years than most men are allowed to live. I will miss him." He stiffened his shoulders and drew a great breath, then turned to face Sir William, every inch the Admiral of the Fleet whose personal concerns must always be subject to the dictates of his duty. "But I fear I may be forced to postpone my mourning until later. I have been told you come bearing urgent tidings, Sir William. Tidings from Master de Molay himself."

"I do, Admiral."

St. Valéry swept out an arm to indicate the room in which they stood. "Do they have any bearing on this obscenity that took place here?"

Sir William glanced at Tam Sinclair, who merely nodded, his lips pursed.

"Yes and no, Admiral. I believe there's a very real connection between what happened here and the tidings I carry, but I cannot yet be sure. I have no proof—merely suspicions. Tam agrees with me."

"Hmm." St. Valéry grasped the back of his chair and pulled it away from the roaring fire. "Then we had best be seated where you can deliver your charges in comfort."

The other two men took the armchairs flanking the admiral, although in normal circumstances Tam would never have thought of doing such a thing. As a mere sergeant, he seldom mixed directly with the knightly brethren, but he had known Charles de St. Valéry for so long that his own conduct had earned him the right to both sit and speak up in the admiral's presence, at St. Valéry's own insistence.

"There is little of comfort in what I have to say this night, my lord Admiral," Will Sinclair said as he sat down.

"Aye, well, that's appropriate, Sir William. There is little of comfort anywhere this night. Tell me what you have. I presume it is in writing?"

"Aye, Admiral, in the Master's own words. Tam?"

Tam Sinclair removed the heavy leather satchel that was slung across his chest. Then, holding it on his knees, he opened the buckle and withdrew two thick parchment-wrapped packages, one of which he handed to St. Valéry, who hefted it thoughtfully in his hand while he eyed the other package that Tam was returning to his satchel.

"The Master had much to say, it appears. Who is the other for, if I am permitted to ask?"

"Aye, Admiral." Sir William waved a hand, and Tam passed the second package to the admiral as well.

St. Valéry looked at the inscription, and his eyebrows rose high on his forehead. "'For Sir William Sinclair. To be opened on the

Feast of the Epiphany, Anno Domini 1308. Jacques de Molay, Master.'" St. Valéry looked at Sir William. "The Epiphany?"

Will Sinclair shrugged, opening his hands to indicate his ignorance. St. Valéry grunted as he handed the bulky package back to Tam and took a fresh grip on his own, making no attempt to break the seal.

"Are you aware of what this contains?" Will Sinclair nodded. "And your own?"

"I have no idea, sir. The Master made no effort to tell me. He merely drew my attention to the inscription, so I shall find out on the Epiphany."

"That sounds ominous. Frightening, even, since this is October. Three months for you to wait, in which time much could happen to affect your instructions—if instructions they be. Give me the gist, if you will, of what this one of mine contains. I'll read it afterwards."

Sir William inhaled sharply and stood up, moving to stand by the side of the fireplace, where he could look directly at the admiral. "As you know, the Pope himself summoned the Master home to France from Cyprus more than eight months ago, giving Monsieur de Molay no hint of why he was called or what was expected of him other than that he was to meet with Pope and King on matters pertaining to the future welfare of the Order and the proposed amalgamation of the Orders of the Temple and the Hospitallers, which Master de Molay has always vehemently opposed on several grounds."

St. Valéry grunted. "I am familiar with the Master's objections. Are you opposed?"

Sinclair nodded. "I am, Admiral. The Master fears the loss of our identity were we to join with Hospital. We all do, to some extent."

"Tell me more, then."

The younger knight brought his hands together in front of him. "Well, for one thing, the Hospital is far larger and more complex than our own Order—more diverse in its activities and less strict in its interpretation of its role and its duties. The Hospitallers have never been warriors before all else, and the Master fears we would lose our imperative need to win back the Holy Land in consequence. He also fears the duplication of installations in the cities—who would survive the amalgamation of those, Temple or Hospital? And who—which administration—would survive the consolidation? All of these things concern him, and he has found little satisfaction in the course of several meetings with Pope Clement in Poitiers and with King Philip in Paris, but nothing concrete has resulted in either case. And so our Master has sat waiting in Paris these two months past, wondering what might be afoot, but obedient to the King's will. But then, less than a month ago, Master de Molay received a warning of a plot against the Order, which he treated with the utmost urgency. I have no idea whence it came, but I received the strong impression, purely through listening to what was and was not said, that it sprang from a trustworthy source close to King Philip himself, or to his minister and chief lawyer, de Nogaret."

St. Valéry nodded, his expression serene. "I see. And to what end does this plot exist? Our money, obviously, and a move to confiscate it, since de Nogaret is in charge. What is involved, and how extensive is it?"

"More than you could possibly imagine, Sir Charles. When I found myself sitting across from Master de Molay and being entrusted with this secret, the scope of it appalled me to the point of thinking the Master had gone mad and was seeing demons everywhere. But in fact he had known of the plot for ten days by then and had had doubts of his own on first hearing of it. The source, he told me, was unimpeachable, and that had caused him sufficient concern to begin making arrangements, just in case the threat proved real.

"The warning was confirmed the very morning of the day I saw the Master, less than two weeks ago now. A second, more detailed report had arrived from the same trusted source. By the time the Master called me into his presence, his plans were in place, and I have been working at them ever since."

St. Valéry was now frowning. "You make it sound like the end of the world."

"It is, as far as we are concerned." Sir William's response was that of a commander to a subordinate, and St. Valéry took note of it. "It is the end of our world, here in France. Philip Capet, our beloved King, has his armies poised to act against us. His *armies*, Sir Charles. And his minions. The entire assembled powers of the Kingdom of France are being brought to bear upon us in one single, unprecedented coup. His creature, William de Nogaret, has issued instructions from his monarch to his army to arrest every Templar in the realm of France at daybreak on the morning of Friday, the thirteenth of October."

St. Valéry stiffened. "That … that is simply unbelievable!"

"Aye, it is. It is also tomorrow."

"This is preposterous."

"I agree. No argument on that from me. But it is also true. The King's men will be hammering at these doors tomorrow morning at first light."

St. Valéry sat dumbstruck, and Sir William could guess the thoughts that must be surging through his head. Every Templar in the realm of France, arrested and imprisoned in one day? That *was* preposterous. There were thousands of Temple brethren in France, from one end of it to the other, and very few of them were soldiers. For the past hundred years the vast majority of so-called Templars had never borne arms of any kind. In reality they were honorary or associate brethren: merchants and bankers, clerics and shopkeepers, traders and artisans, guildsmen and local governors; the men who made the massive empire of the Temple function smoothly. The Order of the Temple was the richest civil institution in the world, and for two hundred years its military arm had been the standing army of the Church, the only regular fighting force in all of Christendom, with never a blemish on its record of probity and service. The vaunted Hospitallers were rivals nowadays, but beside the Templars, the original military order, their record was unimpressive. Small wonder that the admiral was stricken dumb by the mere idea that such an edifice as the Temple could be even threatened, let alone toppled, by a single, greedy King.

St. Valéry, however, was showing his mettle. Rather than fulminating in disbelief, he had brought his attention to bear on the situation with which he was faced. He looked now at Sir William, his jaw set in a hard line. "So what are my instructions? Am I to surrender my fleet?"

Will Sinclair actually smiled. "Never. You are to work all night tonight, in preparation for tomorrow, and then withdraw your laden vessels to safety offshore, where they cannot be reached. There is still some doubt in the Master's mind about whether the warning is real or not, but there is none in mine.

"If tomorrow brings disaster, as I expect it to, you are to take your fleet out of France to safety, to await a resolution of this affair, for reason demands that it must be resolved eventually. But until it is, and reparations have been made by either side, you will remain at sea if need be, husbanding your resources. And you will take me with you, as escort to our Order's Treasure."

The admiral's jaw dropped. "You have the Treasure here? The Templar Treasure?"

"Not here in La Rochelle, but close by."

"How did you get it out of Paris?"

"It was not in Paris, has not been for the past ten years. It has been buried safely in a cavern in the forest of Fontainebleau since then. The Master ordered it moved secretly at that time, to keep it safe."

"Ten years ago? Safe from whom, in God's holy name?"

"From the men now seeking it, Sir Charles. From Philip Capet and William de Nogaret. There was no threat at that time. Master de Molay was merely being a careful steward, as is his duty."

"So …" St. Valéry cleared his throat. "Am I to understand that you two men, accompanied by a small group of sergeant brothers, transported the entire Treasure of the Temple half the length of France unaided? How large is this treasure? Has it grown much since last you saw it?"

Sir William shook his head. "Not at all, Commander. The Templar Treasure is not the Order's worldly wealth. Those are two different things. I saw the same four chests that were shipped out from the siege of Acre, and as closely as I could calculate, they contained the same bone-crunching weight they owned formerly."

St. Valéry looked directly at the younger knight and posed the question foremost in his mind. "What *do* they hold? Did you ever learn?"

Sir William smiled. "You know I am bound by oath to tell no one anything on that subject, Sir Charles. Even so, I know no more than you."

St. Valéry nodded. "Of course. And yet neither I nor my dear friend Arnold, God rest his soul, after our lifetimes of service, ever set eyes on the Treasure, whereas you have been entrusted with its safety twice now."

"Not quite, Admiral. I have *accompanied* the Treasure twice and seen the chests containing it on both occasions. But the responsibility for its safety on the first occasion lay with our late Master Tibauld Gaudin. His was the charge to bear it northward to safety from Acre to Sidon. I merely sailed with him."

"But this time the charge is yours. How *did* you transport it here?"

"Under heavy escort. I told you the Master had been planning ever since he first heard of this plot. He summoned me to Paris as soon as he received the first warning, and at the same time he began assembling a substantial force for the duty of protecting the Treasure."

St. Valéry sat forward intently. "Substantial? How many?"

"Five score, a hundred of our brotherhood, fully equipped and supplied: horses, armor, weapons, squires, grooms, smiths, everything."

"A hundred knights? Where did you find so many at one time?"

"In one place, you mean? We didn't. Forty of the hundred are knights, Admiral. The remaining three score are sergeants, and the force was summoned in secrecy from all across the country. Master de Molay sent out the word a month ago for volunteers to assemble immediately, but discreetly and in small numbers, at several gathering points, and from those points they made their way to the forest of Fontainebleau, where my brother Kenneth was waiting to marshal them. Tam and I joined Kenneth in the forest and recovered the Treasure, and once our expected men were all assembled, we led them here to the coast by routes that kept us hidden from hostile eyes."

"And the Treasure is safe now?"

"Completely, Admiral. Else I would not be here. It is safe, and my brother and his men have it secure."

"And if they are betrayed? Such things can happen."

Sir William Sinclair nodded. "True, they can. That is why we are here today with such appalling tidings. Treachery is bred of greed. But betrayal's barely possible in this case. A thief would have to know in advance where the Treasure had lain hidden, in which case it would have been gone when we arrived to dig it up. Failing that, he would have to know that we have it, that we recovered it from Fontainebleau, and that we would then go where we went to hide it again. We scarce knew that ourselves until the last possible moment."

"I see. And what will become of your hundred brethren should events come to pass as predicted tomorrow?"

"They will escape to fight another day."

"On my galleys." St. Valéry's voice was wry. "Sufficient of them to transport a hundred armed men and their mounts."

"Aye, and all their gear, grooms, and smiths, together with the Templar Treasure. Of course, Admiral. Those are the Master's specific instructions."

St. Valéry grunted, then grinned. "Of course. So, if we have to leave, we will take more than one treasure in our train ..."

"That is the truth, Sir Charles. But any of your vessels that we leave behind will quickly be put to his own uses by the King of France, and that, I think, would please none of us."

The admiral nodded, and then waggled the package he still held. "You know, had you come to me yesterday with this tale, I would have thought you as mad as you thought de Molay. But with the murder of my friend Arnold tonight, and the fact that someone sent assassins into this commandery, I believe your tale as told. And now I must read these documents."

"Not some*one*, Sir Charles. There's no question of identity here—no doubt concerning who is responsible. It was William de Nogaret himself who sent these people. Tam and I saw him talking with the Englishman Godwinson in Paris not two weeks ago."

"Then may God damn his black and grasping heart to Hell. But it makes no sense. Why would he do such a thing? He would have arrested de Thierry and me tomorrow anyway, if what you say is true."

Sir William returned to his chair. "True enough. But it makes grim and frightening sense to me when I consider the fact that La Rochelle is the strongest commandery in France, and it houses the fleet. And consider that no battle plan ever devised has gone unchanged after battle begins. Things go wrong. But if you and the preceptor had been killed tonight, what kind of chaos would have reigned here inside the Commandery? Discipline would have gone by the board, confusion and fear and speculation would have been rampant, and there would have been no organized resistance to tomorrow's coup."

"Aye, I take your point. Pardon me then, for a moment, while I read my orders."

For the next quarter of an hour the only sounds in the vast room were the roaring crackle of the fire and the occasional slither of paper as St. Valéry shifted the pages in his hands. Finally he sat up straight again and waved the papers in the air, looking at William Sinclair with a speculative expression on his face. "Do you know everything this contains?"

The younger man shook his head. "No, sir. The Master told me what he believed I needed to know, no more than that."

"Aye, well … you may learn more tomorrow, but let us hope that won't be necessary." He brandished the papers in his hand again. "In any case, my deputies must know of this, de Berenger and Montrichard. Guard!"

When the summoned guard stepped into the room, the admiral sent him to find the two deputies at once. As the man closed the doors behind him, St. Valéry hesitated and turned back to Sir William.

"What would you have done had I been killed tonight? Would you have delivered the Master's instructions to de Berenger?"

Sir William nodded. "Of course. And to the other man, Sir Arnold's deputy Montrichard. They would have assumed command immediately, and so the orders would have applied to them."

"You have been very tactful, Sir William, but it is clear that I am now your subordinate. Only a member of the Governing Council would be entrusted with the safety of the Treasure."

Sir William merely inclined his head in response to that.

St. Valéry pursed his lips slightly. "May I be curious, then, while we await the arrival of the others? Where do you intend to go when we leave here? Where will you take the Treasure for safety? Do you have orders from Master de Molay?"

"No, Sir Charles. At this moment, all I know is that we will go to sea, and I am still hoping against hope that this is all some kind of elaborate hoax." He held up his hands to indicate that he knew nothing more. "To sea. That is all I know. Master de Molay originally wished me to sail to England, to the court of Edward Plantagenet, but word reached us while I was in Paris that King Edward died several months ago, on his way to invade my homeland again. So that changed everything, since Edward's son is manifestly not to be trusted."

"The King of England is not to be trusted, even before he assumes the Crown? How so? And how can I know nothing of this? Am I so insulated, here in La Rochelle, that I know nothing of the outside world?" St. Valéry's voice betrayed genuine surprise.

Sir William looked directly at the older man and shrugged his wide shoulders. "The Order *is* your world, Admiral. You have had no time to waste on lesser things, and the nature of the new King of England is not something that would interest you at the best of times. The fellow is unnatural, sir. A pederast who would rather play the woman than the man. He flaunts his deviance openly in front of his barons, uncaring what they think, and he is notoriously indiscreet in matters of state. He parades his lovers shamelessly, showering them with gifts and privileges and bestowing rank upon them that they are not qualified to exercise. His barons have neither respect not tolerance for the man, and it is anticipated that he will not be long for this life unless he mends his ways. In the meantime, he is certainly of no value to us in this affair of ours."

"I see. Then be equally blunt about this, if you will: where *will* you go, should things come to pass as you predict? You must have some idea."

Sinclair straightened his shoulders and pushed himself up from his chair, drawing himself up to his full, imposing height. "To Scotland," he said, as though issuing a challenge.

A long silence followed his words as the admiral absorbed what he had said, weighing his words against those he had uttered mere moments earlier about England. Finally, St. Valéry exhaled loudly and exchanged an expressionless glance with Tam before turning his head towards Sir William.

"Scotland … Aye, indeed. We have a strong fraternity in Scotland." There was no discernible hesitancy or uncertainty in the older man's voice, and yet his words somehow conveyed both.

"Aye, we do," Sir William said, "and it has flourished these two hundred years. Our black and white baucent has been a common sight the length and breadth of the land, most recently engaged against the English Plantagenet on behalf of the people of Scotland. We will be welcome there."

"Aye, by our brethren in the Order, certainly. But what of this new King of theirs, this Robert … ?"

"Robert Bruce, King of Scots. I know him. He will not turn us away."

"You know him?" St. Valéry frowned. "How so, as a friend, or as a king?"

"Need there be a difference?"

The admiral's frown deepened in annoyance. "No, my lord Sinclair, there need not, but all too frequently there is. Kings are not ordinary men, and even I, immured in my ignorance, have heard that this new King of Scots is wild—rash and headstrong, and a sacrilegious murderer to boot, killing a man on the steps of God's own altar."

"Aye, Admiral, I know all that, and much of it, although not all of it, was as you say. But I know whereof I speak. The provocation was dire, and I doubt the Bruce was even aware of where he was at the time. I dare say the blow was struck and beyond recall before he even took note of his surroundings. Yet it was not a killing blow, and it was not Robert Bruce who killed the Comyn Lord of Badenoch. He stabbed him, certainly—struck him down with a dagger and then fled from the church, distraught at what had happened. But it was his men who, hearing him tell what he had done, rushed back inside and killed the Comyn. The killing was done, and there's no denying that, but I would hesitate to call the Bruce himself a murderer."

"You would? For the killing of a man on the steps of the altar? How can you say such a thing?"

Sir William cocked one eyebrow. "It was not I who said it, my lord Admiral. It was the Church in Scotland, in the person of Robert Wishart, the Bishop of Glasgow, with the full backing of William Lamberton, Bishop of St. Andrew's and Primate of the Realm, who absolved Robert Bruce of the taint of murder less than a week after the event and thereafter had him crowned King of Scots. The Bruce had few possessions of his own at the time, and clothing was the least of those. He was crowned King wearing Bishop Wishart's own ceremonial robes, lent to him by the Bishop himself for the occasion."

He paused to let that sink home. "I would submit that no churchman, even the most venal and corrupt, would dare to align himself so openly and publicly with a man he truly suspected of the crime of murder, in a church or anywhere else.

"I would remind you of your own words, Sir Charles," said Sir William as he crossed to sit in the armchair again. "Kings are not ordinary men … nor was this killing an ordinary matter. It was not a petty quarrel, a squabble that went wrong. It was a confrontation between two strong, proud, ambitious men, each of them jointly Lords Protector of the Realm of Scotland, each of whom believed the crown rightly belonged to him alone. Bitter, angry words led to sudden blows. One man left the chancel, and thereafter the other died.

"It was John Comyn's supporters, one of them Pope Clement himself, who called the outcome murder at the hands of Bruce. What, I wonder, would they have called it had it been Bruce who died on the altar steps? Would John Comyn, Lord of Badenoch and the Pope's favorite, now stand condemned? He would be King, certes, but would he be papally damned and excommunicate? Bear in mind, this is the same pope who now colludes to permit Philip Capet and de Nogaret to destroy our brotherhood. Was this pope, I wonder, less greedy and more honest last year than he is today?"

St. Valéry cleared his throat. "By your own admission, we do not really know if that is true or not, Sir William. The destruction of our brotherhood, I mean. It is merely what we have been told, and it may yet be proved false."

"Aye, well, we will know tomorrow, beyond doubt, but I know what I believe this night." Sir William stood up again suddenly, clapping his hands together decisively. "Robert Bruce is a true man, Sir Charles. He is young, I will grant, and he is rash and he tends to be hot-headed when provoked, which is not the greatest attribute a king may have. But he learns quickly and he never makes an error twice. Fundamentally, I trust the man and hold great hopes for him. But I firmly believe that we, our Order, may trust him. We have been strong in Scotland these two hundred years, but most recently we have been stronger than ever, in Scotland's cause and for the King himself against the English. The Bruce will acknowledge that and give us refuge."

St. Valéry grunted. "Does Jacques de Molay know you intend to go to Scotland?"

The Scots knight hesitated. "No, sir, he does not, although, to be truthful, I suspect he might anticipate my going there. But we did not speak of it, and the name of Scotland was never mentioned between us. Master de Molay left the choice of finding sanctuary to me and made no attempt to influence my judgment. It is my belief that he himself is not really convinced that the events we are preparing for here will actually take place. He is hoping the warnings that have come to us are false, but as a prudent warden, he has taken steps to avoid the worst of outcomes. In the event that tomorrow proves to be the day we have been warned against, he told me that God will make clear to me where I should go when the time is right, and he instructed me to require of you, as I have now done, that you hold yourself prepared, with all your fleet, to safeguard my flight."

"But … ? I hear a 'but' in your tone."

"Aye, you do. It is my own belief the Master had no wish to know my destination. In ignorance of that, I think he believes he could not divulge it under torture."

"Torture! Torture the Grand Master of the Order of the Temple? They would never dare commit such an outrage. The Pope would condemn them publicly."

Sir William's expression did not change. "The Pope, Sir Charles, will do whatever Philip Capet requires of him. Philip made him pope. He can unmake him just as quickly. And as for outrages and condemnation, de Nogaret already stands excommunicate for having kidnapped the last pope at King Philip's behest. The old pope died of that outrage, but de Nogaret does not seem to be unduly inconvenienced by the consequences."

They sat silent for a moment, and then Sir William spoke again.

"What will you do about the Englishman, Admiral? The assassin Godwinson."

"Do about him? He will be brought to justice, condemned for murder."

"When? And by whom, my lord? Come dawn, de Nogaret will set him free, and Godwinson will laugh as our own men file past him into his present cell. Little justice there, it seems to me."

The admiral turned a little paler. He sat blinking for a moment and then shook his head in bewilderment. "What would you have me do, then? Kill him out of hand? That would be murder."

"No, Sir Charles, I would merely remind you of your own words spoken earlier. As a member of the Governing Council, I hold higher rank than you. Thus the responsibility for such decisions is mine, not yours."

"And what will you do?"

"I will see justice done. And I will do it now, tonight. I should have done it earlier. Godwinson forfeited his life when he left Paris with this deed in mind, and to allow him to evade just punishment would be a travesty. Tam, gather our men who witnessed what occurred in here and bring them to the cells. I'll join you there."

Tam nodded and left without a word, leaving the two senior men alone.

"You really intend to do this, to kill the man?" St. Valéry's question was matter-of-fact.

"What option have I, Sir Charles? To let him live to boast about his triumph? You may wait here, if you so wish. No need for you to see this. We have sufficient witnesses to bear testimony to the man's crimes."

The admiral stood up and arranged his mantle carefully, then stepped forward to Sir William and did the same for the younger knight, adjusting the white garment so that it hung perfectly, the emblem of the Order pristine upon the left breast. He stepped back and examined his efforts critically, and then nodded, satisfied. "Good. And now I will bear witness with the rest of your tribunal. I owe it to Arnold's memory and to his lingering soul. Lead on, Sir William."

4

The judicial proceedings did not take long. Tam Sinclair and his sergeants were waiting at the entrance to the cells when Sir William and the admiral arrived, and Tam led the way into the gallery lined with individual cells, those on the left equipped with solid, iron-studded wooden doors with tiny inset grilles, and those on the right open cages, with thick iron bars on three sides and a solid stone wall at the rear. Godwinson was in one of the latter, sitting in deep shadow on the edge of a narrow wooden bunk and shackled hand and foot. His two guards sprang to attention and backed away as Sir William, St. Valéry, and their companions entered and then grouped together, looking into the prisoner's barred cage. The Englishman grinned at them and spat sullenly.

"Come to gloat, have you? Gloat away, then, and be damned to you. But don't take too long about it, for I won't be here much longer." He spoke in French but he was unmistakably English, his broad-voweled accent butchering the French words.

Sir William ignored the man after his first glance and looked about the space between the cells. It was a narrow, dark, windowless coffin of a place, with a high, peaked roof of red clay tiles over bare rafters, and it was filled with chill drafts that would, Sir William knew, keep it cold and dank even in the heat of summer. The walls were bare, uneven stone, chinked with plaster or dried mud, and the only furnishings were a long, narrow table of plain wood, three chairs, and a smoldering charcoal brazier set on a stone slab against the wall by one end of the table.

He crossed to the brazier and examined it, ignoring the awestruck silence of the two garrison guards. The charcoal had burned past its prime, and a hard, brittle crust of cinders covered the glowing ashes beneath. Behind him, Godwinson was still ranting, his raucous voice sounding more and more guttural as his diatribe grew more intense. Sir William picked up one of the iron pokers from its place by the fire basket and thrust it through the crust of clinker, breaking the carapace and sending up a shower of sparks. He stirred the embers hard, churning them into a sullen mass of flames, then left that poker in the fire and grasped the second one, forcing it into the burning embers beside its twin. That done, he hoisted up the guards' bucket of fresh charcoal, using both hands to tip it forward and fill the brazier with fresh fuel, and as he did so, Admiral St. Valéry stepped beside him.

"What are you doing, Sir William?"

"I am remaking the fire, Sir Charles. It is cold tonight, and this place is drafty. Can you not feel it?" He moved away, to the front of Godwinson's cell, where he crossed his arms over his chest, tucked in his chin, and then stood silently, staring at the raging man on the other side of the cage's bars.

It seemed to take a long time before Godwinson realized that his rage and scorn were making no impression on the tall, white-robed knight who was obviously the one in charge of this party, but eventually his ravings died away and he sneered contemptuously at Sir William, who gazed back at him stonily, his face betraying nothing of his thoughts. Then, just as the silence in the high, dark chamber approached the absolute, he stalked away again, towards the table.

"Bring him out here."

Godwinson fought strongly as they laid hands on him, but he was shackled and his struggles were useless against the six men who picked him up bodily and carried him out to where Sir William now sat at one end of the long table, his hands flat on the boards in front of him.

"Sit him there," the knight said, pointing to the chair at the table's other end. "Wrap his chains around the chair legs, lest he try to rise."

Once again, Godwinson was powerless to resist, and quickly accepted it as two sergeants knelt by his sides and looped his leg chains around the legs of his chair. As soon as they had finished, however, he spoke to Sir William, his heavy voice filled with disdain.

"Who are you, whoreson? I promise you—"

"Stifle him."

Tam had been standing by with a piece of filth-stained, wrinkled cloth in his hands, awaiting this command, and now he ripped the cloth in two, wadding one piece and forcing it into the Englishman's mouth before tying it in place with the other half.

William Sinclair sat forward, resting his weight on his elbows, his chin on his raised fists. "Now, Englishman, listen to me. That man there," he said, pointing to St. Valéry, "is the other man you came to kill tonight. Sir Charles de St. Valéry, Admiral of the Temple Fleet. You failed, failed even to wound him, and your master will not be pleased by that. But you succeeded in killing his oldest friend, the preceptor of this commandery, a man who was a hundred times more worthy of life than you have ever been. You murdered him, and every man here will bear witness to that. And you shot down two garrison guards, also brothers of the Temple. For any one of those, you deserve death, and were I your sole judge you would die here and now.

"For reasons of his own, however, Admiral St. Valéry does not wish me to kill you out of hand."

He was watching Godwinson closely and saw the man's eyes widen involuntarily as hope surged into him with the realization that he was not to die this night, for if he could survive the night, he knew he would walk free come the dawn. Sir William took grim satisfaction in stepping on that newborn hope before it could burgeon. He sat back in his chair and folded his arms across his breast again.

"I have fought men among the Turkish Sultan's Mamelukes who know more of honor than you do, Englishman. Heathens they may be, and beyond redemption, but at least they fight in defense and belief of their God and his false prophet. Your only inspiration is greed." He saw the assassin's eyes narrow down to slits.

"Do you really think de Nogaret expected you to survive this day's events? That would make you a fool, as well as a murderer. And do you think he will welcome you back, knowing you failed in what he set you to do? William de Nogaret is a hard man, Englishman. He will not raise a hand to help you now.

"Oh, I know ..." Sinclair held up one hand, palm outward. "I know he will be here tomorrow. At dawn. I know that." He saw consternation blossom in the Englishman's eyes, but he kept talking, spacing his words evenly and allowing each thing he said to register before he said more. "But how think you he will react when he discovers that the admiral yet lives, and that the fleet is at anchor offshore, out of his clutches? Will he be happy with you?

"Of course, you may tell him that I arrived here in time to thwart you, and that I was aware of the festering plot he has dreamed up with the Capetian King and had come to remove the fleet from their greasy grasp. But will he take the time to listen, Godwinson? Will he let you speak?

"If he does, then I would wish you to tell him that I, William Sinclair, Knight of the Temple and member of the Order's Inner Circle, have removed the fleet from France, and with it the fabled Templar's Treasure for which he and his malevolent master lust so avidly. I would wish you to tell him that from me, and I would also wish you joy of his reward for your faithful service."

Sir William stood up then, aware that Godwinson's eyes were very different now above the gag that stifled him, and tipped his chair forward so that its back rested against the table's end.

"Of course, that is only what I *would* wish, if I believed you would be able to tell him anything. Hear me now, assassin, for I am passing judgment on you, in my capacity as senior member of our noble Order and duly witnessed by these assembled here. You are thrice condemned for foul and cowardly murder, carried out under the concealment of the robes of this Order, which adds blasphemy to your crimes. At the request of Sir Charles de St. Valéry you may live on, but you will never thank us for that. You will never kill a man again, Godwinson, unless you choose to kill yourself. And you will never speak to anyone, ever, of what you did this day."

He turned to Tam. "Hold him steady. Now, two of you seize the manacle chains and pull his arms straight, towards me. Good. Now tie the slack around the back of this chair. Make the chains secure."

In moments, Godwinson was stretched face down along the table, incapable of struggling, his hands secured against the chair at one end, his feet restrained by the chair he was in. Sinclair's face remained expressionless as he turned to one of his veteran sergeants, pointing to the heavy battle-axe that hung as always from the man's belt and then extending his hand to receive it.

The sergeant fumbled at his belt and unclipped the weapon. Sinclair took it with a nod, testing its edge with the ball of his thumb. From the table, Godwinson began to moan, stifled by his gag and knowing what was coming. Sinclair pressed his lips together, and then intoned, "For the triple crime of murder you will lose the hands that killed. For the heinous sin of plotting those same murders, you will lose the tongue that accepted the task and thereby sealed your fate. So mote it be."

The two heavy, chopping blows from the razor-sharp axe silenced Godwinson's muffled screams.

"There are irons in the fire. Cauterize the stumps. Quickly. Now remove the gag." He laid the axe down and drew the dagger from his belt, then bent down to open the unconscious man's mouth and insert the point of his knife.

A moment later, he straightened up again, his face white, his mouth a lipless line. "Take him to the surgeons, as quickly as you may. And carry him face downward, lest he choke on his own blood." He dropped his dagger into the heart of the fire in the brazier, then wiped his bloody fingers on the cloth of the maimed man's gag.

"So mote it be," he said again, mouthing the Templars' ancient invocation, and then he turned and walked from the cell block.

5

"Sir William!"

Sir William stopped on the threshold of the Day Room. "I have summoned de Berenger and de Montrichard," said the admiral, hurrying towards him, "but I want to talk with you before they come. So if you will wait for me in the Day Room, I shall be but a moment."

St. Valéry vanished into another doorway, and before Sinclair even had time to settle into a chair by the fire in the Day Room, the admiral had returned, clutching a plain, shiny black bottle and a pair of small glass tumblers. He set down the glasses and poured two measures of liquid into them, measuring them with a squinting eye.

"Here, I want you to taste this … It is a wonderful elixir, but I have to keep it safely hidden, lest it tempt my brethren. God knows, I have been tempted by it myself on a few occasions, and Arnold, may God rest his noble soul, had a marked taste for it. Sit you down. Sit anywhere, but choose a soft chair. We have very few of those, but that one over there, I'm told, is very comfortable. Pull it up to the fire."

He picked up the brimming tumblers and brought them to Sinclair. "Here, drink. You will find it interesting."

Sir William, wordless, took the proffered glass and raised it to his lips, but at the first taste from it, he broke into a fit of coughing.

The admiral chuckled. "Aye. Careful now, don't spill it! It is a fiery potion, is it not? Made by the Benedictines in their abbey not far east of here. But persevere with it. The burning does not last, and I find that the essence is calming in times of severe stress. And as God is my judge, Sir William, I have seldom seen anyone more in need of calming than you are at this moment. You're wound tight as a windlass. Drink, drink more."

As Sinclair sipped again, more cautiously this time, the admiral drank from his own cup, watching him over the rim. The younger knight was deathly white, his cheeks drawn with strain, the lines about his mouth starkly evident. Clearly his ministration of justice had cost him dearly, and St. Valéry's heart went out to him. True leadership by example was never easy, the old man knew from a lifetime of experience, but at times such as this, the assumption of personal responsibility for demonstrating leadership could be cripplingly painful.

"And more, Sir William. Drink again. It does grow easier, I promise you."

Sinclair sipped again, more deeply this time, and closed his eyes, holding the sweet and fiery liquid in his mouth for a moment before allowing it to trickle down his throat. St. Valéry watched him and nodded slowly.

"Now, tell me, how do you feel?"

The eyes opened. "How do I feel? How should I feel? I have just maimed a man. I chopped off his hands and cut out his tongue with my own hands. How would you feel, Admiral, after such a glowing feat of arms? I feel soiled and befouled, as inhuman as the wretch I have just destroyed."

"You meted out justice, and in a most admirable fashion, my lord Sinclair. You have no reason to feel soiled in any way. Had you done nothing, the fellow would have walked away tomorrow, unscathed and laughing, as you so rightly said. Now he will have a lifetime to repent his sins."

"Repent? Hmm. Not that one, Admiral. I doubt he will repent of anything, save that he did not kill me when we first crossed swords."

"But he will never hold a sword again. Or a crossbow. Yet he will have his life."

"Perhaps. Or he may die of those wounds."

"Not as long as he is in the hands of our surgeon brothers. They are highly skilled."

"Aye, but tomorrow they will be arrested, and their skills may prove useless in protecting them."

That made the admiral thoughtful. "Sir William, in all that you have told me you have said not a word about the garrison here, about what you wish them to do."

"I am aware of that. But you read the Master's instructions, Sir Charles. They must do nothing but submit to whatever tomorrow brings. Resistance would bring chaos and would give de Nogaret free rein to wreak havoc. He would claim insurrection and rebellion, and heads would roll. Your garrison will surrender upon demand. They will be taken into custody, but little else will happen to them. Their main purpose will be to present a semblance of normality at first, thereby providing us with time to make our way to sea without hindrance. And their victory will lie in the salvation of the fleet and our Treasure, although they will not know about the latter." He sipped again at his drink. "This brew is excellent. What is it called?"

The admiral shrugged. "It has no name that I know of. It is merely the drink developed by the Benedictines, distilled from wine and flavored with pungent and pleasant-tasting herbs and spices. May I ask you a question that is personal, Sir William?"

"Aye, ask away." Sinclair's face was regaining some of its color and the lines around his mouth were less evident than they had been a short time earlier.

St. Valéry cleared his throat, feeling the taste of the liquor on the back of his tongue. "It is on this matter of Scotland. How long has it been since you were last there?"

Sinclair emptied his cup, then placed it on the floor and stood up. He leaned his ever-present sword against the back of his chair, then cupped his hands over his face, dragging his fingertips down his cheeks as though wiping away fatigue. "Too long, I fear, Admiral.

I have not set foot in Scotland these twelve years and more. Why do you ask?"

"I expected your answer must be something of that nature, and yet you are remarkably aware of what is happening there, and your tidings are recent. How does that come about?"

"I have a sister there, Admiral. A younger sister, Margaret, who insists, in spite of not knowing her elder brother well, upon keeping him informed of all that is happening to his family. She sees it as her God-given duty to instruct me in the fortunes of all my clan, and I have been grateful for it these past five years, for she is clever and witty, her letters easy to read and filled with welcome and humorous tales of life at home."

"I see. And how do you receive these letters?"

"Through our Order. She has them sent regularly from the Temple in Edinburgh to the Temple here in Paris. I received the latest bundle, eleven letters, when Master de Molay summoned me to Paris to instruct me in this current matter. The newest of them was less than three months old."

"And this is your source of knowledge about the King of Scots? Is your sister privy to such matters?"

"Aye, she is, to a degree. In some of the letters, Peggy—we call her Peggy—spoke of King Robert and his troubles, and how they were affecting her and Edward. That is how I know of the events and the rumors surrounding the King's accession to the throne last year."

"Is this Edward, then, your brother?"

"No, Admiral, he is my good-brother, wed to my sister. His name is Edward Randolph. *Sir* Edward Randolph."

St. Valéry raised his chin, startled. "Sir Edward *Randolph*? Is he kin in any way to Sir Thomas Randolph?"

"Aye. His brother."

"Good God! Then your ... your sister ..."

"My sister is Lady Margaret Randolph. What of her?"

"She must then be a sister by marriage to Lady Jessica Randolph."

Sinclair shrugged. "I know of no Lady Jessica Randolph. Peggy has never mentioned the name. But then, I don't know Sir Edward, either. His elder brother Tom and I were boyhood friends—childhood friends would be more accurate—and the second brother, James, was a mere tad then, no more than seven or eight. Edward was born after I left home, so I suppose there may also have been a sister or two I never met."

"No, you would not have met Lady Jessica, nor might your sister, I suspect, although each of them would certainly know of the other." St. Valéry had spoken quietly and was frowning strangely. "The Lady Jessica is, as you say, much younger, and she seldom visits Scotland. She is a widow who has lived much of her life here in France and then in England, where her husband was an agent of King Philip. His name was Etienne de St. Valéry—Baron Etienne de St. Valéry. He was my younger brother. The Lady Jessica is *la baronne* Jessica de St. Valéry. Thus it would seem we are related through some complexity of marriages, you and I."

Sir William blinked in surprise, not knowing how to respond to this. "Then I rejoice in calling you cousin, Admiral. It sometimes seems God placed us in a tiny world, for all its size. So I will be unlikely to encounter this Lady Jessica in Scotland?"

"No. She is here."

"What do you mean, sir, she is here?"

"What I said. Lady Jessica Randolph is here."

"Here in France?"

"Here in La Rochelle, in this commandery, and she is in grave peril. She has claimed sanctuary from William de Nogaret. Tam Sinclair saved her life this day."

Seeing the utter incomprehension on his companion's face, St. Valéry nodded. "Aye, you heard me rightly. The woman Tam brought through the city gates this afternoon is my brother's wife ... My brother's widow. She has been asleep upstairs since just before you arrived. She had been on the road, hunted, for days, and she was exhausted. I decided that she would be better off asleep than awake this night. But everything has changed since then, and I wanted to tell you that she was here, and why. What is the hour?"

Sinclair shrugged. "Nigh on midnight by now, I'd think."

"Aye, it must be. And thus today has been the first time in the history of this preceptory that Vespers has gone unsung beneath its roof. As I said, this news you brought us has changed everything. And Lady Jessica has no idea of it."

"Why should she have any idea of it, Admiral? She is a woman, and we are speaking of Temple matters. Since when has any of that had significance for any woman?"

The admiral glanced at him sharply, as though on the point of rebuking him. "That particular aspect of our situation has no relevance for her, obviously, but there are other aspects of our circumstances here that do concern her, and directly so. She has placed her trust, her mission, and her very self in our hands, in the hands of the Temple, which has been protecting her interests for a long time now." He glanced towards the door to the passageway outside, and the gesture reminded Sinclair that the two deputies would soon be coming to join them.

The admiral tilted his cup to drain the last precious drops, then peered into it through narrowed eyes, licking his lips fastidiously before he continued. "Jessica's is a long story, but not directly concerned with our current plight, although there is some overlap ..." Again he glanced at the door, then turned back, dismissing for a second time whatever had sprung into his mind. "She must be rested now. She has been sleeping for hours. Would you like another small dram before de Berenger and Montrichard come?"

"Aye, I would."

"Excellent. And so would I. But just a small one. The beverage, delicious though it is, is potent beyond belief." He returned to the table and poured a small amount more of the amber liquid into each of their cups. Then he sealed the bottle carefully before returning and touching his cup to Sinclair's. "Since I first discovered this potion, Sir William, I have come to appreciate that we no longer tip in libation from our cups. That would truly be a waste of Heaven's nectar. Let us drink to tomorrow and damnation to de Nogaret."

"Gladly. Damnation to de Nogaret. But tell me more about your good-sister, for her situation intrigues me. Why is she here at all, and why is de Nogaret hunting her? Did you not say she lives in England?"

"She did. And as her story involves William de Nogaret, if this warning you have brought to us proves valid, her life will be in grave danger, for that devil will put her to the torture to gain what he is after."

Sinclair had no illusions about de Nogaret's malevolence. "He will indeed, if he catches her. No doubt of that. But what *is* he after? And why is she even here in France if she is on de Nogaret's black list?"

"Money, Sir William. The King's minister smells money. What else ever motivates that man, other than hatred?" St. Valéry sighed. "I told you my brother Etienne was an agent of the King, sent to live in England to administer Philip's affairs there at the English court of Edward Plantagenet." He sat down in the nearest chair and leaned back, his fingers laced over his midriff. "He found opportunities for himself, there in England, opportunities for trade, all of them legitimate and of the kind he judged would hold no interest for his master. And on an early return visit to France, he traveled south into the Languedoc before returning to England, specifically, as I have discovered, to set up a trading venture there with a man whom he had befriended years earlier, a Jewish merchant in the coastal town of Béziers, called Yeshua Bar Simeon.

"Etienne said nothing of this to anyone at the time, not even to us, his own family, preferring, as he ever did, to keep his own affairs secret and safely shielded from the eyes of others. He then went back to England, leaving the running of their activities in the hands of this Bar Simeon, and their venture prospered beyond belief, it would appear, for almost twenty years, until Bar Simeon fell ill two years ago. He was very old by then, a full score and more years older than Etienne. He knew that he was dying, and the nature of his agreement with my brother forbade him from delegating the work or passing it on to anyone else to execute.

"And so the old man sold off all their holdings everywhere and deposited the entire proceeds with our brethren, in the preceptory at Marseille. The preceptor there at the time, a fine man called Theodoric de Champagne, issued all the proper recordings of the transaction, but instead of taking them into his own possession, Yeshua Bar Simeon requested that the documents—the principal one being a letter of credit to be drawn on the Preceptory of Marseille—be sent directly to Etienne in London."

St. Valéry set his tumbler down carefully beside him on the floor and then rose from his chair and began to pace the room, his hands now clasped at his back and his head bent to splay his long, forked beard against his chest. "Unfortunately, that was a request that could not be met, because it contravened our rules … the rules of our system."

He stopped pacing and glanced sideways at Sir William. "You are a man of action, Sir William, a knight and a member of the Governing Council, but I suspect you may have had little experience in the commercial side of our undertakings, and so I know not if you are familiar with the precise way in which these things work." He stopped, waiting for Sinclair to respond, and when the other man shook his head and waved for him to continue, he resumed his pacing, holding one hand still behind his back and gesturing with the other to emphasize the points he was making.

"Above all else, and I know you are aware of this, it is fundamentally simple. A man facing a long and dangerous journey brings his money to whatever Temple or commandery is closest to him. We take the specie into custody and issue him with a document, a formal letter of credit attesting to the amount of the deposit he has made, and he then carries that on his person and presents it to the nearest Templar presence when he arrives at his destination. In the meantime, using our own fleet as a direct courier, we have supplied a record of the transaction, including an enciphered code word for recognition, to whatever preceptory the man has decided to use at his journey's end.

"Once there, our traveler presents his *bona fides* and proves his identity—a necessary precaution against fraud—and provides the code word, upon which he receives the full value of his letter of credit, minus a small administrative fee. It works very well as a system, but it has limitations. The man designated in the letter of credit must carry it and present himself in person. The letter of credit cannot be transferable to anyone else—no deputies, no assignees— for if that were possible, the system would break down, with no one truly able to verify anyone's right to claim the monies involved.

"Thus, in this particular case, an impasse had been reached. Bar Simeon knew he was dying. He suffered a virulent attack of some kind, there in the preceptory, and was convinced he would last no more than a few days. He told de Champagne he had been ill for months, growing worse all the time, and did not expect to live to see his home again, and from the look of him, and the convulsions he had witnessed for himself, de Champagne knew it was the truth. Thus it would be useless for the old man to have the letter issued in his own name, for with his death the unclaimed deposit would be lost forever, declared forfeit and absorbed into our system. And for the same reason, he was in no condition to withdraw his funds again from Marseille and take them away with him. That left Theodoric in a moral quandary."

"Aye, it would. So what did he do?"

St. Valéry had stopped pacing and now stood staring into the fire basket. "He prayed. And then he made a decision that ignored the rules that were impeding him, in this instance, from doing what he knew to be morally correct …

"Old Bar Simeon had told him the entire story, probably in desperation, once he realized that he had placed himself unwittingly in a cleft stick, so de Champagne knew that the monies belonged rightly and legally to my brother Etienne. He therefore acted upon his own authority, defying all our rules, and wrote the letter of credit in Etienne's name. He then sent the documents to me under seal, accompanied by a letter explaining the situation and informing me that Bar Simeon had assured him that Etienne would know the code word involved, because it had been a password between the two of them since their first collaboration. De Champagne and I have known each other for many years and he trusted me to respect his confidence. Yeshua Bar Simeon was dead by then, of course. He died within two days of completing the transaction."

"Hmm." Sir William had been sitting forward in his chair, listening closely, and now he was impatient to hear more. "And what did you do?"

"Nothing at first. I was caught unprepared, never having known about, or even suspected, Etienne's venture with the Jew, whom he evidently—and with good reason, it transpired—held in the highest esteem. But once I had thought about it for a time, I conferred with my friend and colleague here, Sir Arnold de Thierry, as the Preceptor of La Rochelle, because although I thought I knew what must be done, it seemed an arrogant and prideful course for me to steer, so far outside the confines of our rules. But Arnold believed I would be doing the right thing, and he encouraged me to proceed."

"So you sent the letter to your brother in England."

"No. That I could not do. That would have been flagrant defiance of our law. I held it in trust for him, here, where he must collect it in person. But I wrote to him in England, informing him that I had the documents in my possession.

"It must have been around that point that de Nogaret got wind of it, although we did not know that at the time. But until that transaction took place, and the documents were sent to me, no one, including myself and the rest of our family, had ever known that Bar Simeon and Etienne were connected in any way. None of us had even been aware of Bar Simeon's existence. So the betrayal must have come from within our own ranks—from one of our brethren in Marseille, a corrupt knight or a sergeant in the pay of de Nogaret. It hardly seems believable, and it galls me more than I can say, but I can find no other explanation. But be that as it may, the word was out—de Nogaret was informed, and the reputation of our Order was besmirched."

"How do you know the information was betrayed from Marseille? The spy might have been quartered here and read your letter before you ever sent it."

"Not possible, Sir William, because I wrote and sealed the letter myself, at my own desk, and sent it off the same day aboard one of our galleys headed directly for London. And by the time it arrived in England my brother had already sailed for France on an urgent summons from the King. He had been preparing to come back anyway, and to bring the Lady Jessica with him, to visit our mother, who loves her dearly, so he merely advanced his plans and left as soon as he received the King's summons. Fortunately for the Lady Jessica, and thanks to the urgency of his recall, he left her on the coast on making landfall, in the care of the Temple at Le Havre, and went directly to Paris on his own. He was arrested upon his arrival, we learned later, and thrown into prison, where he was tortured at great length and eventually died."

Sir William sat silent, mulling over what he had been told, and then he slumped backwards, chin in hand, his elbow propped on the arm of his chair. "So why has de Nogaret not been beating down our doors? If they put your brother to the torture for an extended time, he must have told them everything he knew."

"Aye, true, but he knew nothing … at least nothing that de Nogaret could use. Etienne left England before my letter arrived there. He had not received it and did not even know that Bar Simeon had been sick, or that he was dead. He certainly did not know that all his assets had been sold and the proceeds lodged with us. All he could tell the torturers was what he knew up to the time before the old man fell sick. De Nogaret had blundered badly; he had moved too soon. He knew the funds were in our hands, because of the report he had received from his spy among us, but he was powerless to do anything about that without the letter of entitlement, and he did not know where that was. Thanks be to God in His wisdom, our laws are clear on such things. The letter of credit goes to the depositor and no copies are made of it. The Temple holds the funds in trust, and no king or king's henchman holds jurisdiction over our Order. It would never have occurred to de Nogaret that one of our preceptors might contravene the laws of our system and do what de Champagne actually did in sending the documents to me.

"And so he assumed the obvious: that the letter still existed and that Bar Simeon had passed it for safekeeping to another of his race."

"A Jew, you mean. Wait you now, wait just a minute." Sinclair sat frowning, his thoughts tumbling over each other. "When did all this occur?"

"More than a year ago and probably closer to two."

"Before the purge."

"Immediately before it. The plans for that event must have been well in hand already, for it was a massive operation."

"Aye, it was, and there is not a single Jew left alive in France today to denounce it, even if anyone would listen. It was seen as right and fitting that the confiscated Jewish money—the riches of the Christ-killers—should enrich the French treasury."

"You sound as if you disagree with that."

"I do. Are you surprised, knowing the roots of our own ancient brotherhood in Sion? I have no truck with anti-Jewish hatred. I find it despicable and demeaning, involving willful denial of the fact that Jesus himself was Jew."

"True, he was." St. Valéry sat down again and retrieved his tumbler from beside his chair. "But none of the Jews in France— apart from Yeshua Bar Simeon, of course—had anything to do with Etienne's money. Only we, the Temple, knew anything of that ..." He sipped at his drink. "Has it occurred to you that we might arguably be considered usurers?"

Sinclair eyed the admiral askance. "No, because we are no such thing. We levy a small fee to cover the costs of doing what we do, safeguarding and transferring funds, but that is far from usury."

"Aye, that is what we claim, but is it true? So much of us is little known, even among ourselves, that I fear much truth might have been lost since first the Temple was conceived in Outremer. Can you, for example, cite me the true meaning of the Order's first medallion, the one with two knights mounted on a single horse?"

"*Sigillum Militum Christi*? It merely represents the fact that in the Order's earliest days the knights were so impoverished that two men would often have to share one horse."

St. Valéry's lips twisted with disdain. "Again, that is what is said. I choose to doubt it. Think about it, Sir William. The original nine members of Hugh de Payens's cadre were all members of the Order of Sion—the Order of Rebirth in Sion, as it was then known. After their discovery in the Temple ruins, their numbers swelled and the Temple was born, full of Christian fire and zealotry and underpinned with bigotry and bloodthirsty passion. It pleases me to believe that the first symbol they adopted—the two-man medallion—was an irony, developed, I tend to think, by de Payens himself, the founder of the Temple Order. To me, it depicts the fundamental duality of the transformed organization—not two men on one horse, but two men within each of the founding knights, the first of them the knight of the Temple Mount, the other the far more ancient Brother of Sion. That may be nonsense, born of my own solitude and too much thought, but I take comfort from it."

His listener nodded slowly. "That would never have occurred to me," he said eventually, his voice filled with admiration. "Not if I lived to be a hundred years old. But having heard it from your mouth, I believe it might be true." He smiled, then stooped to pick up his own tumbler, draining it and savoring its fiery potency for long moments, and when he spoke again his voice was lower than it had been. "We never really learn much of anything, do we? Most of us cannot wait to forget all that we know. But what were we talking about before that?"

"About the Jewish purge, how well it succeeded."

"Ah yes." He hefted the empty glass in his cupped hand. "Those Benedictine monks must deal in magic. I have never had the likes of this before … my head is swimming." He waved his hand, dismissing that topic. "And that was nigh on two years ago. What happened to the Baroness at that time?"

"Her people saved her."

"What people, and how?"

"She and Etienne traveled at all times with a bodyguard of Scots, assigned to them by Lord Thomas Randolph himself. They were as loyal as wolfhounds, and as savage. Etienne took half of them with him when he went to Paris. They were with him when he was arrested and were cut down by the King's Guard when they tried to intervene. But they trusted no one and had posted a rear guard outside the gates to keep watch. The watchers saw what happened and returned directly to Le Havre, where they commandeered a ship and took their lady off to safety. To her home in Scotland, though, not in England. As I say, they trusted no one, and Edward of England had been waging his war against the Scots for years, so the Baroness's bodyguard chose to return her to her home and not to risk the goodwill of the English. I knew nothing of any of this at the time.

"Eventually, the letter I had sent to Etienne was forwarded to the Temple in Edinburgh from the Temple in London, but by then a good six months had elapsed. And then, completely unexpectedly, Lady Jessica sailed into La Rochelle, just over a month ago, to reclaim the treasure we held in trust for her, as my brother's widow."

"It must be a deal of money." Sinclair's tone was ironic, but St. Valéry nodded.

"It is. Six large chests of gold, in bars and coin, and five more of silver, bars and coin. Sufficient to ransom a king ... or to support one in a time of desperate need ...

"The Lady Jessica is quite open about her intentions. She intends to give the gold to Robert Bruce, your King of Scots. That is her absolute right, of course, but it entailed another problem that I had not foreseen. I required a password to release the money properly, and only Etienne could have known what that might have been. And so I sent another letter to Theodoric de Champagne in Marseille, explaining my dilemma and requesting the word from him, since he had the only duplicate. He sent it without commentary or demur, having been instrumental in launching this entire adventure, but in the interim the Lady Jessica decided that while waiting, she would visit my mother in Tours. My brother's widow is a strong-willed woman and was convinced there would be no danger entailed, provided she went alone with only the smallest escort for protection."

"And?"

"She was denounced and betrayed. A steward in my mother's household was in the pay of de Nogaret. He sent off a messenger to Paris, but then was foolish and arrogant enough to demand that the Lady Jessica stay where she was when she prepared to leave. My youngest brother, Gilbert, killed the man and fled, leaving a trail and allowing Lady Jessica to make her escape." St. Valéry paused, then continued in a level voice. "We have not heard from Gilbert since he disappeared, but we hope he is still alive. In the meantime, the Lady Jessica has been hunted all over France, and had it not been for your kinsman Tam Sinclair and his assistance today, she would have been captured trying to enter La Rochelle. The three men you saw killed were with her. She had hired them to smuggle her into the city, but they panicked when the guards began to check their handcart a second time, for they knew they were discovered."

"So now you wish me to escort this lady back to Scotland."

St. Valéry looked straight at Sinclair. "I do, but not alone. I will be coming with you, bear in mind. And with her you will accompany and safeguard the treasure for the King of Scots. It is my good-sister's, and it is of incalculable value, and if it remains here, de Nogaret will seize it and he will have won a sizable victory even should he fail in all else." He hesitated. "It is already loaded aboard my galley, along with a lesser treasure of our own."

"A lesser treasure? May I ask what that is?"

"Aye, there is nothing secret about it. It is our own reserve of specie, gold and silver bars and coin, stored against redemption of letters of credit. I cannot leave that behind for de Nogaret, either, for it would be the first thing he seized in his master's name, and Philip Capet already has more than enough of the Temple's funds."

"Of course, I had forgotten the funds each commandery holds in trust. How much is there?"

"Not as much as in the Baroness's treasure, but far too much to leave behind. Six large chests, containing twelve thousand gold bezants."

Will whistled. "We will be the most treasure-laden fleet on the seas."

"Aye, we will indeed … provided, of course, that events tomorrow fit with your warning."

"Aye, well they will, my lord Admiral. This atrocity with God-winson has convinced me of that."

"I agree with you. But I am beginning to wonder what is detaining de Berenger and Montrichard. Is that empty? Good. Give it to me, then, and I'll hide it from sight, along with the bottle."

No sooner had St. Valéry moved to do so than there was a knock at the door, and a young monk admitted the admiral's two deputies. The admiral bade them welcome and then instructed the young monk to go upstairs and awaken his female guest, bidding him to say nothing of the events that had occurred while she slept, and to ask the lady to be good enough to join him as soon as she could make ready.

Behind him, Sir William stared straight ahead into the fire, his head spinning strangely, his thoughts dominated by the image of the wide-eyed woman at the city gates.

THE DEVIL'S WORK

1

Jessie Randolph came awake instantly, and her heart began to race with fear the moment she realized she had no idea where she was. Wherever it was, it was cold and stygian black, not a glimmer of light to dispel the darkness or cast the faintest shadow, and the surface she was lying on was rock hard. Her head was raised, because her neck was uncomfortably angled, so she knew there was a pillow of some kind there, but it, too, was rigid, unyielding.

I'm on the floor. In a dungeon. They found me. De Nogaret's men.

Fighting down the panic, clenching her teeth against the overpowering urge to scream, she reached out cautiously on both sides of her and almost sobbed with relief to discover, first, that there were no manacles about her wrists, no chains, and then the rough fabric of a pallet beneath her hands. She reached farther and found the edges of a narrow cot.

Where am I?

And then there came a knocking at a door very close to her, and she knew that was what had awakened her. Still she lay rigid, not knowing what to expect, and felt the fear that filled her settling into the pit of her stomach, icy and heavy as a ball of lead.

"My lady? Are you awake, my lady?"

The questioning voice was soft but urgent, as though its owner feared to make too much noise. It did not sound the least bit threatening. Her hands touched her clothing, exploring, feeling her body's warmth beneath the garments.

I still have my clothes, and there's no pain anywhere.

"My lady?" Another knock, louder this time. Jessie drew a deep breath and tried to keep her voice steady.

"I am here. What is it?"

"Admiral St. Valéry requests that you join him downstairs. Immediately, my lady, if it pleases you."

Charles! Of course, I'm in the commandery at La Rochelle.

The knowledge washed over her instantly, banishing all her terror, and she pushed herself upright, swinging her feet over the edge of the cot to the stone floor and thrilling to the shocking coldness of the surface against her soles. So great was her relief from fear that she felt like throwing open the door and kissing the man outside. She was in La Rochelle! Safe!

She felt herself grinning as she imagined the look on the face of the fellow outside if she *had* thrown open the door and kissed him. He must be a monk. He might have dropped dead at her feet. She tried to swallow her euphoria and to keep her voice calm as she answered, "My thanks. Tell the admiral I shall be there directly."

"I shall, my lady." There was a line of light at the bottom of the unseen door, and as the man turned to leave it was blotted out.

"Wait! Please, wait. Stay where you are." She hurried to the door, watching the line of brightening light for guidance and fumbling for the handle. When she found it she stopped, ran her hands rapidly over her bodice and shook out her skirts, making sure she was decently covered before pulling open the heavy door.

The man outside was young, his tonsured scalp gleaming even in the dimness of the torch-lit passageway. He wore the brown surcoat of a Templar sergeant, and he stood peering at her, clutching a fat wax candle in a sconce. As he saw her, his eyes widened, and she realized her hair must be in disarray. The poor fellow probably saw few women in his life and here he was confronted by one with her hair in what must have seemed like scandalously intimate disrepair. She held out her hand to him.

"Forgive me if I startled you, Brother, but will you leave me that light? There is no light in my chamber and I must make myself presentable before I meet with my brother."

The earnest young man stepped forward, holding out his candle. "Of course, my lady. Is one light enough? I can bring more if you have need of them."

"God bless you, Brother. Yes, if it please you. One can never have too much of light. Bring as many as you can, and you will have earned great gratitude."

The young man bobbed his head and hurried away, and Jessie went back into her chamber, looking about her now that she could see. The room was tiny, containing nothing more than the narrow cot on which she had slept, a wooden crucifix on the wall beneath a tiny slit of a window, and a prie-dieu directly beneath it. She moved to the cot and bent to press her fingers into it. It did not yield, and the pillow at its head was a shaped block of wood covered with sailcloth.

God! I thought I was in a dungeon, but it is a monk's cell. Of course it is. But there is little difference between the two. Yet I was glad enough of it when I arrived, I remember. These men have no comforts as we ordinary mortals know such things. Their lives consist of prayer and more prayer, hardship and privation and sacrifice. And fighting, from time to time. Oh, dear God, what must I look like? And no mirrors in this place. Not even a table. Where is my bag?

She found it where she had dropped it behind the cot, and soon she was rummaging deep within it, aided only slightly by the single candle's light. She found the small leather satchel that was her most important possession and pulled it out, then loosened the drawstring and tipped the contents onto the top of the narrow bed: hairbrush, combs, a folded chamois square containing hairnets, another, bulkier, containing small solid articles that knocked against one another, and a soft square of woolen cloth that held a hand-sized rectangular mirror of smoothly polished silver. She used the mirror first, polishing it gently with its cloth before holding it up to examine her face and hair by the light of the candle in her other hand, and her mouth twisted as she saw what several days without her maid could do to her. But then she set the mirror and the candle down on the bed's hard surface and set to work to repair the ravages she had counted so swiftly.

She reached into her piled hair with both hands, finding and removing the pins placed there to hold her thick locks in check, and then, when her questing fingers told her there were no more to be found, she bent her head and shook out her heavy tresses, combing them with her fingers and fluffing them, searching for knots and tangles. She found none that were not swiftly manageable and she immediately took up her hairbrush, drawing it in long, smooth sweeps to straighten her hair from her crown to her waist, holding individual hanks in one hand while she tugged the bristles through the rebellious end clumps, grinding her teeth impatiently and attacking remorselessly whenever she encountered a stubborn knot.

She had eradicated all the tangles and was brushing smoothly by the time the young monk knocked again. She opened the door quickly and beckoned for him to enter, aware of the automatic way his eyes fastened on her unbound hair. He was carrying an armload of short, fat candles in the crook of his elbow and a freshly lit one in his free hand. He stepped inside the chamber door and stopped, his eyes roaming around the tiny room, looking for someplace to deposit his burden. Jessie waved an arm to indicate the space in which they stood.

"There is no room for anything in here. Is there by chance a larger room nearby? One with a table?"

The young guard blinked at her, his eyes vacant in thought, and then he nodded. "Brother Preceptor's cell is larger, my lady, and it has a table. And a chair."

She waited, but he said no more, so she prompted him. "And is it nearby? Do you think I might use it for a short time?"

He frowned slightly, clearly not knowing what to make of her request, and so she prodded him again.

"I will not take long. And you did say my good-brother asked that I join him quickly, did you not?"

"Aye, my lady."

"Well then, the quicker I can make myself presentable, the quicker I can meet him. Where is the Brother Preceptor's cell?"

"This way, my lady." He stepped out into the passageway and waited while she bundled up the contents of her little satchel and replaced them to take with her. When she was ready, he led her along the passageway to the left, where he stopped outside a door that stood ajar. "This is it, my lady."

She held her candle high, peering around the preceptor's cell. It was just as Spartan as the one she had left, and barely larger, no more than one third again as long, but it had two small tables ranged against the end wall, opposite the foot of the narrow bed. One of them was only large enough to hold the wash bowl and tall ewer that stood on it, but the other was larger, with an elaborate little ink horn and a matching horn cup containing several goose quills placed neatly on one side, and a plain wooden chair set in front of it.

"Perfect," Jessie said, crossing quickly to the table with the wash bowl. "Oh, it's empty." She turned back to the monk, who had set down his own candle and was carefully placing the six fresh ones he had brought side by side, upright, on the table's surface. "Would it be possible for you to find me some water, Brother, and a towel? I would dearly love to wash my face."

The man was evidently growing accustomed to her requests, for he simply nodded this time and reached over to pick up the ewer. He hesitated.

"I will have to go to the kitchens for the water, my lady. Would you like me to have it heated for you?"

"I would mention your name in my prayers for a month if you could do that for me."

"Thank you, my lady. It is Giles. I will return directly."

As the door closed behind him, Jessie used her candle to light the others he had brought, and when they were all burning she ranged them along the back of the table before sitting down and spreading the contents of her little bag across the tabletop. She peered at herself again in the small mirror, tilting its shining surface this way and that to take full advantage of the increased brightness, and then she propped it against one of the candles and used her brush to part her hair carefully down the center of her scalp and pull it forward to hang in front of her. That done, she began to braid, her fingers moving quickly and with the confidence of years of practice. When she had completed the second braid, she checked them with the aid of the mirror and then rolled each one up in a flat coil, fastening it in place with long hairpins she thrust through the coiled braids, and she finally secured the entire mass to the sides of her head with long, curved, and intricately carved combs of tortoiseshell. She shook her head tentatively, watching in the small mirror, and then again more firmly. Satisfied when nothing moved, she then covered the entire mass with a delicate net of gold wire studded with tiny beads of amber, and pinned the net into place with four more small hairpins. Her next examination in the mirror was highly critical, but she could find nothing wrong. Not a single stray wisp of hair marred her work.

Now she stood up and began the almost impossible task of checking the appearance of her clothing. She had slept in her gown and accepted that there was nothing she could do about the wrinkles in the fabric, so she set about looking for stains and marks, scrubbing at the material with her hairbrush whenever she found anything she thought might be improved, and while she was doing that Brother Giles reappeared, carrying a pitcher of steaming water wrapped in a towel. He was accompanied this time by a second brother, this one wearing a cook's apron and carrying a second, similar burden, the rolled towel held under one arm.

"I brought both hot and cold, my lady, which will permit you to mix the waters to your pleasure."

"God bless you, Brother Giles, and you, Brother Cook. And two towels. And even soap! You have saved my life and my sanity between you."

Both men beamed with pleasure, but neither one made any move to leave, and Jessie smiled at them. "Now I require but two more things of you, Brother Giles: a few moments of privacy in which to bathe my hands and face, and then the pleasure of your company as I go to find my husband's noble brother, for I confess I have no slightest notion of where to find the admiral. Will you wait for me and attend me?"

"Most certainly, my lady." Brother Giles looked at his companion and jerked his head towards the door, and both men left the room, closing the door behind them.

Jessie poured hot water into the bowl and then splashed in a little of the cold. She soaked one of the towels and rubbed some of the harsh, lye-scented soap into it, and wrung it out again before washing her face, hands, and arms with it, reveling in the clean, tingling sensation produced by the hot, astringently soapy water and the feel of the heated cloth against her skin. She dried herself with the second towel, then hesitated, and quickly undid the bindings of her bodice, pulling the laces wide and shrugging out of the garment so that it hung about her waist. The tips of her breasts tingled pleasurably as she wiped them with the hot, soapy towel, and a rash of goose bumps sprang up along her arms as the cloth brushed her nipples. She reminded herself where she was then, and that her brother-in-law was waiting for her. She wrung out the soap and wrapped the hot towel about her neck, sighing as she reached up to knead her nape beneath the tightly bound mass of her hair. She stood there for a few seconds, her head tilted back and her eyes closed in pleasure.

But then she reminded herself a second time of where she was, half smiling at the impropriety of being half-naked in a monk's cell, and quickly dried herself and shrugged into her clothes, tightening the laces carefully and decorously. From her satchel she selected a small round, flat black box, and removed a short, thick piece of twig with frayed and shredded ends that lay on a bed of whitish-gray powder. She sucked on the frayed end, wetting it with saliva, then dipped it into the powder and used it to scrub her teeth and gums. She rinsed her mouth with a cupped palm of water from the cold jug and spat into the bowl, then rubbed her tongue over her teeth, dislodging the gritty residue before rinsing and spitting again. That done, she sat down one last time to peer into the mirror.

I look like death. No color at all. God, Marie, where are you when I need your skills? You're safe, I pray, but you're not here, so I must serve myself. Quickly now, but sparingly. It would not do to look the harlot in this place.

She opened the last of her packages and took out a number of small decorated wooden boxes with tight-fitting lids. She opened each one and arranged the differently colored pastes in front of her. Holding the mirror in one hand, she worked swiftly and deftly with the other, rubbing the pad of her middle finger lightly against the surface of one paste and then applying the merest trace of bluish color to her eyelids, smoothing the substance in until the only noticeable effect was a heightening of the color and light reflected in her eyes. She wiped her fingertip quickly on the damp towel and selected another box, applying a reddish paste to the skin over her cheekbones and blending it into her skin until there was no sign of it apart from the faintest hint of a flush on her cheeks. From a third box she added a tinge of deeper redness to her full, wide lips, then pressed them together, biting them gently. Lastly she reached for the tiny glass bottle that contained her single greatest assurance of self-respect. Working carefully, she extracted the tiny wooden stopper from the precious vial and upended the container until a single drop of viscous liquid dripped onto the pad of her middle finger. She raised it to her nostrils, inhaling the essence eagerly and fully aware that, once she had applied it, she would not be able to smell it again. That was a sacrifice she could live with, however, for she knew everyone else around her would be aware of it. She dabbed two tiny spots of the liquid beneath each of her ears and then smeared what was left into the hollow at the base of her neck, smoothing it into the soft skin there.

And finally she was done. She tucked all her devices into her small bag before blowing out the six candles, and then, clutching the bag beneath her arm, she went and opened the door.

Young Brother Giles raised his candle reflexively to throw more light on her, his jaw dropping as his eyes went wide. "My lady ..." He gulped audibly. "You look— Are you ... are you prepared now?"

She favored him with her sweetest smile. "I am, Brother Giles, and I have kept you waiting for an unforgivably long time. But I feel new born now, thanks to your kindness. I do not know what I would have done had you not been here to aid me. We women, as you must know, are notoriously different from men. We place much importance on appearances, most particularly our own, and thus I thank you again for being so considerate of my needs. I have but one more question: should we leave the six new candles here?"

The young monk smiled, but then his face quickly sobered again. "I see no need for that, my lady. Brother Preceptor would be most unsettled to find such a profusion of luxury in his cell. He might think he had been visited by supernatural agencies. But—" He looked down the passageway towards the stairs, and then continued in a firmer voice. "I shall take you down to the admiral now, if you are ready."

As they began to walk side by side along the passageway, Jessie noticed the profound silence all around them.

"What hour of night is it, Brother? It seems like the very middle of it."

"It is, my lady. Nigh on midnight."

"And will you stay on duty all night long?"

"Oh no, my lady. I am due to be relieved at any moment. I may even have been relieved by now. The guard changes at midnight."

Jessie stopped walking, right at the top of the stairs, and looked at him, her face full of concern. "Oh! Then I must beg your pardon for delaying you. Will you be punished for not being at your post?"

He half smiled again and shook his head. "Not tonight, my lady. The admiral himself sent me to see to you. It has been a most pleasant task."

"Thank you once again, Brother Giles, that is a lovely compliment. But I wonder still about those candles. Could you leave them in the other room for me, and one of them alight? I fear I may have to return at some point, before the day breaks."

A look of concern flickered on the young monk's face. "There really is no need of that, my lady. No one will disturb them." He started down the stairs ahead of her, speaking back over his shoulder as she followed him. "The preceptor will not be seeking rest tonight. Too many untoward things are happening. Do you know that we missed Vespers tonight? That has never happened before."

"All of you, the entire fraternity? That is most unusual. What is going on, do you know?"

"No, my lady. I am a simple brother, privy to nothing of import. There is talk, and I have heard some of it, but nothing that is believable or worthy of repeating." They had reached the bottom of the stairs. "Here we are. I will ask you to wait here, if it pleases you, while I announce you."

He left Jessie standing at the foot of the long flight of stairs, in a high and narrow hallway that stretched off on both sides of her, lit with flickering wall-mounted torches. He knocked at a set of high double doors in the opposite wall and stepped inside.

Jessie stood very straight and tugged at her clothing, making sure once more that she was decently arrayed, and then raised her hands to pat her hair beneath its golden net. She felt nervous, for some inexplicable reason, and attributed it to the concern stirred in her by Brother Giles's tale of missing Vespers. This was a monastic order, and the lives of its members were governed absolutely by the Templars' Rule, which specified prayers at regular and immutable hours, except in times of war. Nothing but war and the need to fight could ever disrupt the schedule of daily prayers, and yet tonight they had missed Vespers. Something grave must be afoot.

2

Charles St. Valéry himself came through the doors to welcome her.

"Jessica, my dear sister, please, come in, come in. I trust you slept well?" He took her fingertips between his own thumb and forefingers and bowed her into the room, and she swept through the doorway, smiling widely as she crossed the threshold, then stopped abruptly as she saw there were a number of men already there. She counted three white robes, besides the admiral's, and one brown-clad sergeant. She knew none of them.

Oh, dear God, a gathering of knights. Rigid pomposity, unwashed bodies, and reeking sanctimony. And what is that awful smell? Not sanctimony, certes. My God, they must have painted the entire room with lye soap! I have no need of this, at midnight.

She pivoted to face the admiral. "Forgive me, Charles, I did not know you were in conference. I understood that you had called for me, but I fear I should have waited before disturbing you."

She had no way of knowing it, but the sound of her voice suggested broad, deep, gently vibrating silver Saracen cymbals to one of the room's occupants, who shivered and was startled at the thought, and could think of no reason why it should have occurred to him.

Admiral St. Valéry laughed. "Not at all, dear sister." He continued to hold her hand gently in his as he stepped gracefully by her on the right, turning her with him, and waved with his other hand to indicate the other men in the room. "Permit me to introduce my fellows. Two of them are the reason for my need to disturb your rest."

Jessie scanned the assembled men. She glanced at Sir William cursorily before her eyes moved on to the brown-coated sergeant beside him. Her eyes narrowed briefly, and then flared with recognition.

"Tam Sinclair!" Her face lit up with the radiance of her smile. "This is the man I told you about, Charles—" But then she broke off and turned back to Tam, her brow wrinkling as she took in his surcoat with its Templar blazon. "But you were a carter ... I had no idea you were of the Temple."

"Nor had anyone else, my dear," her brother-in-law said. "Tam came to us in secrecy, escorting Sir William here, with tidings from our Grand Master in Paris. Brothers, this is my brother's widow, Lady Jessica Randolph, the Baroness St. Valéry."

The woman nodded pleasantly to the assembly and then looked more closely at Sir William.

Great Heavens, he is big. Such shoulders. And he has no beard. I thought every Templar must wear a beard. They consider it a sin to go unshaven, though God Himself might wonder why. A good face, strong and clean, square jawline and a cleft chin. And wondrous eyes, so bright and yet so pale. And angry. Is he angry at me?

"I have never seen a Templar's chin before," she said, and watched his eyes flare. Someone laughed and quickly turned the sound into a cough. "Forgive me for being blunt," she continued, "but it is the truth. Every Templar I have ever seen has been bearded." She glanced again at Tam. "Tam there is Sinclair," she said, pronouncing it the Scots way, and then looked back at the knight. "And therefore you must be his kinsman, the formidable Sir William Sinclair, Knight of the Temple of Solomon."

Sir William continued to glare at her, but he was completely lost in the certain and unwelcome knowledge that the eyes in his mind would never change color again, and that the formless features he had grappled with were now etched into his soul.

What have I done to deserve his anger? Or is it merely that he is one of those woman haters?

"You know Sir William, my dear?" St. Valéry sounded astonished.

"No, brother dear, but I know *of* him. Sir William's exploits are legendary." She was smiling, and there was a hint of mockery in her disturbing blue-gray eyes as she turned her gaze back to Sir William and saw the hot blood of confusion and humiliation flushing his cheeks and spreading to the very tips of his ears.

In God's holy name, he is not angry at me at all. The man is afraid of me. But for what? Because I am a woman? Can it be that simple and that sad? He can't even find words. No, it must be something deeper than mere fear.

For his part, Sir William was cursing himself for blushing like a tongue-tied farm boy, and fighting to find suitable words with which to reply to her mockery, but all he could achieve was a single short sentence that almost choked him as it stumbled, stiff and surly, from his lips.

"You mock me, Lady."

Jessie felt her eyes widening, but her smile remained in place. "No, sir, upon my word I do not." *I truly do not, I swear.* But then she smoothed her face so that both her smile and the hint of raillery were gone and she looked him straight in the eye and spoke in the tongue of their native Scotland.

"I knew your sister Peggy, Sir William, when I was a wee girl, living at home. We spent much time together and were very close, she and I, and she regaled me all the time with stories about you: the things you did, the deeds that you performed." She switched effortlessly back to French. "Peggy sang your praises constantly. You were her paragon, her shimmering, mail-clad brother, Soldier of the Temple and Defender of the True Cross. And yet she barely knew you, having met you only twice, and very briefly both times. Nonetheless, she could not have thought more highly of you."

The big man frowned and his lips parted but nothing emerged, and so he tried again, in Scots. "She was but a lassie then, and silly."

That earned him a swift, tart rejoinder, in French: "Is silliness *always* the way of lassies, Sir William? Peggy is a woman now, and I would wager her opinion of you has not changed. Would you still deem her silly?"

"I would not know." He cursed himself for the transparent lie, for he had already admitted his admiration of his sister to the admiral, but he charged ahead, compounding his folly, incapable of doing otherwise and sounding more hostile than ever. "I know nothing of women, Lady."

"That is plain to see, Sir William." Jessie's voice was noticeably cooler.

"Aye, well. I am a simple soldier—"

"Aye, and a humble monk. Quite so. I have heard that before, Master Sinclair. But it seems to me there is little of the simpleton about you, and far less of the humility you claim." *There, now chew upon that, Sir Churlish.*

She turned away from the white-mantled knight, dismissing him coolly as she directed her attention back to the admiral, who was staring in consternation at what he had heard. She laid her fingertips on his arm, smiling at him as she indicated the other two men in the room. "I thought Commander de Thierry might be here. Am I to see him?"

St. Valéry cleared his throat, and when he spoke, he was careful not to look at anyone else. "Sir Arnold, I fear, is no longer among us, Sister. He died but a short time ago." He paused, allowing her to express her grief and concern, but made no attempt to explain how short the time had, in fact, been. Little benefit, he thought, in upsetting the woman needlessly. He forced a smile onto his lips, and continued smoothly. "I am sure he would wish me, however, to apologize for his failure to be here to welcome you." He paused again, clearly struggling with something, then continued. "May I present you to his successor, Sir Richard de Montrichard, and to my own vice-admiral, Sir Edward de Berenger?"

Both men bowed, and Jessie gave them her most winning smile, unaware that William Sinclair stood stupefied with anger, glaring wildly at her, his skin crawling with embarrassment at the way she had dismissed him, while his mind grappled with an acute and frightening awareness, as he took in every line and movement of her lithe and supple body, that he was looking at Temptation herself, the Devil's work personified. The woman was simply more beautiful and far more disturbing than any other single person he had met in his thirty-odd years of existence.

Even as he looked and fumed, however, he saw how the woman was demonstrating her mastery over mere men. De Berenger, hard-bitten knight that he was, appeared to be besotted with her smiling radiance and her conversation, hanging on her every word and grinning like a fool who ought not to be loose without a keeper to watch over him. And even the dour deputy preceptor, Richard de Montrichard, was smiling and nodding at her every word, his eyes moving from her to de Berenger as he followed their conversation avidly. Will felt Tam's eyes on him and turned towards the other man, scowling, but Tam refused to meet his gaze, looking away quickly before Will could read the expression in his eyes.

And still Will wanted to say something, to step forward, albeit too late, and put the woman firmly in her place with a few appropriately chosen words, letting her know that her wiles and guiles, no matter how indirect or how cloaked in sweetness, would be wasted in the present company. But nothing came to him—no barbed comment, no inspired witticisms, nothing at all that he could articulate—and he was reduced to standing impotently, shamed and humiliated yet knowing neither how nor why, staring at the back of her neck and shoulders and at the way her clothing clung to her caressingly and adjusted to her body's slightest movement.

It was the admiral who rescued him from his agonizing immobility by calling all of them to come and sit by the fire. He held Lady Jessica's chair for her and then sat on her right, waving to Sir William to take the chair on her other side as the other men took their seats. Sinclair moved forward reluctantly to sit where the admiral had indicated, in the only chair left vacant, and close enough to the woman to be able to smell her presence as the faintest suggestion of something warm and sweet and delightfully aromatic. Having spent his boyhood in Scotland and the remainder of his life in monastic garrisons throughout Christendom and the Holy Lands, Sinclair had never encountered perfume before, and so he had no suspicion that he was smelling anything other than Jessie Randolph's natural scent. Despite his disapproval of the woman, he found himself perversely enjoying the tumult the subtle aroma caused in his breast.

Jessie Randolph betrayed absolutely no sign that she was aware of his presence, keeping her shoulder turned against him as she spoke softly to her brother-in-law. St. Valéry finally nodded and patted her hand reassuringly before clearing his throat and calling all of them to attention. But they were immediately interrupted by a loud knocking at the door, which opened to reveal an apprehensive guard.

Two women, the fellow explained falteringly, almost cringing in the face of the admiral's angry frown, had come to the gates some time soon after dark, seeking the Baroness St. Valéry.

Jessie leapt to her feet. *Marie and Janette! Thank you, dear Jesus, for this deliverance.*

The guard said they had been lodged in the guardhouse, in one of the cells, because Sergeant Tescar had been ordered to permit no one to enter or leave the Commandery. But the two women had grown increasingly insistent that they must be permitted to see the Baroness, and so the Sergeant of the Guard had sent to ask for guidance.

Jessie swung to face St. Valéry, grasping his arm. "These are my women, Charles. My servants, Marie and Janette. We had to part on the road when we were warned that de Nogaret's soldiers were looking for three women. I sent them on ahead, to await my arrival here and then come to me when we were all safe. I must go to them. Will you pardon me?"

Sir William had noted her obvious elation on hearing this news, and he had been warmed, in spite of himself, by the gladness in her eyes and the flush on her high cheekbones that signaled genuine concern for the women, so he was surprised when St. Valéry shook his head.

"No, my dear, I cannot release you." He looked about at the other men, and waved his hand in frustration. "I have urgent information that you must hear now … information that even my deputies here know nothing of. Much has happened this day, and much more is about to take place, and we are running out of time, so I cannot afford to tell this sorry tale twice." He glanced at de Berenger and Montrichard, seeing the incomprehension in their faces. "Your women are safe, Lady Jessica. They are in good hands and will not suffer by remaining where they are for a little longer. We will make them warmer and more comfortable now that we know who they are, but I cannot permit them to enter the Commandery without your presence. This is a monastery. We have no place to put them, and the mere presence of two unattended women might cause some consternation among our brethren. I beg you, send word to them to await your coming."

Jessie was glaring at him through narrowed eyes, but she pursed her lips and nodded her head. "These tidings must be grave indeed, Brother, to cause you all to seal your gates and miss Vespers. I can scarce wait to hear them." She turned to the guard. "Have my women eaten anything tonight?"

The fellow shrugged. "I don't know, my lady. They were there when I came on watch. They may have eaten earlier."

"Feed them now, then, if you will, and tell them I am pleased to hear of their arrival. Explain that I am held in conference here but will join them as soon as I am able. And give my thanks to the Sergeant of the Guard for heeding them."

As soon as the guard had left, the Baroness returned to her seat. "Very well, Admiral," she said with great dignity. "Tell us these mighty tidings of yours."

The admiral stood up and turned to face them all, his back to the fire. "Mighty tidings they are, my friends. Grave, momentous, and well nigh incredible. Our Master, Jacques de Molay, sent warning and instructions to us today with Sir William here. He has been advised, he tells me, that this day that has now passed might well have been our last day of freedom in France."

He looked from face to face—his sister-in-law the Baroness, Edward de Berenger, and Richard de Montrichard.

"Master de Molay believes the King wishes to be rid of us, us and our Order. There is no simpler way of putting it. Word came to him at the Commandery in Paris, from a source he trusts implicitly, that King Philip has issued a mandate for every Templar in the realm of France to be arrested at dawn tomorrow, taken into custody, and held prisoner. The plans were laid in place by William de Nogaret, chief lawyer of France, acting upon the King's personal instructions."

"But that is ludicrous!" Montrichard was on his feet in a single bound. "Why would the King do such a thing? *How* could he do it? It would be impossible. This makes no sense."

"It might, Sir Richard, were you Philip Capet."

All five men turned to stare at Jessica Randolph, astonished that she would speak out so boldly to contradict a man among a gathering of men, but Jessie remained unruffled, raising her hand, bidding them wait.

"Philip Capet rules by divine right, does he not? Of course he does. All men know that, since he has made no secret of his conviction on that matter. He is King by God's will. And he has ruled now in France these what, twenty-two years?" She allowed the silence to stretch now, knowing that she had their attention. "Aye, he was crowned that long ago. Two and twenty years. And he is now thirty-nine, so he has spent more than half his lifetime as King of France. But what do we really know of him, after so long a time?"

She left them waiting, then asked again, "What does any man know of Philip Capet? They know his title: Philip the Fourth." She looked around the group. "They know his unofficial name: Philip the Fair. But what more than that?

"And what does any woman know of him, for that matter? His wife, Queen Jeanne, died these two years ago, after being married to the man for one and twenty years, and all she had to say about him on her deathbed was that she once wished he might have warmed to her."

Again she allowed the silence to linger, then added, "Once, my lords. She had *once* wished it. But she no longer cared."

Sir William stirred, as though preparing to speak, but Jessie waved him to silence almost unconsciously.

"I know you are thinking that I am a mere woman and have no right to speak up here like this, addressing you on men's affairs. Well, sirs, I know whereof I speak. This King knows no curb to his wishes—never has and never will. He will not be withstood, in anything to which he sets his mind. He rules, in his own eyes, by divine right, and considers himself answerable to God alone. Philip Capet, this monarch without a soul, a King without a conscience, slew my husband merely because he was displeased with him. Philip the Fair …" She looked around at her listeners once again, her eyes moving slowly, knowing no one of them would interrupt her now. "I have set eyes on him but once, but he is fair. Fairer by far to look at than my late husband was. Fair as a statue of the finest marble."

Now she stood up and moved to the front of the fire, and as she did so St. Valéry stepped away and sat down again. She acknowledged the courtesy with a brief nod, but she was far from finished speaking.

"A statue, my lords. That is the extent of this King's humanity. A statue rules in France—beautiful to look at, perhaps, but stone cold and lacking any vestige of the compassion we expect in mankind. Aloof in all respects, completely unapproachable and unknowable, devoid of human traits or weaknesses. This man surrounds himself with coldness and with silence. He never smiles, never invites or shares a confidence, never permits a casual approach to his presence. No one knows what he thinks, or what he believes, other than that he sees himself as a divinely ordained King of the Capet dynasty, as God's own regent on earth, superior to the Pope and the Church and any other human power.

"And of the few human attributes we do know he possesses, none are admirable, none commendable. He is capricious, grasping, cunning, and ambitious. The lives of other people mean nothing to him. And he surrounds himself with creatures who will do his bidding, no matter what that bidding be.

"William de Nogaret reigns over all of those, the King's favored minion. De Nogaret, who will stop at nothing to carry out the King's wishes. Four years ago, you may remember, he rode with a band of men from Paris to Rome, eight hundred miles, to abduct a reigning pope, Boniface IV, on the eve of a pronouncement of excommunication for the whole of France. It was the most blatant crime against the papacy ever carried out, and he did it with impunity.

"The Pope, as we all know, died within the month, too old at eighty to survive abduction and outrage. And when his successor, Pope Benedict, dared to condemn de Nogaret publicly, and through de Nogaret the crowned King of France, he too died, of excruciating belly pains, and also within a month. He was poisoned, my lords. We all know that, but no one speaks of it because no one dare speak out and no one can prove anything. In the aftermath, though, thanks to his minion's work, Philip had eighteen months to arrange the election of a French pope of his own, this Clement.

"And thus de Nogaret proved his daring, his brilliance, and his loyalty to Philip. And his reward was to be appointed the King's chief lawyer. A man of brilliant mind and abilities—none will deny him that. But a thief, a murderer, a blasphemer, and an abductor of popes … The chief lawyer of France."

"The Jews."

The voice, dull and strangely lacking in resonance, was de Berenger's, and all eyes swung to him.

"The Jews," he said again, more strongly this time. "Last year, last July. It's true, what Master de Molay says about tomorrow."

St. Valéry sucked in his breath. "What about the Jews, man? What are you talking about?"

De Berenger shrugged. "Unannounced plots, my lord. Last year, on the morning of the twenty-first of July and without warning of any kind, every single Jew in France was arrested and imprisoned, then expelled from the country within the month, their holdings and possessions confiscated by the Crown for the good of the realm. I had forgotten it until now, and few people paid any attention at the time, for those arrested were Jews, after all, and our empty Christian coffers needed their Jewish money. But think you, my lord Admiral, that there might have been as many Jews in France that day as there are Templars now?" He looked at Jessica Randolph before his eyes moved on from man to man, engaging each of them in turn as he continued speaking.

"The planning and the execution of that coup against the Jews, with all the secrecy and coordination that was involved, was the sole responsibility of William de Nogaret. The same William de Nogaret, I must now remind you, whose parents are reputed to have burned at the stake in Toulouse as Cathar heretics, under the scrutinizing eyes of the Knights Templar, when we presided there as invigilators for a time, at the behest of the Dominican Inquisitors."

"Mary, Mother of God!" No one so much as glanced at St. Valéry when he breathed the words.

De Berenger made a face. "It makes perfect sense now, even though it didn't seem to make much at the time … I believe now that the Jewish arrests last year were a rehearsal for what is to take place tomorrow. There is not the slightest doubt of it in my mind." He nodded his head slowly and deliberately. "The Grand Master's warning is genuine, and he does not exaggerate the peril in which we stand. This thing has been long in the planning, but it has been done before. I think tomorrow will be a day of much terror and upheaval for our Order."

He sat up straighter. "I am not suggesting that we will see slaughter in the streets, nor am I accepting that this will be or even could be the end of us. We are a military and religious order, when all is said and done, not a scattering of disconnected and defenseless Jews, so we will survive this travesty with more success than they were able to achieve. Besides, we have numbers on our side—not overwhelmingly so, but perhaps adequately—and we have our history of service, which is exemplary. Interference and interruption of our affairs may come out of tomorrow's doings, but I seriously doubt there can be any chance of the total dissolution of our Order. Not even Pope Clement, weak vessel though he be, would countenance such a bare-faced travesty."

The Baroness spoke again, her voice cold. "Pope Clement will countenance whatever he is told to countenance. He is every bit as much Philip's creature as is de Nogaret, but he is worse, weaker and even more dangerous, because he fears for his own position. Therefore you must look for no help from him. Before Philip himself elevated him to the papacy, Clement was plain Bernard de Bot, an obscure nonentity who had somehow managed to have himself appointed Archbishop of Bordeaux. Philip found him there and promoted him because de Bot was known even then to be a greedy weakling, much given to vanity and flattery, and easily manipulated. He was greatly over-fond of worldly honors and recognition, and was notorious for his procrastination, so timorous and spineless that he would rather crawl a hundred miles on his belly than make a firm decision. He will offer you neither assistance nor hope, believe me, for he lives in terror of being un-poped by Philip."

De Berenger shook his head. "Even were we to believe that implicitly, my lady, it would matter little in the long term. And the long term is what we must look to here. It may take months or even years for this matter to go through whatever kind of arbitration may be arranged, and in the meantime it may hit our coffers hard, but our holy Order will survive. It would be insanity to think otherwise. There will be—must be—some kind of resolution eventually, some form of reparation, and when—"

"Reparation? Spare me your arrogant and silly male certainty, sir!" Jessie's face flushed with sudden, flaring anger, and de Berenger sat

back, as open-mouthed as the others, none of whom had ever witnessed such behavior from a woman.

"Have you not listened to a word I've said? In God's holy
name, when will you people learn that you are not dealing with
men hidebound by the concept of honor like yourselves? You call
yourselves men of goodwill, and believe all others must be just
like you. Men of honor and goodwill! Pah! This King believes
himself ordained by *God*. He believes himself God's Anointed,
incapable of being wrong or doing wrong. He *has* no honor, as you
think of it, and no goodwill or any need of it. God save us all from
the blindness of men of honor!

"The man is *desperate*, see you! He is consumed and driven by
the need for *money*. It is all he ever thinks of and all he ever strives
for. He is mired in debt and his treasury is a bottomless pit. He will
tax, take, steal, snatch, and tear funds from the hands of anyone and
everyone he suspects of having money or of hiding it. His greed and
his needs are insatiable, and he believes that God understands his
needs completely and has given him carte blanche to satisfy those
needs according to whatever remedies occur to him."

"You sound as though you know the King passing well, Baroness,
for one who has met him but once." The voice was Montrichard's,
and it emerged as a condescending drawl.

She rounded on him like a lioness, her eyes seeming to spit fire.
"I said I *saw* him once, sir knight. I never met him, so spare me your
disdain. My husband was for years the King's agent at the Court of
England, laboring endlessly and thanklessly to generate funds in any
way he could to throw into the Capet's treasury. The result was not
sufficient to please Capet, and so he had my husband killed. Rely
upon it, sir, I speak not out of ignorance."

De Montrichard appeared undaunted, but he was flushing, and
his voice was less certain as he responded, "Your husband discussed
the King's affairs with you, madam?"

"My husband trusted me, *monsieur*. Far more so than his exalted
monarch trusted him. The King received reports that the Baron had
funds of his own and set de Nogaret to hunt them down. He failed,

but Philip the Fair killed my husband in the searching." She turned away as if to walk from the room, but then spun back again, her skirts swirling, her eyes flashing, and her hand chopping at the air in exasperation before coming back up to point straight at de Berenger.

"And he will kill all of you, if he sees need, to lay his greedy hands on your Order's wealth. Do you *truly* think there will be reparations made in the future? Reparations for what? The royal confiscation of your wealth by divine right? Do you really think Philip Capet will give back what he takes, or settle for taking less than everything, once the die is cast? If you do, sir, you are a fool, vice-admiral or not. I am merely amazed that he has not taken action against you before now."

Since the woman first began to speak, Sinclair had been sitting entranced, slack mouthed and unaware that he was staring at her openly. She was a superb woman, wide hipped and broad shouldered, with a narrow waist, long, clean-lined legs, and high, proud breasts that were emphasized by what she wore. He had never seen anything like her and was hypnotized and fascinated by the way she looked and moved, her bosom heaving, eyes scintillating, and her cheeks flushed a hectic red, but far less red than her wide and mobile mouth.

It was only when she called the vice-admiral a fool that he regained his composure, snapping his mouth shut and sitting up straighter in his chair, flushing again at the awareness of what he had been watching and thinking about. But her last words were still ringing in his ears, and he suddenly found himself speaking.

"I am not," he said.

It was the first time he had spoken since belittling his sister, and he felt all their eyes come upon him at once, but now he was in command of himself. The Baroness had thrust herself into a discussion among men, and had demonstrated her superiority to all of them, but here, among his peers, Sinclair's voice was supreme. As a woman, Lady Jessica Randolph unsettled him. As a Baroness, however, she had intruded upon his domain and could be summarily dealt with like any other subordinate.

"Not what, Sir William?" St. Valéry asked.

"I am not surprised, Admiral. The Baroness said she is amazed the King has not moved against us until now. It came to me then that I am not at all amazed. It has taken him until now to arrange a suitable reaction."

There was a long pause before St. Valéry responded. "A suitable reaction to what? Forgive me, Sir William, but your meaning escapes me."

"Aye, and so it should." Sinclair sat back in his chair, gripping its arms and pushing his shoulders against the wood at his back, his face twisted into a grimace as he debated whether to explain, but then he realized how ludicrous it was, under the present circumstances, to worry about the confidential nature of what he had to say. "King Philip made application to join our Order, a year and a half ago, after the death of his wife, Queen Jeanne."

St. Valéry's eyebrows rose. "He did? I knew nothing of that."

"Few did, Sir Charles. It was not common knowledge. Being the King he is, he could hardly take the common path, and so he approached the Governing Council directly."

"And? What happened?"

"We considered his application, in accordance with our laws and customs, and the matter went to secret ballot."

The admiral nodded. "Common practice, even at the Inner Circle level, I suppose."

"Aye, but Philip was blackballed."

St. Valéry and the other knights gasped.

"Blackballed!" the admiral repeated. "Someone voted him the black ball?"

Sinclair shook his head. "No, Admiral. Eleven of us voted that day. There were eight black balls."

"What does this mean, this talk of black balls?" The Baroness was standing over them, frowning.

St. Valéry looked up at her. "We use two balls in voting on important questions within our Order. One is black, one white. Each man places one of the two, unseen, inside a bag that passes from hand to hand in secret ballot. The white ball means yea, the black, nay. In the overall vote, a single black ball holds the veto, the denial."

Now it was the Baroness who appeared nonplussed. She blinked at Sinclair. "You are a member of the Inner Circle?"

He dipped his head. "The Governing Council. I am."

"And you refused the King admission to your ranks? You denied Philip Capet?"

Sinclair nodded again. "Aye, we did. Eight of our Council members that day believed, as had been discussed in our preliminary hearing, that the King was seeking to join us for the wrong reasons: not to serve our brotherhood but to avail himself of the opportunity to assess and gain access to the Order's wealth."

Oh, you honest, self-deluding fool. You have no idea of what you did, do you? "You turned away the King of France and yet you did not foresee this day?" She shook her head, keeping her face expressionless. "Well, you were correct, both in your assessment and in your honorable behavior thereafter, but your insult was a fatal one. The Order of the Temple was destroyed that day by eight black balls. It ceased to exist the moment Philip Capet found out you had rejected him. It has merely taken all the time from then until now for the word to reach you."

Sinclair nodded mutely, accepting the truth of what she had said, and she turned then to St. Valéry.

"So what will you do now, my lord?"

The admiral smiled at her, although his face was tired and drawn. "God bless you, my dear sister. How typical it is that you should have no thought of yourself, with de Nogaret approaching our doors." He shrugged his shoulders and looked from her to the other men before continuing. "We will do much, have done much already. The fleet has been provisioning for sea these past five hours and more, allegedly preparing for an exercise tomorrow morning. Your funds are safe, tallied and loaded already on my galley. You will sail with me and we will see you and your gold delivered safe to Scotland. Go you now and find your women, if you will. Tam will go with you and see the three of you set safe aboard. You will not find your quarters wide or spacious, for our galleys are built for war, with little thought of comfort, but they will be sound and safe, and warmer than any of de Nogaret's dungeons. Once aboard, you should try to sleep, although that may prove difficult, with all the comings and goings tonight. We will set sail on the morning tide, and later, if weather, time, and chance permit, we may transfer you to one of the larger cargo vessels, depending upon how fully they are laden. Tam, will you take Lady Jessica to her women?"

3

"I was surprised to find Sir William in agreement with me." Jessie Randolph spoke in Scots, and Tam Sinclair, walking ahead of her, was taken by surprise at her unexpected words and looked back over his shoulder at her.

"How so, my lady?"

"How so? Because he obviously does not like me. Is he like that with all women? Ill mannered and surly?"

Tam stopped walking and turned back to stare at her for a moment, and she stopped, too, waiting for his answer. Then his mouth crinkled into a wry grin and he bobbed his head once. "Aye, you could say that. In every conversation I have heard him have with a woman in the last twenty years, he has been exactly like that. Ill mannered and surly soundin'."

"Is he a woman hater, then? I would not have thought so before speaking with him."

Tam's grin grew wider. "No, Lady Jessica, Will's no woman hater."

"What's wrong with him, then? You said he is like that with all women."

"He's just rusty, my lady. Very rusty. What I said is he has been like that with every woman I've heard him speak wi' in twenty years. But you're the first and the last of them."

"The fir—? In twenty years? That is impossible."

"Aye, so *you* might think, but it's far frae impossible, lass. It's both possible and true. The last woman I heard Will Sinclair talk to was his mother, Lady Ellen, and that was on the day he left home for good, dreaming even then of joining the Order … thirty years ago, that was. Will avoids women. Always has. He's fanatical in that, and his life as a Templar monk makes it easy to do. It's an extension of his vow o' chastity, no more than that. And he's very conscientious."

They were still standing in the long passageway outside the Day Room, and now Jessie looked both ways along the empty hall, for no other reason than to give herself time to adapt to this staggering piece of information. Tam began walking again, and she followed.

"He is a monk. I can accept that. But he does not live in cloisters. He is a knight, too, so he moves about the world."

"Aye, he travels constantly, especially since this business wi' the Governing Council. But can you no' see that that's how he keeps himsel' chaste? He never stops working, except to pray."

"Then he must be a saint … an anchorite."

"No, my lady, he's a man. He's no smooth-tongued troubadour, I'll grant ye that. If it's charm and courtly wit you're lookin' for, you're lookin' in the wrong place in Will Sinclair. But he's the finest man I know, and I've been wi' him since the outset. He was just a lad of sixteen when he left Scotland, and he went directly to the Holy Land. Spent years fighting there and was one o' the few men to survive the siege o' Acre."

"He was at Acre? I did not know that. Were you there, too?"

"Aye, I was."

"How did you get out?"

"Wi' Will. I was his sergeant. He went nowhere without me."

"But he escaped, and you with him. How did that happen? Everyone else in Acre died, did they not?"

Tam Sinclair heaved a deep sigh. "Aye, Lady, that they did … Not everyone, exactly, but close to it."

"So why not you and he? How did you manage to escape?"

"He left under orders, lass. Ordered out, wi' Tibauld Gaudin, who was commander of the Temple at that time—second in command

there to the Marshal, Peter of Sevrey. The Marshal, y' unnerstand, is
the supreme military commander o' the Order in time o' war."

"Who's who is not important, Tam. Why was William Sinclair
chosen to be saved?"

Tam shrugged his wide shoulders. "Because he was. He was
chosen. It's that simple, lass. Gaudin the commander liked him.
Will had saved the commander's life a couple o' times, in skir-
mishes wi' the Heathen. Besides, Will was very good at what he
did—a natural leader and a bonny fighter. When Gaudin got his
orders to take the Treasure o' the Order into his charge, an' to take
it away to safety on one of the Temple war galleys, from Acre to
Sidon, he wanted men around him he could trust. Will was the
foremost o' all o' those."

"And you took the Treasure to Sidon?"

"Aye, in Asia Minor."

"And what then? Where did you go after that?"

Tam shrugged again. "We came back here to Christendom, and
Will began to be moved around from one garrison to another, always
being given higher rank and more and more responsibility, in
Scotland first, then in France, Spain, Italy, Cyprus, Spain again and
back to France. And then, a few years ago, he began studying for his
advancement to the Council of Governors. If honor and loyalty,
trustworthiness an' bravery mean anything to ye, then ye'll never
find a greater store o' any of them than in this one man."

She stopped again, and turned to face Tam. "You have heard me
voice my opinions on honor and bravery to the others. They are
manly virtues, and therefore to a woman's eyes they are useless and
futile. Find me a woman who wants to be married to a dead hero and
I will show you a woman who is unhappily wed. Dead men provide
no comfort or love in a harsh winter or any other time." She paused.
"Mind you, I find there are living men who offer little more, and it
strikes me that your Will Sinclair is one of them … I can only pray
his manners will improve when we are aboard ship. It is a long
passage to Scotland, and I would not enjoy spending all of the time
with a great boor."

The tone of her voice had changed, losing its quick and urgent intimacy, and Tam responded to the difference, becoming more formal. "You'll be on different ships, my lady. You will be wi' the admiral, and unless I miss my guess, Will's place will be wi' the vice-admiral, Maister de Berenger."

Jessica Randolph nodded. "Aye, that makes sense. The galleys are war ships, as Charles said, not fitted for comfort or for idle passengers, so you are probably right, we will be aboard separate vessels, you and I. Now take me to my women, Tam, if you would. I've kept them waiting long enough."

"We're nearly there, my lady. Come away."

4

After Jessie Randolph and Tam had left the room, William Sinclair sat still for a few moments, watching the door that had closed behind them, and then he turned to Edward de Berenger.

"Forgive me, Admiral," he said. "I had to cozen you earlier about the naval exercise tomorrow, but I had no choice at the time. Sir Charles had not yet read his instructions from the Grand Master."

De Berenger nodded, affably enough, and turned to St. Valéry. "What about the other elements of the fleet, Admiral? Is there hope for them?"

"Yes, some hope. Master de Molay dispatched word to our Commanderies in Brest and Le Havre, bidding them take all available galleys and set sail last night, on the same exercise you thought you were to join. The fleet commander in Marseille received similar orders a week ago, to set sail with his galleys immediately and make his way down through the Straits of Gibraltar and then north to Cape Finisterre in northern Spain. We will all come together there, and sail wherever we must go."

"How many vessels altogether, Admiral?"

St. Valéry shook his head. "We have no way of knowing, Edward. It depends entirely upon who was in port when the orders arrived. There may have been a score of keels in each, or none at all. But only our fleet here will have transport vessels attached. The other elements, whatever they turn out to be, will be all galleys, but we have another task to see to before we sail for Finisterre, and I will explain that to you tomorrow. Go now and see to your preparations. We are finished here."

"And what of my men, sir?" De Montrichard, who was now the Preceptor of La Rochelle and had been standing beside Sinclair, listening quietly, spoke up as de Berenger left.

The admiral glanced at Sinclair. "The Master's orders were specific. You are to remain in the Commandery and surrender when requested, offering no resistance even under the direst provocation. You must not resist arrest. The consequences could be immeasurable."

De Montrichard nodded, his face inscrutable. "I shall instruct my men, sir."

"Do so, but wait you just a moment. Sir William, I have need of your advice. When Master de Molay wrote his instructions, he was most specific."

"Yes." The rising inflection in Sinclair's response turned the agreement into a question.

"But yet he was unsure of the truth of what he was preparing for, is that not so?"

"It is."

"Had he been here with us tonight, sharing our discussion, think you he might have been convinced the warning was true?"

"I have no doubt of it. Why do you ask?"

"Because I am concerned about this need for our garrison to offer no resistance. How many men have you under arms, Sir Richard?"

"A hundred and fifty-four, Admiral, including the medical staff."

"Five score and more … It seems to me, Sir William, that there could be much temptation to resist, among so many men."

"There could be, were the men not Templars. What are you really saying, Admiral?"

"Why, that we might eliminate the temptation and thereby guarantee obedience to the Master's wishes. A hundred and four absent men could offer no resistance ..."

Sinclair blew out his breath through pursed lips. "You have room for them?"

"I will make room."

Sinclair nodded. "So mote it be. Do it," he said. "We'll leave de Nogaret an empty shell."

"Thank you, my friend." St. Valéry was smiling now. "Sir Richard, remove all the guards and lock and bar the gates, then assemble your command with whatever gear they can carry on their backs, but no more than that. Start boarding them immediately."

The preceptor saluted crisply and marched away with a spring in his step and a new set to his shoulders.

"And now, Will, my friend," the admiral said, "it remains only for me to protect my own priceless treasure here, which I almost forgot. But that big black bottle is very heavy and I find myself growing weak. Will you help me to lighten it before we go outside?"

A short time later, now thoroughly fortified with a third measure of the wondrous liquor of the Benedictine monks, they emerged from the building together and walked down to the wharves, where everything was awash in the flickering light of hundreds of pitch-soaked torches, more than Will could ever remember seeing in any one place. The flares, beacon-like in their intensity, were mounted in baskets atop high, solidly footed wooden poles, and laid out in lanes and alleys, clearly defining the routes from warehouses and stockpiles to the gangplanks of the galleys lining the wharfsides. Will whistled softly in surprise.

"Where did all these torches come from?"

The admiral glanced at him, then looked back at the wharves. "From storage. We sometimes have no choice over when to load or unload a vessel, so we keep the torches ready at all times for night work. There's a good source of pitch not far from here, an open pit by Touchemarin, the nearest village along the southeastern road. We bring it in by the wagonload, in barrels, and store it in a giant vat that has been here longer than I have, so we never run low on fuel."

"I'm impressed. I've never seen anything like this." He turned his back to the activities on the waterside and looked from left to right, gazing at the buildings that extended to either side beyond the Commandery itself, stretching in dark ranks as far as he could see. The only lights to be seen among the massed shapes were those in the Commandery, which at this time of night was unsurprising. "Who owns the buildings on each side of you?"

"We do. They are all Temple establishments, the entire length of the quay on this side of the harbor. They are run by lay and associate brethren: merchants, traders, chandlers, and the like. Of the Temple, but hardly what you and I think of as Templars."

Sinclair nodded knowingly. In his mind, as in the minds of the entire military brotherhood, the word *Templars* applied only to themselves, the fighting monks of the Order. All the other so-called Templars, and there were thousands of them throughout Christendom, were supernumeraries, laymen functionaries of all kinds conscripted from all walks of life as associate brothers, their prime purpose being the daily administration and maintenance of the sprawling commercial empire of the Order's nonmilitary activities. Like most of his fraternity, Sir William viewed them with ambivalence verging, at times, upon detestation. He could acknowledge, however grudgingly, that they were necessary, sometimes even essential, but he harbored a deep resentment of their claims to be *bona fide* Templars, believing that their all too frequent abuse of the name, not to mention the privileges associated with it, were the central cause of the Order's fall from popularity and esteem in the eyes of the world. A greedy and unscrupulous merchant or banker would forever be disdained, but when such malignity was exercised in the name of the Order, then the Order itself inevitably suffered, and the arrogance and malfeasance of the miscreant were perceived, *ipso facto*, as being condoned by the Temple.

It was a conundrum that Sinclair and others like him had debated for decades now and had declared to be unsolvable, and now he dismissed it again, knowing there was nothing he could do. "I wonder what will happen to them tomorrow." He did not expect an answer and turned away to look again at the activity surrounding them. The entire wharf was swarming with movement, all of it disciplined and well ordered, with every man moving purposefully and almost silently, concentrating upon the task at hand. Files of men formed long chains, passing sacks of grain, fodder, and other provisions from shoulder to shoulder to be piled at the edge of the wharf, where lading gangs transferred them into nets to be hoisted aboard ship. Other groups went in single file, carrying goods that were too awkward, fragile, heavy, or precious to be passed easily from hand to hand. Still others manned the hoists that lined the wharves, transferring cargo from the dockside to work crews aboard the ships, who removed the goods from the cargo nets and passed them belowdecks to be stowed. And among them all moved horse-drawn wagons, carrying items that were simply too large to be taken to stowage by any other means. As he watched the constant coming and going, Sinclair was unaware that St. Valéry was watching him, and when the admiral saw the hint of a smile tugging at the younger man's mouth, he spoke up.

"You are smiling, Sir William … Do you find this sight enjoyable?"

"What? Enjoyable? God, no, at least not in the sense you appear to mean, my lord. I find no amusement in it at all." The slight smile lingered on his face. "But there is always enjoyment in watching disciplined men performing well … My smile came out of gratitude that our toilers here are real Templars and not Temple brethren. Were they not, I should shudder to think of the chaos that would be reflected here tonight. I thought to walk among them now, to let them know their work is well thought of. Will you join me?"

FEELING THE LIFT OF THE KEEL beneath his feet as the galley backed away from the quay under oars towards its anchorage, William Sinclair lodged his long sword in a corner where it would not fall, then shrugged off his mantle and hung it from a peg before he allowed himself to fall face down on the narrow bunk that would be his sole resting place for the next few weeks or months, and the last thing he remembered was a vision of Jessica Randolph's eyes flashing with anger, and the words *The Order of the Temple was destroyed by eight black balls.*

A QUEST OF FAITH

1

"Why are we even waiting here? We know they're going to come."

Will Sinclair glanced sideways to where the speaker, Vice-Admiral Sir Edward de Berenger, stood gripping the rail of the galley's narrow stern deck, his knuckles white with the pressure of the grip he was exerting as he stared wide eyed into the thin mist that veiled the nearby wharf.

"Knowing a thing and witnessing the truth of it are two different matters, Edward," he replied. "Were we not to see this with our own eyes before we sail away, we could never be sure it had happened as we expected."

He turned his head to where Admiral St. Valéry's galley rode beside them. It was a larger version of their own, indeed, the largest in the fleet; its oars, forty two-man sweeps ranged in double banks of ten on each side, were like theirs, unshipped, the long blades resting in the waters that lapped against the hull. He could not see St. Valéry himself because the naval commander was surrounded by a knot of other figures on the high stern deck, but he could see that all of them were staring as fixedly towards the fort as was de Berenger.

"And so we wait," he added. "I like it no more than—" He stood straighter. "There they are."

Sinclair knew that every watching eye aboard the two ships had seen what he had seen. Figures moved among the mists ashore, running men, spreading everywhere, and now he could hear the shouts, echoing strangely in the emptiness. The running figures came closer, becoming more easily discernible in the drifting, dissipating fog, until they reached the edge of the wharf, where they came to a halt, lining the edge, their voices rising louder.

"I think they are dismayed," Will murmured, watching the growing throng.

Behind the two galleys that held the admiral and the vice-admiral, the normally crowded harbor of La Rochelle lay empty, save for a cluster of twelve vessels that lay close together near the southern breakwater, bound to each other by stout ropes. Every other vessel that had been anchored there the night before had withdrawn beyond the harbor entrance, where they were now waiting in deep water to see what morning would bring, and it had brought William de Nogaret, as expected. Now Sinclair turned his head in time to see the naval baucent, the white skull and crossed thighbones on a field of black, rise fluttering to the top of the admiral's mast in a prearranged signal. Even the soldiery thronging the wharf fell into silence as they watched the flag's slow ascent, wondering what it signified, but as the silence stretched and grew, nothing appeared to happen. The admiral's galley remained motionless.

An excited shout broke the silence as someone on shore saw what Will Sinclair had already turned to watch, and the clamor spread as the far right side of the crowd lining the wharf eddied and began to run towards the southern breakwater, but they were already too late. The fires on the cluster of moored ships, fueled with oil and carefully prepared, were exploding in fury, spreading with a rapidity that was awe inspiring, and from the sides of the doomed craft men were scrambling down into the boats that waited below.

"Pick them up," Will said quietly, and de Berenger began to issue orders to bring the galley under way and intercept the approaching boats.

On the breakwater the foremost runners had already halted, their arms upraised to cover their faces from the blasting heat of the burning vessels. These twelve ships, all of them cargo carriers, had been the oldest and least seaworthy of the entire fleet, and rather than leaving them behind intact, St. Valéry had decided to burn them where they lay, denying them to King Philip and his henchman in one highly visible act of defiance. As the deck moved beneath his feet in response to the first pull on the right-hand bank of oars, Sinclair saw a different stir of movement ashore, at the point closest to him, and now he fastened his gaze on the figure of one man who stood out from all the others surrounding him, polished armor and a bright red cloak marking him clearly as someone of importance.

"Is that de Nogaret? Would he come here himself?" He answered his own question, aware that de Berenger was not listening. "Aye, he would, the diseased mongrel. He would want to take La Rochelle in person. Now I regret mooring beyond crossbow range. I could shoot him down from here."

A banging against the hull announced the arrival of the boats bearing the arsonists, and as soon as they were all safely aboard, de Berenger issued the orders to bring the galley about and head to sea. As the galley's prow swung around, Sinclair moved against it, revolving slowly until he was gazing out over the stern, his eyes never leaving the distant figure he knew was de Nogaret. Between them, a rain of crossbow bolts was falling uselessly into the waters of the harbor, and he had the pleasure of seeing the King's minister strike out at someone standing beside him and then spin away, vanishing into the crowd, plainly headed into the empty Commandery.

Will turned his back on the scene then, filled with a turmoil of anger and fighting to empty his mind and heart of what was done. He had no time for useless imprecations, for he must now think to the future, to what must happen next and in the time to come. Ahead of him, framed by the entrance to the harbor, the admiral's massive galley was slicing through the last of the calm waters, its sweeping oars throwing liquid diamonds into the rays of the sun that was now rising astern of them, above the walls and towers of La Rochelle, as the sleek, swift craft bore its double cargo of treasure and escapees away from the menace of the King of France. And on the stern, gazing back to the land, he could see the cloaked and hooded figure of the woman, the Baroness St. Valéry.

2

S ix hours later, they were at anchor again, this time within the tiny harbor of a nameless fishing village, four leagues south along the coast from their starting point. The village had no name and few inhabitants, but it had a stout and solid stone quay, and ample flat ground at the base of the cliffs that towered above it to accommodate a host even larger than the small army that had descended upon the hamlet with this morning's earliest light.

Will Sinclair stood with his arms crossed over his chest as he leaned back against the galley's low stern rail, watching the activity taking place all about him and learning much about the way naval matters differed from army activities. Both involved logistics in the use, feeding, and transportation of armed men, but Will knew he could never have begun to achieve the smoothness and ease of transference between land and sea that he was seeing here. Nor could his brother, he knew. He had caught sight of Kenneth on the wharf earlier, but had soon lost him again and was unsurprised, knowing that his brother, younger than himself by three years, was clever enough to stand away without interfering, and to let the seamen do what they did best.

St. Valéry and de Berenger had planned some of the details of this afternoon's activities the previous night, before leaving La Rochelle, but their efforts had been limited by the fact that neither of them knew the village they would visit and both knew they would be constrained by the size and limitations of an unfamiliar wharf. Sinclair could have told them, for he it was who had chosen the place, remembered from a visit years earlier, but he had had duties of his own that night, and they had not thought to seek him out. In the event, the wharf was very small, accommodating only two vessels at a time, but the moorage was secure and the wharf had hoists and pulleys for lifting fishing boats into and out of the water, and now de Berenger was ashore, coordinating the activities there.

Will was watching a pair of horses being lowered, suspended in slings, into the waist of one of the cargo ships. He was growing more and more impressed, both by the handling abilities of the lading and receiving crews and by the swift ease with which the ships alongside the wharf were being rotated, one pair of keels waiting to warp into position as soon as the newly laden pair pulled out. These ships, the Order's trading vessels, were very different in both appearance and function from the admiral's galleys. Built with an eye to maximum storage capacity and solid seaworthiness, they were two-masted for the most part, although three of them had triple masts. They were uniformly broad in the beam and belly and rode low in the water when laden, so that they appeared bulky and ungainly when compared to the naval vessels that accompanied and guarded them. Watching them as they took on cargo, however, Sinclair acknowledged to himself that they possessed a beauty of their own, and he found himself admiring the skill with which their seasoned crews, Temple associates to a man, maneuvered them into and away from the small quay.

The crews of the Temple galleys were equally skilled, he knew, but to different effect and with far greater discipline. The transport ships were manned by professional mariners, employed by or belonging to the Temple; the galleys were manned by fighting seamen, sergeants of the Order whose natural tastes led them to seafaring duties rather than land-based. All of the latter lived, sailed, and fought under military and monastic discipline, their lives governed by a maritime version of the Order's Rule, so that they prayed and performed monastic chores each day, although the off-watch crew were permitted to sleep after their labors and husband their strength at night. Their primary duty, above and beyond all else, was to protect the Order's enormous trading fleet.

Sinclair looked down into the waist of the galley on which he stood, his eyes scanning the ranks of oarsmen at their benches, the nearest of them a good twelve feet below the stern deck. This craft was noticeably smaller than the admiral's, with eighteen oars to a side where St. Valéry's had twenty, but the oars were the same on all galleys, long, heavy, yet graceful sweeps that could propel the vessels over the water at astonishing speeds, even without the massive square sail.

He heard his name being shouted and looked over the rail to where a long, narrow boat rowed by eight oarsmen was taking up position directly beneath him. From its stern seats, Admiral St. Valéry was gazing up at him, and when he caught Sinclair's eye he waved towards the village and shouted, "Join me ashore. I'm going to speak with de Berenger."

Once again, Will was made aware of the difference between moving on water as opposed to land. His galley—de Berenger's—was moored less than a tenth of a mile from the landward end of the wharf, perhaps two hundred paces on land, a distance that Will would have covered in a matter of minutes, even had he had to saddle his horse beforehand. On this occasion, however, he had to call for a boat and a crew of rowers, and then transfer himself from the galley to the boat, with the extreme caution of a landsman distrustful of the behavior of water and the vessels that bobbed about on it, and be rowed over to the end of the wharf. By the time he eventually caught up with St. Valéry, three-quarters of an hour had elapsed.

His brother Kenneth was waiting to greet him as Will climbed from the boat to the top of the breakwater, and threw his arms around him, squeezing him in a great bear hug. As Will prized himself away, grinning, he ran his fingertips over Kenneth's chain-mail hauberk.

"Well met, Brother. I'll presume, from the absence o' tears and wailing, that everything went as it was supposed to. The goods are safe?"

"Safe and sound, Will. They're *all* here."

"You make that sound as though there was more than you bargained for."

"There was! It filled five four-wheeled wagons and a cart. There was far more there than we thought there would be, but not too much to transport. There were four main chests, of course, the big ones—we loaded those onto two wagons, as planned—but then there was a fine collection of gold and silver I didn't expect, in boxes—bars and coinage of both—and seven whole chests of jewels, two of them small, the other five almost as large as the main treasure chests.

They're closed wi' straps for the most part, so a few of them were easy to open and I took a look inside, just to see what we were lugging. They're stuffed wi' studded chalices and crucifixes and church vessels, that kind of thing. Clearly the Master didn't want them falling into de Nogaret's hands. We had to turn the country upside down to find more wagons to carry them."

"You—you did not wreak havoc in taking them, I hope?"

"D'you take me for a fool, Brother? I sent out pairs of men in every direction, with silver coin, to find me anything that they could buy within a day and to buy no more than one wagon and team at any place ... And before you think to ask, none of them wore anything that might identify them to strange eyes as Templars."

"Hmm." Sinclair absorbed that for a moment, then nodded decisively. "Excellent. You have done well, Kenneth. We'll get everything aboard quickly and see that all is safely stowed. In the meantime, promise me you'll take that armor off before you try to board a ship, Brother, and have your men do the same. You'll notice this dagger is the heaviest thing I'm wearing. I've almost gone swimming several times, simply climbing in and out of boats. You fall in wearing any of that gear and you'll sink like a stone. Where are your men, by the way?"

Kenneth pointed a thumb back over his shoulder, and Will climbed up onto a stony outcrop and peered over the top of all the surrounding activity to see the hundred knights and sergeants drawn up on foot, in orderly ranks at the base of the high cliff. The sergeants formed a solid, disciplined bank of brown and black shapes, and the forty knights, most of them wearing their red-crossed white cloth surcoats over chain mail, were grouped to their left. One glance was all he required to see that the men were waiting patiently, and he jumped down again.

"They look good. Their horses are being loaded now. I'll have de Berenger, the vice-admiral, send you instructions as to where and when your men should board—and here he is, the very man."

Sir Edward de Berenger had approached, unnoticed until that moment, and Sinclair introduced him to Kenneth, then asked where the admiral had gone. De Berenger smiled and waved towards a single large tent, a hundred yards from where they stood, and as William glanced towards it he noticed a knot of people he identified by their dress as villagers, standing huddled off to one side, well clear of the activities on the beach. He indicated them with a nod.

"What about the village folk there? Did you have any problems with them?"

"Nah!" Kenneth shook his head. "They were terrified when we came down on them from the cliffs, but once they saw that we meant them no harm but were interested only in their wharf, they threw up their hands and left us to it. The head man is a fellow called Pierre. He calmed them down. I told him to keep them well out of our way and gave him a purse of silver for their trouble. I did it publicly, too, so he won't be able to keep it for himself. None of them has said a word since then. Oh, I told him, too, that if anyone comes questioning them, to hold nothing back, but tell about everything they saw. It won't make any difference to us by then."

"Hmm." His brother twisted his mouth wryly. "If anyone comes looking for us here, it won't matter what these people say. Their lives will be forfeit. I'm sure they know that, too." He turned to de Berenger. "Well, Sir Edward, we should join the admiral, since he called us here in person. Kenneth, you should rejoin your men."

Kenneth nodded to both of them and turned away as de Berenger raised a finger to Sinclair.

"I cannot join you yet. I have another matter of some urgency—a problem with one of the hoists—and it will not wait. Present my apologies to Sir Charles, if you will, and I will come to you presently."

Sinclair was chagrined, as he headed for the admiral's tent, to see the Baroness St. Valéry already there, sitting on the pebbled foreshore beside her good-brother, and his heart seemed to sink into the pit of his stomach. He found himself wondering if she intended to participate in every discussion that was to take place, and the thought set him immediately on edge. He saw St. Valéry take note of his arrival only to turn away, distracted by someone who had approached him with tidings of some kind.

St. Valéry rose to his feet and said something to the Baroness, flipped a hand in salute to the still-approaching Sinclair, and followed the messenger, disappearing quickly among the throng of bodies behind him. Less than half a hundred paces now separated Sinclair from where the Baroness sat gazing out at the shipping in the small harbor, and as he struggled to walk quickly over the yielding mass of the pebbled beach that seemed to drag at the soles of his boots, he lowered his eyes to watch his feet, thus avoiding looking at her. Despite his exhaustion, or perhaps because of it, he had not been able to sleep aboard ship the previous night and had spent a long time thinking about the woman, once he had finally accepted that he was unable not to think about her.

Lady Jessica Randolph unsettled him deeply, and lying on his rocking bunk in the hours before dawn, he had understood that for him, she was the embodiment of something utterly beyond his experience, the essence of everything he had willingly abandoned upon joining the Brotherhood of the Temple and undertaking his solemn vows of monkhood. As monk, soldier, and Crusader, his had been a life of purely masculine concerns: combat, training, and campaigning in times of war; garrison duties, unrelenting discipline, and the incessant prayer schedule of the Templars' Rule in times of peace. Even in recent years, while undergoing intensive training for his future role as a member of the Governing Council of the Order, he had been held separate from the affairs of the world outside the brotherhood, his time dedicated to the staggeringly complex task of learning the esoteric secrets shared only by the privileged elite of the Temple's highest initiates, that knowledge referred to—although not often and never publicly—as the Higher Mysteries of the Ancient Order of Sion. That task had consumed him, and as his comprehension of its immensity grew, it had even frightened him at times, forcing him to review the entire sum of knowledge and beliefs that he had acquired in a lifetime of total ignorance of the Mysteries' existence.

And then had come this woman to distract him with the sound of her voice, the sight of her body, the smell of her presence, and the awareness of her femininity.

When no more than twenty paces separated them, she saw him coming, and her face cleared, losing the slight air of preoccupation it had worn and taking on an expression of … what? Disinterest? No, Sinclair corrected himself. Plain emptiness was what it was. As though he were beneath her notice. Well, he thought, that would earn her no displeasure from him. If she wanted to behave as she thought a man behaved, then so be it; she would be treated as a man could expect to be treated … a lesser man, of course. An underling. Sinclair felt himself grinding his teeth and made a conscious effort to relax.

She looked up at him as he arrived beside her and he nodded stiffly, in a tacit, perfunctory greeting.

"Good day, Sir William." Her voice, while not welcoming, conveyed no hint of displeasure. "Sir Charles will join us directly. Please sit down."

It may have been the "us" that angered him, her assumption that she would share whatever he might have to say to St. Valéry, or vice versa, or it may have been the cool air of impenetrable self-possession with which she invited him to sit and plainly expected him to obey, but whatever the reason, he felt the ire flare up in him, outrage and humiliation vying with each other to undo him equally—for he knew beyond doubt, even then, that he would be in the wrong no matter what he said or did, and so he stood there mute for long moments, unable either to move or to speak. Fortunately for him, the woman misinterpreted his inaction and looked up at him with a shade more warmth in her gaze.

"Please, sit, if you will. Charles saw you coming but was called away before he could greet you. Something to do with the loading of livestock. I must admit to being surprised at the number of your brother's company here. I had expected a score or so of men and horses, but there must be more than a hundred of each. Please, sit you down here. My ladies have gone looking for firewood, to take the chill off the afternoon air, but they should soon be back, and we'll be warmer once the fire is lit."

Bemused by her easy openness and lack of apparent guile, Sinclair found himself moving to comply with her wishes, even though he had no slightest idea of what to say to her. But she simply kept talking as he lowered himself to perch on a boulder across from her, and he found himself listening and preparing to answer in spite of himself.

"I confess, were it not for my ladies, I should freeze and die of exposure, for I have no notion of how to light a fire in the open air, do you? Are you adept with flint and steel? I suppose you must be, being a Temple Knight. I am told there is nothing practical that you and your fellows cannot do."

"No, that's a nonsense," he heard himself say, and nearly winced at his own brusqueness. "I have a tinder box, wi' flint and steel, but a' God's name, Lady, I cannot remember when I last used it, if I ever did. Tam does all that, and I am grateful to him for it. He starts our fires and keeps them alight, and he keeps me fed, for else I would most likely starve. I have little attention for such things."

Well, at least you are capable of speaking like a reasonably normal person. From what I've seen and learned of you until now, that is a very important development in your status vis-à-vis women—

Sinclair was already rising to his feet again. "Here come your women now, madam. I'll leave you with them." Sinclair nodded towards the only two other women on the beach, who were bearing armloads of logs and followed by a group of sergeants carrying more.

Jessica stood up, too, as the armloads of logs clattered to the pebbles, one after the other, and called to Sinclair as he was on the point of walking away.

"Wait, Sir William, if you will. I will walk with you until the fire is lit."

Dismayed, Will stood hesitantly as she approached him and managed not to flinch as she reached out and laid one hand on his forearm.

"There," she said, "and you have my thanks. These pebbles are grossly difficult and dangerous to walk upon."

He made no response, but held his bent arm stiffly and began to walk with exaggerated slowness, clearly braced to prevent her from falling. She fought back the smile that threatened to break out upon her face and made herself walk beside him slowly and with great decorum, visualizing what his shocked reaction might be were she to break into anything resembling a dance while walking with her hand upon his arm. And such was her temptation to break into giggles that she had to raise her free hand to her mouth and pretend to cough. She stopped, obliging him to stop, too, and wait for her as she made an elaborate show of examining the fishing hamlet and the cliffs behind it.

"What a perfect place for the task you have in hand, Sir William. This spot must be completely hidden here beneath the cliffs from anyone above, and I vow it could never be seen from a passing ship, were the people aboard unaware of its existence. How did you ever come to find it?"

Sinclair followed her gaze to where the beetling cliffs loomed over the tiny settlement. "By chance, Lady," he said, avoiding looking at her. "Purely by chance, a score and more years ago."

"What kind of chance might have brought you here? This is not a friendly coastline."

"Wind and weather brought me. I was on a ship that foundered when a winter squall blew us onto a shoal to the south of here. Tam and I were among the very few to survive, him in a boat of sorts with three other lads, and me clinging to a spar with another man who was dead when the current cast us ashore in this inlet. Tam came ashore a mile or so farther north and thought me dead, too, as I did him, but we found each other by chance the following day."

"And this village was here then?"

He glanced at her sidelong, as though surprised by the naivety of the question. "Aye, it was. It is a natural haven. There have been fisher folk living here since the land was created, I am sure."

"And you remembered it."

"Aye, I did. I always try to remember the good and the bad. It is folly not to remember both ends of the range of things. Most of the ruck is forgettable … unimportant … but the knowledge of a safe haven, or of a dangerous killing ground, can be priceless at times."

She had been watching him with her head tilted to one side, and now she began to walk again, her hand still resting on his arm. "I confess, Sir William, the concept of killing grounds is one I seldom entertain, but I understand what you are saying and I agree with the principle behind it."

She said nothing more for a short time, continuing to walk with lowered eyes, leaving him to grapple with the idea that a mere woman had expressed an understanding of a principle. He wanted to pursue that thought, but had no slightest notion of how to go about it, and so he waited instead, hoping she would say more on the topic. But she continued in silence, and then, just as he was deciding that she might say no more, she continued as though there had been no lapse in what she was saying.

"It will be amusing, think you not"—and here she paused to dart a smile at him—"to see how your views might change from now on, given the safe havens and dangerous grounds of your new life henceforth."

"My new life?" His voice hardened instantly as he sensed her threatening to intrude where she had no right to go. "I have no new life, Lady, nor will I."

"But I—" Jessie was flustered by the sudden hostility in his voice and spoke without really thinking. "I was but referring to the events of this morning … the King's obvious enmity and de Nogaret's duplicity. That has changed everythi—"

"Nothing has changed, Baroness." His voice was harsh, peremptory. "There has been a misunderstanding of some kind, some form of miscommunication, but it will be soon resolved, let me assure you. The Temple Order is the strongest of its kind anywhere. It is far greater than any one man. And it is incapable of being seriously disrupted by the greedy scheming of lesser men, be they kings and kings' ministers or no. So there will be no lasting changes made to my life."

She was staring wide eyed at him before he had come close to finishing, the color already flaring up in her cheeks, and she swept in to the attack.

"Misunderstandings? Soon to be resolved? Were you not in the room last night when I spoke on that very topic? Did you not hear a single word I said? Or did you simply dismiss me for being a woman and decide that my opinions are worthless and unfounded?"

The two stood glaring at each other as Jessie waited for his response, but when it came it was not in the form of words. His face simply froze into a baleful mask of disapproval and he swung away, rigid with outraged dignity, leaving her standing alone on the strand as her good-brother the admiral approached, his face clearly betraying astonishment at what he was seeing.

"In God's name, what happened, Sister? What did you to offend Sir William so? I have never seen him so angry. What did you say to him to make him charge away like that?"

She did not even glance at him, her eyes fixed on Sinclair as he vanished among the bustle of people on the beach.

She swung to face her questioner. "As God may judge me, I said nothing to cause offense to any reasonable man. But your obdurate Sir William shows few signs of being reasonable in dealing with anyone he cannot dominate and bully. The offense, and the anger that accompanies it, arise from sources other than from me. Search you inside Sir William Sinclair for the root of it, for I will have no part of him or his anger. He is naught but a great truculent, ill-mannered oaf." And having delivered herself of that opinion, she swept away in turn, leaving the highly perplexed admiral to gaze after her, shaking his head several times, before he turned to move quickly in pursuit of Sinclair.

3

Will Sinclair was standing at the edge of the quay when St. Valéry caught up to him, watching the loading activity in the tiny harbor, his lips pursed and his brow furrowed in deep thought as he tossed a smooth pebble listlessly from hand to hand.

"Sir William. I require some of your time, in order to discuss several matters of import. May we return to my tent on the beach?"

Sinclair nodded wordlessly.

"Excellent." St. Valéry hesitated, then continued. "Look, Sir William, I know not what transpired between you and my good-sister back there, but I know it angered you, and I cannot afford to have you angry at this point. So empty your mind of what displeases you, if you can, and let us talk, you and I, of the priorities facing us in this endeavor. Can you do that?"

"Of course I can, Sir Charles. It vexes me that you should even have to ask. Lead on, if you will. You have all my attention."

"Excellent, for we have much to discuss, first among all the disposition of the treasure brought by your brother, of which there is far more than we at first supposed. The two largest and most seaworthy vessels we possess are our two main command galleys, my own and de Berenger's, which is substantially smaller but newer, and I find myself disliking the thought of entrusting the treasure to any other ship, even though the larger cargo vessels have more space in them. I firmly believe that we would be foolish to stow the chests anywhere else but where we can keep watch on them—not because I distrust our men but purely because I distrust the weather. The winter storms could set in now at any time and our fleet could be scattered to the ends of the ocean, dependent upon the whims and ferocity of the winds. And so I propose splitting the main treasure between your vessel— de Berenger's—and mine. You already have the Lady Jessica's gold aboard your ship, and your own personal responsibility entails the protection of the Templar Treasure. I will therefore have the four main chests containing your charge loaded aboard your ship as well. I myself will take the lesser treasure aboard mine. What think you?"

Sinclair agreed, relieved to know that he would not be parted from the main Treasure, the primary responsibility settled upon him by Master de Molay. For the next half hour the two commanders walked together up and down the beach, observing the work in progress as they went over the details of their plans, such as they were, for the coming few days.

As soon as the treasure was safely aboard ship, they would put to sea again, sailing south, between the mainland and the island called the Isle of Oleron, passing the wide entrance to the Gironde inlet on their port side to follow the French coastline south along the Bay of Biscay until they reached the westward-jutting Iberian peninsula. From there they would make their way west along the Iberian coast of the bay until they reached the headland of Corunna, where they would turn south again for several days to collect whatever elements of the Templar fleet might have gathered off Cape Finisterre. They had no means of divining how many vessels might have escaped from other French ports ahead of the seizures and sailed to await a rendezvous, or how punctual those might be, but once there, the La Rochelle contingent would wait on station, safely offshore, for seven days, to ensure that every vessel that had been en route to join them, prior to Friday the thirteenth, had arrived. Thereafter, the assembly would sail as one fleet wherever William Sinclair, as senior representative of the Order of the Temple, ordered them.

At last St. Valéry appeared to have run out of things to discuss. They were approaching the wharf again, and the piles of material on the beach by the quay had dwindled greatly.

"It looks as though they have almost finished," Will said, nodding towards the wharfside activity. The four great chests of the main Treasure still sat on the wharf together with the remaining contents of Kenneth's wagons, but the wagons themselves had been dismantled and stowed, Kenneth's men had been shipped aboard a number of vessels, and the majority of their horses, along with their saddlery and weapons, had already been slung aboard the ships assigned to them.

St. Valéry barely glanced up before he asked, "Are you completely set on sailing to Scotland, Sir William?"

Sinclair looked at him in surprise. "Set upon it? Aye, I suppose I am … But it comes to me that you are not. Have you something else in mind? If you have, spit it out and we will talk about it. Shall I send for de Berenger?"

"No! No, that will not be necessary ... What is in my mind is ... well, it is something that has been there for a long time now ... Something more concerned with what we are and where we should be rather than with who we are and where we ought to go ... if you see what I mean."

"No, Sir Charles, I do not." He was smiling slightly, shaking his head. "And to tell truth, that marks the first time I have ever heard you be less than clearly explicit, so it makes me most curious." He glanced quickly around to see if anyone was nearby, but they were out of earshot of the closest group of workers. "Walk with me again, then, so we may keep from being overheard, for I have the feeling that you have no wish to say what's in your mind to anyone but me. Not even to Vice-Admiral de Berenger. Come then, as friend, not admiral, and tell me what is in your mind."

He moved away, and St. Valéry fell into step beside him, his head lowered. Sinclair walked in silence, remembering his own difficulties with the tidings he had had to bring to La Rochelle the previous day, and therefore content to wait until the right words came to the older man. Finally, St. Valéry uttered a snort and squared his shoulders.

"Very well then, Sir William, but before I begin, may I ask what befell between you and my good-sister? You were notably out of countenance. That was plain to see."

"Aye, I was, and I think I may have been wrong." He nibbled on his stubbly upper lip. "She asked me what I intended to do with my new life, now that the Order has been betrayed."

"And that angered you?"

"Aye, it did, for it made me contemplate, for a moment but against my will, a world in which our Order would have ceased to exist. And that is close to inconceivable. The Temple, under the guidance of our ancient Order of Sion, has become the most power-ful fraternity in the world. So differences will be straightened out and compromises will be made, in one fashion or another. But above all, our Order will continue. It was the sudden thought of my life being changed, without my having any opportunity to challenge such an outcome, that made me angry. I was ill prepared for that idea and I had no intention of discussing it with your good-sister. There was no more to it than that. As I said, I was probably wrong to react as I did."

"Aye, well, Sir William, the right and wrong of it I cannot judge, but I am as one with you in the judgment that, above all else and despite what men may do to thwart it, our ancient Order will continue. The outward form of it may change beyond our credence, may even disappear completely from the ken of man and revert to what it was before Hugh de Payens and his fellows ever went to Outremer in search of what they found. But the Order of Sion will survive as long as any of us, sworn to its propagation, retains the ability to pass on its tenets to another generation. For at its deepest root, our Order is an idea, Sir William, a system of belief, and ideas are immortal and indestructible ..."

St. Valéry's voice died away into silence, but Sinclair could tell he had not yet finished talking, and sure enough he began again after a space of heartbeats.

"It is precisely that train of thought that has stirred this other matter in my mind." He took Sinclair's arm suddenly and turned sharply left to walk inland, in order to avoid another gang of seamen piling weapons into nets for hoisting. "It seems to me that the fundamental idea underlying our Order might benefit in future from some practical demonstration of the truth underlying our lore."

Sinclair frowned. "What do you mean, a practical demonstration? That has already taken place, nigh on two hundred years ago, when the Order was reborn in the bowels of the temple tunnels and the truth of its lore was proved beyond dispute. What could be more practical than that? At that point we changed our name from the Order of Rebirth in Sion to the simple Order of Sion. We had *achieved* rebirth, then and there. The Order of the Temple came into existence only after that."

"I know that, Sir William, as well as you do, but the ordinary brethren of today's Temple, those who have no knowledge of our ancient Order, do not. And lacking that knowledge, that proof, they stand to be bereft of hope and subject to despair because of these upheavals in France."

"So?"

"So I refuse to accept the notion that the Order of the Temple should simply be allowed to die."

"And why should it not?" Sinclair's rejoinder came without the slightest hesitation. "It is *our* Order that is important here, Sir Charles, the Order of Sion, not the Order of the Temple. Since the fall of Acre and the loss of Outremer more than a decade ago, the Order of the Temple appears to have lost the regard of the people who once revered it. That loss is real, but the lesser loss, the loss of Acre, cannot account for it. The loss of Acre was tragic, but it was honorable. The Temple's knights and sergeants there were wiped out with the fall of the city, leaving no survivors. They did their duty alongside the other defenders of the faith in Outremer, and they performed their task and died as martyrs, against insuperable odds. So it is unjust to lay the Temple's fall from grace upon the shoulders of its dead. The Temple of Solomon has earned its own disfavor down the years, and in full measure, beginning from the day the Order lowered its standards and decreed that monkhood was not the sole prerequisite for membership. *That* is when the rot first set in—the very day the Temple first permitted laymen and merchants to join its ranks and granted them the privilege of calling themselves Templars. Since then, through the behavior of its associate brethren, the Temple that the ordinary people see from day to day has clutched its arrogance and privilege about itself and gone out of its way to alienate everyone who deals with it."

He stopped short and pursed his lips, almost defiant in the way he gazed at St. Valéry, as if challenging him. "Come now, Sir Charles, let us set surface loyalties aside, we two, and admit that the Temple has always had boors, strutters, and pigheaded fools among its brethren from the very outset. But those were fighting knights, and even their worst excesses were held close among the brethren. That is not the kind of behavior that I am condemning

here. The Order of the Temple of Solomon today bears no resemblance to the brotherhood it once was, save for those few of us
who serve its military arm. It has become a tradesmen's guild, full
of braggarts, cheats, bombasts, and unsavory creatures, none of
whom pay taxes, and all of whom, exulting in their privilege and
status, have embodied all the arrogance, pride, folly, and weaknesses to which man is heir.

"And yet within the Temple structure itself, carefully
concealed, are our brethren, the Brotherhood of Sion, forming the
living sinews that coordinate the muscles of the corpus and keep
the body functioning. Remove those brethren, and the lore they
live to perpetuate, and the Temple itself will fall and pass into
history to no one's great regret, while the Brotherhood of the
Order of Sion will continue."

St. Valéry stood frowning, pinching at the hair on his chin, then
nodded. "Aye, you have the right of it. Reluctant though I find myself
to admit that it is true, I will not dispute you. The Order of the Temple
is corrupt, and if it falls or is transformed in any way, our brotherhood
will survive. But at what cost, Sir William? We will be forced to live
and work in secrecy again, constrained to be clandestine in all things,
to the detriment of our Order's designs. That alone, I believe, must
give us pause. The Temple brotherhood, and the very fabric of the
Temple itself, provide us with a mantle of invisibility. Existing within
the outer shell, we are unnoticed and anonymous. I believe we must
do all in our power to maintain that mantle, and in order to do so, we
need to give the rank and file of the Templar brethren something to
believe in, something from their own lore that will encourage them
to endure in the face of these present troubles."

A cold gust of wind swept in across the beach, buffeting them,
and St. Valéry glanced up at the rack of scudding cloud that had
begun to gather as they made landfall and now darkened the sky.
"Squalls," he said, pulling his light cloak more securely around him.
"Let's hope they blow over quickly. If the weather worsens, we could
be caught in here, unable to beat out to sea." He looked back to where
Sinclair was adjusting his own clothing against the sudden wind.

"The Temple *has* no lore of its own, Admiral," the Scots knight said, as though St. Valéry had made no mention of the weather. "It is too new to have developed lore."

"True, I know that." St. Valéry was eyeing the cloud banks again. "I doubt this will turn to much, but if need be, we can use our oars to tow the transports out into deep water. But as I said, if it becomes too bad, we may have to bide here awhile."

"Too close to La Rochelle for my liking," was Sinclair's response. "Barely thirty miles by road from there to here. De Nogaret's men could catch us sitting here helpless."

"They could, if they knew where to look, but they don't. There's cause for gratitude in that thought, my friend." St. Valéry looked at the sky once more, then turned to look about him at the activity in the tiny harbor. "But things appear to be going smoothly, and the tide will not begin to ebb for several hours. The laden vessels are already standing out to safety, well clear of land and in the lee of Oleron Isle, and there are very few remaining. We should be well enough. The Treasure is all shipped, and most of the livestock. All that remains is materiel that we could leave behind, if pushed."

He dismissed the weather with a wave of his hand. "About this lore, or the lack of it … There is one piece, one fragment of the ancient lore of Sion, that escaped somehow and was long since adopted by the Temple."

"The Merica matter."

"Aye, precisely. No one has ever discovered the source of the betrayal, or how the information was divulged, but it was the only instance, ever, of such a thing occurring. Personally, I began some years ago to suspect that Hugh de Payens himself may have released it deliberately, early on in the Jerusalem growth of the Order of the Temple, believing it to be harmless, yet valuable as an earnest of a need for secrecy within the new-established Order. A seed, perhaps, from which to grow a tradition. Do you think that fanciful?"

Sinclair jutted his jaw. "No, not at all. It makes perfect sense now that you mention it. The Merica rumor never had much substance to it, and had been unimportant to our objectives. It was regarded as trivial by everyone who knew of it. Its disclosure was certainly not the kind of thing that could ever threaten our Order. So yes, I think that Hugh de Payens might have borrowed it, in a time of need."

"Merica is no rumor, Sir William. It is an accepted and ratified segment of our ancient teachings and beliefs."

"Yes, I know the substance of it, Admiral: that there exists, beyond the Western Sea, a fabled land of plenty, vast and endless, watched over by a brilliant evening star that the people who live there call Merica. I have even studied what there is to know of it, though that is very limited. But no matter what any of us might wish to believe, it remains no more than a fable, rooted, as you say, in our lore. We may speculate on it, but we have no proof that it exists, or that it ever was."

"I agree, but that is what I was thinking about …"

"Sir Charles, you are not making sense."

"On the contrary, Sir William, I believe I am. How many vessels would you say we have in our fleet?"

Another gust of wind drove icy drops of rain against their faces, and Sinclair raised a hand to wipe his cheek, surprised to feel the coldness of the skin against his fingers. "You know that better than I, Admiral. It is your fleet. I have made no attempt to count them, but the number twenty is in my mind."

St. Valéry dipped his head. "That is a fair estimate. We have seven naval galleys and fourteen cargo vessels—twenty-one in all. In addition, by this time next week, dependent upon what we may find off Finisterre, we could have half as many ships again."

"But the newcomers would not be cargo carriers."

"No, that is unlikely. If any vessels reach the rendezvous at all, they will be naval galleys, simply by virtue of the word sent out to the ports."

"How many fighting men do you have at your disposal?" Sir William asked.

"At *my* disposal, as opposed to yours?"

"Aye, seamen and landsmen."

"Hmm … Landsmen, not counting your brother's contingent, one hundred fifty-four from the garrison at La Rochelle, of whom thirty

and six are serving lay brothers and therefore noncombatant ..."
St. Valéry made a grimace while he calculated in his head. "One
hundred and eighteen fighting men of all ranks, therefore, under de
Montrichard. Seamen? The crews of the cargo ships, about four
hundred men in total, are not fighters. The galley crews are all fighting
men, and they range in size from forty oars to twenty. Two men to an
oar, with a relief crew of one to two extra men per oar on each craft ...
That could total seven hundred men, but it is a misleading tally because
the number of relief oarsmen varies widely from galley to galley, no
matter how hard we try to sustain them." He shrugged. "But there you
have it. A large force, on the face of it. It could be formidable."

"Aye, it could. And it will be. So whence comes all this talk of
Merica, and what has it to do with this fleet?"

St. Valéry stopped walking and turned to him. "Would you need
that many ships in Scotland, a foreign land? Seven to perhaps twenty
galleys and a fleet of cargo vessels? For if you do not, I should like
to take a few of the ships, manned only by men who wish to go with
me, and sail in search of this fabled place."

"Merica?"

St. Valéry showed no reaction to the incredulity in Sinclair's
voice, and the two men stood eyeing each other.

"This is not tomfoolery," Sinclair said at last, his voice without
inflection. "You mean what you say."

The admiral shrugged very slightly. "I do not deal in tomfoolery.
I never have; a lifelong habit. I have always been careful to say what
I mean ... and in consequence, to mean what I say."

Another silence ensued, this one shorter, until Sinclair spoke
again. "You are aware, I presume, of how absurd that sounds.
You are proposing to sail off with a portion of our fleet, for vast
distances and through uncharted waters, in the hope of finding a
place no man has sought in more than a millennium—a place that
may never even have existed. And you will ask for volunteers to go
with you, into almost certain death."

St. Valéry shrugged again. "Essentially, yes. But I would not call
it insane."

"Of course you would not—it's your idea," Sinclair said with a grin. "You know, of course, that the name of the place where we will rendezvous, Finisterre, means the end of the world, the end of land?"

St. Valéry smiled. "I do. But I suspect that name was given the place by men who had never found land beyond that point ... because they had never sailed far enough westward. The ancients knew nothing of navigation beyond sight of land." The admiral cocked his head, gauging his companion's concern. "Look you," he continued. "Hear me out, if only as a man. Listen to what I have to say, and then think about it before you come to any decision. We have ten days at least, and probably more, before we will have to decide. And then, if you decide against my request, I shall obey your wishes, as I am bound by oath. It will be reluctantly, but I will obey ..."

"Go on."

"Think first on what I said about the need for some sign for the men involved in whatever events are happening in France today. If things are truly as bad as they appear to be, and all the brethren of senior status have been taken and imprisoned, then those rank-and-file members who have survived the initial purge, or attack, or whatever it may turn out to be, will feel abandoned and lost, like a rudderless ship in a high sea ... And if that is the case, then matters will only grow worse."

Sinclair frowned as he thought about that, then shook his head. "I can't accept that, Admiral—that things will grow worse. I have to believe that whatever has happened to our brethren in France will be temporary, no matter how traumatic. I believe Master de Molay himself believed that when last I spoke to him, and logic itself demands that it must be so, simply because of our size, if nothing else—"

"The Holy, Catholic, and Apostolic Church is bigger," St. Valéry interrupted, sardonically, leaving the younger man blinking. "Surely you would not dispute that?"

"Well, no, not in terms of numbers. There is no denying that strength, but—"

"But we must suspect the active participation of the Church in what has happened to our Order, Sir William. Philip the Fair, for all his arrogance, would never dare to move against us as he has without the Pope's permission. Such an action would require papal sanction, since we of the knighthood are monks. And need I remind you that Pope Clement is generally accepted to be Philip's puppet, indebted to Capet for his position?"

Sinclair's features had settled into a deep scowl. "Why did you not mention this last night?"

"Because I have thought of it only since then, though I have thought of little else since it occurred to me. Besides, there was no time last night. Too much had to be done in too little time. But today, having failed to win an hour of sleep because my thoughts kept me awake, I find myself having grave and well-considered doubts about the future of our Order in France. There may be compromises and accommodations, as you say, but I fear our Temple will never again enjoy the influence it had in France even one week ago. It is outdated, and in recent years has incurred great resentment, perceived as waxing fat and paying no taxes, if for no other reason. When Acre fortress fell and the Latin Kingdom of Outremer was lost, the Temple lost its *raison d'être* … and there are no few in France and elsewhere who lay the blame for that loss at the Temple's door, unjust and insupportable though that charge may be. And thus I fear our place in France itself is lost. King Philip is a hard and callous man, and his ambitions know no bounds, other than those imposed by lack of funds. He will not return one silver mark of what his lawyers seize from us."

The frown slowly faded from Sinclair's face, to be replaced by an expression of thoughtfulness. "A rudderless ship, you said. But if you are correct, there will *be* no ship … no Order. How, then, could matters grow worse?"

St. Valéry waved a hand as though dismissing the obvious. "Well, let us suppose for a moment that Philip and de Nogaret are successful, and they wrest control of the Order's wealth and assets from our hands—those assets that are left within the realm of France, I mean. That will bring instant and enormous benefits to their treasury—freedom from debts, and real funds with which to operate … my greatest reason for doubting that this matter will be settled to our satisfaction. But if that does occur and goes unchallenged, condoned by Holy Church, think you the other Christian monarchs will hang back from behaving similarly against the Temple in their own lands? I doubt it."

The Scots knight turned his back to the chill rain that had begun to slant inland. "I agree with you on that, at least. The same thought had already occurred to me earlier. And yet … you describe a bleak prospect, my lord Admiral. Unwilling as I may be to concede to it entirely, however, I fear you may be right. But again, what has this to do with your Merica?"

"Everything, William, and nothing. I believe the other kings of Christendom will flock like ravens to a carcass once Philip has shown the way. And I choose not to live in such a world. I am an old man, all at once and unexpectedly, coming to the end of my usefulness precisely at a time when I have most need to be capable of great things, and that awareness galls me. I know the time has come to hand my duties and my admiral's rank and badge of office to a younger man, and I know, too, that de Berenger will be an excellent successor—so be it there is something left to which he can succeed." He paused, then shook his head. "I would languish and die in this Scotland of yours, my friend. It is your home, and Lady Jessica's, but it is far from mine. And besides, you are a landsman, bred to horsemanship. I am a seaman, trained in navigation, and I have been a mariner my entire life. It comes to me that I would rather die at sea, in a worthwhile quest for something I believe in, than wither away in a strange, cold land among folk with whom I cannot even converse.

"Be that as it may, you have ships aplenty here for your needs and mine, and who is to say this Scottish king of yours will not see more than a score of strange vessels as a threat? I—" The admiral cocked his head. "Someone is calling you." He glanced around and then pointed. "Over there, on the quay."

Sinclair saw a man waving at him. "Your ears are better than mine, Sir Charles. It's Tam, and that cannot be good. He would not interrupt me here without cause."

"Then go to him. But first, let me leave you with this in mind: I may sail off and die hundreds of miles from land of any kind, and I will be content, as I have said. And the men who come with me will have made the choice to do so of their own free will. But think, Sir William ... what if the lore of Merica should prove as true as that of Jerusalem and the Treasure that lay hidden there? What if I were to find the place? And what then were I to return to you bearing proofs of what I found? Would that not serve to rally all our brethren, of Sion and the Temple both?" He spread his hands, palms upward. "It is no more strange than digging for the ruins of a Temple no one knew was there. Is it?"

Sinclair raised a hand to Tam to indicate that he should wait a little. "No, it is not, Admiral, when you say it like that. So be it. I will think on this between now and our arrival off Cape Finisterre. But now, if you will permit me, I must see what Tam requires of me."

Charles St. Valéry watched him walk away, then scratched idly at his beard with the tip of one finger. He was surprised when his young superior stopped and turned back.

"Tam seems to want you to come with me," Sir William called. "If his tidings are important they will probably affect you, too."

St. Valéry began to walk again, digging his heavy soles into the yielding pebbles with renewed purpose.

4

"What is it, Tam?"

"I'm not sure." The sergeant wasted no time on formalities, nodding in greeting to St. Valéry and then addressing him directly. "One of your captains just arrived, Admiral. One of the two you turned back this morning. He asked me to deliver his respects and to ask you to board his galley to speak with him."

St. Valéry and Sinclair exchanged questioning glances, and then St. Valéry turned his eyes towards the harbor entrance, where a sleek galley floated at anchor, closer than any other of its kind but concealed from where they had stood by the bulk of the ship at the quay.

"It's Parmaison. But where is de Lisle? And why would he not come to me directly?"

"There's urgency involved. Great urgency," Sinclair said. "Look at the oars. He's ready to put out to sea again immediately, once he has spoken with you."

"Hmm. Find us a boat, Sergeant."

"I have one ready, Admiral, at the end of the pier."

After quitting La Rochelle that morning, St. Valéry, with Sinclair's concurrence, had sent two of his swiftest galleys to return to the roads approaching the harbor and to remain there for the remainder of that day, keeping watch to see what might develop. It had been an afterthought, no more than a precautionary measure, for they had been under way for more than two hours before the thought occurred to either man, and although they considered it highly unlikely that anything untoward might actually take place, since they had burned the only ships remaining in the harbor, they had agreed that it might be a good idea to keep a watchful eye on the fort and the headlands flanking it. But now one of the delegated vessels had caught up to them, far ahead of schedule.

The captain of the returned galley, Sir Geoffrey Parmaison, watched them pull alongside from the narrow forecastle, then helped the two senior officers aboard in person before leading them to a small folding table and three chairs he had set up beneath an awning on the upper foredeck. He dismissed the watchman at the prow, and then all three men sat down.

"Tell us, Sir Geoffrey," St. Valéry began without preamble.

Parmaison nodded and then spoke tersely. "We returned to La Rochelle as ordered, Admiral, and arrived in sight of it just in time to see three of our own galleys entering the harbor. We saw them, I say, but we were too far away to attract their attention and could do nothing to stop them sailing into La Rochelle."

"Who were they? Do you know?"

"Aye, Admiral. De Lisle was closer to them than I was, and swears he recognized one of the galleys as being Antoine de l'Armentière's."

"De l'Armentière? He is supposed to be in Cyprus."

"That's what I thought, sir, but de Lisle is cousin to him, and he swears it was Antoine's galley that he saw leading the flotilla. Apparently it differs from any other."

"Aye, it does. It is Moorish, a prize of war—a pirate vessel, captured off Gibraltar some years ago. De Lisle was sure of this?"

"As sure as he could be from a distance of miles, but whoever it was, he took three Temple galleys into La Rochelle and stayed there."

"Hmm. Where is Captain de Lisle now?"

"On station, Admiral, waiting for whatever might happen. He sent me back to bring you the word."

"And you saw nothing more than you have described?"

"Nothing, sir. They went in, and they did not come out."

"Very well. Thank you, Captain Parmaison. Return to your station, rejoin Captain de Lisle, and bid him remain where he is until he has something more to report." He held up one hand to stay the man and turned to Sinclair. "Do you have anything to add, Sir William?"

"No, Admiral, because I think you and I are considering the same eventuality. Were either of us in de Nogaret's shoes in this, we would impound all three vessels, imprison the commanders and their crews, then take the galleys out to sea again, crewed by our own men, to pursue this fleet. Is that what you are thinking?"

"Aye, it is. Captain Parmaison, you can see for yourself that we have no time to waste. Rejoin de Lisle as quickly as you may and bid him wait, well out of reach, to see if those galleys emerge from La Rochelle again. If they do, at the first sign of them, you are to make all speed to return and let us know. Understood?" Parmaison nodded, and St. Valéry rose to his feet. "Then may God be with you and grant you all speed. Wind and oars, Sir Geoffrey, wind and oars. Sir William, we must inform Admiral de Berenger of this at once."

They could hear Parmaison shouting orders to his crew before they reached the entry port where Tam and their boat waited for them, and before they arrived back at the wharf his galley had already veered away from its anchorage.

5

Vice-Admiral de Berenger's administrative and organizational skills were beyond dispute; his crews had every piece of Sir Kenneth Sinclair's convoy—wagons, livestock, and cargo— sorted, dismantled where necessary, and stowed aboard ship in ample time to sail upon the evening tide, leaving the tiny village looking abandoned behind them. Sinclair, who had not really expected that they would complete everything in time to catch the tide, made a point of seeking out the vice-admiral before returning to his galley, which had already shipped the Templar Treasure, and congratulated him on the speed and efficiency of the entire operation. De Berenger, still preoccupied with the final details of dismantling their lading gear and leaving the small wharf clear of debris, thanked him with a slightly distracted smile and told him he would see him aboard within the hour. Sir William left him to it, returning to where Tam Sinclair awaited him patiently in a boat at the end of the wharf. As soon as he was safely aboard, Tam gave the order to the four oarsmen to take them back to the galley, about a hundred yards away.

It was only as they crossed the water that Sinclair realized that he had not seen the Baroness leave the beach, and that he had not thought of her in several hours, and he grunted to himself in satisfaction. Intense concentration on other things had obviously shut her out of his awareness for some time, and he resolved to remember that technique and apply it to her in future. He could see Admiral St. Valéry's galley already disappearing hull down on the horizon, and the few ships left in the small inlet were all in the final stages of preparing to leave the land again. Sinclair's galley, de Berenger's own command, would be the last to go, and Will found himself hoping that the villagers they were leaving behind would waste no time in erasing all sign that they had ever been visited this day.

By the time he boarded the galley, the last members of de Berenger's party were already climbing into two boats tied to the wharf. The surface of the pier at their back had been swept clean, not a single piece of debris remaining that might be linked to their visit, and after seeing the boats' oars bite into the water, Will turned away and went in search of his cramped quarters in the forecastle. There he cast off his outer clothing and dropped onto his narrow bunk, remaining there as the ship rocked to and fro before finally putting out to sea. At some point, because there was no urgency for him in anything that was happening, he nodded off to sleep, aware, just before he lost consciousness, that in his mind's eye he was staring at Lady Jessica Randolph's face and that she was meeting his gaze, her eyes wide but expressionless, noncommittal, masking whatever she was thinking.

Seven days later, out of sight of land and clinging to a straining rigging rope in the waist of the ship in a howling storm, he was thinking of the woman again and straining to catch sight of the admiral's galley on the port side, where he had last seen it days before, but he could see nothing. Whatever might be out there, it was hidden from his sight by swooping waves, wind-whipped spume, and horizontally driven rain that stung exposed skin like needles of ice. Twice since leaving the fishing village, and both times on the first day, he had seen her muffled figure looking out over the galley's rail, once from the stern and once from the prow, but since the weather had begun to worsen on their second day at sea, he had seen no sign of her and had not expected to.

The Bay of Biscay was renowned for the ferocity of its storms, and most especially so at this time of year, with the inexorable approach of winter. Sinclair was well aware of that, just as he knew that the vessel in which he was riding had been designed to survive such storms, and that they would be safe as long as they held far enough out to sea to preclude any possibility of their being blown onto the rocks along the shoreline. His intellect knew that; his heart and his brain knew it; but there was some other part of his being that remained staunchly unconvinced. That part of him had been telling him for days now that he had no business being here on a heaving ship in the middle of nowhere, confronting a successive chain of storms and howling gales; that he should be safe ashore some place, on solid ground, with a strong horse under him and his feet firmly planted in the stirrups.

As he thought about that yet again, he heard his name being shouted, and clutching his anchoring rope, he turned to see Tam Sinclair within arm's reach. He let go of the rope with one hand and reached out, suddenly conscious of the weight of his sodden mantle, to grasp Tam's wrist and pull him to where he, too, could grasp the rigging and turn his hunched back to the gale.

"De Berenger sent me to get you," Tam shouted into Sinclair's ear through a cupped hand. "He's in his cabin."

Sinclair felt his heart sink into his boots as he heard the summons. He was up here on the galley's central deck for one reason: he had survived his first attacks of seasickness several days earlier, although he could still hardly credit the violent misery he had endured, but even so, the minor degree of tolerance he had since developed for the lurching, pitching, and yawing movements of the ship could not survive in the fetid atmosphere, the darkness, and the chaotic, unpredictable motion belowdecks. The galley's crew appeared to think nothing of it, and knew the layout of the ship so well that they could find their way about down there in total darkness, but Will Sinclair knew that was a skill he would never possess, and the mere thought of remaining aboard for long enough to develop it appalled him. Now, knowing that he had no alternative but to go aft and belowdecks, he turned and looked back towards the high stern of the ship, where he could see a pair of helmsmen straining against the weight of the tiller, struggling to keep the ship headed directly into the wind and the incessant line of combers bearing down on them from the northwest. Below, in the waist of the vessel, the oarsmen sat huddled and miserable on their benches, waiting patiently, their oars shipped and secured vertically, ready to be deployed at the shout of an order.

"What's happening, d'you know?"

Tam shook his head. "He came up on deck and sent me to fetch you. Something's up, but I've no more idea than you."

"Well, let's find out. I'll be glad to get out of this."

"Aye, and so will I. Off this whoreson box and back on dry land. Sooner the better."

Together, choosing each step with great care, they fought their way back to the stern, where Tam crouched down out of the wind, in the shelter of the ship's side, while Sir William approached one of three doors in the wall below the stern deck where the helmsmen stood. He knocked, and without waiting for a response, swung the door open and leaned inside. De Berenger was sitting on one side of his sleeping cabin, facing the ship's wall, in front of a small tabletop that was hinged to the vessel's timbers so that it could be folded away when it was not in use. He had been writing, for his fingers were stained with ink.

"You sent for me, Sir Edward?"

"I did, Sir William. Come inside, if you will, and close the door."

Sinclair did as he was bidden, relieved to see that at least there was light in here. Three fat candles hung in heavy sconces, intricately suspended, although he could not quite see how, from a device that hung from the beams of the overhead deck, and although the shadows they cast swung and swooped disconcertingly, their light was nonetheless extremely welcome, projecting an illusion of warmth.

"Sit on the bunk if you wish, or on the stool." De Berenger glanced at him sympathetically, noting the haggard lines around his eyes and mouth. "How are you feeling, all things considered? Will you last, think you?" There was the merest hint of smile around his eyes.

Sinclair perched himself carefully on the three-legged stool with his spread feet firmly planted on the decking, his back to the door, and one hand clutching an iron bracket that was anchored in the ship's timbers. "Aye, I'll last. I know that now, after five days of this. But I warn you, I'm like to vomit without warning. I can barely manage to control myself on deck, in the fresh air, but I cannot stay confined for any length of time without being able to see the horizon."

De Berenger's little smile widened to a grin. "Aye, that's common with seasickness. But don't worry about vomiting in here. I don't imagine you have much in you to spew up, after five days. And there's no shortage of seawater with which to wash it out." He pointed a thumb towards the papers spilling from the open leather wallet on the table beside him. "I wanted to talk to you about these. Haven't had much time since they came aboard, and only started reading them this forenoon ... But they are thought provoking, and the admiral has obviously taken great pains over what he had to say." He paused briefly. "They came to me, of course, from admiral to vice-admiral, one shipmaster to another. But you hold higher rank within our Order than either of us ever could, and thus I know that what's contained in there concerns you primarily. The admiral has suggested that there will be grave decisions to consider, and he suggests, too, what they might entail ... I read what he had to say with great interest, but I found myself glad the decisions are not mine to make."

Sinclair nodded, glancing sideways at the open wallet and its contents. He had watched the wallet come aboard, on the first day of the bad weather, during a brief lull between the passing of one storm and the onset of the next, when St. Valéry's galley had approached close enough through treacherous waters to shoot a crossbow bolt safely into their ship's side, close by the entry port. It had taken several attempts, but a bolt had eventually thumped home. A length of fishing line had been tied to it, and attached to the far end of that had been a thicker cord, securing a pitch-covered basket, like a tiny boat, that held a waterproofed package of heavily waxed cloth containing the wallet of dispatches. He had watched the recovery process with interest, coming close to forgetting his own discomfort as he admired the monkeylike dexterity of the seamen who had carried it out, and he had presumed that whatever was involved in the hazardous delivery, it had to be a purely naval matter, since they had been far from land for days by then and nothing had occurred during that time that might involve him in his capacity as a member of the Order's Council.

Now he looked back at de Berenger, raising one eyebrow. "You wish me to read them?"

"Aye, Sir William. I do. But I suspect you might find the task impossible, given your seasickness. You would have to sit here, head down, and concentrate on reading while everything around you seems to move. And so, if I may make a suggestion?"

"Of course. What is it?"

De Berenger indicated the table again with a wave of his hand. "I have already read everything here, and have been thinking of it for the past few hours. I can tell you what is involved, and outline the admiral's suggestions. Then, afterwards, if you so wish, you may read anything you choose more carefully, without having to wade through the entire wallet."

"Excellent suggestion. Do that. Give me the gist of it."

The vice-admiral picked up a substantial pile of papers and held them up in one hand. "Much of what's here, naturally enough, is straightforward naval records work—copies of bills of lading, cargo lists, disciplinary reports, that kind of thing. None of that interests us in this instance." He squared the edges of the papers and aligned them carefully against the bulkhead before picking up a second, much smaller pile that had been set apart. "This is what concerns us. These papers deal with the two main areas that the admiral is concerned about. The first of those is the matter of the three galleys that sailed into La Rochelle after we left. What happened to them, and where are they now?"

"Do we know any of that? I have heard nothing since the admiral delegated those two other galleys to keep an eye on them."

"Admiral St. Valéry detached two more vessels to hang back and position themselves separately between us and Parmaison and de Lisle. That was five days ago, before the storms came down on us."

"Separately. You mean separate from each other, or separate from de Lisle's ships?"

"Both. The second pair, commanded by André du Bois and Charles Vitrier, were to station themselves within view of each other but far enough away from the first two to be able to pass the word to us quickly if they saw any signs of trouble."

"And?"

"We don't know. The weather has been too bad for us to know what's going on out there."

"But. I can hear a 'but' in your tone."

"Yes, you can. The admiral has been proceeding in the belief that the three galleys have been seized and will come after us."

"That was our first assumption, and until we find out more, it will remain valid. So what does Admiral St. Valéry propose?"

A tiny frown ticked between the other man's brows. "That is where his logic evades me … or confuses me … and it is why I decided to talk to you." He hesitated, then plunged on. "Has Admiral St. Valéry spoken to you of what he would like to do once we are clear of Cape Finisterre and outward bound?"

Sinclair cocked an eyebrow. "Aye. He has some idea of sailing off to the west, across the great sea, in search of something he believes is there."

"The Merica legend."

"Ah … He has spoken of it to you, has he?"

"No, not spoken of it exactly." De Berenger looked troubled, as though he might be betraying a confidence. "He mentioned it, last time we spoke together in private. Hinted that he might like to go in search of it when he resigns as admiral. Said he had dreamed of finding it for years and that there's nothing to stop him now, if he can find a crew of volunteers …"

Sinclair grunted. "He said much of the same to me. Asked me to consider giving him leave to go. He has no wish to travel with us to Scotland. He made that clear … What think you of the idea?"

De Berenger's blink revealed his confusion before he asked, "What idea? Merica, or going to Scotland?"

"Merica."

A play of expressions crossed de Berenger's face until he shrugged. "Truthfully, I don't know what to think of it, because the Order never really *told* us what to think of it, did it? On so many things the teachings are specific: this is what we know, that is a lie promulgated by Rome, that is true, this is foolish superstition. We always knew where we stood in the matter of most of the Order's lore, and if we misunderstood or disagreed with any part of it, we could ask questions and debate the answers. But this Merica legend … no guidance was ever offered on it."

Sinclair drew a deep breath and held it, steeling himself against a surge of nausea. When it abated, he continued. "There was none to offer. Nothing is known of it, even within our own Order of Sion, let alone within the Temple. The only thing we know is that the legend exists, and that it is based upon a few obscure references within the earliest records. I asked my sponsors and my mentors about it, each in turn, but none of them had paid it any attention, dismissing it for what it appeared to be—a simple legend, not worth wondering about. Later, though, when I was dispatched to Carcassonne to study, one of my tutors told me to seek out a Brother Anselm while I was there. He was the oldest living member of the Order at that time, and a wellspring of information on the more obscure aspects of the lore. He died only last year."

He stopped and tilted his head to one side, as though listening, and his anchoring grip on the iron wall bracket eased slightly. "Am I imagining things, or has the pitching lessened?"

De Berenger nodded. "The storm may have blown itself out, or we may be in another lull between onsets. So what did you get from this Brother Anselm?"

"He offered me a different way of thinking about, and looking at, such things, a different approach to obscure lore." He stopped, listening. "I believe the wind is dying, too. Would you object to stepping outside with me, and continuing our talk out there? Forgive me, but I find the confines of this cabin every bit as stifling as the holds belowdecks."

De Berenger sprang to his feet, perfectly at ease with the ship's motion. "Of course, Sir William. Forgive me. I had not realized how much discomfort you were in." He threw open the cabin door, then stepped aside as Sinclair lurched past him and groped his way to the rail, where he stood with his feet apart and his head thrown back, sucking in great gulps of cold sea air. It really did appear as though the storm had passed, for the wind had dropped and was no longer howling and whipping spume from the wave tops, and the waves themselves had lost their ragged crests. The seas were still huge, propelling the craft in great, swooping surges, but they were noticeably less violent, the sides of the rolling waves now long and smooth, streaked with trailing remnants of the spume that had filled the air such a short time before. De Berenger busied himself looking at the cloud wrack and gauging the extent of the weather change while he waited for his superior to collect himself, and after a short time Sinclair turned back to him, clearly in command of himself again.

"There, I feel better now, much better. I appreciate your concern, Sir Edward, for both my stomach and my well-being … Now, what was I saying before my head started to spin?"

"Brother Anselm, how he offered you a different way of looking at things."

"Aye, he did …" Sinclair thought for a moment longer, then resumed. "He made it very clear to me that I should never ignore anything simply because I cannot understand it immediately. That sounds obvious, but the truth is that most of us do exactly the opposite most of the time. Anselm had found, as had everyone else who cared to look, that there is nothing in our few references to support the Merica legend. But he had gone one step further than anyone else. He had gone looking for the source of our sources, if you see what I mean."

De Berenger frowned. "No, I don't. That sounds impossible. A source is a source. There's nothing beyond that."

"Hmm." William Sinclair looked out at the surging seas, and spoke out towards where he was looking. "That is almost exactly what I said to him, and I remember how he smiled at me before correcting the error in my logic." He looked at de Berenger and ducked his head slightly, almost apologetically. "I was speaking of *our* sources, he pointed out—the sources from which the forefathers in our Order originally developed our lore. And that little word, *our*, has influenced the Order's perceptions down through the ages. And speaking of perceptions, incidentally, were you surprised when I slipped you the fist grip that night in La Rochelle?"

"Aye, I was," de Berenger said. "It has been some time since last I met a senior Templar who was also one of our brotherhood."

"Are you saying you saw me as more of a Temple Boar than a member of the brotherhood?" Sinclair grinned and held up a hand, waving away the chagrin that had immediately shown on de Berenger's face. "Forget it, man, I was but jesting in order to make a point about the ways in which what we see, or think we see, can influence what we think thereafter. For that is exactly what has happened, Brother Anselm assured me, on this matter of the Merica legend."

De Berenger inclined his head, clearly waiting to hear more, and Sinclair continued. "Secrecy, we all know, has been paramount in all we have done since the very beginnings of our Order, more than a millennium ago. But those few of us who think of such things today tend to think that the secrecy was originally based upon the need to hide our Jewish identity from the threat of Rome's vengeance." He gave the lie to his own words with a tiny jerk of the head. "Not so. Rome was never a threat to us since the earliest days of our settlement in southern Gaul, when we concealed our true roots and blended into the local structure, eventually becoming Christian. No, our need for secrecy was far more than that, and far older. The priesthood of ancient Judea, we know from our own records, was a secret, closed society long before Rome began to stir beyond its seven hills. Its roots went all the way back to Egypt at the dawn of time, in the era of the early Pharaohs, when the Israelites were enslaved for hundreds of years until Moses led them out in search of the Promised Land.

"I know you know all this, so forgive me if I seem to preach, but what comes next is the important part: our earliest forefathers brought their knowledge out of Egypt with them, and much of that knowledge was deeply rooted, after so many generations, in the religion of Egypt, with its worship of Isis and Osiris. That lore they took to Jerusalem, where Solomon built his Temple, and the priests were the sacred guardians of its secrets. They—*our* early forefathers—had their own lore, just as we have ours, but *their* sources were Egyptian, unutterably ancient."

Sinclair stopped to watch a young seaman, carrying a bucket, make his way down the ladder from the steering platform above their heads, and when the youth had passed and vanished from view, he continued. "What Anselm enabled me to see then—and I would never have thought of it had he not directed me—was that our more recent forefathers, the fugitive priests from the sack of Jerusalem, had been unable to bring all of that with them. They had escaped with only what they could carry, and had concealed the rest, hoping to return for it later. We found it eventually, when Hugh de Payens and his friends unearthed it, but twelve hundred years had passed by then, and throughout that time, our Order had formed itself around the lore salvaged from Palestine ... Naturally, being human and dedicated to their eventual return to their true home, the earliest brethren gave the greater part of their attentions to those parts of the lore that offered most towards that end. And other, seemingly lesser parts they neglected and allowed to fall into disuse, so that their origins were forgotten and all that remained was the original mention of such things. And most prominent and mystifying among those was—and it remains so to this day—the element that we know as the legend of Merica."

Listening to Sinclair, Sir Edward de Berenger had moved to lean against the ship's side, where he remained now, staring wordlessly at his young superior.

Sinclair smiled at him. "Do you find that hard to credit?"

The vice-admiral shook his head. "Not at all. I believe it makes perfect sense. What you see in my face as doubt is mere amazement, born of my own disbelief that no one, myself included, has ever thought of this before."

"Why should you have—you or anyone else? It is an obscure legend, forgotten by everyone except a few. It was by merest accident that I found out about the ancient Egyptian roots. Had Brother Anselm not been who he was—and had he not been in Carcassonne when I went there—I would never have been able to envision such antiquity." He straightened his shoulders and turned towards the sea again, spreading his arms and leaning his hands on the galley's rail as he gazed towards the southwest, where a rift had occurred among the clouds and a single brilliant shaft of light shone down clear edged, illuminating one patch of water.

"Look at that. A single ray of sunshine changing the world as we see it. What petty, ineffectual things we are, we men. We vaunt our prowess and our power, thinking to alter the world, building empires and Orders, only to watch them scattered and destroyed by things we can never hope to control ... Three days ago, we had a fleet at our command—nigh on thirty ships. A month before that, we had an enterprise, a mighty Order, that we thought inviolable, invincible. And what do we have now?" He scanned the seas around them. "I count three ships. And none of them, I think, is Admiral St. Valéry's." He grimaced wryly at de Berenger. "I have a fear, in my heart, Edward, that we may be lost out here, helplessly witnessing the ending of an era. The ending of the world we have known."

"Not so, Sir William, in God's holy name. Our ships will reassemble when the winds die down, I promise you."

"Aye, I'm sure they will. But will our fortunes do the same? Philip Capet and his creature de Nogaret have wrought great things within these past few days, evil things, to be sure, from where we stand, but they have achieved them nonetheless. And I cannot foresee them giving up what they have won. They hold La Rochelle, our Order's chief stronghold, the center of our worldwide naval power, and I fear that we—this fleet—are all that is left of the Order of the Temple within France. I say I fear it, but I mean I believe it in my heart, for by the time de Nogaret took La Rochelle, the Temple in Paris had already fallen, all its adherents taken into the King's custody."

De Berenger had nothing to say to that, and Sinclair continued. "Until the very moment when we broke into that room in the Commandery and found the assassins waiting for the admiral, I had regarded the truth of what was happening as unthinkable, a monstrous misunderstanding. But it was the truth that was monstrous ... and our wide-eyed disbelief that was unthinkable. France has become a dungeon, an *oubliette*, not merely for the bodies of our brethren but for the ideals and the principles that we stood for. I believe that. And because I do, I find myself considering giving Admiral St. Valéry my permission to sail upon the quest he thinks to undertake."

The vice-admiral stirred, shifting from foot to foot, his face settling into a frown of puzzlement. The silence between the two men was broken only by the sounds of the ship and the surging waters.

"Well, what think you?" Sinclair said. "Your face is black with your thoughts, so spit them out. Talk to me."

Tam, who had been huddled in a corner beneath the deck rail, was no longer where he had been, and Sinclair assumed he had gone belowdecks again. He closed his eyes, concentrating upon the freshness of the air blowing against his face.

De Berenger shook his head. "I know not what to say, Sir William. At first glance, the idea seems like folly ... and yet, having listened to what you said about the legend, I find myself unsure that it is, after all. But there has been no record, anywhere or at any time, of any living person—other than our own brethren who have heard of the legend—having heard tell of such a place, such a land, and the Western Sea is limitless. To permit Sir Charles to sail off thus would be to send him to his death."

Will Sinclair grinned, beginning to enjoy himself for the first time in days, now that the wind had died and the sea was less turbulent. "The sea can not be limitless, Edward. Think of what that would involve. There must be some kind of rim to it, somewhere, else the ocean waters would pour off into the Abyss and the seas themselves would run dry. That is logical, is it not ... even though it be incredible?"

His companion only blinked at him, and Sinclair laughed out loud. "Do not despair, Sir Edward, I have not said I will let the admiral go, for what you argue is self-evidently true. It would be tantamount to sending him off to die." He sobered as quickly as he had broken into mirth. "And yet, I feel it would be a kindness to indulge St. Valéry in this, when he most needs indulgence. In the space of a few days, without warning of any kind, he has lost everything he holds most dear—his oldest friend and companion foully murdered, his command usurped and rendered useless, and the instrument to which he dedicated his entire life snuffed out and perhaps destroyed by forces against which he is impotent. Now, without superiors to guide him, he faces a life he must perceive as futile, exiled in a foreign land about which he knows nothing. What can he have to look forward to in such circumstances, an admiral with no purpose? He has these ships, and whatever vessels may join us off Finisterre, but what ends will that serve? He has nowhere to go."

"With respect, Sir William, that is not really so. The admiral would be welcome in any other country. We have Temples and commanderies throughout Christendom and across the world. It is in France alone that we are beset."

Sinclair looked at him levelly. "True, at this moment. But how long, think you, before other kings follow Philip Capet's example? Capet has his tame pope on his side, which means his blessing will extend to all who wish to move against our Order and seize its wealth for themselves. Any king, Edward, and with one exception that I know of, they are all that greedy. Robert Bruce alone, the King of Scots, stands excommunicate, and more because of that than for any other reason, he is the sole man—the sole king—whom I might be prepared to judge as trustworthy in this matter, for I am told the Scots Templars number strongly among his staunchest supporters. You mark my words, my friend. It will happen, and it will happen quickly. And when it does, we, all of us, the admiral included, will have no place where we can go in safety, other than the dubious sanctuary we may find in Scotland."

"You paint a grim picture, Sir William."

"No grimmer than it truly is, Edward." Sinclair looked around him again, noting that the patch of blue sky had widened greatly.

"It really looks as though the weather might be clearing. If we meet up with the admiral again, I will talk to him at more length on this subject. Mayhap he will convince me to let him go off on his quest, but his arguments will need to be more solid than they are at this point."

POISONED

1

S everal miles from where the two knights were discoursing and scanning the horizon, Jessie Randolph had been among the first of the fleet's passengers to notice the storm dying down, although she paid it little heed for some time, her attention fully taken up with more urgent matters. Now she finished what she was doing and straightened up over the sleeping form of her serving woman Marie, using the back of her wrist to push her hair out of her eyes as she dug with the fingers of her other hand into the small of her back, probing at the nagging pain caused by stooping for too long over both of the women whose sole duty supposedly consisted of looking after her. That thought made her smile, for all her tiredness, and she looked down again at the two faithful souls who lay there, drained and sleeping by her feet, their bedding open to the air but protected overhead and on the sides by a number of tightly stretched and skillfully bound leather screens. The beds themselves, though no more than piles of skins and blankets, were set in the angle of the stern bulkhead, barely enough space separating them to allow her to step between them.

Both women were prostrate from seasickness, as were most of the other people aboard the galley, and they had been so since the sudden onset of the storm five days earlier. Jessie, astonished by her ability to tolerate the violent motions of both ship and sea, had nursed both of them throughout the ordeal, patiently ministering to their every need, aware that both of them would have been horrified even to imagine her doing so. But they had been too sick to know anything of that, and Jessie was too grateful to have been spared the torments that devastated them to waste time thinking about the reversal of their roles.

She had no notion of why or how she should have been able to survive the storms unscathed and with a solid, unshakable calm, but she knew that she was one of very few in the ship's entire complement to have done so. Even her good-brother the admiral, a veteran of decades at sea, had succumbed early to the fury of the incessant squalls and the constantly raging seas, as had his shipmaster and officers, all of them rendered incapable of running the ship, or even of maintaining a semblance of order and discipline aboard, since the ship could not *be* run under such conditions. The oars, save for the massive steering oar that formed a rudder, had not touched water since the first storm broke, and the men who crewed them had been largely useless for anything else, so that the responsibility of temporary command had been taken over by the sergeant called Tescar, who had commanded the guard at the Commandery of La Rochelle the night Jessie arrived there.

Tescar had never been to sea at all, whereas Jessie had made several voyages, all of them short and blessed with fair weather, and like Jessie, he was unable to understand why he should be able to withstand the fury of the elements when experienced seamen of all ranks had fallen victim all about him. But, being Tescar and accustomed to making the best of things wherever he found himself, he had contrived to keep himself, Jessie, and everyone else alive, foraging for food and drink among the ship's supplies and finding ample amounts of both. Thus fortified, the two of them, along with fewer than a score of other men in like condition, had been able to tend, at least fundamentally, to the sick throughout the vessel. Not all of those sick were completely immobilized—many of them continued to function at some degree of normalcy and varying levels of impairment—but all were debilitated beyond dispute, so that it had become commonplace to see them stand vacant eyed and wavering at times, as though waiting for someone to shout an order at them, to tell them what to do next.

Now Jessie found herself looking at one such fellow, noting the way he braced himself against the swell as he trudged forward, blank eyed and whey faced, towards the galley's prow. This was the fourth time she had seen the man, idly aware of him moving from stem to stern and back, and although she had no idea what he was about, she knew he was not without purpose. This time, however, she took more notice of him, aware suddenly that he walked now without clutching at ropes for support, and as she noticed that, she observed, too, that the ship's crashing, tumultuous momentum had eased, albeit but slightly, and that the vessel's forward swoop was now more of a glide than a staggering lurch. A gleam of light attracted her eye, and she looked up to see a ray of sunlight glaring in the near distance, clear edged and brilliant, through a break in the cloud cover. It vanished almost as soon as she saw it, but another broke through the wrack not far beyond, followed by another farther off, and she felt her spirits surge for the first time in days, elated by the possibility of an end to the incessant parade of gales and storms that had battered them for so long.

She bent forward and drew a supple leather satchel from between the two sleeping women. She opened it slowly and withdrew a folded blanket that she shook out and tested against her face for dryness before she swirled it up, over her head and across her shoulders. Then, moving carefully lest she disturb her charges, she lowered herself with great care to sit between them, leaning her back into the angle of the bulkhead and tugging gently at the material of the blanket until it covered her completely. Moments later, she was asleep, head tilted back, her lips smiling at some errant thought that had come to her as she sank into slumber.

2

She was dreaming that someone was calling her name from a vast distance when she opened her eyes to find Brother Thomas the sacristan standing over her, his pale, widely set eyes staring at her disapprovingly. She blinked in disbelief, attempting to raise her hands to rub at her eyes, but her arms were hampered by the folds of the blanket wrapped about her, and before she could free them she had become fully aware of her surroundings again, remembering that she was sitting between Marie and Janette in the angle of the forward bulwark. Both women were still soundly asleep, and she pressed one finger emphatically to her lips, frowning fiercely in warning to the sacristan to be quiet lest he awaken them.

The man recoiled slightly at her gesture, his face showing a faint repugnance, but she paid him no more attention as she set about raising herself to her feet, with great care for her decorum under his disdainful sneer. He had no regard for her, she knew that; it had been clear from their first encounter that he resented her presence among the brotherhood he regarded as being sacrosanct. She took no real offense from that, for she knew it was not personal; she knew, in fairness, that his reaction would have been no different to any other woman. Her own disapproval of him, however, had been equally spontaneous and obdurate. Sensing his antipathy and intolerance from the way he watched her even before she met him, she had dismissed him from the outset as a vermin-ridden, sanctimonious nonentity with the rankly sour, feral odor of a wild goat, and had refused to recognize his existence thereafter.

Unfortunately for both of them, it transpired that they could neither ignore nor avoid each other, for upon the death of his former master the preceptor, Brother Thomas's duties and loyalty had been transferred, in accordance with his years of rank and seniority within the La Rochelle commandery, to assuring the welfare of Admiral St. Valéry, the next in rank to the former preceptor, and he was being as assiduous in his new duties as he had been in his old ones.

That meant that in the narrow confines of the admiral's galley, he was never beyond sight or hearing of his primary charge, and since he considered Jessie, like all women, to be the Devil's own device for the temptation of all decent men, he had refused her entry to the admiral's tiny cabin since Charles first fell sick. Jessie railed inwardly at the sacristan's smug presumption, but she took care to hide her anger, since there was nothing she could do to gainsay him at that point, and she refused to give him the satisfaction of seeing that he had managed to upset her.

Satisfied now that her dress was in order, she turned back to face the fellow. "What do you want?"

Brother Thomas flushed slightly. "Brother Admiral would like to speak with you."

"Brother Admiral, eh?" Jessie eyed the sacristan squarely, making no attempt to mask her dislike. "I wonder whether, in his heart of hearts, Sir Charles enjoys such a degree of familial intimacy? My late, dear husband used to say that we may choose our friends, but our relatives are an imposition at birth." She paused, watching him closely, and had the pleasure of seeing his face flush even more sullenly as the insult sank home, but she gave him no time to retaliate, stepping past him and starting out towards the admiral's quarters at the galley's stern. "I have time now. I will attend him."

She strode rearward, moving effortlessly in concert with the heaving of the deck, taking delight in the sudden, growing brightness of the afternoon, in the growing patches of blue above her, and in the hasty scampering sound of the sacristan's feet as he scuttled to catch up with her. By the time she reached the small doorway to the tiny space that was the admiral's quarters, Thomas had fallen several paces behind her, and she had knocked and pulled the door open before he could interfere.

Inside the dark little cabin, fully dressed and propped up among a welter of bed coverings, Charles St. Valéry squinted painfully and raised a spread hand to his eyes in protest against the glaring brightness of the light now pouring in on him. He was unkempt and disheveled, his eyes sunken and his face haggard with deep-graven lines, and Jessie felt herself wince in sympathy at the sight of him. Fortunately, she thought, he had not seen her do it, blinded as he was. Brother Thomas arrived at her shoulder and began to speak, his voice raised in protest, but Jessie cut him short with a savage movement of her hand, then spoke to her good-brother, smiling and attempting to infuse her voice with friendly amusement.

"Brother Charles, I am happy to see you have survived the storm, though I fail to see how you managed it, cooped up in this black little box. Might I induce you to step outside and breathe in God's clean air? It will do you good, I'll warrant you."

The admiral lowered his shielding hand slowly, blinking yet against the glare of the afternoon, then squeezed his eyes shut and grasped the bridge of his nose between finger and thumb, wrenching it from side to side as though attempting to break it loose from his face. Finally he took his hand away and shook his head hard from side to side, like a dog ridding itself of water, after which he opened his eyes wide and blinked again, owlishly this time, before asking, "What day is it?"

"It is Friday, Admiral. We have been beset by storms these past five days." *And you look as though you have been dead for four of those*, she added silently; this was the first time she had ever seen him less than perfectly coiffed and trimmed.

He sat peering at her, his mouth working silently as though chewing, and an expression of distaste growing on his face. "My mouth tastes like death itself." His gaze went by her to where the sacristan hovered at her back. "Thomas, fetch me some water, will you?"

She smelled the sacristan's departure, the air sweetening immediately as he took his sour stench away with him.

"A seasick admiral," St. Valéry murmured. "That is most unusual, even for me, with all my human weaknesses. I am … unused to seasickness. Unused to any kind of sickness, truth be told. It has been years since I last felt this way. And may God grant me many more before I feel this way again." He pounded the flat of his hand against his breastbone, coughing at the congestion in his chest, then made a sucking sound before continuing. "Friday, you say? A week since La Rochelle already? And where are we now?"

"Still afloat, thanks be to God, but I can tell you no more than that. Sergeant Tescar and I, although we have no right to be, are the two healthiest beings aboard this vessel. Landsmen or not, he and I have been unfazed by the storms, our stomachs calm and our legs solidly beneath us … It's strange, but after a while the smell of vomit seems to lose its strength. There are fifteen more like us, also in good health, but not a one of them knows any more of the sea than we do, and so we have no idea where we are. We are upon the waters and not beneath them, and for that, at least, we are grateful."

"What are you saying, Sister? What nonsense is this? Where are my officers?"

"Abed, sir, all of them as sick as you."

"But that is … that is unthinkable. What of my men?"

"In the same condition. Sick. All but a score or so. And Tescar told me three have died in the storm."

"How, in God's name?"

"Of the sickness … the seasickness."

"The—" St. Valéry stopped and shook his head. "Seasickness does not kill, Jessie. I have never known anyone die of seasickness, although at times everyone afflicted by it expects to die and might even wish to. Do you recall, did all the men fall sick at once?"

Jessie frowned. "Aye, I think so, but I was sick myself for half a day and night, the first day the storm struck, and by the time I began to mend, everyone else was down with it, including you."

St. Valéry's head tilted slightly back as he stared into the distance. "There is something more afoot here, something sinister. This sounds to me like poisoning. I lived through something of the kind before, off Araby … That meat, the first night out. I thought at the time there was a taint to it." His gaze sharpened, returning to Jessie. "Tell me, that first night at sea, after we picked up the Treasure. Did you eat anything that night? And did Tescar?"

"No." Jessie shook her head slowly. "I lost all desire to eat as soon as the seas started to rise, and I spent the next hours in agony, so I cannot speak for Tescar, although I know he fell sick, too, that first afternoon, even before I did."

"Then that must be the cause of what ails the rest of us. We had salted pork. The bread with it was fresh baked in La Rochelle the previous day. Would that the meat had been as fresh!" He looked around the cabin, taking in its condition. "I had best be up and about." St. Valéry pulled himself slowly to his feet, although he was unable to stand upright beneath the low ceiling. He grimaced again and flexed his shoulders cautiously in the cramped space. "What of the others, the rest of the fleet? Are they in view?"

Jessie shrugged as Brother Thomas came bustling back, carrying a horn cup and a bag of water. "I have not looked recently, but the last time I did, and that must have been this morning—it was daylight, certainly—we were alone, nothing visible in any direction. Mind you, we were still being wildly tossed about, so I could not see far."

"My thanks for this," St. Valéry said to Brother Thomas, stepping out onto the deck and holding the cup while the sacristan poured for him. "Tell me, Thomas, have you been sick like the others?"

The sacristan shook his head slowly. "No, Brother Admiral, thanks be to God."

"Did you not eat of the meat the day the storms came up on us?"

"I ate nothing, Brother. It was the anniversary of my mother's death, and so I fasted for the entire day."

"Hmm." St. Valéry drank the contents of his cup in one quaff and held it out again, taking time to look about him this time as the water was being poured. "It's broken," he said, plainly talking about the storm. "Visibility's about four miles." He then straightened up to his full height, peering off the horizon before beckoning to Jessie. "Look, there's one mast, over there, and where there's one, there will be more." He glanced around at his ship, noting the displaced coils of rope, a broken spar and other detritus of the storm caught in the scuppers on both sides of the deck. "First things first, though. I have to rally my crew and bring this ship back into working condition. Thomas, find Captain de Narremat for me. I care not what his condition may be, so be it he is breathing. If he is, bring him to me here … And find the other officers, as well. If they were poisoned, as I suspect, it will be wearing off now and they'll recover more quickly working than they will lying around feeling sorry for themselves. I know I shall."

3

The admiral and his honored guest, the Lady Jessica, had dined upon a meal similar in every detail to that eaten by the lowest-ranking oarsman on the ship: a thin slice of dried, salted beef, carefully checked for freshness this time, with smoked dried sausage, hard goat cheese, and all the hard-baked bannock one wished to eat, sweetened with a handful of dried grapes. But he and his brother's wife had enjoyed the privilege of eating on the tiny stern deck, where they were able to enjoy at least an illusion of privacy, and, rank having its privilege as always, they were able to share a cup of wine from the admiral's own stock. The great single sail was now set above their heads, bearing them steadily westward, along the northern coast of the Iberian landmass.

Jessica swallowed the last, thoroughly chewed mouthful of the tasteless bannock and allowed herself to think for a moment of the crusty French bread that she had loved so much when she lived in France. But she was concerned for her host more than anything else, for St. Valéry had been sitting silent now for the better part of half an hour, gazing vacantly out at the sea, and his face was lined and tired looking in a way that she now thought had little to do with his sickness.

"You miss him greatly." She had spoken in her own tongue, but St. Valéry had understood the idiom and responded in his heavily accented, almost distorted English.

"Hmm?" He looked at her with one eyebrow slightly raised. "Miss whom?"

She reverted to French. "Forgive me. I thought … for a moment there, I was convinced you were thinking of your friend Master de Thierry. But I spoke without thinking and I had no wish to intrude upon—"

He smiled, his eyes clouded with what she decided was regret. "There is no need. You are correct. I was thinking of Arnold. Such a cruel end to a noble life …"

"Tell me about him, for I did not know him well. What I knew, I admired, but you and he were friends for a long time, no?"

His smile remained in place and he dipped his head gently to one side. "Yes, we were, for a very long time …" She was beginning to think he would say no more, but then he continued, as though musing aloud. "They called us the Twins—*les jumeaux*—did you know that?"

Her eyes widened. "No. Why?"

He turned his hands in towards each other in a very Gallic gesture denoting bemusement and ignorance at once. "Because we looked alike, I suppose, for so many years. We wore the same mantle, as commanders of the Temple, and the same armor beneath it. Our personal insignia were different but not noticeably so, and I have been told many times that we were often indistinguishable from a distance, both of the same height and physique, with the same bearing—the result of many years of the Order's training and discipline. And naturally, both of us wore the same tonsure and were gray-bearded these past ten years and more …" His smile became a grin. "Of course, we were not supposed to know what the brethren called us. None of them would ever have dared to refer to us as the Twins within the hearing of either one of us, so we pretended to be unaware.

"We joined the Order together on the same day, you know. On the island of Cyprus, the fourth day of July in 1276, thirty-one years ago … And we had met each other for the first time mere days before that, aboard the galley that took us there as postulants. It picked us up in Rhodes and carried us to Limassol, and from the moment we met, we became, and we remained, close friends."

He turned and stretched out his booted legs on his own side of the table, twisting his body to sit up straighter and drawing the folds of his heavy mantle around him. "Arnold was twenty-one years old at that time—I myself was five and twenty—and he was already widowed, having lost both wife and son in childbirth. But he was filled with fire and zeal for our Order and its mission, and he became one of the Temple's most honored knights, spending fifteen years on constant campaign in the Holy Land before taking part in the final siege of Acre in 1291."

"He was at Acre and survived?"

"Yes and no. He was gravely wounded in the earliest stages of the fighting, long before the end, and was shipped out by sea to the island of Rhodes, where he eventually recovered under the care of the Hospitallers. But in the meantime, Acre fell and our presence in the Holy Land came to an end."

"And what about you, Admiral? Where were you when all this was going on?"

"I was at sea, where else? I spent my entire life at sea before becoming shore-based in La Rochelle. I was born into a powerful mercantile family, as you know, since you were wed into it, and because of that, when I joined the Order at five-and-twenty, I was assigned to the fleet. And there I remained."

"So how did you come to La Rochelle?"

"Because of my friendship with Arnold. And then, too, since we are speaking the truth here, there was the matter of our superiors' collective common sense. It was a matter of compatibility, at root. La Rochelle is the Order's primary base, its center of operations, and it serves two masters *in situ*, two commanders who must interact with each other from day to day—the land-based preceptor and his naval counterpart. Ideally, these two should know, like, respect, and admire each other and be equally dedicated, above all else, to the ongoing welfare of the Order.

"Unfortunately, because such is human nature, that is not always possible to achieve. There are very few highly placed equals, it appears, who genuinely like, respect, and admire each other to the extent that they can share command without jealousy. Personal ambition has a way of confounding such arrangements." He shrugged again, in self-deprecation. "Because of that, the long-standing friendship between Arnold and myself—together with the reputations we had each achieved, of course—recommended us to our superiors. There was no jealousy between us, and we enjoyed joint stewardship in La Rochelle for more than ten years. Ten wonderful years."

He glanced out into the body of the ship and raised a hand to summon a crewman, signaling to him to clear away the remains of their meal, and both of them sat watching as the man removed the leftovers and another folded the small table and took it away.

When they were alone again, facing each other across the space where the table had been, Jessica asked, "What will you do now?"

He looked at her levelly. "I am considering a quest."

"A quest? We are already on a quest, to deliver your Order's Treasure to safety in Scotland, and to deliver *my* treasure safely to the King of Scots."

His lips quirked in what might have been the beginnings of a smile, but he shook his head. "What you are defining is a task, not a quest, and that particular task can be effectively carried out by others, without my participation."

He left that hanging in the air, tantalizing her and piquing her curiosity so that she frowned slightly, trying to decipher his meaning.

"That is … cryptic."

The admiral met her gaze without blinking, his intelligent blue eyes revealing nothing except their own brilliant color. She waited for a moment, to see if he would respond, and then decided that he was waiting for her to continue. She cleared her throat and glanced away for a moment, looking out towards the horizon to give herself time to think of what she should say next. If he had a quest in mind, it must lie at their journey's end.

"This quest you speak of must then lie ahead of you, in Scotland … Have you been in Scotland?"

St. Valéry smiled slowly, the crow's-foot wrinkles at the edges of his eyes the only sign that he was doing so, for the wind was ruffling the hair of his beard and moustache, obscuring his mouth.

"I have never been in Scotland, and I have no wish to go there now. I have been to England, twice, and have no wish to go there, either. I speak a very small amount of English, very badly, as you know, but the Scots tongue to me is unintelligible gibberish."

She knew he was teasing her, for she had heard him say the same thing to her husband, years earlier, but she chose to humor him. "That is not unusual. Many of the people in Scotland speak gibberish in the ears of the others. We have several languages, and several different groups of so-called Scots—Northmen, Gaels, Norwayans, and the oldest of all, the ones the Romans called the Picti, the Painted People."

"Do any of your differing groups ever talk to one another?"

"All the time, Admiral, though seldom in friendly tones, I fear. King Robert is trying to change that, to unite the country against Edward's England and his lust to own our land."

"Edward is dead, Jessie. You heard Master Sinclair."

"He may be dead, but his barons are not, and his iron hand was the sole thing that kept them in check. The son that follows him onto the English throne will be the worst thing that could ever happen to Scotland, for he is a weakling and his own barons will trample over his wishes and please themselves in what they do. And what they will do is invade Scotland." She checked herself, then set her jaw. "But that is neither here nor there for you, is it?" She paused for a moment, then forged on. "So if you have no wish to remain in Scotland, where will you go thereafter? Unless you intend to return directly to France?"

"That is what my heart tells me I would love to do most, but my head tells me that it could be years before our Order sees the light of day again in France, if indeed it ever does. So no, I will not be returning to France." He fell silent, staring out over the rail, then turned to gaze off to his right, over the stern, before standing and crossing the small deck to where he could examine the entire horizon.

"Look," he said, beckoning her to rise and join him. "Did I not say that where there was one there would be more? There are eleven masts now, you see? And three more vessels in plain sight. When we can see only the mast, like that, we say the ships beneath them are hull down. Our fleet still exists."

Jessica stood beside him for some time, scanning the horizon as he had and counting the masts. The sky was almost bare of clouds now and the sun was close to setting. She took notice, too, of the orderly calm aboard their own vessel and the unmistakable air of discipline and renewal that was evident in the posture of the steersman behind them. She was pleased with all she saw, and she moved back to resume her seat and the conversation that had been interrupted.

"Then what is this quest of yours to be?" she asked, talking to his back. "Where will it take you?" She hesitated as he turned to face her, then went on. "I know I am probably being intolerably inquisitive, but I do not think you would have brought the matter up at all had you not wanted me to be aware of it."

Richard St. Valéry nodded his head slowly, and she saw that his eyes had changed upon hearing her question; now they looked troubled. "Do you know that you constitute the last family I possess?" He saw her eyebrows rise and waved a hand to silence her before she could begin to protest. "Oh, I know there are others, cousins and distant kin, I know that, but I was speaking of close family, people who matter to me. I am the eldest and last of four brothers, two of whom I knew and loved well, and a squad of sisters, none of whom I ever knew well." His teeth flashed suddenly through the thicket of his beard, and she remarked, as she often had before, on the whiteness and strength of them. "You, dear sister, constitute my entire adult knowledge of the feminine world, and for a time, when I first met you, you frightened me greatly—"

"Frightened you? Why, in God's name?"

"Because, in God's name as you accurately suggest, I am a monk, sworn to chastity and solitude, and as my brother's wife, without willing it or being in any way blameworthy, you made me see how fragile could be the wall of chastity behind which I and all my peers crouch. You were, and you remain, a creature of great beauty, Jessica, and that beauty unnerved me, unused as I was to associating with women in any way. I seek not to flatter you—I have neither need nor desire to do that. I speak the simple truth. Your beauty frightened me, just as it does Sir William."

Jessica Randolph missed what her good-brother said next, because her mind was instantly full of what he had said last about William Sinclair. The idea that Will might be afraid of her took her aback. Jessie was not at all naïve, but what experience did she have in dealing with the knights of the Temple brotherhood? The few

Templars she had known as a child had all been relatives or family friends, warriors who treated her as what she was: a small girl to be ignored or patted on the head in passing. By the time she grew to be a woman, she seldom saw any of them at all, and as a married woman, living in France and England, she had glimpsed them only occasionally and from a distance, recognizing them by their dress and insignia. Her husband's affairs, as a King's agent, had all been conducted at the court of Philip Capet, and there she had quickly learned how to contend with salacious approaches from indolent courtiers and the importunings of men of all ranks and stations, and she had become adept in deflecting their attentions, when she could not avoid them altogether, but with the sole exception of her good-brother Charles St. Valéry, she had never really encountered, or had any dealings with, the knights of the Temple. That they were distant and disdainful she had taken for granted, accepting it as a consequence of their secretive mystique, but the possibility that they might live in fear of her and of all women had never crossed her mind. So that was it: William Sinclair was afraid of her, simply because she was an attractive woman.

"… and so I find little pleasure in contemplating new beginnings at my age."

"Pardon me, my dear Charles," she interjected, bluntly honest as she always was. "I was distracted for a moment and missed something of what you were saying. What new beginnings are you talking about?" The look he directed at her might have been a tolerant smile, but she could not be sure.

"All of them," he said quietly. "There are several facing me at this point, all of which, save one, I would prefer to avoid." He saw from the quirk of her eyebrow that she was waiting and would not interrupt him.

"First, and most important, dear sister, I am too old to find pleasure in the prospect of starting a new life in a new country. My time in France has been cut short, and I had no control over the events that brought us here. I would, however, like to have some control over what I do from this point onward."

"And can you do that? Exercise control over your future?"

He made his familiar Gallic shrug. "Easily, if God permits it and if I can obtain permission from Sir William, who now appears to be my sole remaining superior. But I doubt he may be willing to grant me that permission, simply because so few of us are left free."

He turned his back on her again, staring out into the gathering darkness for some time, before returning to face her, bracing himself against the rail. "If he chooses to deny my request, then I shall accept his decision, learn to live with my regrets, and do my duty to the best of my abilities, in Scotland or elsewhere, as need arises. If he does permit me to go, on the other hand, then I shall be in my element again, doing what I was born to do, and my life thenceforth will be under my own control."

"Thenceforth? You mean forever?"

"For as long as remains to me."

"You say this quest would remove you from the authority of your superiors. How may that be? Where would you have to go to achieve that?"

"Beyond the seas."

"To Outremer, you mean? But Outremer is lost now. There is no Christian presence in the Holy Land today. To travel back to Outremer would be suicide."

"I am not speaking of Outremer ..."

"Where, then? Where else is there?"

He faced her squarely, and now there was no hint of levity in his gaze. "Nowhere," he said. "At least, nowhere in the known world."

She was genuinely bewildered. "Are you suggesting that there may be *un*known places in the world?"

"I am." He watched her struggle to absorb what he had said, seeing the play of her thoughts clearly mirrored on her face. "Such places may exist. My quest will be to find them."

"But ... how? Where?"

"Far to the west. Have you ever heard the word 'Merica'?"

"No, never. Should I have?"

"No, not at all. I can think of no good reason why you should have, and several excellent reasons why you could not have. Merica is a mystical and legendary place, and I suppose I will be breaking some vow or other in telling you of it, although I cannot think where the transgression might lie."

He lapsed into silence, and Jessie waited avidly, careful to make no move that might distract him. Eventually he cleared his throat and moved back to sit beside her again.

"As I said, you are the sole remaining member of my close family, and so I am going to tell you something that perhaps I ought not to mention. Our sacred Order is secretive. I know you are already aware of that, as is all the world, but the truth is even greater than the appearance of secrecy. The Order, the Brotherhood of the Temple, is founded upon a necessary secrecy, the substance of which is"—and here he flashed her a dazzling grin—"of course, a secret. There are many aspects of our code and our beliefs about which we are completely forbidden to speak, under oath and upon penalty of the most grievous punishment. There are other elements, however, that are less stringently circumscribed. Do you understand the distinction?" When she nodded he continued.

"Excellent ... Among our ancient lore, which is extensive, there are several areas that lack coherency and proof of ... what is the word? Authenticity, I suppose, covers it best. And one of those areas, a fragment, a report, the merest shadow of a tale, perhaps a legend, deals with a place that lies beyond the Western Sea, the ocean we call the Atlantic. It is a vast expanse of land, according to the fragmentary documents we possess, that is overlooked by a brilliant evening star that the natives—and apparently there are native peoples there—call Merica. But there is no proof, from any source, that such a place exists. As I said, it is a shadow."

"How ancient?" She saw the lifting of his eyebrows and pushed ahead. "You spoke of your ancient lore, but your Order was founded less than two hundred years ago, when the Armies of Christ first took Jerusalem. That is old, but it is not ancient, and you spoke with the authority of belief when you spoke of ancient lore."

"Bravo, dear sister." He dipped his head slowly to one side in an obvious gesture of admiration and respect. "Few men I know would be sufficiently astute to make that observation, and women are not supposed to be capable of such objective reasoning—a supposition, I am beginning to suspect, that allows men to cling to their illusions of superiority. I am impressed, and you are correct. Our Temple Order is measurably old, but the lore upon which its core was formed is ancient. I can say no more than that without violating my oath."

Jessica nodded again, accepting that, although the suggestion of a frown remained on her face. "So … an ancient record, an unsupported allegation, the merest fragment of a tale that by your own admission might have no basis in reality … and you intend to dedicate the remainder of your life to the search for this place? Forgive me, but that seems like the most obvious kind of folly. Where would you begin, and how? And who would go with you?"

"It may turn out that no one would, in which case I could not go … But I hope and believe that there will be enough intrepid souls among my men to fill out a sufficiently large crew to undertake the venture."

"You mean to sail with you into almost certain death?"

"Yes, if you wish to put it that way. But the certainty of death would not be nearly as great as your tone implies. Our brotherhood is founded upon faith … faith in God, and faith in ourselves and in our mission. The great Treasure that we are shipping with Sir William is proof, in itself, of the validity and reality of our lore. Until it was discovered in the bowels of the Temple Mount in Jerusalem, its existence was uncertain, its discovery predicated upon the faith of the men who would spend years searching for it. Our founder, Hugh de Payens, had nothing more to guide him than the instructions contained in ancient documents, yet his faith and certainty enabled him, with his eight companions, to dig down into the living rock of the Temple Mount for nine long years before they found it. It had been there all the time, despite all the odds dictated by logic and reason."

"What is it? What does it contain? It is obviously very precious."

"Aye, it is, and with potency to match its value. But above all else, it is a secret, and I can tell you with absolute honesty that I, even as admiral of the Temple fleet, have no idea what it comprises. Until the moment I saw it on the wharf of that fishing village a week ago, waiting to be loaded, I had never set eyes on it, and to the best of my knowledge, no one that I know within the Order has ever seen the chests opened. The last I heard of the Treasure was when it was shipped to safety from the fortress at Acre, just before the city fell to the Saracens. That was nigh on twenty years ago."

"Hmm. I have heard that tale and it is a striking one. But the Treasure is an established fact, dear Charles, its existence long since known. The matter you are describing, on the other hand, is altogether different. Even were you to find a crew as loyal as those who supported your founder in his search, I would be surprised that men would give up everything to leave the world they know and go with you on such a quest, sailing out into the Western Sea in the hope of finding an end to it. They would risk falling into the Abyss."

"All men risk falling into the Abyss, Sister, simply by living in this world. I have no doubt that if I can find the right kind of men—and I believe they are already aboard my own galley—they will come with me."

"And what of your superior? Why should Sir William Sinclair permit you to sail off with some of his few remaining men, on what most people would deem a fool's errand?"

The admiral shrugged. "On the face of it there is no reason, but I believe I might be able to offer him something of value as a *quid pro quo* for granting me leave to go … As you know, we are currently being pursued by some of our own ships, three galleys that we believe were captured by de Nogaret's men in La Rochelle. They are several days behind us, for I doubt that they could have gained on us during the storms, and that gap of days would permit us to do what needs to be done. I would require one day to unload my portion of the Treasure and stow it aboard another ship. After that, while the remainder of this fleet moved to concealment along the westward-facing coastline of Portugal, I would fall back and await the vessels pursuing us, then lead them in a merry chase out into the Atlantic."

"What makes you think they would follow you, a single ship?"

"Because they will know no different. All they will see of me when they arrive is my shape, and perhaps that of one of my escorts, if I have any, disappearing below the horizon. They will assume that I am the rearward lookout that has been ahead of them since they left port, and that the remainder of the fleet lies beyond me, below the horizon. By the time they discover the ruse, Sir William, along with you and the remainder of the fleet, will have vanished into the northern seas, bound for Scotland, with no one the wiser."

Jessica Randolph stared at her good-brother through narrowed eyes as she mulled over what he had told her. "You really believe you can find this Merica, don't you?"

"If it exists, I believe I will find it. And I believe it exists." He hesitated. "Of course, I have no idea how long it will take, so we will have to carry provisions for the entire crew for … probably two to three months."

"Is that possible?"

"Barely, but yes. It would be easier with two ships, though. I asked originally for several vessels, but I see now that three might be too many, simply from the viewpoint of finding crews."

Jessica sat up straight and blew her breath out sharply. "Then you must ask Sir William for two ships, and be prepared to man them both with only one full crew. Would that be enough for your needs?"

St. Valéry grinned. "Aye, it would, easily. But why are you so suddenly convinced Sinclair will let me go?"

"Because it makes sense. You can rid him of the threat of being followed to Scotland. And besides, if you succeed, and find this place—"

"And manage to return—"

She shot him a glance that was almost a frown. "Oh, if you find it you will come back to brag of it, I have no doubt. And when you do that, you will have provided Sir William Sinclair and all his Order with a place of refuge that, should such a thing ever be required, would be unassailable … a place that no one knows, beyond the end of the world. You must speak to him as soon as possible, and with more conviction than you have ever used in your life."

The admiral inclined his head, his beard masking his smile again. "So mote it be," he murmured. "I will do so, rely upon it. But it occurs to me that my task will be much simpler—convincing him to permit me, I mean—if you appear to have no knowledge of my proposal and no interest in supporting me."

She stared at him. "You mean you want me to pretend I know nothing of this."

"I do. Sir William distrusts women—all women—instinctively. It is part of his training and he has not yet learned to cope with other ... accommodations."

Her face hardened and then she nodded. "That is true. I deplore it and I think him foolish and pigheaded in that, but I will say nothing and keep my distance while you plead with him."

"Thank you, dear sister. I am in your debt."

4

To the considerable amazement of both plotters, Sir William Sinclair raised no insuperable objections to the admiral's proposal when he had listened to it in its entirety, but then, although he said nothing at the time to St. Valéry, he had been mulling over the admiral's idea for several days by then and could see nothing objectionable or unworthy in it. He accepted that a churchman might argue, on the grounds of morality, that Sir Charles might be seeking and risking suicide in such a venture, but Will Sinclair was a realist and had decided that the Order owed Sir Charles, after a lifetime of faithful and outstanding service, an opportunity to spend his final days in dedication to a quest he believed to be important.

But it was not until St. Valéry mentioned the notion expressed by his good-sister the Baroness, that success would provide a new haven in a new land to the survivors of the Order should it ever be needed, that Sinclair became convinced of the soundness of the admiral's idea. The idea of hoodwinking the pursuing galleys and leading them out into the ocean appealed to him, too, for he was concerned about keeping the whereabouts of the fleet concealed from de Nogaret and his grasping master, but that faded to insignificance beside the potential outlined by the admiral. Charles St. Valéry was no man's fool, and Sinclair trusted the older man's instinct and judgment as he would his own. If St. Valéry believed this place called Merica was out there within reach, then it was a conviction arrived at only after much thought and grave deliberation over the pros and contras of what he was considering, and it was simply not in the admiral's nature to lead any man dependent upon him into certain death. That truth, more than any other, led to Will's conclusion that he should grant permission to St. Valéry's request. Once that was decided, plans to implement the venture were quickly drawn up.

The weather had been perfect for sailing since the abatement of the storms, and the fleet sailed smoothly and swiftly along the northern coastline of Navarre towards Cape Corunna, where it would round the headland within the following two days and sail south by west again thereafter to Cape Finisterre. The fleet had reassembled on the second day after the last of the storms, with not a single vessel lost, an outcome that Brother Thomas the sacristan attributed to a miracle but which the admiral attributed to the skills of his captains and the seaworthiness of his ships.

Sir William kept the admiral and his men hard at work on the details of what had to be done if St. Valéry's scheme were to have a hope of working. The following morning, a fifth galley was sent back to contact the four that already screened the fleet from the pursuing galleys from La Rochelle. Its captain's orders were to gather information on the current situation vis-à-vis the pursuit craft; to discover the distance and sailing time separating the suspect galleys from the main fleet; and to return with that information as quickly as possible, but not before instructing the senior officer of the four screening galleys, Sir Charles de Lisle, to abandon his strategy of keeping distant and to determine the true status of the three galleys from La Rochelle, be they friend or foe. As soon as he knew beyond doubt, he was to send word immediately to Admiral St. Valéry.

In the meantime, taking advantage of the fine weather, St. Valéry sent out messages by boat asking any man who had intimate or special knowledge of the coastal waters between the two capes of Corunna and Finisterre to report to him in person. Three men responded, rowing from other ships to join him on his galley, where he awaited them on the small foredeck with Vice-Admiral de Berenger, Will Sinclair, and Captain de Narremat, the admiral's shipmaster, in attendance. Two of the newcomers were sergeants, both veteran mariners, and the third a knight who had been born and raised on that harsh coastline. The admiral instructed them to decide upon a sheltered spot, if there were such a place along that ocean-battered littoral, where he could safely send at least some of his fleet ashore for a day.

There was one such place, they told him: a natural harbor that lay approximately forty miles south of Cape Corunna. It was close to where the knight had grown up and it was uninhabited, because the cliffs surrounding it were high and dangerous, undercut by thousands of years of relentless attacks by breaking waves so that they now loomed outwards above the beach, threatening any vessel foolhardy enough to linger in the bay below. All three men agreed that the bay was large and spacious and would easily accommodate the entire fleet in safety and secrecy for as long as they wished to remain there, but acknowledged that it could also be unpredictably dangerous because of falling rocks. The knight, whose name was Escobar, was confident that their pursuers, if they were really French and employed by de Nogaret, would be unlikely to know of the bay's existence, since the only use he knew it served, and in this he was backed by one of the two mariners, was for the beaching of the occasional ship in order to scrape the barnacles from its hull.

St. Valéry looked at Sinclair, who nodded. "It sounds as though it might suit our purposes, but you are the seaman, so what think you? How long will you require to do what must be done?"

St. Valéry glanced at de Berenger, whose face showed nothing of his thoughts. "A few hours to transfer the remaining treasure from my hold to whichever vessel you select to take it, and then to transfer as many provisions as we might need from other ships. Half a day at most."

When St. Valéry asked for distance and sailing time to the bay from where they now were, the two mariners conferred again and offered an estimate of three, perhaps four days, depending upon winds and offshore tides. They did not yet know exactly where they were in relation to the shore, but estimated that they were within two to three days' sail of Cape Corunna, with another day beyond that to reach the bay.

Sinclair was still thinking about the length of time they would spend there. "How many ships do you wish to take with you, Admiral? Much will depend on that. I am thinking of your estimate of half a day's work." Sinclair saw the hesitancy in the admiral's eyes and continued. "The length of time does not concern me; the sufficiency does. I think we will need a full day to see this thing well done. You may be at sea for months, and it would be galling to run out of something simply because we did not take the time to load sufficient supplies. Now that we have made the decision to proceed in this, I want you to do it properly."

St. Valéry shrugged and looked up at the sail above him with its great painted cross of black on white. "Ships would be better than galleys, sturdier ... with more storage room. Galleys would be worse than useless out on there on the ocean, months at a stretch ... Cargo ships, Sir William. Four of them, if you can spare so many."

"We can. We have four spare and available now, according to your own tally, so you may have them—given that you can find the men to crew them voluntarily. Think you that would be sufficient to ensure your success, as far as you can ensure anything in this venture?" He was aware of the three visitors standing close by, their eyes moving from one speaker to the other, their faces alive with curiosity, and he held up a hand to St. Valéry. "Wait, if you will." He turned his attention to the three watching men. "Have you all heard of the legend of Merica, spoken of in the Order's lore?"

The three men nodded, but looked mystified.

"Admiral St. Valéry has decided to sail in search of it, to find out once and for all whether it be there or not beyond the Western Sea where it is supposed to be, and I have given him the blessings of our Master, Sir Jacques de Molay, to do so. In finding it, he and the men who sail with him will prove the truth of another great piece of our ancient lore, just as Hugh de Payens and his companions did with the discovery of the Temple Treasure. He will be seeking volunteers to sail with him into the unknown upon a great and daunting quest. How think you his request might be received by your fellows?"

The three men stood for a few moments, looking at each other, rank apparently forgotten, and then the knight spoke up. "I can speak for no one but myself, my lord Admiral, but I can think of nothing I would rather do than sail on your quest with you."

St. Valéry inclined his head graciously, but said nothing, and Sinclair intervened. "What is your name, sir? We have not met before, have we?"

"Antonio Escobar, Sir William, and no, we have not met before now."

"Well, sir, I shall remember you as the first knight of the Temple to join Sir Charles's quest. And what of you two men?"

The elder of the two sergeants spoke up at once, saying he might think about going since he had no family to concern himself about, but the second man shook his head regretfully and declined.

"Well, Sir Charles, two out of three at first sweep. If you continue thus you will take full two-thirds of my strength."

"No chance of that, Sir William. I seek but to crew four ships. If I have more than that number, I shall select those I need and wish the others well with you."

"What about water? You'll need as much as you can carry."

The knight Escobar raised a hand, and when Sinclair looked at him he said, "There is sweet, fresh water in the bay we spoke of, sir. A spring-fed stream near the top of the cliffs falls to the beach."

"Good, then we'll use it. Thank you, gentlemen. Which of you knows the coastline best? We need only one of you to lead us in; the other two may return to your ships."

"Then it should be one of these two men, sir, since I am not a mariner," Escobar said, and drew himself up to attention. The other two muttered briefly to each other, and the younger of the two turned to St. Valéry. "I will stay, Admiral."

St. Valéry thanked all three men before dismissing them, sending the one who would remain behind to the stern with the galley's captain, and when the four senior officers were alone again Sinclair struck straight to the heart of the matter at hand.

"Very well, then. We will have half a day to effect our changes, perhaps longer, depending upon how closely we are being pursued. Now we have much planning to do, and we need to send out the word to all our ships of what we are about in this endeavor. Can you attend to that, Sir Charles? We should do it quickly and clear our minds for other things. Among which is the disposition of your passenger and her cargo. I presume the Baroness will not be accompanying you on your quest ... What, then, are we to do with her?"

St. Valéry shrugged his shoulders. "She will remain aboard my galley, which will become de Berenger's command. Captain de Narremat here will assume the rank of vice-admiral and take over Sir Edward's present command." He glanced at de Narremat, whose face was flushing with surprised pleasure. "Before doing that, Captain, you will appoint another from your own officers here to fill your present position as admiral's shipmaster." He broke off, turning to Sinclair. "Unless you object to any of that, Sir William?"

The inflexion of the admiral's voice turned that last statement into a question, but Sinclair shook his head. "You are still admiral, Sir Charles, and you know your people far better than I do. The choice of captains is yours. I will remain aboard the vice-admiral's galley for now, if the new vice-admiral has no objection. And now, gentlemen, we have other matters to deal with. Shall we begin?"

But at that moment a hail from the lookout on the cross-spar at the mast top announced that he had seen another vessel bearing down on them, and even as they absorbed that, they heard him counting aloud as more distant sails became discernible far behind them to the northeast.

"Five galleys!" the lookout shouted. "One ahead of four! And ... and more behind those ... Two, three more in pursuit."

St. Valéry looked at Will Sinclair. "Five Temple galleys, fleeing from pursuit by three? That is not possible. There must be another explanation ... The three rearward galleys must be our own, escaped from La Rochelle before they could be taken."

WITHIN TWO HOURS of the first distant sighting, Will Sinclair stood on the upper deck of the admiral's stern castle, watching the approach of the three strange galleys, and he could see plainly why the naval officers had spoken earlier of de l'Armentière's galley, the leading one, as being unmistakably different. The Templar galleys, irrespective of individual size, were all modeled upon the massive biremes of Roman times and built in the shipyards around Genoa, where generations of shipwright families had been building the same kind of vessels for hundreds of years. Huge and solid, with double banks of oars and an elongated ram beneath the prow, they had been virtually unchanged since the days of the Roman navies, the single difference being that now the sails were made of heavy cloth rather than of leather. De l'Armentière's was different; longer, lower, and sleeker, it shipped thirty-six oars, he saw, but in two long, single banks of eighteen a side. The mast, too, was different, neither as tall nor as thick as those on the Temple's vessels, but there was no mistaking the fact that this vessel had been designed for speed and battle. Its long battering ram, clad in copper sheeting, curved up and projected from the water ahead of the craft like the horn of some ferocious beast.

Behind the strange-looking galley, its two escorting craft were standard Temple vessels, each of them shipping eighteen double-banked oars to a side, so that he estimated their fighting force to be anywhere from eighty to a hundred men apiece, dependent upon the size of their relief crews, and his guess was that they would not have sailed from Cyprus without a full complement. So another two to three hundred fighting men had been added to their force, and from the look of them, they were all veteran Temple sergeants.

He stood watching until he saw boats being lowered from the strange-looking leader, and then, as he turned away, he spotted the Baroness St. Valéry watching the newcomers from the corresponding deck on the ship's forecastle. Inexplicably flustered by the sudden sight of her and feeling slightly breathless despite having known he would probably see her somewhere during his visit, he averted his eyes and went below, moving very deliberately, to await the new arrivals in the ship's main cabin.

5

The commander of the leading galley, Sir Antoine de l'Armentière, was precisely the kind of man Will Sinclair had expected him to be, the kind of Templar he thought of as a Temple Boar: a fighting monk, largely devoid of humor and thoroughly dedicated to the affairs of the Temple to the exclusion of all else. Not that there was anything amiss with that, Will thought, examining the captain as he arrived. Such men served a necessary function, and their loyalty to the Order was unassailable. De l'Armentière strode into the cabin as if it were his personal domain and came to attention in front of the admiral, ignoring everyone else.

St. Valéry greeted him courteously, then introduced him to the others in attendance, most of whom de l'Armentière already knew. Finally he brought him forward to introduce him to Will.

"May I present Sir William Sinclair, Sir Antoine. He is a member of the Governing Council, here on direct business for Master de Molay himself concerning the recent matters of which you may or not be aware." He turned to Will. "Sir Antoine is from Burgundy, Sir William. His family has provided members for our Order since its beginnings in Jerusalem." And having delivered his message that de l'Armentière was definitely not of the Order of Sion, the admiral gestured to everyone to be seated. "Shall we begin, gentlemen?"

Sinclair and de l'Armentière exchanged nods, and then the men took their places around the long, narrow table that filled up most of the main cabin.

As soon as they were all seated, St. Valéry motioned to de l'Armentière. "Your report, if you please, Sir Antoine. We know you arrived in La Rochelle mere hours after our departure, but our lookouts were too far away to prevent you from entering the harbor. Since then, we had thought your galleys confiscated. When they emerged again, we had no choice but to assume them crewed by the enemy. Plainly we were mistaken. Please tell us what occurred."

De l'Armentière knew how to savor a moment of attention. He sat frowning for some time, looking at no one, as though gazing inwardly, making a display of collecting his thoughts, then looked slowly from man to man around the table. "Who *is* the enemy?" he asked eventually. "We arrived directly from Cyprus, after ten days at sea, and we saw the King's colors among the men on the quays. But even before that we had seen a pyre of burning ships and a harbor devoid of Temple shipping. And the Order's banners were missing from the battlements, something I had never seen before.

"And so I gave orders to drop anchor out of bowshot from the quay. But once they had seen that we were not going to approach them any closer, they fired upon us uselessly nonetheless. I waited to see if anyone would approach us, but not a single boat was launched towards us, and it soon became quite obvious that the crowds on the quay were leaderless and there was no one willing to assume the authority to deal with us. And so I remained at anchor, to see if someone might return to assume command. But no one did. I waited for three hours, by which time the tide was in full ebb, and then I took my ships out of there under oars … truthfully, with no idea of what I should do next."

"So what did you do, Captain?" Sir William asked him.

De l'Armentière offered a half smile to his questioner. "As soon as we had cleared the harbor mouth, my lookouts reported masts on the horizon to the south, and so I set a course to follow them. I did not know who had occupied La Rochelle, but if these ships were coming in support of whoever it was, then I intended to debate with them. But as it turned out, they were sailing away from us and keeping their distance."

St. Valéry cleared his throat politely. "And you had no suspicion that these vessels you were pursuing might be your own? Temple galleys?"

The other smiled again, more broadly this time. "I had many suspicions, Admiral, but not that one. The thought of Temple galleys fleeing a fight simply did not occur to me. Besides, they were hull down on the horizon most of the time, no matter how we sought to catch them … which told me, indeed, that they were in fact galleys of one kind or another. Not all galleys are alike, as you may see by looking at my own."

He looked again around the table, meeting each man's eye before continuing. "I accepted that they had no wish to close with us, but neither had I any wish to abandon the chase. We had returned from a long voyage, our stores depleted, to find our own harbor closed to us, and so I found myself loath to give up and turn away. And so their flight became our pursuit … until, of course, they approached and identified themselves, early yesterday. Since then I have gathered some information, enough to form some notion of what has been happening recently, but my sources were mainly officers and sergeants who knew little or nothing of what is really involved. And so, if I may ask without being ruled impertinent, will someone tell me what has been going on in my absence?"

The question brought about a general surge of noise that the admiral quelled by thumping on the table, and when silence had returned he himself spoke to de l'Armentière.

"Folly and chaos and treachery has been going on," he said, his voice flat. "Suffice for now to say that the King's chief minister, William de Nogaret, has moved against our Order with the full support of the King himself and, it would seem, the Pope. The atrocity was perpetrated the morning you arrived, and it is our understanding that it occurred on a massive scale, throughout France. You will learn all about it later. For the moment, we have other things to discuss.

"We were forewarned by Sir William here, who came to us with the written authority of Master de Molay, and it was the Master himself who first learned of the plot against us. He issued orders for us to embark on the night of the twelfth and to await whatever might develop the following morning, for even he was unsure of the truth of the warnings he had received. We waited, and de Nogaret's men arrived as predicted. And now we are making our way in search of sanctuary elsewhere, away from France."

"Where, in God's holy name?"

St. Valéry glanced at Sinclair, who responded, "In Scotland, where the King is excommunicate and therefore unlikely to be influenced by the Pope."

"Unless," de l'Armentière said, "the Pope offers to lift the excommunication in return for our capture. Have you thought of that?"

The response verged on insolence, and in fact Will Sinclair had not thought of that at all. He bit back an angry response and busied himself in leaning back in his chair and stretching his muscles for a moment to give himself time to think.

"That thought had occurred to me," he drawled after a moment, knowing somehow that it was important to lie. "But I dismissed it as irrelevant, particularly since we now know you were not de Nogaret's spies pursuing us. We also know that no one can possibly know where we have disappeared to. Had you, in fact, been enemies, we would have led you out into the ocean beyond Finisterre and either lost you or destroyed you. Relieved of the need to waste time doing either of those things, we may now head directly for Scotland, where we will deliver a treasure of gold and silver bars and coins to the King of Scots on behalf of one of his most loyal subjects. That should win us his gratitude for as long as we require it. The Temple is secure in Scotland, so we will be doubly welcome. If de Nogaret traces us there eventually, it will no longer matter, for this unpleasantness will have dried up and blown away by then, all differences settled."

The Burgundian knight sat mulling that for a moment, then dipped his head and smiled. "So mote it be. Then I am content, and at your service, Sir William." He stopped short and looked around the table, one eyebrow raised but this time without giving offense. "I am correct in assuming, am I not, that your rank supersedes all others here?"

Will Sinclair nodded. "Aye, technically you are. In fact, though, the admiral continues to be God at sea, and I am a mere passenger aboard his craft. And having said that, gentlemen, I will leave you to your planning, for you have much yet to do. Admiral, should you need me at all, I shall be in my quarters. It remains to me to commend you, Captain de l'Armentière, on your actions in La Rochelle. You did well. And now, a good day to you all."

6

William was already looking around for Tam as soon as he left the cabin and he saw him quickly, standing by the ship's entry port deep in conversation with Baroness St. Valéry. She was wearing a dark green hooded cloak, and the hood's high peak made it look as though she was taller than Tam. His heartbeat was suddenly loud in his head and his gut twisted in—what? he asked himself. He felt a stirring of pleasure, then a formless guilt quickly smothered in rising anger.

What in God's name are you doing talking to that woman? was the first clear thought that came to him, and then he drew a deep breath, forcing himself to swallow his anger, which he knew was utterly unreasonable, and to take the time to think about how he could make the inevitable encounter with the woman both courteous and harmless. He made his way towards them, and his spoken order was the first inkling either of them had that he was there.

"Tam. My boat, if you will. Good day to you, Baroness."

As Tam swung away towards the stern with a grunt, Jessica Randolph turned to smile at Sinclair.

"Sir William," she said, unperturbed. "We expected you to be detained far longer than this, with all the comings and goings that have taken place today. Are you feeling unwell?"

He forced himself to answer graciously. "No, madam, I am very well. I merely have some matters of my own to attend to, and Sir Charles and his officers have more knowledge of what they are about than I could ever have. And so I left them to it. You and Tam were deep in discussion."

"Tam is a dear man … Is it true you have granted Charles leave to sail away and leave us in search of some hidden land?"

Damn the woman! "I see Tam has been saying more than his prayers."

"Untrue, sir. My good-brother himself told me he would seek your leave to go. Tam merely responded when I asked him about it."

He felt relieved to know that Tam had said nothing untoward, for Will had discussed the plan with him as a matter of course, before making his decision. He had never known Tam to betray a confidence, and to know that this remained unchanged made him feel a glow of warmth inside. But then he realized that the Baroness was gazing at him expectantly.

"Aye," he said, making a harrumphing sound in his throat, "well, the admiral made his request, and I responded. He will be leaving shortly."

"In search of this unknown place, this Merica." It was not a question, and it took him aback.

"He mentioned this to you?"

"He did. Should he not have?"

"No, I am merely surprised."

"That he should share such confidence with a mere woman, or that he should speak of it at all?"

Sinclair shook his head. "Neither, madam. I meant no offense."

The woman stared at him through narrowed eyes, but at that moment a bumping sound from close beneath them announced the arrival of the boat Tam had summoned. He glanced over the side to make sure it was indeed his boat, then bowed slightly to the Baroness.

"My boat is here, madam, so you must excuse me. I have much to do."

"I am sure you have, sir."

The Baroness dipped her head graciously and turned away, and he had to steel himself not to watch her as she made her way forward, although he could hear the crew members greeting her as she went. Instead, he braced himself and stepped forward to the entry port, eyeing the moving ladder that awaited his cautious descent.

When he was safely in the boat he tucked his cloak about him before looking up to see Tam watching him, his face unreadable.

"What? What means that look?" he growled, speaking Scots so their conversation would be unintelligible to any listening ears among the oarsmen. Tam looked away, saying nothing, but Will was in no mood to leave it there. "You two were having a deal to say to each other, I noticed. What else did you tell her, other than that I had granted the admiral's request?"

"We were but passin' the time o' day. She asked me right out and I answered, but no' without thinking. She would find out within a day or two, when it comes time for him to leave, so I thought it no harm." He twitched an eyebrow. "Are ye vexed wi' me?"

Will watched the oarsmen's back muscles clench and unclench as they drove the boat away from the admiral's galley and turned it skillfully towards his own, but finally he sighed. "No, I'm no' vexed, Tam … It's just that that woman … upsets me."

Tam offered no comment on that, asking instead, "What d'ye think o' the new fellow, wi' the fancy galley? What's his name, de l'Armentière?" He pronounced it *Arminteer* in the Scots fashion. "A Temple Boar if ever I saw one."

"Aye, he is, but I think he'll be a good man to have wi' us, ne'er the less. He has a quick mind on him, and 'gin we can keep him happy and gi'e him lots to fight over, I think he'll be well enough. His three ships are grand enough, and he'll have two or three hundred men aboard them. Fine enough if we get into a tulzie at sea, but we'll ha'e to feed and shelter them once we make land."

"Aye, right enough," Tam agreed, low-voiced. They were approaching their own ship now and its hull loomed above them.

Their lead oarsman stood up and reached out with a long, hooked pole to catch the rope that would allow them to pull themselves to where the ladder from the entry port hung just astern of the rearmost of the galley's long oars, and as he did so Tam mused, still in Scots, "But speakin' o' twa, three hundred extra men, forbye the ones we had, you said the admiral wondered whether the King o' Scots will be glad to see a fleet sail into his ken … D'ye no' think he might be right?"

Will grunted, preparing himself to stand up once the boat had been secured. "He might be, Tam. You never know. But from what I hear, King Robert's troubles are all land based. He'll ha'e little use for galleys, I'm thinking, but he'll be hungry for fighting men. But that reminds me, I meant to ask you if there are other Scots among our fleet. D'you know that, or can you find out?"

"I can ask. But what are ye lookin' for?"

Will stood up and braced himself cautiously against the choppy motion of the moored boat. "Any man who knows anything at all about Arran Isle, for I know nothing of it. I've seen it often, but only frae the mainland. I've never set foot there, and it came to me that there might be men, even one man, among the fleet who knows the place."

"Aye, I'll try to find out. Mind your step now and dinna fa' in. I ha'e nae need to spend hours cleanin' salt and rust off your blades."

7

"**S**tep back here and stay away from the edge o' that cliff. You're the one who pointed out to me that it's a' crumbled away underneath. All we would need now is for it to gi'e way and send you and half a mountain straight down onto the tops o' our ships."

Will threw his head back and laughed loud, but at the same time he did as Tam bade him, turning back onto more solid ground, lowering himself to sit on a tussock of grass by his kinsman's side and gazing out to the west, where the Atlantic Ocean stretched ahead of them.

"Look at that vista, Tam. Have you ever seen the like? No, you ha'e not, because you have never seen siccan a vast body of water, and neither have I. We ha'e traveled far, you and I, these past years, but when you think of it, I doubt we ha'e ever been completely out of sight of land, it's aey been there, behind us or in front of us or on either side but somewhere within sight. But out there, where the admiral will be heading tomorrow, there is nothing. We'll be going over that way, more northward, towards Ireland and then Scotland, and again we'll never really be out of sight of land." He pointed due west. "But over there, beyond the rim o' that sky, there lies nothing but more water, and within a matter of a day or two's outward sailing, he and his men will be lost in an ocean so vast that his only hope of reaching land will be to turn around and sail back."

"He's no' an admiral now. Just plain Sir Charles."

That was true. In the two days since the appearance of de l'Armentière and his galleys, the Temple ships had made their way from Cape Corunna to the sheltered, nameless bay they had chosen, and as soon as they had anchored safely and started the transfer of goods and the provisioning of the four vessels he would now take in search of Merica, Sir Charles had resigned his admiral's rank and bestowed it upon Edward de Berenger, the transfer of title and power of admiral of the Temple fleet witnessed and ratified by Sir William Sinclair. The ceremony had been brief, carried out on the beach of the bay without pomp, in the course of a brief Mass concelebrated by the four bishops who had sailed with them from La Rochelle, and as soon as the rites were concluded, everyone scattered to see to the redistribution of the various cargoes.

Sir Charles's guest had captured the imagination of the men, and he had no difficulty raising a party of 110 willing volunteers to sail with him in search of the fabled new land, more than enough to crew his small fleet of ships. His party, however, would take no horses with them, an announcement that astonished Sir William Sinclair when he first heard it, although he realized at once that sound reasoning underlay the decision. No one knew how long the voyage would take, or if it would even end in success, but St. Valéry's belief was that it might take anywhere up to three months of sailing, and the impossibility of carrying sufficient fodder rendered such a thing impractical. Atop that, there was the well-known fact that horses did not take well to sea voyages; after a voyage of mere weeks, it required at least one full day and frequently two to permit the animals to adjust to having solid land beneath their feet. No one cared to think of the effect a journey months in length might have on the creatures. And so St. Valéry's expedition would disembark in the new land and proceed afoot, unless they were fortunate enough to find replacement mounts in Merica.

"How long will Sir Charles stay wi' us before he strikes away?"

"Not long. He'll probably wave us away before we're out of sight of land."

"You sound very sure, for a landsman ..."

"As sure as any man may be of anything. Aye, I'm sure of it. And in the meantime all's well below on the beach, and we ha'e nothing to do but wait a while."

Tam made no response to that. Matters were well in hand on the beach far below them, cargo being transferred from one ship to another so that St. Valéry's small squadron could set out, at least, with as much as possible of anything they might require on their voyage. Will and Tam had had nothing to do among all the activity and so they had taken advantage of the opportunity to stretch their legs and had ended up climbing the beetling cliffs, by a roundabout route that avoided the perilous overhang, so that now they sat at their ease far above the bustling activities below.

Will smiled and lay back, his eyes closed in enjoyment of the sun, but Tam had more questions.

"What about the ships waitin' for us off Finisterre?"

"Already taken care of. De Lisle's already on his way to meet them, if there are any there. They'll follow us, hugging the coastline until they reach Cape Corunna, then they'll head north and west for Scotland. We'll wait for them off the Mull of Kintyre." He turned

his head. "Were you able to find out if there are any other Scots in
the fleet?"

"Aye, but only this mornin'. There's two, one o' them a graybeard
frae Galloway called Mungo MacDowal. I havena seen him or spoken
to him, but I left word for him to come and see ye when he was
finished workin' this afternoon. If he's frae Galloway, he'll ha'e
grown up lookin' at Arran, maist like. He'll probably be there by the
time we get back down to the beach … Tell me, why did ye have us
change ships, you and me? I was just beginning to grow used to where
we were."

His companion opened one eye, squinting against the light, and
looked at him as though he were mad. "We haven't changed ships."

"No, but we could have. We've changed captains, and I liked de
Berenger."

"That is neither here nor there. I had no choice. The admiral's
galley is the only one big enough for the Baroness and her women.
Would you have had me throw them out? De Berenger's transfer
aboard changed nothing, with Sir Charles gone, but had you and I
moved over, it would have been too crowded. So we stayed. Besides,
I could not abide being on that ship with all those women."

Tam started to respond but then merely lay back on the grass, his
fingers interlaced behind his head. "No," he muttered, "you couldna,
could you? That would ha' been too human. Ye winna thole the
women."

Will did not dignify that with a response, for despite his Scots
sarcasm, Tam was correct: Will Sinclair would not, indeed, tolerate
the presence of the women and had thus chosen to remain where he
was, since de Berenger's former galley was more than adequate to
his needs. The fact that the Temple Treasure was already in the
vessel's modest hold was justification enough to allow him to avoid
being saddled with the presence and too-close proximity of the
distracting and infuriating Baroness St. Valéry all the way to
Scotland.

Tam, unsurprised by the lack of response, lay quiet for a long
time after that, feeling the sun's warmth on his face, then asked,

"What are you thinkin' to do once we reach Scotland? Will you go directly to the King?"

Sir Charles had asked him the same pair of questions, almost word for word, that very morning, and although he had answered straightforwardly at the time, he had been thinking about it ever since, and now he gave a slightly different answer to Tam.

"I don't rightly know, Tam. Much will depend on what we find when we arrive. I told Sir Charles this morning that I would first seek a safe anchorage—for I can't be sure Arran will be safe—then make enquiries about the King—his whereabouts, for one thing. But since then I have come to think that neither of those might be as simple as I thought … For one thing, I doubt that I'll be able to strike out towards the King immediately. There's too much to be done first among our own. Our party is too large, and many of the knights too proud and stiff-necked to be left too suddenly to their own devices. It comes to me that I might have to spend some time laying down the rules and asserting my authority before I ride away leaving them behind.

"And then again, there is the matter of the King of Scots himself. The last I heard, he was sore beset with troubles, his own lords and barons being as bad as the English. Particularly the Comyns, in the north. They claim the kingship as their right and name Bruce usurper, so the land is steeped in civil war. And then the threat from England atop all of that. Edward Plantagenet may be dead, but his earls and barons are no less hungry than before to subdue the Scots. For all I know, the Bruce may not even be alive by now, although I pray God that that be not the case. It must be considered, nevertheless, and other plans made against the possibility. Thus I must think about approaching Sir Thomas Randolph and the other members of the Temple in Scotland. They will receive me, I know, but whether they will have the power to succor us must remain to be seen."

"So where will you seek safe anchorage?"

"On Arran first, I think. It has been Scots-held, part of the Bruce holdings, since King Alexander thrashed the Norwayans and dislodged them at Largs Battle. We will go there, find out what holds sway. It lies within the Firth of Clyde but is remote enough to hide us. I doubt it will be much occupied nowadays, for as I recall it is a barren place, yet suited to our purpose well enough."

"There will be folk there, nonetheless."

"Aye, probably, but we will talk with them. We mean them no harm."

"Mayhap. But they'll no' know that. They'll see a fleet o' foreign ships and they'll hide in the hills … Scots folk—and Islanders mair than most—ha'e little trust o' foreigners."

Will sat mum for a moment, then shrugged. "Well, that's a bridge we'll have to cross when we reach it …"

Neither man had any more to say and they lay quiet for a while, enjoying their inactivity and the solid ground beneath them, dozing on the grass as they waited for time to pass, and it seemed to Tam Sinclair that he had barely closed his eyes when the slap of Will's hand against his thigh startled him awake.

"Come, you, let's away. The man Mungo should be waiting for us by now. Scotland awaits us, and the tide is rising."

Tam rolled over and pushed himself to his feet, but before they set out along the winding cliff-top path that would lead them down the long and difficult descent to the beach, he looked out again at the vastness of the waters. "D'you think Sir Charles will find his Merica?"

"No, Tam, I don't. No more than I believe, in my heart, that King Robert the Bruce is dead. Pray God that neither should turn out to be the case."

Wordlessly, Tam turned almost a quarter circle and gazed to the north, where the sea looked just as vast and limitless, but he knew that in that direction lay his homeland, and that, weather permitting, they would find it in mere days.

THE ISLAND
OF ARRAN

THE HOLY ISLE

1

T"here's folk up there, watchin' us."

Tam Sinclair's voice was little more than a murmur, but all three of the men standing with him turned their eyes to look where he was pointing.

The bearded, barrel-chested sergeant called Mungo MacDowal hawked and spat cleanly over the side. "We're on Eilean Molaise," he said, his voice little more than an elongated grunt. "It's a holy place, folk say, so they'll be monks, friars mair likely. There's aey three or fower o' them up there, livin' in caves like wild beasts. They'll no' bother us."

"Not even when we land?" This was Will Sinclair, and Mungo barely favored him with a glance.

"No' even if we kill them," he growled, moving away to the ship's rail, where he continued peering up towards the distant watchers.

Will turned with a lopsided grin to Admiral de Berenger, who stood slightly behind him. "Did you understand that?"

De Berenger blinked. "I heard the grunting of a boar. Should I have understood?"

Sinclair's grin grew wider. "Mungo was saying that the men up there are friars, monks without a community, living as they can. The islet here is called Eilean Molaise, Saint Molaise's Island, in honor of a Celtic saint who once lived here. He says they live in caves up there, like wild beasts, but they will offer us no ill."

The admiral cleared his throat. "I shall accept that ... the recommendation of one wild beast concerning another. I find it hard to believe the man is one of our sergeants."

"Aye, well he is, and has been for two decades, earning himself his captain's trust sufficiently to hold officer's rank for more than twelve of those. He knows his work, and he knows these islands and their people. I do not. And he speaks Scots by choice because he is with Scots today and has not had the opportunity to speak it for many years." Will grinned again, to take the potential sting out of his next words. "Show him some tolerance, Edward, and try not to be so disdainful when you look at him. He is a good man, merely uncouth by your standards."

De Berenger nodded. "You like the fellow. Very well, then, I shall take you at your word and be more tolerant. When do you want to move on?"

Will's face grew pensive. "Not yet, I think." He turned to gaze up to where the men on the hill yet stood, clearly illuminated by the rising sun. Between them and him, however, closer inshore, the sea mist still hung thick above the water, obscuring the land. "We could be up there in an hour or two," he mused, "given that we had a place to land. From the top, we would have a clear view of what's over there, behind the bay on the far side." He raised his voice. "Mungo, could we see the Arran mainland from the top?"

"Aye, ye could count the deer. It's no' even a mile across the bay."

"Excellent, then that's where we'll go. Is there a beach ahead of us where we could land?"

"No, it's sheer cliff, but there's a slopin' beach farther back, on the edge we passed comin' in."

"Edward, can you find us a place to land and still remain hidden from the main island?"

"No, but my captain will." De Berenger called over his newly promoted subordinate and began issuing instructions to bring the galley under way, and as he did so Will glanced back to where Tam Sinclair and Mungo stood beyond earshot, talking together in a blend of Scots and Gaelic, and again a half-formed grin plucked at the corner of his mouth.

Mungo MacDowal had turned out to be a treasure beyond price, for Tam had been wrong in thinking the man came from the MacDowal territory of Galloway on the mainland. He had spent time there as a boy, but he was a native Islesman, born on Arran itself. He'd traveled widely throughout the Isles before his father's death, after which, at the age of fourteen, he had moved with his uncle to the mainland. His gruff, surly façade was no more than that, and once he had accepted Will as a worthwhile companion—mere worldly rank had no significance for him—Mungo had lent himself willingly to their endeavors, proving his value immediately.

He it was who had suggested that they conceal the entire fleet on the southeastern side of a tiny islet called Sanda, itself off the southeastern tip of the headland called the Mull of Kintyre, where it might remain for weeks or even months without being seen from the headland. There, he had pointed out, the fleet would be close enough to Arran to reach it quickly, in less than a day, but anyone on Arran would remain unaware of its presence. Seeing the good sense in his proposal, Will had instructed de Berenger to take his ships north and then east around the coast of Ireland, taking care to steer well clear of the island of Rathlin, off the northern Irish coast, and had they anchored unseen, they believed, in the shelter of Sanda. They had been joined there within the week by Captain de Lisle and three more midsized galleys, each of thirty-two oars, that had sailed to Finisterre from Marseille, the sole members of the Templar fleet to survive from that part of France.

As soon as the newcomers were safely gathered, Will had wanted to proceed with a small squadron to Arran, but once again it was Mungo who had offered the best advice on that. Take a single galley, he had said. The biggest one, to inspire respect and discourage interference yet prevent the inhabitants from flying into a panic thinking they were being invaded. There was a sheltered anchorage on the southeast side of Arran, he had added, a place called Lamlash Bay, and an island offshore, less than a mile away, that could serve the same purpose for them as Sanda had for the fleet, concealing them until they were ready to approach Arran under favorable conditions. Will had followed the man's advice precisely, marveling at his own readiness to do so, yet trusting him instinctively.

Before leaving Sanda, however, and probably to the lady's great displeasure, Baroness St. Valéry and her women had changed galleys, going to occupy the quarters formerly held by Will and Tam, while those two transferred all their possessions aboard the admiral's larger galley for the journey to Arran. The treasures were now split the wrong way—the Baroness's specie in Will's care, while the Temple Treasure itself remained with the Baroness—but there was nothing Will could do about that for the time being.

Tam and Mungo were looking at him now, plainly expecting him to say something, and he pointed up towards the top of the hill. "The admiral's taking the galley back to the beach you mentioned, Mungo, and I'm thinking of taking a wee climb up there, to see what's to be seen. I hope you both feel well enough to come with me. How long, think you, will it take us to get to the top?"

Tam tilted his head back and looked up at the slope on the flank of the hill as the galley began to turn within its own length, propelled into a sharp spin by the skilled oarsmen. As the ship revolved, Tam turned against its swing, keeping his eyes on the hilltop. The oars on both sides bit into the water, stopping the vessel's turn and then driving it forward, slowly at first but gathering speed with every stroke. Tam turned back to Will. "We should be there by mid-morning, if we land and strike out without wastin' time. We might go quicker, but I'm recallin' the fight you had to make it to the top of the cliff above the bay that day Sir Charles changed ships. You could hardly catch your breath after that, and yon climb was nothin' compared to the wee stroll ye'll be facin' up there."

Will kept his face expressionless, stifling the urge to laugh at the familiar insolence, and looked at Mungo, tipping his head sideways to indicate his kinsman. "Would you listen to the man's ravings. I practically had to carry him that time, he was so weak in the legs and wind. Too much time at sea and too little drill to keep him fit. I'm going to get ready. See you if you can find us some food to take with us. I'll meet you here when I'm done." He walked away, grinning openly as soon as his back was turned, and hearing Tam muttering behind his back.

A short time later he was back on deck, wearing a long, heavy cloak of dark green wool over a plain but quilted knee-length tunic and a leather jerkin, his only weapon a single-edged dirk in a sheath by his side. His legs were wrapped in thick knitted leggings, and he wore heavy campaigning boots, tightly laced to mid-calf. The other two were waiting for him, similarly dressed and armed, since there was little likelihood of trouble on the Holy Isle and they had no wish to appear belligerent, even to the watching friars up on the hill. Tam carried a worn leather satchel slung across his chest.

"Food," he said, when he saw Will glance at it.

"Fine. We'll be hungry when we reach the top. Did you find us a boat?"

2

From where they stood now, facing west on the highest point of the islet, all of the east side of Arran stretched out in front of them, across the waters of Lamlash Bay. The morning was crisp but still, so that not all the sea mist had yet gone from the bay beneath them, odd pockets lingering like earthbound clouds. The sky was cloudy, but the covering was broken, holding no threat of rain for the time being, and myriad gulls swooped and dived all about them, their raucous cries drowning all other sounds.

"There's not much moving over there."

"No, but that doesna mean there's nobody there. It's a fine mornin', so there'll be somebody about sooner or later. It's a bonny sight, though, is it no'?"

"Aye, Mungo, it is. How long has it been since you were last here?"

"God! It's been a while ... I was just a bit o' a boy when I was last here, didna even ha'e a beard. So that's a score o' year, at least, afore I lost count. Mind you, I dinna think I've ever set foot on Eilean Molaise afore now. But seein' this, I canna think why."

Sinclair felt no urge to argue that point.

Arran island, he had known, was approximately egg shaped, its narrow end now stretching on their left, sloping gently down to the sea. Directly across from them, on the far side of the bay, shelving beaches led up to a crescent-shaped plateau that stretched inland for what looked like a couple of miles, rising gradually north and west into what appeared to be high moorlands on the horizon. Farther north yet, on their extreme right, the ground sloped more severely until the gentle hills became high, distant mountains, several of them snow capped from the early-winter storms.

He turned to his left, staring at the southernmost point of land, straining to see signs of the fortification they had passed the previous night on their way in. They had made the approach in darkness, using oars and keeping well out from the shoreline, their great sail lowered to prevent any reflection that might betray their passing, and they had seen several balefires flickering in the night as they passed by. Mungo had said they burned on the heights of Kildonan, a natural cliff-top stronghold that had been occupied continuously since men first came to Arran. A stone tower was being built there now, he said, started by the Norwayans decades earlier, before King Alexander had defeated them at the Largs fight and ended Norway's rule in Scotland's west, but the place had always been used as a defensive point. Gazing in that direction now, Will could see nothing and assumed the tower, if such it was nowadays, lay out of sight, around the promontory.

He turned back to the view ahead of him, thinking of how peaceful it appeared and wondering how many men might be concealed there.

"Can either of you see any signs of life?" he asked, knowing that if they could they would already have said so. He was surprised when Tam spoke up.

"Aye, and close by—one of yon holy caterans is coming over here."

Will stifled a groan, for sure enough, one of the watchers from earlier was standing no more than fifty paces distant, staring at them from a fold in the ground that concealed all but his chest and head.

"Well, so much for your saying they would not bother us."

Mungo grunted. "Pay him nae heed and he'll go awa'. As Tam says, he's just a cateran, half mad, mayhap mair ... ye'd have to be, to live up here."

The watching friar, or whatever he might be, stood motionless, staring at them, and it occurred to Will that Mungo's description of him as a cateran, a wandering ragamuffin, might be an accurate one. Ignore him, Will thought, or approach him? The fellow, half mad or not, might have information they could use, and if he had, then learning of it would be far from a waste of time.

He straightened up and turned to face the man directly, catching his eye and holding it in silence, making no other move or gesture. The fellow tilted his head slightly to one side in an unmistakable inquiry. Will nodded and beckoned him forward, then watched in growing amazement as the stranger approached. The man was enormously tall, Will realized as he breasted the rise that had concealed him, and as he drew closer, it became clear, too, that he was old enough to be considered ancient. He was also incredibly ragged and indescribably filthy, his hair and beard a matted, singular tangle that had known neither water nor comb for years, and his only clothing an ankle-length black robe so tattered and torn that large patches of skin were exposed on his chest and legs. He carried a tall walking staff of blackthorn, its thick end towering above his head, and a single, empty-looking leather pouch or scrip hung from the frayed old length of rope that served him as a girdle. His enormously long legs were bare and skinny, and his feet were thrust into two much-scuffed flaps of what might once have been goat skin, bound into place with strips of leather thong.

The visitor stepped forward slowly, advanced to within two paces of where Will stood, and stopped short, meeting him eye to eye. He did not acknowledge the presence of Tam and Mungo, both of whom, Will knew, were gazing at him wide eyed.

Will nodded to the old man. "A fine morning," he said in Scots, not knowing what to expect.

The apparition nodded in return, and then turned his head to look down to where their galley floated offshore at Will's back. When he spoke, it was in flawless French. "It is, a fine morning indeed. What brings the admiral of the Temple to Eilean Molaise?"

Will was stunned for a moment, taken aback as much by the purity of the liquidly fluent French coming from such a raddled hulk of a man as by the question he had asked, and all he could think to say was, "You are familiar with the Temple?"

The ancient's deep-sunk eyes, dark and strangely brilliant beneath their bushy, unkempt brows, swung back to him. "I was, upon a time … familiar enough to recognize the admiral's baucent. But that was long ago."

"And how … whence came your familiarity?"

The old man nodded and shrugged at the same time. "From involvement. I belonged once, until I perceived it for what it was."

"You … perceived it … the Temple … for what it was." Will could hear himself being banal and fought to recapture his self-possession. "And what, sir, did you perceive?"

"A whited sepulcher, rotting from within."

There was no rational response to such a statement, but Will took a deep breath, searching for words with which to continue this bizarre conversation. "You say you … belonged … In what capacity?"

"I was a knight. But as I said, that was long ago."

"A Temple knight? What is your name, sir?"

The aged features cracked in a smile, revealing toothless gums behind the riotous hair that masked much of the gaunt face beneath. "My brethren call me Gaspard."

"No, I meant, what was your name when you served the Temple?"

"That is of no import. It was a former life and I have abandoned it."

"You left the Temple … you mean you broke your vows? You are apostate? How then—?"

"I broke no vows. I merely walked away. I was sworn to poverty, chastity, and obedience and so I remain—in poverty, as befits a seeker of the Way, in chastity, which has never been threatened, and in obedience to my superior, the abbot of our small community here."

Sinclair frowned. "A seeker of the way. What way is that?"

The old man looked at him, quirking one eyebrow. "There is only one Way."

Will Sinclair shivered, unwilling to countenance the outrageous thought that had formed within his mind, but once it had occurred to him, he had no other choice than to pursue it, yea or nay, no matter how outlandish or incredible it might appear. He glanced towards Tam and Mungo, then jerked his head, indicating that they should move away. As they obeyed, looking mystified, he reached out his right hand to the old man, who took it in his own and met grip with countergrip, the strength sand confidence with which he did both surprising Will. This eldritch, tatterdemalion apparition was a member of the Brotherhood of Sion. Will kept hold of his hand and gazed at the old man, shaking his head and smiling in amazement.

"Well met, Brother," he said eventually. "I would never have believed I would find one of my brethren here, in such a place … I hope now that you were not referring to our brotherhood when you spoke of whited sepulchers."

"One of your *elder* brethren," the other answered wryly. "And no, I was not referring to our own, solely to the Temple, another creature altogether. An edifice, built to the glory of God, that has not merely forgotten its own roots but denies its God in its daily mercantile activities. The Temple was built by men, in unseemly haste and for purposes of gathering worldly wealth and power. Small wonder that its members have become as corrupt as their commerce … But you still have not told me what brings the Temple to Eilean Molaise."

"I will, but first you must tell me your name and what brought you to speak to us."

"How old are *you*, Brother, and what is *your* name?"

"I am William Sinclair of Roslin, and I am six and forty years old."

"Well, William Sinclair of Roslin, the man I once was died while you yet lacked the use of reason, and his name died with him. Even were I to tell you who that man was, it would mean nothing to you.

Suffice to say that I wandered for years thereafter, before I found this little island, more than thirty years ago. I have been here ever since, and here I shall die, someday." He tilted his head. "It was when I mentioned the Way that you began to think me what I was, was it not?"

"Aye, it was. But what led you to approach us? I have the feeling you speak to few folk nowadays."

The old man smiled again. "Curiosity. After all this time, I still cannot restrain it. Are you the admiral?"

"No, Brother, not I."

"But you have influence, I think. You are no simple knight. What brings you here?"

"Need," Will answered. "My companions, as you will have guessed, are not of our brotherhood, but they themselves have heard you say you were a Temple knight, so if you would like to break bread with us, we may talk of matters that contain no secrecy. Will you eat?"

The man called Gaspard tilted his head to one side again, in what Will took to be an unconscious gesture. "Aye, and gladly. Goat's milk and ground oats grows tedious after thirty years. I hope you have some meat?"

Will was tempted to ask how he would chew it with no teeth, but he turned instead and waved Tam and Mungo forward again, then introduced them. "Brother Gaspard here will share our noonday meal with us, for we have much to talk about, I think. What have we to eat?"

"No' much," Tam said. "Some bannock, dried venison, a bite o' cheese."

Will looked at the old man, who nodded eagerly, and Tam began unpacking the food from his leather satchel, while Mungo arranged some stones for them to sit upon while they ate.

In the event, the toothless old man had no trouble eating the dried venison, chewing it with gusto between hardened gums and making small noises from time to time with the pleasure of it, and while he did so, Will told him all about the events of the previous month in France. Gaspard showed no surprise, merely grunting and nodding in acknowledgment; it was the natural ending of a whited sepulcher, from his viewpoint, an inevitability that might have been postponed, but not for long. What then, he wanted to know, did Will and his friends seek to achieve in Scotland?

When Will told him he had been charged personally with the safety of the Order's Treasure, the old man's eyebrows rose in genuine surprise. He offered no comment, however, since he knew, but could not say so in front of the others, that the Treasure was the Treasure of their own Order, protected by, but never really belonging to, the Order of the Temple.

"So what will you do now?" he asked when they had finished eating. "Whom do you seek?"

Will sniffed. "We seek the King of Scots."

There was a long silence during which the old man stared at Will, then glanced slowly at each of the others before asking, "You seek the King of Scots on Eilean Molaise?"

Will laughed. "Well, no. Not here. We are hoping to find safe anchorage in Arran. From there, we will cross to the mainland to seek the King."

"You will leave your galley here? How then will you cross over?"

"We'll take this galley, but we have other ships with us. At present they are awaiting word from us, off the Mull of Kintyre at an island called Sanda."

"I see, and you now wish to know who, and with what force, might be on Arran?"

"That is correct. Can you help us? Have you been there recently?"

"To Arran? I was there two years ago."

"Two *years* ago?"

The old man spread his hands. "I have little need to travel."

"But surely you must go there for food and supplies?"

"Why surely? God supplies us with all the food and goods we require, right here. We have sheep, goats, and birds and their eggs, water aplenty for drinking, oats in our little field, and the sea is full of fish. What more could we need?"

There appeared to be no answer to that, and Will shrugged. "So you can tell us nothing?"

"I did not say that. I said I was there two years ago. There were English soldiers there, building a fortification not far up the coast from here. You see the other bay there, to the north?" All three of his listeners turned to look where the old man was pointing and saw the spur of land jutting out into the sea, concealing another, deeper bay behind it. "That is where they were, scurrying about like ants, building a motte and bailey. Mind you, the motte was there before they came—a flat-topped knoll of stone atop the cliff. But they were fortifying it, erecting palisades and digging a defensive bailey in the soft ground to the fore, above the beach. It would be a strong place, I thought, when they were done."

"How many were there? Are they still there?"

"There were a hundred men, perhaps more. I took no time to count them and I spoke to none of them. But they are not there now. A fleet of galleys attacked them and burned their ships a year and more ago. In the late summer or early autumn. We saw the galleys come at dawn, and then we heard the sounds of a great fight carried on the wind. We saw much smoke, and no English ships sailed out of the bay afterwards, so that made us think the smoke came from burning ships."

"How many galleys did you see?"

The old friar thought for a moment. "Seven went in. Five came out again afterwards."

"So there may still be two crewed galleys there? Who owned them, could you tell?"

"How would I tell such a thing? They meant nothing to us. But the fact that they were galleys, in this part of the world, means they would have come from the Isles, to the northwest. As to whether they are still there, I know nothing. They might have sailed away at any time, unknown to us. But two more craft—perhaps the same ones—sailed in about a week ago and have not come out since. We seldom look at such things, you understand, and we pay attention only if something takes place that we can see openly. Otherwise, we tend to our beasts and our prayers."

"Aye, of course." Will sat silent for a spell, then sighed. "Well, Brother, thank you for telling us. I suppose we will have to go and find out for ourselves if any remain."

"Aye … This King of Scots, who is he? King Alexander died long since, I know, and we heard once of a new King called Bailleul, something French-sounding, but that was some years ago, and he had already gone by then, I think. Or does he still reign?"

"King John Balliol. His name was French once, like my own and many others. No, he no longer reigns. He lives in exile in France, a prisoner of King Philip for all intents and purposes. He abdicated the throne when he could not dispute the dominance of England's embittered King, Edward, who died this year."

"Edward Plantagenet is dead? He was a great man."

Will raised an eyebrow. "Aye, so I have heard said of him, when he was young. Men named him among the foremost knights of Christendom. But as he grew older, he grew vicious, I am told, laying claim to Scotland as its liege lord. You will hear few Scots speak highly of him."

"Few common Scots, you mean, I think?"

"Do I? I believe I disagree with you there. What did you mean by that, Brother?"

The old man clawed at the thick hair on the back of his head. "What should I mean?" he said, scratching harder. "Edward's claim to Scotland was a just and dispassionate one in the eyes of many. He demanded allegiance from the Scots nobles, most of them of Norman descent and holding their lands and titles from the English Crown. Where is the vice in that? Their allegiance was to him, as King of England, and had been so since the first Norman landholdings were granted here. And until recently, before the death of King Alexander, it was freely paid. That is the way of the world, Brother William. The feudal code takes precedence over all, and the Scots nobles have been ever bound by it. If they fight against it now, it is for venal reasons of their own—a lust for power, the whitening on sepulchers."

Will cleared his throat. "I hope you will forgive my saying so, Brother Gaspard, but for a man who claims to have forsaken the profane world you are most well informed."

The elder let out a delighted cackle. "Blame that curiosity of mine again. It might be a sin of pride, but I seem unable to keep my mind from being inquisitive, and thus when I meet someone who can converse beyond a series of grunts, I listen and I learn." He cackled again. "And from time to time, I even speak, like now!"

Mungo, whose French was less fluent than the old man's but perfectly adequate to understanding, could sit quiet no longer. "That's a' very well," he growled in Scots, "what ye were sayin' about the English claims, but we had kings in this land while the English were still worshippin' emperors in Rome. That was then, and this is now. The Scots folk dinna want foreign Englishry in Scotland," he growled.

"Ah, the Scots folk ..." The old monk's face sobered and he turned to Mungo, including Tam in what he was to say with a lift of one bushy brow. "That is another matter altogether. The Scots people are like any other. If they do not own land, they have no voice—they are chattels, dependent upon the landholders for what little they may have. Faceless and lacking identity or cohesion, they are therefore weak and worthless for anything in the way of protest. And as long as they cannot unite, they remain constantly at risk from those to whom they are beholden." He drew himself erect and inhaled a great draft of air, and at that moment no man there saw him as old or impotent. "Unless and until they organize themselves, the common folk of any land will count as nothing in the affairs of kings and noblemen."

He paused to allow that to sink home, then went on. "There was a man called Wallace of whom we heard, even here on Eilean Molaise. He, and some others like him, organized the Scots people as never before and united them against their oppressors for the first time in memory. But he and his people saw their oppressors not only to be the English but the Scots nobility as well. And the Scots nobles regarded him as they would vermin, naming him brigand and outlaw."

"How do you know so much about Wallace?" Will asked.

"Three of his supporters sought refuge with us here, some six, perhaps seven years ago. That was when we heard that King Balliol was gone. They were being hunted by their own lords, as well as by the English. One of them, a knight called Menteith, who I suppose was a renegade against his own kind, was well spoken and possessed a keen mind. I spoke often with him during the month or so they remained with us, but I know not what became of him thereafter … nor of the man Wallace."

"Wallace is dead," Mungo growled. "Eight years ago. Sold for English favor. They took him to London and hanged him there, for the pleasure of the crowd—cut him down alive, then gutted him and burned his entrails while he watched. Then they cut off his head, arms, and legs."

Will was looking curiously at Mungo. "And how do *you* know so much of Wallace, master mariner?"

The sergeant shrugged. "We were in Leith a while ago, on business wi' the Temple in Edinburgh. We couldna go anywhere beyond the port, for the English armies were everywhere, but I heard folk talkin' about it in the taverns in the toun. It was the Bruce, they said—the young earl, no' the old man—who dubbed the Wallace knight, so that he could be Guardian of the Realm, but he did it to spite the Comyns, rather than to honor Wallace … At least, that's what folk were sayin'. It was the Bruces and the Comyns and the others like them, the noble families, as they ca' themsel's, who brought Scotland to where she fell and forced the Wallace to do what he did. Them and their bickerin' and girnin', changin' sides frae day to day—now for Edward, now against him, but for themsel's at a' times … Oh, aye, they're for themsel's without pause."

He spat, eloquently, and Will, spurred by a sudden thought, added, "It is the Bruce who rules in Scotland now, did you know that?" Seeing the flaring disbelief in the other man's eyes, he carried on. "No, it's true. The young Bruce, former Earl of Carrick. He seized the throne last year, in the name of the realm of Scotland. He is now King Robert, first of that name."

Mungo stared back at him, unimpressed, to judge by his lack of expression. "Oh aye?" he said, his tone turning the statement into a question. "That must have pleased the Comyns. And does he rule there *still*, d'ye ken?"

Will shook his head. "I know not. I cannot even say if he is still alive. That is what I have to find out."

Mungo folded up the clasp knife he had been using on his meat and slipped it into his tunic before wiping his hands on his leggings and moving to stand up. "So mote it be," he said. "Ye'll no find any o' that out if ye keep sittin' here. Are we awa'?"

The veteran monk was already rising effortlessly to his feet, and Will and Tam rose with him. "It would appear we are," Will said. "Can we land in the bay by tonight?"

"We can land there by the middle o' the afternoon, 'gin we start now."

Will thanked Gaspard for his information and hoped that they might meet again, and the old man smiled and nodded.

"May God be with you across the bay," he said. "I will be watching, but I can be of no help to you. But if you do find anyone over there, they will be Scots, and they may be able to tell you what you need to know about the King. Farewell, and walk in God's Way."

3

"Well, Admiral, what do you think? Did anyone see us?" Admiral Edward de Berenger grunted, glancing up at the billowing sail with its enormous black Templar cross. "If they did, it makes no difference—we'll be around the headland before they have a chance to warn anyone."

Taking advantage of the straining sail, the oarsmen in the waist of the ship were rowing at attack speed, driving the large galley over the waves at its top speed, a pace no other ship in their own fleet could match. They had swept along the entire length of the bay of Lamlash, where they had first thought to anchor, and were now bearing down on the point of land that stretched out ahead of them, separating them from their new objective. Will Sinclair took note of the speed with which the point was approaching and grunted, deep in his chest.

"As soon as we round the point you'll need to make some quick decisions, Edward. How big is the bay, and how deep? And if there are galleys there, as the old man said there might be, whether there be two or four, how far away from them should we remain, without leaving ourselves too far from land or vulnerable to attack. Thank God you are the mariner, for I would not even know where to begin any of that."

De Berenger's normally stern face cracked into a grin. "Put your mind at ease, then. I'll do nothing to endanger us. This is my ship, after all. I have no intention of risking it to chance. Now ..." He raised one arm high. "Get ready!" he shouted to his shipmaster, a stolid but dependable Norman called Boulanger.

The great galley hissed by within spitting distance of the rocks at the tip of the point, and as it did so de Berenger lowered his arm, the signal to Boulanger and his waiting crew to lower the sail. As the billows of heavy cloth were lowered and restrained by skilled seamen, the oarsmen maintained their driving rhythm, propelling them towards the closest point, where the entire bay would lie open to their sight. The basin was larger than Will had expected, cutting farther into the land than its neighbor, and from the color of the water, it was deeper, too, but it was less than half as wide as the Lamlash inlet and its shoreline shelved more steeply. Two galleys lay at anchor close inshore, sails furled and spars lashed down at an angle, no signs of anyone aboard them, and from perhaps one hundred feet above the water's edge, on a flat-topped but natural outcrop of stone, a fortification glowered down upon the entire anchorage from behind a palisaded wall of logs. The place was far from being enormous, but it looked formidable, and the incomplete earthworks in front of it, exposing newly scarred rock and even streaks of fresh clay, proclaimed its newness.

There were men everywhere: on the beach and its approaches, on the hillside among the earthworks, and on the walls or parapets of the fortress itself, and even as Will began to absorb the sight of them, he saw them, in turn, becoming aware of his ship. Where before had been industry and hard work there was now stillness as men straightened up and turned to look at the apparition in their quiet bay. And then, in the blinking of an eye, everything changed as a concerted roar went up and men scrambled everywhere in search of weapons.

Behind Will, de Berenger gave the order to ship oars, and the galley's momentum slackened immediately as the dripping sweeps rose in unison, leaving the vessel to drift to a halt. Another order brought the oars back down into the water, but this time with the intent of holding the ship in place, against the tug of the current.

De Berenger stepped to Will's side. "Well, my friend, they know we have arrived. What now?"

"We wait, Edward. We have made our announcement and caught them flat-footed, it appears. Now we must simply wait and see how they choose to respond to us. The response, in itself, will give us some estimate of the worth of whoever turns out to be in charge. How many men did you count?"

"At least a hundred but probably closer to two hundred ... They were too spread out for accuracy."

"That's much as I thought, close to two hundred. But there might be others inland, out of sight. So, we wait. I will be in my cabin. Call me when something begins to happen."

He barely had time to shrug out of his green woolen cloak before Tam knocked on his door and thrust his head inside. "Ye're wanted on deck, Will. There's somebody comin' out, a party o' three, wi' a white flag."

Back on deck, Will walked directly to join de Berenger and Boulanger the shipmaster, who were standing side by side, observing the events on the shore. The narrow strand was crowded with armed men watching a small boat fighting its way out towards their galley, six oarsmen pulling hard against the current. Three men stood in the stern of the boat, behind the rowers, one of them holding aloft what was probably a spear, with a white cloth attached.

"A parley," Will murmured to the admiral. "Well, that tells us at least that the leader here is no hotheaded fool, whatever else he might be ..."

They watched the boat approach in silence after that, crossing to the entry port in the side rail only when the small craft disappeared beneath their own side. The rowers shipped their oars, and the man at the prow snared the dangling rope, all eyes looking up to where Will stood with his companions. Finally, one of the three standing men, a red-bearded bantam of a man shrouded in the single, voluminous garment that the Gaels called a plaid, tilted his head back and called out in execrable French, "Is this a Temple galley?"

Will leaned forward over the rail. "It is. Who asks?"

"I am Alexander Menteith of Lochranza, Chieftain of Arran. I bring greetings and invite you to come ashore in peace."

Will hesitated for a mere moment, then called, "Greetings from whom, Master Menteith? You said you *bring* greetings, rather than offer them as your own, so on whose behalf do you speak?"

Menteith pointed backwards with his thumb. "I am sent by Sir James Douglas, King Robert's custodian in Arran," he shouted back.

Will fought down the urge to look at de Berenger beside him, for fear of betraying that the name meant nothing to him. He had heard of one Sir William Douglas, a noted knight with a reputation for gallantry and hotheadedness, but had never heard of a James Douglas. Perhaps his son? But William Douglas was not an old man, and therefore any son he had must be too young, surely, to be a King's officer.

Awaiting an answer, Menteith glanced at his companions before shouting again. "Will ye come?"

Will had no choice; this was what he had been hoping for. Surely the King's custodian would know where the King was to be found. He nodded. "We will. Tell Sir James we will follow you. How many men may we bring?"

The question clearly surprised the Scot. "As many as you like," he shouted back, then gave an order to the leadsman, who released the gaff and sat down at his oar again, using it to push the bow off strongly from the side of the galley until his fellow crewmen could lower their oars into the water again.

Will turned to Edward de Berenger. "Will you come with us?"

"If you want me to. Is it important?"

Will sniffed and wiped a bead of moisture from his nose with the back of his hand. "It might be … Could be. Tell me, do your sergeants have surcoats?"

"They do, but they are kept in storage at sea. In chests."

"Can you retrieve them easily? I want your oarsmen to look like Templars when they take us ashore, so have them uniformly dressed, if you will—black or brown, it makes no difference, so be it they are all the same." Without waiting for an answer he turned to where Tam Sinclair stood listening. "You too, Tam. Put on your surcoat and bring Mungo with you, in his. But first ask Captain Boulanger to prepare the admiral's boat for launching."

As Tam turned away to obey, Will spoke again to de Berenger. "Edward, it's mantles for us. Full regalia and all decorations—surcoats, belts, swords, and shields … but no mail, I think. We may be asked to lay aside our weapons, but I think I would rather not be pent up in chain mail all the time we are here. But comb your beard, for Heaven's sake. You are supposed to be a Temple knight, an admiral, not a seaborne hermit."

4

The silence was oppressive, broken only by the lapping of the waves against the shore and the distant crying of gulls. Gazing at the watchers thronging the beach in the final moments before his longboat grounded, Will realized that he could hear the water dripping from the upraised oars, and found himself wondering how so many men could be so utterly quiet for such a length of time. He took time, too, to admire how distinctive his crewmen appeared. Facing him where he stood in the stern with de Berenger, Tam Sinclair, and Mungo MacDowal, the twelve oarsmen looked appropriately impressive: veteran, tightly disciplined sergeants of the Temple, the scarlet crosses on their black surcoats glowing richly in the afternoon sun. Tam and Mungo wore the same black surcoats, borrowed from de Berenger's men purely for effect, but bearing badges of rank equivalent to their own. Both men wore helmets and were fully armed, the black, equal-armed cross pattée of the Order emblazoned on their white shields. Every eye on the crowded beach, however, was fastened upon himself and de Berenger, their thick, snowy mantles of felted wool proclaiming them as knights of the Order.

As the boat crunched into the gravel of the shore, the four lead oarsmen leapt nimbly over the sides, waited for the next incoming wave, then hauled the longboat bodily up and onto the shelving beach. The remaining oarsmen leaned sideways to permit Will and his party to walk forward and leap down to the pebbled beach dry shod. Will was in the lead, and as his feet struck the land, the crowd ahead of him parted, opening a lane to where the chieftain called Menteith stood waiting for them, flanked by three others, one of whom, tall and broad shouldered, wore the same kind of single garment as Menteith, wrapped about him from neck to knees.

The other two members of the group, a man and a boy, he decided, were much different, dressed in tunic and leggings, the elder of them wearing a shirt of much-used chain mail beneath a plain brown cloak that was thrown back over his shoulders to leave his arms free. He stood watching Will approach, his face inscrutable, idly flexing the fingers of his right hand, the palm of which rested on the end of a short, heavy battle-axe hanging from his waist. Will's eyes missed nothing, his mind racing as he sought to identify and rank the men before he reached them.

The plaid-wrapped man on Menteith's right towered over the Arran chieftain, his bulk emphasizing Menteith's slightness, and he was a picture of barbaric splendor, so that Will immediately suspected this might be the King's custodian, Douglas. His plaid was the color of fresh honey, and he wore it kilted like a tunic to just above the knees and then wrapped about his upper body to hang down his back from his left shoulder. It was held in place at the waist by a heavy belt of intricately fashioned silver links, and at the shoulder by a massive, ring-shaped brooch of hammered silver. He wore a loose cap of some kind on his head, arranged to one side, another silver ring brooch gleaming at the left temple and securing a large, decorative eagle feather, and his feet were encased in leather brogans, the straps wound crosswise about his long, bare legs. Beneath the tight, leather-bound brim of the cap, the eyes were bright and challenging, a pale, luminescent yellow-brown that was enhanced by the color of his clothing. The long hair that spilled down to his left shoulder from beneath the cap was golden red, as were his eyebrows and beard, the latter close-trimmed, and the entire face was defined by high, cleanly chiseled cheekbones. Clearly a leader and a man to be reckoned with, Will thought, and then eyed the last of the waiting quartet.

This was a man, too, he could see now, and not the boy he had taken him to be at first. He, too, was set apart by his dress and bearing, but even more so by his youth. He wore a plain but rich and costly quilted tunic of bright blue, cinched at the waist with a heavy leather belt from which dangled a plain, unadorned dirk. There was an emblem of some kind on his tunic, still too far away to be discerned, but clearly embroidered in white upon the left breast. His legs, solid and muscular, were encased in thick, knitted leggings of a paler blue than his tunic, and were wound about with black leather bindings that rose up from heavy, thick-soled boots. He wore no cloak, this one, and he stood comfortably on spread feet, brawny forearms exposed by the elbow-length sleeves of his tunic, his hands loosely clasped about the cross-guards of a large broadsword sheathed in a highly decorated scabbard.

Will and his party halted just short of the four and Will inclined his head courteously, the gesture one of equality containing no hint of subservience. "I bid you good day, gentlemen," he said, allowing his voice full resonance. "I am William Sinclair, Knight Commander of the Order of the Temple in France. My companion here is Sir Edward de Berenger, Admiral of the Temple Fleet."

Menteith nodded, graciously enough. "Welcome to Arran, so be it you come in peace." His French was so poor that his words were barely understandable, which made his next question almost inevitable. "Sinclair, you say? Do you speak Scots then?"

Will smiled. "I do. Sir Edward does not."

The young man in the blue tunic cut in before Menteith could say anything more. "Then we will speak in French, through common courtesy—those of us who can—lest we embarrass an honored guest. Sir Edward, you are welcome here in Scotland, as knight, if less so as admiral. May we ask what brings you here? Forgive me. I beg your pardon. Here is no place to be asking such questions. Will you come with us up to the fort? We can scarce call it a castle yet, since it is incomplete. But there, at least, we can be comfortable … and private. Not to mention warm. An ill wind is rising, and it looks as though we are about to be rained upon."

De Berenger glanced at Will, who nodded, and then both men looked up at the clouds; thick and angry looking, they were lower and more menacing than they had been earlier in the day. "Yes, sir, we will," the admiral said.

"And what of your men? Do you wish us to send them back to your galley? They can return later."

The admiral barely hesitated, then called to the lead sergeant on his boat, which was still drawn up on the strand less than fifteen paces behind them. When the man had run up the slope and snapped smartly to attention, de Berenger instructed him to return with his crew to the galley and await his further summons, and then he turned back to his hosts. "My thanks," he said, smiling easily. "The men will be far more comfortable aboard ship."

"They could have stayed here," the young man in the blue tunic said. "They would have been welcome to eat with our own men."

"True, sir, but they might have been uncomfortable … as might your own. My men do not speak your language."

The young man nodded. "True. That had not occurred to me." He paused, then gestured to his three companions. "Some names, gentlemen. Menteith, here, you know already. The other fellow there, the big, fierce one, speaks no French at all. He is Colin, son of Malcolm MacGregor of Glenorchy, chief of Clan Alpine, and he likes to claim that his race is royal, directly descended from Kenneth MacAlpin, first King of Alba." He was smiling as he spoke, and the MacGregor, having heard his own name mentioned, inclined his head, his face unreadable. "Beside me here is Sir Robert Boyd of Noddsdale, who accompanied me here on the King's business, and I am James Douglas, son of Sir William Douglas of Douglasdale. I am nominally the King's custodian in Arran, but for the past year I have been more than glad to leave the running of the place to Sir Alexander here, who is hereditary chieftain of the Menteiths of Arran." As he finished speaking, a gust of chill wind blustered around them, and he raised his eyes to the clouds overhead. "As I thought, and just when expected. Let's away from here, my friends. Others you will meet later. Come, if you will."

He turned and walked away without another word, swinging his sheathed sword up to rest over his right shoulder. They followed him, the four Templars flanked by the MacGregor and Menteith on one side and Sir Robert Boyd on the other, and the entire assembly, some two hundred men, tailing after them in an undisciplined herd, albeit a noisy, talkative herd now that it seemed the formalities were dealt with.

Will walked in silence, his eyes on the man ahead of him, surprised for the second time that day by finding perfect French spoken where he had least expected such a thing. James Douglas was young, indeed—Will guessed his age as barely twenty, if he was that old—but the young man's self-assurance was nothing short of astonishing, and nothing about him, other than his youth, suggested to Will that he might be unworthy of holding the post of King's custodian. Now, as he followed Douglas up the steep slope to the motte, watching the lithe, easy step so similar to his own at the same age, he found himself wondering where and how the young nobleman could have learned such flawless French, for there was nothing of the guttural Norman accent—the accent of most of the English and Scots descendants of the Conqueror—in his voice.

The motte was crowned by a large, rectangular building, the massive-walled ground floor built of heavy stones. Windowless and fireproof, it was intended purely for defense and storage, the only means of entrance being a heavy portcullis of wrist-thick wrought-iron latticework set into a tunnel-like doorway, more than two paces deep, that had been cut through the wall itself. The portcullis, Will knew, would be controlled from the winding room in the hall overhead. On each side of the portcullis entrance, heavy, serviceable wooden stairs led up to the great hall above, which appeared to have been built from alternating panels of stone and heavy logs, although the gable walls at either end were of solid stone, too, rising from the walls of the storage rooms beneath and chimneyed to hold flues. Moments later, climbing the sturdy wooden stairs and seeing the collection of men awaiting them beyond the hall's open doors, he realized that the formalities that he had assumed were over had barely begun.

5

Sir James Douglas's hospitality, albeit unplanned in the middle of the day, was unstinting if plain. Tuns of both wine and ale had been broached, supplied, Will suspected, from the stores of the former English garrison, and fresh bread and cheese were brought to the tables that lined one wall. The men refreshed themselves liberally, the sound of their voices increasing in volume as they drank. There was no hot food, for the supper hour was still far ahead, but the rituals that went hand in glove with the hospitality lasted for more than two hours and involved a constant procession of greeters, all of them curious and eager to meet the Temple knights. The seemingly endless parade of names and faces, most of them Highlanders and Islesmen wearing a bewildering array of brightly colored clothing, had a stultifying effect on Will, and he knew, without a word being said, that de Berenger felt exactly the same way. Tam Sinclair and Mungo MacDowal stood apart, their backs to the wall by the entrance door, and took no part in the activities.

Leaving de Berenger deep in conversation with a couple of French-speaking Scots who had engaged him, probably because they enjoyed the opportunity merely to speak the tongue, Will took advantage of a temporary lull to look around the room more carefully than he had before, scanning the gathering as a gathering rather than as a chain of unknown faces. Several men present among the throng had impressed him, a few of them favorably, and he watched two of those now from across the hall. One was a Highlander, the chief of Clan Campbell of Argyll, whose first name had escaped Will for the moment, and he was deep in conversation with one of Douglas's commanders, a tall, broad-shouldered fellow with a close-cropped beard who was evidently a cousin of the knight Boyd, since both men bore the same name. The Robert Boyd on the beach had been Boyd of Noddsdale, and the one talking to the Campbell was Boyd of Annandale, another Robert. Will had met him some time close to the start of all the greetings, and he had been struck by the fellow's eyes: the sheer brightness of them, a blazing, silvery gray, and the way they bored like augers into his own. They had not said much to each other on meeting, but Will had believed the man when Boyd said he would look forward to speaking with him later, when there would be more time and space.

"You are deep in thought, Sir William. Should I banish everyone?"

Will turned, startled, to see James Douglas standing by his side, and he felt himself flushing because he did not know how long the young knight had been standing there, watching him.

"Your pardon, Sir James, I was woolgathering ... It is a habit of which I ought to rid myself."

"Oh, I would not do that, if I were you." Douglas's smile was open and sincere. "The ability to lose yourself in thought among so many clacking tongues is an uncommon one ... valuable. I think were it my fortune to have such a gift, I should treasure it." He tilted his head to one side, his eyes narrowing as he tried to gauge Will's expression. "What is it? Come, walk with me as far as the door. The rain may have stopped by now and the fresh air will be cool and welcome."

As they picked their way through the crowd towards the doors, the Scots knight glanced sideways at the emblem that hung about Will's neck.

"That is a pretty bauble," the young man said. "And plainly it's a potent one, judging from the look and heft of it. What does it represent?"

Will fingered the piece, looking down his nose to where it dangled heavily on his breast. "It is my badge of rank within the Order, probably the best known but least seen symbol of the Temple. Some members may live full lives and die without ever setting eyes on one of these." He grasped the emblem between fingers and thumb, feeling its thick, solid, highly polished smoothness. "This is the emblem worn by serving members of the Governing Council of the Temple—the Inner Circle, as some call it. But in reality it serves no other purpose than to set its wearer visibly apart and mark him as the entitled representative and deputy of the Grand Master."

They had stopped, and Douglas was leaning forward, gazing at the medallion, and Will knew it was worth gazing at. It hung suspended from his neck by a thick chain of intricately carved, S-shaped links of solid silver, each one a thumb's length and thickness, carved to represent a thick cable of rope. The emblem itself, of thick, glossy enamel, was mounted on a heavy silver oblong lozenge that hung suspended from two of the lowest links and portrayed the cross pattée on a square field of white, surrounded by another field of brilliant red, the color of the Savior's blood worn for so long by the Temple knights. He waited patiently, allowing Douglas to gaze his fill, and the young knight reached out a hand as if to touch the emblem, but he stopped at the last moment and lowered his hand, dipping his head quickly to one side in a nod of admiration.

"Beautiful piece" was all he said.

"I have been marveling, Sir James—evidently too openly—at the way you speak. Your French is perfect—flawless—and I was wondering where you learned it."

Douglas laughed. "In France, of course. Can you think of any better place to learn it? I spent five years in Paris when I was a boy."

It was on the tip of Will's tongue to point out that the young knight was still little more than a boy, but he thought better of it and allowed Douglas to pull the doors open for him, waving aside the guards who stepped forward to attend him.

"We'll go down to the wall, there." He pointed and moved on, leading the way down the wide wooden stairs for a few paces before stopping halfway and looking about him. The rain had stopped long since, although a cold wind was still blowing fitfully from the northwest, but the few remaining clouds were scattered now, glowing pink and golden in the late-afternoon sun, and both men inhaled the clean, briny air.

The young knight continued where he had left off. "I came home three years ago, just before my eighteenth birthday."

"What sent you there, may I ask?"

"Not what, Sir William—*who*. Edward Plantagenet did. He liked to call himself *Malleus Scottorum*, the Hammer of the Scots. And he did not like the idea of my remaining alive after the death of my father." He glanced sidewise at Sinclair and his face twisted into a humorless grin. "Another Sir William, my father, and a rebel, dyed in the wool. Sir William Douglas was no man's puppet. He died in London's Tower, some say of grief at being caged. Others say he died demented. And there are others, well placed and of good character, who have told me Edward had him murdered. I may never know the truth of that. But the truth in force at the time led to my family sending me to France, for my education and safety, and there I spent five formative years in the household of William Lamberton, Archbishop of St. Andrews and Primate of Scotland. Do you know the Archbishop?"

Will shook his head. "I have heard his name spoken, but have never met the man."

Douglas set off again, down the steps to the courtyard of packed earth and across to the earthen parapet that backed the fronting palisades of recently hewn logs. There were others about, talking in twos and threes, but none of them paid the two newcomers any attention, and Douglas kept moving to where they could stand alone on the top of the defensive wall, their view over the bay uninterrupted. Will laid one hand on the sharpened top of one of the heavy log palisades, then turned from the sea to look about him.

"Where did the trees come from?"

"The English cut them and hauled them here from the uplands above the moor on the west side of the island. There's a forest there on the slopes—or there was, before they cut down all the biggest trees. They must have shipped the logs down around the south coast ..." He fell silent, crossing his arms on his chest, then looked at Will speculatively. "So tell me, Sir William, how does a Knight Commander gain superiority over the admiral of the Order?"

Will smiled. "It is all a matter of degree, Sir James. I am a member of the Governing Council of our Order, and was sent here by our Grand Master, Sir James de Molay himself."

"Which means you stand high in the Master's esteem, even if it says little else that I can understand." Douglas inclined his head, then asked, "Why are you here, Sir William, in King Robert's Scotland, accompanied by the admiral of the Temple fleet? You may speak plainly, for we are alone here and I command on Arran."

Will looked at the young man, pondering his next words, and Sir James Douglas seemed content to let him take his time. "I will tell you, bluntly," Will said eventually. "But before I do, I would appreciate your courtesy were you to answer several questions that you might think impertinent." The younger man cocked his head. "How come you to hold the command in Arran?"

"I hold command in all the southwest, at King Robert's pleasure. But as to Arran, I took it in January of this year—both the island and the title. We came to steal supplies, but the garrison of Englishry here was busy building the fort. We threw them out, then captured the ships that came to reprovision them and declared Arran ours, a part of the realm of Scotland. Merely reinforcing a point ... Arran has been a possession of the house of Bruce since King Alexander defeated Haakon and his Norwayans at Largs, forty years ago. The English may come back, but we'll be ready for them, and they'll be less confident than they were before. The King has made some notable advances here in the south these past few months, and elsewhere as well."

"So where do you keep your prisoners?"

"What prisoners? We have none."

"I—" Will caught himself. He chose his words carefully. "You sent them home? To England?"

"No. There were no prisoners." He saw the disbelief in Will's eyes and added, "We took none."

"You ... took none." Will could think of nothing more to say for several moments, but then he cleared his throat. "This may offend you, my lord Douglas, but it seems to me you are very young to be so ..."

"What, cynical?"

"I was about to say merciless."

"Ah. Merciless." The young man grinned again, the same humorless grin with which he had spoken of his father's rebelliousness. "How long have you been gone from Scotland, Sir William?"

"Many years, now, more than twenty."

"And in France throughout that time?"

"Most recently, yes. But I served throughout the world before that ... before we lost the Holy Land."

"And how closely informed have you been about matters in Scotland during that time?"

Will shrugged. "Barely at all. My duties and my concerns have been with the Temple throughout, in accordance with my vows. My sole source of information has been a younger sister. She writes to me sometimes. Those letters, I fear, contain my entire knowledge of the state of affairs in Scotland, their contents filtered through a woman's eyes."

"I see ... Well, sir, believe me when I tell you Scotland has seen savagery during those years the like of which was seldom seen in the

Holy Land, even at the sack of Jerusalem. Unforgivable savagery, right here in this small kingdom, meted out against helpless folk by a man once known as the foremost knight in Christendom. Edward of England taught me and mine all about mercy and its uses. And his barons and their armies refined my education. We Scots are small in numbers and at the mercy of the English when they choose to march against us, as they have these past ten years and more. And in the years to come, more than ever and despite the death of the Plantagenet, they will come for us again, in ever greater strength and with ever greater hatred.

"You think me merciless. Well, I admit I am now. For I have learnt, in a hard and bitter school, that showing mercy to these enemies gains nothing for us but contempt, and ultimately death. The Englishry, be they king, barons, or earls, have no regard for us as people, let alone as a race. To them we are vermin, and they treat us as such, burning, raping, hanging, and plundering, slaughtering our folk wholesale without regard to their own humanity or ours."

He held up a restraining hand, although Sinclair had made no attempt to interrupt. "I know what you are thinking, because I myself once thought the same way ... long ages ago, when I was eighteen. You believe I am defiling the knightly code. Well I, too, once thought that way—jousting and tilting in the lists, making grand gestures, living my life according to the code. But once I returned to Scotland, England and its minions quickly taught me the error of my ways. There is no knightly code in Scotland today, my friend—certainly not among the English in Scotland. Oh, they all pay it lip service, and it fuels the fires of their outrage against what they call our atrocities." He flung up his hand again, this time to interrupt himself. "Ach! There is no point in talking of such things. It only makes me angrier."

He fell silent for a space of heartbeats, his young face dark and scowling, then resumed. "Let me say but one thing more, and then I will leave off. I have released English prisoners before—men of good birth and fair repute—and I have seen those self-same men come back and vent their spleen on helpless innocents—women and children and old men too spent to fight. And I have known whole towns, like Berwick, razed to the ground and all their burghers and their people slain, scores of them burned alive, walled up within a church where they had sought sanctuary. And all of this for no crime other than jeering at the Plantagenet when he brought his armies to their walls. So, if it please you, speak no more to me of mercy and the lack of it."

He spun on his heel and glared at the small number of curious onlookers attracted by his raised voice, even though they understood not a word of what he had said. Abashed by his obvious anger, they scuttled away guiltily, and he turned back at length to Sinclair, who had barely moved. But Douglas had mastered himself by then, and the grin he offered this time was genuine, if rueful.

"I know what you are thinking, sir, and I acknowledge it. I am young." He spoke in Scots now, as though that language were more suited to a gentler mood. "Hotheaded, King Robert says. But I swear to you, Sir William, I am bent on learning better." He squared his shoulders suddenly, raising his head as though dismissing such intimacies. "Now, it strikes me we have business to conduct, you and I, and here I have been wasting your time. My question to you was, why have you come to Scotland, with an admiral at your command?"

Will turned away from the sea and leaned back against the palisades, crossing his arms over his chest, and he, too, spoke in Scots, keeping his voice low. "I come in search of your King, in hope of finding sanctuary."

Douglas's mouth fell open, and it was clear that nothing William Sinclair had said could have surprised and confounded him more. But before he could find words, the hall doors opened above them and noisy men came spilling out, among them the knight called Robert Boyd of Noddsdale. Facing them as he was, Will saw immediately that although the men around him were gone in drink, the Scots knight was sober, and his eyes found Douglas immediately.

"Sir James," he called. "A word with you."

Douglas beckoned him forward, and Boyd came down the stairs, nodding to Will as he arrived. He was concerned, he informed them, that instructions to the cooks should be issued now if, as he suspected,

Sir James was to entertain his guests that night. Douglas agreed, and issued crisp instructions to dismiss the crowd above, bidding them return that night to eat as usual, and then to offer his apologies to the admiral and explain that he and Sir William would return very soon now. In the meantime, he added, Boyd should also ask the admiral if he would care to invite his men ashore, to share in the food and festivities. He watched Boyd hurry away, then turned to face Will again. The knot of men who had left the hall with Boyd were now drifting down to where Will and Douglas stood, and they were followed by others, voices raised in good-natured argument. Douglas ignored them, confident that they would not interrupt him.

"Sanctuary. You seek sanctuary in Scotland. Amid a civil war. Are you mad? And from what would the Temple require sanctuary?"

"It is a long story, but quickly told, once we have rejoined Sir Edward and the crowd has broken up. Where may I find His Grace the King, do you know?"

Douglas shook his head, glancing at the crowd. "That I cannot tell you. The King finds little comfort in his own realm nowadays. There's a price on his head, and he has more enemies among the Scots, it seems, than among the English. He has been campaigning in the north, east, and west these past few months."

"Against the Comyns."

"Yes and no. Not yet against the Comyns, though their time is coming. And yet yes, against the Comyns and their ilk, John MacDougall of Lorn and the MacDowals of Galloway among them. The MacDowals are cowed for now, but not yet finished. Their land of Galloway is a smoking ruin, but they might yet rise again. Part of my task is to make sure they do not. His Grace spent much of his time in the past avoiding them while trying to raise an army with which to fight them, but he is ever sore pressed for funds and ye canna buy many good men with mere promises. But for much of the past autumn the MacDowal lands have paid the price of treachery."

Will made a quick decision. "Aye, well I might help him there, could I but find him."

Douglas was instantly alert. "What mean you, help him *there*? In Galloway?"

"No, with funds. I have a treasure for him, aboard one of my ships."

"*One* of your—?" But Douglas had already jumped forward in his mind to the meat of what he had heard. "What kind of treasure?"

"A substantial one, of the kind that will buy men and weapons. Six chests of gold, in bars and coin, and five of silver, likewise divided, brought to him by one of his most leal subjects, the Baroness St. Valéry, youngest sister to Sir Thomas Randolph."

"The King's nephew? That cannot be. Sir Thomas is in England, captured at Methven fight last year—" He shook his head. "But he has no younger sister old enough to be a baroness."

"No, sir, you are mistaken. Sir Thomas is my age, perhaps five years older. He was never nephew to Bruce and he has a brood of sisters."

"Ah! Two different men. That Sir Thomas is dead, I fear. His son is now Sir Thomas Randolph."

"His son? Then he cannot be much older than you."

A smile flickered at the corner of Douglas's mouth. "Younger, I believe. I have never met him, but I've heard tell he is a young man with the spirit of chivalry burning pure in him. You'll never find him refusing mercy to an enemy."

Will was unsure how to respond to that, so he ignored it, saying instead, "Sir Thomas the elder. He had a younger brother, Edward. Know you ought of him?"

Douglas looked at him with raised eyebrows. "Aye. He, too, is dead. Killed at Methven."

"Ah!" There was pain in the soft exhalation. "Then Peggy is alone … My sister. She was Sir Edward's wife."

"So, I am the bearer of bad news again then, even unwittingly …" It was clear from his saddened expression that he was thinking of a number of other times when he had delivered similar tidings to women awaiting word of their menfolk.

Will cleared his throat and changed the subject. "You speak of this Methven fight as though I should know of it. But I know nothing. What happened at Methven?"

Douglas's blue eyes met Will's eyes squarely, and it occurred to Will that here was a singularly honest young man, who could accept his own shortcomings and proceed with what he had to do in spite of them.

"You know nothing of Methven? Forgive me if I appear to disbelieve you, but it seems incredible to me that there could be a knight alive, let alone a Scots knight, who has never heard of the Methven fight. Plainly I was wrong … Well, we received a lesson in English honor, chivalry, and the knightly code there. Do you know the place?"

"No."

"It is close by the town of Perth, the first English-held stronghold King Robert challenged after his coronation. You'll have heard of Perth, I hope?" Will nodded, but the younger man was being facetious and had not waited for a response. "Aymer de Valence, Earl of Pembroke and commander-in-chief of the English in Scotland, was occupying the town and was caught unprepared for our arrival. He had been harrying the countryside in a punitive campaign and had merely stopped at Perth in passing and hence was in no great condition to withstand a siege. We arrived in front of the town on a Sunday afternoon to find it shut and fortified against us, and the King, in the spirit of the knightly code, rode forward alone and challenged de Valence to come out and fight. De Valence declined, since it was the Sabbath, but said he would meet us on the following day. His response was reasonable, and we withdrew as far as Methven, about five miles away, to set up camp for the night … And as we were settling down, our horses unsaddled and in picket lines, our army preparing for sleep, the English attacked in the dark—a full cavalry attack. It was a rout and the attack was dastardly, devoid of any trace of honorable conduct or the knightly code. We lost hundreds of good men, and King Robert, sorely wounded, barely escaped alive, carried out by a few others and myself."

"Where did you go, with the King wounded?"

"We ran into the forest. Once we were assured the King would live, we spent the next three weeks making our way north and east in secret, towards Inverness.

"Why Inverness? That is a long way from Perth."

"Aye, but it was also a long way from Aymer de Valence. But the King had made arrangements to meet his womenfolk there."

"His *women*folk?"

Douglas nodded. "Aye. The Queen was there, and the King's daughter Marjory, along with his sister Mary and Isobel, the Countess of Buchan, who crowned King Robert when her brother the Earl, whose duty it was, refused to do so. He is a Comyn, of course. The Countess herself is a MacDuff, of the ancient lineage who crowned the kings of Scotland since the days of Kenneth MacAlpine. Aye, we had a dozen women in our train after that day."

"That surprises me … that the King should take his women with his army, I mean."

Douglas looked at him wide eyed. "What else could he do? Where could he leave them in safety, when all the southern regions of his realm were either in English or in Comyn hands? The only place they might be truly safe was by his side."

Will nodded, beginning to have an inkling of what Douglas had been saying earlier about the conditions in the land. "I see. So what happened then?"

"Folly, treachery, and more dastardy. Less than two weeks after Inverness, we rode into a trap in the Valley of Glenfillan, near Glen Dochart in Macnab country at a place called Dal Righ. Alexander MacDougall of Argyll, good-brother to the Comyns, had sent a thousand men there from his own lands to gut us, with the blessing of Macnab, whose land it was. But we fought our way out, though it lost us four-fifths of our strength. Suffice it to say that we split what was left of our small party after that. The King and a dozen others of us took to the heather afoot. The Queen's party, much larger and stronger, took the horses and rode north and east to safety in Kildrummy, in the earldom of Mar, escorted by the King's brother, Sir Nigel Bruce. With them went David, the Bishop of Moray; John de Strathbogie, the Earl of Atholl; Sir Robert Boyd; and divers others."

"How long ago was this?"

"Last July. More than a year ago."

"And what has the King being doing since then?"

"He played the cateran among the Isles last winter, raising support from the Islesmen, living off the land and fighting to consolidate his kingdom. And all the while straining to stay unbowed while new burdens afflict him daily."

"Burdens such as what?"

Douglas looked away, clasping his hands about his upper arms, so that Will thought he was not going to answer, but no sooner had he thought that than the young nobleman spoke. "Oh, the loss of three of his four brothers, Nigel, Alec, and Thomas, all of them betrayed by Scots nobles and sent to Edward in England to be hanged, drawn, and quartered like brigands. And the capture of his wife, Queen Elizabeth, his daughter, Marjory, his sisters Mary and Christina, Countess of Mar, and the Countess of Buchan. All of them taken and sent to England likewise, this time by John Comyn, the Earl of Ross. The Queen, we have been told, is being held prisoner somewhere in the north of England. The Princess Marjory, at thirteen, is forbidden to be spoken to by anyone and is hung in an open cage from the outer wall of London's Tower. The Lady Mary Bruce, the King's sister, hung in a similar cage from the walls of Roxburgh Castle. The Lady Christina of Mar, his other sister, locked up in a nunnery. And Isobel, Countess of Buchan, hangs in an another cage from the walls of Berwick."

"Good God! And this was Edward's doing? But surely, now that he is dead—"

"Nothing has changed. Nor will it. Edward of Caernarvon is not the man his father was, but he hates just as hard. He left this land last August, with nigh on two hundred thousand men in his train. We thought for a while he would march north in search of us, for that would have been the end of everything, but thanks be to God his coronation had been scheduled for September in London. He had dallied too long without striking at us and marched away leaving us with the knowledge of the size of the force he had fielded. Two hundred thousand men, against our three thousand. They came and they left, but they'll be back one of these days, though we have had word from England, from a trusted source, that he has problems enough with his own barons to keep his mind away from us for a spell.

"And that gave King Robert opportunity to turn to cleaning his own realm of turncoats and traitors. He took the MacDowals first, in Galloway, and gave them a taste of what treason entails. And then he turned to the MacDougalls in Argyll, and wrung a truce from them, from their chief's son, Lame John MacDougall of Lorn. The father, old Alexander, can no longer march or fight, so Lame John rules there in all but name now. But the King made a truce. No more hostilities between now and June of next year. I fear he should have finished it then and there, but he was loath to risk losing too many men in formal battle. We are not yet strong enough for that. But then he headed north and east, marching along the Great Glen, and took the castle at Inverness—the first such victory he has won since taking up the crown. All the other castles in the realm remain in English hands."

Sinclair struggled to encompass the enormity of what he had been told, trying to imagine the effect such a progression of family catastrophes must have had on the man Bruce. How had he managed to survive such things without losing his ability to function as a man, let alone a king? He shook his head, trying to clear it, and Douglas spoke again, quietly, as if he had read Will's thoughts.

"His family's losses hit him hard, but they strengthened him too. A lesser man would have been beaten to his knees. I know I would. But not King Robert … Even so, I sometimes wonder how he restrains himself from hunting down his enemies, one by one, and killing each one privily, in person. But he will not do so. He sees himself as Monarch first, responsible for his people, and only after that, his duty done, as family man, responsible for kinsmen and friends.

"And yet, within these past few months, we have seen signs that the tide is turning. Not sufficiently, not yet. But there is hope, increasing all the time. We have won a few tulzies, and folk are coming to our cause more and more all the time—not the great nobles, but the common folk—and we have more strength now than we have had since Methven. But King Robert will not hear of set battles, not when he can field fewer than three thousand men against English and Comyn hosts of tens of thousands … But that will change, once he carries the fight to the Comyns."

"Then how come you to be here, in Arran, Sir James? I would have thought your place is with the King."

"No, my place is here, holding the southwest and maintaining it against the King's return. I have it safe for now, but every castle in the land is still manned by English garrisons. Above us, to the north and east, the MacDougalls and the MacDowals still swarm like maggots in Lorn and Galloway, nursing their hatred. We are safely based here on Arran, for the time being, but that could change with the next sail that comes over the horizon … Speaking of which," he added, taking a new tack, "you said *ships* when you spoke of your treasure—*one* of your ships. I see but one, so plainly you have others." Will pursed his lips and nodded, and Douglas's eyes came close to squinting. "How many, and where are they?"

"They are nearby, awaiting word from me. I told you I came seeking sanctuary, but I knew not how I might be received or what, if anything, I might find here. I left my ships behind, in a safe anchorage, whence they might come or go without hindrance whatever we found."

Douglas was nibbling on his upper lip now, deep in thought as the noise and horseplay nearby swelled in volume. But then he straightened and drew a deep breath. "Come you with me, if you will. There are others who should hear what you have to say … and many others who should not. So mind you, guard your tongue henceforth until I give the nod. Will you agree to that?"

Will Sinclair smiled widely, unable to resist his inexplicable liking for this dark-skinned young man with the brilliant and expressive blue eyes. "Happily," he said, and then followed Douglas back across the wide forecourt and up the flight of sturdy wooden steps to the castle hall.

6

The vast room was almost empty now and, pausing just inside the threshold, Will was surprised to see that it was not as he had first perceived it. In the crush of people who had filled it earlier, he had taken it to be a single great space, its high roof supported by pillars and huge beams, but now he saw that there were doors at each end, leading to two more full-width chambers, and that wide stairways against the wall facing the main entry doors led up to partitioned spaces above both. The platform on his left held several rooms, each curtained off and served by a common passage-way along the gallery they formed. The one on the right, presumably similar in layout, was fronted by a wooden wall, affording privacy to whoever lived there, and he supposed that it would be occupied by the commander.

The place was new, and crudely but strongly built, its wooden beams still showing the fresh cuts of axe and adze, but already he saw signs that carpenters had been at work, smoothing and finishing the main surfaces, particularly the wall that fronted the upper space reserved for the commander. A fire blazed in a great, open stone fireplace against the rear wall, too, between the two flights of steps, and by just looking at it and smelling the gently drifting haze of smoke from it he could tell that it was freshly lit. Along the walls to his immediate right and left, a small army of men was starting to prepare tables and benches for the coming feast, manhandling them from where they had been piled on end in the far corners and carrying them out into the middle of the floor, laying them out in rows from there.

All of this he absorbed in moments, along with the awareness that the place now seemed to be full of large dogs—lean, rangy, spike-coated hounds that he remembered from his boyhood but had seldom seen in France. Three knots of men, the largest of them a quartet, were talking quietly in various parts of the main room, each far enough away from the others to remain unheard. De Berenger was there, too, standing about ten paces ahead of Will in the middle of the floor and turning to look at him. He had been talking to one of the Scots knights Will had met earlier, although the man's name was long since beyond recall, and as Will focused on the stranger he felt Douglas place a hand on his elbow.

"Come, I see your admiral has met Bishop Moray. I will leave you with them for a while, with your permission, for I have things to do before we can continue."

He started to move forward, but Will restrained him with a touch on his arm and a question. "Bishop Moray. Is he the same one who rode north with the Queen and her ladies?"

"The same."

"And is he one of those you trust, or no?"

Douglas grinned, a flash of brightness in the gloom. "David is one to trust, believe me."

He led Will forward then to join the other two, introducing him again to the Bishop, who looked less like a bishop than any other Will had ever seen or known. David de Moray, Bishop of Moray, was not a tall man, but he was enormously broad and deep across shoulders and chest, and he was self-evidently a practicing member of the Church Militant, armored from head to foot. The open skirts of his calf-length coat of rusting but still pliable chain mail clearly showed three bright scars where they had recently been struck by hard-swung weapons. Beneath the coat he wore leggings of the same mail, and on his feet, sturdy, well-worn boots with thick, many-layered soles. His head was covered by a close-fitting hood of felted wool, the bindings at its chin undone, and the mailed cap that would cover it dangled between his shoulders. A long, plain-hilted dirk hung from a sheath at his waist, and a broad belt slung across his chest from his right shoulder supported a heavy broadsword in a scuffed scabbard.

"I am glad you're here, David," Douglas said, speaking in French again and nodding to the admiral as he did so. "Sir William has been asking me about the state of King Robert's realm today. But I thought it better he should speak with you, to hear the Church's reasoned view of things, rather than my bloody-handed version of what is going on and who deserves to die." He turned to Will. "David has been one of our King's staunchest supporters since the beginning. He can tell you all you need to know—things I could not tell you. He is less priest than fighter, as the dints in his mail will attest, but priest he is, nonetheless, with views more sober and long-headed than mine, so I will leave you with him." He pointed at one particularly bright slash of silver on the Bishop's rusted skirts. "You were lucky with that one, David. That could have taken your leg off."

"It almost did," Moray drawled, smiling. "But God was watching at the time, even if I was not."

"Of course He was. I'll leave you to it, then, and be back as soon as I can be."

Moray turned to Will. "Well, sir, what think you of our young Jamie?"

Will watched the younger man bound up the stairs leading to the upper floor two steps at a time. "A remarkable young man ... and *very* young, it seems, to hold the trust he evidently holds."

The Bishop laughed. "Granted, he's young indeed, but Jamie is a Paladin. For all his youth, he's one of our best commanders, and if he lives, he will become *the* best. The lad learns quickly and he never makes the same mistake twice. But he has grown from boy to man in desperately short time, and it shows on him to those of us who know him. He is also become one of the King's closest and most trusted friends and advisers, despite his having been unknown to any of us until last year. King Robert knighted him in person upon meeting him, the day before his coronation at Scone." His hand fell naturally to toy with the dirk at his waist. "So, you have questions. Ask away, then, and I will answer them as well as I may."

"Thank you, my lord Bishop. I scarce know where to begin."

"Begin by calling me David, then, and go forward from there. As Jamie said, I am become more fighter than bishop these past two years, and outside the chancel, away from my cope and miter, I find I prefer my name to my title ... Mind you, it took me months before I could convince Jamie Douglas to call me by name. What do you need to know most?"

"About the King and his status. He is excommunicate, I heard."

"Hmm. In the eyes of some, he is. But there is more of politics than of theology in that belief. Within the Church in Scotland, there are those, thank God, who can see things from another viewpoint, and prime among those are our Primate, Archbishop Lamberton, and Bishop Wishart of Glasgow, who is second in seniority and influence after the Archbishop. These two, in good conscience and for the good of the realm of Scotland, believe sincerely that the Holy Father has been misinformed about what came to pass between the two guardians that day in the chapel at Dumfries. They believe that His understanding of the situation has been warped and twisted by advisers desirous of promoting their own visions. Pope Clement passed his judgment *in absentia*, far removed from Scotland and its troubles, and it is the devout hope of the Archbishop that the Holy Father may be convinced of this someday soon and lift his interdiction. In the meantime, the Primate has refused, still in good conscience, to prosecute the excommunication ... and that, in turn, permits the King to govern the realm in its time of sorest need."

Will frowned. "Think you, then, that Archbishop Lamberton might know where the King is to be found?"

"No. On that I can be definite. The Archbishop is in England, a prisoner of the English, as is Wishart of Glasgow. Once again, betrayed and sold by fellow Scots. We are told they are well enough treated, as befits their station, but they are held fast nonetheless."

"I see. And what of the other bishops of the realm? Is all the Church in Scotland united behind the Archbishop?"

Moray snorted in disgust. "No. As I said, there's more politics here than theology. The bishops who support the Comyn faction stand against the King, united in treason. They hope still to see him overthrown and their own candidate anointed in his place."

Will nodded, accepting the Bishop's explanation. "I have already told Sir James Douglas this, but no one else. I am a member of the Governing Council of our Order, appointed to my current task by our Grand Master, Sir Jacques de Molay, and I am entrusted with a large sum of gold and silver, although not from the Temple's treasury, intended for King Robert's use. Did you know Sir Thomas Randolph, the former Sir Thomas?"

"Tom? I knew him well. Why?"

"Knew you then his youngest sister, the Lady Jessica?"

"Aye, but not well at all. I met her but once, long since. She was wed to a Frenchman … a baron, I believe."

"The Baron Etienne de St. Valéry. He is dead, too, but he amassed a sum of wealth ere he died, and through a long chain of circumstances it was entrusted to our keeping in the Temple. His widow, the Baroness, is here aboard one of my ships, at anchor off the isle of Sanda, on Kintyre coast, and she wishes to donate this treasure to the King of Scots. And if ever we can find him, we will deliver it."

The Bishop scratched his beard. "How large is it?"

"Large enough to buy an army. Six chests of gold and five of silver."

"That is a great treasure …" Moray's eyes narrowed shrewdly. "Depending, of course, upon the size of the chests. Yet I find myself wondering whether it be large enough to warrant accompaniment by a Knight Commander and the admiral of the Temple fleet?"

Will had trusted Douglas instinctively, and now he decided to trust this bishop, too. "You have not heard all of it—nor yet one-tenth of any part of it. We barely managed to bring the treasure out of France ahead of King Philip's grasping fingers. And the reason we were able to do so was that we were warned in advance."

"You were warned that the King of France was coming for the Baroness's gold?"

"No. The Baroness's gold was already in La Rochelle. Our saving it was mere good fortune. We had received warning that the King's chief lawyer and first minister, William de Nogaret, planned to attack and interdict the Temple in France on the morning of October thirteenth."

The silence that followed seemed long, and Moray's face was a picture as he grappled with what he had heard. Finally he shook his head. "Tell me that again. What exactly did you say?"

"At dawn on the morning of Friday, October thirteenth, mere weeks ago, the French army, acting under the instructions of William de Nogaret, the chief lawyer of France, moved concertedly against every commandery and every Temple installation in the country. All the occupants—knights, sergeants, brethren, and lay brethren—were arrested and imprisoned. All of them, at one swoop."

The Bishop's mouth was hanging open. "That is ... that is inconceivable. But how then come you here?"

"I have said—we were warned. Our Master, Sir Jacques de Molay, had word of it more than a month before. He scarce believed what he was told, but he took steps to safeguard the fleet against such treachery, should it be true. At the last moment, in the increasing belief that it *might* be true, he sent me to La Rochelle, to warn the garrison and make preparations to secure the fleet and take it safely offshore the night before the threatened raid."

"And it came to pass?"

"We stand here as witnesses. From all we understand, the Temple in France no longer exists."

"That defies belief. The Temple no longer *exists*?"

"Not in France, at least not for the time being. That is what we believe. We did not linger long enough to verify the extent of the attack, but we saw what we saw in La Rochelle, and that was the Order's operational headquarters in France.

"We have been through all the explanations we can think of— that it might have been a misunderstanding of some kind, that it might be no more than a gambit by the King to frighten the Order into making funds available to him, that whatever the root cause, negotiations will follow and all will be resolved ..."

"But you believe none of it."

Will's headshake was barely noticeable. "No. I do not. I believe King Philip did what he did deliberately, with malice aforethought, and with the precise intention of seizing the Order's wealth for himself. And I do not believe he will relent. In truth, he cannot. He owed the Temple too much money and he was bankrupt. With the Temple gone he will be solvent again, debt-free and with money to do whatever he desires. The Temple in France is finished." He glanced at de Berenger, whose face was unreadable. "Forgive my bluntness, Edward, but the truth of that has just come home to me."

De Berenger nodded. "No forgiveness required, my friend. I agree with you. But that leaves the question, what do we do now?"

Moray was still thinking about what Will had last said, his face wrinkled in perplexity. "Such blatant aggression would require papal sanction, at least, if not outright support."

"Aye, it would," Will agreed. "And as you said, Pope Clement is not the strongest of the strong. He is a vacillator, notoriously weak and open to manipulation, and in France, under Philip the pope-maker, he is but potter's clay in the King's hands."

Moray drew in his breath with a hiss, straightening up to his full height, but before he could say anything more Sir Robert Boyd of Noddsdale, whom Will had seen descending the stairs mere moments earlier, appeared at de Berenger's shoulder.

"My lord Bishop," he said to Moray. "Sir James requires your presence. You are to come with me and bring these two gentlemen with you."

Moray looked from de Berenger to Will. "Were I not a bishop I might be inclined to wager that the two of you are going to have to sing for your supper."

OF LOYALTY AND FRIENDS

1

S ix men waited in the room behind the wooden wall that
screened the upper platform from the hall beneath. The room
was well lit with candles and high ceilinged, its right wall,
wood paneled, rising to the height of a tall man, then assuming the
steep slope of the roof. In the corner to one side of the door a pile of
discarded armaments stood propped against the wall; shields and
swords, axes and dirks. A stone fireplace was built into the gable
wall, and a pair of small, high-set windows on either side of the
chimney face allowed the fading evening light to shine in from
outside.

Most of the room's length was taken up by a long, narrow table,
bare except for three candles in sconces, and the occupants were
sitting around it in a variety of poses, all of them looking at the
newcomers as they filed in. Douglas sat at the far end, facing the
door, and on each side of him Will recognized the Campbell chief—
Sir Neil Campbell of Lochawe, he remembered now—and the other
Sir Robert Boyd, of Annandale. The young MacGregor chieftain
from Glenorchy sat beside Boyd, and across from him sat a stern-
looking man Will remembered as being called de Hay. An empty
chair sat beside de Hay, and next to it, at about the middle of the
table, lounged another, even grimmer-looking fellow whom Will
gauged to be in his late twenties, younger than all of them except
Douglas and MacGregor. He was thin faced, black bearded and
glowering. Will had no recollection of meeting him before. The
sixth man at the table was Menteith of Arran, who appeared even
smaller than before among so many large companions.

As David Moray stopped by the foot of the table, Will and de Berenger moved to stand beside him, while Boyd of Noddsdale took his own seat. Douglas greeted the two white-mantled knights with a wide smile that showed his strong white teeth.

"Welcome, gentlemen," he began, and then spoke to de Berenger in French. "You will pardon, I hope, what may seem to be an ill-mannered summons, Admiral, but in talking with Sir William I decided that others here, as noblemen of Scotland, should hear what he has to say, particularly on this matter of the gold you bring for our King's coffers. Good tidings indeed, on the face of it, but creating a need for a certain … circumspection. Sit, if it please you, and, Sir William, I trust you will not mind repeating your tale. All present here enjoy the King's trust."

Will started towards the nearest seat, but Bishop Moray restrained him with a light hand on his arm.

"Before we begin, Sir James, I think you should know there is more to Sir William's visit than you have heard." Will sensed an immediate heightening of interest among those at the table.

"How so?" Douglas leaned forward slightly as he spoke, and Moray looked at Will.

"Would you like to speak, or shall I try to explain it?"

Will felt a deep calmness unfold inside him, and smiled easily. "As you wish, my lord Bishop. But if you tell it, I will know, at least, how closely you listened."

Moray nodded, the hint of a smile flickering at one corner of his mouth, then looked at de Berenger, serious again. "You will forgive me, Admiral, if I speak now in Scots, for there are several here who have no knowledge of your tongue. You are already familiar with everything I will talk about, but Sir William will translate anything new you need to hear."

Moray turned back to face the others. "Sir William tells me there are grave matters unfolding beyond our realm—matters of import that could ill affect us here. Let me be clear, for we have little time to waste here in idle talk. What I have to say next will set you all agog, clackin' with curiosity, but I must ask you simply to accept what I have to say. It is all true, but here and now is not the place to debate it." He looked at each of the men seated around the table, and then concisely described the King's move against the Temple a mere two weeks before. "It is the opinion of both of these knights who stand before you—Sir William of the Governing Council and Sir Edward, the admiral of the Temple fleet—that they are the sole members of the French Temple not held in custody by the French King and his people."

Despite the Bishop's warning, a buzz of comment broke out around the table, and he fell silent to allow it to subside. When he spoke again, his words brought instant silence. "None of us here could have imagined such a thing, the Temple bein' what it is, but no man present should suppose, even for an instant, that this does not concern us, that's it's none o' our affair. It is, and it concerns us deeply, and on mair than a few levels, the first o' those being that these men come here in search o' sanctuary—temporary, right enough, but nae less real for that. What they don't know, and couldna know, is that ..." He hesitated. "King Robert is engaged at this time with the King of France, seeking an alliance against England. This request o' theirs could set all that at naught."

Again Moray stopped, to let that sink in, aware that Will was whispering behind him, translating to de Berenger.

"And forbye," he continued, "King Philip wouldna have dared do what he has done without the approval o' the Pope, for the Temple, nae matter what ye may think of it in your own mind, is a religious Order. I'm sure I needna remind anybody here that there's only one Pope— the same one Archbishop Lamberton is trying to persuade to lift the excommunication against King Robert. So there are two stringy mouthfuls o' gristle for us to chew, and that's just the start o' it."

The black-bearded man at the middle of the table grunted. "Send them home, then," he drawled. "Back whence they came. We have enough to occupy us now, with what we have in hand, without seeking further troubles."

"Oh aye? And take the treasure off them first, is that what you mean? Just relieve them o' the gold they bring in our time o' need and then wave them farewell?" The Bishop's voice was cold, filled with dislike of the man to whom he spoke, and the two glared at each other until Sir Robert Boyd of Annandale sat forward, raising a hand.

"A word, if I may." He scratched slowly at his close-trimmed beard. "Our black-bearded friend is but newly arrived, from Rathlin island, so he knows but little of who you are. He bears an unfortunate English name, too—Edward—and the burden makes him unmannerly at times. But he is chief captain of his clan and brother to the chief himself. Sir William, were you aware of any of these things—the things the Bishop mentioned—before you came here?"

Will shook his head. "This is the first I have heard of any treaty with King Philip. It surprises me in a way, knowing the kind of man Philip is, but I can see how the need for it might arise. As for the writ of excommunication, I was aware of it." He shrugged his shoulders. "But I admit I had not seen the connection between King Robert's case and our own." He hesitated. "Not quite true—I had seen it, but thought the connection to be a common ground, one which might lead your King to grant our wish. It had not occurred to me that there would be plans in place to acquire a dispensation, or that we might cause embarrassment to King Robert because of it."

Boyd pursed his lips and sniffed. "Sir James was saying you have been long away from Scotland. Tell us, then, what, if anything, do you know about our King, Robert Bruce?"

Again Will was prompted to smile, even knowing as acutely as he did that he was on trial here. He bent his head slightly sideways, the smile widening. "I think it might be easier and less troublesome were you to ask me to reveal the inner secrets of the Temple, Sir Robert." No one smiled in return, and he continued. "In truth I know little of your King, and most of what I have learned before today came from two single sources, both of them women. My life and my duties, these past decades, have been dedicated to the Temple, bound thereto by oath, by duty, and by loyalty. I was born in Roslin and spent my boyhood there, and when I left Scotland as a lad, there was no strife between this realm and England. I have lived in ignorance of all that has transpired here since then, but I feel no guilt over that, for I renounced the world when I entered the Order, and the Temple owes allegiance to no temporal lord or monarch other than the Pope.

"My sister Margaret wed Sir Edward Randolph, long after I left home, and she was the prime source of my knowledge of the troubles here in Scotland, and of the travails of King Robert when he was yet the young Earl of Carrick. In her letters, she spoke very highly of the man, and of the esteem and love her husband held for him and his cause. And since she was always a levelheaded lass, I accepted her judgment. The second woman of whom I spoke is Lady Jessica Randolph, the Baroness St. Valéry. I do not know that lady well at all, but her determination to deliver her dead husband's wealth into the hands of Robert Bruce, together with her belief in the man's righteousness and his destiny as King of Scots, was a persuasive argument that fitted well with my sister's opinion. And so I am here."

"Hmm. What else do you know of him—the man, if not the king?"

"Little enough. I have never set eyes on him. But from what Sir James has told me in a very brief time, I have formed ... opinions of my own. He must be a man of extraordinary fortitude and honor to generate such reverence among his friends."

"Aye, that may be. But what of his enemies? Have you not heard it said that the King's numbered friends are few, less than it would take to fill up both sides of a table?"

Sir James Douglas broke in, smiling. "Or that his enemies abound like fleas on a moudiewort, leaping over and across each other to infest him?"

Will stood staring from one man to the other, perplexed, aware that all eyes around the table were fixed on him and that he was suddenly unsure of what was happening here. Not knowing what to say next, he gave in to his instincts and shrugged. "I have no doubt that must be what folk say, if, as you say, you have heard it said ... But I think you need no reminding that folk are great tellers of lies. Being recently arrived, I have heard nothing of the kind myself—nothing, that is, from 'they' who hold so many opinions. For myself,

I would choose to believe things differently. If your King has, as they say, so few friends, then you would do him honor to add the word *remaining*, for he strikes me as a man who holds friends close. But even more, above that, he seems to me to be a man—and perhaps even a king—who brings out the best in those who love him. Therefore either his friends die willingly, in support of his cause, or they are easy to identify and find ... and kill thereafter. He may indeed have but few friends remaining, but I am sure he never forgets those friends whom he has lost. That must grieve the man day and night, from what I have heard of him, and in enduring it, tholing it all and moving on, he must be like a blade tempered in fire and blood, and withal a king worthy of the name." Again he was aware of the silence as he concluded. "That is my opinion of your King, gentlemen, no matter if he or you send me on my way or not. It is a judgment newly formed, but it is in my heart, and should I ever come face-to-face with him, I will believe myself honored to do so."

Looking back on it, Will would see that it had been an astonishing statement, one that he had not known he was going to make until the words were spilling from his mouth, evoked by a deep and formless, unsuspected anger that had left him trembling with tension by the time he finished. He could sense, without looking, that even de Berenger, who could barely have understood a word of what he said, was staring at him in surprise. It must have been something in his tone, he thought.

He sucked in a deep breath and held it, looking straight ahead and waiting for a reaction from the motionless group around the table, three of whom had not spoken a word since he and his companions entered the room, but when one came he could scarcely believe what he was seeing. It was a tiny glimmer of light, trembling almost unseen at the edge of his vision, and when he sought the source of it, it sprang sharply into focus: a single teardrop, reflecting the glow of one of the candles on the table, had welled up in the eye of the stern-faced knight called de Hay. The man sat rigid but unapologetic, making no attempt to wipe the drop away before it spilled over and ran down his cheek into his beard. Only then did he blink and glance at Will, both eyes awash, before looking over at Sir Robert Boyd of Noddsdale, then turning his head further, to look at the other Boyd, of Annandale, who was already watching him.

The expression on Annandale's face was hard to define, but there was no hint of pity or derision in it as he gazed at the mail-clad veteran, tears now running openly down both cheeks. He held de Hay's eyes a moment longer, then looked down the table to where the Temple knights stood waiting.

"Well, Sir William, your sentiments have won the approval of Sir Gilbert." The noise his chair made as he pushed it back and stood up was loud in the quiet room, and from somewhere down below a loud crash echoed it as someone dropped what sounded like a heavy table. "So be it—no more subterfuge. I am Robert Bruce, King of Scots, and I regret the mummery. Suffice to say, alas, it was not uncalled for. My presence here is not for common knowledge and few, even downstairs, know who I am."

Will Sinclair stood stunned, his senses swimming at the unexpected revelation, but the King seemed unaware of it and was still speaking.

"Jamie told me I could trust you. He has a keen nose for such things. But I had to judge for myself. It may be the single greatest curse of this life I live nowadays, but I always have to judge for myself." He stood even straighter, drawing himself erect and seeming to collect his thoughts. "But that is neither here nor there. The die is cast and we have work to do—atop the work we gathered here to do." He turned to de Berenger, then waved a hand in invitation and spoke in serviceable Norman French. "My lord Admiral, you are welcome here. Take off your mantle, if you will, and sit with us. We have much to discuss, though I fear the brunt of it will be done in Scots. Sir William will serve as translator to both of us when the need arises."

As the two knights began to divest themselves of their heavy capes, he spoke to Will. "Your ships, Sir William—where are they now and in what strength?"

Will stopped, his mantle halfway off. "They are Sir Edward's ships, Majesty—the galleys at least—not mine."

The Bruce looked him straight in the eye, one eyebrow slightly raised. "Yours or his, it matters not. They are the Temple's ships, and they are in my waters. And save the *Majesty* for England's King, should ever you be misfortunate enough to meet him. Here in Scotland we speak of the King's grace, not majesty."

"Of course. Forgive me, my lord King, I had forgotten."

Bruce nodded. "Off with that coat, then, and sit ye down." He groped for the back of his own chair, waving Douglas back into his seat at the table's head as the young man made to stand up, and as the two knights and Bishop Moray settled themselves at the table, he pointed with his thumb towards the black-bearded scowler at the center of the table. "This is my brother, Edward Bruce, Earl of Carrick. The others I believe you know, but just in case, here is Sir Neil Campbell of Lochawe, chief of Clan Campbell, and here Colin, son of Malcolm MacGregor of Glenorchy. The man you made weep is Sir Gilbert de Hay, my standard-bearer, and Sir Robert Boyd of Noddsdale has been with me since Dumfries, lending me his support, as well as his name in time of need. And now, about your ships ..."

Will cleared his throat and rephrased the comment in French for the admiral's benefit before continuing in Scots. "We have a mixed fleet, Your Grace, made up of the ships that were in La Rochelle on the day of the ... the strike, plus three that joined us from Marseille. In all, we have a score of vessels, ten of them galleys, the others cargo ships."

Across from the King, Sir Neil Campbell whistled softly, and Bruce leaned back in his chair. "Those would be Temple galleys, I'm thinking—naval ships. How big?"

"They are all different, Your Grace. The three largest, the admiral's included, are of twenty oars a side—two-man sweeps, arranged in the ancient fashion of double banks."

"Biremes."

"Aye, my lord, biremes—all save one, built in Araby and captured by the man who captains it today. It has eighteen sweeps to a side, in two single ranks. All told, we have four ships of thirty-two oars, three of forty, and three of thirty-six."

"Impressive. How many men in all?"

"In total, perhaps five hundred men. We have not made a formal tally."

Bruce looked impressed. "A strong force," he said quietly.

"Aye, Sire, but a naval force."

"What mean you by that?"

"Nothing, save that they are mariners, not men-at-arms. But we have more. We brought the entire garrison from La Rochelle, snatched from beneath the nose of de Nogaret."

"You mean the French King's henchman?"

"Aye, a good word."

"You dislike the man, I jalouse."

"Sire, the measure of my dislike of him could scarce be comprehended."

"How many men there, then?"

"One hundred and fifty-four, of whom thirty and six are serving lay brothers. Of knights and sergeants, therefore, one hundred and eighteen."

The monarch's eyes, silver-gray and piercing, narrowed perceptibly. "And you were hoping to gain my permission to lodge these many men within my realm?"

"More than that, Your Grace. I also have a complement of Temple knights and sergeants, under the command of my own brother, Sir Kenneth Sinclair. Twenty full knights and four score regular sergeants."

Sir Edward Bruce stirred in his chair, but everyone else sat motionless while the King pursed his lips and nodded slowly. "And the cargo vessels?"

"Ten of them, all trading vessels. Seven of them carry my brother's men and horses, with all of their gear and supplies. Two more carry the garrison from La Rochelle and their equipment. The last of them contains general supplies."

"Horses, you say? You bring horses in your train?"

"We do. We scarce could leave them all behind to benefit King Philip and de Nogaret."

"And so you brought them here with you. In ships. Where do you hope to keep them?"

Will shrugged his shoulders, dipping his head at the same time. "I confess, my lord, I had not thought of that. I simply knew I had no wish to leave them stranded in France, and I presumed you might advise me on where to keep them. Some of them, the knights' mounts, are destriers, bred to the fight. The rest are common stock, sturdy and versatile."

The King leaned an elbow on his wrist, plucking at his lower lip. "We are going to have to talk, you and I, Sir William, about loyalties and *quid pro quo*. In the meantime, though, there is a problem that must be resolved without delay. Jamie tells me you left your ships off Sanda, close to Kintyre's Mull. That is MacDonald country, and should they espy your ships, they would come running, which would serve no useful purpose to me. I will need you to fetch your fleet, as quick as you may, and bring them to Arran. They may shelter in the wide bay to the south of us, the bay of Lamlash. Will you do that?"

"Aye, at once. But might they not be more easily seen coming here than they would remaining there?"

"They might, but if they sail at night they should be fine. Off Kintyre, they might be open to attack by MacDonald, but here in Arran they will be safe. Who will you send?"

"Sir Edward, of course." Will turned to the admiral and repeated the entire conversation between himself and the King, and de Berenger immediately stood and reached for his mantle.

"I'll go at once," he said, "under oars. It is a four-hour journey—"

"Wait!" said Bruce, holding up his hand. "No need for such haste. Not now. Your crew has been invited ashore, Sir Edward. Let them eat first, rest for an hour, then put them to work. What difference between leaving at nightfall and leaving at midnight? The journey will still be in darkness, and it will pass more quickly on a full stomach than on a cramped and empty one. Bide ye, then, until midnight. In the meantime, we'll go down and eat. But bear in mind my name is simple Rob this night, plain Robert Boyd of Annandale. When we ha'e supped, then we, too, will return to work."

2

For Will Sinclair the banquet—it seemed more elaborate to him than a normal daily meal must be—passed by in a blur of raised voices—there were no women present—roasted meats including venison and mutton, a vague awareness of free-flowing drink, and the strident music of the Scots Highlands and Isles, harps and bagpipes and the seemingly interminable sagas of a string of bards and singers, all of them mouthing unintelligible Erse, or the Gaelic, as they called it. Will sat with Douglas and de Berenger at what was nominally the head table, but few there paid attention to it, its other occupants scattering to sit with their own friends as soon as the main meal was eaten, leaving the high dais to the three French speakers. Will's mind was still reeling with the unspoken implications of the Bruce's presence, and he found it inconceivable that the monarch could sit out there among his own followers and not be recognized. He said as much to Douglas, and the young man smiled.

"It must seem strange to you, I'll grant you, coming from France where all is civilized. But the truth is simple. Every man in Scotland knows the Bruce by name and by repute. But when they think of him they see the former Earl of Carrick in their minds, and the Earl was much the … what's the word? the prodigal, in his youth. Aye, that's it. He was known for it, his prodigality—the newest, brightest fashions in clothes and armor, the finest horses, the loveliest ladies, and of course, the smiling, sparkling wit. He spent money lavishly. Although his father, the Lord of Annandale, never gave him much to spend, he was Edward Plantagenet's favorite when the Earl was yet a youngster. Most thought him a wastrel and a waste of time, seeing nothing in him beyond his youth, his wantonness and seeming irresponsibility. Mind you, that was before my time, for I was but a child when the Earl of Carrick was at his brilliant best, or worst … But that was the portrait he presented, before King Edward taught him to hate the leash."

"Hate the leash?"

"Aye, the ties that bound him to the Plantagenet's will. When Edward's plans to annex Scotland to his realm failed to work out to his satisfaction, he sought to make the Earl of Carrick his whipping boy."

"How so?"

"By requiring him to perform acts and deeds that seemed to mark him as Edward's lackey—and therefore England's. He made life barely tolerable for the Earl."

"What manner of acts and deeds? Though you were a boy at the time, you must have heard examples of such things."

"Heard of such things? I witnessed one of them: the Earl of Carrick's first rebellion. My father, as I told you, was a rebel, one of the more contentious souls with whom Edward had to contend. He was involved in an uprising and outlawed by Edward, ten years ago. I was twelve at the time. Edward sent English troops to burn our castle and take my mother and me captive, but my mother barred the gates against them and refused to surrender. The Earl of Carrick was there, as part of the English force, but purely for the sake of appearances. He held the highest rank there but had no authority and was accorded no respect—a mere figurehead, a Scottish lordling dispatched to give the English raiding force a semblance of legitimacy. The English commander, whose name has long escaped me, brought up some children, one of them a friend of mine, and threatened to hang them then and there, in front of my mother's eyes, believing her to be too weak to withstand such horror."

Will had to prompt him. "And was she?"

Douglas chuckled. "We never did find out. The Earl of Carrick defied the English commander and drove him and his men away. Then he released the three children and begged my mother's pardon. And thereafter he led us to my father in the north and joined in the rebellion, declaring himself a Scot and vowing to stand or fall with his own people. That was the first solid step along the course that led the Bruce to Scone and the Scots Crown." He smiled. "It also marked the first step of my pursuit of knighthood, for the man that I saw that day became my ideal of honor and of chivalry. I wanted to be like Robert Bruce, the Earl of Carrick."

He paused, and then held up his hands. "Which brings me around, full-circle. That is the man—the armored knight, the fighting King—whose portrait people still envision when they think of Robert Bruce. The man you see sitting over there among them now, unrecognized, is the man he has become—a Highland cateran, hardened to living like an Erse clansman on the open heath in all kinds of weather, sleeping in caves wrapped in a wet and dirty plaid and often afraid to make a fire lest the smoke betray him, snaring hares or guddling fish to eat, begging bread from cottagers and paying for it when he can, and sleeping with a dirk in his hand each night. No armor, no spurs, no sword, no knightly robes. And there's another thing that comes between him and being recognized ... the beard. King Robert Bruce goes everywhere clean shaven. Everyone knows that. But for the past year, he has not had the time or opportunity to shave. Thus, when he decided to come back down here to Arran, he trimmed his beard but kept it. The King of Scots now lives among his Scots as no other ever has, and when he speaks with them, they do not know him."

"Hmm." Will Sinclair shook his head. "Strange how events occur ... Edward of England had no plans to annex Scotland when I was a lad. What happened?"

"Who knows? Things changed. Some people think it was the success of his campaign in Wales that did it. He defeated Llewellyn, subjugated the Welsh, and even made his son Prince of Wales to mark his conquest. Ten years it took him to defeat the Welsh, but he increased his kingdom hugely. Thereafter, some men think, he turned his mind to Scotland, seeking to unite the entire island of Britain under his Crown ... but he underestimated the temper of the Scots."

De Berenger spoke for the first time since the discussion had begun. "But all the Scots nobles are Norman French, are they not? They all owed him fealty and, from what Sir William has told me, they tendered it. Was that not enough? What need had he of conquering them?"

"No, not so, Admiral. Not all Scots nobles are Norman French. The great earldoms of Scotland descend from the Celtic kingdoms, the Erse-speaking clans who lived here ere the Normans came. And besides, how long must a family live in a land before they can belong to it? The Bruce family has been here since the days of William the Conqueror. Sir William's own family were once St. Clair, but they have been Sinclairs for many a year now. I would suggest that when your great-grandsires and dames were born and bred in Scotland, then you yourself might think yourself a Scot."

There was disturbance in the body of the hall, and Will looked over to see tables being drawn aside. Then two men stepped out from the ruck, eyeing each other inimically and stripping off their clothing, preparing to fight. Bets were being laid and sides taken, and amid all the pushing and shoving, Robert Bruce was grinning, his teeth gleaming through the short beard that masked his face.

"Look at the King," de Berenger murmured. "He is loving every moment of this."

"Aye, of course he is. His tastes have changed this past year."

"You told me the King was campaigning in the northeast."

"And I did not lie. His presence here will be brief, but necessary."

"Why *is* he here?" Will asked.

"To discuss strategy." Douglas grinned. "On what, you will have to wait to find out. But I have the feeling that you are going to become involved in it … to some extent. I heard King Robert mention *quid pro quo*, but it is not for me to guess at what he meant by it. You will just have to wait until he raises the matter."

De Berenger stood up. "Talking of raising matters, I ought to go and check that my men are behaving themselves. I gave word that there was to be no drink served to them beyond one cup of wine with their meal. Now I should see to it that all is well and make sure they are ready to go back aboard, if we are to sail with the night tide. Pardon me."

Will held up a hand. "Before you go, Edward—something else has just occurred to me. When you bring back the fleet, you will take them into Lamlash Bay." De Berenger nodded. "I will still be here, there is no road between here and Lamlash. So when you reach Lamlash, I want you to leave the fleet at anchor there, with strict instructions that no one is to go ashore without my personal order. You will then come directly here to pick me up. I will be waiting for you. Is that clear?"

"Completely, Sir William. It shall be as you say. Pardon me again, gentlemen." He bowed from the waist to Douglas, including Will in the salute with a wave of one hand.

"He is a good man, but how can he expect to do that?" Douglas asked as the admiral marched away towards his men. "I wouldna dare leave my men within smellin' distance o' a drink if I had work for them to do. What kind of power does he hold over them?"

"The power of God, my friend. Don't forget that they are monks of the Temple, every one. They fight like demons, but they live like anchorites and pray like priests."

He followed de Berenger with his eyes as he spoke, watching him head directly to the table where the four knights who were his ship's officers sat with the six senior sergeants who actually ran the galley's crew. The differences between knights and sergeants were clear, even could one disregard the white surcoats of the knights and the black of the others. The knights, to a man, wore the forked beards that marked them as Temple knights, an affectation that sometimes amused Will but more frequently annoyed him as typifying, it seemed to him, the elitist arrogance within their ranks that so offended outsiders. The sergeants were more sober in their demeanor, although their uniform close-clipped beards were equally a mark of belonging to the Temple.

The wrestling match was still going on in the middle of the room. One man had already been thrown off his feet, and a shifting circle of onlookers milled about them, variously shouting oaths and encouragement. The Bruce had vanished, no sign of him to be seen, although he might simply have been hidden by the press of bodies.

Looking at the array of clothing in the room, Will supposed that he might have seen a more riotous confusion of colors in France at some time, but he doubted it. Most of the men present were Highland Gaels, wrapped in plaids, their hair and beards unshorn, many of them even plaited into strips, and they were tricked out with barbaric jewelry and decorations ranging from eagle feathers to brightly woven sashes of startling hues.

Will did not know what it was that captured his attention, but once aware of the man, he observed the fellow keenly. The man was too busy watching others to think of being noted himself. He was unremarkable, apart from being one of the few among the common throng who was not dressed as a Gael. Will could not see what he had on below the waist, but the man wore a plain thick tunic beneath a worn leather vest, and his head was bare, showing a balding scalp and stringy, nape-length brown hair. He had a beard and mustache, but both appeared sparse, as though his facial growth was light enough to deny or defy masculinity. But he was very interested in de Berenger and what the admiral was saying to his men … so interested that he was bending sideways from his chair to hear, while ludicrously attempting not to seem so.

Will nudged Douglas to distract his attention from the brawl. "Don't be obvious about it, but take a look over there, where de Berenger is talking to his men. See you the fellow craning to overhear them? Bare headed, balding, in the leather jerkin. Do you know him?"

Douglas's eyes slitted in concentration. "No, I don't, but he is one of ours. From the mainland, I mean—a Lowlander, by his clothes. He must have come with Rob Boyd or one of the others. What about him?"

"I don't know, except something about him set my teeth on edge … the way he's bent on hearing everything that's being said over there. De Berenger is probably telling his men what he expects of them when they pull out later tonight, and it's plain he has seen no reason to be secretive … but that made me think of what our friend from Annandale was saying, about how spies, traitors, and informers are everywhere in this land. If someone were to slip away from here with information on what is happening on Arran, he might earn a fine supply of English silver."

"Aye. Like Judas. I will ask about this fellow. And in the meantime, I will watch him like a hawk. They're speaking French, are they not?"

"What else? They're all Frenchmen."

"Aye … so how then does a ragged Borders moss-trooper gain the skills to understand what they are saying? Dougald!"

A huge man stood up from the table in front of the dais and lowered his head to what Douglas had to say. After a whispered monologue, he turned casually, glanced at the man Douglas had described, and nodded before sauntering away.

Douglas turned back to Will. "You have a good eye, Sir William. By this time tomorrow morning we will know everything there is to know about our long-eared friend. Dougald's lads will count the number of his breaths between now and then." His eyes focused beyond Will's shoulder. "I think we are about to be summoned."

3

Only Will had been summoned, and he left Douglas at the dais and followed the man who had been sent to fetch him. They made their way up the wooden stairs to the gallery, threading their way between two burly characters who sat indolently on the stairs themselves, one above the other, and pulled their knees aside to let them pass.

King Robert was waiting for him in the chamber they had met in earlier, sitting alone by the table, close to the replenished fire in the iron grate and staring into the flames as he scratched the head of a big, gray-haired wolfhound. He pushed the dog's head away with a muttered command as Will entered, and it lay down at his feet. When the King stood and turned to face him, Will was immediately struck by the air of exhaustion that emanated from the man, but then the monarch drew himself erect, casting weariness aside like a discarded cloak, so that even the etched lines in his face seemed to recede and fill out.

The King addressed the other man. "See to it that we are undisturbed. No one to come up here except David Moray, and him not for at least the next half hour." He waited until the doors had closed before he next addressed Will. "De Moray's a doughty fighter, but his head is even longer and sharper than his sword, so we'll be glad of his advice."

The King hauled his heavy chair to one side of the fire. "Throw your coat on the table and sit with me, Sir William. Pull a chair up to the fire. It gets cold these nights, with the wind off the water, and I find myself being grateful to the English for their need to build sound flues to hold big fires. Were it left to my Scots, we would be squatting now in the open air, wishing for firewood. There is some wine on the sideboard. Help yourself and sit down, sit down. Is the admiral away?"

"Preparing to leave, Sire. I left him chivvying his men. He will be at sea within the hour, or close to it." Will eschewed the offer of wine and did as bidden, tossing his folded mantle onto the tabletop and dragging a heavy chair close to the fire.

"Good, that pleases me," the King said. "I like that man. Now, before anything else, tell me about this treasure that you bring to me. Jamie was agog with it, but wouldn't tell me of amounts, probably for fear of listening ears. He's aey canny that way. You say it has been sent by Lady Jessica Randolph?"

"Aye, Sire, the Baroness St. Valéry. But it was not sent. It was brought."

"What? She is in Scotland?"

"She is, aboard one of our galleys. We did not expect to find you on Arran, you understand. I merely came in search of a safe anchorage and, I hoped, a tolerant reception. Once we knew what we were doing, I would have headed to the mainland in search of you, and the Baroness would have come with me, making her way homeward from wherever we landed."

"Then it was fortunate that I was here, for you would have found scant welcome in Scotland. Every castle left standing, save Inverness, and every single harbor is in English hands, though by the will of God, this money you have brought may make it possible to change such things. How much is there?"

"Eleven heavy chests of specie, Sire, six of gold and five of silver, each in bars and coin."

"Glory be!"

"It should meet your needs, for a while at least."

"And it could not have come at a better time. I have broadswords to buy, forbye fighting men to wield them. But we will talk more of this later. In the meantime, we have other matters to discuss." He broke off and stared into the fire for some moments before continuing. "Davie Moray was right when he said that your presence here brings me problems, but I have been neck deep in problems since the day I took the Crown, and they are seldom insoluble—albeit time is the one thing I never have enough of.

"If I remember rightly, you have somewhere in the range of a thousand men with you—galley crews, mariners, the garrison from La Rochelle, and your brother's men. A round thousand, give or take, am I correct?" Will nodded, and the Bruce did, too. "Aye. Tell me, then, if I were to suspend all my concerns and give you leave to stay and shelter here in Arran, what would you do next?" Perhaps to give Will time to think, he bent forward to throw a fresh log on the fire, then pressed it into place with one foot before sitting back in his chair. "I ask that for a reason, for the first thing I learned commanding men in war was that as easy it as it may be to raise an army, the task of feeding them for any length of time will break your heart and wear you out. Have you thought of that? For let me tell you, you could hide your men from all the world on Arran, but there is precious little here to eat. There are trees and stones to build huts and shelters, and sedge for thatching them, and peat to burn in their hearths, but there is little land suitable for farming, and less in the way of creature comforts. How would you feed your people, were you free to bide here?"

Will had been thinking of little else since leaving La Rochelle, and he nodded in acknowledgment of the other man's point. "I've thought much on that, Your Grace, and I believe I have the means to deal with it, using my ships." He saw Bruce's eyebrows twitch, and he half smiled. "Not the galleys. I am not intending to go raiding. I mean the trading ships. We have ten of them, and I would send them off to ply their trade, purchasing foodstuff and basic living supplies—tools, not weapons. We have enough weapons for our needs. But once we have unloaded our horses and few kine, we will be able to buy more and ship them here … cows, sheep, swine, goats, and the like."

"Where would you buy them, and with what?"

"Wherever they are to be found. In Ireland at first, I think, but then in England and even in France. My trading ships are able to come and go wherever cargo may be available. They bear no insignia, nothing to mark them as belonging to the Temple, but they are crewed by Templar mariners for all that. And to pay for them, we would use gold. It is a potent aid to commerce, I have found."

"Aye, and it's scarce. Whence would it come, this gold?"

Will grinned, sensing the monarch's fear for his own funds. "From the Temple, the funds I have in trust in my own holds. When we left La Rochelle we took all that it held belonging to our Order, and, as you doubtless know, every commandery has its own vaults, wherein is kept the specie required by our trading system, which, if I may digress, reminds me of my duties here. Can you tell me who is now the Master of the Temple in Scotland?"

The King of Scots hitched himself around in his seat to look directly at Will, scanning the Templar's face with steady eyes. "The Master of the Temple here died soon after I was crowned. He was old, and he was not replaced. You'll find a commandery in Edinburgh, if you go looking for it, but it lies empty." He gazed down at his hands, aware that what he was saying would not be welcome news to his listener. "There is no Temple now in Scotland. It could not maintain neutrality in a civil war." He looked at Will directly, almost defiantly. "There are Temple knights here, certainly, but they are Scots first nowadays, of the old houses, and they stand with me as Scots. The others are all in England, recalled by the Temple there."

He saw Will's frown and grimaced in return. "Politics, Sir William … The need to politick is ever stronger than the need to pray, it seems, and men of God can always find a way to shape God's needs to reflect theirs. The Temple knights in Scotland were mainly French and Normans, their primary duties owed to the

London Temple and to the Order in France. They saw less trouble in placating Edward Plantagenet than in defying or offending him ... Longshanks was ever easy to offend. And thus the Temple quit Scotland. Does that cause difficulties for you?"

Will released pent-up breath in a loud hiss. "No, Your Grace," he said. "It is a disappointment, but no more than that, and your explanation makes sense. You have the right of it on the matter of prayers and politics. It's just that ..."

"Just that what?"

"Loyalties, Sire, and the way they shift ... It leaves me wondering if there is any sense, any logic or reason, to life itself once we step out of our own small concerns. Here am I at this moment, for example, calling you Sire and coming within a breath thereby of breaking my own oath as a Temple knight, for I swore to pay obedience and fealty to no one but our Order's Master."

"And the Pope ... not so? Do not forget the Pope."

Will's mind returned unbidden to the conversation he had had mere weeks earlier with the former admiral St. Valéry, about the duality of their role as members of both Orders, the Temple and the Brotherhood of Sion, and how, at bottom, they lived a lie in even appearing to be loyal to the papacy. "Aye," he agreed reluctantly, "and to the Pope ... although but to a lesser degree. Our own Master comes first in our loyalties."

"And your Master is now in prison, betrayed by that same Pope— by the man in Saint Peter's chair, if not by the office itself." The King fell silent for a moment, then resumed. "Well, we can ease your mind on part of that, at least the Sire thing. Call me Robert when we are alone. I'll call you Will, for I heard your kinsman Sinclair call you by that name. When others are around, add you the 'Sir,' for I am plain Sir Robert Boyd of Annandale here on Arran. Tell me now, though, and speak plain as your conscience will allow: what do you plan to do with your galleys while you are here as guest of the King of Scots?"

Will grinned. "*Quid pro quo*?"

Bruce spread his hands. "What would you? It will come up soon or late, but soon would be my guess."

"No doubt, and you are right. Here is what has been in my mind since we set out from France. From what I have gleaned from Douglas, listening as much to what was left unsaid, you have been seeking aid from the clans of the West, the Highlands, and the Isles, so far with some success, but not as much as you would wish. I gather, too, that many of the chiefs with whom you have been dealing think of themselves as kings of their own little realms. Am I correct?"

"Aye, you are." Bruce sniffed and crossed his legs, turning away from the fire that was now blazing fiercely. "Angus Og MacDonald is the most active local chief here in the southwest. His territory is mainly Kintyre but stretches north, and he has a base in Islay nowadays. He likes to call himself Lord of the Isles, and he is working hard— and to this point successfully—to become the acknowledged head of a federation of neighboring clans, the MacNeills, MacCruaries, and McNaughtons prominent among them." He grinned. "He has been known to call himself King of the Isles, too, and although the rank far outstrips his true status, that is, in effect, how he sees himself at this time. He calls me King Bruce, an equal with no claim upon his loyalty other than that which he chooses to grant, or that which I buy in the form of mercenaries … galloglasses, they call them in these parts."

"You count this man among your enemies?"

"No, I do not. But neither do I number him among my friends, although he has helped me much in the past. It was thanks to him last year, and to Campbell of Lochawe, that I was able to withdraw into the Isles when I was hunted like an animal. And he covered my seaward flank when I marched northwest recently, into Argyll, to argue cases with Lame John MacDougall of Lorn—an expedition that worked out little to the MacDonald's liking, since it ended in a truce instead of the bloodbath he was seeking. He is … different, Angus Og, from all the others. Ambitious; but he stands by his word, as befits a self-styled king, and he has been—and continues to be—of great use to me, knowing that I may be of equal or even greater use to him."

"He holds the power in the Isles, then?"

"No, but he wants to. The power is held at this time by Alexander MacDougall of Argyll, with whom we have the truce of which I spoke. The MacDougall is old now, and he holds no love for me or mine. His son, though, Lame John MacDougall of Lorn, wields the power nowadays in truth, albeit not in name. They are kinsmen by marriage to the Comyns. John Comyn the Red, the man I killed in Dumfries, was good-brother to Lame John. Angus Og hates the pair of them beyond reason, and since he knows I am still determined to destroy them, he is prepared to help me."

"Why do you wish to destroy them, may I ask?"

Bruce rubbed his palms together hard, grinding them one against the other. "For the same reason I destroyed the MacDowals of Galloway. Because they have left me no choice. Their enmity I could overcome without rancor—that is a king's task. But Lame John's treachery has cost the lives of hundreds of good men, including several loyal friends whom I held close as brothers. He is an evil man, a creature beyond redemption. The Galloway MacDowals were similar, if less evil. Their treachery cost me two brothers, Thomas and Alexander, taken in war and sent to England to a felon's death, merely for being my brothers. MacDougall worked on the betrayal with the MacDowals, knew what their end would be before they were sent off. It was done with intent. That I cannot, will not, forgive. A blood debt, you may call it. I care not what men may think or say of me afterwards, but the MacDougalls' days of power in Scotland are at an end. We have a truce with them today, with no term set upon it—convenient to us both. But when it ends, Lame John of Lorn will have to pay his debts, and those he owes to me and to this realm will see the end of him."

"Why did you even offer truce? Douglas says you had a strong force with you, and MacDonald threatening MacDougall from the sea. Why not press home then, with your advantage?"

"I did. I pressed it home to the point of gaining a truce I needed badly. Lorn had more than a thousand broadswords at his back, with another thousand waiting to be called. I had six hundred men. So instead of fighting, I took my army up the Great Glen to Inverness, gathering men to me all the way. I took the castle there, then headed northwest again, into Comyn territory, harried the place and wrung another welcome truce, this one for nine months, from Ross, the Earl, who ranks among my greatest enemies. He, too, has much to answer for, and come June, he will rue the day he chose to abduct and sell the Queen of Scots …" He fell silent then, his gaze unfocused, but quickly shook the thoughts off the way a dog might rid itself of water.

"Forbye, the Argyll fight would have been a set battle and I'll have none o' those. Scotland will not be won by set battles, not after a decade of being culled and stripped of its best men by England and by internal wars. Wallace proved that beyond dispute. Even at Stirling Brig, where he destroyed the English host, he fought by his own rules, like a brigand, according to the nobles talking down their noses. But he won. The only other time he committed to a battle was at Falkirk, and there he was betrayed by Scotland's own knights, who led their cavalry off the field before the fight began, but too late for Wallace to react to their turncoat behavior. Falkirk cost Wallace dearly, and he never played by knightly rules again. But he united Scotland in a way that had never been known before. And I have taken up his ways. I would rather fight by guile and terror and win than be hanged, drawn, and quartered because I fought by England's rules …" He frowned slightly. "But why are you asking me these things? They have little to do with you."

"I know. I set out to ask something else, but your answers fascinated me and I lost track of my question … which was, do any of these island chiefs own galleys?"

"Of course they do. They all do. They are Islesmen—they go everywhere by boat. MacDonald has more than any other. His is the largest fleet."

"How large?"

Bruce shook his head. "I know not … but I have seen him summon more than a hundred at one time, all fully manned, to Islay. What are you thinking?"

"I was thinking that my galleys will serve no one well floating in Lamlash Bay. They will gather barnacles and my men will lose their fighting edge. Therefore, I thought to keep them in condition by lending them to you … a loan, you understand, for appearances only. No fighting involved. No naval battles. Merely the sight of not-too-distant force. We can remove the crosses from their sails, or replace the sails completely, but they will remain Temple galleys. Could you use them?"

The King's eyes narrowed almost to slits as he weighed the offer. "I could use one of them, for my own transportation from time to time, whene'er I have to travel to or through the Isles. But if they cannot fight—"

"Oh, those ones would fight—your crew, I mean—were you aboard in person. They would be King's Escort and Guard in that case, and would do battle on your personal behalf if ever that were required. The others would be in different case."

"I would not need the others. One craft would suffice, for I seldom travel by sea."

Will cocked his head. "Perhaps because you have never had the means to hand before … a galley of your own?"

Bruce smiled. "Perhaps, but nonetheless, I would seldom use it. My greatest concerns are always on the mainland, where the English swarm, the true realm of Scotland. And I would not need the others."

"Then that leaves my fine galleys unemployed …" Will hesitated. "Think you this Angus Og could find a use for them, in gift from you?" He held up a hand before Bruce could respond. "Think, for a moment, from your kingly needs. Might you not have much to gain from offering Angus Og the use of five fine galleys? You could make the stipulation plain at the outset: he would have them for display and demonstration and, of course, they ship at least four hundred men, closer to five hundred. It strikes me that an ambitious man like him, taunting a stronger force like the MacDougalls, might be glad to take advantage of even the appearance of greater strength than he can field."

The King grunted deep in his chest, pinching the hair on his upper lip, thinking over what Will had said, but as he made to speak, there came a knock at the door, and Bishop David de Moray stepped into the room.

"You sent for me, Sire."

Bruce rose to greet the Bishop, glancing at Will in wonder as he did so. "Aye, Davie, I did. I gave word to send you up in half an hour, but it feels as though scarce the half of that has gone. Come in. Pour yourself a cup of wine and sit you down. Master Sinclair and I have not yet finished our discussion, but you needna leave. Sit and listen. I'll tell you later what we have discussed till now."

He sat down again and turned back to Will. "Offer them as a gift, you say ... from me to Angus Og. That is a wondrous fine idea. The man will jump at it like a trout after a fly. But why only the five galleys? You have ten, you said."

"Aye, and one of them's mine and another yours, and I'll feel safer keeping three more reserved for our own use, should the need arise. That leaves five."

"Of course it does. I had forgot those first two." The King smiled, and his entire face was transformed, appearing years younger. But then the smile faded. "So now you will have but half as many men to feed and house, since Angus Og will have the keeping of your oarsmen. What about the rest of your men?"

"Kenneth's party, plus the garrison from La Rochelle—two hundred and thirty, all told, not counting the galley crews. The same needs apply to them. Stuck here on Arran for months on end, they will grow soft. Now clearly you need good men. I can lend you mine—not all at once, mind you, but in rotating groups, knights and sergeants both. Three groups of five-and-seventy, say, all of them mounted and equipped, the complement changing every four months."

"You would do that?"

Will shrugged. "Without hesitation. But there would be conditions."

The King held up his hand. "Before you say another word, I cannot undertake to keep them from the fighting—"

"Nor would I ask you to. War is war. I make exceptions for the galleys because they are all that remains, at this time, of the Temple fleet and they are my responsibility. Regular fighting men are another matter altogether. I will ask for volunteers, then select the first group of seventy-five from among those. Every man I have will volunteer, no doubt of that, but they will fight as Temple sergeants, under their own officers. That is the single stipulation I will make there. What say you?"

"I say aye. What else could I say? But what do you expect to gain from this?"

"The King's blessing upon our use of Arran, and a free rein while we are here. Also the King's open and freely bestowed goodwill in speaking for us with our neighbors, on Kintyre and the Isles if not the mainland, so that our ships will be free to come and go for as long as we remain. I hope our stay will not be long, that we will return to France one day soon, but in the meantime we would have a place to live and to think of as our own."

Bruce nodded and slapped his hands on his thighs, then turned to Moray, who had been listening intently. "There, we're done. And now it is your turn, David, as representative of Mother Church. D'ye want to stay back there or will we make room here by the fire?"

Moray had been working with the fastening of his mail coat and now he stood up and shrugged out of it, tossing it to the tabletop where it landed with a heavy crunching of links. "I'll come by the fire, Your Grace." He set his wine on the table's end as the three of them rearranged themselves around the heavy iron grate. Will took it upon himself to add fuel to the fire while the King summarized all that they had talked of for the Bishop's information.

"So," the Bishop said eventually, looking into the fire rather than at the King, "you have considered all I had to say o' this and decided to ignore it."

"I ignored nothing, merely sought ways around it. Besides, you were but stating the obvious that first time."

"No, Sire. The *obvious* is that you have decided to proceed despite my warnings. It is the *needful* wi' which we now have to deal." David de Moray, Prince of the Church, had no compunction about risking the displeasure of his monarch. Bruce, however, showed no sign of disapproval. He merely sat with his chin on his breast, peering sidewise at the Bishop from beneath raised brows, and when he spoke his words came from the corner of his mouth, directed to Will, seated on his right.

"He can be testy when he's crossed, our Davie, but he's a solid lad. Very well, my lord Bishop, explain this *needful* ..."

Moray huffed in exasperation, and Will was sure that this was not the first time he had done so in his dealings with the King. "I would to God Archbishop Lamberton were here at times like this."

"As do I, Davie." There was no hint of levity now in Bruce's voice. "Our superior in Christ, William, is sorely missed, and by far more folk than you and me. But that canna be helped. God has decreed, for reasons of His own, that the Archbishop spend these days in England, and until England releases him to return to his flock there is nothing we can do about it—for the present, at least. But in the meantime, you know as do I that he believes my temporal and spiritual welfare to be well served at your hands, so an end to this moaning. It's your counsel I need, not your complaints."

"I have had a thought or two on that." Moray raised both hands in front of his face and turned them back and forth, scrutinizing them, then bent forward to look across the King to where Will sat. "Sir William, you have no beard."

Will raised a hand to scratch at his stubbly chin. "I will have, soon enough. I had to shave it off a few weeks ago."

"And why would you do that? I thought a Templar's beard was sacrosanct."

Will almost grinned, his lips twisting in wry agreement. "Most people think so, my lord, but it is merely an affectation. The tonsure is sacrosanct, but the forked beard is no more than a tradition born out of the desert wars in Outremer, and it is one to which I refuse to subscribe. I wear a plain beard, uncut, but unforked, too. I shaved it off with scarce a thought when necessity demanded it."

"Necessity?"

"I had a need to pass unnoticed among de Nogaret's men."

"Ah!" Moray sat back in his chair, apparently satisfied, but Bruce was not.

"What was all that about?" He glared from one of them to the other.

Moray merely glanced at him. "Did you not hear? I was asking Sir William about his beard."

"I know that, man, but why?"

The Bishop raised his eyebrows. "Because I need to think, and pray over the thoughts. I shall tell you all about it tomorrow." He leaned forward to address Will again. "I meant what I said earlier, you know, about the Pope and the King of France. Neither of them will be happy when they learn that you are here and that King Robert has granted you sanctuary. King Philip will be greatly vexed, if what you say is true. Perhaps even more than the Pope."

"Why do you say that, my lord?"

"Because if he and his man de Nogaret were as successful in his coup against the Temple as you suspect, then your escape with the fleet would, in all probability, be the single greatest error of that day. Philip Capet is not a man to enjoy failure—especially so public a failure, with the plain proof of it abroad in other lands. He will not look kindly upon the King of Scots—a suitor for his assistance— granting any kind of clemency to his quarry."

"Not clemency, my lord Bishop. Sanctuary."

"Think you King Capet will see the difference?" Moray's eyebrows had risen even higher with his astonishment.

Will looked crestfallen. "No, sir, he will not." He hesitated, looking at Moray. "*King Capet*, you called him. Have you met the man?"

"Aye, three times. I still believe him more statue than flesh and blood. But that is neither here nor there. This sanctuary you have won may cost King Robert dearly."

"Let King Robert fret over that," the monarch answered. "Tell us about the Pope. You said he would be more vexed than Philip. How could that be?"

Moray twisted sideways in his seat to look at his friend. "Do you really have to ask that? He has declared you excommunicate, Robert, and with you all the people of this realm. That means damned: condemned and excluded from the affairs of Christian men and from the sacraments of Holy Church. No Eucharist. No penance, absolution, or salvation. No marriages, nor burials in consecrated ground. And withal a complete lack of hope." He looked over to Will. "The sole thing standing between His Grace here and the weight of that anathema is the intervention of the body of the Church itself in Scotland. We, the bishops of the realm, are his only shield, and we ourselves are divided by loyalties, for and against the Bruce claim to the Crown. Mind you, the dispute of that claim is impious, since His Grace is now God's Anointed, duly crowned and ratified at Scone by the senior prelates in the realm, the Primate himself, Archbishop of St. Andrews, presiding."

He turned back to Bruce, who was rubbing a knuckle against the tip of his nose. "Can you not see it, Sire? If Pope Clement has permitted this outrage against a vested Order of Holy Church, then he will feel his guilt, but being the weak man that he is, he will do nothing to stop the travesty. He dare not take a stance against the King—he never has and never will—unless and until Philip does something to push even him beyond endurance. And even then, Clement might submit. But we in Scotland here, the bishops of the realm, are too convenient a target for his guilty wrath. We have managed to placate him to this point, and to stay him with sound arguments, submitting that he could have been misled and that the events in question were deliberately misrepresented by your enemies for political gain. And we have been able to do that because all of us believe what we say—Lamberton, Wishart, myself, and the other bishops who stand with us. But if Clement hears of this sanctuary he will see it as sheer defiance of his authority and he will be greatly tempted to make example of us, claiming disobedience to his papal will and citing this sanctuary, plus our former arguments on your behalf, as evidence. Our voices and our powers would be then annulled ... and you can rest assured the King of France will see to it that Clement vents his anger on us. And once that happens—the which may God forbid—your entire realm will lie under anathema, condemned to Hell in this life." He allowed his words to hang in the air, then concluded, "And *that* is why I spoke of dealing with the *needful* rather than the obvious."

He rose abruptly to his feet, moving to collect his sword from where it stood in the corner, then slinging it by its belt over one shoulder before crossing to gather up his coat of mail from the table, speaking over his shoulder as he did so. "I am going to pray for a while, and then to sleep. Do you both the same. Tomorrow, in the bright of God's daylight, I shall tell you what is needful and, pray God, what might be possible. Until then, a peaceful night to both of you."

"Wait you, Davie." Moray had opened the door to leave, but turned on the threshold, looking back at the monarch. "I would be greatly obliged were you to postpone your prayers for a wee bit longer. There is still much to be said between us this night, and it would vex me to lose the gist of what I am thinking. Bide a while longer, if you will." Moray closed the door again, shutting out the muted sounds of music and raised voices that drifted up from downstairs, and the Bruce, listening to it idly, raised an eyebrow in mild surprise.

"Well, they're still going strong down there. It must be less late than I thought …" He turned again to Will. "Sir William, what think you of our warrior bishop? Did I not say he has a long head on him?"

Will looked a little bemused. "You did, Your Grace." He turned then to Moray. "Forgive me, my lord Bishop, but the last part of what you said was lost to me. What were you talking about, if I am permitted to ask?"

Bruce grinned and bent forward from the waist, his eyes on Moray but his words meant for Will. "Needful things, he said. Davie's clever." His grin widened at the frown on Moray's face. "And, Davie, truth to tell, I ha'e little more idea than Will of what you meant." He winked at Will. "But if we dinna deal with it tonight, he will tell us when he thinks fit, sometime tomorrow. Your fleet will be here the morning after that, but in the meantime, I'll be away again. Another will be coming in tomorrow, from the north."

"Another fleet?"

"Aye. Angus Og's. Good sense, as we see it, might dictate that he come alone, or wi' a small escort, but Angus Og willna play that game. He will bring his fleet, you mark my words. His Highland pride will not permit him to do otherwise. He willna stoop to be seen as scuttling about in his own domain, God save his wit. Anyway, he's on his way to pick me up again and carry me around the south end of Kintyre, then up the coastal passage through the Firth of Lorn and Loch Linne to the start of the great Glen. We hold it now, and Moray's men are waiting there for us, along with Neil Campbell's and a contingent of MacGregors. Davie here has raised the whole o' Moray country to my cause, more men than I could find in all my own ruined lands of Annandale and Ayr. So we'll march up the Glen again to Inverness, where we'll join with the men of Mar and Atholl, and with the grace of God, Clan Fraser. From there we will strike east, into the Comyn country of Buchan. The Earl of Buchan is a proud, unbending man, arrogant and filled wi' self-righteous scorn, but he will pay me fealty, or he will die, for good and ample cause."

"When will you leave?"

"Tomorrow, as soon as may be." He smiled again, fleetingly, but generating the same lightening of lines and years as earlier. "But not before Davie tells us what is needful. I have little time these days, and none at all to waste. I came back here to reaffirm James Douglas as Guardian of the Southwest, and to give him further instructions on what I shall require of him these coming weeks. That is done. He has a full eight hundred men now under his command, two hundred here, the rest awaiting him near Turnberry, on the mainland. He'll pick up more as he moves inland through my own country, now that the word of our recent successes has had time to spread. His foremost task will be to keep the King's peace, mainly by keeping the MacDowals on their toes, though he'll harass the English garrisons forbye."

"And will he leave a holding force here on Arran?"

"Aye, he will."

"No need for that if we are here. He could take all his men with him in that case."

"He could if he had room for them."

"He could use a couple of my ships in addition to his own."

"Aye, there is that." Bruce paused, considering. "You understand that there is still a chance that I might needs refuse your request? If Davie comes up with some difficulty that canna be set aside, I may have to heed him."

Will nodded. "I understand that."

The King ignored Moray's gathering scowl. "But let us suppose he does no such thing. Then I will inform Sir James that you have my permission to remain on Arran, under sanctuary. But what will you do after that?"

"I have my work cut out for me, my lord. My men have been cooped up aboard ship for weeks on end. By the time they land, they will be unruly and ripe for mischief. My first task will be to rein them in. And I have more than twenty Temple knights in my care—no small responsibility and no laughing matter. Our sergeants can be quickly disciplined, but Temple knights, as you may or may not know, can be ... difficult. They have a tendency to arrogance and pride. They are contentious and overbearing at the best of times, and they may think, some of them, at least, that the recent events in France and the removal of their superiors' authority, no matter how temporary, absolved them of responsibility to their sworn duties. My first task will be to curb them and remind them of their solemn vows, and then I will have to break them to renewed monastic discipline, re-establish life according to the Temple Rule. And then there are the lay brothers, a score and a half of them. I must set them busy, too, building a house for us and setting up a core about which the monastic discipline can revolve."

"You can use this place for the time being. It has kitchens, and most of Jamie's men already sleep in it, but it will lie empty when they leave. Do you have builders with you?"

"House builders and masons? A few, but we have ships' carpenters and willing workers and men who know how to erect a shelter. We will manage."

"Make sure they build your stables first. Your horses will need shelter from the winter storms. Will you hold my treasure here for me?"

Will looked over in surprise. "Of course. You will be gone when it arrives."

"I will, but even were I not, I would be loath to take it with me aboard MacDonald's galleys. Too visible, too much temptation. Forbye, I'm sailing first, but then I'll be afoot, marching through hostile country towards war … an ill time and place to be carrying heavy treasure."

"I'll see it kept safe for you, Sir King."

"Good man. I'll have Jamie collect it at some future date, when I can tend to it as it deserves." He yawned and stretched, then looked at the dying fire. "I need to sleep, my friend, and so do you. There's a room next door ready for you, though you'll have to share wi' Jamie Douglas." He smiled again. "But it has two cots. And now I'll bid ye a good night, for I do have vexing matters to discuss wi' his Lordship Davie here. We will deal wi' his needful things tomorrow, the three of us. Sleep well, Sir William Sinclair."

4

Will rolled from his cot long before dawn to find a candle burning in a sconce, and no sign of Douglas, who had shared the room with him. He doused his face with ice-cold water from the pitcher on the table, then realized that there was no toweling with which to dry himself. Containing his annoyance, he dried his hands and face on his bedding, thinking it strange that he had not heard Douglas rise or leave, but when he thrust a hand into the bedding on the young knight's cot he found no trace of warmth. Surprised, he dressed himself fully and made his way downstairs, expecting to find Douglas there, but there was no sign of him. Aside from a busy work crew, the place was empty, its erstwhile inhabitants already scattered to meet the working day.

The great hall, lit by flickering torches and a replenished fire, had already been cleared of any sign that it had ever been a dormitory. The main doors were propped open to let in the cold, pre-dawn air, and the tables and benches had been hauled aside and stacked in their storage spaces. A crew of cleaners was clearing out the old, dried rushes from the floor, sending up clouds of dust, and at their backs another group was spreading a fresh mat of green rushes underfoot. The far side room to the left of the main doors had tables in it and had already been much used as a breakfast room, and Will was grateful to see that there was still food available and helped himself to a bowl of thick, hot oatmeal porridge that he cooled liberally with fresh goat's milk.

Afterwards, seeing no one that he recognized, and feeling unaccountably lost and lonely as the only Templar among so many strangers, he went outside at daybreak and walked down to the parapet overlooking the bay, where he saw one of the men he had met the previous night, one of the Gaelic chieftains of the Campbell party who had spoken to him in Scots rather than the unintelligible Gaelic. The fellow was peering intently out to sea and muttering to himself as Will approached, and when he looked to see what the man had noticed in the strengthening light, he was alarmed to see a pair of boats half a mile away, dancing dangerously in turbulent waves and far too close to the rocks at the base of the cliffside that dropped steeply into the sea.

"In God's name," he asked, "what are they doing over there?"

The fellow looked at him askance. "Ah," he said in Scots. "It's yourself. They're fishing."

"In that sea? They'll be killed."

"Nah, they're finished now, coming back in. They found a shoal. We'll eat well tonight."

"What kind of shoal?"

"Fish!" The man looked at him as if he were soft in the head, then turned away to shout—uselessly, Will thought—at the men in the distant boats, who, it transpired, were his own.

Will watched with him for a long time as the boats fought their way back to the beach below, wallowing heavily in the choppy swell, and then he went down through the wall gate with the Gael and gazed in stupefaction at the sight of thousands of foot-long silver fish being unloaded from among the feet of the rowers, scooped and shoveled from the bottom of the two craft and thrown onto the graveled beach, their shed scales leaving the wooden interiors of both craft shimmering and crusted with a metallic coating. It was a miraculous catch. He could tell that from the excitement of the men working around him as they scrambled knee deep in breaking waves to keep the fish from escaping back into the water. They were throwing and scooping the squirming, leaping creatures high, tossing them up onto drier land away from the water's edge, where others, whooping wildly, caught them and threw them into sturdy baskets hurriedly brought down from the kitchens. Will found himself responding to the excitement and had to restrain himself from leaping into their midst like a small boy and joining in the frenzy of collection.

When the last basket of fish was carried away he was left standing alone on the beach's silvered edge, lost in a swirling torrent of thoughts that tumbled over one another and swept his mind along without rhyme or reason. The boyhood memories that the fisher folk had evoked gave way to memories of joining the Order of Sion at boyhood's end, at the age of eighteen, of being sent to join the Temple, and of how he had begun to struggle with the lore and the advanced mysteries of the Order of Sion, all the time advancing through the Temple hierarchy. For a while he found himself plunged back into the struggles they had had in trying, vainly, to stop the spread of Islam from northern Africa across the narrow seas into Iberia.

The waves swirled around his soles, shifting the pebbles on which he stood, and he turned away to climb the sloping foreshore towards the palisaded fort. He was through the gate and just starting up the flight of stone steps that led up to the forecourt of the hall when he heard yet another commotion erupt ahead of him, beyond the stairs. The sounds cut through the drifting eddies in his mind and snapped him back to the present. He lengthened his step and bounded up the stairs, fearing what he would find up there, and sure enough, a mile beyond where the fishing boats had been, the line between sea and sky was obscured by an irregular mass of angular shapes: masts and billowing sails upon which he could clearly see the emblem Bruce had described the night before, the galley symbol of Angus Og MacDonald, stark in its blackness against the whitened sails that bore it.

More and more men were crowding around him, obscuring his vision as they bobbed and weaved for a sight of the distant fleet, and he saw Tam Sinclair among them. He waited to catch his kinsman's eye, then waved him over.

"Good day to you," he growled when Tam reached his side. "You look … fresh. What were you up to last night?"

Tam grinned down at the thronging clansmen. "Among this crew? What would you think? I supped well, played a few games of dice and lost, then had the best night's sleep I've had since leaving La Rochelle. On a tabletop on a floor that didna budge or sway once in the whole night. Whose ships are those?"

"Islanders. They are expected. Where's Mungo?"

Tam shrugged. "He's here somewhere. I saw him just a while ago. What's going on?"

"I'll tell you everything later. For now, I need to see what's happening out there."

The crowd had ringed them in while they stood talking, and now Will began to weave among them, trying to find a vantage point of his own, but a hand pulled at his sleeve and he heard his name being spoken. It was David de Moray at his side, with the taller figure of Bruce looming just behind him.

"A word, if it please you," the Bishop said, and beckoned him to come with them.

They crossed the crowded yard and mounted the wooden stairs to the hall, picking their way through the press of craning bodies that jammed the steps. Inside, the building was deserted, and Bruce led the way quickly across the rush-strewn floor and up the stairs to the room they had been in the night before. As he climbed the steps, Will was surprised to realize that for a period of hours he had managed to escape the tension and uncertainty that had kept him awake for most of the night. It had all returned now, filling his breast, and he had not yet spoken a word since being summoned. The Bishop pulled the door shut behind them.

The room was dim, lit only by thin November daylight from the small windows high in the gable wall, and the King was already seating himself next to the long dead fire in the iron grate. He waved Will to a seat across from him, and as the Temple knight obeyed, Moray lowered himself carefully into the chair next to Bruce. The King looked at Will and scratched his chin.

"Davie here has been praying all morning," he said.

"*Thinking* and praying," the Bishop amended. "And I have some suggestions to propose … some provisos."

There came a deep-throated roar from outside and Bruce glanced up at the windows. "Angus Og is giving them something to react to," he said quietly. "A great believer in spectacle, is Angus. But," he drew himself upright in his chair, his entire demeanor changing, "we will have an hour before he approaches the beach, so we can talk—" He broke off, his eyebrows rising slightly, then asked, "What is it?"

Will flapped a hand to indicate that what he had to say was unimportant. "Forgive me, Your Grace, but it occurred to me that when your guest arrives, he might address you as King Bruce openly, in front of all … and I know you are here secretly. That is all."

The King nodded. "Well said, but Angus will not come ashore. He will merely send a boat for Davie, Boyd, de Hay, and me. He and I talked of this but days ago and he knows I am plain Boyd of Annandale here. Now, let's listen to what my lord Bishop has to say. Davie?"

The Bishop sat back and leveled his bright, hazel eyes at Will. "Fine," he said, speaking in clearly enunciated Scots. "Fine. I'll not bore you with what you already know, Sir William, but get right to the heart of things. We have … difficulties … possible and serious discomfiture and embarrassment for King Robert and his entire realm should your presence here become public knowledge—and with the arrival of the fleet you expect tomorrow, that knowledge can scarcely be avoided. But on the other hand, there could be—there *are*—equally potent benefits available to both Crown and realm through your presence here, not the least of those being the treasure you carry in your hold for the King's purse. But there is also the matter of your galleys to consider, the goodwill and advantages those offer us. And forbye, there is the real, appreciable worth of the trained, disciplined, mounted, and fully equipped manpower you have promised in King Robert's support should you be permitted to remain here. Those things are known, and in many respects, they counterbalance each the other, pro and contra.

"The difficulty lies in finding the means—some *practical* and valid method—whereby we, the Church in Scotland, as much as the King's military and civil advisers, could justifiably grant the sanctuary you seek, while keeping the dangers entailed from overwhelming everything. The losses we would court in doing so are not to be made light of. They involve the excommunication and eternal damnation of an entire people on the one hand, and the loss of a powerful ally on the other. And even the threatened loss of that ally's neutrality is to be feared, since the absence of neutrality entails his espousal of England's cause in the wars we face."

He cleared his throat, glancing away towards a distant corner. "I prayed long and hard last night, searching for some guidance, some oracle, I suppose, to tell me what Archbishop Lamberton and Bishop Wishart would wish to say, were either of them able to be here. But of course they cannot be here, and I must act in their stead, for my sins. And so I tossed and turned much of the night, and thought ... thought about the idea, no more than a flashing notion, that had come to me last night. We talked briefly of beards."

"I remember."

"You told us that the full, forked beards were an affectation. That was the word you used."

"Aye. It is an affectation. It began in the Holy Lands, during the wars there. All men went bearded there, Muslim and Christian alike. And at some point, no one knows when now, the knights of the Temple began to wear their beards forked, to differentiate themselves from others."

"How do you know that? You sound certain of it."

Will frowned, wondering where this was leading. Bruce was saying nothing, plucking at the tuft of beard beneath his nether lip and studying the Bishop through narrowed eyes.

"I am certain of it. It was referred to in—" Will caught himself. "In some documents I read ... while preparing for advancement within the Order. It was of no importance, but it stuck in my memory for some reason." He shrugged. "My mind works like that sometimes, retaining things of which I have no need. Why do you ask? Is it important?"

"I think so. How does one man look at another and know he belongs to the Temple?"

Will's frown deepened, reflecting his growing bewilderment. "Several different ways. By the clothes he wears, and the insignia he bears—the cross pattée, the various marks of rank."

"And the beard?"

"Aye, certainly, if the wearer is a knight, but not so the sergeants. The knights all wear forked beards, highly distinctive, as you pointed out, but the sergeants simply go bearded ... and tonsured, of course."

"Of course," the Bishop agreed, nodding. "They all wear the tonsure of the Church's most privileged Order." He paused for barely a heartbeat, then continued on a different tack. "You said your first task would be to remind your people of who they are and what they represent, no?"

Thoroughly perplexed now, Will glanced at the King, seeking some guidance. But the monarch's steel-gray eyes stared back at him levelly, offering nothing in the way of enlightenment, and so he looked again at Moray, only to find the same level, noncommittal gaze. He flapped a hand impatiently and nodded. "I did say that, yes. And I meant it."

"I know you did, because you named your reasons and your fears: that their morale might have been threatened by the events in France, because after weeks cooped up at sea they might be feeling mutinous, angry, and resentful and thus prone to unpredictable behavior. Am I correct or have I missed something?"

"No, Bishop, you were listening well." Something like a small hard-edged grin flickered at the corner of Will's mouth. "You may have overstated the case slightly, but the gist of what I said is there."

"You said you must remind them of their vows and make them aware of the obligations they undertook in joining the Order. Those would be poverty, chastity, and obedience." Moray smiled now. "Poverty, it seems to me, has never been a difficulty for your brethren, would you not agree? And chastity becomes a way of life in a religious Order, free of the fleshly temptations that beset the ruck of men. But obedience is another matter altogether, and in this instance of what occurred in France, the deterrent to obedience, the fear of punishment, has been removed by the incarceration of the Order's leaders and commanders. That, I believe, must be your first priority: to re-establish the concept of obedience, and your own authority, before all else. How will you do that, should the need arise?" He extended his hand, fingers spread, inviting a response.

Will gazed at the tabletop, seeing the grain in the long slabs of wood that had been used to make it. Across from him, his audience of two sat patiently. He could feel their eyes watching him, waiting.

"This ... this potential for rebellion, as you put it, *could* present a novel situation," he said finally, speaking almost to himself, so that the others leaned closer. "The chances are strong that it will not arise, but if it should, I will have to deal with it."

He looked from one to the other of them, then continued in a louder voice. "You must understand that the matter of the punishment of brethren who offend the Rule is one that is strictly held, and privily, among the Order. It is not, nor can it ever be, a matter for discussion or debate outside of chapter gatherings. But I can see why it is you ask." He stopped again, wrestling with words. "When we ... disembark ... and reassemble from our ships, we will be a community again—a single entity and a self-contained chapter. My first duty, as a representative of the Governing Council within that community, will be to convene a gathering of the chapter and give blessings and prayers for our deliverance from the perils thrust upon us by King Philip and de Nogaret." He smiled, briefly.

"Not that I will officiate myself in the praying. We have three of the Order's own bishops with us, by the grace of God. But, that done, and the specific requirements, regulations, and obligations of the Order and its sacred Rule completed in this, our new communal home—for no matter how temporary our stay here might be, the obligations are unchangeable—it will remain for me to supervise the election of the community's officers, and with them, to define the brethren's tasks and duties in this place. And by that time, with the establishment of a community again and the reinforcement of our duties, the threat of disobedience should be slight. It ought to be unthinkable, in fact, but … it will be slight."

He sighed, then twisted his head, loosening his neck, which had grown stiff from the force of his concentration. "And if it is not, then I will have to build some kind of jail, some means of holding the miscreants apart, for the good of the community and the salvaging of their own souls. The value of a month of enforced solitude, existing on bread and water, is an inestimable thing."

Bruce spoke into the silence that followed. "There are storehouses on the ground floor with stone walls and stout iron bars. Jail cells, if you need them."

Will looked at him and nodded. "Thank you for that. Those would serve in the short term … and that is all we should need, a short-term solution. But we would have to build a Chapter House of our own for the duration of our stay. A religious community cannot share common lodgings with laymen. I trust you can see that?"

The King nodded slowly, then turned to the Bishop. "Davie, you must have more?"

"I do, Your Grace." Moray drew both palms down his face from forehead to chin, then leaned forward towards Will. "Here then, Sir William, is the gist of my thinking, and before I say it I must make a point, not to insult or demean anyone or anything, but simply to make myself clear. Were you to enter this room and look at me now, for the first time, what kind of man would you take me to be?" He saw the puzzled look on Will's face and stood up from the table, dragging his chair aside and stepping back so that he could be clearly seen. "Come now, what would you take me for?"

Will shrugged, his eyes taking in the figure facing him: short hair, enormously strong shoulders, a solid, confident posture, large, capable hands, a well-worn shirt of rusted mail, and a sheathed dirk hanging from a belt about his waist. "A knight," he said. "A well-born fighting knight in need of a new shirt of mail."

"Aha! And were I to walk out and come back in wearing miter and chasuble? What then?"

"I would see a bishop."

"Yes, you would, and though both warrior and bishop would be accurate descriptions, you would be hard put to see either one in the other, am I right?"

"You are."

"And I am right in this matter of the beards, for at the heart of that lies the solution we require. If you can make the manner of your people's dress and appearance a matter of obedience, then you and yours might remain here in perpetuity." He raised a swift hand to cut short Will's reaction, pressing on with what he had to say. "Strip off the outer marks of what you are and you will not be seen, will be perceived as being other than you are. Command your knights to cut off their forked beards, to leave their tonsures to grow out, and dress them commonly, like ordinary men. Remove the Templar crosses and visible emblems from their clothing and military devices— armor, shields, and surcoats—and above all, be careful with your horses. Keep them apart and well concealed from casual view, and permit no displays of chivalry for idle folk to gawk at and talk about later. Become ordinary men, to outward view at least, even farming the little land that's there to till, and you may rest secure here, as we may rest secure knowing you are here, unseen.

"Unseen? But we *will* be seen. God knows there are enough of us, and this is a small island. How can you think that we will not be seen?"

"I don't. I am not talking about sorcery or magic. You will be seen, but you'll be seen as ordinary men—soldiers and men at arms.

We are at war here in Scotland. There are men in arms everywhere throughout the realm, and no one pays them any notice until it comes time to fight. But a strong force of disciplined men, religious, well-horsed fighting men in red Crusader crosses and the black cross of the Temple Mount, based upon the Isle of Arran? Think you not that would be remarked, a topic for discussion throughout the land?"

Will's mind reeled as he grappled with what the Bishop was suggesting. Here, he thought, was blasphemy, issuing from the mouth of a bishop of Holy Church. His every instinct told him to rise up against it. And yet, even as he contemplated doing so, seeking the words that would reject the notion, the edge of his outrage softened and he began to think more logically, and to perceive that the outrage might be confined to his own mind alone.

"This could not be," he said, his voice sounding strange to his own ears. "It is too much—"

"Too much of what?" Moray asked. "It was you who said the beards were but an affectation."

"And they are. The matter of the beards is nothing. But the tonsure …"

"Do you know whence came the tonsure, Sir William?"

"Whence … ? No, I do not."

The Bishop of Moray smiled, as though he were enjoying himself. "Well I do. Like you, I have a mind that retains such trivial, meaningless things. Eight hundred years ago, in the dying days of Rome's empire, a shaved head was the symbol of slavery. Slaves were forbidden to wear hair, lest it make them indistinguishable from ordinary citizens. And so their heads were shaved bald, shaved unnaturally in a square, to mark them as slaves for all the world to see. And those were the days in which the first monastic Orders were being formed. The early monks took up the practice of shaving their heads, too, to demonstrate that they chose to be the lowest of the low, the very slaves of Christ." The Bishop paused. "Few people know that today, and fewer still regard the tonsure as what it has become, now that its true meaning has been lost to history. It is an affectation. No more than that. Just like your full, forked beards." He

waited for a reaction from Will, and when he saw the knight's jaw
sag in amazement, he changed course, his voice deeper and more
conciliatory.

"Look you," he said. "You will establish a new community here
on Arran. It will have a new chapter, new appointments, and new
rules befitting the new reality you face here. Believe me, there will
be nothing sinful or slothful in what results from banning tonsures
and forked beards as part of those new rules." He bent farther
forward. "It is your *community* that is important here, Sir William,
your very survival that is at stake. Your community will not fall
about your ears because its members grow hair on the crowns of
their heads. Discuss it with your chapter if you like, but if you
explain the situation as it stands, and then propose your solution and
its goals, I am certain that few complaints will be uttered. And if any
are, I am equally sure you will rise to the task of meeting them. Prior
to that time, though, King Robert and I will be long gone from here,
and we'll require an answer ere we go. What say you?"

Will looked from Moray to the King and shook his head, still
unsteady from the shock of what the Bishop had proposed. King
Robert spoke.

"There is pasture aplenty on the high moor, inland, the one called
Machrie. Your horses would thrive there, I think, and there is ample
space to separate them and stable them apart, in glens and woods.
And to the north of that, the forest stands. It is no Ettrick Forest, but
it will furnish logs enow to help you with your building. The moor
is bottomless peat, rich fuel."

Will barely heard him, though he recognized the kindness in the
voice. "But our weapons," he began. "We will need—"

The Bishop cut him off again, his voice dry and matter-of-fact.
"What about them? I said nothing about weapons. You'll need those.
I said that you should conceal the *visible* signs of who you are—the
white mantles and the sergeants' surcoats and all your visible badges
and emblems of Temple rank. Conceal them, Sir William. Paint over
the crosses on your shields and on your helms, but there is no need
to destroy any of them. Store them away until you have a need for

them again, on your return to France. Then your men may shave their heads and even fork their beards again before riding home with fresh new crosses painted on their gear."

Will thought more about it, seeing the possibilities, the shape of it at last. A vision of the fleet grew in his mind, de Berenger's mighty galley at its front, and then he nodded, all at once convinced. "Aye, I can see that. Hide ourselves in plain view. And the same must go for our sails."

Bruce spoke up again, smiling now. "Angus Og will help you there. He'll have no emblem but his own on any sail that goes with him. He will provide you with new sails, never fear. And at no cost."

Will felt as though a great weight had been lifted from him. "So be it, Robert, King of Scots. I will make it so." He turned to Moray. "My lord Bishop, I can scarce find words to thank you. I believe your solution may be perfect to all our needs and I am deeply, personally in your debt."

"Then here's my royal hand on it, if we're agreed," Bruce said, standing up and stretching out his hand. The others laid their own upon his and they shook once, twice, and thrice. "Done!" said the King.

"Aye, but there's still a lot to do." Moray was already turning towards the door. "We have to arrange to ship your first contingent of men to join King Robert when he needs them—the where of it, if not the when—and we have yet to broach the matter of your galleys and your presence to MacDonald. We'd better see to that now. Come with us, Sir William, and we'll row you out to meet Angus Og. He'll send you back in a boat."

"I'll enjoy meeting him. But I must ask, where is Sir James today? He was gone long before I awoke this morning."

"He's hunting," the Bruce answered, clasping a hand over Will's shoulder. "Hunting for information, it seems, somewhere at the north end of the island. He left word with de Hay before he went, sometime in the dead of night. Something about a French-speaking spy, he said. Not one of your men, though. This one, whoever he is, was among our own. Anyway, Jamie will tell us all when he returns. Now, let's see what Angus Og has brought for us."

He made to leave, then hesitated. "Wait, though. One more thing has just occurred to me. I will not have the opportunity to thank my lady Randolph, the Baroness St. Valéry. By the time she arrives tomorrow morning, I will be long at sea, and mayhap even ashore again. Will you, therefore, thank her sincerely on my behalf? You need ha'e no fear of being too effusive. My gratitude in this matter would be impossible to overstate. Assure the lady of my personal gratitude and tell her I will look forward to thanking her in person and at great length in days to come." He paused, thinking deeply. "And ask her, if you would, to consider returning to her home in Moray. I will have Jamie prepare a strong escort for her, and they can drop off her treasure for me at St. Andrews as they pass by. Now, Davie, let's away."

A GATHERING ON ARRAN

1

W ill Sinclair was sitting on the edge of his cot, rubbing his eyes, when Tam came to rouse him the next morning. Tam carried a lit candle in a sconce in one hand and a ewer of warm water in the other, a towel folded over the arm holding the candle. He grunted a greeting, used the candle to light another on the room's single table, and set the ewer inside the earthen bowl on the tabletop before arranging the candles one on either side of the bowl and dropping the towel beside one of them. Then, his duty done, he turned and left the room again, well aware of the folly of attempting to talk about anything with Will before his friend had had time to collect himself and wash the sleep from his eyes.

On this particular morning, however, Will was wide awake and preparing to meet a very busy day. He had met the MacDonald leader, Angus Og, aboard his galley the previous afternoon and had made the necessary arrangements to secure permission for his vessels to sail unchallenged in these waters, in return for the loan, ostensibly through the medium of King Robert, of five of his galleys. He had then borrowed writing materials from Bishop de Moray before making his farewells to the King of Scots and returning ashore. There he had met with the dour Lowlander who was Douglas's quartermaster and made arrangements with him for a group of cooks to travel to Lamlash the following morning, to cook a simple hot meal for the incoming Temple fleet. After that, he had returned to the upper room assigned to him and worked alone late into the night, acting as his own scribe and making list after list of things that needed to be done this day. When he was satisfied that he had forgotten nothing, he had rolled into bed and slept soundly and peacefully, recouping all the losses of the night before.

Downstairs now in the anteroom of the main hall, surrounded by sleepy men who paid no attention at all to his knight's mantle or the heavy silver chain he wore beneath it, he poured goat's milk over a bowl of the daily porridge made by the garrison's cooks and ate it in silence at a table shared by a group of Highlanders as quiet as himself. When he was done, he crossed to the serving table again, where he cut a slice from a cold joint of meat, sprinkled it with salt from a jar, and wrapped it in a slab of bread that was still warm from the ovens.

"That looks good," Tam said from behind him. "I'll have some o' that, too. Here, I've brought your things."

Will nodded his thanks and bit off a mouthful of the bread and meat before setting it down and taking the sword and shield Tam was holding. He shrugged out of his mantle and settled the sword belt across his shoulders, adjusting the hang of the long, sheathed weapon, then replacing the mantle over it while Tam looked to his own feeding.

"Did you sleep well?" he asked as they headed for the main doors.

"Aye, well enough. I'm still enjoying having a bed that doesna move under me. We'll ha'e much to do this day, I'm thinking?"

"More than enough. Sir Edward should be here waiting for us by the time we reach the water. He was to come in last night, under cover of the dark."

It was still dark when they reached the beach, but the admiral's longboat was waiting for them, its prow drawn up on the pebbles, and the two men barely had time to seat themselves before four of the rowers jumped into the waves and hauled the boat out into deeper water again. Ten minutes later, Sir Edward de Berenger himself welcomed them as they climbed aboard his galley, then issued orders to get under way as soon as the longboat had been hauled aboard. Once the rhythmic sweep of the oars had settled into a steady beat, Will finally saw the admiral relax.

"Well, Commander," de Berenger said eventually. "How was your visit with the King of Scots?"

"Good enough. We have permission to stay here, with certain provisos. What about you? Any difficulties, going or coming?"

The light was strengthening now, and De Berenger was clearly visible as he turned to face Will, twisting his mouth into an expression that brought a swift frown to Will's face. "No difficulties going either way," the admiral said. "But there were difficulties nonetheless. They were brought to my attention, and I was very glad that I could leave them for yours."

"What happened?"

"Some of your garrison knights decided that they wished to go ashore, on the peninsula behind the island. They overrode the opposition of the ship's captain, a good man but a mere sergeant, awed by four bullying knights. Fortunately he had the sense to send word by boat to de Narremat, who sent de l'Armentière after them at once. He caught them in the channel between Sanda and the peninsula and threatened to run them down if they did not turn back upon his order. When they defied him, he sank their boat with that wicked ram of his. None of them were lost, for they were in the shallows at the time and de l'Armentière was very skillful, but they were four very wet and angry ranting knights when they were hauled aboard and taken straight to de Narremat's galley. He confined them belowdecks, in chains, and they are still there, rusting in their hauberks."

"Damnation. Who are they, do you know?"

"No, I did not think to ask their names. But they are Temple knights, cooped up too long at sea and little liking having no voice in their own affairs. It is fortunate, perhaps, that there were only the four of them aboard that ship. There were no other incidents among the knights aboard the remaining vessels."

"Nor will there be from this time on, for I intend to bring all of them to heel again and remind them of who they are and the vows they took." Will reached into his scrip and pulled out the folded sheet of vellum that he had written his lists on the night before, and held it up for de Berenger to see. "This arrogant nonsense of your four knights was foreseen yesterday, or some version of it was, by Bishop Moray, and I set myself to thinking how to deal with it before anything serious can develop. How long to reach the others from here?"

De Berenger looked forward, to where the Temple fleet could already be seen crowding the waters of the bay of Lamlash, which were motionless as a sheet of glass in the still morning light. "We are almost there now ... a quarter of an hour."

"And you bade them wait for our arrival before starting to disembark?"

"I did. Look! What's that over there on the island? There are people there. Who in blazes are they?"

Will picked out the small procession wending its way across the hills towards Lamlash Bay, perhaps forty men in all, pulling an assortment of lurching, high-wheeled handcarts loaded with cargo.

"Cooks and workmen," he said. "Douglas's men, courtesy of his quartermaster. They'll set up fires and prepare food for us to eat later, after the ceremonies." De Berenger raised an eyebrow at Will's mention of ceremonies, but said nothing. "Before we do anything else, we need to find the ship my brother is on and summon him to join me here. I'm going to need his hundred men ashore before anyone else moves towards land. Can you take us within hailing distance?"

The admiral smiled. "I can do better than that. With the water as still as it is, I can lay us alongside and he can jump down to us. I know his ship. In fact, I can see it from here." He turned to the ship-master behind him and issued quiet instructions, pointing out the vessel that held Kenneth Sinclair, and the man moved quickly away and began issuing orders.

"My thanks, Edward," Will said. "Now, look at this." He bowed his head to the parchment and began to run a finger down his long list of things to do, directing de Berenger's attention to the items that concerned him and explaining what he needed to have done and in what order, and as they drew steadily closer to the waiting fleet, Sir Edward, too, became absorbed in the importance of the day that stretched ahead. Before he did anything else, however, de Berenger had one question to ask, and it was one Will had been anticipating with some discomfort.

"What will you do with the Baroness while all this is going on?"

"Do with her? I shall do nothing with her, or to her. She will remain aboard her ship with her women until our business ashore is complete. After that, I care not what she may do ... she may disembark, if she so wishes."

"You would deny her the privilege of attending Mass?"

"Aye, I would, in this instance. The lady lives surrounded by priests and may have any one of them celebrate Mass for her at any time, in her own quarters, if she wishes. But today's Mass on the island will be a chapter Mass, the first such event celebrated by the brethren since we left La Rochelle. It will be a solemn ritual, its content dictated by the Rule of the Order, and you and I both know there is no place for women in any element of the Rule's applications. Her ladyship may be displeased, but there is no alternative open to any of us. She remains on board ship until we are done, and there's an end to it. Now, let's go and find my brother.

2

S ir Kenneth Sinclair clung grimly to a rope on the bulging side of the ship that lay alongside the galley, his face taut as he gauged the timing of his leap, and then he launched himself outwards, between the vertical sweeps of the galley's port-side oarsmen, the fingers of both hands spread wide in the hope of catching something—anything—to break his fall. There were willing hands aplenty to catch him, and he landed gently, his knees bent and his shoulders sagging with relief. He let out his breath with a great whoosh and stood upright, bracing himself for a moment before stepping forward to embrace his brother and pay his respects to Admiral de Berenger. As soon as the greetings were over, he swung back to Will.

"What's wrong?"

"Nothing is wrong. Why would you think otherwise?"

Kenneth's eyebrows rose up in mock delight. "You mean you came all this way just to wish me well, and tied your ship to ours with grappling hooks only to make me risk my life leaping down here for an embrace?" He sobered and his voice dropped to a lower register. "There's *something* happening—something in the wind, Brother—and I suspect that I'm a part of it."

Will nodded. "Right. You are. But nothing is wrong. I merely need you to do some things for me. Important things."

"I'm your man, then. What d'you need?"

Will glanced at de Berenger, then looked around to see if anyone else was listening. No one was close enough to hear, and he took his brother by the elbow and turned him to face the land above Lamlash Bay. "I want your men ashore within the hour, Kenneth, every one of them, in full mail and surcoats. Sir Edward will see that you have everything you need in order to do that. You see that shelf of land there, just above the bay? It stretches back for almost half a mile and most of it is level, and there's a knoll in the middle of it, a round-topped outcrop of rock, not high, but high enough to serve our purposes. Can you see it?"

Kenneth nodded.

"Good. That knoll will hold our altar. By the time you arrive on the beach, there will be a work party there from Brodick—that's where I have been staying, in the next bay to the north. The head man's name is Harkin and he is expecting you. He has an extra table for you, with trestles, for an altar. Set it up on the knoll there. All the altar cloths and vessels are aboard one of the other ships, and Bishop Formadieu will see to their disposal. But you'll need to find a site close behind the altar to hold the tocsin—" He turned to de Berenger. "Admiral, can you supply a party of ships' carpenters with rope and spars to erect a tripod for the tocsin? It might tax their skills, but we'll need the bell in place before noon."

De Berenger nodded, and Will continued his instructions to Kenneth. "I'll want your men in a perimeter around a space that's large enough to hold all our people in an orderly assembly, with room enough to stand comfortably but not to encourage movement or commingling. Define the area yourself, then mark it, sides and rear. Leave the beach end open. Post twenty of your four score sergeants on each of three sides—rear, right, and left. The score remaining, plus your score of knights, will serve as ushers. I will permit no one else to go ashore until you have marked the bounds and posted your men, but waste no time. Mass will begin as close to noon as may be. Have your people marshal the others as they come ashore." He told his brother how he wanted the men arranged in front of the altar.

"What then?"

"Then we will celebrate our first Mass as an assembled community in weeks, and I will address the brethren."

Kenneth was looking down at the massive medallion on his brother's chest, smiling again. "I've never seen one of those before, though I know what it is. But aren't you supposed to wear it *over* your mantle?"

"I am, and I will, and after today you may never see it again. Now, away with you and do what I've told you. Some of the admiral's lads will hoist you back up to your ship, and as soon as you get there your every minute will be precious."

Ropes and grappling hooks were being cast loose even before Kenneth was hauled back aboard his ship, and the forward oarsmen of the right banks were straining to push the galley's bow around and away from the other vessel, a widening gap spreading between the two craft. Normally, Will would have been watching the operations avidly, for he was endlessly fascinated by the skills of the Temple's seamen, but on this occasion he had neither time nor interest and was already scanning his lists again, allocating a degree of importance to each item and deciding upon how to proceed.

He eventually became aware of the sound of the oars pulling in unison again and looked up briefly to find himself already among the fleet, ships and galleys ranged in disciplined lines on both sides of him. The sound of ropes squealing through a pulley attracted his eye, and he watched the admiral's rigidly framed standard, the naval baucent with its skull and crossed bones on a black field, being hauled to the top of the mast. Its sighting was a signal to all ships' captains to assemble, and it had clearly been awaited, for within minutes boats were pulling towards the galley from all directions.

By the time all the captains were assembled, the stern deck was crammed with men, and de Berenger swung himself up onto the deck's rail to address them, bracing himself easily against the rigging. He waited until he had all their attention and then launched into a crisp series of succinct orders, consulting Will's list from time to time and missing nothing. He named each captain and listed his individual requirements from each one: personnel and equipment to be unloaded and shipped ashore, and the precise order, ship by ship, in which the business was to proceed. He named several senior officers from each of his galleys, none of them present there, to be delegated by their captains as quartermasters for the disembarkation, to handle the logistics of the landward exodus, and he emphasized that only a minimal crew should remain aboard each vessel when the landing was complete. When he was finished, he asked for questions and was grimly pleased when none materialized. He dismissed them all to return to their ships, then made his way, accompanied by Will, to his own cabin.

As Will followed him he saw several boatloads of Sir Kenneth's men already close to the beach, while above their heads, clearly visible on the hillside leading down towards the plateau, the contingent of cooks and workmen was struggling with the weight of the laden carts they had brought with them from Douglas's place at Brodick.

3

Noon came and went without the Mass being celebrated, but arrangements were well enough in hand by then that Will was content simply to wait in the concealment and privacy of his massive pavilion, paying close attention to the proceedings by looking through small observation slits in the pavilion's walls.

The lay brothers from the preceptory of La Rochelle had been the second party to land, following Sir Kenneth Sinclair's group, and had been working hard since they arrived. They had begun by setting up two large pavilions behind the central square, one facing the beach on the right of the altar, for use by the bishops who would conduct the ceremonies, and the other on the left, where Will now stood, for Sir William Sinclair himself as senior officer of the Order in attendance. That done, they had then erected the altar on the knoll above the beach and were still fussing around it so that now its gold and silver vessels and candlesticks stood out against the snowy white cloths and napery and the surrounding natural colors of the grassy bench above the beach, while above and behind the altar the looming shape of the tocsin, suspended from a tripod of ships' spars, added an air of even greater solemnity for the participants.

The tocsin was a symbol of the Temple that was almost as old as the Order itself, a great bronze bell taken in battle against the Seljuk Turks almost two centuries earlier and used ever since to summon the brotherhood to assemble. Its last use in battle had been at the siege of Acre, more than two decades earlier, when it had roused the rapidly dwindling garrison of the doomed fortress to face the relentless attacks of the Muslim hordes each day. It had been shipped out of the fortress to safety along with the Temple Treasure mere days before the final collapse of the stronghold and the loss of the Templars' last presence in the Holy Lands. It had lain concealed and almost forgotten since then, until it came to light in the activities surrounding the removal of the Temple Treasure from the forest of Fontainebleau before the events of October thirteenth. Now it sat high above the waters of a Scottish island, ready again to stir the hearts of the Temple brethren.

Sixty of Kenneth's people, knights and sergeants, now lined three sides of the venue; the remaining forty were meeting the incoming brethren as they came ashore and directing them to their assigned positions around the altar. The ships and galleys had almost finished disgorging their personnel now and the assembly was close to being complete. Knights from the various ships stood shoulder to shoulder in four ranks, facing the altar with their backs to the sea, and behind them were ranged the remaining members of the garrison of La Rochelle. On the left side, ranked laterally behind the cordon of Sir Kenneth's men and facing inward, stood the crews of the fleet's trading vessels, the nonmilitary mariners, while opposite them on the other side of the central space, the crews of the naval galleys stood easily, waiting for whatever might develop. The lay brethren of the former garrison of La Rochelle were formed up in a black-robed block to the right of and slightly behind the altar on the knoll.

"They're coming, Will."

Will grunted in acknowledgment, the opening chord of plain-song from the lay brothers almost drowning out Tam's comment and rendering it unnecessary. It signaled the departure of the last longboat from the fleet, with a full cargo of robed churchmen, and the chanting would continue until the three green-robed Templar bishops, Bishop Formadieu of La Rochelle senior among them, had disembarked and made their way in procession, accompanied by their cadre of canons, deacons, and subdeacons, to the altar.

He turned away and stood in silence for a spell, his chin sunk on his breast as he reviewed what he would say to the assembly when his turn came. The Mass would take precedence, as it must, and the churchmen would, as always, have the ordering of the rites, but when it came time to address the urgencies and realities of what faced the displaced community beyond this tent as a whole, Will knew that his would be the words most closely heeded, and his the voice that would be either obeyed or ignored. He pursed his lips, absently rehearsing what he would say, and his fingers toyed idly with the heavy pendant hanging at his breast, supported by the massive chain of silver links. He had laid aside his white knight's mantle for this rigidly formal occasion and now stood vested in the stark regalia of the Governing Council of his Order: black chain-mail armor surmounted and covered by a formal garment of incalculable value, an elaborately embroidered heraldic surcoat known as a tabard. It was fashioned of multiple hand-worked, coruscating layers of black upon black—beadwork and shell work of contrasting hues and textures; beadwork upon shaved sable fleece and blackened silver wire—its dark magnificence illumined by a single equal-armed cross pattée appliquéd in tiny white seashells upon the left breast, and by the heavy silver chain about Will's neck and shoulders, with its thumb-thick lozenge of red and white enameled metal. A massive shield hung from his left arm, black with a blazoned cross pattée in white at its center, and his long two-handed sword hung at his side from the black-buckled, polished leather belt slung across his chest.

He stood patiently throughout the events that followed, unseen in his pavilion and unaware that he was frowning, and remained practically motionless as the bishops and their acolytes landed on the beach and made their way in procession to the altar knoll. There they launched immediately into the celebration of the High Mass, concelebrated by the three bishops and supported by the massed voices of the choir of lay brothers, assisted by the congregation of monks. He was unaware that he stirred only three times during the entire ceremony, flexing the fingers of his right hand each time as he changed his grip upon the enormous black war helm that rested against his hip bone.

Eventually the ceremonies at the altar ended, and as the bishops and their acolytes filed off, Admiral de Berenger stepped forward to address the assembled company. As he did so, Will raised his arms and lowered the great war helmet into place on his head. The silence that greeted de Berenger's arrival was absolute and respectful, and he stood silently for several moments as his eyes roamed across the assembled throng. Finally he nodded and raised his right hand, palm forward.

"Brethren," he said, "I know you have been awaiting this moment, so I will make no attempt to delay it. Pray silence for our superior and sole representative of the Grand Master and the Governing Council of the Order of the Temple of Solomon."

He stepped back and gestured towards the large tent where Will stood waiting, and as he did so, Tam Sinclair pulled strongly on the cords that controlled the tent flaps, and Will strode through the opening to mount the knoll and stand in front of the altar, flanked on either side by the two senior knights of the chapter of La Rochelle in their formal regalia. The sound that greeted Will's appearance was more a sigh than anything else, for few among the assembly had ever actually seen the ceremonial garb worn by the members of the Governing Council, and this richly black and glossy apparition was more than most of them could have visualized. Its mere presence before them emphasized, more than anything any of them had seen before, the power represented by and vested in the organization that controlled their entire lives. The great crested helmet of shiny black steel with its towering black and white plumes concealed the identity of the man beneath the costume, but in these opening moments of the drama that was to unfold, the man within was unimportant; the embodiment of power that was the black apparition with its crested shield, its heavy chain of office, and elaborate enameled medallion was paramount.

Will waited patiently until the silence of the crowd was absolute, and then, feeling every eye focused upon him, he lowered his shield and raised his clenched fist to his left breast in a formal salute, and the entire assembly snapped to attention and returned it in a rattling roll of sound as metal struck upon metal. The senior knight on Will's left, the veteran Reynald de Pairaud, stepped forward one pace and relieved him of the heavy shield, while his companion on the right, an equally grizzled elder called Raphael de Vitune, reached out to take possession of Will's sword belt and weapons as Will released the heavy black buckles. Then, free of encumbrances, Will reached up slowly and undid the clasps securing his helm before lifting it slowly from his head and settling it in the crook of his right elbow, its rim against his hip bone once again.

"Hail, Brethren," he intoned, and "Hail, Brother," came the response. Will raised his voice. "In the name of Master de Molay, I summon you to chapter here in this fair place."

"So mote it be!"

The response was deep and sustained, and when it faded away, Will turned and waved his hand to indicate the great bronze bell that hung behind the altar. "You all know the tocsin, though few of you have ever seen it before now. For nigh on two hundred years its tone has called our brotherhood to assemble in times of dire need. Now it will sound again, here in this new land, for the first time since it left the fortress of Acre, for once again our Order's need is dire." He nodded to his brother Kenneth, who had been waiting for the signal, and two men swung a heavy log between them until its end struck the tocsin and a thunderous bronze tone crashed out and echoed across the waters of the bay, sending birds flying in fright. No one moved or spoke until its echoes had died away.

"This island is called Arran, and it will be our new home for the next while, a temporary base for our operations, extended through the good graces of Robert Bruce, King of Scots. Here we will establish ourselves as a community again, for as long as may be required of us, while we do all that we must do to discover what is happening to our Order and its brethren in France and elsewhere. Until such times as we discover the truth and the effect it will have upon our future, we will conduct ourselves here exactly as though we were in our community in La Rochelle … save that we will have to build ourselves a home before we can enjoy it."

He swept his eyes from side to side, watching the reactions among his listeners and gauging their temper. Most, he could see, were calm, almost fatalistic, waiting to see what would come next, but there were others who looked angry and others yet who looked merely perplexed. He raised his hand high and waited for silence again.

"I know that most of you know little of what happened back in La Rochelle on the day we left, and while we have been at sea there has been no opportunity to tell you what occurred or why. And thus you have been unable to distinguish truth from rumor or from wild imaginings. I intend now to tell you what we know, though even we, your senior officers, have had to bolster the little knowledge we have with intelligently formed opinions and theories. For the time being, here is the gist of what we know …"

For the quarter hour that followed, Will held his audience rapt as he related everything he knew of the events of Friday, October thirteenth, including his summons to Paris by Master de Molay, the Master's doubts about the veracity of the warnings he had received, and the struggle de Molay had had with his own conscience in deliberating whether to break his solemn vow of loyalty to the Pope for the future welfare of the Order. He spoke, too, with clarity and openness about his own reactions to de Molay's tidings, and about the uncertainties he had experienced thereafter, despite knowing that the Master himself was acting against his own instincts and solely in the best interests of the Order. He also told them about his brother's mission to assemble one hundred men in secrecy and then lead them, in great secrecy, to collect the Order's Treasure from its hiding place in the caverns of the great forest of Fontainebleau and transport it to the coast.

His listeners knew of the success of that venture, of course, for they themselves had picked the Treasure up and stowed it safely aboard their ships, but Will saw the benefit of permitting them to tie themselves into the arrangements that had been made to survive in the face of the French King's duplicity; it would do no harm, he knew, to encourage them to believe that, even unwittingly, they had each been a part of the operation to ensure their Order's survival.

When he had finished, he stood facing them for several moments, half expecting that someone would dare to ask a question, but the discipline of two centuries held strong and no man spoke. Finally Will nodded and took one step back, extending an arm to where Tam Sinclair stood behind his left shoulder, a package ready in his hand. Will hefted it twice before tightening his grip and raising it in both hands. It was a large wallet of leather, evidently of solid weight, its bulk approaching a foot in length and breadth, by half as much in depth, and he brandished it high, turning from side to side so that everyone could see its solid substance.

"What happens now?" His voice rang out clearly. "Every man of you out there is asking yourself the same question, are you not? What happens now? What do we do next? Where do we go from this point forward?" He turned again as he shouted out each question, shaking the wallet above his head so that every eye in the assembly was fixed on it, and when he had finished asking, he lowered his arms and tucked the package beneath his left arm.

"Well, now I will make a start on answering those questions for you, and the answer to the first question, *What happens now?* is that we *eat!*" He waited for the storm of cheering to subside. "The cooks whose work you smell now behind us are sent to feed us by Sir James Douglas, guardian of this island and deputy of Robert, King of Scots, our host in days ahead."

The men cheered again, for they had been aboard ship for weeks and the prospect of fresh-cooked meat must have been the stuff of fantasy to them since they left France. As the noise began to subside Will raised his arm again, the wallet firmly clutched in his hand. He had judged his timing perfectly and the crowd fell silent again, poised for his next words.

"As to what happens next, we have guidance here, inside this wallet. Look you now." He lowered his arm and loosened the buckled straps binding the pouch, extracting a heavy bundle as large as the container itself. "I have here a package of documents sent under the seal of our Grand Master himself, Sir Jacques de Molay. Inside it are Master de Molay's instructions for our conduct from this time forth, entrusted to me, on your behalf, on the occasion when I saw him last. I call now upon the senior knight here, Sir Reynald de Pairaud of the former garrison of La Rochelle, to examine the seal and to attest that it is, in fact, the seal of our Grand Master and that it is intact and undisturbed."

He stood with his arms extended, holding the bundle in both hands until the veteran knight had turned and examined the seal on the documents, nodding his head profoundly and bowing from the waist, pronouncing himself satisfied that the seal was intact. Only then did Will return the package to Tam Sinclair and raise his voice to the assembly again.

"And so for the remainder of this day we will feast and give thanks for our deliverance, and tomorrow our senior brethren will convene for their first chapter meeting here in our new home. Therein, they will examine the instructions from our Master and will decide, in commune, what must be done henceforth to concur with the wishes of the Council as expressed therein.

"In the meantime, there will be much to do for all the rest of us, I promise you, for we are greatly exposed and at risk here on this open beach, and we shall remain so until we have secured our foothold. Go then in peace, all of you, and set about the task of becoming a devout community again after so long a disruption of our way of life. Our friends from Brodick will summon you to the tables when it comes time to eat, and I suspect you might be ready to attend when that occurs. Go with God."

As the assembly began to break up, Will nodded his thanks to the two veteran knights who had assisted him and turned back to his pavilion, aware that Tam Sinclair, who still clutched the wallet with its sealed package, was watching him closely.

"What is it?" he asked as soon as they were inside and the tent flaps were closed behind them. "Did I forget something?"

"No," Tam growled. "Nothing except the women. You've left them stuck aboard ship all day while everyone else was allowed to go ashore. Can I invite them to come ashore now and eat on land, or will I have something sent to them?"

"Damnation, I had forgotten about them." Will frowned, quickly rejecting the possibility, tempting as it was, of keeping the three women aboard ship. He made a grunting sound, part disgust and part denial. "Aye, go ahead and bring them ashore. Our business for the day is largely done. But see you set them well apart from the brethren. I have enough difficulties to face in dealing with men too long away from the discipline of the Rule. I see no point in adding to them by parading women where they can be seen and talked about. Keep them hidden, Tam."

4

While all the knightly Templar rigmarole had been going on ashore, Jessie Randolph had been far from unhappy. She had, in fact, been rejoicing in the freedom to set aside her role as Baroness St. Valéry for the first time since leaving La Rochelle, and to make and enjoy a more thorough and extensive toilette than she would formerly have believed possible aboard a Temple galley. That she could do so at all, of course, was the result of the complete absence of Templar personnel aboard the ship for the duration of the shore-based ceremonies. Every man in the expedition, it appeared, was crowding onto the beach in front of the rows of ships anchored in the bay, and all of them had their backs to her, their entire attention taken up by whatever was unfolding in front of them. Jessie could hear the massed voices of the Temple monks raised in ritualistic chant, and she knew that there would be no swift return to the ships for anyone on the beach that day. And as that awareness dawned on her, she recognized her opportunity and made a decision that would have greatly shocked the brethren assembled ashore, could any of them have known of it.

Calling her two women to attend on her, she ordered them to have the few crew members remaining on the galley start heating water for a bath for her, using the craft's cooking fires. And then, glorying in the almost total absence of men, she took possession of the great cabin for her own needs, laying out her entire wardrobe, scant though it was, for examination and repairs. Thereafter, while the solemn and secretive rituals of the Temple were carried out on the beach, the far less solemn but no less secretive rituals of womanhood were observed and celebrated by Jessie and her two women, Marie and Janette, so that by the time the solemnities on land were concluded and the first men began to head for the cooking fires in search of food, the three women were ready to join them, newly bathed, coiffed, groomed, and attired, and feeling cleaner, fresher, and more attractive than they had since the beginnings of this venture.

"Wait!" she called to Tam mere moments after landing from the boat.

Tam stopped and looked back at her, waiting. Accompanied by two of the oarsmen from the boat who were now carrying the women's baggage, he had been leading them obliquely towards the far edge of the main assembly.

"So, we women are to sit farthest from everything, behind the clowns and jesters, behind the harpists and jongleurs, even behind the camp followers and mendicants, were any such here? We are to be fed last, with cold food? Where is Sir William? I really must offer him my thanks and appreciation for such consideration."

Tam knew Jessie well enough by then to ignore her tone of voice, and he responded as though she had merely made a passing comment. "Your food will no' be cold, my lady. I'll see to it mysel'. I made arrangements for it to be served and covered and set aside before I left to fetch you. And before you say anything more, I told them to wait an hour before doing anything, so they should just be about ready to look to it now." He pointed off in the direction they were heading. "See, Mungo's ower there, waiting for us. I don't think you'll ha'e met him yet, but he's a good man, born and bred in these parts. He's dour, and he doesna say much, but ye'll like him. He'll have a fire built by now, and fresh wood to hand to keep it going. We'll get you seated and comfortable, wi' a good fire, and then I'll go and bring your food back … with wine, the yellow kind you like, from Anjou. Now come away and let's get you settled, or none of us will ever get to eat. And when you've finished dining, why then ye may go and find Will Sinclair and thank him yourself … as long as I'm no' there."

A short time later, he had made them as comfortable as they could be on an open heath above a beach, and the taciturn Mungo was piling the fire high with well-seasoned driftwood. When both men were ready to leave, Jessie thanked them courteously, then watched them as they quickly vanished among the crowds of men up ahead.

Before Tam returned, she became aware of a commotion among the crowd and stood up to see what was happening, but even on tiptoe, standing on the highest stone around, she could see nothing beyond the packed mass of men ahead of her. She dispatched Janette to find out what was happening, and the servant soon returned, shaking her head.

"I do not know what has happened, madam. A ship arrived, it seems, from the north, but no one knows whence it came or to whom it belongs."

Moments later, against the darkening skies of the late-November afternoon, Jessie saw Tam, Mungo, and another man returning towards them, each carrying a covered, flat-bottomed bundle that proved to be boards holding food and drink in sufficient amounts to feed all six of them, men and women. There were platters of succulent, thickly sliced lamb and goat, bowls of diced savory turnip, and dishes of boiled green leafy vegetables, along with fresh-baked crusty bread served with wild honey and unsweetened oat cakes with hard, tangy goat cheese. After weeks at sea and the scant, uninspiring food associated with long sea journeys, this was a royal feast, and Jessie and her women paid it the homage it merited, matching even Tam and Mungo in their voracity and making no attempt to speak until their appetites had been sated. Eventually, however, Jessie pushed a rind of cheese away with her fingertips and held her hands up in front of her, fingers spread.

"That was sinfully good, Tam. Well done."

Tam grunted, then used a fingernail to pick a morsel from between his teeth before he answered. "Don't thank me, my lady. I but brought it here. It came wi' the blessings o' the island's quartermaster, who takes his instructions from the Douglas. Sir William made the arrangements for it last night, while he was with the garrison at Brodick, whence he came this morning."

"Then I shall thank the quartermaster if I ever meet him. But speaking of garrisons, someone said a new ship had arrived. Do you know anything of that?"

"Aye." Tam swept some scraps from his wooden platter into the fire, then placed the platter by his feet. "It was a galley. Highlanders from the north. Mungo said it bore the standard of MacDonald.

I didna see it myself. But whoever landed from it came ashore wi' banners flying ... blue and white banners, so it might have been the Douglas himself."

"Might have been? Are you not sure?"

Tam looked at her reproachfully. "No, Lady, I am not sure. I can think of five noble houses whose colors are blue and white, or white and blue. Douglas is but one of those, though he's the likeliest to be here in person, seeing that he holds the island at the King's pleasure."

"What does that mean?"

"He is in charge here in Arran."

"Who is this man?"

"A personal friend of the King. The two are close, I'm told."

"Then I must meet him, as soon as may be. He is the one will know where to find King Robert."

Tam hesitated, on the point of telling the Baroness that King Robert already knew about her gift, but then he decided to hold his tongue. This was none of his affair, he knew, and he would earn no gratitude from either Will or her ladyship by admitting any knowledge of what was going on. He merely dipped his head. "Of course, my lady," he said. "That should present ye with no difficulty, providing that this *was* the Douglas who sailed in ... As I said, I didna see him. But if he's here, you'll doubtless find him wi' Sir William."

"So be it. Let us find him with Sir William, then." Jessie rose to her feet, gazing with narrowed eyes towards the spot where she imagined Sir William Sinclair and his noble guest might be found.

5

Will Sinclair, stripped of his ceremonial finery and wearing his white knight's mantle again, had finished his dinner and was deep in conversation with Sir Reynald de Pairaud, a personality with whom Will knew he would have to deal very carefully during these first days on Arran. De Pairaud was widely known—although *assumed* would probably have been more accurate, Will decided—to have powerful connections within the Order's hierarchy. His brother, the redoubtable Sir Hugh de Pairaud, had been one of the highest-ranked members of the Governing Council, holding the positions of both Treasurer of the Temple and Visitor of the Priory of France, and had presumably been arrested with his fellow Council members in October.

Will knew, and presumed that de Pairaud must know, too, that any influence the veteran knight might once have had was now moot, set at naught by the removal of his brother. But he knew, too, that among the other knights the perception of de Pairaud's influence remained, and might conceivably be used to channel resistance to the changes Will would suggest in the coming days. It was in de Pairaud's nature to resist change of any kind, to maintain with stubborn, mindless ferocity that continuity equated to tradition and inherent rightness. It went without saying that he would be loud and self-righteous in his condemnation of the changes that Will was about to implement, involving, as they did, some of the most cherished shibboleths of the ultra-conservative group known as the Temple Boars, which included de Pairaud among its stubborn, headstrong number. Will was deter- mined nonetheless to attempt to lessen the older man's resistance through simple courtesy, and he was trying hard to remain amiable in the face of the other's humorlessness.

He had just fallen silent, having failed to engage Sir Reynald in a discussion of new beginnings and the opportunity for change, when he looked up to see men standing on their toes all about him, straining to see towards the bay beyond the beach. He heard raised voices, too, loudly wondering what they were looking at and who this newcomer might be. He rose quickly and easily to his feet. Even standing, though, he could see nothing, and so he made his way through the crowd to the top of the gradient on his left, growling to the people there ahead of him to make way and give him room.

Below him, its mast and rigging limned by the fast-setting sun, and rapidly approaching the shelving shoreline, a great galley was hurtling forward, plainly about to drive itself ashore, but even as he saw it and began to marvel at its suicidal speed, its rowers shipped oars as one, raising their long sweeps vertically in a concerted movement that demonstrated long and uncountable hours of practice. Then, under the propulsion of that last, hard, precisely executed stroke, the ship glided forward, its speed bleeding away rapidly as it nosed towards the shingled strand and came to rest exactly where its captain had wished to place it—far enough on land for its passengers to leap down safely and dry shod from the prow, yet sufficiently afloat for its rowers to be able to pull it free again without great difficulty. It was a superbly executed maneuver, and Will responded to it as he did to any example of demonstrated excellence, fighting the urge to applaud.

He had already recognized the slim figure of Sir James Douglas by then, clearly identifiable by the bright blue, white-striped sash that crossed his breast beneath the paler blue covering of his cloak. Douglas was helmed and armored, standing alone in the prow of the grounded vessel despite being surrounded by others, and as Will watched, the first members of the incoming group leapt out and down, to land softly and dry shod as expected before stepping out of the way of those who followed. Will counted three men dressed in white tunics bearing the device of a black galley on their chests, and two of those carried the bagpipes so beloved of the Highland Gaels, while the third held a long pole bearing a banner with the same emblem, the black galley on a field of white that he knew to be the standard of MacDonald. The two pipers inflated their bags immediately and began to play, sustaining their melody as the remainder of the landing party jumped down after them. Two of the last ones bore the standard of the house of Douglas, in blue and white, while the remaining eight, plain men-at-arms, wore simple chain mail over padded leather tunics. Douglas himself jumped down last, and the MacDonald standard-bearer began leading him up from the beach, followed by the two pipers, to where Sir William Sinclair, having climbed down from his high viewpoint and away from the crowd, awaited them.

Since they had no hope of making themselves heard over the noise of the pipes, both men exchanged nods when they met, then stood smiling and waited for the tune to end. When it did, the strange, wailing music falling away with unexpected swiftness into a final, dying bleat, both were aware of the silent throng surrounding them, waiting for them to speak. Will moved first, nodding to the younger man and greeting him quietly in the Scots tongue.

"Good day to you, Sir James, although the day appears to have gone already. Welcome to our camp, temporary as it is."

"Aye, my thanks." Douglas nodded in return, grinning slightly, then lifted the heavy metal helmet from his head and tossed it to one of his men, before pulling a soft cloth cap with an affixed blackcock feather from under his cloak where it had been folded over his shoulder. He tugged it onto his head, adjusting it until it felt comfortable, then swung away to look back over his left shoulder at the fleet ranged in the bay. "I am impressed, I must say. You told us you had a fleet with you, but I had pictured nothing this grand. It gives you … a certain presence, shall we say?" He turned back, his eyes scanning the crowd around them. "The admiral is not here?"

"Oh, he is here … simply not *here*, if you take my meaning. He ate with me, but left some time ago to speak with some of his captains, now that they have all filled their bellies and are capable of speaking without pleading to be fed. Do you require to speak with him?"

"No, I was merely curious. And what of my people from Brodick? Are any of them here in your camp?"

Will shook his head, surprised by the question. "No, none at all. We have been about our own affairs all day, coming ashore and finding our land legs, then rededicating ourselves to our Order and our way of life." He shrugged his shoulders. "Knowing it would be thus, therefore, I invited no one from among your captains. Of course, the exceptions are the men you can see behind the fires—the cooks and scullions who prepared the food—and incidentally on that matter, our thanks to you for that service are heartfelt."

He switched smoothly into French and raised his voice for the benefit of the Templars standing all around them.

"Brethren, my friend here is Sir James Douglas, Guardian of this Island of Arran in the name of Robert, King of Scots. Sir James is the man responsible for providing the food on which we have just dined this day, and the cooks who prepared it for us, so it would be meet to offer him thanks." His last words were drowned out by a concerted roar, and when it died away Will raised a hand to recapture their attention. "If any of you speak the Scots tongue, you will already have heard me welcome Sir James to our temporary encampment. I would like to promise him now that by the time he visits us again, he will not have to sit on the rocks of the beach to talk with me." That earned a shout of laughter. "In the meantime, though, he and I have matters of some delicacy to discuss, so if you will permit us, I should like to take him up to my pavilion and speak with him there. Remain you where you are and continue to enjoy yourselves for a while. But get you then to your beds. Our new lives will begin right here on this beach tomorrow with Matins, hours before the sun rolls around to shine on us again. Come, Sir James."

He ignored the chorus of groans stirred up by his last announcement and led the Douglas chief away, followed by his escorting party. He took them along the shelf above the beach, to where his large pavilion had been erected earlier that day. They walked in silence, because of the need to watch their footing in the dark on the uneven ground, and as they went Will wondered what had brought the Douglas here at this particular time, and aboard a galley.

Even in his absence, it was clear that someone had plainly had an eye to his welfare for the evening, for Will could see the glow of a bright fire inside the pavilion from a long way distant, and the intensity of the light told him it was burning in a brazier on the stone slab at the center of the tent.

"That fire is going to feel good," Douglas remarked, but Will stumbled then, misjudging a step, and the jarring impact drove the breath from his lungs, so that he made no further attempt to speak until he and Douglas were safely inside the pavilion. They handed their heavy cloaks to a waiting lay brother and made their way directly to stand on either side of the blazing brazier, hands outstretched to the heat. Douglas's men-at-arms had melted away silently as they approached the great tent, distributed themselves around the outside of it, and although Will had said nothing at that time, he was curious enough to speak of it now.

"Why the escort, today of all days, and here in front of all my men?" He grinned, taking the sting out of what he was saying. "I warrant you, if we wished to harm you or molest you, there are sufficient of us to overcome your eight guards without a deal of trouble."

"You think so? There's only a few hundred of you, and you're all French at that, so don't be too cocksure." He paused then, and when he spoke again all humor had been set aside. "The guards are an official escort, Will, just in case of need, and nothing to do with you or yours. I came to bring you a gift."

Will looked at the young Scots chief in surprise. "Gifts are always welcome, my friend, but what kind of need would require you to keep guards at hand here, among your own folk?"

Douglas shrugged. "Dire need, if only on occasion, and always unpredictable. I have come here directly from the north end of the island. I remembered that your fleet was to put in today and so I thought to find you among them. I was right, and I am glad."

"You came seeking me directly? Why?"

"To offer thanks for your keen sight."

Will shook his head. "I have no idea what you are talking about."

"Your keen insight, perhaps I should say. Remember the long-eared fellow with the need to eavesdrop on French conversations? Well, I set two of my men to watching him and he left here that same night, in something of a hurry, but fortunately unaware that he was being watched. One of my men followed him while the other waited for me. He headed northeast, across the hills and through the mountain glens, clearly headed for Lochranza, since there is nowhere else up there. It was difficult to follow him though, without being seen— that is empty country up there—but we had ample grounds for suspecting him of deviltry and so we picked him up that afternoon and asked him a few questions."

Will was well aware of the euphemism, but when Douglas showed no signs of continuing, Will asked him outright. "And what did you discover from your … questions?"

"That you had detected a plot … against the King, as all such plottings are."

"And this fellow was the ringleader?"

"God's blood no! He was but a messenger—an observer and a spy. He was on his way to his master with tidings of the arrival of a large body of French soldiery in Arran."

"So who was his master, did you find out?"

"MacDougall of Lorn. The old chief's son, Lame John himself. Nothing surprising there, the dastard being who and what he is, but what *was* surprising was the next piece of information our songbird spat out, concerning his most recent employer. It transpires that Menteith himself, our beloved and much-trusted hereditary chieftain of Arran, has made alliance with MacDougall, upon the understanding that he will be given the rule of both Arran *and* Kintyre once the Bruce is dead and the MacDonald upstarts crushed. More fool him for believing any word from Lame John's mouth, but the deed was done, the alliance made, and now he himself has been betrayed and his fate is sealed. Menteith will see no mercy from our King for this piece of treachery, I'll warrant you. There have been too many like matters, and far too many foresworn traitors set free to rebel again."

Will felt his chest constrict in dismay, thinking about the slightly built chieftain of Menteith, whom he had found to be pleasant and unassuming. If that innocuous little man could be a traitor, he realized, then anyone could. He grunted. "So where is Menteith now? What have you done with him?"

"Nothing. He still sits in Brodick, unknowing that his bolt is shot before ever he had a chance to raise a hand. I told you, I came straight here from the north. There was a MacDonald galley in the bay beneath the western moor, and we were able to use it, since its captain was already on his way here to Brodick. We came around the north coast of the island, checking for skulking MacDougalls among the bays and inlets, then made our way directly here. Our next move will be to put into Brodick, where we'll arrest Menteith and keep him under guard until the King can deal with him. That is why I travel with an escort this day. We did not know where we might find

Menteith, nor did we know who might attempt to defend him when we arrest him. Thus my men-at-arms, and thus, too, my gift to you, well earned."

"What gift to me?"

"Lochranza, man! Menteith's stronghold. Did you not say you would need a solid base here on the island? Well, now you have one. Lochranza is yours, from this time on, to use as you see fit. God knows Menteith will have no further use for it. Its castle is solid stone, easily defended, and it has the best sheltered harbor on the entire island, apart from this bay. Your galleys will be able to lie there unseen from any but the closest approaches, and there's ample room in the castle and the land beyond it for your men. More than that, there is probably ample grazing for half of your horses, too, in the glens between the mountains—they're lush and well watered. You'll have the high mountains at your back and the sea lanes at your feet. You could do far worse. And from my point of view, of course, the castle could be in far worse hands than yours. Sitting empty, in fact, it could be a drain and a curse. But now you will use it for your Order's purposes, and while you are about that, you will defend it for me and the King, thereby relieving me of the need to worry over it. *Quid pro quo*. It's perfect."

Will, open mouthed with astonishment, was thinking exactly the same thing, but he never had the chance to say so, for there came the sound of female voices approaching outside the pavilion, followed by male voices raised in challenge and response. And then the secondary, curtained entrance to the body of the tent was pulled open and Tam Sinclair stepped in, looking decidedly put out.

"Sir William," he growled, making no attempt to be polite or amiable. "The Baroness St. Valéry wants to speak to you, and she winna take no for an answer, so I have brought her." And with that, he turned on his heel and stalked away, letting the curtain fall behind him.

Will and Douglas stood staring at each other as a silence fell abruptly beyond the curtained doorway. Neither man made any attempt to move, each of them wondering, for different reasons, what would happen next, and then came a discreet cough and the fabric of the heavy curtain swayed as someone groped at it, then pulled it aside. Jessica Randolph, Baroness St. Valéry, stood there alone, staring at the two knights who stood watching her warily.

"My lady Baroness," Will greeted her, after what felt to him like an age of gawping at her like some foolish boy. He pulled himself up straighter until he began to feel ridiculous, then waved a hand limply towards the young man across the fire from him. "You will not yet have met Sir James Douglas, I think …"

Douglas's face broke into a delighted smile as he swept off his bonnet with a flourish and bowed deeply from the waist in the grand manner he had learned during his boyhood sojourn in Paris, and because of that he failed to see the astonished widening of Jessie Randolph's eyes as she heard the flawless French of his greeting.

"Madame la Baronne de St. Valéry," he said, head down, pointing his toe and sweeping the blackcock feather in his cap along the floor at arm's length. "I am honored and delighted to meet you, for I have heard much of you and yours." He straightened up and looked her straight in the eye. "I knew your brother Sir Thomas, by repute, as did all of Scotland. I never had the honor of meeting him, but my father held him always in the highest regard. I am familiar, too, with the name of your late husband, the Baron St. Valéry, for he ranked high in the esteem of Master William Lamberton, my Lord Archbishop of St. Andrews, who was my patron and protector during my stay in France. I have heard the Archbishop speak admiringly, on several occasions, of your late husband's exploits and achievements as agent general of King Philip to the court of England."

Jessie merely nodded in response to that, acknowledging his courtesy and marveling at the self-possession he displayed for one so young, but she continued to study him, trying to take his true measure as he continued. "I understand from Sir William that you have not set foot in Scotland for some time, so may I say that I am delighted that you should be guided to this isle of Arran as your landing place, and use my status as its guardian to extend the warm and willing welcome of my liege lord Robert, King of Scots?"

God's blood, did he say guardian? The legal King's Guardian of this isle? He's but a laddie.

Jessie felt herself frowning severely, the wind of her self-righteousness snatched completely from her sails. She had practically forced her way into this pavilion, bullying Tam Sinclair mercilessly until he threw up his hands and yielded to her determination, and she had hesitated only once, very briefly, before pulling back the shielding curtain between the entranceway and the interior of the great tent, prepared to confront the redoubtable and intolerant Sir William Sinclair and to demand the recognition and the consideration that she believed her sumptuous and voluntary gift to the King of Scots had earned for her. She had entered the arena fully prepared for battle, her mind filled with imaginings and visions of what she would say to him, and he to her, when she vented her righteous anger at him over his treatment of her and her women. The very last thing she had expected was the sheepish, guilt-tinged, almost shame-faced diffidence of Sinclair's greeting, and the unforeseen presence of the very young and distinguished-looking nobleman now addressing her merely added to her confusion and rendered her speechless.

Who was this popinjay, she wondered now, and whence had he sprung? Douglas was a common enough name in southern Scotland, but it held no great resonance for her. There had been a notorious Douglas in southern parts when she was first married, she remembered, a hothead and a rebel who had been imprisoned in England for his crimes. Could this man be a relative? Certainly, if the young fellow was as important as he clearly appeared to be, and judging by Sinclair's deference to him she was prepared to accept that he was, then it would not do to offend him. And so Jessie bit back the snappish retort that had sprung to her lips and instead inclined her head graciously, summoning a smile, though a small one, from somewhere deep inside her and speaking gently and decorously.

"Thank you, my lord … Douglas, is it? You are most civil."

"Some people attract civility without effort, my lady." The young man smiled and bowed again, less deeply this time. "James Douglas of Douglasdale, but no lord. The lordship was held by my late father,

Sir William Douglas, and is now gripped jealously by the English, who maintain that my father died a rebel and a traitor. My opinion differs from theirs, as does all of Scotland's, but Castle Douglas, my family home, with all its people, now lies in the hands of Sir William Clifford, one of England's so-called governors in Scotland." He shrugged, still smiling faintly. "It will not always be thus, but for the time being it is and there is nothing to be done for it."

Jessie had been watching him closely as he spoke, her eyes absorbing every nuance she could discern of his character and personality. Her initial anger and irritation now abated, she could see that he had much, on the surface at least, to recommend him, beginning with the cleanly brushed tumble of glossy black hair that hung, unusually long, to his wide shoulders. His face, long and wide jawed, clean shaven and angular, could not, she thought, be called handsome in the classical sense, because his eyes, deep set beneath black brows, were slightly too close together. But they were large and wide nonetheless, the irises dark enough to appear black, and the whites were clear and healthy, almost blue tinged in their purity. They would, she decided, have been perfectly beautiful had it not been for that single, discernible lack of space, a mere hair's breadth, on either side of the long, bony nose that dominated the rest of his face. His mouth was wide and mobile, and his teeth, thanks to his youth and good health, were even and brilliantly white, showing up starkly against the naturally saturnine color of his skin. He wore a blue tunic over blue trews of a different hue, and a long, heavy blue and white cloak, thrown back from his shoulders, hung to his ankles. His feet and lower legs were sturdily booted, and a long, serviceable sword hung from a belt across his chest. All in all, she decided, he looked ingratiating: young and vibrantly pleasant and enthusiastic; fit, friendly, open countenanced, self-confident and well put together … he would make a fine and worthwhile mate for some enterprising young woman in the not too distant future.

Having catalogued the young man in the space of a few heartbeats, Jessie now favored him with her most charming smile. "Plain knight or belted lord, Sir James, you are clearly a man of distinction, and I thank you for your courtesy." She then turned her attention to Will Sinclair, who had been hovering uncomfortably at the edge of her vision.

"Forgive me for interrupting you in conference, Sir William, but since I have heard nothing from you for several days on the matter of the gift I bear for the King of Scots—you have clearly had other matters on your mind since arriving here in Arran—I thought it might be to the benefit of everyone concerned were I to press my own urgencies and make arrangements to have myself and my women, along with the King's gift, transferred from here to the mainland, where I will doubtless have a far greater chance of finding King Robert than seems possible here on this island."

Will stood bemused for a few moments, gazing blankly back at her, but then his eyes widened and he stood up straighter, stung by her air of haughtiness. "Really, madam," he answered, his voice devoid of any attempt at pleasantness. "Instruct me then, if you will. How, precisely, would you achieve that, on this island, and what steps would you take to protect yourself and your women, not to mention the treasure you carry? Where would you find trustworthy men to accompany you from here, knowing that all *my* men are bound by sacred oath to the service of the Temple and may not leave without permission?"

Jessie was incensed by his careless mention of the treasure when she had been at pains to speak of it only as a gift, and her anger came through in her reply.

"It was in my mind that you might see fit to provide a suitable escort for us from among your men, sir." Her voice, too, was cold, her tone contemptuous, and that fanned the flames of Will's own irritation.

"As it was in mine, madam," he snapped. "And ever has been, since the day we left La Rochelle. But the choice of time and suitability is also mine, and dependent upon the conclusion of my duties and responsibilities to the Temple. Those criteria are not to be abandoned at the whim of anyone outside the Temple Order."

Douglas was standing open mouthed, dismayed by Will's hostility and searching for a cause. This was the first time in his dealings with the Templar knight that he had perceived him as being anything less than utterly self-possessed and amiable, although he did not doubt that Sir William Sinclair could be a martinet when that was called for. On this occasion, however, Sinclair was being rude and boorish to the St. Valéry woman without provocation. Douglas could see no reason for such truculence, and he looked from one to the other of them as they spoke. It took him some time, nevertheless, to realize that it was Sinclair who was losing this confrontation, despite all his hectoring and his offended dignity.

"If I may make a suggestion," Douglas said, smiling, "I may have the perfect solution to both your problems." Both of them turned to glare at him, and he broadened his smile and waved towards a nearby table. "Come," he said. "It is a cold November evening, growing colder by the minute, and this has been a long day, for me at least. My lady, I am about to set sail—tomorrow, in fact—to join King Robert, and he has already expressed a wish to greet you and express his gratitude for your timely and much-needed gift. Nothing would be more simple than for me to take you, your ladies, and your treasure with me. So why should we not sit down here by the fire in friendship—I will pull up some chairs—and discuss how and when this arrangement may be made?"

Jessie barely heard his last words, all her attention focused upon what he had said about the King's gratitude. Her brow wrinkled, but as the only explanation of what he had said became clear to her she nodded, grim faced. Slowly then, her entire body stiff with outrage, she looked across at Sinclair and spoke in words that dripped withering sarcasm. "The King has expressed a wish to meet me and thank me for my gift? How can this be possible, sir? I am but newly arrived, so how can the King already know of my coming and the gift I bring? Who might have told him? Can you tell me that?"

A deep red flush suffused Sir William's cheeks as he realized how he had been made to look. His hand fluttered and he attempted to speak but nothing came out, and the look of sheer gratitude on his face when James Douglas intervened again might have been laughable at another time.

"My lady," Douglas interjected, reclaiming Jessie's attention, albeit unwillingly. "My lady, forgive me, but King Robert was already here on Arran when Sir William arrived. His Grace remained for less than a day, having pressing matters of state that demanded his royal presence elsewhere, but while he was here, he took time to meet with Sir William on the matters underlying the arrival of the Temple fleet here in Scotland. I was present at that meeting, and in the course of it, the matter of your presence among the fleet, your escape from France, and your generous gift emerged. Sir William spoke of it in good faith, unaware that by the time you arrived in person from your anchorage off Kintyre, His Grace must be gone, about the business of the realm.

"King Robert left last night, and you arrived this morning. But in the here and now I am to follow him immediately, as I have said, though by another route, and I will be happy to escort you to wherever you might wish to go." He laughed, waving one hand airily. "So be it, of course, that we remain well clear of any Englishry who might seek to throw me into a dungeon for my sins. But steer you safely home we will, and with great pleasure. In the meantime, though, my lady, you must not be angry at Sir William. I see your displeasure clearly, but William Sinclair did not betray your trust, nor did he demean your gift. He had no choice in this matter, and he acted honorably, as ever, with great care for your name and reputation."

Jessie could not but be mollified by such an explanation, and she looked from Douglas to Sinclair, standing close beside her. She tilted her head to one side, well aware that he was waiting for her response although he could not bring himself to look at her, and she nodded once, and then again more slowly.

"So be it, then. I accept your explanation, Sir James, and I thank you for it. Sir William Sinclair, I fear I may have wronged you, in this at least." Then, accepting that he might be absolutely incapable of looking at her, she reached out and prodded his forearm gently with the tip of one finger. "Will you forgive me, Sir William?"

Will stood stock-still, fighting an overwhelming urge to lean towards her, more aware of her proximity than he had ever been of anything else he could remember in his life. The warmth of her physical closeness in the radiant glow of the fire's light was a palpable thing, making him want to reach out and touch her, and the sweetness of her body's haunting perfume filled his nostrils and even his mouth, making his head swim. He knew he had to answer her, and he wanted to respond graciously, but his senses were awash with sensuous and guilty pleasure and he could not collect himself sufficiently to answer her directly. And presently the silence, brief as it was, had stretched to the point where even young Douglas became aware of it.

"Sir William?" he inquired, and Will drew himself erect, forcing himself to address the moment.

"Forgive me, Baroness," he muttered, in what amounted to a growl, glancing sideways at Jessie and hearing the slurred quality of his own words, "I was ... woolgathering, my thoughts far from here ... I beg your pardon. Something you said ... I know not what now, reminded me of my sister Peggy ..." He drew in a great breath and spoke again with more strength and conviction. "As for what you may have thought about my conduct, think no more on it, for it was understandable, given what happened. I merely regret that I could not bring you to the presence of King Robert, to make your own presentation to him." Somehow, he found the strength to enable him to turn his head and look her straight in the eye, and he spoke now with absolute conviction. "I swear, though, that had you been here to witness his receipt of your tidings, you would have been much gratified. He was deeply moved and greatly honored by the *substance* of your decision to do what you have done, and by your devotion and loyalty, supporting him so openly and generously. That much I heard him say, and in those words, and I had no doubt of his sincerity."

Jessie was gazing at him in surprise, for this was the most she had heard him say in one breath since the occasion of their first meeting in La Rochelle, when he had been talking to his equals in the Order. But even in her astonishment, she saw that he was on the point of swinging away from her again, impatient with her scrutiny, and so she spun quickly, before he could move, and spoke again to Sir James Douglas.

"In that case, Sir James, I will accept both of your offers ... a seat by the fire *and* safe transport. Pull up those chairs, if you will, and let us talk of what must be done and how it can be achieved."

WITHIN THE FOLLOWING QUARTER HOUR, everything needful had been arranged to the satisfaction of all three participants. Will would arrange for the Baroness's belongings, including the chests destined for the royal treasury, to be transferred the next day from Admiral de Berenger's galley to the craft now commanded by Vice-Admiral de Narremat, which would be placed at the disposal of Sir James for the month to come. The procedure would be both straightforward and complicated, Douglas suspected, requiring each of the two great galleys to be warped, in its turn, close up to the single small quay in the bay below the castle at Brodick, the first to unload its valuable cargo from its holds onto the wharf, and the second to reload it safely in its own hold. When the Baroness asked why it should be so difficult, it was Will who answered her, pointing out that the sheer weight of the bullion chests made it too dangerous to attempt the transfer from hold to hold on open water using ropes and pulleys. A single slip, he pointed out, could lose a chest forever and might easily damage, or even maim, a ship.

While the transfer was taking place, Douglas, for his part, would delegate a handpicked crew of his most capable and trustworthy men to act as escorts and bodyguards to Jessie and her women until they were safely lodged within the security of her own family lands, for he and they would probably have to part company as soon as they made landfall on the mainland of Scotland, dependent, of course, upon whatever concentration of English soldiery and military readiness they found nearby upon landing.

Will had made but little contribution to this discussion aside from his comments on the weight of the treasure. He was content to leave it to the other two, who were more closely involved than he, to work out the details. He merely listened and nodded his agreement from time to time, staring steadily into the fire for the most part in order to avoid looking at Jessie Randolph, for although he had grown inured, to a minor degree, to dealing with Baroness St. Valéry on a surface level, it was her disconcerting alter ego, the mercurial Jessie, who confounded him and set his pulse racing while his chest constricted and butterflies of tension fluttered beneath his ribs.

When their conversation lapsed eventually, all arrangements concluded, they sat silent for a while, enjoying the soporific heat of the fire in the brazier, until Jessie turned slightly sideways and spoke to Sinclair in what he thought of as her "baroness" tone.

"And you, Sir William, what will you find to occupy your time here in this lonely place once we are gone and you are alone and fancy-free at last?"

The question was so ludicrous in its banality that Will was shocked into responding openly. "My time? You ask me how I will spend my time? I have no time, madam. No time to spare, I mean, for any other purpose than that to which I stand committed—the care and sustenance of our Order in these difficult times."

"Ah! Of course. I should have known that without asking." Jessie was almost smiling at him, her lips barely quivering at the edges, her eyes alight with mischief. "The great and massy responsibilities to which you are forever tied. But surely, after several hundreds of years, your men and your people are sufficiently set in their ways that they are able to function successfully under any circumstances? I should have thought that, once safely delivered here to their new premises, they would be able to set themselves up and establish their disciplines afresh without the need for direct supervision. Am I to understand that this is not so, that they require your stern and guiding eye at every stage?"

Will knew she was trying to goad him into anger, and so he bit down the retort that first sprang to his lips and forced himself to sit silently as he shaped an appropriate response, one that she would not be able to rip apart and ridicule at first exposure. Douglas sat silent, too, watching both of them and awaiting developments.

Will finally nodded. "You are partially correct, Baroness," he said, still stiffly. "Under normal circumstances, matters would proceed as you describe. But the circumstances in effect today are most unusual, and I may speak of them to you because you are already aware of what I mean. The recent events in France have created havoc among our normal means of doing things, and I am faced with a situation that has no precedent ... to call it novel would be gross understatement. And I am the one who must adapt to it and deal with the outcome, since I appear to be the highest-ranking member of the Order here. King Robert and Sir James have both informed me that there is no Master in Scotland today, and no official Temple outpost, since most of the knights of the Scottish Temple were in fact English, adherents of the former king, Edward, and withdrew to London during the wars. Thus, it appears that I am in sole charge of our Temple affairs here."

You poor man, can you not see how hopeless your case is? What will you do when you discover that you are not merely the sole commander but the last? Where will you turn? Jessie allowed nothing of her concern to show on her face as she continued, solicitously, "And what will that involve? I know there are many things of which you cannot speak, but there are other matters that are more open ... things that even I can see. What are the tasks that face you here on Arran, to demand all your time?"

"Housing and feeding my men and livestock, first and foremost, madam, although, thanks to Sir James, that will be much easier than it might have been."

Jessie turned to Douglas. "What does that mean? What did you do?"

The young nobleman smiled, showing his strong white teeth. "I merely gave Sir William the use of a place here on the island, one forfeited this very day by its owner, who has plotted against King Robert and been caught. It is the other castle, Lochranza, on the northern coast, and it will suit Sir William's needs. It has a fine harbor, deep and safe, and ample grazing for his beasts in the mountain valleys."

If it is so fine, then why are you giving it to a stranger? She turned back to Sinclair. "And what will you eat there?"

"We can survive for the coming month on the rations we brought with us, and there are fish in the sea, wildfowl in profusion, and plenty of fresh water. After that we will be supplied regularly by our own trading ships. We will send a number of them out at once, with gold and silver coin, to purchase supplies for the short term in Ireland and in England and explore opportunities for future trade. Others we will send farther afield, to purchase trade goods in the English ports, and then to go and trade legitimately elsewhere."

"Elsewhere?"

"In France, most particularly, where their primary task will be to bring back information on what is happening to our Order there."

"But surely they will be denounced and thrown into prison as soon as they start asking questions."

For the first time since she had met Sinclair a month earlier, Jessie saw him smile easily and spontaneously, sure of himself and full of confidence in what he was saying to her, and the transformation in him that the smile generated almost made her exclaim aloud, for his entire being seemed illuminated by its radiance and his habitual sternness vanished instantly, making him look ten years younger. "Who will denounce them, Baroness? And for what, curiosity? How will their questions stand out, when the entire country will be abuzz with talk of what is happening? Bear in mind that our people will not be recognizable as Templars. Nor as anything else, for that matter, other than mariners new into port and hungry for gossip and the latest news."

"But ... months will have passed by then. The story will be old. Surely, then, to bring it up again will attract attention?"

Sinclair's smile remained in place as he glanced at Douglas and then shook his head. "Bring it up again? Baroness, the Order of the Temple has been a pillar in France, supporting and strengthening it for nearly two hundred years. Next to the Church, and the monarchy, of course, it is the most prominent institution in the country. The Temple and its influence—in land holdings, trading centers, buildings, estates, manufactories, farms, orchards, equipment, and livestock—are everywhere, flourishing throughout the countryside in every duchy, county, and region. I can imagine no circumstance under which the Order's demise—even should it amount to total dissolution or annihilation—could be brought about, let alone that the Order be forgotten from human memory, within a matter of mere months. It is simply inconceivable."

He waited for a comment of some kind, but when Jessie remained silent he continued in the same matter-of-fact, confident voice. "Which means that, no matter what has happened to our Order, no matter what fate might have befallen our brethren in France, the scope of the events of October thirteenth and the period that followed must be sufficiently significant to remain uppermost in the minds of Frenchmen and most worthy of discussion for a long, long time to come. Our mariners will land in ports around the coast, on both littorals, the Atlantic and the Mediterranean, and they will be perceived solely as mariners, behaving as mariners always do, and avid for information on what has been happening ashore while they were at sea."

He said nothing of his plans to send envoys and messengers to make contact with the Brotherhood of the Order of Sion, but he had already discussed that matter with de Berenger and the few other members of that Order who had accompanied him here. The ancient Order would continue to function as it had for fourteen centuries, sacrosanct in its secrecy, and no more than slightly inconvenienced by the vicissitudes of the Temple and its adherents. Indeed it would already have begun to adjust to the loss of the public interface provided by the far younger Order of the Temple, and to revert to its time-proven system of functioning smoothly beyond the ken of ordinary men. It was guidance from the Sion fraternity that Will required most urgently.

Jessie had been observing him closely, watching the play of emotions on his face, and now she nodded slowly. In the face of his earnest sincerity she found she had lost all desire to bait him. Instead, and to her own great surprise, she found herself gazing at him with a new stirring of interest, a pleasing sensation of warmth and affection akin to her feelings towards her brother-in-law Charles. She was honest enough, however, to admit even in that moment that the affection was bolstered by a considerable attraction of the kind Charles would never inspire, and she took hold of herself sharply, shying away from the thought, vestigial though it was.

"I see you have thought this matter through. And it is plain that you will have much to occupy your mind and hands here in Arran, so I will wish you well with all of it, Sir William, and remove myself from your affairs." She rose smoothly to her feet and nodded first to Will, then to Douglas. "Sir James, I thank you for your courtesy and consideration. If you will send a man in search of me tomorrow morning, I shall have my belongings brought ashore and will place myself at your disposal while you make the arrangements for our journey to the mainland. And now I will bid you both a good night."

Will stood up wordlessly, feeling once again like an awkward, tongue-tied boy. But as James Douglas began to walk with her towards the entrance of the tent—a courtesy Will recognized as one he should have tendered—he pulled himself together.

"Wait!"

She stopped at once and turned back to him, one eyebrow slightly raised and an unreadable expression on her face, and he felt his own face suffuse with blood, appalled by the madness that had induced him to call out to her so brusquely. But he had done it, and now she was waiting, the woman and Douglas both unaware that his tongue had turned to dry wood. And then a memory stirred and inspiration touched him and he gestured vaguely towards the depths of the pavilion at his back, using the movement to counteract the urge to sway on his feet.

"There is ..." He cleared his throat, willing his voice to steady itself. "I have a ... a kindness I would ... would ask of you, if you would honor me with your favor."

Jessie had to stifle the unkind urge to grin at him and so increase his difficulties, for she had no doubt of what an unexpected smile from her would do to his stern demeanor. Instead, she inclined her head demurely. "It would be my pleasure to grant any favor you might ask of me, Sir William." *There, and think upon the subtleties of that, if you will, Will St. Clair, while you lie on your hardwood cot tonight.*

Will stood blinking at her for several more moments, and then she watched as he moved into the dimness at the rear of the great tent, where he stopped by a table of some kind against the rear wall. She thought she saw him open the lid of a small chest, and then he bent over, rummaging inside it. He came back to them, and she knew he had something clutched in his hand and her curiosity was difficult to control, but she willed herself to stand still and wait for him to approach. When he reached them, he kept his eyes fixed on Jessie as he reached out awkwardly and opened his hand to show her what he held. It was a small amulet, looking as though it might be made of gold and very old, buttery ivory, and it lay atop a long curl of gold chain, part of which was looped around one finger.

"You are for Scotland, Baroness, to see your own people, and it came to me that you might see your good-sister—my own sister, Peggy—while you are there. I have no wish to impose upon you, but this is ... I bought this bauble for her some years ago in Navarre. She had recently written to me, and when I saw this I thought she might enjoy it ... but then we became involved in campaigning against the Moors there, and I neglected to send it to her when I returned to France. It is but a trinket, purchased upon a whim, and in truth I had forgotten it until I found it recently, when preparing to leave on this journey. It is Arabian, I believe, but it is well made, and the colors are those Peggy has ever loved. If you would take it to her as a gift from me, I would be greatly obliged."

Now Jessie smiled. "I will be happy to do so, Sir William. That is no imposition at all. And Peggy will love it." She held out her hand.

On the point of dropping the pendant into her open palm, he hesitated, frowning, then quickly reached deep into his tunic and pulled out a folded square of cloth. It was a simple kerchief, clean and white, and he shook it open in his left hand, then dropped the pendant into the center of it and folded the thing into a compact package that he passed to Jessie, who took it from him without touching his fingers. It was warm with his body heat and she closed her fingers over it tightly, feeling his warmth. She was about to tuck it demurely into a concealed pocket in her bodice, but on the spur of a sudden thought she moved to lodge the little packet securely between her breasts, highly aware that both men followed the movements of her hand beneath the fabric of her shawl.

There now, Master St. Clair! I have you close to my breast. And see how you flush with the mere knowledge! Remember it, poor monk man, though it stir the need in you to seek confession. She smiled at him again, knowing he was seeing the narrow dimple in her left cheek, and then dipped her head in salute and left him there.

Douglas moved quickly to escort her again, and when they reached the main entrance he dispatched two of his own guards to escort the lady and her two companions back to the beach, to where they could find a boat to take them back to the admiral's galley for the night.

When he returned, and saw Will standing forlornly by the fire, he grinned.

"She's a well-made woman, that one, eh? A fine lady. More French than Scots, though ... probably because she has spent so much time in France, married to a Frenchman. Don't you think?"

Will Sinclair, as was usual in his happenchance dealings with Baroness St. Valéry, did not know what to think, so he merely nodded and sank back into his chair, feeling slightly deprived, although he could not have said why.

"So you'll sail tomorrow?"

"Aye, on the high tide," Douglas answered. "But tonight I have to take Menteith into custody, and it's already dark. So, if you'll forgive my discourtesy I think I'll go now, and strike overland with my small band of guards. It's only two miles, and the men I have with me will suffice for the task at hand. I can be there and have Menteith in chains before he has time to finish dining." He adjusted his sword belt before tugging his cap with its blackcock feather back into place on his brow and adjusting the hang of his cloak, shaking out its thick folds in anticipation of the chill of the evening. Then he nodded in salute and turned to leave, but stopped before reaching the flap to the outer door.

"The Baroness was right," he said over his shoulder. "You do have a wealth of matters to keep you busy here. You will no' be bored. A good night to you, Sir William, and I'll return for my galley in the morning."

Those parting words came back to Will the following afternoon, as he watched the vice-admiral's galley bearing Douglas and the Randolph woman eastwards across the narrow waters of the Firth of Clyde towards the Scottish mainland and the Bruce lands of Ayr and Carrick: *You do have a wealth of matters to keep you busy here. You will no' be bored.*

Will knew Douglas was right. He would have no time to be bored; no time to waste at all; and certainly no time to waste in thinking about that Randolph woman, who was now safely, and definitively, gone from his life.

OBEDIENCE

1

The upheaval took Will Sinclair completely by surprise, although, looking back on it, he could see that all the signs of its imminence had been there and he had merely chosen not to see them. Some of the brethren muttered about it afterwards as a revolt, or a mutiny, but Will himself was never sure what to call it. If revolt it actually was, it was not widespread, and it was quickly quelled, but its ramifications were profound because it ran counter to the Temple's centuries-old traditions of brotherhood, tolerance, and obedience to authority within the Order, and it demonstrated the extent to which discipline had declined in the preceding years. Those truths alone made the events of that day, the Eve of the Feast of the Epiphany, significant enough to trigger an explosion of displeasure from Sir William Sinclair the likes of which none of his chapter had ever seen.

He literally walked into the fight that began and ended the affair, and for several moments he stood blinking, unable to come to terms with what he was seeing. But then, as awareness swept over him, so too did anger, and the unexpectedness of both combined to propel him instantly from deep concentration into cold and implacable fury.

He had been awake since the wee hours of that cold January morning, roused long before Vespers with the news that Sir James Douglas, newly arrived from the mainland in pitch darkness and a raging storm, sought urgent audience with him. Those words had banished all sleepiness from his mind, and within the quarter hour he had created a stir that had serving brothers bustling everywhere—lighting fresh fires and refueling old ones against the bitter winter chill; preparing tables, chairs, candles, and tapers for instant use;

and arranging for hot food and dry clothing to be provided for the famished newcomers. Douglas's visit would be brief, Will had learned, for his ship had not come to Arran apurpose. He and his men were on their way to Ireland, carrying messages for King Robert's brother Edward Bruce, who was there attempting to raise mercenaries and create alliances on his brother's behalf with some of the Irish kings. But they had run afoul of a squadron of English ships soon after leaving the sea arm of Loch Awe, and although they had evaded them with relative ease, the maneuvers of the night chase had left them at the mercy of the storm in the Firth of Clyde, with little option but to run for Arran, which they had expected to visit only on their return journey.

By and large, though, the tidings that Douglas brought with him were good: Bruce's progress through the Highlands of his realm was going well and, as Douglas gleefully declared in the course of the short time he was able to spend with Will, the house of Comyn had fallen upon ill times long overdue. The proud Earls of Buchan and Ross had surrendered and bowed the knee to Bruce, he reported, almost crowing with satisfaction, and the seething Comyn brood, including the contentious MacDougalls of Lorn and Argyll, would never again pose a danger to King Robert.

For all of Bruce's successes, though, attrition had been high. The King had called a halt to his progress in order to refresh and refurbish his following, and to begin his drive to introduce some order and signs of coming prosperity into his beleaguered realm. The news of his increasing successes had worked wonders among the common folk, and recruits were joining his standard in increasing numbers every day. Still, the King would not be happy, Douglas said, until he could convene a legal Parliament—the first to be held in Scotland in more than a decade—and begin to enact new laws for the governance of the land and the protection of its people. In the meantime, he added, the end of the first tour of duty for Will's mounted Arran contingent was drawing close, and King Robert was so pleased with its performance that he was hoping, and had asked Douglas to suggest, that for this single occasion the schedule of changeover might be accelerated slightly, in order to provide him with a fresh armed and mounted escort to accompany him on his travels throughout the land now that it was at peace.

Will found King Robert's request reasonable and had ordered the necessary changes in scheduling, and it was about that change that he was thinking as he made his way down the spiral staircase from the tower room where he had sat thinking since Douglas's departure. The sun had been up for more than two hours by then and the storm had finally died down, but the occasional glimpses of the weather that Will caught from the slit windows of the staircase were enough to show him that no sunshine would break through the clouds this day.

He reached the bottom of the tightly winding stairway and stepped out of the tower into daylight, pulling his cloak about him against the mid-morning chill. As he did so he heard the ringing of steel close by, accompanied by upraised voices, but he paid little attention, assuming them to be the sounds of training men, drifting in from the yard beyond the gate. He shivered in the drab light and looked absently around him, noting the drops of moisture hanging from the open mesh of the heavy wrought-iron gate that served as the tower door, and then he spun to his left and made his way around the base of the building, intending to visit the latrines beyond the gate. Halfway around, though, on the roughly level walkway at the foot of the wall, he was confronted by a knot of struggling men in the yard below, or so he thought. But then he saw that there were only two men struggling, chest to chest, while the others, wide eyed and noisy, clustered around them, shouting encouragement to one or the other.

He stood staring for a moment longer, open mouthed with incredulity, and then his outrage set in, for this was no training bout. These men were set to maim or kill each other, and one of them was already bleeding from a deep gash in his leg. The two were nose to nose, their blades locked between them and grating together as they struggled, each straining to hold the other's blade captive and gain the advantage, but even as Will began to move, the deadlock broke and the two sprang apart, the wounded man, less agile than the other, catching his heel on the rough ground and staggering backwards, arms outflung in an effort to retain his balance. He kept his grip on his sword, but it was point down and useless for the crucial moment that it took his opponent to rally himself and leap forward, sword already sweeping in a downward slash.

Neither man had heard Will's shout ordering them to stop, and even the watchers were unaware of his presence as he launched himself down from the low parapet. He was less than two feet above them when he jumped, but that was high enough to suit his purposes. He landed within striking distance of the charging knight and kicked out hard in a straight-legged blow that took the unsuspecting man high on the left hip and sent him crashing sideways to fall full-length on his back in a clatter of armor. By the time the first of the spectators had swung around to protest the interference, Will's own long sword was screeching from its scabbard. They froze in mid-movement, assessing the threat, and then, as they recognized Will, they blanched, assuming the collective, shamefaced look of miscreants caught in the act.

Not so the fellow on the ground. He knew only that he had been knocked down, and neither knew nor cared by whom. He came up with a roar and threw himself towards Will, hungry for blood and vengeance, his sword upraised and his helmet slightly askew, so that the eye slits of his visor were visibly off kilter. That detail saved his life later, for it enabled the man's official defender at the ensuing trial to claim that the fellow had not been able to see who had struck him and so had been unaware he was attacking a superior officer. As it was, Will merely threw down his sword, stepped aside, and pivoted, grasping his assailant with both hands, elbow and neck, as he hurtled past. He then leaned backwards, pulled the fellow off balance, and kicked the back of his knee, driving the leg from beneath him and sending him crashing to the ground once again. He then bent down to pick up his sword.

Dazed but unyielding, the fellow fought stubbornly to stand up, failing the first time but then rallying himself until he was on his feet again, weaving unsteadily. Will, still furious, stepped in close, hooked the fingers of one hand into the neck of the fellow's cuirass, and jerked him violently forward to his knees and then to all fours, where he finished the matter by chopping down onto the man's helmet with the hilt end of his sword, felling him like a slaughtered ox.

He stepped away and turned to face the others, blade raised towards them, his teeth bared in a rictus of fury. But when he spoke, his voice was low and sibilant, dripping with scorn. "Are you all mad? Are you insane? Have you forgotten your vows along with your discipline? Well then, by the living Christ, I will reintroduce you to the penalties you swore to undergo for laxity and lassitude and disobedience." He pointed his raised blade at one of them he knew by sight. "You, Duplassy. Go now at the run and find Sir Richard de Montrichard. Find him quickly, if you value your skin, and bring him back here to me. I have no care what he may be doing—interrupt him if you must. But bring him here *now*. Run!"

As the pale-faced Duplassy hurried away, Will turned to the next man in line. "You, Talressin. Find Tam Sinclair. Tell him I need a squadron of his best men here, for guard duty, and then bring him to me. Go. Now!"

Four of the erstwhile spectators remained, plus the two combatants, the first of whom had now risen to his feet and was hovering nearby, hunched over as he tried to stanch the flow of blood from his leg with a dirty cloth, holding himself apart from his companions and evidently well aware of the trouble he was in. Will looked from man to man, his thunderous expression ensuring that none of them would dare to speak to him, but finally he sheathed his sword and spoke again in that same flat, menacing voice.

"Throw your weapons at my feet. All of them. And one of you strip the sleeping assassin of his." He waited until the last weapon had clattered onto the pile, then nodded. "Now, on your knees in a row, facing me, and prop the prisoner up between two of you. You will remain where you are, in silence, until you are taken into custody and caged in the cells to await your trial. In *silence*," he barked as one of the men opened his mouth to speak. "Mark me. You are in dire case now. Do not be foolish enough to compound your grief by disobeying further."

He still had no idea who the unconscious and still-helmeted man was, but at this stage he did not want to know and nor did he care. If Justice was blind, as the ancients maintained, then Will, as the arbiter of justice and punishment in this small community, was quite prepared to remain blind to the identity of the miscreant in front of him.

Moments later he heard the sound of approaching footsteps, and Tam Sinclair came around the base of the tower, followed by the man Talressin. Tam drew up short as soon as he came into view, his gaze sweeping along the kneeling men and coming to rest on the pile of weapons at Will's feet.

"You want them locked up, Sir William?"

"I do. And in chains, hand and foot."

Tam nodded abruptly, his face expressionless. "Aye. My men will be here quickly, and we'll have these fellows out o' here." He stepped smartly backwards as Sir Richard de Montrichard came hurrying towards them, accompanied by two of his officers, all three of them bareheaded and wearing the new, closely trimmed beards that signified the new order. De Montrichard held up a hand to stop his two companions and made his way directly to Will, although he never took his eyes from the kneeling men in front of them. The helmeted one was recovering quickly, reeling drunkenly but still propped up by his neighbors on each side.

"What has been happening here, Sir William?" De Montrichard spoke from the corner of his mouth, his eyes on the prisoners, and still distant, Will heard nailed boot soles thumping in double time, Tam's hastily summoned guards approaching.

"A breach of discipline," Will answered, his voice a monotone. "Fighting among themselves, with full intent to kill. One of them, as you can see, sustained a wound. His assailant attacked me when I sought to stop them, and I had to deal with him."

De Montrichard gasped. "Are you injured?"

"No, I am well enough. He caused me no difficulty."

"I'll have him flogged for this. Who is he?"

"No, Sir Richard." Will took de Montrichard by the arm and led him aside to where they could not be overheard. "You will not punish him, nor will I. This transgression goes well beyond the bounds of normal punishment within the ranks. What happened here was an assault against the Rule that binds us all, and it must be dealt with formally, in full chapter, as soon as may be arranged. The brethren in chapter, after due process, may decide to have him flogged, but that decision is beyond the jurisdiction of you or me."

De Montrichard glanced sidelong at Will, then nodded and turned back to face the brawlers, clasping his hands at his back as the arriving guards clattered up and were ordered by Tam Sinclair to take the eight prisoners into custody. But before they moved away, De Montrichard stepped forward and held up a hand to stay them, then indicated the knight in the helmet.

"That man. Remove his helmet and show his face."

One of the guards unlaced the tight cap covering the prisoner's head and pushed it back to reveal the fellow's face, freeing the unkempt mass of the beard that had been concealed beneath it in defiance of Will's recent order that all beards should be close-trimmed if not completely shaven. Will looked closely at the man but felt no stir of recognition. The prisoner was clearly one of the garrison knights from La Rochelle, and most of those were still unknown to him, despite the close quarters in which they had all lived for more than a month now.

De Montrichard, on the other hand, clearly knew the man now standing before them.

"Martelet," he said, his voice cold with distaste. "I should have known. The rest of you, show your faces."

One by one, the group surrounding the man called Martelet loosened the thongs binding their armored caps and pushed them back to expose their bearded faces. Without exception, they were closely shorn, all of them showing varying degrees of recentness in their barbering.

De Montrichard nodded. "Take them away," he ordered.

Tam barked a string of commands, and the entire column of prisoners and guards straightened in response and was soon following him away towards the building in the inner bailey that held the iron storage cages that served as temporary cells. Will watched them go, one arm across his waist, its wrist supporting his other elbow as he stroked his lower lip with the side of his finger.

"What should I know of this Martelet, Sir Richard?"

De Montrichard sniffed. "A malcontent and a hothead. Did you hear about the affair off the Isle of Sanda, when several knights tried to go ashore and their boat had to be sunk in order to stop them?" Will nodded. "Well, that was Martelet, the ringleader as always. It is good that he be tried in chapter. Perhaps the seriousness of that will have an effect on him."

Will straightened, dropping his hand from his mouth to his shoulder. "I doubt it. He strikes me as being too arrogant, and too far gone from the way of the Rule, to change his ways now without … redirection. A flogging and a month of bread and water might bring him to heel, but it might not. And if not, what then? We will have to deal with him according to the Rule. When was the last time we walled up one of our own to die, can you remember? I can't. It must have been fifty years ago at least. Not since the fighting years in the Holy Land, as far as I know. But that could be what we are facing here …" He paused, considering what he had said, then nodded. "Thank you for coming, Sir Richard. I regret having had to summon you, but I thought it best you should be informed, as preceptor."

"And you were correct. You spoke of convening a chapter meeting. When will that be?"

"The day after tomorrow, in Brodick Hall, if that suits you. But I know it is your right to choose the time and place, so if you wish—"

"Not at all. You are the senior here, and charges of this seriousness cannot be made to wait on convenience. I am content."

"My thanks, then. I will make the arrangements today and send off word to Brodick, so that they'll be ready. We ourselves, the entire garrison, will march down there tomorrow at dawn. Can you be ready by then?"

"I'm ready now, but tomorrow is the Feast of the Epiphany. The bishops will not be happy to forgo their ceremonies."

"Regrettable, but they have no choice. We will march before daybreak, and if Fortune serves us well, we will get to Brodick Hall by nightfall. The bishops can then have their postponed ceremonies that day, prior to chapter opening. A day late, certainly, but no less sincere ... God knows what we are about, and knows the difficulties that we face here. I have no doubt He will accept the necessity of what we have to do, and will make allowances for us."

De Montrichard nodded, his face somber. "I agree with you completely. So mote it be. And now I will leave you to your arrangements ... Unless you have some other use for me?"

"My thanks, Richard. I will not hesitate to call on you if I do have need of you."

Will watched as the other man rejoined his officers and went away. Sir Richard de Montrichard was nominally in charge of all garrison affairs, as his rank of preceptor decreed, but he had been a major disappointment to Will, for he had turned out, under pressure, to be a weak reed. As vice-preceptor in La Rochelle, working under the redoubtable Arnold de Thierry, he had shown all the necessary promise of becoming an excellent commander in due time, but in the event—perhaps because of the murder of his superior, or perhaps because of the unsettling events of October thirteenth—he had fallen far short of his promise and had been largely ineffectual as a leader and commander. Will could find nothing to put his finger on that would justify replacing him with someone else, but he felt, nonetheless, that de Montrichard might be better off, to the advantage of everyone else involved, relieved of his responsibilities and relocated, indeed relegated, to a more contemplative and less active role in the Order's affairs on Arran. It was a problem Will had spent time considering in the month since their arrival on the island, but as yet he found himself unable to decide upon a satisfactory resolution. There was no one at this point, at least no one obvious, whom he could promote to fill de Montrichard's position satisfactorily, and that troubled him.

Now he found himself having to reassess all his thinking on the matter, for he had seen in de Montrichard more life, and more initiative, and more willingness to become involved in things than he had seen in the previous two and a half months. He resolved to take advantage of the signs, and to test the matter further in the hope that the preceptor might be consigning the safe haven of his earlier life to a previous existence. If that were the case, no one would be happier, more relieved, or more eager to reinstate de Montrichard to his former status than Will Sinclair himself.

He was interrupted in his reverie by the sound of approaching footsteps as Tam returned, carrying a ring of heavy keys. He held them up for Will to see. "I thought it might be just as well to keep these under close guard, if what I saw here was what I think it was." He tucked the large metal ring securely down behind his belt, leaving the keys themselves to dangle at his waist, and Will smiled wearily, amused and touched, as always, by his kinsman's concern for him.

"And what was it you thought you saw?"

Tam grunted eloquently and lapsed into the dialect he and Will had spoken as boys. "Well, for one thing, I saw you girnin' like a madman, mair angry than I've seen you in many a month. You had that 'dinna dare look at me or I'll cut your heart out' glower that ye sometimes get on your face. And then there was that Martley fellow, still wi' a long beard. That tell't me he wasna about to take your word for anythin' and that wee bit o' defiance was his way o' showin' it, even though he didna ha'e the guts to dae it openly, where you could see it. He needs to be taken down a peg or two, that yin."

Will started to respond, but then waited when he saw that Tam was not yet done.

"Forbye," the other continued, "I didna like the way his cronies there were lookin' at him for support, even though he'd nane to gi'e them. I didna like that at all … They're whiners, every whey-faced one o' them, no' a real set o' balls among them, and he's recruited them to whatever he's up to … So I thought, if there's any more o' their ilk about, I'd save them from bein' tempted to let him out. And so I kept the keys. Now, will ye be convenin' a chapter meeting? An' if so, where and when?"

"What made you think I might?"

Will's question produced an almost exasperated look. "Because it's owerdue. Tomorrow's the Epiphany feast, so there will need to be a full Mass wi' all the rites an' ceremonies, the bishops dressed up in their finery. So it seemed as good a time as any, and better than most, wi' all the work ye have everybody slavin' on. Besides, it seems to me ye've forgotten Master de Molay's wallet ..."

Will frowned. "No, I have not, I've merely been preoccupied. But what about the wallet?"

"The date on it, Will. It's to be opened tomorrow, on the sixth o' January."

"I know that, Tam. Did you really think I might have forgotten something so important?"

"No ... but ye've had other things to occupy ye. What's to be done about it?"

The question nettled Will, for it was one he had been struggling with, on and off, for weeks. What, indeed, was to be done about it? The Grand Master's missive would have to be opened and read on the date named, he knew; he had no choice on that aspect of things. But the ramifications of reading it and the speculations arising from that had been keeping him awake in recent weeks. The possibility of the letter's containing anything good was less than slight. It had been written months before, predating the events with which it must now deal, and those events had been more appalling, more sweeping, and far more destructive than de Molay could possibly have envisioned. Within the intervening months, on the other hand, Will had managed to establish an equilibrium among his charges, focusing tightly on the creation of a new community and their shared need to create order out of the chaos into which they had been thrown. His greatest fear now, barely admitted even to himself, was that Master de Molay's words might undo all that Will had worked so hard to achieve here. He had had nightmares about opening the letter to find orders instructing him to return to La Rochelle with his companions and their ships; orders written in complete ignorance that such a move would be suicidal after four months of persecution and banishment.

He realized that Tam was waiting for a response, and nodded brusquely. "Aye, well, I'll read it tomorrow, and all we can do is hope that what it contains has not been rendered senseless by what's happened since it was written. I had already decided on that, while you were locking up the prisoners. Their case is too urgent to be set aside, Tam. It needs to be dealt with as soon as may be. So I have called a chapter meeting for the day after tomorrow. Depending upon what the wallet contains by way of instructions, it might make my task less difficult."

Tam shrugged. "Aye, or more so. Ye never ken, wi' superiors ... If ye unnerstand what I'm sayin'."

Will ignored the comment and the mischievous grin that went with it, and answered seriously. "Well, so be it, if that's what comes. So, now I need you horsed and on your way to Brodick with these tidings. Will you take Mungo with you? No? Then get yourself some food and oats from the commissary and be ready to leave within the hour. By then I'll have written dispatches for Kenneth and Bishop Formadieu, and they'll be waiting for you to collect on your way out."

Will walked quickly back to his quarters, aware that the hour he had claimed for writing his dispatches would be barely long enough to accommodate all he required of it.

On the day of the Baroness's departure—Will had scarcely thought of her since, and when she did happen into his thoughts, he could manage a tiny smile at her memory before turning determinedly to other things—he had addressed a plenary gathering of his men and expressed his wishes concerning their conduct from that day on. He made no attempt to underplay his concerns, and clearly described the threat that they now represented to the monarch through their very presence in his realm. The brethren listened in silence, heeding everything he had to say, and no one made any demur when he issued commands that, henceforth, all forked and therefore recognizably

Templar beards should be cut severely, all heraldic symbols and devices bearing Temple associations were to be painted out or otherwise concealed, and their distinctive armor was to be stored away. They faced no danger of pitched battle here in the safety of their island refuge, he pointed out, and therefore plain armor—mailed shirts and leggings, with hammered leather guards—would be more than ample henceforth. Horses were not to be ridden in disciplined formations, and were to be stabled in small groups of eight or fewer, far enough apart from their neighbors to offer no curious stranger an opportunity to assess their type or overall numbers.

He had then split his entire force, leaving his brother Kenneth in command of his own one-hundred-strong contingent of knights and sergeants, to occupy the great English hall at Brodick, assisted by the veteran knight Reynald de Pairaud as adjutant and by Sir Edward de Berenger as naval adviser whenever he was in residence. Brodick would become the *de facto* headquarters of the Temple force on Arran, and as such would become the home of Bishop Formadieu and his chancel of clerics and lay brethren. Their task would be to establish the community that would nourish the Brotherhood of the Order. The neighboring bay of Lamlash would serve as anchorage for the trading vessels of their little fleet, and the majority of their horseflesh, mainly the lighter breeds, would be scattered throughout the rolling moorland inland from Brodick.

The remainder of the land-based fighting men, approximately a hundred plus one score, would be relocated to the northwest coast of the island, to Lochranza, the castle formerly owned by the disgraced chieftain of Menteith. The castle there sat high above a secure and easily defensible harbor that would serve as the home base of the galley fleet, and its garrison would be the former garrison of La Rochelle. More than half of the heavy horseflesh would be taken up there, too, and kept in the steep-sided, amply grassed mountain valleys surrounding the castle, as secure as they could possibly be from prying eyes.

There had been other details, and not all of them had been well received by the brethren. There had been muttering and disgruntlement among the ranks in the days that followed, but apart from keep an ear cocked for real trouble, in which he was unobtrusively assisted by Tam and Mungo, Will had ignored the grumblings, content to let time and habit erode the resistance to his changes. Clearly, though, he had missed at least one pocket of willful resistance, and that was what he intended to stamp out.

Finding writing materials at his work table, he quickly wrote out his instructions to Kenneth regarding victualing and accommodations for the arriving garrison from Lochranza. They would be arriving after a twenty-mile march and would be hungry and weary, perhaps more so than usual, he warned his brother, because Will intended to push them harder on this occasion than he normally would, testing their endurance for the first time since their landing, and using the opportunity to remind them of the discipline they might have been tempted to neglect.

The second missive he penned was to Bishop Formadieu, ordering immediate preparations for a chapter gathering to be held the day after Epiphany. The gathering of the knights would take place in darkness, as always, and under guard, shut off from outside eyes and ears. It would begin before Vespers and would last until all the business of the chapter was concluded. Although it was uncommon for chapter meetings to extend beyond the break of day, it was not unknown, and certainly on this occasion Will was concerned over the amount that had to be accomplished in this one session, even without the additional drama of a trial for disobedience, conspiracy, mutiny, and assault upon a superior. He took greater pains with his instructions to the Bishop than he had with those to his brother, despite knowing that the cleric needed no instruction in the details of what was required in chapter, because he wished to be as precise as he could be, and he had no desire to have the clerical contingent of the chapter overreach itself in seeking to gain too much influence over the flow of things. Will had had enough of that nonsense, although he knew it would never stop as long as there remained a priest who aspired to wear a miter someday. But the ambition of bishops, prelates, and clerics in general he could handle with ease. Because he had no fear of any of their threats, they were powerless to browbeat or manipulate him. The law of the Order stated that, in chapter, all men's voices were equal; the newest knight among them could raise his voice in argument with the most august Archbishop, and that was the equality that Will wanted to safeguard most.

From that viewpoint, he wanted the trial of Martelet and his associates out of the way first. Then, once they had been removed, he wanted to read the parchments from the Grand Master, in the hope that the contents would provide instruction for their group at this most difficult time. After that, once all the judgments were ratified and the instructions from the Master had been admitted to the records of the chapter, there would come a plenary assembly of all the members of the Order, irrespective of rank, at which the instructions of the Master and the wishes of the chapter would be made known.

By the time he had finished that second letter, signing and sealing both documents, Tam was already there, waiting to take possession of the dispatches. He left immediately, buckling them carefully into the scrip that hung from his belt as he went. Will sat for a moment, scrubbing at his eyes with the heels of his hands, then rose to his feet and went to talk to Bishop Bruno, the senior cleric in Lochranza, and then to review the final details of the preparations being made by de Montrichard's officers for the gathering of troops and livestock for the following day's journey.

2

Ever since joining the Order at the age of eighteen, one of Will's greatest pleasures had been listening to the plainsong chants of the assembled brotherhood in chapter. The heavy resonance of massed adult male voices singing within the confines of a vaulted church filled with the aroma of precious incense and illuminated only by candles and tapers in the dark hours before the dawn provided him with an experience that was as close to mystical as anything he had ever known. The amalgam of song, echoes, incense, and flickering light encouraged him to believe, although infrequently, that God was up there somewhere, looking down on such activities with benign approval.

At Brodick Hall, however, there was no vaulted ceiling over their heads. The chapter was convened in the large southern antechamber, and armed men guarded the doors against intrusion. The music was as deep and resonant as ever, but the high-ceilinged room dwarfed the proceedings and muted the effect. Now, as the last notes of the antiphon died away into silence, the assembled knights began to shuffle their feet and clear their throats, but before anyone could speak, Sir Reynald de Pairaud rose to his feet and stood in plain view, one hand upraised in the traditional plea to be given leave to speak in chapter. The old man, whom Will had fully expected to oppose him on the changes he wished to make, had in fact been surprisingly supportive and, according to his brother, had been performing admirably as Kenneth's adjutant in the month since Will's departure for the north.

Will, as the sole representative of the Governing Council, was the senior member in chapter, superseding the preceptor, de Montrichard, who would normally occupy the Chair in the East. And so Will sat alone on the dais on the east side of the darkened chamber, with the preceptor on the Northern dais to his right and Vice-Admiral de Narremat, representing the naval presence in the absence of Sir Edward de Berenger, on the South, to his left. Bishop Formadieu, the green-robed senior prelate of the Order, sat facing Will at the far end of the floor, on the Western dais, and behind him sat the clerical members of the secretariat who would record every word of the proceedings. The brotherhood of the chapter at large sat ranged on chairs on the northern and southern sides of the squared floor.

It fell to Will, as Master-in-Chapter, to recognize the speakers and to decide whether they should be allowed to speak when they wished. He glanced around the chapter chamber, taking note of where the accused mutineer, Martelet, stood to his left with his co-accused, in chains and under guard. Will could not see the man's face, but the length of his beard, defiantly pulled into a forked split with bare fingers, underlined his obduracy. Will turned his gaze back upon de Pairaud.

"Brother Reynald, Brother Preceptor has informed me that you wish to address the brethren."

"I do, Brother William." De Pairaud turned deliberately to look at Martelet, then turned to face Will again. "It concerns the matter of the letter from our beloved Master de Molay that is to be read here today, Brother. I raised the point with Brother Preceptor when it first occurred to me, and he was most insistent that I bring it your attention here in chapter, deferring to your senior rank." He cleared his throat. "The sequence of events for our deliberations in chapter has traditionally been to deal with disciplinary matters before moving on to the business of the community at large." He hesitated, glancing down at his hands, and then looked back at Will again. "It has occurred to me—and I emphasize that what I am about to suggest is no more than that, a suggestion—that it might be of value, in this present instance, to read the letter from the Master now, in the presence of the accused miscreants." The stillness in the large room was absolute, with every pair of eyes fixed upon the aging knight, who now scratched his beard delicately before continuing.

"We have had no guidance of any kind from our superiors within the Order since leaving France, and it seems clear to me that we stand in grave need of such guidance. I know that the letter in question does not truly fit that need, since it was written prior to the events that led to our leaving France. But it is, at least, a message from our Master, and one can only presume that it was written in the light of the dilemma in which Master de Molay found himself at the time of writing." Again he stopped, as though waiting to be interrupted, but no one sought to question him or challenge what he was saying, and eventually he shrugged his shoulders. "I merely feel, in my heart, that the accused here, all eight of them, should be permitted to hear whatever the Master might have said to us before they go on trial. It might be that the advice and guidance therein, intended for all of us, could have some effect on them and their behavior. That is all I wished to say."

Will had known what the veteran knight was going to say, for he had discussed it with de Montrichard the previous night, and now he merely inclined his head in agreement towards de Pairaud before rising to his feet and moving to stand behind his ceremonial chair.

"So mote it be. In recognition of Sir Reynald's eloquence and plea, the prisoners will be permitted this privilege on this unique occasion. And unique it is, for it will never be repeated." He picked up the heavy leather wallet that had been lying on the small table beside his chair.

"This is the first occasion of our gathering as a community in this new land. Not the first *gathering*, for that was on the beach in Lamlash, but certainly the first gathering we have had as a community beginning to establish itself. I know I have no need to tell any of you how difficult a task we face, attempting our own rebirth here on Arran, and particularly so since we must do it without guidance, solving our own problems for the first time in two hundred years without recourse to our annals, records, and histories. But we are not without resources of our own. We may not have our complete written records in our possession, but thanks be to Almighty God, we have our memories, our lessons, our awareness of how things ought to be according to the Rule by which we are sworn to live. We have sufficiency of all of those, working together in concert and in mutual goodwill, to achieve what we must achieve, and to begin again, if need be."

The mention of beginning again, of starting over, brought a chorus of muttering and speculation, and Will held up one hand to quell it.

"I know what all of you are thinking, and it is all contained in those last words of mine ... *if need be*. We might have no such need, but at this time we do not know, one way or the other. We have ships homeward bound at sea, and by this time, God willing, they are on their way back from France, and they will bring us tidings of how things are for our brethren there. But until they come we cannot know the truth, and it has been three months now, lacking but six days, since we left in obedience to the Master's command. But the

Master gave me this to bring with us, and commanded that it be opened this day ... well, yesterday, in fact. But here it is, and since our good Brother Reynald reads better than most of us and has a loud, clear voice, I will invite him to come here to me, in the East, and to deliver the tidings of our Master to your ears. Brother Reynald, will you come forward?"

De Pairaud stood and walked the length of the chamber to where Will, who had opened the leather wallet by that time, handed him the letter it had contained.

"Check that the seal remains intact, if you will, and then announce it to everyone, so there is no misunderstanding."

De Pairaud glanced at the inscription and then, slightly baffled, looked up at Will from beneath bushy gray brows. "But this is for you, Sir William. Your name is clearly inscribed here."

"It is addressed to me because I am the conduit between Master de Molay and the brethren here. Open it and read it to them. There will be nothing contained therein that was not meant for other eyes to read."

The knight addressed himself to examining the package. He held the seal close to his eyes, peering at it intently, then held the package high in the air.

"Brethren, I have here, as you can see, a sealed package inscribed to Sir William Sinclair and bearing the unbroken seal of our Master, Jacques de Molay, and although it is addressed to himself directly, Sir William has requested that I read it now to you, from the Eastern Chair, in earnest of the importance of the tidings, guidance, and instructions that it may contain. Thus, if you will grant me a few moments, I shall do what Sir William asks of me."

He inserted his thumb beneath the seal, scattering shards of wax as he opened the wrappings and took the contents in his free hand. It fell into three parts, the first a rolled letter, loosely bound with a leather string and written on several heavy sheets of hand-cut parchment, the second another letter, more tightly rolled and bearing the Master's personal seal. The third piece was an oblong packet tightly encased in thick waxed cloth, again bearing Will's name but clearly marked as being for his eyes alone. De Pairaud set it down wordlessly on the table by Will's chair, where it landed with a solid, heavy sound. De Pairaud held the second, smaller letter out to Will, who shrugged but made no attempt to take it. De Pairaud shrugged in return and set the sealed missive down on the table, too, and then pulled open the primary letter, clearing his throat reflexively as he held the text up, turning it towards the light.

"It says here—" He stopped, recognizing the banality of what he was saying, then began to read the letter aloud in a high, clear voice.

The Temple in Paris

To our good and faithful brother, William Sinclair, Honorable Member of the Governing Council of the Order of the Knights of the Poor Fellow Soldiers of Christ and the Temple of Solomon; Greetings from Jacques de Molay, Master.

My Dear Brother,

Having delivered my instructions to you on the matters currently unfolding here in our Homeland of France, and in the full and confident knowledge that you will obey them in their entirety, I now feel a need to enlarge upon my thoughts, expressed to you in our recent colloquy, in order to ensure that no man, of any rank or station, might be enabled to question you regarding the propriety of anything that you might here-after pursue or attempt in my name or in the name of our Holy Order.

Accordingly, I have decided to confide in you at greater length, explaining some elements of my thoughts and beliefs that I have not thought appropriate to reveal to my fellow Councilors for reasons that will become apparent as I continue.

I have now come to believe, with great reluctance and frus-trated incredulity, that the warnings I have received are correct in every aspect, and that our Holy Order, despite its well-accredited record of exemplary service and unstinting support for the Church and its Christian beliefs and objectives, has become the target for an unscrupulous campaign of calumny and perfidious lies aimed at destroying our reputation and the credibility we achieved over two hundred years of faithful service.

I am equally convinced that the source of this scurrilous campaign is the King himself, Philip, the fourth of that name of the House of Capet, and for the first time in a lifetime of service to this Order, I am experiencing both fear and despair, because in our coming hour of need there is no source of succor and support to which we may safely turn. The world-wide resources of our Order are of no use to us in this extremity, since we have insufficient time to marshal those resources and broadcast what we know, and even were that not the case, we have no proof to offer in the area of our suspicions: nothing has yet occurred to justify our misgivings, and by the time it does, we will be faced with a *fait accompli.*

My despair stems from our loyalty to, and support of, the Pope, the Vicar of Christ and the See of Rome. We swear our sacred oath of loyalty and obedience, as an Order, to the reigning pope, and have done so ever since our founding, and for more than one hundred and fifty years, our Brotherhood has stood staunchly by that oath and formed the standing army of the Church, dedicated to enforcing and supporting the will of the pontiff.

But now I fear we have a pontiff who is more concerned with pleasing and propitiating the King of France than he is with safeguarding the welfare of the Church of Rome and its faithful adherents. Clement V was created by Philip Capet, for all intents and purposes, and may be just as quickly uncreated. All men of conscience know, within themselves, that Philip, through the machinations of his chief lawyer, William de Nogaret, has already effected the certain death of one pope who displeased him, and is suspected of having poisoned that one's successor, clearing the way for Clement's accession to the Throne of Peter. Clement himself requires no reminders of that truth, and so will bend to the wishes of his grasping, money-hungry master.

These words I can say to you alone, knowing from our discussions that you are of like mind. What then can we do, who are bound by oath and honor itself, to escape the malevolence, or even in this case the indifference, of our titular earthly Master, when he chooses to accept the case being argued against us *in absentia*?

In that light, I must assume that the events foretold for Friday the thirteenth of October will come to pass, and that you, God willing, will read these words of mine three months thereafter, on the Feast of the Epiphany in the coming year. Within those three months, one of two things will have—must have—taken place.

The first, most reasonable, and devoutly wished of those is that the King of France will have admitted himself to be in error in suspecting our noble Order of whatever might have precipitated his actions in the first place, and will be in consultation with the senior Administrative Council of the Order to seek a resolution to the entire affair. The sole alternative, failing that, is that the Crown will have completed its machinations against the Order, and the Holy Inquisition will be in full pursuit of the adherents of the Temple at every level of French society, in every stratum of involvement, and the State, allied with the Church, will be immersed in the process of confiscating all the assets, liquid and fixed, real estate and specie, of the Order of the Temple in France.

It is a bleak and dismal prospect that lies stretched ahead of us, dear Brother, but should the former instance prove to be the case, and our Order be judicially and morally absolved of sedition and treasonous intent, then it is not unreasonable to assume that word of such amicable resolution might not yet have come to you in whatever place you happen to be. Therefore you should bestir yourself, for the good of all, to ship envoys back to France as soon as may be practicable, taking care that they bear no mark, insignia, or rank that might identify them as Temple adherents and thus endanger them. These men should go ashore, comporting themselves as simple merchants with no interest in the affairs of France, and should discover for themselves the condition of the Temple fraternity within the French state.

The second alternative is far less pleasant to contemplate and will demand great fortitude from you since, by definition, it entails the virtual extinction of the Order of the Temple in France—and I must add that this is now my personal expectation of what is about to happen. Capet, I firmly believe, is heart-set upon the destruction of the Temple. It may be because we refused him entrance to our own ranks—a slur his pride will not let him digest—but I believe that is but a contributory factor. Morally and financially bankrupt, Capet is envious of our wealth, and his treasury is permanently empty. In our hands he sees the great accumulation of lands and holdings, shipping and trading specie on earth, forever unavailable to him without indebting himself further, and the thought of it has been too overwhelming for him to contemplate without lusting to possess it.

Should that come to pass, Brother William, then the Order of which I am the twenty-third consecutive and duly conse-crated Master will in all probability cease to exist within this land. And if that be the sin of Despair, then I know not how to avoid it, for I am become sufficient of a Cynic to recognize another such, and this one of overwhelming capacity, in the distant, unapproachable, and inhuman personality of our anointed King, Philip IV of France.

Despite our power and strength, Philip will win this struggle, for he has the Church at his beck and call, the Pope securely in his pocket. With that support, the compliance and even the complicity of the Pope himself, he is become invincible against us. And only such support would embolden him, powerful as he is, to mount such an obviously avaricious and covetous attack against the first and greatest and most honored of the Church's military Orders. And Philip will do his worst. I anticipate torture and coercion, to gain our secrets, besmirch our honor, and establish our guilt—albeit for what, and to what end, remains to be seen. And therein lies the reason for my reluctance to share these thoughts with any other. Such thoughts are treasonous. But no man may reveal, under torture, things that he does not know. And for that good and sufficient reason, rather than endanger any of my clerics with the possession of such knowledge, I have seen fit to entrust the writing of these lines to a trusted scribe who will have returned to his home in Cyprus before the date of which we speak and will thus be safe from whatever might take place in France.

It is my belief that we will be fortunate to retain anything tangible at the end of the purge that lies ahead. Everything our Order holds will vanish into the coffers of Philip's treasury and the Vatican's vaults—not necessarily in evenly divided portions. Thereafter, if any of our brethren remain alive, they will face a return to the earliest days of the Order itself, when each knight personally and voluntarily abandoned normal life in search of spiritual satisfaction and salvation, swearing the three Great Oaths and accepting utter poverty, laying claim to possession solely of those things, such as weapons, clothing, and horseflesh, that the Order and its adherents held in common. Our days of power and influence within France, at least, are strictly numbered, but my greatest fear is that, beyond the shores of France, the other kings of Christendom will follow Philip's example, seduced by the prospect of uncountable wealth, there for the taking and unprotected by the Church.

Such matters are beyond my control, Brother William; I merely register them here as matters of concern to me. I myself will stand or fall with our Order in France, wherein it was conceived and brought forth, and since my own vows prevent me from raising a weapon of any kind against my legal superiors, I will submit to whatever judgment or action may be prosecuted against me, irrespective of what I may perceive as its moral worth.

One thing yet lies within my control, my jurisdiction, and my grant as I write this: the delegation of authority within our Order wherever I think fit. To that end I have included with this missive a formal letter of appointment and recognition, duly witnessed by the senior members of the Governing Council and signed and sealed with my official seal as Grand Master of the Order of the Temple, naming our faithful subordinate, Brother William Sinclair, Knight of the Order of the Poor Fellow Soldiers of Christ and the Temple of Solomon, as Master of the said Order within Scotland, or wheresoever said William Sinclair might find himself upon the cessation of his travels, so be it that he is still among a company of the knights and sergeants of the Order and remains dedicated to the preservation of the ancient secrets and rites of the Order duly passed down to him by his peers, brethren and companions within the Order.

That missive accompanies this letter. Read it aloud in chapter when the time is right, and proceed with my full blessing. May the God of our Fathers watch over and protect you and yours.

In humble fraternity, this seventh day
of October, Anno Domini 1307
Jacques de Molay, Knight and Grand Master

For some time after de Pairaud fell silent no one moved, and there was absolute silence. But then from somewhere among the men on the right of the Eastern dais came a slow and rhythmic sound as one of the knights began to beat his right palm against the side of his leg, in a seldom-used tradition that had become known over the years as the chapter applause. The beat was at once taken up by others and spread quickly until the entire assembly was clapping, the sound of their mailed arms striking the heavy chain mail on their armored sides adding a pronounced, heavily metallic background to the clapping of their open palms against their legs.

Will had experienced similar approval only twice before in all his years in the Order, and on both occasions he had contributed to it in support of others. Twice in a lifetime had now become thrice, and this time he felt the neck hair stirring on his nape, for knights in chapter were more than simply sparing in such applause; the conferral of the honor indicated wholehearted approval of some signal development or deed. Strictly speaking, it went against the rules of chapter, since no voice was ever to be heard therein that did not belong to an approved speaker, but technically, no voice had spoken, and so the point was moot.

Will felt his face flush with pleasure, and he had to fight to maintain his composure, allowing no trace of his feelings to show on his face while he thought about what he should do now. The applause, flattering though it was, was illegal and had to be stopped, but he was loath to curtail it abruptly, for the circumstances of this chapter meeting were already unusual. He glanced sideways to where Martelet and the other prisoners stood in chains, and took note that the ringleader was standing stiffly upright, arms unmoving at his sides, glowering with disdain.

Will looked back at the assembled brothers and raised his hands to shoulder height, slowly and steadily, palms outwards in a request for order, and was glad to hear the steady, pounding beat diminish slowly until it died completely. That way, the silence he had gained was voluntary, not commanded. He stood then and looked out at them, aware of their eyes and their expectancy, but for long moments no words came to him. And then he knew, in a flicker of understanding, what he wanted to say, and he cleared his throat and spoke out clearly.

"This chapter meeting is unique, Brethren, as is our celebration here today. Unique … incomparable and unprecedented. Think upon that word and what it means … Unique. It means singular in all respects; it means unequalled and without parallel. It means new and never previously experienced. And as a word to describe this gathering, it is in every way appropriate.

"Within the history of our Order, there has never been a letter penned that has approached the one that you have heard read here today, or one that has more clearly demonstrated the inner beliefs of our Grand Master concerning the status and welfare of this organization, the safety and propagation of which had been entrusted to his care. That, in itself, is unique.

"Since the birth of our Order, two centuries ago, even in the seething chaos of the campaigns in Outremer against the Seljuk Turks and against the Syrian Sultan Saladin and his Muslim hosts, there has never been a time when any new preceptory of our Order has had to set down roots without any guidance or support from the senior authorities of the Governing Council. We here in this chapter are the first such instance. And that, more solemnly and somberly, more chasteningly and more regrettably than anything else imagination might encompass, is unique."

He looked around at the assembled faces of the brotherhood as he gave them time to absorb what he had said, seeing the frowns of consternation spreading as his words sank home.

"We are alone here, Brethren, in a situation and place that half a year ago would have been inconceivable. And so we must govern and constrain ourselves. Without hope of help from any source. Our closest associates, the Brethren of the Temple in England, are shut off from us, unaware of our existence here, and I fear, because of politics and our obligation to King Robert, we dare not trust them with the knowledge of our presence. Therefore we must govern ourselves. And we must begin now, today, this minute."

He paused again and turned his head to cast a meaningful look towards where the prisoners stood watching him disconsolately, and no man there misunderstood the solemnity of that gesture.

"Before we move to trial, though, we must address the matter of the Master's solemn charge, as contained in the second document that accompanied his letter." He turned to de Pairaud again. "Brother

Reynald, will you be good enough to break the Master's seal and read his announcement to our chapter?"

De Pairaud was ready this time, and nodded curtly before taking up the second letter, breaking the seal firmly and without hesitation, so that the sound of pieces of the shattered sealing wax hitting the wooden floor were clearly audible. He then held the tightly rolled parchment up in front of him and pulled it open with his other hand, scanning the contents for a few moments before he harrumphed and began to read again.

To All Brethren and Adherents of the Order of the Poor Fellow Soldiers of Christ and the Temple of Solomon, and to All Men at large, of whatever Rank or Station:

Be It Known that I, Jacques de Molay, three-and-twentieth Grand Master of the aforesaid Order, with full approval and support of the Brotherhood of the Governing Council of the said Order, do hereby announce the Appointment and Elevation of our well-beloved and distinguished Brother, Sir William Edward Alexander Sinclair of Roslin in the Realm of Scotland, to the position of Master in Scotland.

And be it further known that should it come to pass that I, as Grand Master, along with my senior Brethren of the Order in France, be prevented, either by death or incarceration, from performing our Duties or Appointing suitable Successors to Our Offices, then the aforesaid William Edward Alexander Sinclair, Master in Scotland, will be Raised, ipso facto, into the Title and Entitlements, Responsibilities and Duties of Grand Master of the Order, becoming the four-and-twentieth Holder and Executor of that High Station.

So Mote It Be
By My Hand, this fourth day of
October, Anno Domini 1307
De Molay, Grand Master

Will Sinclair was as stunned as any man present. Master in Scotland had been surprise enough; he had never dreamed, even fleetingly, of such an honor. But elevation to the Grand Master's Chair defied belief. But as he recovered and his thoughts began to race again, he saw this elevation for what it was—the strongest possible gesture of support from de Molay, who well understood the task facing Will.

The thump of hands began again, but this time Will was quick to wave it into silence with a single slash of his hand. "I thank you for your support, Brethren," he said. "But it is misguided. There is nothing *to* support at this time, and pray God there never will be. Master de Molay, to the best of our knowledge, is alive and well, along with the other officers of our Order. It has been nigh on a month since we sent off four of our ships to trade along the coasts of France in the Atlantic and the Mediterranean seas. I expect the return of any or all of them daily now. But tidings we will have, very soon. Only then, armed with sound knowledge, will we be able to do anything realistic to address the situation in our homeland. In the meantime, we have more than enough to occupy us in building a home for ourselves here, temporary though we hope it might be. I shall speak more of that later, but at this time we have graver matters to consider." He pointed without looking towards the clump of prisoners on his left.

"Mutiny and disobedience." The words reverberated in the silence they produced. "Eight men stand here in chains, accused of both these sins against the most basic tenet of our Brotherhood. Some might argue that their infringements are but minor, in the overall view of what has happened recently. That is for you to decide here in chapter. I will take no part in this trial. Brother de Montrichard will sit in charge, as is his right as preceptor. But regarding the serious nature of the accusations, I must say this. All of us, every man here present, swore the triple oath upon entering the Order: to adhere to poverty, chastity, and obedience to our superiors in all things. And obedience is primary among those, because without obedience, to the Rule and to our superiors, we are but a rabble, a mob more dangerous than any other, for we are trained to fight and kill, and as a mob, we threaten mayhem to ourselves and all around us."

He turned deliberately and swept the ranks on either side of him with eyes that held no trace of humor. "Heed me. I speak now as a man, not as the senior member present but as a brother among brethren and a veteran member of this Order, and I speak from my heart. We have been too long away from our daily discipline these past few months—that is a simple truth that you will all acknowledge. But the truth is far greater than that, and far more disquieting. We have drifted too far from our beginnings in recent years. We have grown lax and lazy, all of us, and I can say so loudly and openly here in chapter knowing that the only ears to hear that truth are ours alone.

"Since the fall of Acre and the loss of our holdings in Outremer, we, the knights and sergeants of the Order, have in many respects become a rudderless ship, because our *raison d'être*, for more than a hundred and fifty years, was the defense and protection of the faith and the Church in the Holy Land. When we lost the struggle there, we lost our way, and, I regret to say, we lost our status in the eyes of men. The fall of Acre fortress, which had been seen as invulnerable and indestructible, was attributed to us, the fault laid at our door. We were the custodian of the Church's interests in Outremer, and we are seen now as having been negligent in caring for our charges. That is untrue, as every man here knows, but people *think* it true, and we can now do nothing to change that. Too many decades have elapsed. No one cares about the roll of honor we have earned since we began. No one remembers our successes or the valor of our exploits in bygone days. All they see is failure and the loss of Outremer."

He lifted his voice to a shout on his next words, seeing the impact of the unexpected sound among the suddenly stiffening ranks. "And we encourage this! The Temple encourages it, through its policies past and current! We make it easy for our scowling enemies to hate us. The Temple pays no taxes, anywhere, and neither do its adherents— the merchants, moneylenders, and guildsmen who gouge and steal for profit under the Temple's auspices, calling themselves Templars in defiance of the fact that they have never owned a sword or swung a blow in defense of anything other than their own greed ... And that includes the so-called Brethren of the Temple, none of whom serve as we do.

"Think upon that, and how it looks to others less fortunate. They see us as laden with privilege, tax free and wealthy beyond credence, while they struggle daily to survive. They see our trading empire and resent it. The churchmen see our letters of marque and credit, and the bullion in our vaults, and the fees we charge, and they think of us as usurers. And *all* men see us—and rightly so, I fear—as arrogant, intolerant bullies, swaggering about in our forked beards, with rich clothing and the finest horseflesh, behaving with ingrained smugness towards everyone we see as lesser than ourselves, which means they themselves—all of them, everywhere, who are not Templars."

He stopped, his voice fading as quickly as it had swelled, and then resumed in a quieter, more solemn tone. "That is the truth. And that, at root, is what has undone us in France, and possibly elsewhere. Men may give it different names and ascribe what happened to other causes, but at the bottom of it all, we brought our troubles upon ourselves in recent years by giving people reason to be envious, and resentful, and angry at us for what they perceive us to be. No man here, I believe, can deny the truth of what I have said, if he but takes the times to think on it in conscience.

"But we are here in Scotland now, where, thanks to the efforts and goodwill of our predecessors in this troubled realm, our Order remains highly regarded. I intend to maintain that high regard while we are here. I will explain my plans and issue my commands as Master in Scotland when I return, but for now, I will withdraw and leave it to this chapter to conduct the trial of these men with only one advisory from me: past misdeeds may be forgiven in good conscience and goodwill, but in this instance forgiveness, if such you choose, should be weighed judiciously against the prospects of future behavior. I will say no more. You know the procedures, and you know the punishments involved should your judgment go against them. Commander de Montrichard, if you will send for me when your deliberations on this matter are concluded, I shall then conclude what I wish to say to chapter. In the meantime, the East is yours."

Will stepped down from the dais and marched swiftly from the chapter meeting, returning directly to his chamber on the second level. Tam Sinclair, just leaving the chamber with an empty basket, having replenished the log supply by the fireplace, stopped as Will came into view and stood, lips pursed, eyes asquint in the dim light.

"Well, are they for entombment?"

Will barely paused. "D'you think they should be?"

"That's no' for me to say, but I think a man would have to ha'e done something awfu' terrible before I'd sentence him to that … bein' sealed up in a hole in the wall, wi' no fresh air to breathe. I canna think o' a worse way to die—ither than bein' buried alive in a coffin. Come to think o' it, it's the same damn thing, except that you gi'e the prisoner bread and water to keep him alive while's he's waitin' to die o' suffocation. An' just because he wouldna shave off his beard?"

Will stopped in his tracks and stood motionless for the length of several heartbeats before he shook his head and turned to look at his kinsman.

"No. No, no, no, Tam, that has little to do with it. The beard is unimportant in the overall. It's the mutiny that's important—the arrogance, the pride, the example that they set for others by such willful misheed. That is what needs to be nipped in the bud before it can flower and seed itself. And besides, entombment is not an option in this instance. Entombment is the last resort against intransigence. These fellows will probably be sentenced to a month of confinement with bread and water. Martelet might get two months or even three. But he won't be walled up."

"You hope," Tam grunted. "You're no' even there to keep an eye on the trial. What if he defies them an' some idiot loses his head and condemns him? Stranger things have happened."

"Then I will veto the punishment. But now I have to write, while the trial's going on. Is there ink ready?"

Tam looked sideways at him, scowling, and did not even deign to answer such a silly question as he swept out, bearing his empty basket.

3

Less than an hour had gone by when Will was summoned back to the chapter meeting, and he strode into the assembly carrying the sheet of parchment on which he had listed the points he wished to address in the aftermath of the Master's letter. He saw at a glance that the prisoners had been removed and that the remaining brethren were standing at attention, awaiting his arrival, but he showed no curiosity about what had transpired. Instead he nodded courteously to the preceptor, who was also on his feet, waiting to relinquish the Eastern dais and command of the chapter gathering to him, but invited him to remain on the dais, in a chair by his side. As soon as de Montrichard was seated, Will invited the brotherhood to be seated.

"Brethren, I will take little more of your time, for this assembly has already been prolonged, but hear my words now, spoken with the authority bestowed upon me as Master in Scotland by the hand of our Grand Master, Jacques de Molay. I have spoken before of my wishes with regard to our deportment while we reside here. I will now repeat them as solemn charges, with, on this sole occasion, some explanation of my reasons, for I cannot underestimate the importance of what you must all understand from this day forth.

"We have been given sanctuary in this land by the grace of its monarch, Robert Bruce, King of Scots, and I have accepted, on behalf of all of us, a firm and moral obligation in return for the privilege of being here." He paused, aware that every man before him was listening intently. "King Robert stands excommunicate in the eyes of Pope Clement and his adherents in Rome. But he stands thus with the firm and unwavering support of the senior bishops of the Church in Scotland, headed by the Primate of Scotland himself, William Lamberton, Archbishop of St. Andrews in Fife, and William Wishart, Bishop of the See of Glasgow. Such support, in defiance of the papal writ of excommunication, is without equal in the annals of the Church in Christendom, and the most surprising outcome of that support is that the Scottish bishops themselves have not been condemned in their turn by the Curia in Avignon for disobedience. But the reason for that is straightforward enough: the King, through the intermediation of the Scottish bishops, has friends in the Curia, and the excommunication was obtained by the King's political enemies, arguably for their own ends and for reasons far more political than religious. Accordingly, the writ lies under dispute, and Bishop Moray, acting for Archbishop Lamberton, who is held prisoner in England as a supporter of King Robert, remains confident that the excommunication is reversible in canon law and that the ban will be lifted.

"But here is our dilemma, and the King's: the excommunication of the King applies to all his people. Under canon law, held in abeyance here by the goodwill of the bishops of the land, all the people of the realm of Scotland stand excommunicate with their King, until such times as they renounce and depose him. Until they do so, no Sacraments may be dispensed to the people of Scotland. But the King is duly and solemnly crowned as Robert I, the crown laid on his brow according to the oldest and most hallowed traditions of this ancient kingdom, and is legally recognized as monarch by the ancient Scottish families of the realm and the noble houses of the Norman French.

"By our simple presence here on this island, we in this chapter pose a greater threat to the eventual resolution of this excommunication than any other source, now that King Robert is well on his way to establishing peace with his enemies. We, the surviving brotherhood of the Temple in France, are a potential embarrassment and an impediment to the King and his bishops, for we ourselves are fugitives, fleeing papal displeasure. We know not, at this point, to what degree we stand formally condemned in the eyes of Holy Church, although we will discover that truth in the days that lie ahead, but we know beyond a doubt that Pope Clement sided with King Philip to bring about the downfall of our Order in our homeland.

"And based upon that, we may know with certainty how great the danger we represent to the King. Should it become known that we are on Arran, under the protection of the King of Scots, his enemies will make great use of our presence here to discomfit him and blacken his character in the eyes of the Church. They will claim that he openly and willfully defies the Pope and militates against the King of France. How can we deny the truth of that, having undergone this baseless royal purge and our ensuing exile these three months past? When matters of state and untold wealth are at stake, men of power may be relied upon to bend their strongest wills towards the confounding of justice and the corruption of truth and moral right. And Robert Bruce stands in defiance of powerful men, here and in England and in the Roman Church itself. That is the stark and simple truth, Brethren."

He stopped again, and his silence lasted long enough for men to start stirring in their chairs, glancing at one another, the expressions on their faces as different and distinguishable as the faces themselves. And as he watched them he found himself wondering at his own ability to hold them and to speak as he had spoken, aware that he had said more, and more eloquently, than he could ever recall.

"So here is my decision, as Master here, and I announce it now as a resolution in chapter, to be observed and obeyed by this community. We have been working towards this end already, but the need now clearly exists for me to change my previously expressed wishes to an absolute command, enjoining every one of you to absolute obedience, so hear me clearly. As of this day, the Order of the Poor Fellow Soldiers of Christ and the Temple of Solomon will vanish from the eyes of men upon this isle of Arran." He waited for the shock of his words to register and start to dissipate. "It will be simply done.

"Our task, indeed our obligation, from this moment on is to disguise our presence here, protecting ourselves and our identity and in so doing, ensuring the welfare of our gracious host, the King of Scots, from our hands, at least. Therefore the matter of the beards will henceforth stand as law. In addition, all our brethren, save only our bishops and their acolytes, will abandon the monkish tonsure, permitting it to grow out naturally. That is another affectation, dating from the early days of the Church, to distinguish monastics as the slaves of God. We know who we are, we know our duties and responsibilities, and that is all that is required of us. Everything else that could mark us as Templars will be concealed from sight. We will have weapons enough, and we have no enemies here. If enemies do come, we will not lack the means to arm ourselves quickly and prevail, but we will do so as fighting men defending themselves and their possessions, not as armored knights massing in disciplined French squadrons … though there will be time for that, as well, should the need occur.

"We will become invisible, Brethren. Certainly we are many, and we have no womenfolk, but that will pass notice by all but the most inquisitive eyes, and we can deal with those. Scotland is a land at war, and Arran is part of the King's own personal lands—a safe place to raise and train fresh troops and to house mercenaries. The fact that we are French may become known, but we will be seen as hired warriors, not as Temple brethren. But let me be clear, Brethren, there is nothing in any of what I have said that will change, or contravene, our strict adherence to the Rule that is our way of life. All rites and ceremonies, duties and obligations will continue as before, and strict adherence to the Rule will remain sacrosanct.

"In the matter of battle readiness, training will continue as before, but in small groups, with major exercises and maneuvers regularly scheduled in locations where they may be carried out without being observed by hostile eyes."

He stood up. "That is the gist of it, Brethren. The recording clerics here will work out all the details and present them to you as they complete them. But there is one thing more that I require of you, and it springs directly from all I have said until now. It is needful, I believe, that we take steps to split our community, in order to lessen the need to travel north and south in noticeable numbers in the prosecution of our tasks, and so I would like to see a subsidiary commandery established in the north, at Lochranza, with its own duly appointed chapter." He looked down the length of the hall to the assembly of green-clad bishops around the Western dais. "Brother Bishop Formadieu, may I request that you direct your attention towards the completion of that task? I will leave it in your hands to arrange the division of forces and the appointment of a sub-preceptor and officers." The Bishop stood up and bowed in formal acceptance of the task, and Will looked quickly around the assembly.

"So mote it be. And now, my lord Bishop, if you will lead us in the closing rites, the brethren may depart and think upon all that has been said here today. Senior officers and brethren will join me thereafter in my quarters."

4

"I have never heard you say so much at one time in all my life, Brother, and I confess, you said it remarkably well. You gave the brethren sufficient food for thought to keep them chewing at the cud for days. What are we drinking?"

Kenneth Sinclair was the first arrival, following Will into his quarters less than a minute after his brother's own arrival. Will grinned and waved towards the table where Tam had set out cups and jugs of wine.

"I was ever the clever one in the family. What happened at the trial?"

Kenneth busied himself pouring wine for both of them and handed a cup to Will just as approaching footsteps announced the arrival of others. "Solitary time, on bread and water. Two months for Martelet, who showed not a whit of remorse, and one month for the others, including the wounded man, Gilbert de Sangpur. Some think they got off lightly."

"Enter!" Will shouted as someone rapped on the door, and as de Narremat, de Montrichard, and several others began to come in, he turned back to his brother. "And you, what do you think?"

"I agree, particularly in the case of Martelet. That one is a bad apple that could corrupt the whole barrel. He'll not be broken and he will not change easily."

"He will, when he finds himself alone and obvious in his truculence. He will stand out like a splinted limb and will start to behave himself soon afterwards, you mark my words. Gentlemen! Make yourselves comfortable."

Will moved away to welcome his guests and busied himself pouring wine for each of them in turn, the simple courtesy of his gesture betraying, his brother thought, that special quality that made Will Sinclair who he was. Will himself, on the other hand, was already regretting having invited his guests to come here, his mind full of curiosity about the third package from the Master's wallet. The realization that he might now have to wait several hours to open it filled him with a sudden impatience that he sought to neutralize by being attentive to his officers, who appeared both tentative and diffident, plainly uncertain of what he might expect from them and probably of what they might now expect of him after the dramatic announcements he had made in chapter.

It was the preceptor, Richard de Montrichard, who asked the question that, on reflection, Will wryly acknowledged must be bothering all of them. They all had cups of wine in their hands and were at ease, talking among themselves, some sitting, others standing by the roaring fire, and several leaning idly against walls and tables as they discussed the chapter meeting. Will was standing slightly apart, watching all of them and making no attempt to assert himself, when he saw de Montrichard turn and seek him out with his eyes, then raise a hand to indicate he wished to speak.

"Sir William, I have a question to ask, if you will permit me."

"You have no need of permission, Sir Richard. We are at leisure here, for the moment. Ask away."

"Well, sir, it concerns the matter of our raiment ... our habiliments ..."

Will smiled. "You mean our clothing."

"Exactly. I agree with everything you said this morning on that topic. It makes perfect sense, for both our own protection and King Robert's cause. We must become invisible, as you said. But ... if we set aside our mantles and surcoats as you suggest, along with our mailed coats and blazoned armor, what will we wear instead?"

Will had to fight the urge to laugh, reminding himself that these were men whose every movement and behavior, from dawn to dusk through each day of their lives, had been dictated by the Rule that governed them all. They possessed no concept of personal liberty in matters of clothing or deportment; they had spent their lives wearing the clothing issued to them by the Order. Solid but stolid men for the most part, they lacked the imagination to conceive of anything different from what they had always known. And so he nodded solemnly, accepting the question gravely.

"Why, Brother Richard, we will wear what we have always worn— plain, simple tunics, unadorned, and comfortable leggings against the chill. We will merely set aside our outer clothing, replacing it with the plain cloth or waxed woolen cloaks and other overgarments worn by the common folk in these parts—leather jerkins, and bossed leather armor of boiled and hammer-beaten hides. We shall not freeze from exposure, I promise you. And if your next question be, where will we obtain these things, then I will tell you they are here already. There is a large family of weavers along the southern coast, who supply clothing for all weathers to the local fishermen. And another family of tanners, in the cove below Lochranza. I have spoken with the tanners, although not with the weavers, but I am sure that both families will be eager to work hard to clothe and equip us in return for solid silver coin … and most particularly so if we provide them with hides and woolen yarn, which our ships are already collecting abroad. So set your mind at rest on that, Brother." Yet he saw confusion lingering in the preceptor's face. "You appear unconvinced. Was I unclear?"

"No, Sir William, not at all." The protestation was almost apologetic. "I was merely wondering how we will distinguish ourselves … in rank, I mean."

Will's eyebrows shot up in astonishment. "Why would we need to? We are less than two hundred here at any time. Is there a man in your commandery whose name and ranking you do not yet know?"

"No, of course not."

"And is there any among them who would fail to recognize you, or any other here?"

De Montrichard began to look slightly crestfallen, and Vice-Admiral de Narremat came to his rescue. "I think Brother Preceptor might have been referring to procedures in time of conflict or battle, Sir William. I confess the same thought had occurred to me, for all men look alike in the midst of action. An admiral needs to be recognizable to his men as does a land commander."

Will nodded. "A valid point, and one that had already occurred to me. But we were speaking here of normal activities, and there is little need for detailed recognition in the daily grind. We have our regimen of daily prayers and ritual, and that alone will suffice to maintain discipline now that it is re-established. In times of war, though, should such ever arrive on Arran, we shall identify ourselves by using colored patches and plain colored banners." He glanced at the preceptor again. "That is already in hand, Sir Richard, the preparations being set in place, and all men will know the colors before a month has elapsed from now."

De Montrichard nodded his acceptance, and from there the conversation became general, with questions coming from everyone present, requiring Will's illumination on all points raised. In consequence, the hours passed quickly, and when his fellows left him alone at last, Will felt great satisfaction. He had achieved more than he had hoped, and had encountered no opposition even on the details he had expected would be thorny.

Tam had come in to replenish the fire as soon as the last visitor had left, and he cast a glance at the unopened package on the table where Will had laid it.

"What's that?"

"I don't know. I haven't opened it yet. Part of the package from Master de Molay, for my personal attention."

"So when are ye goin' to open it?"

"Once you've gone. I told you, it's for me alone at this point."

"Hmm. What would it be like, I wonder, to be a Templar without secrets? I jalouse ye'll be itchin' to be rid o' me then, seein' as how you're no' noted for your patience when it comes to bein' kept waitin' … well, let me finish here an' I'll leave ye to your business. Oh—what was the verdict in the trial?"

Will told him.

"So we'll all ha'e bare faces from now on?"

"No, not bare. You sergeants won't have to change your hair or beards at all, except for letting your tonsures grow out. But the knights will trim their fabled forks. And all the signs that we are Templars will be hidden."

Tam grunted, pressing the last of an armload of logs into the fire with the sole of his heavy boot, and dusted off his hands. "Well, I'll be interested to see what changes that will make."

"It will make very little difference to who and what we are, Tam. But it should fool a casual eye from a distance. We don't want to hide ourselves, but we do want to hide our identity, as you well know. Now, out of here and leave me to my labors."

Tam merely nodded amiably, then closed the door firmly behind him as he went out.

Will reached for the heavy, cloth-wrapped packet on the table. It felt slick in his grasp, for the entire thing had been dipped in sealing wax, forming a smooth, solid, yet brittle protective skin. He hefted it for a moment, gauging its weight and wondering what it could contain, then took his dagger from its sheath and rapped the hilt down hard against the wax covering, pieces of which scattered across the floor. But wax adheres strongly to coarse-woven cloth, and he had a minor struggle to free the contents, finally resorting to his dagger's edge to cut through the packaging.

A plain black slender iron key fell onto the table before he could catch it, and he sat still for a moment, staring down at it. It was slimmer than most such keys, almost delicate in appearance, and as long as his hand from heel to fingertips, its only decorative feature being that the handle formed the unadorned cross pattée of the Temple. He gazed at it, frowning slightly, then looked inside the wrappings in his hand to see the edge of a piece of parchment. He pulled it out and unfolded it, and as he read it he felt the small hairs stirring on his neck.

William

Should you become my successor you may have need to access the contents of the chests in your possession, for reasons yet to be discovered. There is among them one smaller than the rest, bound in brass and with a single padlock, sealed in wax. This fits that lock. Guard it well. It is the Master's Charge. The chest contains the keys to all the others. Open them alone, in your own time, and view the vindication of our ancient Order of Sion, so that you may know what must be done to safeguard them, intact or apart, should a time of great need arrive. May God keep you, and all of us, in safety and in health.

D.M.

Will sat back heavily, aware only now that he should have been expecting this development, since it made no sense that he should be permitted to transport the fabled Temple Treasure without the means to open it. But the mere thought of now being able to do so, possessing the right to open the great chests and gaze upon their legendary contents, shrouded for so long in mystery, made him reel with dizziness.

Contemplating that reminded him that the Treasure itself was still floating aboard one of their remaining ships in the bay of Lamlash, awaiting the discovery of a safe hiding place. It was covered in sailcloth and not even under formal guard, and by now most people there had been kept busy enough to forget its existence. But more than a month had elapsed and no good hiding place had been discovered by any of the trusted men assigned to the task. That, he now saw clearly, was neither acceptable nor even tolerable. And as he thought about the problem, the answer came to him without warning, raising gooseflesh on his shoulders with its aptness. There was no place on Arran safe enough to hold the treasure; several large caves and caverns there were, certainly, but they were far from inaccessible to anyone determined to enter.

The perfect place, and, he instinctively believed, the *only* place made for such a use, lay far from Arran Isle on the Scottish mainland, in his father's own lands of Roslin, deep in the forested hills southwest of Edinburgh and far inland from the sea. To the best of Will's knowledge, no one but he and his brothers, three of whom he had not seen or thought of in many years, were aware of the existence of the place, a vaulted, subterranean cavern with a single narrow slit of an overhead entrance, discovered by sheer accident years before by Will's elder brother Andrew when he fell into it while searching for an errant arrow and found himself rolling down a slope of scree into a vast black, empty space. The brothers had used the cavern as their secret place for several years after that, swearing fearful oaths that they would never reveal the place to others. Will had not thought of the cavern for years, having used the place for no more than two summers during his boyhood, and he would have wagered that his brothers, too, had forgotten about it. But now he recalled it perfectly, its single, narrow entrance, a black slash in the level ground at the base of a hill, invisible beneath an overgrown mass of ancient brambles.

The entrance would have to be enlarged, he knew, for it had barely been wide enough to admit small boys, and it was a fracture in solid rock, not a subsidence of soft soil, but he barely spared a thought for the difficulty involved. The brethren of the Temple had been building fortresses and palatial buildings for more than a century, using mathematical and geometrical methods handed down, by the Order of Sion, from the architects of ancient Egypt. And a result, stonemasonry, the greatest of the builder's arts, both ancient and modern, had become an honored craft among the Temple knights, who referred to their lore as sacred geometry. Will knew a score of expert stonemasons among his own circle within the brotherhood, and there were five of them among his current command. To them, he knew, the task of enlarging the entrance and then concealing it completely afterwards would be a simple one, quickly completed.

He felt his stomach stirring in anticipation, knowing that, as a place of concealment for the Treasure, the cavern would be unbeatable, even safer and more secret than the cavern in the forest of Fontainebleau where the chests had lain in safety for decades.

Now, he decided, his priority must be the safe transportation of the Treasure to his father's land and its proper concealment there. The thought of seeing Roslin again after so many years, of seeing the faces and hearing the beloved voices of his father and siblings and all their broods, brought him to his feet and set him to pacing the room, already busy selecting the party who would ride with him.

"Tam!" he roared, and the door swung wide a moment later to reveal his kinsman, wild eyed at the urgency of Will's summons.

"What? What's wrong?"

"Nothing is wrong, Brother Sergeant! I merely deliver advance warning. Clean yourself up and try to look respectable, and start practicing your manners. We'll be heading home to Roslin within the week!"

5

The days that followed seemed too short for the amount of activity that had to be packed into them, transportation from the island to the mainland being a high priority. Will had a galley at his personal disposal, commanded by de Narremat, but he decided to take along a cargo ship as well, one of the craft partitioned between decks to accommodate livestock, since he had estimated his traveling party at twenty trusted men, ten of them knights and ten sergeants, and all of them would need riding horses. He limited the number of spares to four mounts, but also had to include four dray horses for the wagon that would carry the Treasure chests, which brought the number to twenty-eight animals aboard a ship modified to carry thirty-six. The extra space he dedicated to the men of the expedition, since his galley could not easily carry all of them plus the space-consuming chests, and he was unwilling to leave the chests aboard the ship, where they would be out of his sight and control.

One of the galleys they had lent to Angus Og MacDonald visited Brodick on the second day of their preparations, in the course of a normal patrol of their own waters, and Will took advantage of the opportunity to quiz the MacDonald's captain on the safest route to follow in crossing from Arran en route to Edinburgh. The captain, a wiry-bearded, bushy-eyebrowed veteran with a face weathered to a mass of leathery wrinkles born of years at sea, spoke both Scots and Gaelic and even had a smattering of French at his command.

"You will go by the dear green place," he said, his soft, island-bred accent softening the harshness of the Scots in which he responded. "Straight north from here, up the Firth and then veering to the northeast along Clyde vale as far as you may go before the shallows cut you off. From there, it is journey of four or five days to Edinburgh on a sturdy horse. Where did you say you are going?"

"A place called Roslin. My father's home."

"Aye … I have never heard of the place."

"Why should you have? It is small and lies far inland. But you yourself named a place I have never heard of. What was it, the dear green place? Where is that?"

"Och!" The captain threw back his head and laughed in genuine pleasure. "I forgot you are not from these parts. It is the place founded by the great saint Kentigern, hundreds of years ago—the mainlanders call him Saint Mungo, but he is Kentigern to us of the Isles, and his church town there at the top of the Firth is Glasgow, which is a Gaelic name, o' two words, glas and gow, meaning dear an' green."

"I see. And are Englishmen garrisoned there?"

"I do not know, for I avoid the place. But there might be. It's a strong place, wi' a cathedral, so they'll think it important. Anyway, take no chances. Keep you to the north bank of the Clyde and stay well clear of the town. It's well wooded all along the vale o' the river, and there's few folk about nowadays. Just keep guards out ahead o' you and ye should be fine. Edinburgh will lie about ninety miles to the east o' you. The place you're looking for, I canna help you wi'."

Will thanked the man and left him to his work while he himself went in search of Mungo MacDowal, to whom he repeated the captain's words. Mungo nodded. He knew the route, he said, having traveled it several times as a boy, with his father.

The next day, an hour before sunset, the watch atop Brodick Hall reported sails approaching from the south, and as dusk thickened around them Will was on the beach, awaiting the arrival of the pair of ships returning from the Channel ports of France, but apart from a brief and discouraging indication of the state of affairs there, he had to wait until late in the evening, after the communal prayers and meal, to hear the full extent of their discoveries. Immediately after dinner, he removed himself from the assembly and led the two captains to his quarters.

Trebec, a laughing, amiable man when not on duty, hailed from the Breton port of Brest, and so he had covered the ports to the south of Brest, down as far as the Spanish border, since there was less chance of his being recognized there and remembered as a Temple captain. The younger man, a swarthy native of Navarre in northern Spain, whose name was Ramon Ortega, had visited the northern ports, from la Rochelle itself, where he was unknown, north to Brest and on through Cherbourg as far as Dieppe, calling in to all of them and sending trusted men to find out what they could.

Neither man smiled as he made his report, and Will paced the floor as he listened to them, too tightly wound to be seated. True to the predictions of the original warning to de Molay, it appeared that every senior officer of the Order had been arrested on the appointed day in October and thrown into prison to await interrogation by the Holy Inquisition, the grim-faced Dominicans who called themselves the Hounds of God and whose implacable zealotry for the absolute sanctity of Christian dogma had spread terror and dread among ordinary Christians for the past hundred years, keeping them in abject subjugation through the fear of death by fire and torture. Both captains could attest to the involvement of the Inquisitors from numerous observations. The length and breadth of the coast of France, the tavern talk was all about the imprisonment of the Templars, and rife with speculation as to what was happening to them behind the forbidding walls of the King's prisons.

Will listened in mounting anger and frustration to the reports, his frown deepening until he could stand no more of it and whipped up one hand, cutting both men into silence.

"That's all well and good," he growled, "and plainly there's no lack of it. But where's the sense of it? Where's the meat of the matter? It's one thing to execute a coup like that, but it's another altogether to maintain it in the absence of hard truth. What are our people charged with? What's the nature of the crimes of which they stand accused? You have told me nothing of that."

Both men fidgeted, and neither one would meet his eye.

"Come then, speak out. You must have heard something of the accusations and I can but presume it deals in heresy of some kind. So what is it? What are we accused of? Apostasy? Usury? Both of those I could see, preposterous though they be, but usury in itself could not justify the extent of this malice. What else is there?"

Trebec looked at Ortega, who met his eyes and shrugged as though helpless, and the older man drew in a great breath and straightened his back and shoulders, turning to look Will straight in the eye. "There's more than that, Sir William. Much, much more."

"Then tell me, Captain Trebec. I am not a diviner."

The mariner's face was bleak, his voice flat. "Black arts and Devil worship. Crimes against God and Holy Church. Pederasty. Blasphemous rites and ceremonies involving obscene kisses and acts, man upon man, as part of Temple rites and initiations. Oaths against God, witnessing the Devil's supremacy … The Temple Council and the knights stand accused of worshipping an idol, a mummified head called Baphomet, a creature of Satan, given to them to adore in token of his mastery and carefully kept and treasured in the Order's secret vaults. All that, and many other things I have no wish to mention." He looked down at the table. "Mutilation and abominable sins perpetrated against women … cannibalistic rites involving the sacrifice of

infant children and the eating of their flesh." He drew a deep, shuddering breath. "It seems, Sir William, that there is no sin, cardinal or
mortal, and no crime conceivable, with which the Temple has not
been charged. And the Holy Inquisitors are busy even now, torturing
confessions out of broken men through the entire land of France."

Will Sinclair stood as though thunderstruck, the blood draining
from his face, and then he groped sightlessly for a chair and collapsed
into it, shaking his head in mute denial of what he was being told.
Neither of the captains spoke another word, merely staring at him
wide eyed as they waited for him to gather his scattered wits.

"God damn them all," he said at last, his voice barely audible.
"This is infamy beyond the ken of ordinary men. God damn them to
the deepest, darkest pits of nether Hell. God curse their evil, petty,
miserable, money-grasping souls ... Grasping King and weakling
Pope and mindless, brutal minions—sound, solid, praying
Christians every one ..." He fell silent again, his frown growing
even darker, and the silence stretched until he sat up straight again,
grunting in anger and disgust. "So be it, then. I'll think on that and
decide what we must do. But even so, we still do not know all there
is to know. Two ships are still to come back, from the Mediterranean
coasts, though I doubt their tidings will be any brighter. Tell me, did
you drop St. Thomas and Umfraville off without incident?"

Trebec nodded. "Aye, off the coast by Bordeaux. They were to
head straight to Aix-en-Provence and then make their way south to
Marseille, where Charlot de Navarre was to pick them up. They
would have lots of time, because the outgoing weather was stormy
and de Navarre had to make his way south and around by Gibraltar
to reach Marseille. They should be fine."

Will nodded, keeping his thoughts to himself. Marcel de
St. Thomas and Alexandre d'Umfraville were both members of
the Order of Sion, and would be bringing back information and
instructions from the Order's secret sanctuary in Aix—all of
which would offer better insights than the collected impressions
of the seafarers. He was now trembling with impatience to hear
from them.

"How much longer will the others be, think you? I am no mariner, so I know nothing of wind speeds and journey lengths."

Ortega shrugged one shoulder. "A week to ten days at the very least … but realistically up to twice that long. They are at the mercy of wind and weather, and neither one of those is amiable at this time of year, especially in the south Bay of Biscay. I would expect them in a month. From now."

"That long?" Will could not conceal his chagrin, but then thought better of it. "Well, that may be good, when I think about it. We are bound to leave for Scotland tomorrow, and we should be gone for two or perhaps three weeks. That would make the timing just about right." He gripped the arms of his chair and stood upright, nodding to both captains. "My thanks, Brothers, for your reports. You have done well. Now I must ask you to keep this knowledge to yourselves until I find a means of informing all the brethren simultaneously. In the meantime, I am sure you must have matters of your own to attend to. You may go."

THE CAVES OF ROSLIN

1

The deer had been grazing in the knee-high shrubs since before daybreak, oblivious to the grayness of the strengthening light and the relentless drizzle of chill January rain that seemed to seep down from the clouds hanging just above the treetops. Behind them, the grassy, shrub-scattered meadow sloped gently down towards the rain-swollen stream, and above them, less than ten fleeing leaps away, the forest covered the hillside, ending in a straight line that formed a border to their feeding ground. The motionless air was filled with water sounds, the not-quite-roaring gurgle of the swollen stream melding with the patter of rain on leaves, and the grazing herd, accustomed to the peacefulness, browsed contentedly, secure in the watchful presence of the antlered stag. But then came a distant, different sound, followed by a whir of driving wings as a covey of startled grouse erupted from the edge of the forest, and the entire scene changed in an instant. The stag's head came up, his alarm transmitting itself to the small herd, who raised their heads, too, ears pricking, then froze in place. The stag stood stock-still, staring into the trees, only his twitching ears betraying his concern. And then the distant noise came again, closer this time, and he whirled and bounded away, his entire family at his heels, so that in the space of heartbeats the meadow was empty.

The alien noises drew nearer, recognizable now, had anyone been there to hear, as the metallic jingle of harness, accompanied by the solid thump of hooves on damp, soft ground. Then came a stirring among the branches at the forest's edge, and three mounted men emerged, swathed from head to knees in heavy riding cloaks of greenish-brown, thickly waxed wool. They paused there, barely out of the trees, and all three scanned the meadow beneath until, on an agreed signal, one of them stood up in his stirrups, put two fingers in his mouth, twisted around, and blew a loud, short whistle back into the trees. His companions kicked their horses forward to make room for the file of men and horses that followed them out of the forest.

When they were all assembled, Will Sinclair called for their attention.

"Well, Brethren," he began. "Welcome to Roslin. The sunshine might be less brilliant than you were accustomed to in France, and the air much cooler, but the place has much to recommend it. It was, for many years, the childhood home shared by myself and my brother Kenneth here, and I cannot tell you how pleasing it is to me to see the place. My father's hall lies less than a mile from here, on a rocky knoll by the side of the river there. You cannot see it yet, but I assure you it is there and that you will all be welcome, with a sound roof over your heads tonight, warm bedding, and good, hot food. A pleasant change from the fare and lodgings we have known these past nine days. I brought you through the woods because I knew the way, and knew that, were there English soldiery in the area, the likelihood is that they would be encamped in this meadow, for it is the only place within miles that is suitable for such a thing."

He looked about him, then continued. "And it is as I hoped, serene and calm. But I must caution all of you to bear in mind, from this moment forth, that we are on a mission of secrecy and you must guard your tongues. No one will question you here, for the people are but simple country folk. This valley and these hills are their entire world, and they know nothing of the world beyond a day's journey from their homes. But they are human, and therefore curious, so they might ask you questions. Answer them simply if they do, and say nothing that might prompt them to ask further. We are warriors, on a mission to King Robert. But we are not monks here. There will be no communal prayers and no services. Do you understand me, all of you?" He looked from man to man, waiting for each one to nod, then nodded himself. "So mote it be, then."

He turned to Tam Sinclair. "Tam, take eight men with you and ride back to the byre where we hid the wagon, then bring it around by the road to the main house. We'll be waiting for you. The rest of you, come with us."

The group split into two parties again, Tam Sinclair leading Mungo and seven other sergeants back into the forest while Will and his party of eleven knights, including Kenneth, formed up in pairs and rode down through the meadow, turning at the banks of the swollen little river, which was less than fifteen paces wide, the water tumbling noisily along its narrow, rocky bed. Kenneth and Will rode at the head of the small column, Will whistling tunelessly to himself while Kenneth looked around him, absorbing the familiar details of the countryside as they drew nearer to their home. When they were about halfway there, at a bend in the river that they both recalled from their boyhood, Kenneth glanced behind him to make sure they could not be overheard, and said in a conversational tone, "You can't discuss those two letters you received from France the morning we left, eh? That's a pity."

Will looked at him, surprised. "Why do you say that?"

His brother shrugged, grinning. "Because you're morose. The only time you ever whistle to yourself like that is when you're angry and perplexed, thinking on a difficult problem. And you've been doing it since we left Arran, so it has to be because of those letters, because you were fine before they arrived. What are you going to tell Father?"

"You mean about the situation in France? I'll tell him everything."

"Everything you can, you mean. Will you mention the Treasure?"

"Aye, but to him alone. Father will keep his mouth shut, but I have doubts about anyone else. Treasure is treasure, and the one we have here is legendary. It would be impossible to stop people from talking about it. Besides, without Father knowing what we're about, we would have great difficulties doing what we have to do. Don't forget, we have to open up the entrance to the cavern and then seal it afterwards. I would hate to try to do that on his land without his knowing. In fact, I don't think we *could* do it without raising his suspicions, and then his questions could be awkward ... So I whistle when I'm upset, do I? I wasn't aware of that."

"I know." Kenneth's grin grew broader. "That's why you do it. You always have, even when we were boys, and I never mentioned it because sometimes it saved me from a beating ... You think Tam will be able to get the wagon out of sight without anyone asking questions?"

"Of course, so be it he does it openly. Folk will assume it contains all our gear, and it does. The chests are well covered and tied down. No one will look beneath the wraps, and we'll move them out into hiding tomorrow."

"If you say so, Brother ... you're the man in charge." He stood up in his stirrups and peered ahead to where the path curved, following the riverbank. "We're almost there and I feel like a boy again. I'm going to ride ahead and let them know we're coming. I wonder if Peggy will be here. Father's going to have a fit. I'll have some people ready to take your horses."

He kicked his horse to a gallop, and Will smiled as he watched him disappear around the bend in the track ahead, at the same time regretting that he could not take his brother and his father fully into his confidence. His father knew little of the Temple Order, other than that he had two sons who served it, and neither he nor Kenneth had any inkling of the existence of the other, far more ancient Order of Sion.

He grunted and turned in his saddle to make sure that the column behind him was in good order, since they would come into sight of his father's house within moments. Everything was as it should be, but he gave the hand signal to tighten up the column anyway, then went back to thinking about the reason for his whistling. One of their two ships from the Mediterranean had arrived the morning they left, having left its sister ship behind while it sped home to Arran bearing a large wallet of written reports for Will from the headquarters of the Order of Sion in Aix-en-Provence. Will had spent many hours immersed in those documents on the voyage from Arran and at every opportunity since then, and the information they contained had been more than disquieting, even while he had been anticipating nothing good.

Jacques de Molay and several of his closest advisers, all members of the Governing Council, were being held under close arrest in Paris and subjected to questioning by the functionaries of the Inquisition, and there was a terse report in one of the missives, gained through a Sion brother at the King's court in Paris, that Master de Molay stood condemned, having allegedly admitted to several of the cardinal charges and confessed himself guilty. Will cringed each time he thought of that, because he could only guess at what kinds of atrocities and iniquitous tortures must have been inflicted upon the Master of the Temple to reduce him to the condition in which he would confess to such baseless charges.

In a commentary attached to the report, Seigneur Antoine de St. Omer, the seneschal of the Order of Sion and a direct descendant of Godfrey St. Omer, one of the seven founders of the Temple, had offered solace of his own, remarking that the man had not yet been born who could withstand the torments of the Holy Inquisition, undergoing tortures that encompassed being burned with live coals, stretched on the rack until one's joints separated, having one's bones deliberately smashed and left unset, being lowered into vats of water to the point of drowning and then being revived and resubmerged, and having one's extremities crushed and mangled by the application of screws, all of these torments varying endlessly from day to day. These were the instruments of the Inquisitors ... the Christian God's own tools in the war against heresy. Will had vomited on first reading the litany, and his mind had never been free of morbid fascination since that time, for if a giant of a man like de Molay could be broken by such means, what chance had any other poor, accused soul of finding mercy or salvation?

He saw the roofline of his father's house above the trees that surrounded the knoll on which it was built, and shook his head clear of the images that had been thronging in on him. He could hear voices raised in tumult ahead of him and he raised a fist above his head and kicked his horse to a canter.

2

"**W**hat do you intend to do now?"

Sir Alexander Sinclair of Roslin had sat silent for more than an hour while his two sons told him their tale of the recent events in France and Arran, and now he spoke to Will. It was late at night, and he had led them directly from the great hall of his house after the communal supper into the bedchamber he had shared with their mother since before their births. It was a vast room with comfortable chairs and a huge stone fireplace, and the massive fire burning in the hearth had sunk into embers since their arrival.

Will let the question go unanswered while he gazed at his father for a while, taking stock of the changes he could see in the man. At sixty-eight, Sir Alexander was still a large man, still broad of shoulder and erect in posture, but he had aged greatly, his beard gray-white and his thick, long hair silvered into a halo about his head. His wife had died ten years before, of a sudden sickness that had taken her from her husband before he'd had time to adjust to the possibility that she might die, and the loss had devastated him, leaching much of the bulk and muscle from his giant frame. His mind, however, was unimpaired, and his blue eyes were as bright as Will remembered them.

Will shook his head. "I cannot say, Father."

"Why? Because you know not, or will not? There are few of your Order left in the land, apart from your own soldiery, very few … Sir Alan Moray for one, Sir Robert Randolph, a score or so others. Their observances of your rituals and monkish ceremonials might have been neglected, for we have been at war these past ten years and more, and most of the Temple clergy returned to England years ago. But they will rally to you if you summon them, for they have no idea about this morass of treachery in France, and I dare say they might welcome some solid leadership after so long without it. So which is it, Son, cannot or will not?"

"Cannot, because at this moment I simply do not know. But the need to know consumes me, every waking moment."

"Aye, well that, at least, is as it should be. The rest will come to you. Having heard what you told me, I am not surprised you're undecided. Betrayed on every side, by every superior who should support you, you need to think things through, and from a viewpoint that you might never have contemplated ere this all came to pass … I know little of the Temple, but if I can help you in any way, you've but to ask. You know that."

"I do, and I thank you for it. But there is—"

"What happened to the Treasure?" his father interrupted. "I hope it was well hidden, for the thought of Philip Capet laying his hands on it offends me. Did he find it?"

Will glanced at his brother, who was wide eyed and slack jawed with shock, and had to smile in spite of himself. "That is what I was about to say, Father," he said. "The Treasure was well hidden, and Philip's dogs did not find it." He nodded towards his brother. "Kenneth reached it first, deep in the forest of Fontainebleau, and brought it safely out. It's sitting in your barn right now."

Now it was his father's face that went wide with shock.

"The Treasure is *here*? The Temple Treasure, in Roslin? That seems beyond credence. Most men doubt that it even exists nowadays."

"It exists very solidly, Father, believe me. I'll show it to you tomorrow, but only the chests, I fear. I've never seen them open. Their contents is the most closely held secret of our Order, valuable beyond price. Only the Grand Master is permitted to know what they are. His two closest deputies have access to the keys to the chests, but even they are not permitted to look until one of them becomes Master himself."

"And you've left these chests out in the *barn*?"

Will laughed. "Why not? They'll come to no harm. They've lain untended in a cave in France for ten years, and since then they've been safely stowed in the holds of several ships. They can survive a night in a barn, until we decide on someplace safe to hide them for a while."

Sir Alexander had now had sufficient time to absorb the shock and his expression turned pensive. "What are your plans for it? Plainly you seek to hide it, but why bring it here in the first place?"

"Because here, with your consent, is where we intend to conceal it." Ignoring his father's raised eyebrow, Will quickly told him about the cavern he and his brothers had discovered as boys, and the old man chuckled, his eyes sparkling.

"I know it well," he said. "I played in it with my own friends and brothers as a lad. It's big enough to lose a substantial treasure inside it. But how large are these chests? You'll never get them in if they're too big." His father paused, a peculiar expression on his face, and Will knew his own face must be reflecting his surprise, for Sir Alexander laughed again. "You didn't know I knew about the place," he said. "William, that cave has been there since the beginning of time, long before the first Sinclairs arrived in Roslin. You held the knowledge of it secret, thinking it yours alone—but so did we, my brothers and I, in our own time. And it would surprise me to learn that there was ever a generation of Sinclair boys who did not think the same."

The old man chuckled again, but quietly this time, as though at himself. "We all delude ourselves in youth," he continued finally. "It is the same with babymaking and the joys of doing it ... each of us, each pair of young lovers, believes they have discovered the secret of the ages, now revealed to them alone, the wonder of it. Ah, well. That is the miracle of youth and learning ..."

Will sat blinking, not knowing what to say next in the face of this unprecedented glimpse of his august sire's humanity and fallibility, and his mind filled with the sudden knowledge that, no matter how old he grew or how highly placed he became, his father would always have the ability to put him in his place and make him feel like a child again. The feeling grew into the first stirrings of panic, and he coughed and tried to pull himself together, to return to the business at hand

"Aye ... of course ... But that is why we require your permission, Father, and your aid. Many of the men I brought with me are highly skilled masons, while two are architects. It will be a simple task to enlarge the entrance, then seal it up again with stonework once the Treasure is inside. There, it will be more than safe, since none but you in all Scotland will know its location … That is true, is it not? You will be the only one who knows of it?"

The elder Sinclair smiled. "The only one I can think of … but there were many who knew of it when I was a lad. Today, though, if anyone went back to look for it after your men had finished their work, they wouldna fret about no' finding it … But you have not explained why you need my aid. It sounds to me as though you don't."

"Oh yes we do, Father. We need you to make sure that none of your folk come looking out of idle curiosity, seeking to find out what we are doing out there in the woods."

"Aye. That is easily done. No one will come near you—I can see to that, if nothing else. Now, as soon as day breaks, have some of your men bring the chests in here. They can sit over in that corner, and no one will as much as look at them. Is there anything else you need from me?"

"No, Father, nothing more."

"Good, then tell me about this King of ours. What was your reading of the man? Kenneth, what did you think of him?"

"I never met him, Father. Will was the one who met and talked with him."

Will shrugged. "I found him … regal … and in his dealings with me he was straightforward, noble, magnanimous, and unassuming. I liked him greatly." Sir Alexander made a harrumphing sound, and Will glanced keenly at him. "You sound unimpressed, Father. Do you disagree with my judgment?" His voice was quiet, showing only curiosity and no offense.

"No, no, lad. I believe you well enough, but until hearing you saying it, I would have been inclined to doubt such things. I knew him as a young man, and I was unimpressed by his bearing or his behavior. In those days he was a strutting lordling, a favorite of the Plantagenet, with not a thought in his mind beyond clothing, hunting, gambling, and women … He did not appear to me to be of the stuff from which strong kings are made. My father had supported his grandfather, old Robert Bruce, the Competitor as he was known then, and so I was—with the rest of our family—known as a Bruce man. But this one's father, Robert Bruce the Elder, was a dour and unlikable man, and even his son shunned his company, preferring to spend his time with the Plantagenet crowd. And the father didn't seem to mind, probably thinking that, wastrel or not, the boy had the ear and the patronage of the English King … for what that was worth.

"But from all I hear, and what you've told me from your own experience, it would appear the lordling has grown up well—from Earl of Carrick to King of Scots—and is well thought of, too, by those who know him nowadays. You trust him, then?"

"Aye, Father. I do. He had no need to be generous to us, supplicants for his aid when he was ill beset himself. He was engaging and possessed of a great and unassuming dignity … Regal, I said, and regal I meant. Robert of Scotland is a king in more than name."

"Then I will take your word for it and think no more ill of him. Speaking of which, I hear that he has fallen ill himself and his brother Edward—a hothead, that one—has him under guard near Inverurie. It is mere rumor—I have no proof of the right or wrong of it. You know how people talk, knowing nothing but pretending they know all there is to know." Sir Alexander rose to his feet and crossed to the fireplace, where he picked up a long, narrow log and used it to rake the embers into activity before placing it among the glowing coals and adding several more. He stood there for long moments with his back to his sons, staring into the rekindled flames, then spoke without turning around.

"How will you protect your fleeing brood? And for how long?"

Will had been thinking about the Bruce's illness, concerned by the news of it, and now he was aware that he had lost the thread. He looked over at his brother, puzzled, but Kenneth was looking back at him the same way.

"I don't follow you, Father. What do you mean?"

The old man turned to face them, glancing from one to the other before addressing Will directly. "You are made Master in Scotland, you say … Master of what?"

"Of the Temple Order, I told—"

"I know what you told me, William, but now I am asking you to think on what is involved in that. If your worst fears are realized—as it seems they are bound to be—then the Temple is finished through-out Christendom. The head is already gone, and the rest of the goose will run around flapping its wings for a short time, and then fall dead." He held up a hand to stifle protest, though neither of his sons had responded.

"In all of Christendom, then, your command here—your little outpost of a few hundred souls—will be the sole repository of your Order's history and traditions. Your charge, William, as Master—and yours, Kenneth, as his brother—is to cherish and protect it: knights and sergeants, history and traditions, readiness and manpower. But how long can you sustain it? Where will you find recruits if the Order is abolished? Every man you lose from this time on will be irreplaceable. You cannot even breed sons to fill your ranks, even had you the time, because your people are all monks. Has that occurred to you?"

Will sat staring at his father. "No, Father. It had not. But you are right, and the thought chills me." He sat still again for a moment longer, meeting his father's eye, then added, "I have the feeling you have more to say on that …"

"I have an idea, a thought, nothing more. But it might offend you. How strong is your authority as Master?"

Will blinked, puzzled by the question. "Here in Scotland, it is all-powerful."

"But subject to overruling by the Council, is that not so?"

"It is."

"What if the Council never rules again, on anything? By your own admission, that could happen."

"Aye, it could, but may God forbid it. And yet, if that should turn out to be the case, I already have my duty defined for me, in writing, and by Master de Molay's own hand. I will become Grand Master over all … which may be my own few hundreds and no more."

"Then release them from their vows."

"*What?* Relea— I can't do that, Father. The mere thought is ludicrous. I do not possess that kind of authority. Besides—"

"Who does possess it, then, the Pope?"

"Well, yes."

"The same Pope who set the Inquisition to torture a false confession out of your Grand Master in order to appease the greed of your venal King? That Pope? Is that the one you mean? The Pope who rewards centuries of outstanding service and loyalty to his cause with treachery and vicious lies? The Pope whose craven, pusillanimous nature turns him into an insult against all he is supposed to represent, because he lacks the backbone to confront a king and refute a grievous wrong, and demonstrates his unfitness by turning his back on God Himself?

"Backbone, William—that's what you need in this case, and if you will but think on it, I believe you will see the truth of it. Absolve your people of their vow of chastity. Obedience and the other one they may keep. But give them at least the chance to marry and breed children to your cause."

"That's madness, Father. These men are monks, of long service. They could never adjust to such a change, would see it as sin, as a consignment to damnation."

Sir Alexander dipped his head. "Aye, some of them might … the older ones. But others would not. Their entire world is changed, and will probably remain that way. They will be *personae non gratae* within the Church, and they may even stand excommunicate, as fugitive members of a banned order. By releasing them from their vows, you would be offering them at least a chance to live as men in this new world in which they find themselves. Should even one score of them go on to breed sons, you would have young minds into which to implant your lore and teachings …"

Will sat silent, his mind reeling, seeing only the unconscionable arrogance and hubris of his father's suggestion and completely unequipped to deal with it, coming as it had from his father, the most honorable, righteous, and upstanding man he had ever known outside of the Order of Sion. Kenneth said nothing, refusing to look at either one of them, and for his part, Sir Alexander, too, said no more, merely waiting for his son to collect his obviously scattered wits. Finally Sir Alexander rescued him.

"Another matter altogether: do you have a squire?"

Will blinked. "A squire? No. I had one until several months ago, but he was knighted last July and I have been traveling since then. Why do you ask?"

"Because you have a nephew, your brother Andrew's son, Henry, who recently lost his master, after having lost his father, too. Andrew arranged the placement just before he died, but the knight, Sir Gilles de Mar, a worthy man, was sore wounded in the fight at Methven— he fought for Bruce—and he never recovered his health. He died of his injuries two months ago, and so young Henry's training has been interrupted. He needs a new master. Will you take him?"

"I would, and gladly, but how can I, Father, under the circumstances?"

"Circumstances change. But suitability does not. And I have no doubt your brother here will agree with me when I say that, as Master of your Order in this land, you would be perfect for the lad. He is fourteen and he needs discipline and tolerance, but more than that he needs a good example—integrity, strength and fortitude, and judicious moderation in all things. I can think of no better exemplar than yourself. Such attributes are few and far between, nowadays."

And so after very little more discussion it was agreed that Will would become responsible for his young nephew, Henry Sinclair. But even as he said he would, Will found himself wondering about his dead elder brother, Andrew, whom he could remember only as a boy, six years his senior.

"What happened to Andrew, Father?"

"He died ... ingloriously for a knight so full of virtue and promise." Sir Alexander grimaced ruefully. "Ingloriously, but very humanly. He died of a congestion, three years ago, after a mishap on a winter hunt, while he was separated from his companions. His horse stumbled in a storm-swollen spate and threw him into the rocks in the streambed. By the time his men found him, he had been lying there for hours, half in and half out of the water. They brought him home, but he never woke up. He simply grew weaker and sicker until he could no longer breathe. It was God's will, the priests told me, but I would have seen all of them in Hell to have my son returned to me."

"And what of the lad's mother?"

"She died long since, when he was but a babe. Young Henry never knew her." The old man straightened abruptly. "So, God's will or not, Andrew was gone, but his son remained, and now he will resume his training in good hands. He will make you a fine squire and will be a worthy knight when his time comes."

The talk from that time on was desultory, and soon Sir Alexander declared himself tired, and all three men went in search of sleep, although Will, at least, would lie awake for more than an hour, thinking about his father's astonishing and unsettling suggestion. And thinking about it, about what it might mean were he to do such a thing, he acknowledged that he could do it with impunity, were he so inclined, and were matters in France so bad that the very survival of the Temple knights fell into question. And then as he drifted into sleep he found himself thinking about Jessie Randolph, seeing her smiling at him as though through a distant haze, and too far by then from real awareness even to know that his body was reacting pleasurably to his vague imaginings, and that a succubus was even then coiled on his belly, waiting to drain him later while he slept.

3

It was early afternoon outside and Will could hear a blackbird singing in one of the five majestic elm trees that ringed the front of the big, fortified house that was his ancestral home, but here in the single-windowed interior of the bedchamber in which he had been born, it was almost dark. The single slash of light thrown by the open window illuminated one corner of his father's massive desk and a sharply limned segment of the wooden flooring beneath it, emphasizing the lack of brightness in the remainder of the room.

Will stretched backwards in his chair, digging his thumbs into the flesh of his waist under his lower ribs, and huffed out his breath in a great sigh, looking at the chest that sat on the corner of the desk.

The desk was ancient, acquired by one of his ancestors in the distant past—family legend had it that the piece had once belonged to a Roman governor of Britain, who had left it behind when the Legions left, more than seven hundred years earlier—and it had sat here in this room, huge and immovable, since the house itself was built more than a hundred years before. Its intricately carved oak was blackened and patinaed with unimaginable age. Compared to the objects now concealed behind it, however, the desk was of recent manufacture, and that thought, coming out of nowhere, brought Will out in a rush of gooseflesh and made him focus his attention on the chest again.

Its brass bindings seemed to blaze, throwing reflected sunlight in his face, and he was conscious of the weight of the key to it, hanging from a chain about his neck. It was a slim key, but solid iron, and no one but he knew that the chest it was meant to open contained more keys, one for each of the three large containers that held the bulk of the Temple Treasure, now ranged along the wall at the rear of the desk, and two more for the padlocks on the fourth, smaller and very different from the others. He straightened up and looked at them again, craning his neck to see over the plane of the desk's surface, highly aware that his would be among the few eyes to look at them before they disappeared into obscurity again, for they were to be reburied the next day, far from sight, in the domed cavern beneath the lands of Roslin. He sighed again, then grimaced and tapped a fingernail against his teeth. The chests were his responsibility now, and for the past half hour he had been sitting staring at them, fighting a growing urge to open them up and look at their contents.

He knew he had the right, for the keys were in his trust, but had he the will? Despite knowing, or perhaps because of knowing, what was in them, he found himself afraid of violating their sanctity, of transgressing upon their sacred antiquity. But it was his responsibility, as he had told himself yet again, mere minutes earlier, to make sure that they were undisturbed; that their contents were intact; that they were, in fact, there at all. His was the name that would be attached to them from tomorrow onwards, from the moment of their concealment in their new hiding place, and his was the honor that would be impugned were they to be opened at a later date and found to contain nothing but rubble, their original treasures stolen.

He cursed, and rose to his feet, crossing directly to the door at his back. Outside, at the top of the stairs, Tam Sinclair turned towards him as the door swung wide.

"Are you done?"

"No, not even started. All's well?"

Tam shrugged. "Well enough. What's keeping you?"

"Nothing … Nerves … Right, I'll do it now. If anyone approaches, anyone at all, sing out, then stall them here for long enough for me to close the locks."

Tam's eyebrows twitched. "Who would come up here in daylight? Your father's out and away and there's nobody else in the house except the two o' us. Just do what ye have to do, and let's away."

"Fine. I will." He stepped back into the bedchamber and pulled the door closed behind him, then went immediately to open the brass-bound chest. He removed the keys it held and hefted them in one hand, surprised at the solid weight of them and at the difficulty of grasping all of them at once. Then he looked at the one chest that was different from all the others, the Prime Chest, as he thought of it. He laid the keys on the desktop, then selected the proper pair from the pile, one for each of the two padlocks, before moving towards the Prime Chest. It was the only one of the chests that had iron rings mounted on its sides, for ease of carrying, and a pair of long, thick poles lay on the floor behind it. The poles were threaded through the rings whenever the chest was to be moved, but Will knew, too, because he had been told, that they would fit a second set of rings fixed to the sides of the device inside the chest.

The thought of what that device could be unnerved him slightly, and even as he reached out to grasp the first padlock the hackles rose on his neck and he had to stop. He tried to swallow, but his mouth was suddenly dry and he had to work his tongue before he could open it. He licked his lips and took a firmer grip on himself, then inserted the key, only to find that he had chosen the wrong padlock. Moments later the second lock opened with an oiled click and he reached for the key to the first. The metal hinges of the hasps grated gently as he raised them, and he paused again, drawing a great breath before pulling upwards, gently at first but then much harder than he had anticipated, to lift the heavy, lead-lined lid.

The contents of the chest were covered by a voluminous quilted blanket that he lifted out easily with both hands, dropping it on the floor by his feet as he gazed, open mouthed, at the astonishing object that now lay revealed. It fitted the interior closely, filling almost the entire space, and its ends and corners were wrapped and padded against abrasion by the sides of the chest. The golden glow it emitted seemed to radiate outwards, spilling over the edges of the container, although he knew that was no more than an illusion caused by the brightness of the shaft of sunlight striking the metal-coated surface of the artifact. From the way his skin reacted, though, causing him to shiver and stirring the short hairs at his nape, he had no doubt in his mind that he was looking down at the most compelling object in creation, the single most precious relic on earth: the gold-sheathed coffer made to contain the Covenant between God and His chosen people; the Ark of the Covenant from the Holy of Holies in the Temple of King Solomon.

He lost awareness of how long he had stood there, gazing down at the thing, his senses awash in its beauty, but at one point he found himself reaching out to touch it, his hand coming within inches of the beaten gold surface of the lid before his fingers closed spastically and he jerked his elbow back, holding his forearm out unnaturally in front of him. According to the legends of this thing and the lore of his own Order of Sion, only priests were permitted to touch it. Anyone else who did so died violently, and the ancient scriptures cited examples of such transgressions. He released a shuddering breath and lowered his arm, pushing his hand behind his back, where it might no longer be tempted. And then he allowed himself to look more closely at the two towering golden figures that surmounted the lid of the Ark. They were angels, he knew, Seraphim, but there was little angelic or serene about them. The figures were filled with menace and exuded vigilance and tension, the upper tips of their spread wings almost touching one another as the angels leaned forward, appearing to hover over the lid of the Ark, sheltering the sacred area between them from which the voice of God Himself was said to have spoken to the priests.

Graven images, he thought, and was surprised by the vehemence with which the anomaly thrust its way into his consciousness. The Jews abhorred graven images, believing them idolatrous, and yet here, atop the very repository made to store the stone tablets bearing God's own Law, was an absolute and categorical defiance of their first commandment, for these two images were graven in pure gold. And Aaron's Rod was in there, too, if the ancient lore were true: the sacred rod that turned into a serpent and devoured the serpents set upon it by Pharaoh's priests and sorcerers. Will found himself frowning, for he had always imagined that Aaron's Rod would be at least as long as its bearer's height, but the Ark itself was less than four feet in length and just over half that much in width, and thus, if the Rod was really in there, it must be far less imposing in appearance than his imaginings had led him to believe. But then he had a sudden memory of the heavy rod of state the King of France had carried on the only occasion when Will had seen him; it had been a two-inch-thick, intricately carved baton of ebony wood, ornate and solid and imposing, the embodiment of regal authority. The image in his mind of Capet's Rod, as he thought of it, satisfied him, and he immediately stopped wondering about the size of Aaron's Rod. But still he stood gazing at the golden box, one detached segment of his mind yet playing with the need to reach out and touch the thing with his bare hands.

He shuddered and wrenched his awestruck mind away from the appalling thought as a vision of his own end burst into his mind and he saw and felt himself stricken and overwhelmed by flames of heavenly immolation, and before he even knew what he was going to do, the lid of the great wooden chest slammed shut beneath his hands and he threw his full weight on it, pushing it down, his head hanging and his open mouth working as he struggled to catch his breath. Moving awkwardly, he forced himself to turn away from the Prime Chest and contemplate the other three, finding enormous difficulty in focusing on them and fighting to shut the image of the Ark and its brooding Seraphim out of his mind.

He failed. He filled his lungs with air, turned away from the chests, and began to walk rigidly towards the corner nearest him, looking straight ahead until he reached it, and then he squared the room, marching to each of its corners before turning right and making his way directly along the wall to the next. Three times he made the circuit before stopping again where he had begun, and now he found himself able to look at the remaining chests with something approaching equanimity. He knew what was contained in these three, because he had been told two decades before, when his studies had first touched upon them, but he had been told again, more recently, what they contained, and this latter time, as a senior member of the upper hierarchy of the Order of Sion, he had learned more than he knew before, because now the safety and welfare of the chests had become his personal responsibility.

He went back to his father's desk and collected the remaining keys that lay there, unlocking each of the chests in turn until they all yawned open side by side, their contents on display. Each of them, solidly made from dense, heavy wood and reinforced with iron strapping, was packed to capacity with uniform rows of earthen jars in a double layer, eight above and eight below, all of them made from the same thick, reddish clay, indistinguishable one from another. The tops had been covered with stretched, wet leather centuries before, the coverings then tightly bound in place with wet thongs of rawhide that, when dried, formed an airtight seal as hard as iron.

Will felt no desire to touch these items, and no curiosity about their contents. He was merely happy to see that they were intact, their seals unbroken. He already knew what they contained, because several of the jars had been broken at the time of their discovery in the ruined vaults beneath Jerusalem's Temple Mount, by the nine original knights who had founded the Order of the Temple, two hundred years earlier. The contents of those broken jars had been studied for years thereafter by the scholars of the Order of Sion, and had confirmed the teachings contained in the Order's ancient lore, which had itself emerged from Judea a thousand years before that, at the time of the destruction of Jerusalem by the Romans in the first century Anno Domini. These plain and unimpressive jars, Will knew, were the real Treasure of the Templars, notwithstanding the importance of the Seraphim-crowned Ark in the Prime Chest. The Ark of the Covenant represented religious tradition, awe and the fear of God, but the contents of the jars represented nothing supernatural. It was their simple existence that was awe inspiring and revolutionary, for they contained, on tightly rolled scrolls of papyrus, the written records and history of the original community of the Essenes in Qumran, the community that the man Jesus and his brother, James the Just, had ruled and guided. Their contents proved beyond dispute that the Jesus of Qumran, now known as Jesus of Nazareth, was an ordinary man and not, as Paul had decreed, the Son of God, risen and reborn miraculously from the dead ...

Will was intensely aware that the threat these records posed to the very existence of the Catholic Church could not be underestimated. Their existence was unsuspected, but were they ever to be found by Rome, they would be destroyed immediately, their threat expunged by fire, along with the lives of everyone who knew of their existence. Will knew the truth of that from his own training within the Order of Sion, because the Church's entire edifice was built upon a misunderstanding.

Among their ancient secrets, brought with them from their days of slavery in Egypt and firmly rooted in the age-old rites that had dominated their worship for the centuries of their enslavement, the priests of the Israelites had preserved a ritual involving a symbolic death and resurrection—a rebirth into Enlightenment and the search for Communion with God Himself—that had been passed down through the millennia and now existed as the central ceremony of the Order of Sion. Will himself had undergone the ritual, when being Raised to brotherhood in the ancient fraternity, a ceremony that had roots stretching back into the earliest days of Egypt and the worship of Osiris, the God of Light, and his wife-sister, Isis.

Paul, the Order of Sion believed, had caught wind of this ceremonial—or of the reported fact that Jesus had "died" and been "reborn" decades earlier, before Paul's own time—but being a Gentile and therefore by definition an outsider, he knew nothing of the true Way of the Essenes and thus had been incapable of under-standing the truth of what he had discovered. The result was that he had transposed the ritual "death" in the Raising rite into the actual death of the man Jesus, believing that he had truly risen from the grave as a divine being. And upon that misunderstanding had been born the Catholic Church.

"Will! Are ye *done* in there?"

Will came out of his reverie with a start. "Aye, I'm coming." He moved quickly now to close and lock the chests again, raising the lid of the Prime Chest and replacing the quilted blanket before closing it firmly and slipping the twin padlocks through the hasps. When he was done, he replaced the keys in their chest and locked that one too, lifted it onto one of the large chests, then hung the key around his neck and thrust it down into his tunic. He slapped the dust from his hands and looked around the room, checking that everything was as it should be, and then he walked quickly to the door and rejoined Tam outside.

4

Will and his party were back in Arran within three weeks of their arrival in Roslin, having covered the three-hundred-mile journey there and back without incident. They had met potentially dangerous groups on both legs of the journey, but their own strength of twenty strongly armed and mounted men had been sufficient to discourage anyone from trying to molest them. In the meantime, the Treasure was safely concealed in the underground cavern close to his father's home, and the excavation work had been expertly handled, so quick and thorough in its execution that the great bramble thickets hiding the entrance hid it still— they had been uprooted very carefully and then replanted in their original position when the work of sealing the entrance was completed.

Will was relieved to discover that nothing untoward had occurred during their absence, and that the new program of allocated work had progressed well, the newly structured organization apparently functioning smoothly. The brethren were already almost indistinguishable from the ordinary folk he and his men had encountered on the journey to and from Roslin. Their clothing was drab and sturdy, their beards had all been cropped to be unremarkable, and their scalps were overgrown by new-sprouting hair.

The secondary chapter had been set up at Lochranza mere days after Will's departure, with the senior Temple bishop there, Bruno of Arles, functioning as temporary chaplain and Sir Reynald de Pairaud installed as acting preceptor. This development pleased Will immensely, because the veteran knight, for all his prickliness and his Temple Boar mentality, was utterly reliable when it came to his duty and responsibilities. On his first visit to Lochranza, four days after his return from the mainland, Will was open and sincere with his praises for the work that de Pairaud had already achieved in his new stewardship.

As a castle, with towering mountains in the distance at its back, Lochranza was well established, built upon a high crag overlooking the bay beneath, and very easily defended, but its principal feature was inside: a great, strongly built hall that was both draft free and well lit, two elements that rendered it more hospitable than nine out of any ten other castles Will could think of. De Pairaud had already taken advantage of that, setting skilled carpenters to partitioning the huge hall one-third of the way along its length, leaving ample room for all the necessary daily functions that the garrison required. The partitioned third had been turned into a Temple Chapter House, complete with a single, fortified door; the required celebrants' Chairs, mounted on rostra in the east, west, north, and south; and a squared central floor laid out in alternating foot-square blocks of black- and white-painted boards thickly covered with multiple layers of clear, hard-set varnish. Here, in quarters far more elaborate and sumptuous than those used by their brethren in Brodick, the knights of Lochranza would convene in the hours of darkness to hold their chapter meetings and conduct the rites and ceremonies of their Order.

Beyond the walls, a smithy had been set up in one of the castle outbuildings, and most of the heavy livestock, the knights' big warhorses, had been brought from Brodick and divided into small herds of seven to ten animals, each of them tended by a small team of men and allotted its own grazing territory among the lush valley bottoms that penetrated the highlands and mountain ridges soaring behind the castle. The fisher folk who had lived in the village by the harbor had vanished with the approach of the strange Southrons, as they called the newcomers, and it was generally assumed that they had fled to the high hillsides out of fear, caused more by the treasonous conduct of their former chief, Menteith, than by fear of the newcomers *per se*. De Pairaud believed they would return eventually, as soon as they had convinced themselves that they were being neither hunted nor persecuted, but in the meantime, several of the sergeants had moved into the small stone huts left vacant at the sea's edge and were making themselves valuable to the community by fishing every day, bringing in a constant and varying supply of fresh fish for the castle tables.

Farther out, de Pairaud explained, on the high moors behind the castle and sloping towards the island's western shores, other small teams of men were amassing and drying mountains of peat that would be stocked for the following winter's needs, while yet others were busy felling the remaining trees of the island's only extensive woodland, pillaged beyond salvation by the English garrison that had built the hall at Brodick. A team of men from both chapters had refurbished the old sawpits used by the English soldiery, and sawyers were now hard at work, cutting the green logs into planks, boards, and beams for their construction needs in both Brodick and Lochranza. Those, too, would have to be stacked and dried before they could be used, but Will no longer believed that his party's stay on Arran would be a brief one, and even if it were, the exercise of cutting and stockpiling both the fuel and the green lumber served a worthwhile purpose in keeping the men busy and preoccupied against boredom.

He ended his visit to Lochranza by setting out on a long, south-westward sweep of the high moors on his way back to Brodick, visiting the various worksites and greeting the men involved in person, inspecting their efforts and expressing his satisfaction and encouragement to each group he met. But he found himself fretting more and more about the King's rumored illness, for if Bruce were to be removed from power, he and his men would be in great peril on this island, perhaps even unable—and this thought chilled him— to reclaim their galleys from the MacDonalds. That final thought weighed heavily on him from the moment it occurred to him, and he arrived back at Brodick Hall on a blustery day of wind and chill rain, his mood matching the weather perfectly, bleak and comfortless.

His worst fears were put at rest immediately. Sir James Douglas had called in to Brodick while Will was at Lochranza and had left word that the Bruce was well, and had withdrawn with his brother and all his army to Strathbogie on the Deveron River near Aberdeen, where the local lord was a staunch supporter and where the King was recovering his strength and preparing for a spring campaign against the English forces in the area.

Douglas had left a packet of dispatches for Will, in care of Sir Richard de Montrichard, and Will collected it and took it with him to read while Tam Sinclair supervised the preparation of a hot bath—a weakness, in the eyes of many, that Will had developed in his years of traveling among the Moors in Spain. Whenever he grew chilled or was drenched by cold rainwater, Will would insist on bathing in hot water, and Tam had long since grown inured to the strange behavior. Tam had not accompanied him to Lochranza, opting instead to remain in Brodick to undertake the interrupted training and education of Will's nephew Henry, who, as squire now to a military monk, would need to know far more than was required of the squire of a common knight, and Will had been content to leave them both behind.

Will cut the leather binding on the packet and withdrew two documents. One was a folded note on a scrap of parchment from Douglas himself, written in a bold, looping hand, with the tidings of the Bruce's sickness and mentioning that the King, now much improved, was greatly pleased with the loyalty and dedication of the "Arran" men who rode with him. It ended with a simple, flourished signature, plain "Douglas."

The second missive was entirely different, carefully folded into a neat oblong and sealed at the rear with a waxen stamp that Will had never seen before. His name was written in a small, neat hand in the upper right front corner. Curious, he broke the seal and opened up the letter, aware of the rich and supple texture of the three sheets of fine parchment between his fingers. He turned first to the last page, his eye going directly to the name at the bottom, and the breath caught in his throat as he saw the simple signature of Jessica Randolph de St. Valéry. For long moments he could do nothing, his pulse pounding and his thoughts churning, seeking vainly for reasons why this woman, of all people, should write to him. But eventually, accepting the folly of such feckless thoughts, and acknowledging his own unreasonable excitement with chagrin, he turned back to the first page and began to read the delicately formed Angevin script, whispering the words aloud to himself in the accents of his own boyhood, in the time before the more ubiquitous French overwhelmed his native tongue.

Sir William

I have little doubt but that you will be filled with outrage at my temerity in writing thus to you, but you will be aware, even now, that I am writing in the language of your latter years to some purpose. Should this letter fall into unfriendly hands, it is my sincere wish that it should remain incomprehensible to those who find it.

I write to you from a place in Scotland's northeastern lands, where it has been my honor and privilege, these past two months, to take part in tending to our King, who has been gravely ill but is now mending rapidly and regaining his former strength, to the joy of all around him and the great good fortune of his realm.

I know the countryside is rife with rumors of my Lord's imminent demise, all kinds of lurid tales of grief and disaster being carried far and wide by people who know little of the truth. I know, too, from experience, of your uncomfortable situation on your far-off island there, and I have been concerned lest, hearing such tales, you may fear for the welfare of your charges there. If that has been the case, then put your mind at rest, Sir Knight, and know the truth: His Grace is well. The crisis is long past and the man himself recovering strongly enough to act the man and the King again, planning campaigns for the coming year with all his friends and commanders.

Which leads to the main purpose of this letter: to inform you of affairs being planned. A delegation of powerful Frenchmen has been here. We have no knowledge of how they were able to trace His Grace's whereabouts—a close-held secret—but they arrived in secrecy and departed again directly for France. The substance of their visit was to bruit the notion of an alliance between His Grace and France himself, Philip Capet, with the end of mounting a fresh crusade against the Moors in Spain. His Grace received them courteously, accompanied by only a few of his closest advisers. He told them that he would consider the matter, and that it appealed to him, but that his own realm is yet insufficiently strong to permit his soon departure from its shores. And then, as soon as they were gone, he sent for me and in a private audience told me what had transpired, after which he asked me to write this to you on his behalf, and in your native tongue, learned by me from my late husband's family, explaining his thoughts to you while reassuring you that you and yours need have no immediate concerns, since it is unlikely that this matter will progress further for several years.

From the viewpoint of diplomacy, this development has great political value—an open acknowledgment of His Grace's kingship by the most powerful King in Christendom. It has equal, future value as a weapon against those who would see His Grace's excommunication made permanent, since the joint leader of such a crusade could scarcely be condemned by Holy Church. But it also emphasizes the delicacy of your situation and his own in the face of your status as fugitives from France and Philip's displeasure, for if that knowledge were to become widespread, it would endanger the proposed alliance. Therefore His Grace requests your increased concern in compliance with his wishes in the matter of disguising the identities of your people on the island—an assurance I have already tendered with confidence on your behalf. He has no doubts that you will honor his wishes, but merely wished to draw attention to their increased importance in the face of this approach from France.

I have great respect and liking for this man. I met him, as you might already know, soon after leaving your island, led to do so by Sir James himself, and His Grace honored me at that time by requesting that I accept the guardianship of his young niece, Marjorie, the illegitimate daughter of his beloved brother Nigel, dead at the hands of the English torturers. The child is one of the few remaining female relatives left free in his whole family, and he believes she might remain safe with me, since I am but new-come from France and few know much about me. Accordingly, she has now become my niece, adopted by me in France and brought here in my train, and when we leave here, she will come with me to my family's home in the valley of the River Nith, near Dumfries town.

Thus I am well, and greatly honored on a number of counts, and my task here in the north is almost done, this letter being almost the last of my self-imposed duties. Sir James is here with His Grace for several days and has promised me that he will deliver this to you when next he travels near your place of refuge. I promise you that upon my return to my home in Nithsdale, a mere day's travel from where you are, I will make no further effort to distract you from your humorless and all-consuming duties. But I hope that you might some day think of me, despite all your stern disapproval and imposed restrictions, as your friend,

Jessica Randolph de St. Valéry

5

Will folded the letter up carefully and went to have his bath. From the first words of the letter, he had lost awareness that it had been written by a woman, his entire attention given to the content rather than the sender. The news of the French King's approach to Bruce troubled him only briefly, the generosity of his nature accepting the importance of the gesture to the King of Scots. And he decided that it could do no harm to reinforce his instructions on their need for anonymity on Arran. He owed that much to Bruce, he knew, for any failure by the Arran Templars to achieve complete invisibility in the eyes of the idly curious could cause the King of Scots unnecessary and embarrassing discomfiture.

Then, his decision made, he dressed in fresh, dry clothing and summoned his senior officers into conference. There he outlined what he had been told and asked each of them to think of any difficulties that they might have overlooked in putting his earlier instructions into practice. Did they believe they had they been entirely successful, he asked, in hiding any and all signs that might identify their men as monks of the Order?

There was, he was told, only the matter of the mutinous monk, Martelet, who was still imprisoned, with a full month more of solitary confinement ahead of him. The man, Will was told, was still recalci-trant, refusing to acknowledge that he had done anything wrong.

As soon as the meeting was concluded, Will went down to the cells and confronted Martelet, who looked as he might be expected to look after a month of being confined in a tiny cell, deprived of any means of cleansing himself. Will dismissed the sergeant on guard duty, then crossed the floor in two paces to stand in front of the bars, gazing at the prisoner, who glowered back at him without speaking. Will stared at the man for a long time, watching his eyes and seeing no signs of yielding there—no hint of indecision or regret.

"You look unhappy, and you have served only half your sentence. I will take care to avoid seeing you as you approach the next month's end." He waited then, but Martelet made no sign of having heard a word.

"You are a fool, you know. There is no one here to overhear us, and I am telling you, man to man, that you are a fool. You are also a mutinous, arrogant ingrate and a disgrace to our Order."

That won him a response, as Martelet straightened up and almost spat at him. "You would not dare speak thus were there no bars between us!"

"Twice a fool now. It was I who put you in here, you may recall. I bested you out in the yard when you were armored, with a bare sword in your hand. I have no need to dare anything. You, on the other hand, must dare to change your attitude. I was not present when you were sentenced to be held here, nor had I any voice in what transpired. That decision was made by your peers, the brethren you insulted by your arrogant attitude. But hear my voice in this: you cannot win in this case. You swore three oaths on entering this Order, and the greatest of the three was obedience—obedience to your superiors, and to the Rule that dictates the behavior of each of us. Your breach of that vow brought you here, to this. And your continuing rebellion can have but one sure end, for it will not be tolerated by your brothers—it cannot be, for the good of all. Thus, if you persist in this folly, you will end up being immured, like other disobedient souls before you. Think you to find any satisfaction in being walled up alive and left to die of thirst, and all for foolish pride?"

He waited, expecting some response, but all he saw was a momentary flicker, perhaps doubt or fear, behind the other's angry eyes.

"Wake up, Brother Martelet, and use the wits God gave you. We are not so many here that we can afford to lose a brother so needlessly, and absolution is not yet beyond your reach. Look at me now. No crossed surcoat, no mail, no forked beard, and no tonsure. But I am still the man I was a month ago and have been all my life. And I am Master here … Master in Scotland, as you yourself heard proclaimed. Beyond those doors at my back, your brethren are no different than they were, save that they, too, are dressed and armed and bearded as I am, their tonsures vanished. This was not done upon a whim. You heard the reasons announced before your trial and they are sound and solid, necessary to our continuing welfare. And still you choose to be obdurate, which makes me call you fool for your pride and stubbornness."

He stopped, for the space of a heartbeat, then continued. "Think on this. Promise me that you will never again lift your hand in violence against your brothers of the Order, agree to trim your beard and join your brethren again as an equal, and I will release you in good faith as soon as you summon me and say you will obey and observe the Rule again. But I warn you, Martelet, cross me in this and you will surely die thereafter, bricked up within a wall at the behest of your brethren. Summon me if you decide to be sensible." And with that he spun on his heel and stalked out, signaling the waiting guard to resume his duties.

Two days later, on a bright but cold afternoon, the summons came, brought to him by Tam, young Henry following at his heels like a watchful puppy. "Martelet's asking for you. Will ye go?"

Will set his sword and whetstone against the wall by the step where he had been sitting and stood up. "A bath, Tam, good and hot, as quick as you may."

"A bath? You had a bath three days ago!"

"Not for me, man, for Martelet. He's filthy and foul and hoaching with fleas and lice. Set out fresh clothing for him, too—I have plenty and to spare—then take the ones he will strip off away and burn them, fleas and all. Be quick now. Henry, you help him."

Mere moments later, Will was facing Martelet again though the bars of his cage. The prisoner's face was calm now, showing no trace of the anger or bitterness that had marred it before. Will nodded to him. "Have you decided?"

When Martelet spoke, his voice was as calm as his expression. "I have. I confess I have been arrogant, perhaps slightly mad, and my behavior inexcusable."

"Not inexcusable. It is pardoned."

"My thanks then. I would like you to know that I will not forswear myself in this. I will obey henceforth."

"So mote it be. Guard! Release the prisoner. I'll wait outside, in the fresh air." That last was to Martelet, who merely nodded and waited for the guard to open the door to his cage and unlock his chains.

Several minutes later, he stood cringing in the bright afternoon light, holding both hands up to shield his eyes against the unaccustomed glare. Will gave him time to adjust to the brightness, then led him to his own quarters, where Tam and young Henry already had the wooden tub half full of steaming water.

"Drop your clothing over there in the corner, then cleanse yourself in the bath. Be thorough. Use the soap. Everywhere. It is medicinal and will kill the vermin in your hair, both head and body. And have no fear, the water will not sap your strength or lay you open to the Devil's wiles. There are fresh clothes on the chair there and those boots should fit you … and you'll find trimming shears on that table by the wall. Tam will help you with the trimming, if you need him. When you are cleaned and ready, my squire here will bring you to me. I shall be in the preceptor's quarters, with the preceptor himself, Admiral de Berenger, and Bishop Formadieu attending me. You will address your contrition to them, and they will absolve you of the remainder of your punishment, for you stand lawfully convicted and sentenced according to the Rule, and in seeking clemency you must now convince them, the senior brethren of our community, that your remorse and contrition is real and heartfelt. Farewell then. We will await you."

Within the hour, the thing was done. Martelet, scrubbed and trimmed and combed and freshly dressed in a simple tunic and leggings, looked like an entirely different person from the man they had all come to deplore in recent months, and the tribunal of senior brethren sat emotionlessly as he recanted his former behavior and asked humbly for reinstatement. The tribunal had few questions for him, contenting themselves with reminding him that he lived under oath and now upon their sufferance.

Will was glad to see that de Montrichard, too, had undergone some kind of quiet transformation in the recent past. Gone was the diffidence and the air of indecisiveness that had marked the man and caused Will great concern since their departure from La Rochelle; the knight who stood here now was every inch the Temple precep-tor, crisp, decisive, and authoritative, speaking from the full stature of his office. He reminded Martelet that he would undergo close scrutiny for the month to follow, and that, should his behavior be found wanting, he would return to the cell from which he had been released, to serve out twice the length of his full sentence. He warned him sternly to adhere strictly to the Order's Rule henceforth, and then dismissed the case.

Martelet stood hesitantly for several moments, clearly not quite believing that he had been pardoned and set free, and then he bowed deeply and thanked the tribunal for their clemency, before turning away and marching smartly from their presence. Only then did Will permit himself to relax, subsiding back into his chair and breathing a deep sigh. He would have been reluctant to cause the man's death, but he would have had no option had Martelet chosen to remain obdurate.

He barely noticed when the others began to stand up and move away, and by the time he did, his mind, freed from his concern over Martelet, had already moved on to other, less harrowing things, among them the impending arrival of the ship from the Mediterranean coast of France; the upcoming change of roster for the troops soon due to return from riding with the King on the mainland; the incongruous possibility of releasing his men from their oath of chastity—a thought that recurred to him from time to time nowadays but bore no real onus of consideration; and the troublesome matter of whether to respond to the letter from the Randolph woman. She had gone to considerable trouble to put his mind at ease on the matter of the King's illness, and he felt both grateful that she had and guilty for the pleasure he had taken from it. But then he reminded himself that she had been ordered to do so, for all intents and purposes, by the Bruce himself. His decision not to respond was made as he grasped the wooden fists at the ends of his chair's arms and levered himself up to follow the others to the refectory, only to find that Richard de Montrichard had stopped to wait for him in the doorway.

"May I ask a question?" he asked, as though seriously awaiting a deliberated answer.

"Of course. What is it?"

The preceptor stepped aside to allow Will to pass, then fell into step beside him. "Idle curiosity, you might think, but it is not. How long do you believe it will take us, north and south, to implement all you designed for us before you went away last month? I can judge my own people's progress, but you are the only one with an entire overview, and so I thought to ask you outright. My estimate would be four months from now."

Will looked at him. "For all of it, Lochranza included? No, Sir Richard, I fear you are being optimistic. The best I could guess at, to see this island settled to our satisfaction, would be half a year from now—high summer—and perhaps even longer. We have much to do, and it cannot all be done at once. We have buildings and barracks, bothies and byres to build." He smiled at the preceptor's blank-faced reaction to the Scots words, and kept on speaking. "And they have to be built well—roofed and snug against the weather all the year round. We'll build them out of peat sod, so they'll be solid, but we'll have to dig the sod in the first place. We have to prepare beach sites, too, where our galleys and ships can be hauled ashore and their fouled bottoms scraped clean of barnacles and shellfish.

That will take some work. There are sufficient suitable sites around, but no one has ever had a need to shape them to such purposes, so we will have to start from the very beginnings on that project. The logging you are familiar with, but that will not last six months. De Pairaud's master sawyer tells him we will have used up all the suitable trees within half that time, so after that, we will simply be sawing and stacking the remaining logs. And atop all of that, we have our community obligations and holy days, and our ongoing training to be dealt with, including the revolving roster of the troop accommodations between here and Scotland. No, my friend, trust me—we will be fortunate indeed if we are finished here within six months."

They had arrived at the doors to the refectory and went inside to find themselves late, one of the brothers already reading the day's lesson to the silent assembly as the two most senior members of the community made their way in silence to their places.

A CATALOGUE OF SINS

1

Jessie Randolph sat on a stone outcrop overlooking the vale of Nith, where the river meandered peacefully from the low hills to the north on its way past her home and to the Solway Firth and the English border, several miles to the south. She sat without moving, drinking in the scene before her and listening to the silence of the late-summer afternoon, a stillness broken only by the occasional shouts of the children playing on the hillside behind her and the incessant song of a single thrush perched somewhere on one of the low buildings two hundred paces away to her left. At her back, the sun was well into its decline, casting the shadows of the hillside down in front of her towards the river, and she felt a tingle of excitement stir in her stomach as she reached into the neck of her tunic and pulled out the soft cloth bag that nestled between her breasts, feeling the springy tension of the tightly rolled parchment it contained, and shivering as a sudden rush of gooseflesh swept over her shoulders and arms. The bag contained a letter, and its very existence seemed outrageous, waxing in significance now from moment to moment. Its content, and the tantalizing possibility of actually sending it off, made her stomach flutter in a way she had not experienced in years, since she was a young girl dreaming of her first love.

She looked over her shoulder, almost laughing to herself at the formless guilt she was feeling, and seeing that she was still alone, she loosened the drawstring and pulled the letter out, then untied the silken bow that held it shut. It was written on several sheets of fine, extremely valuable parchment, carefully trimmed to a uniform size, part of the hoard she had begged and won from Master Bernard de Linton, the Abbot of Arbroath who had recently become King Robert's secretary and whom she had met and come to like during her stay in the north, while she was tending to the King's illness. Now she held the scrolled sheets in one hand, her elbow resting on an upraised knee as she gazed down towards the water, her eyes unfocused, completely unaware of the picture she presented.

Had she been aware of it she might have laughed again at the thought, for she was wearing what she thought of as her scandalous suit, since it had scandalized every woman in her district when they first saw her wearing it. In all probability, she had often thought, it had scandalized their menfolk too, but none of those had ever dared to comment on it. In fact, she was wearing men's clothing, altered to her own use, that she had brought with her from France—long, loose-fitting breeches, tight in the seat and flared from the knees and made of chamois leather. The snugness of their fit was disguised by a knee-length wraparound tunic of the same material, belted at the waist and worn over a plain square-necked bodice of soft, finely woven wool, cinched at the waist by a heavy, well-worn, and pliable leather belt from which hung a long, sheathed dagger. Her boots, made by a master craftsman on her late husband's estate, were of the same soft leather, thicker, and heavily soled and heeled, but unmistakably made for her feet and as supple as well-worn gloves.

From a distance, she might pass as a man, but as the distance dwindled there could be no mistaking her startling femininity. Her hair, auburn in the afternoon light, hung down past her shoulders, tied loosely at the back with a leather thong, and her face and arms were tanned with the summer sun so that her wide eyes seemed to flash and sparkle, thrown into prominence by the smooth luster of the taut skin of her cheekbones with its scattering of light freckles. The color of her eyes, and she had been told sufficiently across the years to believe it, defied description by most men. Predominantly gray, they changed according to the light, sometimes pale blue, sometimes dark, and at other times more green than anything else.

A movement by her feet made her glance down to where a vole was scuttling past her, and she watched tolerantly as it darted towards the base of her perch and vanished somewhere behind the crossbow and quiver of bolts that leaned against the rock. The sight of the weapon made her turn her head again and stare briefly towards the Cairn Woods below on her right, one of the few belts of trees in the area, where one of the local men had seen a bear the day before. She did not expect to see the animal, but the possibility had been enough to prompt her to carry the crossbow with her that afternoon. Nothing moved over there, though, and she flapped the parchment in her hand, checked again to be sure there was no one in sight, and then began to read aloud, but quietly, what she had composed painstakingly over the past few days. She read a word or two, hesitated, began again, and after two or three sentences stopped and flapped the letter in frustration.

My God, Will Sinclair, have you any idea of the trouble you put me to? How can I—? No, you have no idea, you stubborn, upright, stupid man. How could you have? You are over there on your silly little island, playing the sanctimonious monk while all your benighted brethren in France rot in Philip Capet's prisons, tortured and abused by the very men who ... Ach! God, give me the strength to be patient!

She rose to her feet, rolling the scrolled parchment sheets tightly again while she looked around for the silk ribbon that had bound them. It had fallen from where she dropped it, lodging deep in a narrow fissure in the stone outcrop, and to reach it she had to place one booted foot on the stone to bear her weight while she bent forward, stretching down into the crack. She retrieved the ribbon with difficulty and straightened up, blowing a stray lock of hair out of her eyes, and as she did so she saw the length of her own outstretched thigh, its shape tightly outlined by the stretched leather of her breeches. It made her laugh.

Sweet Jesus, Will, if you could see me, dressed like this, you would not be able to pray for a fortnight. There would be a sight to interrupt your most chaste thoughts and make your frown like a thundercloud, would it not?

Well, sir knight, I am going to send this letter to you. I'll have my young cousin Hugh take it to Arran in person. Too much time and work have gone into the penning of it to let it go to waste. Besides, why should I not send it? It will bring you tidings of your sister Peggy and the joy your gift brought her. And it will bring you tidings of our King and what he has heard from France concerning your Order. You are in disgrace, Will Sinclair, with all your brotherhood, whether or no the cause be justifiable. Time to forget about return- ing there, and to find yourself a new life here in Scotland. A real life, as a real man, with a wife who would make you happy. Dear God, listen to me! Talking about marriage to a monk! I must be mad ... But 'tis a gladly borne madness, I must say. Now ...

A high-pitched shout made her turn and look up to where twelve- year-old Marjorie Bruce—her supposed niece but in reality King Robert's—had left her friends behind and was bounding down the hillside, calling. Jessie had spoken nothing but French to the child since she first met her, since for their current purposes, and for her own protection, Marjorie was supposed to be French, and the girl, gifted with an ear for sounds, had learned quickly, so that now she spoke the language effortlessly, with no lingering trace of the tongue she had learned from birth. The child was still a distance away, too far for Jessie to make out what she was shouting, but she sensed an urgency. "Wait you there!" she called. "I'm coming up!" She quickly collected her crossbow and quiver, slinging the latter over her shoulder, and started to climb the hillside.

"What is it, child?" she asked when she reached the girl. "What's wrong?"

"There are men coming, Auntie, from over there, beyond the hill."

"From the west? From Annandale? How many?"

"I don't know. They are too far away to count, but they're coming."

"Show me."

The girl turned and started to run up the hill, and Jessie stretched out her pace to keep up with her, remembering when she, too, had been able to treat steep hillsides as though they were flat ground, but she was concerned about who might be coming her way from the west. The Annan lands had belonged to the King's father, Robert Bruce of Annandale, but they, like her own Nithsdale, had always been a major invasion route from the south, and during the wars of the previous few years they had become sparsely populated as the local people fled into the safety of the higher hills to avoid being harried by the ever-present English. The vales of Annan and Nith, with the rest of Scotland's south, had both been burned bare many times in the previous decade in order to deny sustenance to King Edward's armies.

She breasted the top of the hill eventually to find the children hopping up and down with excitement as they jabbered and pointed into the distance. Jessie, fighting for breath, held up her hand to shield her eyes from the glare of the sinking sun ahead of her. The light was fierce, but her eyes adjusted quickly, showing her the unmistakable reflection of light on weapons, armor, and saddlery. They were still more than three miles away, she guessed, not yet having passed the distinctive stone outcrop known locally as the Leopard, which reared up two and a half miles from where she stood. She was aware of Marjorie close beside her, craning on tiptoes as she tried to see all that she could.

"Your eyes are better than mine, child. Can you see how many there are?"

"No, Auntie, but there's a lot of blue among them."

Jessie could see no blue, but she did not question the girl's assertion. The men were coming from Annandale, Bruce country, and James Douglas's colors were blue and white—Douglas, whom the King himself had appointed governor of all the south mere months before. Her mind went at once to what she was wearing. Her scandalous suit was no fitting garb in which to receive the King's young envoy. She spun suddenly, grasping her ward by the shoulder.

"It is Sir James Douglas, here on the King's affairs. I must run back to the house and dress to receive him. I leave it to you to round up all the others and bring them back safely. Can you do that?"

"Of course, Auntie." Marjorie Bruce swung away and began calling to the other children, but Jessie was already striding off, her crossbow balanced on one shoulder as her long legs bore her effortlessly down the slope towards the cluster of houses less than half a mile away.

She was half undressed by the time she entered her own house, but fortunately no one was around to see her remarkable condition. Calling loudly for her companion Marie as she swept inside, she pulled the cloth bag from its resting place between her breasts and dropped it on the table just inside the door of her own room before unlacing the bindings at the front of her leather breeches, pushing them down over her hips, and stepping out of them. The open tunic fell beside them, and she grasped the edges of her undertunic and pulled it swiftly over her head. Then she crossed naked, except for her high boots, to the large French armoire that held most of her more formal clothing.

There were few dresses there to choose from, so her selection did not take long, and before long she was standing erect, tapping her foot impatiently as Marie fussed with the lacings of the bodice of the rich green dress. It was a magnificent gown, as out of place among the women of Nithsdale as a preening peacock would be among a local flock of geese, but it set off her eyes and her hair wondrously well, as she had been told by many an ardent admirer, and she knew it would have the required effect on the King's young warden.

"Your hair, madam," Marie said, concern in her voice. "It needs … something."

"Then do something. But be quick. Our guests will be here at any moment."

During the few minutes that she knew Marie would require to pin up her hair into something resembling what she thought a lady's hair ought to look like, Jessie eyed the cloth bag containing the letter. It was a very special bag, although no one else ever glanced twice at it. But it was his, made from the kerchief he had pulled from within his tunic to wrap the gift he had sent to his sister. Jessie remembered taking it from him, remembered the feel of it in her fingers, warm as it was with the heat of his body and scented, as she discovered moments after leaving his tent, with the clean, intimate odor of his skin. She had delivered the gift to Peggy Sinclair, and taken joy in Peggy's pleasure at receiving it, but she had kept the kerchief, sniffing at it fondly from time to time when she was alone—and foolishly, she sometimes told herself—long after the faint, lingering odor of his presence had faded and died. But she could not bring herself to part with it, and so she had sewn it into a rectangular bag, a reticule that she used to contain the things that were essential to her every day ... her combs; her sachet of rose petals and dried lavender; her needles and fine thread, carefully protected in a tiny etui of flat, polished ebony from some exotic land; a palm-sized mirror of polished silver in a velvet bag; and now the daring letter that broke her promise not to disturb his peace once she had returned to Nithsdale.

"There, madam. It is finished. No one would ever know it newly done. But the boots ..."

"The boots are very comfortable. No one will see them."

Jessie stood up, taking the metal hand mirror that Marie offered. She checked her reflection once, briefly, then nodded her thanks. "You are a miracle, Marie. Now, my reticule from over there, if you please, and we may go and greet our guests."

2

The leading group of the visiting moss-troopers—the garron-mounted raiding Scots horsemen of the long-disputed border country between Scotland and England—was clattering into the courtyard of the farmhouse as Jessie reached the front door, and she had no trouble finding a smile with which to welcome King Robert's dashing young lieutenant. James Douglas saw her immediately as he cantered into the yard, and he grinned, whipping off his bonnet with its blackcock feather and bowing from the saddle.

"Lady Jessica!" he shouted. "Seldom has weary traveler ever beheld such a wondrous sight as you present there in your doorway." He prodded his horse forward until it could approach no closer, then slipped from its back and took her proffered hand in his own, bowing over it. "My lady, you must pardon my arrival unannounced, but I had little choice. We chanced across some Englishry two days ago and they outnumbered us heavily, so we chose to run and hide." He smiled as he said that, but Jessie knew he was quite serious. King Robert had expressly forbidden his commanders to engage the enemy in anything resembling formal battle—a directive, logical and judicious though it was, that did not sit well with many of his staunchest commanders. Among those, young Douglas was the ablest and the most fiery, so she could guess at what it had cost Sir James to run away, as he put it.

She looked him in the eye and nodded. "Then you are welcome here, my lord of Douglas. Are they far behind you?"

"The English?" He laughed. "No, my lady, they are miles away, seeking us in some distant part of Galloway. We gave them the slip easily, left them slaistering through dub and mire last night and heading westward while we doubled back and came this way. I wouldna bring them howling here to bother you. But I have brought another to amuse you … one I picked up last month."

He gestured over his shoulder with a pointing thumb, and Jessie looked to see what he was talking about. There were about forty men crowded into the yard now, climbing down from the garrons and beginning to mill about in the enclosed space, but one of them stood out from all the others, a tall man wearing half armor and the polished steel helmet of a moss-trooper. He stood with his back to her, his eyes apparently looking over the outbuildings around the yard.

"He's shy," Jamie said, then raised his voice. "Thomas, have you no words of greeting for our hostess?"

The tall man seemed to stiffen, and then turned around slowly, and even from a distance Jessie could see the color suffusing his face as Douglas called again. "Come over here, man, and play the civil courtier."

Jessie felt her jaw sag open as she gazed at the stranger, whose eyes only now met hers, clouded with what she could only discern as shame and embarrassment. She knew the man, recognized him easily, but yet her mind seemed incapable of accepting his presence here.

"Thomas?" she said, her voice little more than a whisper. Then, more strongly, "Thomas, is that you?"

The man ducked his head in acknowledgment, then moved forward slowly, his fair-skinned face burning with blood. "Auntie

Jessie," he said. "Forgive me for this. I fear you may not want me 'neath your roof."

Her eyes went wide with astonishment. "*My* roof? What are you talking about? It is your roof, Thomas. This is your house. But you were … I thought … How come you here?"

Sir Thomas Randolph, her eldest brother's son and nephew to the Bruce himself through a half-sister, stepped closer, his face a portrait of misery and shame. "You thought me in England, a willing vassal to the Plantagenet, a traitor to my home and kinsmen. Is that not what you wished to say?"

Jessie gasped, then bridled in protest. "Well, yes and no, in equal measure. In England, certainly. A prisoner of England, willingly or no, taken at Methven field. But traitor? No. That thought never entered my mind. No man who bears the name of Thomas Randolph could ever be traitor. So have done with the self-pity if you would please me, for it ill becomes you. Now, tell me true, how do you come to be here?"

Before the other could answer, Jamie Douglas moved away and began barking orders to his men, bidding them settle down and dispose themselves quietly and without fuss, and Jessie turned to interrupt him.

"How many are you, Sir James?"

"Forty-four, my lady, including ourselves … young Thomas and I."

"Then we can put them all under roofs. There are four bothies behind the farm, apart from the main buildings. They can hold twelve men apiece in comfort. Have your men move into those and set up picket lines for your horses at the rear. There's ample grazing in the paddock back there, and I'll have my people—Sir Thomas's people—start preparing food for everyone. We had to kill a stirk that broke a leg four days ago, so we have ample meat. I had feared much of it might go to waste, but now we'll make good use of it, though it will be well after dark, I fear, before we sup."

She turned back to her nephew to find that the angry color had receded from his face and he was looking at her now with something akin to gratitude and wonder in his eyes. "Well," she said. "Are you going to stand there fidgeting all night, Thomas Randolph? Come you inside. I have been keeping your house clean and warm in your absence, but now that you are home again, I am become your guest."

He threw up his hand immediately, then bowed from the waist, smiling suddenly, and it seemed the sun itself shone from his eyes. "No, Auntie Jess. Do not even say the words. I am ... in transit. No more than that. This house is yours for as long as you may need it. And I am grateful."

"Grateful? For what?"

"For your forbearance ... your goodwill. Sir James has told me you are close in the King's regard. Nursed him while he was sick. I had thought you would bear me ill will for taking arms against him."

"Aye ... Well, you were wrong. We talked of you, the King and I, when word first came to us last winter that you were riding with the English. He bore you no ill will, even then, knowing you for what you are, a knight yet unschooled in the realities of the wars he fights today. He said you reminded him of himself, when he was your age, full of the bright awareness of knighthood and honor and chivalry and not yet dulled by life's realities. He feared that you saw him as a brigand, unfit to bear the title of knighthood. And he grieved for that. But we will talk of that later. I have much to do to feed your company, and the day grows late already. Come you in when you have finished what you have to do, and bring Sir James with you. I will have something more than water to slake your thirst by then. Go now."

His face flushed again, though not so shamefacedly this time, and she felt the beginnings of a smile upon her lips, for she thought he might be quite the most attractive man she had ever seen, tall and broad shouldered and fair of hair and face. He would be more than half her age, she thought, twenty at the most, to her thirty and six, and he had his father's easy, upright carriage and his mother's length of limb and her maternal family's golden hair and bright blue eyes. He shrugged the sword belt from across his chest and over his head as he went from her, and she admired the easy confidence with which he threw the long, sheathed weapon to a waiting, gray-bearded moss-trooper before he strode through the entranceway and out into the fields beyond, headed towards the bothies at the back. And then she remembered what she had to do and spun back to the doorway.

From that moment on until late in the night after the huge but plain supper of spit-roasted beef, fresh oatmeal bread, and boiled greens served with vinegar and butter, Jessie barely had a moment to herself, making herself available and visible everywhere, supervising the details of the meal's preparation and the arrangements for housing more than two score unanticipated visitors. And so it was with great relief that she sank into a solid, upholstered chair by the fire in the farmhouse's main room shortly before midnight, taking pleasure in the fact that her two guests were there already, comfortably seated and awaiting her arrival.

Douglas had been dozing when she came in, but had leapt to his feet as quickly as her nephew and ushered her towards the room's main chair, situated directly in front of the peat fire that glowed in the stone hearth. She thanked him with a smile and murmured word of thanks, then allowed herself to relax into the chair and look around the shadowed, comfortable room. It was spacious but low ceilinged, with a roof of hammered beams, and furnished for comfort, with four massive armchairs and a deep couch, besides the enormous table of ancient, hand-carved black oak and the twelve matching high-backed chairs surrounding it. Candles were scattered throughout, some in sconces, others in scattered holders, and a half score ranged in each of the two candelabra on the old oak table, and their light reflected on all the upright surfaces, casting the four corners of the room into dark, flickering, shadow-filled places. She sighed contentedly and waved away the proffered cup of wine that her nephew held out to her.

"No, Thomas. Too late at night and we must be astir at daybreak. So come and sit down and tell me, for you never did, what brings you here thus unexpectedly."

Randolph grinned. He poured the wine from the cup he had offered her into his own, then gestured with it towards where Douglas had subsided back into his chair. "Sir James, my captor here, thought we should visit you."

Jessie glanced from him to the other man. "Your captor?"

"My captor. He took my sword at Peebles last month. And he now holds my parole that I will not attempt to flee back to England."

Douglas shook his head ruefully. "What you are listening to is guilt and nonsense, Lady Jessica. I captured him, that much is true. But then I took him directly to the King, who forgave him all his follies and received him back into his peace in return for an oath of loyalty. So this of the captivity is but a nonsense. Your nephew is being harder on himself than any other is."

"I see ..." But clearly she did not. "So why is he here with you now?"

Douglas sat straighter and held out his empty cup to Sir Thomas, who carried it to the table and refilled it from a silver jug. "I am his penance, Lady. For his sins, he must bear with me and my brigandage ... until he learns the rules of war."

Jessie was frowning now, more perplexed than before. "Brigandage? I do not understand—"

"It is my lord of Douglas who spouts nonsense now, Auntie." Thomas carried the replenished cup back to Douglas, then sat down again, his forehead creased in a frown.

"I thought to judge my uncle Robert as being unworthy of the name of knight. You know that already, but it is simple truth. When I was captured after Methven fight, they took me to King Edward, who received me with great kindness and treated me with much largesse. And then for the ensuing months he played upon my gullibility and my ... credulity and sinful arrogance. He sought to convince me—and I am ashamed to say he succeeded—that no true king would wage war as this ingrate upstart—that was his name for King Robert, the Ingrate Upstart—sought to do in Scotland, ignoring all the protocols of warfare, burning and pillaging and slaughtering from ambush, then running away to hide in the hills, playing the savage cateran and all the while not daring to stand and fight like a man of honor. And I, to my eternal shame, gave credence to everything he said."

"I see ... And what brought about your change of heart?"

"The sight of the Lady Isobel MacDuff, Countess of Fife and wife of the Earl of Buchan, hanging naked in an open cage from the walls of Berwick." The words hung in the air for a long moment before the young knight continued. "I had not believed it until I saw it with my own eyes … Edward Plantagenet's *chivalry*. The English took great delight in it, their King's vengeance on the woman who crowned Scotland's King in defiance of him and of her whole family. And when I saw her there, a living truth I could not deny, I began to question all I had been told. What kind of a man, be he knight, king, or both, would besmirch the very essentials of honor to stoop to such a thing?" He gazed directly at Jessie, making no attempt to avoid her eyes. "From that point on, I began to take note of what was being done to my fellow countrymen in the name of the King of England's justice, and I soon saw it for what it was: a grasping, willful lust for power in the heart of a once great but now demented man. And so I began to think about returning home, but my shame was too great … My shame and, I fear, my humbled pride. By the time I met Sir James in the field, though, I was prepared to throw down my sword and face the King I had dishonored."

"And so he did, as I have said," Douglas put in. "And spoke most eloquently of his disenchantment. The King believed him, and so did I."

Jessie looked at Douglas. "So why is he now with you, as penance?"

The young man smiled at her. "Because I, too, am what he thought of as a brigand. He rides with me today to complete his education, seeing at first hand how I operate to rid this land of Englishry, and seeing, too, ever more clearly, why it must be so. His Grace thought it more fitting that it should be I, rather than he, who teach young Thomas what is involved in bringing peace to this sad realm of his. We cannot fight the English in pitched battle—a matter of strength rather than willingness or mere determination. We have less than one-tenth their strength and not one-twentieth part of their resources. The reserves they keep at home in England outnumber us beyond counting. And yet we must fight, with everything and every man we have. To do less would be to guarantee their victory. We cannot give them time to rally or opportunity to consolidate their forces. And so we harry them, playing the cateran, as Edward said.

"The old Plantagenet Lion is dead now, thanks be to God, and so the pressure is relieved, but though his son, Caernarvon, will never be fit to cast a shadow like his father's, his barons are more powerful than ever, threatening to rise against him, sensing his weakness and deploring his pederasty. But they want Scotland, too, for the scent of blood and power is rank in them and they seek to rip our realm apart and divide it among themselves. Gloucester and Leicester, Northumberland and Hereford are but the leaders of the pack, and any one of them can field more men from his own earldom within a seven-night spell than we can raise through all this land in a twelvemonth. So Thomas is my student, and I will admit to you he shows great promise. We will make a brigand of your nephew yet, my lady, and the English will take note of where he goes. Believe me."

Jessie nodded slowly. "I do, my lord ... And the King is well? He prospers?"

"Aye, Lady, by the grace of God he does, and fortune smiles upon us for once. All of the northeast is in his hands now, for the people of Aberdeen rose up and cast out the English garrison last month, which means we have a seaport of our own for the first time. And his brother Sir Edward has spent these past two months subduing the MacDowals and their hives in Galloway. And subdue them he did. Aided by Angus Og and his Highlanders, he thrashed the MacDowals and their English levies under Ingram de Umfraville and Aymer St. John. Outnumbered by more than two to one, and with only fifty knights, he swept them into ruin. We have just come from there, with dispatches from Sir Edward to the King, and we must now ride north and west, for the King himself is marching there, against the MacDougalls in Argyll."

Jessie's frown was quick. "There is a truce with the MacDougalls."

"There was, my lady. It expired last month, and the old chief's son, Lame John of Lorn, had spent it raising men in arms to continue his fight to depose His Grace. But the King has men, even among the MacDougalls, who now incline to his cause, and he is well aware of what's afoot. And so he moves to stamp upon the snake, marching to invade Argyll through the Pass of Brander. We ride to join him there, Thomas and I, and are to meet with him in ten days' time, at Loch Awe. If we succeed in Argyll, and Lame John goes down—and he will—then only the Earl of Ross will remain to stand against King Robert in the north. And when that arch schemer sees the error of his ways and recants, as he surely must, Robert Bruce will be King indeed through all of Scotland. Pray that it be so, my lady."

"I will. You need never fear. Now tell me, my lord, have you heard ought of how things progress in Arran?"

Douglas's eyes narrowed as he looked at her and slowly shook his head. "No, Lady Jessica, I have heard nothing. But that must surely mean that there is nothing ill going on there. Bad news travels fast, and had there been cause for such, we would have heard of it. On the dexter side, though, I know the corps of riders from the island was renewed at June's end, and the numbers increased. King Robert is well pleased with the unflinching support he has received from Arran." He hesitated before adding, "And from Sir William." Again he hesitated. "Forgive me for asking, my lady, but do you communicate with the brotherhood there?"

"No, sir, I do not, although I have in the past, on King Robert's behalf. Why would you ask me such a thing?"

Douglas had the grace to look embarrassed, but he shrugged his wide shoulders. "Because I have tidings that the monks on Arran should know of. King Robert has received word privily, from Archbishop Lamberton in England, that the Pope has sent a communication regarding the Temple to all the kings and princes in Christendom. King Robert himself did not receive the missive because he is excommunicate."

Jessie's breath caught in her throat, because she could see from Douglas's expression that this communication would offer no solace to Will Sinclair and his men. "What did it say, this missive?"

Douglas cleared his throat. "It bore a title, *Pastoralis Praeeminentiae*. In it, the Pope asked all who received it to arrest all the Templars in their lands, and to do it—and these the King took to be important words—prudently, discreetly, and secretly. That done, they were to confiscate all their property and hold it in safekeeping for the Church."

"But that is infamous! All Templars, everywhere in Christendom?"

"Aye, my lady."

"So Sir William was right. He foretold this ..." Jessie stopped, thinking hard, then looked at her nephew. "Did you know anything of this, Thomas?"

Randolph merely looked back at her, utterly mystified as to what she meant, and she turned back to Douglas. "When did this happen?"

"The Archbishop wrote that the letter was dated November the twenty-second, last year."

"Barely a month after the arrests in France. Surely they could not have proven any of de Nogaret's lies by then?"

"So it would seem, my lady ... but I know nothing more than I have told you."

Jessie fought to keep her face expressionless, merely nodding in acceptance of what she had been told, but her mind was full of the knowledge that the letter over which she had spent so much time and thought was now outdated and would have to be rewritten.

3

In the north anteroom of the Great Hall at Brodick, Will Sinclair set down his pen on the long refectory table that served him as a desk and stretched, arching his back and rubbing his eyes with the heels of his hands as he grunted aloud with the pleasure of flexing his shoulders and straightening his spine. He had been working without rest since dawn, digging his way through the mountain of papers and parchment that had confronted him after weeks of neglect caused by other priorities. Most he had merely read and marked with his name, as evidence of his examination, before setting them aside on a smaller table to his left. Others he had examined more meticulously, making occasional notes to himself to remind him of their content and what had been achieved in recent months, and these he had also set aside, to his right.

His companions and brethren had achieved great things in a short time. Each of the two Arran chapters now had its own Chapter House, and each of those administered its own affairs and resources, from devotions and ritual procedures to stables, barracks, houses, crude farms, and warehouses. The program of horse breeding, training, and maintenance was now firmly established in both chapters, and military drill, albeit discreet, had come back into its own as a *sine qua non* of their daily practice. A strong and resilient trading schedule had been set in place, too, with their ships coming and going to and from both Brodick and Lochranza at regular intervals, plying the waters of Britain for the most part but venturing into Ireland and France, and occasionally, in the summer months, crossing the northern waters eastward to reach Norway and Denmark and the Germanic coastline to the Low Countries. Food was now plentiful, in sufficient supply to be stored and husbanded, and even livestock had been brought ashore in small numbers—swine, sheep, and goats in the main, but also a few cattle and oxen, tame geese with clipped wings, and fat white ducks whose eggs were a luxurious addition to the island diet, which consisted mainly of fish and oats.

Housing had sprung up throughout the island, but it was hidden in most places, carefully concealed from any stranger looking from a distance. The buildings were long and low, their walls and even their roofs made from peat and sod, their floors frequently excavated to provide the building material for the walls, so that although the height of most roofs was less than that of a man, the tallest man could stand easily inside. The first of the longhouses had been designed and built by a brother called Anselm, who had in better times been one of the Order's most gifted architects and builders, and when Will, surprised by the apparent gracelessness of the construction, had called in the elderly monk to question him, Anselm had looked at him in surprise. Was it not their intent to keep their presence on the island secret, he asked, and was it not also true that they would not be remaining on Arran forever? When Will agreed that it was, the monk had shrugged expressively and spread his hands. That was what he had set out to do, he said: to keep their presence shrouded from strange eyes, and to ensure that they would leave little trace behind when they returned to France. Besides, he said, they had insufficient supplies of wood and lumber to do otherwise. The peat-built buildings could be quickly torn down when the time came to leave, and within a few years their walls would return to the ground from which they were made, leaving no trace of their existence. Will had been unable to argue against the old man's logic, and so he had given his blessing to the project and decreed that all their impermanent buildings would be made from peat thenceforth.

Now he was tired, but he had completed his work and could speak out loud and clear at the chapter gathering in two days' time, giving praise and credit confidently where he felt each was due. He called in his earnest, humorless assistant, Brother Fernando, and instructed him in what he wished done with the different piles of documents, and then he sat thinking while the emaciated cleric bustled around him, collecting all the documents.

As soon as the brother had left, carrying a heavy basket full of scrolls, Will bent forward and took a fresh sheet of parchment from the pile at the back of his desk, then picked up his pen again, playing idly with it while he thought of what he would say in the report he had been planning for his superiors in Aix-en-Provence. He had sent three reports already, in February, April, and June, detailing the progress of the works he had set in motion in Arran, and requesting information on the status of the Temple in France. The third of those, in which he had labored long and hard to outline the dilemma he might face in the bleakest of all possible futures and the possibility of releasing the younger brethren from their vow of chastity, thereby permitting them to marry and procreate, had thus far gone unanswered, to his intense chagrin, for he had been hoping for some solid words of guidance. And the two replies he had received to his initial reports had both been terse, lacking in specifics and generally discouraging.

What he had not done, to this point, was set down in writing a description of what he had discovered when he opened the chests committed to his care upon leaving France. He had sent word, in his third report, that the Treasure now lay safely concealed, and had included a map of its location in the underground vault on his father's lands in Roslin, but he had made no mention of having opened the chests and viewed the contents. Nor had he identified the location shown on the map. That information would be supplied in this next report, once he had confirmation that the map had arrived safely in the hands of the Order in Aix.

Quite simply, as he had long since admitted to himself, much of his failure to describe what he had seen in the chests was based upon fear: his very real fear of betraying the secret by committing anything to writing. Unwritten, the secret was safe in his mind. Written down, it would pose a constant danger of discovery. He knew the contents of the chests were familiar to the highest members of the ancient brotherhood, for it was they, or their forebears from two hundred years before, who had commissioned Hugh de Payens and his small fraternity to find the Treasure, described in minute detail in the Order's ancient lore. He knew, too, that certain portions of the Treasure had been taken back to France for study, to Aix itself, to furbish truth of their ancient records, but he had no idea at all of why the brotherhood had wished to send the Treasure to safety beyond France.

Certainly it made sense that it should be kept away from King Philip and de Nogaret, but neither one of those depraved souls had the slightest scintilla of suspicion that there was such an entity as the Order of Sion, and no senior member of the Order of Sion had any overt connection with the Order of the Temple, for obvious and necessary reasons. No man could reveal under torture what he did not know, and even if any of the lesser brethren, who served both Temple and Sion, were to reveal something under duress, the secrecy and intricacy of the Order's structure was such that nothing could be proved or would be found. The major certainty of Sion's security lay in the fact that the Inquisitors could not possibly conceive of another, far more ancient, secret, and non-Christian structure underlying the Order of the Temple, their sole target. They could not possibly ask questions about something whose existence they did not even suspect.

That knowledge was a more than sufficient reason for Will Sinclair to have grave doubts about committing anything to writing.

Dear God, he thought. *How can I write anything of this?*

He was interrupted, his pen still undipped, by footsteps in the hall outside, and then came a quiet knock. The door swung open, and young Ewan Sinclair leaned into the room, his hand on the door handle.

"Your pardon, Sir William. My father says can you come at once. There's a galley coming in, from the north. It's the admiral."

"What brings him back so soon? Wait you then, and walk with me."

He put his pen down by the inkwell and replaced the sheet of parchment, trying not to think about what the new arrival might bring with it. He glanced from side to side of his table desk, making sure that he had left nothing of importance for idle eyes to scan, then stepped away and turned to where Ewan stood waiting. They crossed the empty hall together to the outer door, Will glancing down and sideways to eye the slight limp with which the younger man favored his right leg.

"How is the leg? Does it still bother you as much?"

"No, sir, it's mending nicely. Brother Anthony seems pleased with it, although he warns me, every time he sees me limping, that I shouldna be so soft on mysel'. The harder I use it, he says, the stronger it will mend." He grinned, a cheerful, infectious grimace. "Mind you, I fancy it easier to tell others how to act when you're not the one bearing the pain."

Will grinned back and resisted the urge to slow his pace. Young Ewan had been warring on the mainland with King Robert, part of the last rotation of fighting men on that duty, and towards the end of his three-month tour, while riding with the King's brother, Sir Edward, in Galloway, he had taken a wicked slashing wound above his right knee from a heavy broadsword wielded by a MacDowal warrior. Luckily for him, he had been well tended immediately after the skirmish by one of their own men, a veteran physician who had spent years in Spain tending to wounds sustained by Templar knights in the wars against the Moors.

"What of your father? Does he have ought to say of your progress?"

Again the young man grinned, but this time he answered in his native tongue, so that Will had to listen closely to understand the fast-flowing rattle of his clipped words. "You know my father, Uncle Will. He glowered like an angry bear when I came back and he first set eyes on me ... but that was to mask his concern. He wasna frowning at me. But that was the extent o' what he'd say. Since then he hasna mentioned anything about it ... Hasna even asked me what happened."

"What did happen?"

"I don't know ... I canna remember. I mean, it was a tulzie ... and there were people everywhere, screamin' and shoutin' and fightin' wi' one another. There was a lot o' spillin' blood, I mind, but to tell ye the truth, I didna know who was who, because they a' looked the same. There was no way o' tellin' Bruce men from MacDowals. So I was sittin' there on my horse, gowpin' around and ready to swing at anyone who came at me, but I didna dare swing at anybody else, for fear o' hitting one o' our own men. And then I felt this big dunt on my leg, and when I looked down, there was a big sword hangin' out o' it. Nobody holdin' the sword, I mind. Nothing holdin' it at all, in fact, except the edges o' the gouge it had made in my leg." He shrugged. "I must ha'e fell off my horse, for I didna mind anythin' after that."

"Passed out. I'm not surprised. Did you kill anyone over there in Scotland?"

"No, Uncle Will, I didna."

Will looked at him sideways. "Have you ever killed anyone?"

"No, sir. But I will, one o' these days."

"Don't wish it on yourself, lad. It's not as thrilling as it's made out to be. Aha, that was quick. De Berenger is wasting no time, so something must have happened."

The admiral's huge galley was still approaching the wharf below the hall, but a boat had already been launched from it and was pulling quickly to the shoreline, its thwarts crammed with people, some of them wearing brightly colored clothes that marked them as strangers to Arran. Will recognized Tam Sinclair among the small crowd of men lining the waterside, waiting to pull it up onto the beach, and although he could recognize none of the newcomers from this distance, he felt an urgency that compelled him to rush down the long flights of steps to meet them.

Less than halfway down, however, he hesitated, slowing to a stop in stunned disbelief as he recognized one and then another of the newcomers. The first ashore, being aided onto the firm shingle by Tam himself, was a stooped, elderly man with a shock of silvery white hair. He looked up as Tam released his arm, saw Will on the steps above him, and waved.

"Stay here," Will said to Ewan, and walked quickly down the remaining steps to the steep pathway that led down to the beach, his mind in a whirl.

Etienne Dutoit, Baron of St. Julien in the province of Aix-en-Provence, was one of the senior and most influential members of the Order of Sion, but he had also been Will's sponsor on the occasion of Will's Raising to the brotherhood, and the second man being helped ashore behind him had been Will's co-sponsor, Simon de Montferrat, seigneur of the distinguished clan that claimed precedence among the federation of ancient bloodlines known as the Friendly Families, whose ancestors had fled Jerusalem before the destruction of the city by the Romans. These two were lineal descendants of the founding fathers of their Order, and the significance of their presence on Arran was so overwhelming that Will was scarcely able to think about what it portended.

He reached them moments later and fell to one knee in front of Etienne Dutoit, but the old man refused his obeisance and seized him by the shoulders, pulling him upright in a flurry of expostulations meant to convey that Will had no need or reason to kneel. Instead, the Baron embraced him closely, murmuring greetings in his ear, then pushed him towards his companion, and de Montferrat greeted Will the same way. Behind them stood two tall, richly dressed young men whose fine weapons and breadth of shoulder pronounced them knights, and whose unmistakable vigilance proclaimed them bodyguards.

Will stepped back from de Montferrat's embrace and looked from one to the other of his former mentors, shaking his head in bewilderment. But then he remembered who and where he was, and spread his arms, smiling at both of them. "My friends and brothers, you are welcome here … how much, I have no words to express. But how came you here? And why? And aboard a galley from the north? You have much to tell me, it seems, But here is no place for it. Come you up to the hall, where we may be at ease. You will find it a far cry from the comfort of your homes in Provence, but it has comfortable chairs and a sound roof to keep out wind and rain." He looked now at the two straight-faced young knights. "You gentlemen are welcome, too, since I presume the safety of my guests here is your prime concern." He held out his hand to each of them. "I am William Sinclair."

The two knights bowed formally and named themselves, and then Will turned to lead them up to the hall, calling up to Ewan Sinclair, who had remained on the steps above, to run ahead and order food and drink to be prepared for their visitors. Will glanced back at his guests. "You will have baggage, I presume?"

"It's all here in the boat, Sir William," Tam Sinclair told him. "I have it in hand. I'll see it safely up as soon as it's unloaded."

"Aye. My thanks, Tam. Take them to the rooms over the hall." Again he hesitated, glancing at each of the newcomers in turn. None of these men were Templars, but everyone in the press surrounding them on the beach was, and Will knew speculation would be lively afterwards with wonderings of who these people were and why they had come here from France. And so he decided to limit the imaginings of his men from the outset.

"Brethren," he cried, seeing how every eye present turned towards him. "These knights are very dear to me, friends and mentors of long standing. I cannot say exactly why they come here today, for I do not yet know, but I suspect they bring us tidings of the welfare of our Order in France." He looked questioningly at Dutoit and de Montferrat, and when both men inclined their heads gravely in acknowledgment, he turned back to his men. "Therefore we will have information we may trust, and as soon as I know of what it consists, I will pass it on to you. Now you may return to your interrupted tasks."

As the small procession began to climb the stairs, with Will leading, flanked by the two elders, the Baron St. Julien answered the first of Will's questions, speaking in the same measured tones that Will remembered from years before, his vibrant baritone unchanged by the years that had elapsed since then.

"We sought you first in the north, at Lochranza, only to find you had already returned here. Admiral de Berenger received us—he had just returned himself, he told us—and seeing our chagrin at having missed you, he brought us south in his galley, much faster than our own ship would have. He will join us as soon as he has put his ship to order."

Will said nothing. De Berenger, too, belonged to the Brotherhood of Sion, and he would be as interested as Will in whatever urgency it was that had brought these two so far from home. But the steps ahead of them were steep for two elderly men, and so he asked no more questions, concentrating instead on assisting his guests to climb the long flights of stairs that had been made for use by men much younger than they were. Time enough for questions and answers once they had refreshed themselves and regained their wind.

4

Aresinous knot exploded loudly in the iron grate, and the burning logs collapsed upon themselves, sending a storm of sparks whirling up to be sucked into the chimney, but ignored by the small group of men who sat ranged around the hearth, staring silently into the roiling flames, each engrossed in his own thoughts. Outside in the cooling night the air was yet warm from the late-August sun, but within the hall the temperature reminded its occupants that they were in Scotland, where the sun's warmth seldom penetrated walls of stone and timber.

Etienne Dutoit, Baron de St. Julien, rose to his feet and picked up a heavy iron poker from the grate, then used it to break down the burning logs further, stirring them into an inferno before moving to select several logs from the pile in the big iron fuel basket and throw them onto the pyre. He pulled them this way and that with the poker until he was satisfied that they would burn properly. That done, he set the poker down again in its place and turned to face the men now watching him.

"You live in a cold country, my friends," he said.

Edward de Berenger grunted and sat up straighter. "It's not so much cold, Baron, as it is damp. Cold you can live with, and you can dress to fight it. But the dampness here is an internal thing … it chills your bones in summer as well as winter. The only way to combat that is from within, with solid, hot food in your belly."

Dutoit smiled. "Aye, well, none can deny we have had our fill of that tonight. Your cooks are remarkably good." He drew himself up to his full height, his back to the fire as he looked at the group facing him in an arc, his eyes shifting from face to face. His traveling companion de Montferrat sat on his far right, combing his fingers idly through his sparse gray beard, and next to him sat Bishop Formadieu, the senior Bishop of the island community. On Formadieu's right sat Admiral de Berenger, and beside him was de Montrichard, the preceptor. Sir Reynald de Pairaud, the acting preceptor of Lochranza, who had accompanied Will to Brodick for the coming chapter meeting, sat next to the preceptor. Will himself made up the last of the gathering, seated next to Dutoit's empty chair on the right end of the arc.

"And so to our affairs, the reasons for our presence," the Baron began. "Neither Sir Simon here nor I myself have any overt association with your Order, so we and our affairs have been largely unaffected by the upheavals in our homeland these past long months. Unaffected, I say, but not unmoved, and I was happy when my dear friend Sir William thought fit to send to me with a request for assistance in gathering information on the status of the continuing investigation into your Order." He held up a hand, palm outwards, to forestall a protest that did not emerge, and when he heard nothing but silence he quirked an eyebrow and nodded briefly.

"So be it ... A request to gather information on the status of the investigation. I will not insult you by offering any opinion on whether or no that investigation is justifiable. I will say only that I myself, along with Sir Simon and many other men of probity and sound mind in France, deplore the actions of our self-righteous King and the creatures with whom he surrounds himself to carry out his bidding. That truth, allied with my long-standing fondness and admiration for Sir William Sinclair and the Order he represents, made it a pleasure rather than a burden to gather all the information available to me and to my friends throughout the land."

He turned slightly to look at Will. "I discovered, though, and Sir Simon agreed with me, that although your questions were exhaustive, Sir William, the answers to them were even more demanding, and the upshot of that, after several wasted weeks of trying to write down an adequate summation of what we had learned, with all the conflicting elements of rumor and conjecture accompanying it, was that we decided the only way to present the information was in person, where we can listen to your reservations and respond to them." He looked around again. "So, before I begin, does anyone wish to ask me anything? Or does anyone wish to challenge my right, as a non-Templar, to speak to you on this?"

Bishop Formadieu cleared his throat. "On the contrary, Baron Dutoit. What you have to tell us will add clarity, both to what we know and what we fear, for you will deal with it through the eyes of a dispassionate observer. I cannot think of any reason why my brethren should object to that." He looked left and right at his brethren. "Does anyone disagree?"

No one did, and Will spoke up. "Proceed, sir. We are eager to hear what you have to say."

The Baron's face remained solemn. "Your eagerness might not outlive the first thing I must tell you," he said somberly, then took a scroll of tight-wound parchment sheets from the scrip at his waist. He loosened the single leather binding and scanned the first page before looking up again.

"Let me begin with the wording of the King's order for the arrest of the Templars in his own domain. He began to read. "'To effect the detention of all members of the Temple for crimes horrible to contemplate, terrible to hear of ... an abominable work, a detestable disgrace, a thing almost inhuman, indeed set apart from all humanity.'" He looked up again. "No mention, you will note, of what this so-called abomination *was* ... But on the one day in October, close to five thousand members of the Temple were taken into the King's custody within his realm of France. Among them were knights, of course, but also sergeants, chaplains, laborers, and servants of the Order. Five thousand souls in one short day."

"Did anyone of note escape the purge?" This was Reynald de Pairaud.

Baron Dutoit shook his head. "From the information I have managed to gather, it appears that, apart from yourselves, about whom nothing has been released, less than a score of knights escaped. Two preceptors managed to avoid the net, but no one knows where they are now."

"Who were they?"

"The Preceptor of France, de Villiers, and Imbert Blanke, Preceptor of the Auvergne."

"Who else?"

Dutoit shook his head again. "Only one other that I know of by name, and he failed. A knight called Peter of Boucle. He shaved off his beard and dressed in common clothes, but someone recognized him and betrayed him. He, too, ended up in prison."

"But on what charges?" Edward de Bergeron was coldly angry. "You yourself pointed out the lack of substance in Capet's orders. This fellow, king or no, has dared to lay hands on an exempt Order—exempt from allegiance to him and answerable only to the Pope. That is sacrilege."

The Baron pursed his lips beneath his mustache, and then he nodded slowly. "You are correct, Sir Edward. But he went even further. He claimed to have proceeded on this path after consulting with, and gaining the permission of, the Pope himself. And that was a lie. A lie that came quickly to the Pope's attention."

Will spoke up. "And what did he do? The Pope, I mean."

"He wrote the King a letter … Here, I have a transcript of it, provided at grave personal risk by a dear friend. Let me see …" The Baron shuffled through the sheets in his hand, then held one out at arm's length, peering down his nose as he read aloud: "'You, our dear son, have, in our absence, violated every rule and laid hands on the persons and properties of the Templars. You have also imprisoned them and, what pains us even more, you have not treated them with due leniency … and have added to the discomfort of imprisonment yet another affliction. You have laid hands on persons and property that are under the direct protection of the Roman Church. Your hasty act is seen by all, and rightly so, as an act of contempt towards ourselves and the Roman Church.'"

"Pardon me, Baron," the Bishop said. "Would you read that again?"

Dutoit read the letter again, and every man there sat frowning as he listened. When he had finished, the Bishop turned to him. "It is as I thought on first hearing it. The Pope deplores the King's actions, but he is more concerned about the flouting of his own authority than he is with the outrage perpetrated upon our Order. But what is this 'other affliction' to which he refers?"

"Torture."

The word dropped into the silence like a stone falling on a wooden floor. "William of Paris," Baron Dutoit continued, "the Chief Inquisitor of France, is King Philip's confessor, and there can be little doubt that he was privy to the King's plans for the Temple long before any action occurred, for his Dominican Inquisitors stood shoulder to shoulder with the King's officers and explained what had occurred at a public meeting in the King's own gardens two days after the arrests."

"What ..." Richard de Montrichard's voice failed him at first and he cleared his throat before trying again. "What kind of ... tortures are we speaking of? What do they do, these priest Inquisitors?"

Bishop Formadieu was the first to answer him. "Nothing too severe. Torture was authorized in defense of Church doctrine fifty years ago, by Pope Innocent IV. The Inquisitors are constrained to stop short of breaking limbs or spilling blood." He stopped, perhaps to continue, but before he could say anything more, Baron Dutoit intervened.

"That is the theory, Bishop, but the reality is far more harsh. The term is torture, not sympathy or compassion. The use of explanations such as yours entails an inclination to believe in the humane and tender mercies of the Inquisitors. But they have none. They use the rack and the strappado to obey the rules. The rack stretches a man's limbs, painfully and slowly, to the point where the joints separate and may be torn asunder. Not broken, but ripped apart. The strappado is even more effective. You tie a man's wrists behind his back, then hoist him into the air by a pulley fastened to the bindings on his wrists. He will talk very quickly after that, provided he is sane enough, and that you have sufficient capacity to decipher his babbling. And then of course there is a third method of loosening unwilling tongues. It has no name, but it is a simple procedure, involving neither broken bones nor bloodshed. You rub fat on a man's feet, then hold his feet to the fire ..." Every man there stared at him. He shrugged and spread his hands. "Bernard de Vado."

"I know Bernard de Vado," de Formadieu said. "He is a priest, one of our own. I ordained him. What know you of him?"

"He came from Albi. Is that the same man?"

"Yes, that is Bernard."

"Well, they roasted him. Forgive me, Bishop, but they did it so badly that they cooked his feet until the bones fell out. It was witnessed by a man who reported the incident to a friend of mine in the Justiciary. In all, my friends and I have gathered reports of a number of deaths, varying from twenty-five to forty-four, resulting from torture administered by the Inquisitors, often assisted by the King's own officers."

"That is … inhuman. Unacceptable to God or man." The Bishop's voice was slack with shock and Sir Simon de Montferrat spoke out for the first time.

"It is, indeed as you say, Bishop, inhuman. But it is being done, and it is being done by churchmen in the name of an all-merciful God. And no less inhuman is the truth that all these prisoners are kept awake at all times, denied sleep, and that they are kept in irons, fed only on bread and water. And it is in that weakened state that they are then submitted to these fiendish tortures."

"Damnation take all clerics and their hypocritical posturings!" De Montrichard's voice was barely audible, but his anger was caustic, and Etienne Dutoit turned to look at him directly. "Why is any of this blasphemous infamy permitted to proceed, at any level, considering the Pope's revulsion to the fact that these things have been done at all?"

The Baron's eyes moved to meet Will's. "Finally," he said quietly. "The correct question."

Will cocked his head. "What do you mean?"

The Baron thought for a moment, his eyes seemingly unfocused, and then said, "Hear me. This much we know of those early accusations of what were called 'crimes set apart from all humanity.' Your Order and its members stand accused of being servants of the Devil, dedicated to the worship and the service of Satan himself." He ignored the sudden hiss of indrawn breath and forged ahead, speaking into the stunned silence that followed. "They say that each of your recruits is taught, and must acknowledge at the moment of his Initiation, that Jesus the Christus was a false prophet. He is then required to proceed through that denial to spit, trample, or urinate upon an image of Christ on the Cross, and then to kiss the Templar who received him into the Order, upon the mouth, the navel, the buttocks, the base of the spine, and sometimes on the penis. And in the aftermath, in the closing ceremonies, the new Initiate is told, *in toto*, that he may freely have carnal relations with his brethren and that it is, in effect, his duty so to do … that he ought to do and submit to this, for it is not sinful for the brotherhood to do this."

The appalled silence stretched until the Baron added, "De Molay confessed."

It took a moment for his words to register, but then the Bishop said, "Confessed? Confessed to what?"

"To everything I have mentioned. Except the matter of the homosexual kisses. Those he denied."

Will finally found his tongue. "That is … That is not possible. Master de Molay would never—"

"In the face of unremitting tortures and torment such as we have been discussing, any man will confess to anything, merely to stop the pain and find some relief. Jacques de Molay is admirable beyond most men, but he is, in the end, a man. He was arrested on the first day of the purge, and within ten days he had confessed to most of the charges against him. He admitted having denied Jesus Christ and confessed that he had spat upon his image at the time of his Initiation—"

"Great God in Heaven! This is infamy!"

"Aye, and it is also blasphemy. But the infamy is not the Master's, though the admission of blasphemy is. They put de Molay to the torture first, bringing all their power to bear on him alone from the moment of his imprisonment, and it is to his credit that he withstood their torments for as long as he did."

"I cannot believe that he confessed to such things." This was de Pairaud, his voice hushed.

"Believe it," Dutoit said. "They broke him. They can break any man. Your Grand Master was the first to confess, but far from the last. I have reliable information that of one hundred and thirty-eight Templars arrested in Paris in October, one hundred and thirty-four had, by January of this year, admitted to at least some of the charges brought against them." He hesitated, then turned his eyes to where de Pairaud sat glowering disbelief at him, his outrage rendering him speechless. "Your brother Hugh, Sir Reynald, Visitor of France, confessed on November ninth, admitting, in addition to many other sins, that he had encouraged brethren troubled by the heat of nature to cool their passions by indulging their lusts with other brothers." He ignored de Pairaud's efforts to rise to his feet in protest and kept speaking in the same expressionless voice. "Sir Geoffrey de Charney, Preceptor of Normandy, was another. John de la Tour, Treasurer of the Temple in Paris, who had been a financial adviser to King Philip, also went down into despair, condemned by his own voice … And with those distinguished names went many others too numerous to mention." He paused again. "That was in January of this year. We are now in August and much has happened in the interim, not all of it bad, but unfortunately none of it is yet resolved."

No one dared ask him what he meant by that, so deep was the disbelief that filled his listeners, but eventually Will coughed to clear his throat. "We have heard tell, through trusted friends who know such things, that the Pope sent out a letter to all the kings and princes of Christendom, requesting them to seize all the Templars in their lands and to sequester their holdings. Can you tell us aught of that?"

"Aye. The *Pastoralis Praeeminentiae*. That was a recent move, designed to assert Clement's control of a situation that has long since passed beyond his grasp. But it was sent, and widely acted upon, and the Temple's assets, beyond France at least, now lie within the jurisdiction of the Church … Which is not, in this instance, necessarily a bad thing."

"How so? If they have been sequestered, they are lost to us."

"Not necessarily. They are within the *jurisdiction* of the Church—not within its coffers. Not *yet* within its coffers, I should say. There is yet hope." The Baron looked from man to man around the arc. "Look at yourselves and take note, and try to imagine for a moment that you are plain French knights, not Templars. Think you that you are the only group to feel this outrage, this disbelief that such things can happen in a time of peace? The Pope *himself* cannot—does not—believe it. And more important than he, nor can his cardinals. Clement is far from being an effective pontiff at this time, and his failure to challenge and stop Philip's depredations are causing him great difficulties, most particularly with his cardinals.

"By January, as I said, de Nogaret had gathered a sufficiency of confessions that Philip could claim a moral victory, emerging as a defender of the faith and a champion of fervid Christianity. Clement could hardly disagree, faced with the existence of the admissions. But in an attempt to wrest control of the investigation from Philip, he dispatched three cardinals to review the findings of the Inquisitors, and when these three prelates, two of whom were French, had de Molay brought before them, he revoked his confession, stripped off his clothes, and showed them the wounds—the scars not yet healed—that had been inflicted upon him during his 'questioning' and had led to his 'confession.'

"It seems that he was very eloquent. The cardinals believed him. And they believed others who followed him with similar retractions—among those your brother Hugh, Sir Reynald. This was still early in January. The three cardinals recommended clemency and refused to confirm the condemnations of the Order. And they convinced their peers. No fewer than ten cardinals of the Curia threatened to resign that spring, in protest against Pope Clement's cowardice in refusing to refute the actions and the arguments of the French King, who, in their opinion, did not have a single justifiable reason for his outrageous and abusive behavior, and certainly none for his sneering disdain of the Church and its institutions, of which the Temple was one."

De Montferrat sat straighter and cleared his throat, and Will's eyes went to him immediately, for he knew that de Montferrat was the more outspoken of his two mentors, the one who could always be trusted to cut to the heart of a contentious issue and say what was truly on his mind, without mincing words. "You wished to add something, Sir Simon?"

The elderly aristocrat harrumphed, but rose to his feet and began to pace the floor with his hands clasped behind his back. "Not add," he began. "Not add … clarify, if anything." He threw a glance to indicate his traveling companion and friend of many years, who was returning to his seat, content to leave the floor to him. "Etienne here has a tendency to dwell on detail. He was about to tell you next that Pope Clement decided in favor of your Order the following month, in February. After conferring with his cardinals, he professed himself convinced that the charges were untenable and that he would rather die than condemn innocent men. So he ordered the Inquisition to suspend its proceedings against the Templars."

"My God! So it is over?" Bishop Formadieu's voice was filled with awe and joy, a mixture that Will himself felt stirring inside him. But before any of his listeners could say another word, the blunt-spoken de Montferrat dashed all their short-lived hopes.

"No, it is not. Believe me when I tell you it is barely begun. But the stakes have now been raised so many times that the original case against the Order has been overshadowed."

"How, in God's holy name? By what?"

"By the realities of politics, Bishop. This is become a war between Philip and the Pope, for dominance, and Clement is afraid of being ousted, if not from the papacy, most certainly from his supremacy in men's minds. Nominally, morally, there should be no question of conflicting jurisdiction—Philip's is temporal; Clement's is spiritual. The division should be clear, and it would have been with any other ruler than Philip Capet. But this is a king unlike any other before. He is ambitious, greedy, and contemptuous of all opinions that are not his own. His malevolence and his greed know no bounds and never have. Ten years ago, he sent his hellhound, de Nogaret, riding nine hundred miles to lay hands upon another pope, at Anagni in Italy—Pope Boniface VIII—and no one doubts he brought about that old man's death by doing so. But he has never betrayed a flicker of contrition. De Nogaret remains excommunicate for that outrage, but as France's chief lawyer he sees no shame—and no hindrance to his arrogance—in that. Nor does his master.

"So here is a war between two men, one of whom has armies, fortified castles, ministers of state who will do his bidding without questioning its morality or justice, and a record of implacable ruthlessness, while the other, despite having the entire wealth of Holy Church at his disposal, owns nothing but a moral right and a record of dithering and procrastination. And the Capet's strongest weapon in this fight is a powerful means of swaying people's minds. He claims to rule by divine right, holding himself answerable to none but God. And he believes that to be true, which makes him truly frightening."

He stopped pacing and looked from man to man. "Heed my advice on this. Take steps from this day on to safeguard yourselves here, for you will never return to France as Templars. Even at the moment when Clement was suspending the Inquisition against you, Philip was already moving to impeach the Pope, threatening to charge him with the same sins of which you stand accused, along with additional charges of heresy for aiding and abetting the Temple's heresies, and for offering support and encouragement to Devil worshippers. And no one doubted he would proceed with that ... including the Pope himself.

"Since then, matters have gone from bad to worse, and the tortures were resumed in April, when Clement submitted to the King's pressures. Now the days are filled with charge and counter-charge, plot and subterfuge, lies and malicious rumors. Campaigns are being waged throughout the land to convince the people that Philip, His Most Christian Majesty, has right on his side and that the people of France themselves are the staunchest guardians of the Christian faith. The Templars have been largely lost sight of, although some are hauled out from time to time to remind the world of how perfidious they were.

"But the struggle, the real struggle, is for the Temple properties ... the Order's wealth. The Church holds it for the time being, since

Philip recently bent the knee, ceremoniously at least, to acknowledge Clement's papacy and power. But even if Clement and his cardinals hold the nominal power over the Templar prisoners, it is Philip the Fair who holds those prisoners in his dungeons. And Philip will win this war. The Temple in France will become nothing but a memory, and even that will fade and die. So look to yourselves. That is the best advice we have to offer you."

The silence stretched long after de Montferrat had finished, the air of gloom around the gathering almost palpable. A few of the Templars looked at each other worriedly, but no one seemed inclined to speak out on anything until Bishop Formadieu muttered, "Well, here is a moral conundrum ..." He said no more than that, however, and no one sought to question him about what he meant, no doubt because each one of them, in his own way, was facing the same realization. The game was over, and their side had been defeated.

It was Baron Etienne Dutoit who brought the meeting to a close, ending the long, embittered silence with a question directed to Will.

"Tell me, Sir William, have you heard aught recently from your aged aunt in Aix?" The term "aged aunt" was commonly used among brothers of the Order of Sion when outsiders were present to refer to their dealings with the Order, and Will responded without a blink.

"No, Baron, I have not, not since before I left Paris. She was well then, but like all of us, she grows daily older. It occurred to me, before we began to speak of these other things, that you might have word for me on her condition. Have you seen her recently?"

"Aye, I have, but—" The Baron hesitated. "I ... the information that I have for you is somewhat personal and ... delicate in nature." He turned to eye the rest of the group, who were all listening. "Would it vex you, my friends, were I to ask your indulgence in this matter? Our business here is concluded, I believe, but I have yet some information to impart privately to Sir William, concerning his relatives in Provence. Would you mind leaving us now?"

5

As soon as the doors swung closed, Will looked directly at Baron Dutoit. "Have you any resolution for me on the matter of releasing men from their vows? Guidance, counsel, opinions, advice? Anything will be welcome, for I confess I am utterly lost in this."

"Words," the Baron responded. "We have words. Nothing more, nothing less. Together, they address all your requests, from guidance to advice. But the decisions to be made are yours alone. You might take comfort, though, from knowing that many of the most astute members of our brotherhood have been working together on your dilemma, seeking to determine the best route for you to follow here in your tiny community in exile. Simon and I have been involved in those discussions, and that, more than any other reason, is why we are here in person. The retelling of the history of this past year was important, certainly. But what we are really here to discuss is the course of action that lies ahead of you, here on your island of Arran and in Scotland. We hear all the time about how things are changing in this modern world we live in, and it is true that many things are changing, visibly and noticeably. But this change we are living through now is epoch making. Our world—*your* world in particular, as a Templar— has changed forever. And the changes are numerous, enormous, widespread, and, we believe, permanent. They are certainly so in France, and the rest of Christendom is bound to follow."

He glanced then at de Montferrat, who grunted and took over from him smoothly. "We are here to remind you of your roots, Will: of where you came from, who you really are. Not because we think you have forgotten any of it, but simply because you have spent so long now with your energies dedicated entirely to the welfare of the Temple and your Templars that we suspect you might have lost your perspective. We are not here to criticize you or your conduct. You have done nothing wrong. But we are here to realign your thinking … your line of sight … and to adjust your mental point of view. Are you prepared for that?"

Will had been leaning forward in his chair, listening intently, a small frown of concentration drawing his brows together. But his gaze had been focused on the long table by the doors, where he had left his sword belt when he entered, and now, instead of answering directly, he stood up and crossed to the table, where he unsheathed his long sword and swung it several times with exaggerated slowness, testing the weight of the weapon and the accuracy of his swings.

"Do you know how long it has been since I last swung a sword in earnest?" He did not wait for an answer. "I'm not exactly sure of what you mean by 'adjusting my mental point of view,' but the prospect does not trouble me. I am prepared for whatever you might wish to put to me."

"Good. Etienne?"

Baron Dutoit stepped forward and held out his hand for Will's sword, which he then proceeded to use in formal exercise, stepping through the prescribed rules of attack and defense in a way that proved he still knew what he was about with a blade in his hand. He stopped after completing a basic pattern of moves and held the weapon upright in his hands, gazing up at its shining tip, then deftly spun it and reversed his grip, pointing the blade downward and grasping it in both hands about a foot below the cross-hilt, so that it resembled a crucifix held up in front of his face, between him and Will.

"Do you remember this? This symbol? Do you remember what you learned of it when you joined our brotherhood—that it was then and is now other than it seems today? Do you recall the teachings you received about our forefathers and whence they came? Do you remember learning, and believing, that the Cross that Christians revere is a fabrication, an appropriation of the Cross of Light that was the symbol of the Roman god Mithras, adopted and adapted to men's use today by other men who knew the power of symbols and sought to convert the followers of Mithras—which was, effectively, every soldier in the legions—to Christianity?

"And do you remember learning, and coming to believe, that Christianity itself is a usurpation and distortion of the Way our ancestors followed? The same sacred Way that the man Jesus and his brother James pursued and the secrets of which they died defending? A usurpation because it was taken from the Jews, then stripped of every vestige of its Jewishness, and a distortion because it was thereafter scrubbed and cleansed and reconstituted free of any Jewish taint that the Romans might find offensive, including the person and character of Jesus himself? Do you remember that? Any of it?"

Will, taken aback by the quiet ferocity of this sudden catechism, could only raise his hands as if in self-defense. "Of course I do. I remember all of it."

"Then the time has come to start living your true life, as one of us, a Brother of the Order of Sion."

"Do you doubt that I have been doing so?"

"No, not at all. But we believe you need to see things afresh, beginning now."

"We. You mean you and Sir Simon?"

"No. I mean we and all your peers in the brotherhood. That is the message we bring to you: it is time to take stock of what remains to you and your people here on Arran."

"All that remains to us, from what you have told us today, is our freedom, and we are fortunate to have that. But what use is freedom if we cannot exercise it?"

"That is true. As things stand now, your freedom is constrained. But that is why we are here, Simon and I. Unless you take steps to alter fate, you will have only the freedom to die off, one by one, until the last of you disappears. You know that already. We were greatly encouraged to see that you had already given this matter much thought before reporting your concerns, because you are correct in thinking that your younger men, at least, should be released from their oath of chastity. Without the ability to procreate, you and your charges will soon be left with no one to whom you can entrust your legacy."

Will frowned again, more deeply now. "What legacy is that?"

"Your legacy as Templars … the last free Templars. After two hundred years, is that not worth preserving?"

Now Will threw up his hands in exasperation. "I certainly think so ... of course I do. But you have just finished telling me it is time to leave all that behind."

"Did I say that? No. What I said was that it is time to start living your true life again, as one of our brotherhood before all else. But that does not entail abandoning any of the responsibilities that are yours. It involves rethinking them and rearranging them, but there can be no question of abandoning your charges."

"No more than there can be of releasing my men from their oaths of chastity and then expecting them to remain on Arran."

Now it was the Baron's turn to frown, tilting his head slightly to one side. "I don't follow."

"I did not expect you to, Baron. But there are no women on Arran. Or only very few, wives of the inhabitants, most of whom have long since crossed to the mainland. There are certainly no young women here, of childbearing age." He shrugged. "Therefore, if we release our monks from their vow of chastity—even ignoring the fact that most would refuse, along with all the other reasons why such a course would be sheer folly—they would have to leave the island in search of wives, which would decrease our numbers and hasten the end of us."

The Baron, clearly in need of guidance, looked at his friend de Montferrat, and Sir Simon spoke up.

"When you say 'the end of us,' you are referring to the Temple brethren here, is that not so?"

"Of course."

"But *us*, to us, refers to our more ancient fraternity of Sion. The Temple, the entire Order since its initiation, has been but a means to an end for us ... a convenient way of masking ourselves and our true endeavors from view. There is no end in sight for us, in that sense. Our existence is undreamed of beyond our own brotherhood and our work remains ongoing. That is why we are here, urging you to take appropriate steps to protect yourselves. Your very presence here, ostensibly as Templars, extends the presence of our true Order in this land, for besides yourself and those brothers here among your number, there are fewer than a score of our brothers in Sion in all Scotland. And yet our dearest and most precious possessions, the source of all our efforts, are now here, under your protection."

"The Treasure chests," Will murmured, then nodded. "Aye, they are, for the time being."

"Of course. They will be returned to France and to safety when the time is right, but in the light of current developments it would be folly to risk bringing them back there today. And so you, my young friend, must stay here. That is your charge from your brothers in Sion. And you must prosper here—that is even more important. Our Order needs you here, enlarging and exercising your influence with the King of Scots and his nobles."

Will shook his head. "But what has that to do with releasing the brethren from the vow of chastity? I fail to see the connection."

De Montferrat grunted, then sucked in a great breath, clearly willing himself to patience. "Templars take three vows, Will. Which of those takes precedence?"

"Obedience."

"Precisely. Now, as Master in Scotland, you have supreme power over all of the Templars here. We will find the proper way to explain the situation to them, and though you may be right and many may refuse to renounce their oath, some of them will. But those who do will yet be constrained to obey your commands as Master, and those commands will instruct them to find wives, wherever they can, and then *return with them to Arran*, where they will still be accepted as members of the community. I am not saying it will be simple to achieve. But I am saying it is necessary."

"No, by God! Think of what you are saying, both of you … By relieving these men of the need to observe *one* vow, we debase all three. How can we say in conscience and with authority that one lifetime vow is less important than another, that we will absolve them of the sin of oath breaking in one instance, yet hold them to the sanctity of the others? It makes no sense. It is illogical."

"Aye, it is. But the lack of logic is not ours. It is the logic of the world within which they have elected to live that has gone awry. We are all sinners. That they know, as Christians. But in this present case they have been punished and condemned by the very authorities they have spent their lives defending: the Church and the society in which they lived and served faithfully. Their priests, from the highest down, have betrayed them mercilessly and callously, and their King, to whom admittedly they swore no allegiance, has declared them treasonous, fit only for torture and the flames of death. If they hold dear to anything now, it must be to themselves and to the thought of survival, for themselves and their ideals. And that survival entails the getting of children to follow them into a new life. These are men who would have gladly died for their beliefs, fighting for Christianity and its beliefs. And now they are declared anathema by the governing body of that Christianity, deprived of any say in their own lives. Believe me, they will listen, and they will understand. And if one-tenth of them accept your absolution, that will make a score of new families here in Scotland. Families who may be taught the truth."

"The Christian truth, you mean."

"Aye. Our own truth is not Christian. But the Templars in Scotland must endure, by whatever means they must employ."

"But still it seems impossible to do what you suggest. There has never been such a thing happen before … the lifting of a collective vow."

"Not true … or not exactly true. Larger changes have been made. Never in history, you may recollect, had any cleric, any priest or monk, been permitted to kill any man prior to the founding of the Temple Order. But when the time was right and circumstances called for drastic change, that law, which had been immutable since the foundation of the Christian Church, was changed to meet the new requirements of the age. And monks and priests acquired a dispensation that required, even encouraged, them to kill in God's name. That change, requiring sweeping alterations to what had been God's own commandment, makes your current dilemma seem very small."

"Aye, when put like that, it does. We must disappear, then …" Will was aware of both men's eyes on him, and shrugged. "Something

I was told by a churchman here … something with which I agreed at the time." He fell silent, musing, then looked from one of his mentors to the other. "So, do you and your Council really believe this is achievable, all that we have talked about?"

It was Etienne Dutoit who answered him. "We do, on the most fundamental level. And we will place the entire resources of our Order at your disposal."

"To save the remnants of the Temple …"

"To save it and preserve it. And we will send you aid, in the form of bright young men from France, the best of the best of the Order of Sion, all of them married men with young families. Scotland and France—*our* France, our *Order's* France—will be allies in this renaissance."

Again Will sat in silence for a long time, but then he straightened his back and nodded resolutely. "Very well, then. It will not be easy, but it will be done. So mote it be!"

6

For perhaps the tenth time in the course of four hours, Will Sinclair flipped over the carefully wrapped oblong packet on the tabletop in front of him. The smooth front bore only his name, written in a hand he recognized with mixed feelings. The reverse bore only a wax seal, impressed with a smooth, blank stamp, and he fought hard against the inclination to break it open and read the letter folded inside. He could not guess why it had been sent, and for some reason he felt reluctant to open it and find out. The woman who had penned it had been in his mind for months, with increasing regularity and utterly against his volition. Her face would appear in his mind unpredictably and at the strangest times, and he had awaked several times from a sound sleep with the memory of her form and the warmth of her skin imprinted on his befuddled awareness. And now, sitting staring at her letter, he acknowledged to himself that his unwilling preoccupation with her had increased since the day when he had released so many of his brethren from their vow of chastity.

He grunted, disgustedly, and flipped the letter again, staring now at the inscription of his own name in the exact center of the flawless vellum sheet. It had been delivered to him that morning by a young man who had arrived aboard de Berenger's galley, returning from the Galloway coast where the admiral had been meeting with Edward Bruce and Douglas for the previous month. Both leaders, Will now knew, had been in the north all that time, campaigning with the King against the MacDougalls of Argyll. De Berenger himself had been up there, sailing the sea lochs in support of the royal forces, and brought word of a recent victory for the King's forces, led by the King himself, with his fiery brother and James Douglas in support, at a mountain pass called Brander—the supposedly impregnable rear entrance to the Argyll lands. The taking of the pass, largely due to the genius and improvisation of Douglas, had permitted the invasion of Argyll itself, and the confusion and confoundment of Lame John of Lorn, who had thought his rear secure.

And with that news had come this other missive: a single package brought by a wide-eyed, earnest, and very young man called Randolph, cousin to the Baroness. He had ridden from Nithsdale, he said, at the behest of his lady cousin, with specific instructions to seek out the acting commander of the Bruce army in the south and secure a passage to Arran aboard the next ship sailing there. He had waited for two weeks on the coast until the admiral's galley returned, and had then crossed the firth aboard it.

Now, with a muttered imprecation, Will pushed himself to his feet, leaving the letter on the tabletop, and crossed to the narrow window, where he leaned on the sill, gazing out at the activities of his men in the yard below.

More than a month had elapsed since the arrival of Dutoit and de Montferrat. In the course of that time, in a closed plenary meeting of the combined Arran chapters, convened in the three-day turnover when one expedition returned from riding with the King of Scots and before their replacements had left for the mainland, Will had outlined his intentions to his Templars. Assisted by Admiral de Berenger and several other senior members of the community, and proceeding slowly and patiently so that even the least gifted of his people could understand what was being said and what it meant, Will had explained the situation now in force in their homeland, with particular and detailed emphasis on exactly how, and how profoundly, those truths had come to affect the life of each and every individual Templar on Arran. And towards what would have been the end of the proceedings, he explained his intentions on the matter of releasing the Arran brethren from their vow of chastity.

He had anticipated strenuous opposition from all sides, but mainly from the three Templar bishops in his community, and from the Boar de Pairaud and his adherents, so he had been at pains to consult with them first, seeking their advice long before making his announcement to the chapter. But to his profound astonishment, not one of them had raised a single quibble. They had asked some penetrating and profoundly concerned questions—particularly on the theological improbability of being able to choose between vows already taken, rejecting one completely while conforming to the others with equanimity—but when he answered all of them straightforwardly, they had, as one man, acceded to his wishes. It was not they who had elected to usurp God's will in the first place, as one of the bishops pointed out. God's own churchly deputy had opted to revise the rules governing the worship of his divine Master, and the Templars had merely responded sanely, in self-preservation.

When he made his presentation to the remainder of the brethren, however, his proposal sparked a debate that went on long into the night before it gained acceptance. The vast majority of those assembled were too firmly set in their ways and had no interest in being released from their vow, for any reason, but fifty-seven of the younger brethren accepted, some of them eagerly, some complacently, most with varying degrees of reluctance. Will had been unsurprised, but slightly disappointed against all logic, that the former rebel Martelet had been among the first to accept, although none of his erstwhile companions joined him.

Will had then reconvened the chapter the following day, wearing his full Master's regalia and formally entreating the blessing of the Old Testament God upon their new course of action and behavior. And the exodus had begun the very next day, with the newly enfranchised brethren having renewed their vow of obedience and undertaken, without exception, to bring new wives back to Arran when they found them. Of the fifty-seven newly released brethren, however, a full thirty had been members of the new rotation of riders to the mainland and King Robert's service, which meant that they either would have to await the end of their tour before seeking a wife, or would spend the tour looking around them at available prospects.

The two delegates from Aix-en-Provence had left to return to their homes soon after that, both of them well pleased with the way things had turned out, and both promising to send young, married men from the Order of Sion as soon as it could be arranged. These newcomers, it had been agreed, would come as Temple sympathizers, their intentions to support and assist the Arran brethren of the outlawed Temple. Will's thinking on that matter had not yet extended to how he would welcome the newcomers or to what use he might put them, but he was unperturbed by the prospect. When the time came, he knew, there would be positions available for them to fill.

He turned back to look at the unopened letter on the tabletop, recognizing that there was no logical reason for his reluctance to open it. It had been delivered openly and innocently, and so he knew it would contain nothing inflammatory or outrageous. The woman had written to him before, and in this letter she would probably continue as she had begun, with personal information on the King's affairs that she had been able to glean through her special, trusted status. He had no fear of any of that; all the fear he felt was for his own reaction to his renewed awareness of Jessie Randolph's existence. The memory of her—even worse, imaginings of her—had disturbed his sleep on too many occasions, and it was only recently that he had been able to forget about her for weeks on end. Now here she was again, chapping at his door, as his Scots friends would say.

He sighed, then sniffed hard, his mind made up, and strode back to the table, where he seated himself and snapped the seal on the missive with a flick of his thumbnail. The pages of the letter, neatly folded and pressed, were folded tightly inside the enveloping cover, and he saw at a glance that the letter, like the previous one, was written in the tongue of his boyhood, Angevin.

Sir William

You may already be better informed of what I am about to tell you than I myself am, but having spoken with SJD as he passed through Nithsdale on a recent journey, and learning that he had intended to visit you but had been unable to do so because of the restrictions of his campaign in Galloway, it has occurred to me that you might not yet be aware of what is happening in the north.

The truce that has been in force with the MacDougalls of Lorn and Argyll is now at an end, and it is obvious that the recalcitrant Lame John, Lord of Lorn, has been using the time of truce to strengthen his position and his forces in order to intensify his efforts to overthrow His Grace Robert. Aware of that, the King has marched north with his army to invade Lorn's lands from the rear, through a natural gateway called the Pass of Brander, and SJD and his command are now on their way to join the royal forces. You may be unaware of those developments, but the outcome of the venture will greatly influence your situation on your island for better or for worse. I pray that it will be the former.

By now your plans for consolidating yourselves upon the island must be well in hand, if not absolutely complete. I trust that you and yours have prospered in that regard. I myself continue to enjoy being an honorary aunt, although "mother" might be the better word for this relationship, all-embracing as it is. Be that as it may, I am finding great pleasure in it and the child is a delight, with a very quick ear for languages. She is already speaking French as though she has never known another tongue, after less than a year of practice.

I hope you will not think too unkindly of me for thrusting myself into your awareness yet again, but I think of you often and was born, my father used to tell me, with far more curiosity than was good for me. Peggy is well, and aging beautifully. You would be proud, could you but see her. And she wears your trinket constantly, her pride in her elder brother a self-evident truth.

The young man who bears this letter to you is a cousin—far younger than he appears to be—so I beg you to ignore his pleadings to remain with you, and to send him home again. He will have plenty of time to go to war once he comes of age for it.

Your friend,
Jessie Randolph

The foray into Argyll and Lorn had been a great success, with Douglas playing a major role in the capture of the supposedly impregnable pass, all of which Will had already learned from de Berenger, whose source was more recent than Jessie Randolph's was when she wrote her letter. But Will was obliged to admit to himself that had her letter arrived by any other means than de Berenger's galley, he would have been grateful and highly pleased to have received it. It was not the Baroness's fault that time and events had overtaken her tidings. Her concern for his welfare—and for that of his men, he added hastily—was genuine, and he had no desire to dispute it. And that, in turn, made him feel guilty for having no intention of acknowledging her letter. To the best of his knowledge he had never, ever written a letter to a woman, and he had no desire to begin now. He had not even written to his sister Peggy in response to the letters she had sent to him, and she was a sibling. The prospect of even attempting to write to Jessica Randolph made him quail. He would not even know where to begin, or how to proceed from there. Better, then, he decided, to continue as he had begun, unresponsive to the woman's blandishments and therefore reasonably safe from ever saying anything he might regret.

He read the letter through again, then folded it carefully and placed it in the small locked chest of sandalwood on his table, atop the woman's first letter, where he knew it would be safe.

THE ROAD TO
LEGEND

THE RETURN

1

Will Sinclair was about his own business on that magnificent June morning in the year of our Lord 1312, and it was business he wished to share with no one. His life as a monastic was generally without privacy, and his activities as Master and commander of the Temple on Arran exacerbated that condition. There was always someone needing to speak to him, seeking his approval or his advice, and any time he was out in plain sight he would end up in the center of a throng. Only in prayer and meditation could he find solitude, and seldom even then, since most of the Templars' daily prayers and the rites surrounding them were communal. Today, however, Will had elected to be alone, for what he considered to be good and sufficient purpose.

He had been told the previous evening, by one of the old mariners off a trading vessel anchored in the bay at Lochranza, that the next day promised to be the finest of the year thus far, and on the spur of the moment, Will had decided to do something that he had been thinking about for more than a month. He sought out Richard de Montrichard, the island's preceptor, and informed him that he was leaving then and there, alone, and would return within two days, on the last day of June. De Montrichard merely nodded, showing neither surprise nor curiosity, but Will knew that even if the preceptor saw nothing strange in the disappearance of the Master without the smallest escort, others would, and so he added, purely for the later benefit of those others, that he had much on his mind and needed time to be alone and to think without distraction. He then went and told Tam Sinclair that he would be sleeping under the sky for the next two nights, and asked him to keep his squire, young Henry, busy while he was away. He had expected an argument from Tam, but his kinsman had just shrugged and wished him joy of his privacy.

Will then packed one saddlebag carefully with all he thought he might need, threw a thick rolled blanket over one shoulder, then made a quick call upon the commissary for food to keep him going for two days. A good, sturdy mountain horse selected from the stables completed his preparations, and he disappeared into the hills just as the sun was beginning to set.

A strong wind came up before he was two miles from Lochranza, but he slept soundly that night on a bed of bracken in a deep, sheltered hollow by a mountain tarn while a howling gale shrieked and whistled above his head without harming him, wrapped warmly as he was in a thick woolen blanket and covered by piled bracken ferns. The wind subsided while he slept, and he was up and about long before dawn began to brighten the sky. He ate a breakfast of cold meat and oatmeal cake in the dark and struck camp before sunrise, heading south and east under the flanks of the great Fells that towered on his right, until he found the coast again. He reached his destination by mid-morning, when the sun was already hot on his face.

Will stood with his back to the sea, peering up at the slopes of the high mountains, searching for signs of human life but not expecting to see any. This was one of the most remote stretches of coastline on Arran, seldom visited because it had high cliffs and no shelving beaches in front, and massive, impassable mountains at its back. It was approachable only from the way he had come, and he had found the place by accident, two years earlier, while following a gut-shot stag.

He took his horse's bridle and led the broad-hoofed beast down towards the cliff, where they descended into a narrow defile cut by a fast-flowing stream and vanished from view. Down there, however, was the jewel of this place. Fifteen paces beneath the lip of the cliff, invisible from every direction but the sea straight ahead and forming one side of the gully housing the cataract, a wide finger of rock jutted out into the sea, its upper surface coated with turf and bracken ferns. Once there, Will unsaddled his horse and left it to graze freely.

Then, carrying his saddlebags and four lengths of alder sapling that he had cut from a grove a mile away to the north, he walked to the farthest point of the rocky finger and gazed down into the sea, less than ten paces beneath him.

The day was perfectly calm, and the sea reflected that, only the gentlest appearance and disappearance of isolated underwater rocks revealing that there was a five- or six-foot swell down there, its presence the only sign that a gale had been howling here mere hours before. The water was so clear and still-looking now, despite the swell, that he could see the occasional large fish glide by. He turned and gazed up again at the cliff top above. Nothing stirred up there; he was alone.

He stepped away from the edge of the rock and shrugged his long-sword belt up and over his head, dropping it and the weapon it bore onto the grass, to be followed by the waist belt holding his scrip and his sheathed dagger. He wore no mail or armor of any kind this day, for those things were never needed on the island. The people of the mainland and Kintyre might not know exactly who the strangers were who had recently occupied Arran, but they knew that they were numerous, they were womanless, and they were warriors, and so they kept their distance and left the islanders in peace.

Moving rapidly now, Will collected the four lengths of alder sapling and tied them together with strips of leather to form a four-foot-high tripod, after which he tied the fourth length across two of the legs. That done, he pulled off the plain brown summer surcoat he wore and folded it loosely before dropping it on top of his discarded weapons. Then he undid yet another narrow belt and removed his knee-length fold-over tunic of rough wool, baring his upper body and spreading his arms wide to embrace the freedom of the air against his skin. Moments later he dropped to his rump and pulled off his heavy riding boots, then eased his loose woolen breeches down until he could kick them off his feet, leaving himself clad only in a single undergarment.

He reached over, bending sideways, and pulled the saddlebags towards him, and from them he withdrew two objects, the first of them a heavy cake of rough, strong-smelling soap from the chapter's laundry, and the other a white, carefully rolled and bound packet that he untied and flapped open. It was a plain rectangular sheet of bleached lambskin, more than twice as broad as it was long. Soft and supple, the inner side was scrubbed brilliantly white and clean, the outer still bearing the fleece, shaven to a depth of less than one quarter of an inch. A long thong of the same white leather was threaded loosely through the first few of a row of punched holes on one end, and the other end was similarly punched. Leaving the thing lying fleece side down on the short grass, Will rolled and swung himself up until he was kneeling. He reached down to his side and tugged at the knotted thong that held a soiled but otherwise identical lambskin wrapping tightly in place about his waist, from hips to just above mid-thigh. It took him some time to undo the bindings, pulling them loose from the eyelets through which they were threaded, and when the garment fell away he swept it up and walked naked to the edge of the promontory to look down at the fast-flowing stream hurtling down its deep gully to the sea. Sighting carefully, he lobbed the garment, and then the cake of soap, down to the one spot on the far bank of the narrow flume where there was sufficient space to do so, and then he turned and walked swiftly to the point of the promontory.

The decision to come to this spot had been precipitated by a recent encounter with Richard de Montrichard's squire, Gareth. Will and de Montrichard had been reviewing the duty roster for the upcoming rotation of troops for King Robert when de Montrichard's squire had come in, bearing a message for his master, and as the burly youth passed close by him Will had had to close his eyes and hold his breath against the sour, fecal stench emanating from him. He was practically immune to the smells of the people he lived among, some of whom gave off a rank and even feral odor, but even among a community of unwashed bodies, this young man stank. Will had forced himself to sit still and breathe only when he had to until the doors had closed behind the young man, and then he'd sucked in a deep breath.

"Sweet Jesus, Richard, that boy of yours stinks like an open latrine. A festering corpse would smell more wholesome. When did he last bathe, do you know?"

De Montrichard looked mystified. "I don't know. At Easter, I suppose, with the rest of us. Three months ago? Should I have him bathe again?"

On the point of uttering an explosive "Yes!" Will shrugged and waved a hand mildly to dismiss the topic. He had already decided upon a course of action regarding the Gareth lad.

As soon as his business with the preceptor was concluded, Will sent word to the training yard to have his own squire, his nephew Henry Sinclair, report to him in his private quarters. He then went to one of the six small chests that lined the rear wall of the room that served him as a cell, pulled out a bar of rough soap, and wrapped it in one of his own towels. When the boy arrived he beckoned young Henry to approach, then bent towards him to sniff, searchingly, and his nose wrinkled.

"When did you last bathe?"

"Two weeks ago, Uncle." The boy did not even blink at the question, having long since grown inured to his uncle's strange regard for, and insistence upon, bodily cleanliness. Bathing was not a requirement of the Rule, so they did not bathe. Regarded as being effete and conducive to carnality, it was officially frowned upon.

"Then I have a task for you. It is high time you went for a swim."

Young Henry smiled, a little uncertainly. He was one of only half a score of the two score squires in the community who could swim, and he loved nothing better than to do so on the very infrequent occasions when his duties granted him the freedom to enjoy it.

Will lobbed the towel and soap towards him and the boy caught it.

"You will take your friends with you—those who swim—and enjoy the afternoon in freedom. But there is a condition. You will take Preceptor de Montrichard's squire, Gareth, as well. He needs a bath, and it is your task to assist him in taking one. That thing you are holding is a bar of soap. You know how to use it. You will use it on Gareth, and to good effect. Do I make myself clear?"

"Yes, Uncle. Very clear. But—?"

"I'm not suggesting you throw Gareth from the cliff, you understand? He does not swim and might drown there. But you can drag him in from the beach and scrub him clean there. Now, let's away."

Will allowed himself a small chuckle now as he imagined the scene he had set in motion, Gareth forced to overcome what was clearly a lifelong aversion to soap and water. Anticipating the pleasure of the same experience, he paused briefly, studying the water below him, and then dived out and down.

The sea was fairly warm, he knew, at the end of June, but the initial shock of plunging into it was enough to drive every vestige of breath from his lungs, and as he fought his way to the surface he found himself thinking how fortunate he was to have no fear of swimming, or of water. Most people did, he knew. They found it an alien and terrifying reality, a threat of death over which they had no control. Will had learned to swim as a small boy, taught by one of his father's men, who had been a fisherman all his life and had learned to swim and to love doing so. Will had been an eager pupil, and though he had had little opportunity to swim since the age of eighteen—he could count the separate occasions on his fingers—he had never forgotten the exhilarating freedom of swimming in deep, clear water.

He swam for what he believed to be a quarter of an hour, feeling at once guilty and liberated, diving down to the sea bottom and then returning to the surface time after time. He could see, down there, the kelp and tangle anchored to the rocks, and the limpets and other shellfish that abounded there, but the salt water stung his eyes and blurred his vision, and when the sensation became uncomfortable he remained on the surface, floating on his back and gazing at the promontory above him, occasionally kicking strongly to counteract the tidal drift that pulled him southward along the coast. He became acutely aware of his genitals, of their freedom in his unaccustomed nakedness. And that awareness made him aware of his reason for being there, so that he struck out strongly towards the shore and dog-paddled his way into the tiny estuary of the freshet that bounded down from the hillside above.

The fresh water, splashing heavily and urgently against his body, was far colder than the sea he had just left. He scampered upwards against its pounding, bent over and using hands and feet to scramble over the rocks in the streambed until he reached the cauldron beneath a six-foot waterfall and climbed onto the shelf beside it, where he had earlier thrown the soap and the sheepskin.

It was cold in the gully, the sun blocked out by the steep sides, and he moved quickly now, spreading the lambskin fleece over a good-sized stone and scrubbing at it with the cake of soap until it began to work up a lather. It was hard going, for the soap was primitive and had little capacity to generate bubbles, but he kept at it and soon was able to knead the fleece, feeling the slickness of the soapy wool under his hands and between his chilled fingers. He worked single-mindedly, kneading and pummeling at the cold fleece to dislodge the accumulated dirt and grime, adding fresh soap occasionally, then repeating the entire process until he was satisfied that he had washed out as much as he could. He gathered up the fleece and went back to the foot of the waterfall. He draped the garment over another, larger stone with a flat surface, where the thunderous deluge from above fell straight onto it, the sheer weight and pressure of the water scouring the soap from the wool until no trace of suds or discoloration could be seen draining into the pool below the rock.

He felt cold to his bones now, and he had difficulty hauling himself up the remainder of the steep gully, carrying the waterlogged fleece over one shoulder to the nearest point at which he could climb safely up onto the sunlit surface of the rocky outthrust. The sun felt wonderful against his bare skin, but he knew it would take some time to burn off the chill that afflicted him. He quickly spread the streaming fleece over the tops of the tripod poles and left it to drip while he launched himself into a familiar series of physical exertions designed to loosen his limbs and increase his heartbeat. And when he felt warm again, he collapsed limply on the grass, luxuriating in the sun's warmth before he fell asleep.

He awoke some time later to find a large, heavy beetle crawling across his torso, its scrabbling claws tickling him awake. He flicked it away and it took to the air, droning heavily as it vanished into the gully by his side. A glance at the tripod told him the fleece had stopped dripping, although it still looked waterlogged. He grunted and rose smoothly to his feet, taking the sheepskin in both hands and shaking it hard, trying to snap the ends of it to expel as much water as possible. That, too, was hard work, but he kept at it, changing his grip from end to end, until he was convinced no more water could be shaken free. He was wet again by then, his skin covered in water droplets, but he was warm this time, too.

He used the white leather binding thongs of the garment itself to tie it securely to the tripod, stretching it and draping one end across the crossbar on two of the three legs. When he was satisfied, he angled its surface directly towards the sun, estimating as he did so that it must be close to midday, and feeling quite sure that by the time the remainder of the day had elapsed—at least eight hours at this time of the year—the sheepskin, if not completely dried, would be at least dry enough to be packed and rolled without damage.

He walked to the edge of the spit of land and turned in a full circle, scanning the cliffs above him and the empty sea ahead of him and seeing no single sign of life anywhere. He might have been the only person alive in the world, and that thought spurred him to urinate, aiming deliberately towards the mainland visible in the distance and watching the arc of his urine rise high into the air before falling into the waves below. But then, suddenly aware of his nakedness, he turned back and scooped up the fresh white garment he had brought with him. It was known as an apron. Every member of the Temple wore one, receiving it as a mark of belonging on the occasion of his being admitted to the fraternity, and none of them wore it easily, for it was intended as a barrier against sexuality—a safeguard against concupiscence—to be worn constantly, day and night. And Will, his face wrinkling involuntarily, conceded to himself that it was effective if only because the majority of the Temple brethren chose to interpret the Rule literally and never thought to remove their apron once it was in place. The stink of the rancid thing was in itself a guarantee of chastity. Thinking this,

Will grunted to himself and, the lacing completed, stepped into the restrictive garment, shrugged and pulled it into place, then laced it up tightly, bidding farewell to naked freedom.

He then collected his weapons and unsheathed both sword and dagger. After examining the blades critically, he dug again in his saddlebags for the small package containing his whetstone and the tiny vial of oil he used to protect the blades against rust, and for a while he worked on the weapons with total concentration, using the stone to burnish the metal wherever he thought he saw a blemish or the threat of one, then honing the edges with great care before applying a thin film of the protective oil to each blade. Throughout it all, he was aware of the tightness and familiar restriction of the fresh, tightly laced apron around his hips,

The real tradition underlying the use of the garment, Will knew, had nothing to do with the Order of the Temple or with the Catholic Church's strictures on sexuality. The apron sprang from far more ancient roots and was a symbol of membership in the Order of Sion, representing the white apron of lambswool worn by the Egyptian priests of Isis and Osiris in the days of the Israelite captivity. Later, when Moses led the Israelites out of Egypt, their priests took that association with them and wore the white lambskin aprons to denote their spiritual purity as servants of the living God, Jehovah, and the original priestly caste of the Temple in Jerusalem wore the aprons long before the advent of Herod's Pharisees, who saw no need to wear them. The white apron had then been taken up by the Essenes, who called themselves the Followers of the Way, the movement espoused by the man Jesus and his brother James, who was known as the Just.

Will knew, too, the tale of how the Templars had come to adopt the tradition of the lambswool apron, and now he smiled as he remembered it. Hugh de Payens and one of his closest friends, Payn Montdidier, had been surprised by some of their fellow knights one day when they were bathing. Asked about the strange garments they were wearing, Montdidier had retorted that it was a penalty they had imposed upon themselves during their years of excavating for the Treasure. It was a form of enforced chastity, he said, because it was sewn in place and could never be removed, and such was the reverence in which he was held that his explanation was accepted immediately, and the apron was worn thereafter by every Templar knight upon joining the Order.

Will smiled again at the thought and began giving his sword blade a final, careful wipe. The Templars wore a lambswool apron, but it was vastly different from the shaved and supple aprons worn by the Brothers of Sion. The Temple apron was a much bulkier apparatus, bearing the entire fleece, almost a thumb's length thick. It was unbearable in hot weather, whereas Will and his fellows in the Brotherhood of Sion suffered no such discomfort.

Satisfied with the edges of his blades, Will replaced them in their sheaths and ate a simple meal of dry, salted fish and fresh bannock, then made his way down to the stream to slake the thirst the food inspired. When he returned to his place he checked the dryness of the washed fleece, then lay down with his back on a wad of his castoff clothing to think in comfort, and perhaps to sleep again, relishing the luxury of being able to do so in broad daylight, and conscious, too, that he might not have much opportunity to sleep anywhere in comfort in the days that lay ahead.

The King of Scots had summoned a Parliament of the Realm to be convened at Ayr, in the heart of Bruce country and just across the Clyde from Arran, in the coming weeks of July, and Will had been invited. He had no idea why, but the word had come to him in the form of a letter telling him that King Robert would be well pleased to have him attend the Parliament. The letter itself came from the Bishop of Moray and had been delivered in person by a Benedictine friar who had made his way from Edinburgh on foot to the west coast and crossed the Firth of Clyde to the island aboard one of the MacDonald galleys. The Parliament, Will knew, would be a glittering assembly, all the finest and strongest in the land in attendance, but he had no slightest pang of regret over being unable to wear his full Templar panoply. Sir William Sinclair would attend the King's gathering as a simple well-armed and clean-smelling knight, and he would leave Arran to do so in three days' time.

A large seabird swooped low over the coast, and Will watched it idly as it reared up in a sudden tilt of wings, then dived into the sea right in front of him to emerge moments later with a fish in its beak, the weight of it forcing the bird to fight hard to climb into the air again. He half smiled in admiration of the beauty of the bird's maneuver, how it had plunged vertically into the water with hardly a splash, and then as he went to lie back again, something caught his eye, a half-recognized anomaly at the edge of his vision, to the south, almost obscured by the reflection of the sun off the water.

He sat up straighter, shading his eyes with one hand and squinting against the glare, and eventually identified the outline of a ship out there, evidently becalmed, miles from where he sat, its shape indistinct against the hills of the mainland at its back. It appeared dilapidated and tawdry, hard worn and ill used, and it seemed to pose no threat. But whom did it belong to, and where was it going? The thought was not alarming, but it was enough to banish his hard-won peace of mind just the same, and Will dressed again, wondering how many more hours he might steal for himself before he was summoned to return and assume his responsibilities once more.

2

David de Moray had been recognizable to Will even from the deck of his ship as it approached the small stone jetty at Ardrossan, the only fishing village on that stretch of mainland coast, near Ayr, that possessed such a feature. As Will Sinclair leapt down onto the small wharf, he was still struggling with his surprise to find the Bishop waiting there, evidently having anticipated his arrival. De Moray shouted his name and waved, then stepped forward from the small group of men with whom he had been talking and came striding towards Will, smiling broadly, looking no more like a bishop of Holy Church than he had the last time they had met.

"Sir William!" he cried. "Welcome to the King's realm. His Grace sends his best wishes and hopes you will be able to join him, even briefly, before our great affairs of state begin to unfold." He threw wide his arms to embrace Will, who, unsure of what behavior might be proper, had been considering kneeling to kiss the episcopal ring Moray wore as the only visible symbol of his ecclesiastical office. Instead, he succumbed to the bear-like hug the armored clergyman bestowed upon him, then stepped away, searching for words.

"Bishop Moray," he managed to say. "I am greatly surprised to see you, sir ... and greatly honored. How did you know when I would be arriving?"

The Bishop grinned and waved a hand towards the heavens. "Dinna forget my office, Sir William. Holy Church has spies and informants everywhere, and was it no' one of my own who brought you my invitation? He came back and sent word to me o' your plans. I was nearby myself, on my way to Ayr, and so I stopped to meet you. Come away, now. I ha'e a horse for you and a roof to shelter you tonight and we ha'e much to talk about."

Will glanced over to where Tam Sinclair and young Henry were already haranguing the ship's crew from the wharf, preparing to supervise the unloading of his party, including the ten horses they had brought with them from Arran.

"Permit me, then, to instruct my steward on what we are about. Where will we be staying tonight?"

"Two leagues from here, on the road south. There's a stone keep there, belonging to my cousin Thomas Moray, and we have the use o' it. Tell them to follow us there. They canna miss it, it's in plain sight o' the road."

Will nodded and went to speak with Tam. There were ten men in his party: himself, Tam and young Henry, three knights, and four sergeants, although by this time no eye, no matter how well trained, could have detected any distinction in the latter seven's appearance. The men were traveling light, each carrying his own bedding and provisions since they anticipated no hardship on this excursion, but all were armed and armored in plain harness.

A few minutes later, Will had been introduced to the men in the Bishop's group and swung himself up into the saddle of the fine bay gelding de Moray had brought for him. He waved a salute to Tam and his squire, then spurred his mount forward with the others, heading inland in a clatter of hooves.

Tam turned to young Henry. "Take note o' that. Our patron is the only Templar left in Christendom who gets welcomed by a prince of Holy Church. Does that no' make ye want to laugh?"

The boy looked after the departing group in surprise. "A prince of … That was a *bishop*?"

Tam barked a laugh. "Aye, that was a bishop. But ye'd never find his like in France. That was David de Moray, though his real name's David de Moravia, and he's Bishop o' Moray. He's a wild man, though, and a warrior, wi' balls as big as a stallion horse. One o' the Bruce's staunchest supporters. Now come on, we have to get this ship unloaded."

He moved towards the gangway, already shouting orders to the men above, but young Henry stood a moment longer, gazing towards where his master and the party of Scots knights had disappeared into the distance. A fighting bishop who wore armor—worn and battered armor—instead of vestments and miter! Henry had never seen the like.

Will Sinclair was thinking approximately the same thing at the same moment as he rode just behind and to the right of David de Moray. De Moray was one of the triumvirate of prelates who had made it possible for Robert Bruce to become King of Scots, supporting him in spite of the writ of excommunication that hung over him after the murder of Sir John Comyn on the altar steps of Dumfries Cathedral in 1306. De Moray's support since then had always been actively militant, his sword constantly bared in support of King and realm, his loyalty to both unwavering and unimpeachable. But apart from the episcopal ring he wore on his finger and the heavy pectoral cross of plain silver at his breast, de Moray looked nothing like a bishop most of the time. There were occasions, Will knew, most of them ceremonial and ritual, when the bishop would don his chasuble and miter, and he expected that the forthcoming Parliament might be one such, but de Moray's normal attire was that of a fighting warrior: plain brown woolen shirt and trousers beneath a leather jerkin, and a much-scarred steel breastplate with armored epaulettes complemented, from time to time, with heavy chain-mail leggings over stout boots with armored toes and ankles. Although not particularly tall, the Bishop was strongly built, with the carriage and demeanor of a fighting knight, broad shouldered and narrow in the hip, and he carried a long sword at all times, sheathed at his back, while a heavy battered and dented shield on which his personal colors had been painted and had faded long ago hung from his saddlebow. As though he had become aware of Will's gaze, de Moray swung around in his saddle, looking back over his shoulder, and beckoned.

"Sir William. Ride with me for a while. I would speak with you."

Will spurred his horse to ride alongside the Bishop as the other men in the party, obedient to their leader's unvoiced wish, slackened their pace to permit the two to draw ahead in privacy. De Moray rode on in silence for a few moments, listening to the receding sounds of their escort's hooves, then turned his head to look Will up and down.

"You look fine, man. No trace of the Templar left visible in you. I'm impressed. And I must tell you that you have made a like impression upon the King himself and those of us who seek to safeguard and guide him. You and your men have made a great contribution to the King's cause, notwithstanding your Order's standing restrictions upon paying service to a king. That has not gone unnoticed." He was speaking polished, fluent, accentless French, and Will noticed that there was no trace now of the rough informality he flaunted so carelessly in speaking Scots. Here, he thought, was the urbane Bishop, trained in diplomacy and statecraft as much as in ecclesiastical administration and procedure.

"We both know, you and I, that your initial commitment here was one of necessity—a *quid pro quo* in return for a place for your people to stay, allied with your need to keep your men in training for their own sakes and the principles of your Order. I will not even say 'belonged to,' but that is the plain truth, I fear. As an officer of the Temple, you held no allegiance to our King or his concerns—and that is as it should be, so no one has tried to convince you otherwise. But you yourself have gone further, and of your own free will, in supporting King Robert's cause than many a Scot I could name. Your contributions, and those of your men, are greatly valued, and that is what has led to this—the King's invitation to attend his Parliament as an honored guest." He glanced at Will. "This will be your first Parliament, I suppose?"

Will smiled. "Aye, my lord Bishop, it will. Philip of France believes he rules by divine right. He sees no need to involve any of his people in that."

De Moray grunted, and Will was encouraged to ask the question that had been on his mind for some time. "Why Ayr, my lord Bishop? For the Parliament, I mean. And why in the height of summer?"

His companion switched the reins to his left hand and scratched idly with gloved fingers at his cheek. "First, I am not your lord Bishop until you see me wearing robes and miter. To you, I am plain Davie otherwise. That is what my friends call me and I would like to count you among those. Second, we are riding to Ayr because the King has chosen Ayr, as is his right. Ayr is King Robert's home, the home of his own folk, and they have been ill used these past years, with armies coming and going over their lands in all directions. And so the King decided that it was high time the people of Ayr and its surrounding lands had the privilege of seeing how their land is governed under the King's stewardship.

"The King of France rules his land and his domains as his personal fiefdom and, as you say, he sees no need to deal with the common folk. But the King of Scots rules his people, not the land. He is the steward of his people, and the folk need governance. Hence our Parliaments—a gathering of the estates of the King's realm, including the common folk since the days of Wallace, to ensure the safety and protection of the people. Scots in general, and in particular." He paused briefly. "Right now the English are at war among themselves, as you must know—Edward of Caernarvon and the Earl of Pembroke against a host of other nobles calling themselves the Lords Ordainer, led by the Earls of Warwick and Lancaster, who would dearly love to ordain the future governance of England *and* Scotland to their own benefit. And long may they wrangle, for while they are at one another's throats, we can have peace in Scotland, free of the threat of invasion, for a while at least. A good opportunity for our Parliament."

He cocked an eyebrow towards Will. "You understand why they are at war?"

"Aye. It was caused by the assassination of Piers Gaveston, in May, was it not?"

"It was. Gaveston had surrendered to Pembroke, upon Pembroke's guarantee that his life would be safe, but Warwick intercepted him on his way south and executed him out of hand, on Lancaster's orders. Assassination is too good a word for that. Murder, blatant murder, is what it was. And Edward was rightly furious, as was Pembroke, whose own honor was impugned, his authority flouted and set at naught. As for the King, I have no time for pederasty, and the last thing any land needs is a womanish king who likes to bed with men, but that is neither here nor there. The King's honor, little as that might be, was besmirched, his puissance, however slight it may have been, sneered at and disdained by greedy, mutinous nobles lusting for power and wealth. And so they are at war. And we are not, for once."

"But there are still Englishmen under arms in Scotland, are there not? Or have they been withdrawn?"

"No, they are still here. But they are garrisons, not armies. They hold our strongest castles for the time being, but King Robert is determined they be ousted soon. Berwick and Dumfries, Caerlaverock, Buitle, Bothwell, Perth, and Stirling and Edinburgh, the strongest of all. We will take them all soon, I have no doubt, but in the meantime the King has neither time nor men to waste besieging them."

"And what of me and mine? Is there a purpose to my presence here, or am I truly no more than an honored guest?"

Now the Bishop turned his head to look at Will directly, a smile wrinkling the skin around his eyes. "Is that cynicism I hear, Sir William Sinclair? Surely you would not suspect our King or any of his representatives of an ulterior motive?"

Will found it easy to smile back. "Certainly not … at least, not with the intent of abusing us. But out of self-interest and concern for the weal of the realm? That I would be foolish to doubt. So, what would King Robert have of me while I am in Ayr?"

De Moray's headshake was brief. "Nothing more than you have freely given until now. Your ongoing support in the King's cause, and the continuance of your successful efforts to conceal your presence here in our realm. That above all, for the reasons you already understand."

"Aye. And how goes the struggle to have Pope Clement lift the ban of excommunication?"

"Poorly." The Bishop's voice was heavy with disgust. "When venal men have the handling of God's affairs, change becomes … difficult … and sometimes nigh impossible. But we persevere. We have ambassadors at the papal court even as we speak, and Archbishop Lamberton continues, even in his captivity in England, to argue strongly on King Robert's behalf by means of letters to the Pope and cardinals, smuggled out in greatest secrecy."

"How is that possible, my lo—? How can he contrive to do that?"

"Because Edward of Caernarvon is not the man his father was. That is how, and why. England's new King has a certain fondness for our Archbishop and so grants him more privacy and freedom than he ever had while the old King was alive. And Lamberton exploits that leniency, his main purpose being to support and indemnify our liege, King Robert, against the false charges of murder and treason leveled against him by unscrupulous enemies."

Again they rode in silence for a while, but this time it was de Moray who broke it with a question.

"Tell me, Sir William, how have you succeeded with your decision to release your men from their vow of chastity? I'm certain they did not take the decision lightly."

"True. Not all my men accepted the new freedom, but a few dozens did, promising to return to Arran with their wives and families as they acquire them."

"But …" De Moray's voice faded away, and Will smiled sadly.

"What would you have had me do, Bishop Moray? Sit there and watch my men die off, one by one, thus failing in my duty to safeguard the traditions and lore of the Temple? That would have been a greater sin than any I could commit by releasing my men from an oath in the interests of self-preservation. I have had a surfeit of betrayal by those to whom I have been loyal all my life and whom my men supported faithfully, honestly, and industriously. We were left with nothing, sir, not even the means of survival as men and monks. I sought to change that. Do you think me wrong?"

"There's the castle. We'll not be long now."

The castle lay below them, perhaps two miles from where they had crested the ridge on which they now rode, on a low knoll dominating the countryside around it, and the ocher of the under-lying earth shone clearly through the sparse grass that covered the surrounding terrain. There were no trees anywhere, just miles and miles of rolling, empty land. It was a bleak-looking spot, Will mused, and it had given de Moray an excuse for not answering his last question, but before he could go any further with that thought, the Bishop spoke again.

"No, Sir William, I cannot say I think you wrong. My training as a cleric and a bishop rails quietly against any usurpation of the right to forgive and nullify an oath, a right belonging only to God or his anointed representatives. And yet my gut convinces me you did the right thing. And have any of your people married?"

"Aye, they have. Eight of them are now wed and living on Arran with their families. Twelve children, between the ages of three months and three years. They are our future, our most precious treasure, and they are well cared for, you may trust my word on that." He grinned. "For they have nigh on two hundred uncles, all of them concerned for their welfare."

"Good. Excellent. We will speak more of this tonight, after we have supped, for I have other reasons to learn more from you about your Templars. For the nonce, enough. Let's reach our destination and take our ease."

He twisted in the saddle and waved to the men behind them, speaking Scots again. "Torrance, MacNeil, here, to me."

He nodded once again to Will, who returned the gesture and then moved aside to let the others coming from behind cluster around their leader.

3

It was late that night by the time supper was over. Bishop Moray ordered his company to bed in preparation for an early start in the morning, but he bade Will stay behind and wait upon him until they were alone in front of the fire in the empty dining hall. The Bishop was by all accounts an abstemious man, but on this occasion, once the two were alone, he reached into a leather satchel that hung over the back of his chair and produced an earthen bottle of the fiery spirits his countrymen distilled from barley grain. He splashed a measure into each of two clay cups and handed one to his guest.

"This comes from near my own country in the north," he growled, raising his cup. "One of the better things to come out of the Comyn lands. We call it *uisquebaugh*, the water of life. Let us drink together to the King's grace."

Will sipped the fiery spirits cautiously, and fought against the urge to catch his breath. "The water of life," he croaked. "It has a potency akin to death, on first tasting."

"It grows on you, you will find." De Moray raised his cup again. "To the King's grace."

"Aye, then. To King Robert, and long may he reign."

"Amen." De Moray sipped and sat for a spell in silence, then set his cup down on the floor by his feet. "I want to talk to you about the Templars, William. Our Templars."

"*Our* Templars … I don't understand. Whose Templars?"

"Ours, in Scotland. I—we, the King and I—want you to talk to them."

"The Scots Templars? You told me all the Scots Templars had withdrawn to England with King Edward."

"You misunderstood me. The Templars who went to England—the majority of the knights in Scotland—were all Norman French, not Scots. The true Scots knights remained, under their old Master, de Soutar. But since he died, five years ago, they have been purposeless—disorganized, to say the least. Now, with all the tidings coming in from France and England, they feel betrayed, even by His Grace, for though they enjoy their freedom here, where none else of their ilk do in Christendom, they know they stand under papal anathema and can expect no help from Holy Church.

"There are not many of them left—full knights, I mean. Between two and three score at most, widely scattered throughout the realm. And they are valuable men, dour fighters and staunch allies in the main who have supported King Robert since the outset. Now the King would like to bind them even closer to him, and he has asked me to seek your help in doing so."

Will sipped again at his drink, finding it less fiery now. "Why would he do that?" He understood why, of course, but decided to make the Bishop explain himself fully.

"Because you will talk to them, letting them know who and what you are."

Will could not conceal the smile that came to his lips. "Wait now … You would have me talk to these men openly, after years of concealing who I am and dissembling our presence in Scotland? That seems illogical, if you will forgive my saying so."

"It might, to you, but it is logical enough seen from our viewpoint. These men are Templars, bound to the Church by oath and loyalty that once forbade them from accepting allegiance to any king. Their support of King Robert has been voluntary. But now they are lost and lacking purpose in their own eyes, abandoned by the Pope to whom they swore allegiance and unable to conduct their offices as monks and members of their Order. They are rudderless, lacking a Chapter House or preceptory. They perceive no return support coming from the King for whom they have fought these long years, and, as you know, because of papal politics, we churchmen can do little overt to assist them."

"And so you fear to lose their loyalty through seeming unwilling to welcome them ... Very well, then, what would you have me do?"

"Convene a special gathering of all the brethren in Scotland, under the aegis of the Grand Chapter of France."

"There no longer is such a thing."

"I beg to differ, lad. You yourself gave the lie to that but moments ago. *You* are now the ultimate Grand Chapter, and you are all French. You may call yourselves Angevins, Poitvins, Gascons, Normans, Bretons, and all the rest of the names you have for yourselves, but you all come from the same land, and Philip Capet has deemed it to be France, and there is no one, it seems, who cares to contradict him. So your community on Arran is now the Grand Chapter of France, for all intents and purposes."

Will gazed at him for several moments, his eyes narrowed to slits. Then he grinned and sipped at his drink again. "That is a dubious and duplicitous argument, Davie Moray, even for a bishop, but I'll accept your case for the moment. Where, then, do we go next? Where do I find these three or four score knights? I have no notion of where to start."

"No matter. I know all of them and will contact them ... or most of them."

"So be it. And where is our venue to be?"

"Is that not obvious? It must be Arran. They need to see that you are established there, a Temple community, and that they can join you and renew their vows, refresh their commitment."

"Bishop, you sound disapproving." There was a hint of a smile on Will's lips as he spoke, and de Moray shrugged.

"That's the Bishop in me, intruding again. The Church dislikes secret societies, and the Temple is the most secretive of all ..."

"Apart from Holy Church herself, you mean."

De Moray narrowed his eyes for a moment, then nodded, reluctantly, Will thought. "As you say. But I can accept that secrecy— your Order's, I mean—so be it the loyalty extended to our cause is heartfelt and sincere."

"Has it not always been so? We served as the standing army of the Church for nearly two hundred years, and none found us wanting, until this French King grew greedy."

"I do not dispute that."

"And what do you hope to achieve through this gathering? There are, you said, a mere few of them."

"Fifty at least … perhaps sixty, mayhap even eighty. But they all have sergeants in their ranks, just as you do, so their sum totals a deal of fighting men."

"And you fear they may be disillusioned and become unreliable."

"Not so much unreliable as unpredictable … You can treat with some certainty with someone who is unreliable, but such certainty vanishes in the face of unpredictability."

"Aye, I see your point. Who are they, these Scots Templars? Are there Highlanders among them?"

"Gaels, you mean? No. They are largely Norman French by descent, but bred here, unlike the men who returned to Edward's England. These men are Randolphs, Morays, Buchans, Boyds, even some Comyns. My clerics have all their names, but I do not. I simply have not yet had time to gather them."

"The names, you mean. And what about the men themselves, how will you gather them?"

"Circuitously. They will have to be approached with some caution. The air is rife with rumors of what has taken place in France, and elsewhere since then, so any direct summons from myself, as a representative of Holy Church, will be viewed with suspicion and might even be ignored. Most of them will be contacted by King's messengers, their instructions delivered from the King himself."

"But you said some of them are Comyns and Buchans, and therefore the King's sworn enemies. They would pay no heed to King Robert's summons, through simple fears for their own safety."

"That is true. And that is why the King hopes that you will be willing to contact such as those yourself … as a French Templar, not as a messenger of his. He hopes that you would issue this summons on your own authority, from within the Temple, using whatever secret means you possess to convince them to attend your gathering."

"I see … And once I have them assembled as brethren, their external enmities set aside under the Temple Rule, I can then press upon all of them, both friends and enemies of Bruce, the reminder of their vow of obedience to their Master and his wishes. Whose idea was this?"

A tiny frown ticked at de Moray's brows. "What mean you, whose idea? I told you, the King—"

"No, Davie, no. There is a longer head behind this than the King's … longer even than yours, I suspect. When did you last see King Robert?"

"A month ago. At Dunfermline."

"And you discussed this at that time?"

"Aye."

"How long were you there?"

"Three days. But what has that to—?"

"It has much to do with everything, Bishop, and you know it. This task you would seek to place on me calls into play my deepest obligations to my brethren and my Order. And the idea behind it did not spring full fledged into place in a matter of days, no matter how hard you might have applied your minds to it. So I will ask you again, whose idea was this?"

De Moray glared at him for a moment, then grunted and smiled, grudgingly. "You are no man's fool, are you? I will answer you, but only on condition that you swear to reveal what I say to no one else."

"You have my solemn word on it."

The Bishop nodded. "The idea was conceived, and the whole thing planned, by the Primate of Scotland."

Will's eyebrows shot up. "Lamberton is in England, a close-held prisoner."

"Aye, and England is at war. The Archbishop took advantage of the chaos and the King of England's laxity. He broke his parole briefly, traveling to Scotland to meet with King Robert and advise him of everything he knew to be happening in England. That is why you must breathe no word of this. Lamberton remained here less than a week, advising King Robert in many areas, then returned to his captivity. It was his idea to hold this gathering and to enlist your aid on King Robert's behalf.

"He yet deems it unwise, on the one hand, to encourage and foster the Temple's welfare officially within the Realm of Scotland, since it could greatly endanger the King's cause in the matter of having the excommunication lifted, but on the other, he sees the necessity to retain the loyalty of the Scots Templars who support the King, and to court the loyalty of those who, in the past, have not. And so he devised this stratagem. Your presence as a community on Arran, living by the Rule of the Order, and your reception and welcome of the Scots Templars, will demonstrate the King's good-will towards your brotherhood. It will also demonstrate that the Temple community can flourish within the King's realm, as long as it proceeds with discretion. And last, but not least, it will subject some of the King's most intransigent enemies among his own folk to the requirements of the brotherhood's obedience. That may not work with all of them, but it should give them grounds for reflection, and if any of them do decide to change their minds, the King will make them welcome to his peace with no demands and no obliga-tions other than their ongoing fealty from that time."

"Hmm." The fiery spirits he had drunk had induced a gentle feeling of tolerant well-being in Will, and now he sat nodding. "Your Archbishop is a clever man. He has impressed me greatly, even on the matter of his interrupted parole … So mote it be. I will convene a chapter, but it will not be soon. This thing will take much planning, much collaboration between you, as the King's spokesman, and myself. And your life is far more demanding nowadays than mine, the way you ride constantly the length and breadth of Scotland. Who, then, will coordinate things between us two?"

"A very clever young cleric from the Abbey of Arbroath, Master Bernard de Linton. He has the King's ear and the absolute trust of Archbishop Lamberton, as well as my own. He will arrange a schedule of messengers, to ply constantly between yourself and him.

Which reminds me that when last I met Bernard, he was escorted by your brother Kenneth. Are you close, you two?"

Will smiled. "Aye, we are, but that renders him useless in approaching these enemies of whom you speak, the Buchans and Comyns and their ilk. He has fought them, so they may know him as a King's man. The people I will send to summon those must be unknown to any of them, so I will select them from our resident brethren on Arran, the stay-at-homes who do not ride with Bruce ..." His voice trailed away.

"What is it? Something new has occurred to you—I saw it in your eyes."

"You did." Will sat thinking for a moment longer, then grunted and looked down at his hands, examining his callused palms. "It came to me that I have good news for you and Lamberton both."

"You do? On what matter?"

"Our presence on Arran, and the embarrassment it could cause you. I will be taking my men away one of these days."

"Away? To where? There is no safer place in Christendom for you. Where would you take them?"

Will thought for a moment longer, then sat back, smiling, his decision made. "To a place far beyond Christendom." He watched now with amusement as a series of expressions swept across the Bishop's face, culminating in pure lack of comprehension.

"Far beyond Christendom ...? That can only mean the Holy Land, for even Spain, swarming with Moors as it is, lies within the bounds of Christendom. But such a course would be suicide. You would be completely alone there, among thousands—countless thousands—of enemies. You would be wiped out as soon as you set foot there."

"Aye, we would, but that is not where I intend to go ..." He looked intently at de Moray, who sat gazing back at him, his face now deeply troubled. "Davie, I gave you my solemn oath of silence mere moments ago on the matter of the Archbishop's parole, and you accepted it. I will now ask the same of you, and if you bind yourself to equally solemn secrecy, I will tell you a tale that you will find hard to credit, though every word of it be true."

De Moray's eyes widened in surprise, but there was no trace of hesitation in his agreement. "You have my oath. Tell me this tale."

"Then pour me some more from that bottle, for this will be thirsty work. And have some more yourself. It will be thirsty listening, too."

HAVING MADE THE UNFORESEEN DECISION to confide in the Bishop, Will sat gathering his thoughts while he watched de Moray replenish their cups, and when the other had finished pouring and returned the clay bottle to its pouch, he sipped the *uisquebaugh* again and launched directly into the tale of Admiral St. Valéry and his wish to take some men and ships and sail in search of the legendary land mentioned in the Templars' lore, the place called Merica that lay beyond the Western Sea.

De Moray sat rapt throughout, his only movement an occasional raising of his cup to his lips, and when Will had finished, detailing his last sighting of the admiral's ships on the western horizon, the Bishop sniffed and sat for a while, scratching at his nether lip.

"This was five years ago, you say?" he asked eventually. "And you have never seen him since?"

"No, I have not. But I had tidings of him four days ago, just before I left to come here."

"Whence came these tidings?"

"From the place he sought."

The Bishop sat up straighter, alert.

"The admiral is dead," Will continued, "but his quest was successful. He found his Merica—or some other, unknown land, though I believe it must be Merica—eight weeks after setting sail. He and his people wintered there, in brutally cold weather, in a wilderness of snow-bound, primal forest that happily teemed with life and game—enormous deer the like of which no man in Christendom has ever seen. In the spring they sailed again, south-ward along a never-ending coast, until they came to warmer climes. And there they formed a settlement, among the dark-skinned people they found living there. A noble, stoic people, it appears, of great charm and warmth. They lived there for two more years and prospered, by and large, until the admiral died last year, struck by a falling tree in a fierce windstorm. They had refurbished one of their four ships before he died, to return home with the word of their discovery. And it found us in Arran, after an arduous and tedious voyage. More than half the crew was lost to tempests and to sickness in the crossing, but they came safe to shore."

"Had you expected them?"

"No. I had thought them all dead long since, after years of hearing nothing. But I was wrong. They had found their new land, a sanctuary far from the world of Christendom with all its madnesses."

"So why did they return, so few in number?"

"Because they *were* so few in number. They came back seeking reinforcements and fresh blood to sustain them in their efforts to survive in their new home."

"And they are now on Arran?"

"They are, regaining their health and strength after their voyage."

"And they have found a new land ... Great God, Sir William, do you know what this means?"

"Aye, I do, and fully, Bishop Moray. It means our Order has found true sanctuary, far removed from the politics and villainy of this sad, present world. It means I have a place to take my charges, where they will be safe to live and worship without threat from the petty princes and prelates of this Christendom, wherein Christ's message has been sorely lost."

"But there are people there, you said. No doubt savage and Godless, ripe for salvation in the form of Holy Church."

"Your thoughts are dancing in your eyes, Davie, and they are a bishop's eyes. But think of this, two things: you are under oath of secrecy on this matter; and we who go to this new land *are* Christian clerics ... bishops, priests, and monks, well suited to the spreading of God's word among the natives there. When we have civilized this place, with God's own help, there will be time to return and announce its existence to the world here. For the time being, it is my belief that it would be sheerest folly, utter madness, to bring this new and unknown land to the attention of the predators who swarm in Christendom. God has revealed this place to us, His faithful servants in the Order of the Temple, for reasons that must be His own. It is ours now, through God's will. It is our refuge, our salvation ... our single hope in the bleak grimness of the undeserved night surrounding us and ours. And therefore we will guard the secret of it with our lives, for as long as may be required, and certainly for the present time, until it is safe and fitting to announce it. The land is there, Davie. It will not disappear."

"And it is vast, you say ..."

"Vast enough that St. Valéry could sail south along its eastern coast for months on end, from one clime to another. That could make it as large as all Christendom ..."

De Moray's eyes were staring into emptiness. "A whole new land," he whispered. "Were word of this to spread, every king and baron in Christendom would be launching fleets to find it and claim it for his own."

"Aye. So the word must not spread ... not before we have taken possession of it."

"In whose name? The King of France?"

Will laughed. "Do you think us mad? Nor in the name of the Pope, for Clement V cannot govern his own see, let alone a new, untested land. We will hold it in the name of our Order, and if the powers here at home should ever vindicate us honestly and make it possible for us to return, we would then dedicate it in good faith to our proper Master at that time. Some other pope, perhaps, but no mere king."

"What of the King of Scots?"

Will expelled an explosive breath and sat frowning at the Bishop. "Why would you even say that? The King of Scots barely has legitimacy here in Scotland. How could he lay claim to a new land?"

"As readily as any other king, and I believe he is a better man than all of them combined. Your new land will need a king someday."

"It might. Who is to know? But if it does, mayhap we will have bred one of our own by then ... a Christian king in his own right, untainted by the stink of politics or corruption."

Unable to restrain himself any longer, Bishop Moray sprang to his feet and went to stare into the heart of the dying fire for so long that Will wondered what he might be seeing in there. When he eventually turned back, his eyes were steady and somber. "You have the right of it, I think, William, and so I will say nothing of this to anyone for now. Not even to the King. But I will expect you to keep me informed of everything you know or learn of this new land. When will you leave?"

Will grinned, relieved to have an ally in this man. "Not for a long time, and certainly not before the convocation you have asked me for. We have ships, but they will have to be refitted for such a long journey—their crews retrained, the lessons of the crossings there and back studied and absorbed and mastered. Two years, at least, I would say, perhaps three ... and four would not surprise me. Can you put up with us for four more years, Bishop Moray?"

"I can, and gladly, and His Grace the King has come to rely heavily on your armed support, so you need have no fears there. Now let us to bed, though God alone knows how I will find sleep this night. It must be nigh on dawn already and tomorrow will be a busy day, with a full Parliament to see to in the coming week and my head filled with wonderings about this strange new land of yours ..."

4

With all his excitement over the discoveries beyond the Western Sea, and the ever-growing possibilities and challenges that entailed, Will found the Parliament at Ayr vaguely disappointing and anticlimactic. He had heard much about the grand and exciting Parliament at St. Andrews, three years before. That gathering, in the ecclesiastical center of the kingdom, had been the first of King Robert's reign, as well as the first formal Parliament to have been assembled in Scotland in more than a decade. This one, in July of 1312, was a far less imposing affair—even though it was attended by all the loyal peers, bishops, abbots, and officers of the realm—because rather than a celebration of the King's advent to the throne, this Parliament was an affair of governmental procedures overshadowed by the preparations for a bold campaign to carry the Bruce's war into the northern reaches of England.

The King himself urged the immediate mounting of a swift thrust into the rich vales of northern England, now that the barons and nobles there were preoccupied with their own war in the south. There were fat, rich priories down there, he emphasized, places like Lanercost and Hexham, and towns like Carlisle, and Durham and Hartlepool in the east, all of which had grown prosperous at Scotland's cost, through serving as staging posts for the assembly of England's armies of invasion before they headed across the border into Scotland. Such places were ripe for chastisement and ransom, he pointed out, and Scotland's coffers were empty. His suggestions were met with unbridled enthusiasm by those assembled, all of whom were excited by the prospect of striking back and carrying the fight to the enemy for once, and the matter was soon settled, the commitment made. Edward Bruce, the King's ferocious brother and the kingdom's most able cavalry commander, would lead a hard, swift-riding strike against the English strongholds and cities in the northwest, starting at Carlisle, while the Bruce himself led a similar raid in strength against Westmoreland, Coupland, and Cumberland.

Will had heard much about Edward's skills and exploits, for his own mounted contingents from Arran had been assigned to the man's command for almost two years, and now he made full use of the opportunity to observe him from a distance. Will remembered the scowling, black-bearded man he had met the same day he had met the King himself. Edward was much more of a hothead than the King; that was plainly visible in his demeanor and his brusque way of dealing with the others around him. The new Earl of Carrick was an imposing but humorless man, swarthy and ever-frowning. Intense and impatient and remarkably unlike his regal brother in those respects, he was renowned for his impetuosity and his intolerance of diplomacy in any form, believing implicitly in the rule of force above the rule of law, to the frequent annoyance of his older brother. But his undoubted talents as a commander of horse—he was far and away the most competent in the Realm of Scotland—enabled him, time after time, to sidestep all but the worst of his royal brother's displeasure. And the Earl made few demands of the Frenchmen—his own dismissive term for the Templars in his train—other than that they be ready and available at all times to carry out his wishes.

Still, Edward was a martinet and an autocrat by nature, and watching him, even from a distance, Will could see how galling it must be to the man to be forever held in check by his elder brother, who possessed a mind far more appropriate for kingship than the volatile, belligerent Edward's. That inability to behave at all times the way he doubtless wanted to behave must have provoked much of the glowering discontent that flashed so often in his dark eyes.

Will was glad, too, to renew his acquaintance with Sir James Douglas, for the two had not met with each other in two years. And he was intrigued to meet Douglas's close friend, the notorious and now famed Sir Thomas Randolph, nephew to both Jessie Randolph and to the King himself. From being a traitorous champion of England and a close-held prisoner after his return, Randolph had reversed his loyalties dramatically, swearing allegiance to his kinsman the King, and had since then distinguished himself in Bruce's service, quickly becoming one of the realm's most able commanders. Will also met the chancellor of Scotland, the High Constable, and several earls and Highland chiefs of whom he had heard but had never met, and to a man they greeted him with dignified respect and civilized tolerance of his alien status as a visitor and a guest of King Robert. They all knew him by name, and knew that he was high in the esteem of the King and his close supporters, but he found himself smiling inwardly on several occasions, wondering what their reaction might have been had they even suspected that he was the highest-ranking Templar left free in Christendom.

The Parliament was brief, a mere three days as dictated by the urgency of the need to mount the raiding campaign into England, and at the end of the third day those in attendance were scurrying from the great Hall of Ayr, relieved that the business was over, while hundreds of clerics swarmed like ants, allocating the mountains of written records to be transcribed. Will, as a mere observer, stood alone by the main doors after the adjournment, watching the nobles and commoners disperse and wondering if anything might be expected of him, or whether he could simply take himself off and return to Arran. Before he could decide on anything, however, he heard his name being called and turned to see Sir James Douglas striding towards him and waving to catch his eye.

"It surprises me to see you still here, Sir James," he said when they met. "Do you not have a war to fight?"

Douglas grinned. "In due time I do, but for the nonce, I remain here. The King wishes to speak with you."

"Now, you mean?"

"Aye, if you have the time."

It was Will's turn to grin. "Or the inclination to ignore a royal command? I'll suspend all my important activities immediately and come with you now. Lead on."

Douglas led him back through the length of the hall and out through a postern door to where a small encampment had been set up for the King's party within a square yard protected by high, sharply pointed palisades. Will glanced at the unexpected fortifications and the heavy presence of guards, but said nothing, and within moments they came to the King's pavilion, where their entrance was barred by a pair of vigilant men-at-arms. They knew the Douglas by sight and stepped aside without comment to let him and his companion pass, and Douglas raised the protective curtain of the large tent's doorway to allow Will to precede him.

The interior of the massive pavilion seemed dim after the sudden brilliance of the July sun outside, and Will was unsurprised to find it crowded with men, most of them nobles and high officers of the realm, standing around in groups, some small, others larger. Will looked about for the King, his eyes moving rapidly from group to group without finding the Bruce. His brother Edward was there, as was Sir Thomas Randolph, the latter conversing with three of the

King's oldest and most trusted friends, Sir Robert Boyd of Noddsdale, Sir Gilbert de Hay the Lord of Erroll, and Sir Neil Campbell of Lochawe. Behind them, huddled together and muttering solemnly, stood a group of mitered prelates, only one of whom Will recognized: Master Nicholas Balmyle, Bishop of Dunblane, a scholarly, ascetic-looking man who had served for years as chancellor of Scotland and must now be close to eighty years old, although he still retained his faculties. Will had never met Bishop Balmyle, but he knew the old man was one of King Robert's most able and respected counselors.

The crowd eddied and parted as a procession of servitors moved among the assembly bearing trays of sweetmeats, and Will saw the King, seated at a table towards the rear of the huge space, deep in an earnest conversation with the Bishop of Moray. His heart skipped a beat the moment he saw the two talking together so privately, for the first thought that leapt into his head was that de Moray was telling the monarch about the discovery of the new land in the west. He dismissed the thought immediately, knowing it was unworthy, and fell in behind Douglas, who was already making his way towards the royal table, beckoning him to follow.

As Douglas reached the table, bowing slightly in greeting, Bruce looked up. The beginnings of a frown ticked between his brows at being interrupted, but his face cleared immediately on recognizing Douglas, and his eyes went immediately to Will, standing close behind Sir James.

"Sir William. Welcome to you, my friend." He rose to his feet at once and stepped around the edge of the table, extending his hand, but as Will was on the point of bending over it, he snatched it away. "It is for clasping as a friend, William, not for kissing. You owe me no liege loyalty and I expect none from you. Your friendship, and the willing support you extend to us without being asked, are more than I could expect, so take my hand as friend and brother." And then he clasped Will by the hand and pulled him into an embrace that was but slightly hampered by the half armor both men wore. Will was aware that every man in the great pavilion was watching this and taking note, and he wondered if any of them might resent him because of it, seeing his reception as a threat to their own situation.

"So, Sir William, did you enjoy our gathering? I swear to you, these Scots crows and peacocks far too seldom come together at one time, save only for our Parliaments. I trust you were impressed."

"I was, Your Grace. I have seldom seen so much achieved so skillfully in so little time."

"Aye, it was well done, I think. And now we must disperse and see to it that all we decided upon is done, too, and quickly. My men are being marshaled as we speak and will move out as soon as I can join them—which is why I sent for you. Would you care to ride with us?"

"Into England, Your Grace?"

"I have an abbot or two down there I intend to press for funds … for charitable work, the rebuilding of this realm of ours after the depredations England has wreaked upon it. Will you come?"

"I will, Your Grace, and gladly. But I have no more than a few men with me—my squire and an escort of four others. We would not contribute greatly to your fighting strength, I fear."

Bruce laughed. "I have no need of your fighting skills, William. It is your company I seek … your conversation on civilized matters that have nothing to do with the ailments that beset my kingdom. Though mind you, if it does come to fighting, five extra swords would be very welcome. What say you?"

"I will be ready to depart when you are, Your Grace, but I will need to warn my people to strike camp and be ready."

"Aye, go then and do that speedily, and meet me in the marshaling yard when you are ready."

5

They had crossed the shallow tidal flats of the Solway several days after leaving Ayr, and had struck first at the wealthy Lanercost Abbey, near the walled town of Carlisle. Bruce had taken great satisfaction in capturing the abbey that had for so long offered sustenance and support to England's King, and within which he himself had almost died at Edward Plantagenet's hands a few years earlier. A vast sum of money in gold and silver coinage had been surrendered by the Abbot to avert the flames of Bruce's vengeful wrath, and Bruce had ordered the chests of coin to be transported back to Scotland and into the care of Master Balmyle at St. Andrews for safekeeping.

The wagons and the treasure they carried were the responsibility of a young knight called Sir Malcolm Seton, another nephew of the King, being the son of his sister Christina, the Countess of Mar. Sir Malcolm's squire was of an age with young Henry Sinclair, Will's own squire, and the two had become fast friends during the short time they had spent together on the ride south, so when Henry had come seeking permission to ride out to watch his friend's departure, Will had granted the permission and then decided, on a moment's whim, finding himself with nothing to do at that time, to accompany the boy.

Henry had changed greatly in the space of four years, shooting upwards and outwards to transform the slight, wide-eyed boy he had been at the outset. Now he was tall and strikingly attractive, with wide shoulders, a narrow waist, and strong, well-formed legs. His face was open and guileless, with a wide-lipped mouth and strong white teeth beneath a long, straight nose and sparkling eyes the color of the bluebells that covered the ground here every spring. He was now a fine young man, and Will had no doubt that in two years he would grace the ranks of knighthood as well as any knight he had ever known.

It was a bright, clear summer's afternoon, and Will and young Henry, both of them glad to be free of responsibilities for a spell, had ridden hard, galloping from time to time to stretch out their horses, to the top of a wooded ridge above the road the treasure party would use. Will thought about the spectacle they might have made, charging uphill like a pair of fools, but quickly decided that on this day he cared nothing about threats to his dignity from cavorting on horseback with his young squire. His dignity had begun to irk him lately, anyway. Having committed so unexpectedly to the excursion across the border into England, he had determined to make the most of it, keenly aware that he had not swung a sword against an enemy in earnest for more than four years. But after ten days of raiding he had not encountered a single Englishman with whom to trade blows, and had now resigned himself to the possibility that he might not find one at all. A linnet sang brilliantly among the trees at the two horsemen's back, and far below them, though not so far as to make recognition and a wave of farewell impossible, the advance contingent of guards led the first of the three loaded wagons up the steeply winding road from the Scottish camp.

Will felt a swelling sense of well-being to be alive and free on such a perfect summer day, the mid-morning sun warm on his armored back and the lazy droning of a fat bumblebee briefly catching his attention. He was aware, as young Henry suddenly spurred his horse higher onto a rocky knoll that crowned the escarpment, that behind him the linnet had stopped singing, but he paid it no heed as he set spurs to his own mount, pulled hard on his reins, and sawed at the bit, wheeling the horse around in a rearing spin for no other reason than that he felt like doing something to express his own high spirits.

He neither heard nor felt the impact of the crossbow bolt that struck the back of his cuirass. The missile glanced off the curved surface of the steel covering at his back, digging a deep gouge into the metal and hammering him from the saddle to crash senseless to the ground.

He regained his wits moments later and opened his eyes, but was unable to draw a single breath, every ounce of wind smashed out of him by his fall, so that he could only splutter and whoop in agony, vainly trying to suck air through the flattened air passages in his breast. His sight was as sharp as ever, nonetheless, and he saw every feature of the four men running towards him, weapons drawn. They were unarmored and poorly dressed, and he assessed them instantly as local peasantry who had seized the opportunity to attack and rob an unescorted knight. One of them carried a crossbow, useless now that it had shot its bolt, but two others carried daggers and the last of them held a long-bladed, single-edged dirk as though it were a sword. Will tried to draw his own blade, but although he held the hilt of it in his hand, the sheath was trapped between his legs, hampering his draw.

Time must have seemed suspended, he realized later, but at that moment he heard the clatter of hooves as a charging horse smashed into the four running men, sending three of them flying. Young Henry Sinclair had no weapon at all, for squires were not allowed to carry a lethal blade before they were knighted, but he spurred into the fight as though he were fully armed. His horse snorted and reared after the collision with the runners, and the man holding the crossbow swung it like a club and caught the young squire on the thigh, drawing a high-pitched shout of pain. He threw down his weapon and grasped Henry by the booted heel, wresting his foot from the stirrup and heaving upwards, unseating the boy, who fell heavily on the other side of the horse, and after that things started happening far too quickly for Will's taste.

He was just beginning to catch his breath. The unmanning pain in his chest had abated and he had managed to untangle his legs and the sheathed sword between them, but he still had not enough strength to rise to his feet, although he was fighting to do so, both hands crossed on the guards of his still-sheathed sword and using it like a crutch to pull and push himself erect. The three downed men righted themselves quickly, little the worse for being knocked aside, and now two of them scrambled towards the supine Henry while the other two scuttled towards Will, splitting to take him from opposite sides like rats converging on a wounded squirrel.

Still gasping for air, Will managed to stand up at last and drew himself as erect as he could, finally stripping the sheath from his sword blade and casting it aside, and even though he was weaving on his feet and plainly weak in the legs, the sight of the long, lethal blade was enough to give his attackers pause. They glanced uncertainly at each other, and Will gave silent thanks, for he could feel the strength flooding back into him with every heartbeat as his breathing steadied towards normal. Looking from one to the other of them, he moved his point from side to side in concert with his eyes, waiting all the while for his breathing to steady, yet trying to give no indication that he was recovering. The two hovered there, now glancing at each other for support and growing more apprehensive by the moment. And then Will saw the other two rush on the boy Henry with their daggers raised.

He exploded into movement, leaping towards the man on his right and felling him with a single angry overhead slash before spinning, sword rising again, towards his companion. As the fellow turned to flee from him, his upraised arms bent over his head for protection, Will hacked around and down, severing the tendons behind the running man's knee and dropping him like a stricken ox, and at once leapt towards the other two men and the unmoving form of his young squire.

One of the two heard him coming and turned to face him, drawing himself up to his full height, but as he did so Will heard a tearing sound in the air and three arrows hit the fellow in the torso at the same time, their combined force clubbing him to the ground. Again Will paid no attention, his entire being focused on what was happening to Henry Sinclair. The ruffian above the boy had him by the hair, and his hand, clutching his long dirk, plunged down even as Will threw himself forward with a despairing howl and stabbed his blade deep into the murderer's back. Raging with grief and disbelief, he wrenched the steel free and struck again, this time at the killer's neck, and as the severed head went bouncing down the slope of the hill, he kicked the torso violently aside and dropped to his knees beside the boy who had saved his life.

He was aware of the sound of hooves galloping towards him, but he could not pull his eyes from young Henry, whose face was the color of whey, his cheek pushed out of shape by the blade of the dirk that thrust upward, dripping blood, from the neck hole in the boy's long shirt of mail. He felt hands grasping him and pulling him up and away, and saw someone else take his place, kneeling above the still form and slicing with a sharp blade at the leather thongs holding the mailed shirt in place from neck to waist, stripping the garment back before cutting the coarse shirt beneath it and ripping it away to expose the boy's white skin and the thumb-wide hole in which the dirk was lodged. Thick blood welled from the wound and spilled sluggishly down the dead boy's chest, coating his skin and soaking into the wadded cloth beneath his armpit.

"My fault, my fault." He heard the voice repeating the words and knew it was his own, but he could do nothing other than keep repeating it. "My fault, my fault."

The hands bracing him gripped him tighter and he felt himself being swung around until he was facing the man who had spoken. It was the King's nephew, Sir Malcolm Seton, and the young knight's face was creased in a deep frown as he looked at Will.

"Sir William, are you hurt? You are covered in blood."

"I killed him."

"You killed more than one of them. You killed two and spared another to hang."

"No, young Henry. I killed him. Brought him up here blindly, without looking."

"Sir William, the lad is not dead. Sore wounded, but not dead, not yet. Look at him. Dead people do not bleed."

The words penetrated the buzzing that filled Will's head and he frowned, then turned and glanced sharply down at his squire, seeing the still-welling blood. The sight of it brought him to his senses immediately, and the strangeness fell away like a discarded cloak.

"Sweet Jesus, he is alive." He swung around, searching the hillside below. The three treasure wagons had halted on the road, guarded by roughly half the men who had set out; the others had come charging up the hill as soon as they saw what was happening. "I have to get him to safety—to where he can be tended. Let me carry him."

"No need for that. We'll make a litter." Seton pointed to the two men closest to him. "You two, use your spears, quickly, and your belts. Tie them across the poles—here, take mine, too—and spread a cloak over them to wrap the lad in. No!" He had turned to where one of the men crouching above the motionless boy was gripping the dirk's hilt securely. The fellow hesitated, caught by the urgency of the knight's shout as young Seton dropped to one knee beside him and caught hold of his wrist. "Leave the blade where it is, Robbie. If you pull it out he'll bleed to death. Leave it there for someone who knows what he is doing. Hurry with that litter, you two."

Moments later, Will stood side by side with Seton, watching as four men carried the boy carefully, moving slowly and taking great pains to keep the litter level on the steep hillside. Will had not spoken since the younger knight had assumed command of the operation, but now he huffed through his nostrils and looked at the other man.

"Thank you, Sir Malcolm, for your assistance."

"Don't thank me, Sir William. You owe your thanks to the sharp eyes of my squire, who was looking up at you when this began. I did not even know you were here, but young Donald saw you knocked from your horse and raised the alarm."

"Where is he now, then? I should like to thank him."

"He's still down there. I ordered him to stay. He'll see enough dead friends once he is knighted, and I doubted you or your squire would be alive by the time we reached you. I thought to spare him the sight of that."

"Then you are a good master, as well as a true knight. You have my deepest gratitude, Sir Malcolm."

Seton cocked his head and eyed Will with concern. "And you yourself are well? Are you sure? You are drenched in blood."

Will looked down at himself and shook his head. "None of it is mine, although it should be. I should be flogged for dereliction, riding up here like a fool without taking a moment to check the woods for enemies."

"That was unfortunate but understandable. These were not soldiers."

"No, but they were enemies. I should have—"

"Pardon me for a moment."

He turned aside to where two of his men had bound the hamstrung survivor's hands in front of him and were holding him upright with a spear shaft thrust across his back between his elbows. No one had made any attempt to stanch the bleeding from his damaged leg. Sir Malcolm looked the man up and down. "We will have the devil of a time getting you down to the camp in that condition, and you might die before we reach it. On the other hand, you will certainly hang if you do reach it, and for good and ample reason. You are guilty of brigandage and the attempted murder of a guest of Robert, King of Scots, and his squire might yet die." He addressed the two men flanking the prisoner. "Take him into the woods and find a tree strong enough to hang him from. And be quick." Seton caught the look on Will's face. "Do you object to that, Sir William?"

Will looked at the prisoner, whose face had blanched on hearing the death sentence Seton had pronounced. The man had not yet begun to scream in protest, but he soon would, and now his eyes fastened imploringly on Will, sensing that his intended victim now had the power to spare his life. Will, however, was not in a forgiving mood. He looked at the fellow and saw again the bloodstained body of his young squire, and he knew the man would hang, one way or the other.

"I doubt there's a tree in there big enough to hang him from," he said. "Hawthorn scrub and stunted trees for the most part. And I think you have the right of it, he could die if we attempt to take him down the hill—to be hanged there anyway. We could leave him here to starve, since he cannot walk, but that would be inhuman." He turned and spoke directly to the prisoner. "There is nothing I can do for you. You condemned yourself when you decided to murder us from ambush, shooting me in the back and slaying my unarmed squire. Now, whatever way things might turn out, you are a dead man. May God have mercy on your soul, for I can have none on you." He shifted his eyes to the senior of the two guardsmen. "Obey your commander. Hang him, but if you can't find a suitable tree, behead him, quick and clean."

THE WOMAN IN THE BYRE

1

Jessie Randolph was flustered. She had fallen asleep on the couch in her own room in the middle of the afternoon, a rarity in itself brought on by the fact that she had been up and laboring since dawn in her garden, attacking the weeds that were threatening to overcome her carefully nurtured little crop of hand-set herbs and vegetables. She had neglected the garden badly in previous weeks, driven to ignore her own concerns by the urgency of an outbreak of fever that had swept the district, threatening the lives of the elderly and the very young. The sickness had not been virulent enough to earn the name of pestilence, but it had nonetheless proved to be a potent and dangerous threat to the welfare of many of her tenants, and it had kept her traveling the countryside with her two women, Marie and Janette, doing what she could for the families under her care, most of whom had lost their menfolk to the King's last, urgent summons to gather for the invasion of England's northern counties.

The sickness had died off in the previous ten days, having taken the life of only one elderly woman for whom nothing could be done, and Jessie had been able, finally, to return to her own home, where she had spent a day resting and recouping her strength before yielding to the urge to go outside and begin inspecting her properties. The morning's work on her garden had stretched long beyond noon, and Jessie had been exhausted to the point where, having sat down on her couch and then lain back to close her eyes for a few moments' rest, she had fallen deeply asleep.

Almost immediately, it seemed to her, she was awoken by her ward, Marjorie, now grown into a strikingly beautiful young woman of almost sixteen, with word that people were approaching from the south. Startled awake, Jessie was at first surprised and then appalled to realize that her hair was unkempt, her hands dirty and her fingernails black with soil, but she quickly stifled the urge to flee and make herself presentable and went instead directly with Marjorie to the roof, where several of the household retainers had already gathered on the fortified central tower to watch the approaching strangers.

She recognized Will Sinclair at once, even from the distance of a mile. His party, and she counted six including himself, was moving slowly, at a walk, accompanying a low-slung wagon pulled by a pair of stocky lowland horses. Jessie quickly estimated that she had time enough, if she made haste, to prepare for their arrival, but just as she was on the point of hurrying back inside the house, she realized that there was something odd about the small group, an air of dejection that she would never have associated with the Will Sinclair she had come to know.

She went inside quickly, down from the tower and through the house to the great wooden entrance doors, which she threw wide before crossing the entrance yard to the high gates in the curtain wall, all thoughts of her appearance banished by her concern over what could be wrong. The gates were open, and she marched out onto the road, where she stood, hands on hips, waiting for the newcomers to reach her. Only then did she realize that young Marjorie had followed her. She sent the girl back inside, telling her she wished to be alone, and although it was obvious that the girl was disappointed, she obeyed meekly enough as Jessie turned her eyes back to the road.

Will Sinclair saw her before any of the others did, and she saw him turn in his saddle and say something to his kinsman Tam, whom she now recognized. He then set the spurs to his horse and came galloping towards her, reining to a halt right in front of her. She said nothing, merely gazing up at him, and he nodded and doffed the plain black cap he was wearing.

"Lady Baroness," he said, frowning, but she knew him well enough by this time to know that this particular frown was not his usual expression of disapproval. "Your pardon, I beg, for disturbing your peace thus unannounced. I would not have done so without great need."

"Sir William. I know that. What is the matter?"

"My squire, my lady. Henry Sinclair, my nephew. He is sore wounded and in need of care. We were in England with King Robert, close by Carlisle, when the lad was almost killed … through my fault, my carelessness. The King himself sent me to find you here and to entreat your aid."

"You did not need the King's backing to enlist my aid, Will Sinclair. How badly is the boy hurt?"

Will did not react to her use of his informal first name and simply waved back over his shoulder. "Badly enough. He needs rest and shelter and is in great pain. We made a bed for him in the wagon, but every movement jars him into crying out, no matter how bravely he fights against it. He has a physician attending him, Brother Matthew, lent to us by the King himself, but even so, the physician's remedies are useless against the roughness of the roads."

"Enough. When they get here, bid them inside and bring the wagon as close to the door as it will go. I see Tam is with you. Have him and his fellows ready to lift the boy out. We have a litter just inside the door. I will send Hector out with it, and then have them load him carefully onto it. By the time they are ready I will have a bed prepared on the ground floor."

She left him standing there and made her way back into the house, where she sent two servants running to bring down a cot from the floor above. She then ordered her two women to fetch clean bedding and bring it into the main room of the house, where they would set up a bed for the young man in one corner, between the enormous fireplace and a shuttered window in the wall. In the meantime, she and Marjorie began clearing space for the bed, a temporary sickroom, separated from the main part of the long, low-ceilinged room by an arrangement of brightly painted folding screens made from hinged frames with reeds woven between top, bottom, and sides.

Within the quarter hour everything was ready, and Tam, Mungo MacDowal, and two other men carried young Henry in, unconscious, and transferred him to the cot. The physician, a kindly eyed young-looking monk, saw to the lad's comfort and then asked Jessie for hot water and clean cloths with which to wash and bind the boy's wounds, and Jessie dispatched Marjorie to the kitchen. She then reached out and touched the monk's shoulder.

"Brother Matthew, I would speak with you." She turned then to where Will and his men stood watching, attended by her steward Hector. "My friends," she said quietly, "I can see you have been at great pains to see to this young man's welfare, but he is here now and will be safe. If you will follow Hector, he will show you where you may refresh yourselves after your journey, and will give you to eat and drink. Sir William, you and I will talk more hereafter ... Hector, will you see to our guests?"

As soon as the men had left, Jessie turned back to the monk. "Now, Brother Matthew, tell me what happened and how bad the wound truly is. Will he survive, or have you brought him here to die?"

The monk, who was yet young enough to be awed in the presence of a baroness, shook his head in protest. "No, no, my lady. He should do well now that he is here and may rest. The wound was not fatal, although it should have been. He was stabbed by a dirk, thrust down at him by a man kneeling over him. But the thrust was hasty— I believe the killer was aware of Sir William bearing down on him— and the blade glanced off the bone here." He touched his own collarbone, then dug one finger down behind it. "The blade, deflected, slid down and backward, slicing through the shoulder muscles and scraping along the lad's shoulder blade before emerging again. It made a nasty cut, deep and ragged, and it bled copiously, but it was never life-threatening, thanks be to God." He smiled, uncertainly. "The greatest danger to the lad's life lay in transporting him here in the wagon, for every bump of each wheel on every stone and unevenness between Lanercost and here cost him dearly, opening his wounds painfully before they could begin to heal."

"But why did they not tend to him in Lanercost?"

"We did, as best we could, but there was no time, my lady. The King's army was raiding, striking for Durham, and he dared not wait, lest word of his arrival came before he did. And they had no wish to leave the lad behind, among the English."

"Hmm. I can understand that ... So you came directly here?"

"Aye, my lady. At the King's bidding. His Grace said this was the safest, closest place. It was hard going, even when we reached the road north, and took us three days. Thus the young man is exhausted and harrowed, and he has lost much blood. But with good food and a sound, stable bed, he should recover quickly enough."

"How long, think you?"

Brother Matthew made a moue. "I cannot answer that, my lady. It is in God's hands. A month, perhaps? Perhaps even more. I simply do not know. But he will recover. His wounds appear to be merely superficial but only time will demonstrate the truth or falsity of that. He should regain full use of his arm and shoulder ... but he might not. In God's hands, as I said, though I believe he should do well. My own teacher studied the methods of the ancients, and most particularly of the great healer Galen, who believed that the prime threat to life in such cases lies not in the wounds themselves—unless of course they be fatally inflicted— but in the inflammation and putrefaction that all too often follow afterwards. He therefore urged the wholesomeness of keeping wounds well drained and clean, in order to avoid the dangers of purulence and contamination from ill humors." He looked down at the squire with a gentle smile. "He must think he is in Heaven now, warm in a soft, unmoving bed after such a long and painful journey. Sleep is God's own blessed cure for many ailments. Let us pray that this is one of those. Leave him to sleep on."

"Thank you, Brother Matthew. Marjorie, would you conduct Brother Matthew to where the others are and then come back to me?"

Jessie stood looking down at the sleeping youth for some time after Marjorie and the monk left. *Well, young man, another Sinclair? You have your uncle's look about you, I think, although it's hard to tell, truly, beneath all that grime. But you have his shoulders, and his hair. Mayhap his eyes will be there, too, once you open them, but they are sunken deep and black with shadows now, and your face is far too white, and gaunt … pain-graven lines already, where none should be in one so young …*

She was interrupted by the return of her niece, and waved her to a chair by the fireplace. "I want you to stay here and watch over the young man while I am gone. He is not likely to awaken, but if he does, bid him lie still, tell him where he is, and then come for me at once. Look at me." She held out her hands, fingers spread to show the black dirt caked beneath her nails. "I must go and make myself presentable to our guests. It will not take me long, but in the meantime I need you to remain here."

"Of course, Auntie." The girl did not look at her; her entire attention was taken up by the pallid young man asleep on the cot.

2

As she swept back into the main room, refreshed and renewed and looking every inch the chatelaine of a fine house, Jessie Randolph found herself smiling inwardly at the thought that neither of her guests—for only Will Sinclair and Tam were there—even appeared to be aware of her transformation. The stained, much-worn green gown she had been wearing in the garden had been replaced with her finest, of soft, rich handwoven wool in a shade of blue that was almost the color of the night sky, more blue than black, and her hair had been carefully brushed and pinned up, allowing only a few errant curls to fall in ringlets by her ears. Her hands, wrists, and forearms, scrubbed clean to the point of rawness, had been softened and smoothed with a sweet-smelling unguent brought with her from France, and she could still detect a lingering trace of the fragrant oil of cloves and cinnamon that she had dabbed into the hollow of her throat before leaving her chambers.

She greeted both men brightly before going directly to look behind the screen that shielded young Henry's cot. There was no sign of Marjorie, which surprised her slightly, for the girl had not come seeking her. The boy was still asleep, his face peaceful and the deep-graven lines of pain already lessened in repose. She pulled the wicker screen back into place and turned to the two men, who were still in quiet but intense conversation, standing with their heads almost together.

"I expected my niece Marjorie to be here. Have either of you seen her?"

Tam answered. "Aye, my lady, she was here when we came in not five minutes ago. She went to find us some ale, for the jug on the table was empty when we arrived."

"Ah, that explains it. Thank you, Tam." She smiled at him. "Will you not sit down? It is drawing on to evening and will soon be cool in here. I will have Hector light the fire for us."

"Thank ye, my lady, but I canna stay. A drink o' ale to wet my throat, and I'm away."

"At this time of day? Where will you go?" She saw the rising of Sir William's eyebrows and spoke on before either man could respond. "Forgive me, I know that is none of my affair. 'Twas but idle curiosity that prompted me." *Oh, Will, still as fierce and disapproving as ever. I had hoped you cured of some of that at least.* "Gone within the hour, you will yet have a good three hours of daylight in which to travel."

"Aye, my lady. I can reach where I'm going within an hour after dark."

And where are you going? Why such a rush?

Will surprised her by speaking into the silence. "He rides on an errand for me, Baroness ... and for the King's grace. King Robert has instructed me ..."

He fell silent as young Marjorie came into the room, clutching a heavy wooden jug of beer in both hands and clearly threatened by the weight of it.

Tam went quickly towards her. "Here, lass, let me take that, and our thanks for your kindness." He grinned. "You could ha'e brought a smaller jug, or carried less in this one ... it would ha'e been less taxing."

The girl smiled back at him and dipped into a curtsey, holding her skirts daintily. "I wouldna ha'e dared, sir," she answered in Scots. "But I couldna carry more. Guests in this house never go thirsty."

"Aye, nor hungry, either." Tam took the heavy jug to the table and busied himself pouring the ale into clay cups, one for Will and one for himself, before he turned to Jessie. "My lady, will you ha'e a cup?"

She glanced at Will. "Have you two finished what you were discussing, or should we leave you to conclude your affairs without interruption?"

Will shook his head and his expression was pleasant and open. "No, madam, our business is concluded."

"Excellent. Then gratefully, Tam, I will have some ale." She turned to Marjorie, who was standing watching her, a tiny smile tugging at her mouth. "But you, young lady, have matters to attend to. We will have Sir William at table tonight, and I would like you to appear as what you are, a proper young woman. Marie is waiting for you upstairs and will help you to prepare, so off with you now, and on your way send Hector to me."

Marjorie curtseyed again, managing to address a smile to all three of them as she did so, and let herself out without word.

Will looked inquiringly at Jessie. "This is the child about whom you wrote? The niece?" Jessie nodded. "I am impressed. She is a young woman. I had expected more of a child."

"She was a child when first she came to me, but that was five years ago, and years have an aging effect on all of us as they pass. Come, sirs, sit ye down." She stopped, struck by a sudden thought. "What became of Brother Matthew, do you know?"

Will Sinclair actually smiled, and Jessie had to will herself to make no remark on it as he waved a hand towards the screens behind her. "I have no idea, but I presume he is in there, asleep, like his charge, exhausted by his journey. He slept even less than the lad did, all the way from Lanercost, so he has earned his rest. But permit me to finish what I was saying when your niece came in." He glanced at Tam, who kept his eyes studiously on the rim of his cup as he raised it again to his lips. "King Robert has requested that I visit St. Andrews, to talk with his friend and adviser Master Nicholas Balmyle."

"Oh, I know Master Nicholas well. We are friends, he and I. Have you met him before?" Will shook his head. "Well, you will like him, I think. He is very old, and very dignified and highly regarded, but he has a wondrous warmth and sense of humor, and I found him unusually pleasing, for a cleric. A man unafraid to speak his own mind. The King sets great store by his advice."

"Aye, so His Grace told me. But the trouble is that Master Nicholas will not remain long in St. Andrews. He is bound from there to Arbroath, and under a certain urgency, to meet with the Abbot there. Therefore I am dispatching Tam and Mungo MacDowal to ride on ahead of me and alert him to my coming and to the King's wishes. They will leave immediately ..." He broke off, frowning.

"You appear unsure of something."

"Aye, madam, I am. I must ask you if you object to being saddled with my young squire while I ride on. It strikes me as a great imposition."

"The alternative does not bear thinking about. You will leave him here and we shall tend to him happily, as part of our duty to King Robert, if for no other reason. You may return for him when he is healed, or when your business is concluded with Master Balmyle. There, the matter is closed."

The door opened quietly after a discreet knock, and Hector the steward thrust his head inside. "You sent for me, my lady. Should I light the fire?" Jessie nodded mutely, and the steward threw wide the doors to admit two men behind him, one of whom carried a thick, burning candle in a sconce while the other lugged a heavy bellows.

Tam Sinclair quaffed off his ale and rose to his feet before asking Will's permission to depart. It was given, and Tam bowed deeply to Jessie, thanked her for her hospitality, and expressed the hope that he would see her again soon. He then nodded cordially to Will and made his way in search of his traveling companion, Mungo.

Neither Jessie nor Will rose as Tam left, and both of them sat watching in silence as Hector's men attended to the fire. The two had crossed rapidly to the big stone fireplace where the first of them had already lit a long, thin wooden taper from his candle and was using it to set light to the fine kindling piled in the grate, stooping to blow gently into the nest of tiny, glowing sticks until they burst gently into flame. The other man had laid down his bellows by the fireplace and stood idly by in the meantime, his fists filled with larger sticks, watching closely and waiting for the flames to catch sufficiently to permit him to add his larger pieces of dried and seasoned firewood, stacking them carefully to allow the air to circulate between them, and when those caught fire he began to use his bellows with great skill, blowing air into and among the burning fuel in just sufficient quantity to feed the hungry flames without blasting sparks and ashes into the air.

"That will do it," Hector said when he was convinced that the fire would no longer be in danger of dying out. "Well done. Now add logs and then be out of here. Will there be anything else, my lady?"

Jessie shook her head and then watched as the two firelighters made their way back towards the bowels of the house, followed by the steward. When the door closed behind them she turned to look again at Will.

"Come, it grows cool in here. Pull a chair close to the fire and I will join you. We have matters to discuss." She half expected him to react angrily to that, but again he surprised her by simply doing as she had asked, rising to pull a heavy chair to the front of the hearth and then bringing a second one for her, and while he was doing so she brought the ale jug and filled his cup again, adding a little to her own as well before returning the jug to the table. He took the cup from her and nodded courteously before sitting down and swallowing a mouthful of the beer.

"This is good. You have a brewer among your tenants?"

"Aye, my steward Hector. It is but one of his talents. But in truth he is *the* steward here, not mine at all. He serves my nephew Sir Thomas Randolph, whose house this is. I live here and care for the place on my nephew's sufferance."

He nodded, amiably. For a fraction of a moment she thought he was going to smile again, but the tic at the corner of his mouth faded before it could grow, although his eyes remained more tolerant than she had ever seen them in regard to her.

"Tell me then, if you will, what matters have we to discuss?"

She turned sideways in her chair to look at him, taking in his entire appearance before she responded. "Several," she said, her voice soft. "And not the least of them your own condition. You look gaunt, Will Sinclair—gaunt and haggard and careworn. When first we met today you told me the boy was injured through your fault, and it is clear, from the look of you, that you believe it to be true. Sh!"

She stood up quickly, setting her ale cup on the seat of her chair, then almost bending to one side as she listened to the silence behind the woven screens. Will had heard nothing, but he had not been listening. She flicked a warning finger at him before gliding out of sight behind the nearest screen. Moments later she emerged again, closing the flap of the screen carefully.

"He sleeps soundly. I thought I heard him move, but if he did, it was unconsciously." She collected her cup and sat back down, cradling it between her hands. "Tell me then, what did you do to endanger the lad and almost get him killed?"

He inhaled sharply, and without preamble told her the whole tale. When he fell silent again, clearly having no more to add, she cocked her head in an unconscious gesture of puzzlement.

"Why *should* you have thought to search the woods there? You said they were sparse."

"And they were, but not too sparse. And they were hostile territory. They concealed men, enemies."

"But not soldiers."

"No, they were farmers. But they wished us ill."

"And why would they wish to attack an unarmed boy?"

"They did not. It was me they wanted. A single knight, lightly armed. Well worth killing and robbing."

"And had you gone looking, do you think you would have found them?"

He jerked his head in a negative. "Perhaps not. They were afoot, and would have hidden when they saw me coming."

"So then, not having seen them, might they have killed you from concealment?"

"They might."

"And had they done so, they would have killed the boy, too, no? Especially since he was unarmed."

"Probably."

"Then why do you berate yourself? You are both here, alive, because you did *not* search those woods. And Henry lives because you were able to rescue him, after he rescued you. Therefore, it seems to me, as a mere woman, that each of you has great cause to be grateful to the other for the way this thing transpired, and no reason at all to be sitting around moping and feeling guilty. The boy is strong, and you are in good health, save for your appearance, which cries out for sleep." She paused, waiting, and then added, "Have I convinced you yet that this guilt you feel is foolish?"

Sweet Jesus, the man is smiling. He is smiling! The first real smile I have ever seen in him ... And what a wondrous change it brings about in him, even with his paleness and those bitter worry lines etched into his face. Why, oh why, dear God, do you not permit this man to smile more often? He could banish storms—expel the clouds and bring the sun back into view.

He shook his head gently. "Perhaps you have," he said. "We shall see ... Now, what else must we discuss?"

"Nothing too grave. I have some questions I would like to ask. Would that vex you?"

His smile grew even wider. "Today, no. I doubt you could ask me anything today that might vex me. The willingness with which you undertook the care of my nephew without question has seen to that. Ask away."

Jessie pursed her lips, another unconscious gesture, and nibbled on the inside of the lower one, thinking carefully before beginning. "Very well then ... I have been told—it matters not by whom and I will not divulge his name—that you released your brethren from their vow of chastity." She saw his eyebrow quirk and prepared herself for a brusque dismissal of her unformed question, but he merely glanced sidelong at her and nodded.

"And so I did. Some of my brethren. Many of them, mainly the older men, had no wish to be released, and so they remain as they were. Others availed themselves of the dispensation."

She looked at him in surprise and spread her hands palms upward. "Why? Why would you do such a thing, you, of all men the most devout and duty bound? Why did you do it, after a lifetime of single-minded obedience to duty and to God?"

"Perhaps because my God is not the same as yours." The words were pitched so low and were so indistinct that she was sure she had misheard them, for they made no sense to her. But she had sufficient wit to say nothing, inexplicably aware that William Sinclair might be about to say more, and of more substance, than she had ever heard him say before without hostility. Instead of continuing, however, he sat staring at her, his eyes strangely distant, as though he were unaware of her, gazing at other things.

Oh, Will Sinclair, I have no idea what is in your mind, but I'll give thanks to God tonight for the absence of scowls on your face and for the smiles you've shown me and for the brightness of those eyes. For only He can know whence that brightness comes, or where and why those scowls lie banished. I would not care were you to say no other word from now until bedtime, if your face remained as open and free of arrogance and disapproval as it is now.

He continued to stare at her, and through her, for so long that she began to suspect he might, in fact, not say another word, but just as she began to draw breath to speak, he broke suddenly into the French tongue of Anjou, his eyes now focused upon hers.

"You know, when first we met I distrusted you." He jerked one hand in the air to cut her off before she could react. "No, pardon me. That is untrue. I never did distrust you. That is the wrong word … and an evasion. I believe … I believe I feared you. That is the truth, and now that it is spoken, I recognize the verity of it. Yes, I feared you. Feared you for what you were and what you represented in my eyes … the undoing of my sacred vows … And even in that I was deluding myself, though I may not tell you how or why. I know both how *and* why, but it is something I cannot explain without jeopardizing matters sacrosanct to me. Be that as it may, you frightened me because I found you … attractive … And that was contrary, and threatening, to all the things to which I had dedicated my life."

There's that smile again, but stifled quickly, as though you thought to laugh at yourself. Ah, Will Sinclair, I can't believe I'm hearing this. You thought me attractive! Do you still think that way of me?

"And do you not fear me now, Sir William?"

There was sly humor in her tone, but Will ignored it and answered forthrightly. "No, Jessie, I do not, not even slightly. Nor did I ever, if the truth be told. It was myself I feared … myself and my own weaknesses that I thought might lead me into sin."

"Sin over me?"

Jessie was scarcely conscious of what she was saying now, as her shock at his confession was amplified by the delighted surprise of hearing him call her by her given name for the first time. But her pleasure increased tenfold when he looked at her, cocking an eyebrow.

"Sin over you … Aye, why not? I am a man, after all, and you are … yourself. The mere contemplation of you stirs temptation, and the sins of the mind are as potent and destructive, we are told, as sins of the flesh."

His admission stunned her, leaving her speechless.

"You once called yourself my friend, in the first letter I received from you. And I am honored by your friendship, undeserved as it was at first. But I was a Temple knight at that time, living within and dedicated to a brotherhood I thought to be immutable and sacrosanct—that is the second time I have used that word within this hour, though I have come to see it nowadays as undeserving of the breath most men require to utter it.

"Still, that was what I believed when you and I first met, and I believed it deeply and sincerely. The knights of the Temple, as all the world once knew, were forbidden to consort with women, even their mothers and sisters, for they were monks, sworn to the cloister albeit they might seldom live there. And so I was outraged—" He snorted, a smothered laugh of scorn, shaking his head at his own remembered folly. "I was outraged and offended at having your company thrust upon me, no matter your peril or your family connection to Admiral de St. Valéry, so I decided to safeguard my own convictions by avoiding and ignoring you as much as possible. I never thought of it as cowardice—not at that time, although I see it as such now—but I soon discovered the impossibility of what I was attempting to achieve."

"Ignoring and avoiding me?" Jessie was smiling gently, and he returned her smile wryly.

"Aye. You are not easy to ignore, and the way things transpired, you were equally difficult to avoid. But I fear I treated you ill, for all that you were guiltless in being who you were."

"And what changed that? May I ask?"

"Time. Time and the aspirations of godless men of God ... And that latter led to my decision, as Master of the Temple in Scotland, to release those of my men who wished it so from the constraints of the oath of chastity."

Jessie sat gazing at him for a long time before she said, "That is ... that is an astonishing leap. I have never heard the like."

"There *has* never been the like since the foundation of our Order. But it was necessary."

"To what, Will? I am trying to understand what you are saying, but I do not even know where to begin. What brought this to your mind? It cannot have been a swift decision."

"No, it was not. Nor was it reached without much searching of my soul and my conscience. But it was the right decision, and events of the past few weeks have proved it so. Jessie ... your husband's brother, Admiral de St. Valéry, is dead."

"I know that. I have known for years. Dear Charles. I hoped, for a year or so, that he might return from wherever he sailed off to, but when that year became two, then three, it became obvious that he had perished somewhere—" She stopped short, her forehead wrinkling.

"But how can you know that with such certainty as I heard in your voice now? You *do* know it beyond doubt, do you not?" He nodded, and she stared at him in perplexity. "The only way would be—"

"If some other man whose word could not be doubted brought home the news." He hesitated, frowning slightly, then made up his mind and spoke more forcefully. "Jessie, I spoke earlier of trusting you. Now I will trust you further, with a secret known to very few … a secret that could be very dangerous were it to be uncovered. Do you remember why the admiral left?"

"Of course. He went in search of some legendary land beyond the Western Sea, some place called …" She frowned.

"Its name matters not," Will said quietly. "But the place is there. The admiral found it. And he died there last year. Most of his people remain there now, living among the native inhabitants, but some sailed back in search of men to join them. Their ship arrived in Arran less than three weeks ago."

"It came back …" She heard the dull incomprehension in her own voice, but the notion he had put into her head defied sane, logical thought. She cleared her throat, suddenly tentative. "This land … it is unknown to Christendom?" She watched him nod his head. "Where is it, then?"

"Where it was said to be, beyond the Western Sea."

She shook her head, trying to comprehend the possibility of such a thing. "Is it large, this land?"

"According to what I have been told, it is enormous. It could be an entire new world, as big as Christendom."

"But that is …That would be … That is why you say the secret of it is so dangerous. Who knows of this?"

"I know. You know. The crew who returned know. And my community in Arran knows. No one else."

"And thus you believe your secret safe? Your community is large."

"Aye, but it is secretive, too. We are all Templars, bound to secrecy and silence and obedience—and to our own survival. Were word of what we know to spread, Christendom, with all its persecution and its follies, would flock to the new shore."

"And would deprive you of the hope of finding a new life in this new land."

"You have the truth of it. A sanctuary unknown to any soul in Christendom save us, who have great need of it."

"The oath of chastity. That is why you did it ... to have your brethren breed sons."

"Sons and daughters, yes."

"Because monks, such monks as yours, can have no women and thus must perish and their Order vanish from the world."

"That has been happening, everywhere but here. There is no Temple left in France, and now the other kings of Christendom are playing Philip's game, exactly as Master de Molay feared they would. Our community in Arran appears to be the last Templar outpost remaining. That is why I released the brethren from the oath. I set them free to wed and to have families, upon their oath that they would bring those families back to live on Arran."

"But is that not ..." Jessica could say no more, still grappling with the idea, and they sat in silence for a while. When Jessie spoke again, a half smile tugged at her mouth. "And you, Will Sinclair, have you renounced your oath?"

He looked directly at her and his face was as unreadable as the tone of voice in which he answered. "No, I have not. I am too ... too set in my lifetime's ways." His right cheek quirked in what might have been the start of a smile. "Not that it would bother me in the least to do so, for those reasons I have named. But I have another oath to plague me in the eyes of other men, and it is far more troublesome than my chastity."

"And what is that?"

"Obedience. When I joined the Temple I swore an oath of obedience to the Pope, and through him to Holy Church. But to whom should I be obedient now? The Pope, and with him Holy Church, have disowned and demeaned our Order, for no other purpose than their own gain, and at the urgings of a greedy despot who now calls himself Philip of France. What an arrogant nonsense! What is this France he speaks of? It is a tiny territory in the north of what was Gaul. But in his delusion he sees it as something vast, and he seeks to authenticate his mad ideas by laying claim to Flanders, Normandy, Brittany, Anjou, Poitou, Burgundy, and Aquitaine. And with his vaunting claims of vastness he has suborned a pope and warped the will of Holy Church to his twisted ambitions. Now"—he held up one hand, as if to emphasize what would come next—"an oath, the priests will tell you, is an oath. Thus, in obedience, I should submit myself and all my brethren to the mercies of the Inquisition …

"Jessie, I swear to you upon my love of life that I will gladly burn in Hell for what they deem my sinful pride before I will submit to such obscenities as those people are now to me. Thus I stand damned by my own pride and obstinacy, alone with my own honor. A loss of chastity would cause me not a moment of concern, were I but interested."

Jessie had heard his last reference to chastity, but startling and cynical as it had seemed in the utterance, she realized that it held little significance by comparison with the other, far more fundamental changes she was discerning in the man beside her.

"You are greatly changed since last we spoke, Sir William." She herself heard the formality of the address, but he seemed unaware of it, gazing now with narrowed eyes into the leaping heart of the fire. "I can scarce bel—"

"Greatly changed?" He made a sound deep in his throat, a stifled sound of bitter, repressed self-mockery. "Greatly changed … Aye, I suppose it must seem that way to you, after so long a lapse of time. The years pass more quickly nowadays, it seems, but the effects they wreak in passing remain with us." He stood up abruptly and stepped towards the fire, leaning against the mantel with one outstretched hand as he spoke down into the flames. "I have not changed at all, Jessie, not one whit, but all the world in which I used to live has changed around me, and I am dispossessed. I have responsibilities and I discharge them to the best of my abilities. I have my honor and my beliefs, and I am true to those. But all the duties I once owned are shrunk to one small sphere—the duty of protecting the community of the brotherhood on Arran."

He turned back to face her again, a lopsided, reluctant grin on his face, although she saw at once how sad his eyes were. "Those changes you referred to are changes forced upon me by the world and its treatment of me and mine. Changes in the way I think, and in the way I perceive the things I may not ignore. Changes in the way I look at grasping kings and venal priests and what they will do in their never-ending greed and lust for power, whether it be power over men's souls or over men themselves and their possessions. But greater than these, I think, are the changes I have accepted in the way men dictate morals and morality and govern them with the threat of God's displeasure to suit their own vicious whims ... and with never a thought of the God in whose name they disgrace themselves. And so I have abjured them all, and all they represent." He shrugged then, twisting his mouth. "If that is what the ancients called hubris, the sin of pride, then so be it. But I know what I believe, and I cannot accept that God will see much that is wrong in my beliefs or my behavior. As for the rest ... no sinful priest can ever again claim the right to define sin in my eyes." He grinned. "The sole exception I will make is for your priests in Scotland, hovering on the edge of damnation with their King. People like Davie Moray, whom I cannot see as priest, for all his rank."

Jessie made no response, sunk deep in thought with her head bowed. Will watched her, seeing the straight slash of white scalp that divided the tresses of her hair, and when she made no move to look at him again he cleared his throat.

"What are you thinking about?"

She sighed and straightened. "About your strange new land. When will you go?"

He inhaled deeply. "Not soon enough to suit me. There is much work to do first."

Now she looked at him. "What kind of work?"

"Ship building and repairs. The ship that returned was battered beyond endurance. It had been repaired before setting out to return here, and when it sailed it was as strong as they could make it, lacking the proper tools. The native people who live there have no skills in building ships. They fear the sea. The only craft they have are hollowed logs, for use in inland waterways. Clumsy things they are, and dangerous to those who ride in them. Without steel, iron, skills in working metal they cannot cut trees properly but must wait until they fall naturally. They cannot split logs with care, or make planks. Therefore they have no ships. Our men had shipwrights with them, but no means of making new tools and therefore no means of teaching others how to use the few they had. So they turned all their efforts to the repair of the single ship they had that was still seaworthy, in the hope of sailing it home. It survived, but barely. The tales I heard of the storms they met at sea seemed scarce believable, except that I saw the damage they suffered." He shook his head, remembering. "So we need new ships, built strong enough to withstand the ocean storms. That will take years, and more resources than we have in hand. There are no oak trees on Arran."

"So what will you do?"

Will smiled without humor. "Find them elsewhere, I suppose. I have not yet thought this thing through … In truth, I have not yet had time to absorb the immensity of the thought."

"And if you find such trees, do you have men with the ability to build these ships?"

"Aye, we have those, enough of them, at least, and they will train others. But it will be slow and will take long."

"How long?"

"As long as a piece of rope." He smiled at her puzzled frown. "I cannot tell you how long, my lady … three years, perhaps four if we are lucky."

"Jessie. Call me Jessie. I am your friend, Will, not your lady. Can you not simply buy new ships? You do not lack for money, do you?"

"No, we do not. But that is not—" He stopped, tipping his head to one side as he thought about what she had said, and she saw a change come over his face. "I was about to scoff at you, but that is a fine idea. It had not yet occurred to me. To buy new ships … We would have to go to Genoa."

"To Genoa! Why there?"

Will smiled again, animated now, and she took pleasure in the novelty of seeing it. "Because they build the finest ships in all the world and have been doing it since Roman times. Until recently, they built all our Temple ships, galleys as well as trading vessels. They may even have some now, waiting to be sold again, now that the Temple no longer requires them … save that it does, here and now." His face darkened. "But that might require all the gold we have, and more. I have no idea how much a strong ship costs, but it must be a massive sum."

"Who *would* know that?"

"Hmm. The seneschal of the Order would, or the draper. All such outgoing expenses must be directed through their offices and are—were—subject to their approval. But the seneschal is entombed in one of Philip's jails, and I have heard the draper, Sir Philip Estinguay, died of the tortures inflicted upon him by the priests. Their people might, the underlings who worked for them, but they are all dispersed and vanished as smoke in a high wind. Thus, no one knows, and I would—I will—have to find out for myself." He smiled again. "One thing is certain. If we can afford the cost, we will meet it though it beggar us, for we will have no need of gold in the new land."

Someone knocked on the door, and Will jerked his hand for silence as it opened to admit Brother Matthew, his face puffy with sleep. He blinked owlishly at Will and then addressed Jessie.

"My lady? Is the boy yet asleep?"

As if in answer to his question there came a stifled groan behind the woven screens, announcing that young Henry was awake, and for a time the former stillness of the room was banished as everyone went to see to him.

3

The following morning, before the sun had risen, and for want of anything better to do to take his mind off the condition of young Henry, Will took his bow, a spear, and a quiver of arrows and went hunting, accompanied by his two remaining sergeants. He had dined with Jessie the night before, but they had had no further chance to speak in private, surrounded as they were by other people. And so they had talked of normal things, sharing the laughter and the conversation of those around them. Only once, at the beginning of their dinner, had she leaned close to him to tell him that she regretted the interruption of their talk earlier, and that she wanted to speak further on the matters they had been discussing.

Will had been surprised, and pleased, to discover that he enjoyed the evening and, to some extent, the novelty of being in the company of so many women—there had been eight of them in all—after so many years of exclusively masculine companionship. Four of the women had been the wives of Jessie's tenants, plain but pleasant farm women whom she had invited to the house, along with their goodmen, on a mischievous whim. Will had caught Jessie watching him and smiling slyly on several occasions when one or the other of the women had engaged him in conversation, and at some point he had begun to suspect what she was watching for. The awareness, instead of annoying him as it would have a mere few months earlier, now simply amused him, and he had entered into the spirit of the enjoyment she was obviously taking from observing him. In spite of his determination to be less rigid, however, a lifetime of training was hard to relinquish, and his disapproval of female company was too deeply ingrained to be so easily set aside. He found the women's conversation inane, trivial, and often unpleasantly inquisitive and personal, punctuated with rather alarming, spontaneous laughter, but he persevered, although his cheeks sometimes ached from smiling and being pleasant, and when it was over he had been glad to have Hector show him to his bed for the night.

He had slept well, but had awakened in full darkness with the memory of Jessie telling him that her people had been unable to hunt recently, thanks to the sickness that had stalked their valleys, and in consequence they were almost bereft of fresh meat. And so he had decided to make it a hunting day.

By mid-morning one of the two sergeants, a taciturn Burgundian called Bernét, had killed a fine young buck with a long crossbow shot that Will knew he himself could never have equaled, and soon after that, carrying the butchered animal back to where they had tethered their horses, they happened upon a rooting boar that promptly charged at them with none of the ground-scraping preliminaries they might have expected. Bernét and his companion were carrying the deer carcass between them and had no time to react, apart from dropping the meat and attempting to draw their blades, and the angry animal was upon them before either man was ready.

Will had been carrying all three hunting spears and barely had the time or the presence of mind to drop two of them and grasp the third firmly in both hands before falling to one knee and thrusting the butt of the weapon hard against the ground, holding it there with one straight arm while he used the other to aim the point at the charging beast, shouting to attract its attention. The boar ignored him, driving straight for Bernét and remaining well out of range of the spear's point, but for some imponderable reason it paused to savage the bloodied carcass of the deer in passing, giving Bernét time to leap away and free his sword while Will leapt to his feet and hurled the heavy spear. He had no time to aim with care, but the boar was large enough, and Will was close enough, for his target to be unmissable. The spear's barbed point plunged deeply into the creature's flank, knocking the thing off balance for the space of a heartbeat before its swinish eyes fastened upon Will as the originator of its new torment, and it lunged towards him, dragging the heavy spear as though it were weightless.

By then, though, Will had snatched up a second spear and set it properly, and the enraged animal ran right onto it, snapping at the wide spearhead and transfixing itself with open mouth, swallowing the metal head with all its charging weight and driving the broad, sharp-edged blade through its own spine.

When their breathing returned to normal, the three men decided they had had enough of hunting for one day, and the two sergeants set about butchering the boar while Will went to collect the horses and bring them back to be loaded with the fresh meat.

They were back at the house by midday and took the meat directly to the kitchens, where they found a visiting priest sitting by the fire in the hearth, wolfing down a bowl of stew left over from the previous night. On seeing Will, the priest set down his bowl and rose to his feet, asking if Will might be the knight Sir William Sinclair. Will admitted that he was, and the priest told him that Master Balmyle awaited him at St. Andrews but requested that Sir William proceed there without delay, since the urgency of the King's business was great and Balmyle must leave to meet with the Abbot of Arbroath as soon as possible.

Will grimaced as he listened, thinking that he could have kept Tam and Mungo close, had he but known this fellow was coming. They must have passed one another along the way. Now he would have to ride through unknown lands with an escort of but two men, when they would have been much safer as a band of five. He thanked the priest for delivering his summons and quickly ate a small bowl of stew himself, not having eaten anything for hours, then left the two sergeants with the grateful cook, warning them to have his horse ready and be prepared to ride out within the hour. He went to look for Jessie and a report on the progress of young Henry.

Henry Sinclair was doing well, he was told by the solicitous Brother Matthew, whom he found in the sickroom after a brief, unsuccessful search for Jessie. The monk motioned him aside and, in a low voice clearly meant to avoid disturbing his sleeping charge, told him that the lad had slept soundly throughout the night. His wounds had been washed and his dressings changed the previous night, and again when he awoke in the morning, and Brother Matthew had been happy with the pus-free condition of the soiled cloths. The wound was still bleeding, but no more than a slight seepage now, and the inflammation around the entrance and exit points of the stabbing blade had subsided visibly, indicating that the danger of putrefaction and disease had been greatly reduced.

"He sleeps soundly after a night of solid rest," Will murmured to the monk. "Is that not unusual?"

"Not in this case. It means he is healing. Were it otherwise, it would mean he is in pain, still suffering and not yet doing well." The monk smiled crookedly. "As I said to the Baroness last night, sleep is the greatest healer of all."

Will nodded. "So be it, then. I will take your word for it and offer you my gratitude in return." He pulled a small bag of coins from his scrip and lobbed it towards the monk, who caught it deftly and hefted its weight without appearing to, and smiling his thanks. "And now I must away. Do you know, perhaps, where I might find the Baroness?"

Brother Matthew raised his eyebrows high and shook his head. "No, Sir William, I do not. I saw her earlier. She, too, came to look at the boy and ask after his health, but I have no idea where she went after that."

"Well, I must bid her farewell. Tell the boy, if he ever wakes, that he is to stay here and grow strong again. I will return for him when he is healed. *Adieu, mon frère.*"

He heard Jessie hailing him as soon as he stepped out into the courtyard and saw her watching him from close by the gates, accompanied by her two women and her niece. Like them, she held a large wicker basket propped against her hip and supported by a straight arm.

"I am told I owe you deeply, Sir William," she called out, "for replenishing my larder. Will you walk with us?"

He crossed quickly to where she waited and bowed to all four women before addressing her. "I fear I may not, my lady. I have been summoned to make haste to St. Andrews, where Master Balmyle awaits me urgently. Thus I must be on the road within this hour."

"So soon? That is a pity." She cocked her head. "I presume you have been in to see young Henry? He is well, Brother Matthew says."

"Aye, thanks be to God, it appears he is."

"I have something I wish to show you. Can you take the time? It will be no more than a few minutes." He bowed again, and she set down her basket, heaving it out with her hip and letting it drop heavily to the ground before she turned to the others. "Go on without me and make a start. I will come soon."

She beckoned to Will with one crooked finger, and he followed her to a long, low, thick-walled stone building that looked and smelled like what it was, a cattle shed. As he stepped inside, he had to duck his head to avoid the low lintel, but he found plenty of room to stand erect beyond the doorway. The stalls were empty, the kine long since turned out into the fields, and the narrow central waste gutter had been recently mucked out. On either side of the scoured channel, the flagstone floor had also been swept clean and covered with fresh straw, and in the far right corner of the byre, raised above the floor itself, he saw a sturdy wooden platform, piled to the rafters with well-made bales of hay. The door at the byre's far end stood open, allowing the brilliant late-July sunlight to glare in, casting the side stalls into darkness. Will blinked his eyes until they adjusted to the shimmering, mote-filled light and darkness, then looked sideways at Jessie.

"You brought me to show me this?" There was a smile in his tone. "It is a byre, a cowshed. We have them in Anjou, too."

"Come." She did not even react to his jibe but led the way towards the hay bales piled in the corner, and he followed dutifully, hoisting himself up easily onto the wooden platform. She pointed to the bales. "Can you move those? Not all of them. The middle ones. There's a fork there."

Curious, but saying nothing, he picked up the heavy hay fork and dug it into the top bale. "Where will I put it?"

"Pile them on the floor. We'll put them back afterwards."

He worked hard and silently for several minutes, then saw what they were searching for. Buried beneath the bales was a long, narrow wooden chest that he recognized immediately.

"Pull it out, but be careful. It took four of us to push it in there."

Will squatted carefully and grasped the thick rope handle on one end of the chest with both hands. He took a few deep breaths, then lifted steadily, pushing upwards with his thighs and keeping his spine straight as he took the weight of the thing. He raised the front edge from the floor and dragged it towards him, and it scraped loudly as it came, resisting him every inch of the way until he was able to lower it to the floor again.

He straightened slowly, breathing heavily and wiping the sweat from his brow with the back of his hand. "That, madam," he drawled, "is heavy. I don't even have to ask what it contains ... Part of the treasure that you brought King Robert?"

"Yes, but my part. I thought to keep it safe, against sudden need. The King has all the rest. Open it."

"I do not need to. It holds bags of gold coins. The weight makes that obvious."

"How many bags, think you?"

He looked down at the box, prodding it with his boot. It was a hand's span wide, approximately nine inches, and he gauged the sides to be a half-inch thick apiece, reducing the interior width to eight inches. In height, it was half as much again, and its length was double that. He stood scratching his chin, trying to picture the size and bulk of the stuffed bags it would contain. Finally he nodded. "Four bags, each half a foot across ... Four *heavy* bags."

"Open it, then. Here is the key."

The oiled padlock opened easily, but as he raised the lid Will sucked in his breath sharply and crouched motionless, awestruck.

"You see? You were wrong by four."

"Great God! No wonder the thing is so heavy."

There were no bags in the chest. Instead, it was packed solid with layers of cloth-covered tubes, each carefully wrapped and sealed at both ends with a wafer of wax. One tube on the top had been sliced along its length with a sharp blade, and the dull gleam of gold showed through the cut. Will squatted beside it, holding the lid open and trying to estimate the chest's contents.

"Gold bezants," Jessie whispered, leaning close to look down with him. "Fifty bezants in each roll, fifteen rolls in each layer, and five layers deep. I didn't count them, but I have the accounting rendered in writing by the Jew Yeshua Bar Simeon of Béziers. He was an honest man, and scrupulous. Etienne could not have found a better or more trustworthy associate. And to think no one knew anything of their affairs, their being so prosperous …"

Will was still staring down into the chest. "I heard those numbers, but what do they amount to? It's too much for my simple knowledge."

"Three thousand seven hundred and fifty bezants."

"Three *thou* … Great God in Heaven … Worth what? Five Scots silver marks to one, at least."

"Closer to ten and perhaps more."

"And there were five more chests like this. Those you gave to the King. And five of silver."

"True, but those five were not all packed like this one and they were not all gold. Some were mixed with silver."

He had turned to stare at her. "Why did you keep this one? This particular one, I mean?"

She raised her hands, a gesture almost of helplessness. "Because it was Bar Simeon's. His own, unconnected to his venture with Etienne. He had no family, and knowing he was dying, he tidied his affairs and left this single chest to Etienne, in whom he had great trust. I have the letter that he sent with it, contained among the documents Sir Charles passed on to me. Thus, I suppose it seemed more personal, somehow—the old man's dying gift to poor Etienne, who was already dead … And so I kept it. I thought that, given ten parts of the treasure, the King would not begrudge me the eleventh, and if it weighed more than the others, that was happenstance … I had no knowledge at that time of what it contained. That I discovered only later, when I had read all the documents. Besides, I had no thought then of what to do with it, other than to hold it in reserve against another day of need … the King's, I mean. Money in hand has a way of being spent out of hand. I thought there might come a time when an extra fund might be welcome."

"Welcome?" He shook his head in wonder. "Jessie, this single chest could ransom a kingdom. It contains more wealth than all the specie I brought out of our commandery in La Rochelle … far more."

She grinned, a quick flash of strong white teeth. "Perhaps so. It might indeed, if you say so, ransom a kingdom. But with the King himself in England, raising ransom from the English towns and abbeys, this kingdom should have no need of it. Whereas I do."

He blinked. "You do? What need is that?" He grinned back at her, lowering one knee to the floor to ease his crouched position. "Do you intend to purchase a kingdom for yourself, then? Be a queen?"

"No, not a kingdom. We have enough of kingdoms here in Christendom. But mayhap I could buy a ship like those you spoke of yesterday, from Genoa. Or even two of them, depending on the cost."

"You could buy a fleet with this small chest ... but from Genoa? What would you do with a Genoese ship?"

She grinned again, a glint of purest mischief in her eyes. "I might do as my dead husband did and go a-trading. Or I could even sail in search of some new land beyond the Western Sea." She saw the sudden consternation in his eyes, the quick stiffening of his posture, and laughed loud. "Oh, Will, Will Sinclair, you can be thick in the head sometimes and easy to predict. I meant the ship for you ... or the fleet, if it can be had."

His mouth dropped open and his slackened fingers lost their hold on the chest's lid, which fell shut with a heavy, solid thunk.

"You are too kind, Baroness. I could not accept such a gift. It is too much."

"Nonsense. Of course you could, and you will. You said yourself last night that you will not need money where you are going. Therefore this chest is worthless, save as a means of reaching the place ... And besides, it is not a gift. It is a payment."

He frowned slightly, suddenly cautious. "In return for what?"

"For taking me with you to your wild new land—me and mine."

His jaw dropped yet again. "You're mad," he whispered.

"How so? I believe I am being rational."

"That is no place for women, and by God's holy elbow it is no place for a well-born lady."

"Will Sinclair, that might be the stupidest thing I have ever heard from your mouth. You will be taking women with you, the wives of your followers. Is that not the point of this whole expedition?"

"Yes, but—"

"But nothing, Will. I want to go with you. I lay awake for hours last night, thinking the whole thing through, and I have decided. I will buy your fleet, or some of it, if this is not enough. In return you will take me to this Merica. I remembered the name."

Will's mouth worked, but no words emerged for a while until, frustrated beyond bearing, he burst from French into Scots. "But ... but, Jessie, how could you even think o' such a thing, to go alone into an unkent world? The folk o'er there are savage ... wild. They dinna even wear clothes, or no' the kind o' clothes you wear. They wear nothin' but the skins and furs o' animals."

"So did the Danes and the very English, no' so long syne. And have you visited the Highlands here? Folk run naked there at times—much o' the time in fact, or so I'm told. Men fight naked, and they take no ill o' it."

"But these folk o'er there across the sea are primitive, did ye no' hear me? They're barbarians—godless."

"Godless barbarians? Would ye mean like the noble King of France, who killed my husband out o' plain greed, then sent de Nogaret to hunt and kill me, too, for the same reason? The same King who claims to be God's anointed, yet drove you and yours out of your homeland to sate his own lust for power, and whose people now torture and maim and kill your own brethren? Or mayhap you mean the English King, the old one who hung highborn women naked in open cages from town walls, just to vent his spleen? Is that no' barbaric?" She added with finality, "Besides I'll no' be on my own."

"Among your women, you mean. Aye, that's what *I* meant, too. Who would protect you there, you and your womenfolk? Ye have no *man*, Jessie, and ye'd need a strong one, and fell."

"I'll ha'e a man, and a strong one, Will Sinclair. You'll be my man."

He flinched as though she had slapped him, then glared at her wild eyed for the space of several heartbeats, before clamping his hands on each side of his forehead and rising to his feet, spinning away from her.

"In Christ's name, woman!" he roared. "Have you lost your wits altogether?"

But then he stopped, the heels of his hands still pressed against his temples, and she saw the tension drain away from him as he turned back to face her. She waited, saying nothing, and he shook his head and slowly lowered his hands. "I shouted at you, in the name of Christ."

"I know." She was almost smiling. "I heard. Was that a special kind of sin for you?"

"No ... no, it wasna, but ... it makes me see how rash and false to himself a man can be when he is vexed."

"I don't understand."

"I know ye don't. Ye couldna. But it means much to me. D' ye think anyone heard us?" He looked around him, as though expecting to see people listening everywhere, and then he shook his head again. "I hinna time for this. I should be far frae here by now." He drew a great sigh, then looked back at her and lowered his voice. "Look, lassie, I would look after ye. I ha'e nae doubts o' that, forbye my oath. But it is just too dangerous, the whole o' it unknown. I would never forgive myself were ye to come to ill ..."

When she spoke again, she spoke in French. "And what of here, Will?" Her voice was calm to match his own now. "How would you feel if ill befell me here? We are at war, and this house built on the high road from England into Scotland. I could be murdered in my bed, right here, at any time, murdered and raped by passing soldiery of either side. Think you to leave me safe behind, when you sail off without me?"

"*Without* you? I never thought of you and me that way at all until you spoke the words!"

"If that is true, then you are a fool, Will Sinclair. A fine one, but a fool nonetheless. Look at yourself. You had become a ship without a sail, a vessel without purpose, betrayed and deceived on every side by men unfit to look you in the eye. But you released your brethren from their oath after you thought the matter through and decided it was justified. That took leadership, determination. And now you will lead them to another land, another life, in search of a new destiny. And so you now have renewed purpose. But incomplete, until you change yourself ... Look, and listen to me, for I know you must go now."

She drew a deep breath and stood upright, looking him in the eye. "We have said much here today, perhaps too much, though I doubt that. But the gist of it is this—I want to help you buy a fleet, and the means is there, at your feet. Think upon that ... the how and why and wherefore of it all. It will take much time and long planning. You will need an agent for the dealings in Genoa. Moray may help you in that. He has many contacts everywhere. In the meantime, think on this ... I will pay for the ships, as many as this chest will provide. You then will use your own funds to lade and equip them with everything you will need in your new land ... including cloth for clothing. And think, too, upon my offer, Will—the offer of myself, my companionship, my loyalty. I do not make it lightly. I know it will be hard for you even to think about it, being who you are. But try, Will. Try to see what could be ..." She smiled again, gently. "Will you do that for me, sir knight?"

He stood staring at her, his right hand grasping the hilt of his long sword, his lips pursed. And then he nodded. "Aye, I will think on it. And we will talk again ... But now I had better hide this chest again and go. Is it safe here?"

"As safe as it would be anywhere, save in your vaults on Arran. It will be safe until you come back for it. Now hurry, and be gone." She turned to leave, then hesitated and looked back at him. "And when you think of all of this, think, too, of me ... and kindly, Will Sinclair."

He growled in his throat, unable to find words to reply to that, and she left him there to bury the chest beneath the bales again.

BISHOPS AND CARDINALS

1

Will had never seen St. Andrews town, and riding in he was awed by the sight of it, dominated as it was by the great unfinished cathedral church that had been more than one hundred and fifty years in the making. It was close to completion now, he knew, and it towered above the surrounding town, close to the sea's edge, its bulk seeming to dwarf even the mighty St. Rule's tower that shared its site and rose above its steeples. The town was also the principal center of the Catholic Church in Scotland, and it seemed filled with priests of all description. There were soldiers there, of course, and burghers, merchants and their families, along with tradesmen and the normal idlers one found in every town of any size, but the overwhelming impression was one of a plethora of priests and clerics. Monks and friars, priests and abbots and bishops bustled everywhere, most of them with parchment scrolls and writing implements about their person. Will inhaled deeply more than once, expecting to smell the bite of incense on the air.

It had taken Will and his two sergeants four days of hard riding in foul weather to cover the distance from Nithsdale, traveling north along the western edge of Ettrick Forest to Lanark, and from there to Stirling, where they crossed the River Forth before turning east on the last leg of their journey. But it was behind them now, the sun was shining again here on the eastern coast, and the prospect of spending the night in a warm bed beneath a sound roof was a cheering one, requiring only the discovery of a tolerable inn.

They found a prosperous-seeming hostelry on the broad main street facing the western façade of the church of St. Rule, and Will led his men into it and arranged lodgings for the three of them and stabling for their horses. He secured their stay with a silver mark to the landlord, then stripped off his cuirass and mailed shirt and left them, along with his shield, spear, and helmet, in the room he had rented, knowing they would be safe in the care of his two companions, who would see to the animals before making themselves at ease in their own shared quarters. He then set out to find Master Nicholas Balmyle, enjoying the sensation of walking the street unrestricted by his mail, though he still wore his sword belt with its weapons.

Bemused by the size and bustle of the place, and by the packed ranks of magnificent gray-stone buildings, he quickly realized that he had no idea where to begin his search, but his first question to a passing man-at-arms brought the answer, and he was directed to the nearby Charter House of the new cathedral. His first thought on seeing its grand entrance and the burnished, liveried men-at-arms on duty was that he might be improperly dressed, but then he remembered the way Davie de Moray dressed, and decided that Master Balmyle would be too pressed for time to take note of what a man summoned in haste might wear.

He presented himself to the guards and asked where he might find the Bishop, and they directed him courteously to where he could report to one of the cathedral's clerical officials. He did so, and a black-robed monk swiftly led him along a number of identical passageways. They eventually stopped outside an immense pair of magnificent doors fully twice Will's height, where his guide knocked twice and opened one of the doors to allow Will to pass through.

The huge room, sumptuous by any standards, was high ceilinged and lit by floor-to-ceiling windows of clear leaded glass. The floor was of broad oak planks, stained towards blackness, and an enormous table of the same wood, with a lectern at one end, filled the central space, surrounded by matching chairs. The chill in the great chamber struck him immediately, and the place appeared to be deserted, but then he glanced to his right and saw a trio of men standing together in discussion in front of a giant fire in a stone hearth that could have housed an entire family. Now all three turned to him silently, and he saw them only as distant shapes, outlined against the great fire at their backs. He began walking towards them; it seemed like a long way, and with every step he felt them gauging him, weighing him. But then one of them came towards him, calling his name and bidding him welcome, and he grinned with relief to recognize David de Moray.

Within moments, feeling Davie's arm about his shoulders, Will's apprehension had vanished, and now it was he who did the weighing and gauging as they approach the other two men. There was no mistaking the former chancellor. Besides, Will had seen him before, although he had not met him, at the Parliament in Ayr mere weeks earlier. Master Balmyle wore a full, ferocious beard of snowy white, and shoulder-length hair the same color hung to his shoulders, but that was the only relief from the uniform black of his vestments. He wore a long black cloak over a priest's cassock, a sash of shiny black cloth about his waist, and a polished pectoral cross of pure jet hung from a black cord around his neck.

His companion, far less richly dressed, somehow achieved the same air of distinction by making no attempt to do so. He, too, wore plain black, but his cassock was of coarse wool and its skirts were much stained and ragged-hemmed. He wore no cloak and no cross, so Will accepted him as a mere priest, although no doubt a powerful one, judging by the company he kept. He was imposing, tall and straight backed, with short-cropped, graying hair receding at the temples. He was clean shaven and had startling eyes, deepset and gray-blue, on either side of a great, formidable beak of a bony nose.

Will nodded affably to the priest as he approached, then bowed low to Balmyle, whose age and reputation alone demanded recognition.

"Master Balmyle," he said, "I am William Sinclair. Forgive my tardiness, but I came as quickly as I could. Did my messenger arrive ahead of me? I hope he did."

The old man smiled in welcome and reached out to take Will's hand in both of his. "He did," he said, in a deep, rolling voice that belied his advanced age. "He and his companion came last night with word that you would follow, but we did not expect you until tomorrow. Welcome, welcome."

"And so we would have come tomorrow, had not your priest found me in Nithsdale and urged me to make haste. And so I left at once and made good time."

"And how is your young squire?"

"Improving, my lord Chancellor. I left him well, in the care of the Baroness St. Valéry."

"Ah, a fine woman. But I am no longer chancellor and have not been these many years. Plain Master Nicholas is all my title now." He turned to the gaunt priest in the stained cassock. "This is the knight of whom you have heard so much, my lord, and I rejoice that you are here to meet with him."

My lord?

Before Will could suppress his surprise, Master Nicholas spoke again. "Sir William Sinclair, may I present you to his Lordship William Lamberton, Archbishop of St. Andrews and Primate of the Realm."

Again! He has broken parole again!

Lamberton smiled, and his austere, gaunt face was transformed into a thing of beauty and shining light as he extended his hand to Will. Sinclair was so taken aback that he caught himself on the point of stooping to kiss the archepiscopal ring. He hesitated, wondering at himself, for he had never willingly kissed even a bishop's ring, but then, seeing the radiant smile on that careworn face, he stooped and kissed the ring nonetheless, as a gesture to the man rather than an obeisance to his rank.

The Archbishop seized his hand warmly and pressed it in his own, then spoke, in the liquid Angevin tongue of Will's former home. "Thank you for your concern," he said, still smiling.

"Concern, my lord?"

The blazing smile widened. "For my immortal soul, over the matter of this breach of my parole."

Will felt his face flush. "My lord, I had no—"

"I saw it in your eyes, my son." Lamberton's face grew solemn again. "I had to seek the quantum of my sins, and weigh the one of leaving my confinement temporarily against the other of neglecting my sworn duties to my church, my King, and this realm of ours. Leaving was thus a minor lie, a venial sin with which I can live. The alternative was far more grave. And so I am here, to meet with you."

"To meet with me?" Confusion made Will more forthright than he might have been. "Why would you wish to meet with me? I mean, I am honored to be here, but to what end? I am a simple knight. I live in obscurity and have no wish to be involved in the affairs of state. Indeed I cannot be, for I am sworn by oath never to bend the knee in allegiance to any king."

Again Lamberton smiled, glancing this time at Balmyle and Moray. "That is precisely why I wanted to meet you," he said. "Because of who and what you are. And here we are, standing when we could be sitting, and fasting while we could be refreshing ourselves. Davie, would you send one of the brethren to find us food and drink? We will sit at the table end there, closest to the fire. Come, Sir William."

As Will unfastened his sword belt and laid it, with the weapons attached, across the table far over to his right, the Archbishop asked him, "Would you object if I called you Will, Sir William?"

"No, my lord, of course not."

"Good, then I shall do so. It is a good name—my own, before they lengthened it to William and thence to Archbishop and My Lord. And in return, you may call me William."

Will half grinned. "That would not be easy, my lord. Your fame and reputation discourages that. I might as lief call the King's grace Rob."

The Primate's eyebrows rose. "And why should you not? He would not be offended. You have proved to be too good a friend and worthy of respect for him to take ill of such a small thing. So you will call me William."

"And I am Nicholas to you," said Balmyle, taking a seat across from Will. "You have earned that right, and by the time we four leave here you might have harder names for us."

"Might I? How so?" Will's eyes were narrowed now.

Moray returned from issuing orders and glanced from Will to his colleagues. "Did I miss something? Ye all look gey dour."

"Young Will is justly concerned over what we might seek from him," Balmyle said, "since he has heard nothing to indicate our reasons for summoning him here. We were about to speak of that when you came back."

"Aha! Well, speak away then, until they bring us to eat. I'll just listen and grunt from time to time to prove I'm no' asleep. Ye both know my mind on it." He crossed his arms on his chest and slumped down into his chair, shifting around until he was as comfortable as he could be. This was the first time Will had ever seen de Moray in his bishop's garb, weaponless and unencumbered by chain mail, and he was surprised to see that the Bishop was less cumbersome, less corpulent than he would have guessed. The man was massive in the shoulders, but his belly was flat and his chest deep and strong, and he looked to be in peak fighting trim.

"Well," the Archbishop said quietly. "Shall we begin?" But no sooner was the question asked than the doors swung open and a column of servitors entered the room, each of them carrying a heavy tray laden with food and drink.

"That was quick," Balmyle observed, and de Moray grunted.

The food was plentiful and hot, a full dinner even though it was but afternoon, the bread fresh baked and crusty, and the ale brewed in the cathedral church's own vaults, which had been in use for decades while awaiting the completion of the roof and façade. Will chose roasted pork with savory crackling and made his meal of that, followed with fresh raspberries and blackberries and strong, rich cheese. He devoured it, aware that his tablemates were eating as devotedly as he. Lamberton also chose the pork, while de Moray demolished a roast duck stuffed with apples and breadcrumbs and chopped berries. Balmyle, perhaps because of his great age, ate sparingly, confining his meal to fresh berries followed by bread and cheese, and he drank milk, which had been provided for him, rather than the ale the others drank.

The Archbishop was the slowest eater of the four, but eventually he pushed the wooden platter from in front of him, took note that the others were finished, and summoned the steward to clear away the remains of the meal. The steward waved his minions forward, and within moments, it seemed to Will, they were gone, the steward himself having taken a clean cloth to wipe the tabletop before departing, leaving the four men with their drinks.

For a moment after the doors closed behind the monks there was silence, and Archbishop Lamberton sat back contentedly, hoisting his ale pot to his mouth, though he did not drink deeply. He set the pot back on the table and looked over at Will.

"So, let us begin. You said, Will, that you had sworn an oath never to bend the knee in fealty to any king, did you not?"

Will crinkled his brows, wondering what was coming. "I did."

"And to whom did you swear that oath?"

"To our Grand Master. I was eighteen, and I have lived by it for two score years and more now."

The Archbishop nodded. "Forgive me for these questions I must ask, for there is no slightest hint of judgment or of condemnation entailed in any of them. But in whose name did you swear your oath?"

"In the name of God."

"Apart from that, I mean, since every oath is to God. In whose *earthly* name did you swear it?"

"In the name of the Master of our Order, the Knights of the Temple."

"Aye. And through him to the Pope, is that not so?"

A jerk of the head was Will's sole response to that.

"Did you ever expect that what has occurred might happen? That your Order might be impeached, its brethren deemed excommunicate?" He raised his eyes now to examine Will's reaction.

"No, my lord," he said, fighting hard to keep his face unreadable. "No thought of such kind ever crossed my mind."

"Why not?"

Will spoke slowly, calmly, digging his nails into the palms of his clenched fists beneath the table. "Because until the moment that such blasphemous infamy first spilled from the sewers that pass for minds in the lickspittle servants of the King of France, no such thought would ever have been possible. For almost two hundred years our Order had stood as the champion of Holy Church. The primary force behind the Christian presence in the Holy Lands and one that never faltered in its duty or its dedication. Its record was spotless, its reputation and integrity unimpeachable. But it became too strong, too rich, too wealthy—too large a target for a rapacious vulture like Philip Capet to resist ..." He wondered if he had gone too far, but none of the other three made any attempt to interrupt him, and so he continued. "He sought to sway us first by seeking entry to our brotherhood, thinking that he could thus gain access to our treasury. Do any of you know the word 'blackball'?"

Lamberton nodded. "A secret ballot. A white ball means approval, black, denial. A single black ball kills the vote."

"Precisely so, my lord. Capet underwent the same close examina-tion of character and morality that every other candidate for brother-hood must undergo. I sat on the Council that voted on his admission. Eight of eleven voted to deny him." He grimaced. "I know a wise woman who, on hearing that story, defined that vote as the moment the Temple began to fall. She said the Temple was destroyed by eight black balls ..."

"She may well have been right," said Master Balmyle. "Who was this woman?"

"It was the Baroness St. Valéry, whose own husband had died by Philip's greed and treachery."

Archbishop Lamberton cleared his throat. "And thus you see the malefactor in this stew as being the King of France? What of the Pope?"

Now is where I give offense, Will thought, and squared his shoul-ders. "What of him? What might I say to you, as princes of the Church, to express my loathing and disdain for a man who will bend the craven knee to the willful spite of an un-Christian king and permit him to commit such an outrageous felony? The blessed Clement vacillates like an inflated bladder in a wind. He changes his mind with every hour that passes. And he unleashed the Inquisition on our Order to flesh out the untenable charges spewed out against us by de Nogaret, himself a murderer of popes. What of the Pope, you ask? He is a disgrace to his faith and to his calling, a spineless panderer to an ambitious monster whom he fears will turn and rend him if displeased … and he is right in that. Capet has caused the death of one pope who displeased him, perhaps two. He will not hesitate a third time, if he deems it justified by his divine right."

"You will hear no contention from me over that matter," the Archbishop said, "but Philip Capet is not of grave concern to us right now. For now, let us remain with the matter of your oath, and others. I am told you have released your men from their oath of chastity." Will nodded, and Lamberton eyed him, twisting his ring around on his finger as he did so. "On whose authority did you do that?"

"On my own authority, as ordained Master in Scotland."

"Your authority is that strong?"

"Of course it is. I am acting Master, and until our Grand Master de Molay is released and reinstated, I have complete responsibility for those brethren under my care. I did not make the decision lightly or suddenly."

"I would not think you could, but would you tell me why you did it? It seems like an intemperate thing to do, to free an entire Order from a sacred oath."

"Pardon me if I seem to contradict you, my lord, but we are speaking of the last surviving remnants of a once-great Order. By freeing my marriageable men from their oath, I have created the possibility, the hope at least, that our Order might survive our deaths."

"Is that not fanciful?" This was Balmyle. David de Moray was sitting listening, his eyes moving from face to face.

Will looked back at the former chancellor and dipped his head slightly. "Perhaps so, Master Nicholas, but the alternative—to do nothing—is the death of our Order, preordained. Therefore I seized the chance to contest the odds."

"I see. So now there are women on Arran? Married women?"

"There are a few, and there are children."

"Tell me," interrupted Lamberton, "to whom do you pay your allegiance now?"

"Not to Pope Clement. I hold my allegiance to Master de Molay, even while he is buried in some unnamed prison. And from him, my allegiance goes directly to my God."

Archbishop Lamberton leaned his elbow on the arm of his chair and pinched the bridge of his great, bony nose. But then he straightened again. "I am told there are French mercenaries on Arran. Sir Edward Bruce relies on them greatly."

"Is that so? Well, my lord, it had to come out sooner or later."

"Aye it did, and I am gratified that it took as long as it did … I am even more amazed, though, to have heard no single report, no slightest whisper, of Templars on Arran. From anyone. I trust you will accept my profound appreciation of that."

"I do, my lord Archbishop. It has been almost five full years since anyone might have recognized us as belonging to the Temple. Now we are simply islanders, French mercenary islanders, kept close enough to be useful but far enough removed to pose no threat to any honest Scot." He stopped, struck by a thought he should have mentioned earlier. "Has Bishop Moray spoken of the convocation we are to assemble there soon?"

"Of course he has, and that is why I am here. We need to plan this carefully, we four, for it is of far greater import than Davie might have realized when he arranged it through your goodwill."

Will twisted sideways in his chair to look at Moray, but the Highland Bishop merely shrugged and waved a hand, as though to say "How could I have known?" and Will turned back to the Archbishop.

"How can it be of greater import? I understood the urgency of what was being asked of us. The King's need was all-important."

Lamberton inclined his head. "And so it was, but it has taken on a far greater significance of late." He sat straighter and smoothed the fabric of his cassock, pressing it flat against his lean belly with one hand before looking Will straight in the eye. "Davie has told me all that I know of you, Will Sinclair, and though I liked all that I heard, I felt I had to see you for myself, judge you with my own eyes."

Will stared back at the Archbishop's unsmiling face, unsure of how to react to that, but eventually he nodded. "And have I passed your scrutiny, my lord Archbishop?"

That startling luminescent smile broke over him again. "None here would think to blackball you, if that is what you are wondering."

"Then ..." Will reached up and scratched the stubble on his left cheek. "Now will you tell me what this is all about?"

The radiant smile faded, replaced with a solemn look. "Aye, and willingly, with no further ado. It is about politics and the struggle for men's souls and freedom ... weighty matters, Will. When first you came here, there was no question of refusing you sanctuary. But Bishop Moray told you of our concerns about your presence in our realm—the difficulties associated with the writ of excommunication against King Robert and the dangers of your presence here becoming known to the King of France, and thereby to the Pope. And you have dealt with that to everyone's great satisfaction, so no more need be said of it.

"Now, I have listened to your opinion concerning our Holy Father, and bluntly, your concerns echo my own, in all respects but one ... one highly distinctive respect. As Primate of this realm, my first responsibility is to its people. If the King of Scots stands excommunicate, then so does all of Scotland. If his excommunication is confirmed, then all the land goes down with him into perdition. No sacraments may be bestowed on anyone who does not abjure King Robert's kingship instantly, and there will be many who abjure him thus—some out of fear for their immortal souls, and some through jealousy and envy, for their own ends. And if that happens, Scotland will fall." His voice dropped in volume. "It is unthinkable, but the threat of it is very real and waxes stronger every day."

Will sat frowning, having heard all of this before, but never stated so bluntly or so passionately, and now he raised a hand. "Pardon me, my lord Archbishop, but is not the ban supposedly in place? I know it to be in abeyance, but is it not a fact?"

Lamberton took a deep breath, and Will found himself holding his breath as he waited for the Archbishop to respond.

"In existence, yes, but not in abeyance ... not really that. The matter lies under canonical dispute, at the instigation of myself and the senior prelates of Scotland, among whom is numbered Wishart of Glasgow, now a prisoner, like myself, in English hands. But Robert Wishart is an old, old man, and sick, expected not to live much longer ..." He made the sign of the cross before resuming. "But the dispute is coming to a resolution. Master Nicholas can tell you more of this, since the coordination of our case before the Pope and the Curia is largely in his hands today, now that I am unable to see to it in person. He and Master de Linton of Arbroath share joint responsibility for the conduct of the affair. Nicholas?"

The former chancellor grunted deep in his chest and took up the explanation where Lamberton had left off, his sonorous voice solemn, his words clear and precise. "The original excommunication was for the sin of murder—murder aggravated by its commission in a church, on the very steps of the high altar. But there was ever a question of intent and culpability. The charges came from the enemies of Bruce, from the relatives of the man he supposedly slew, John Comyn, Laird of Badenoch. The house of Comyn, as you know, Sir William, was very powerful six years ago—more powerful than the Bruce faction by far, and very well connected, with several bishops among the family who added their official voices to the plaints being sent to Rome. And they moved quickly, lodging their accusations while yet the confusion here was unresolved. They deemed Bruce in rebellion against the true King, John Balliol.

"That was a specious nonsense, for John Balliol had abdicated by then and removed himself to France and the protection of King Philip, and the truth was that they had a claim to the throne almost as strong as Bruce's was. Whatever, they were heeded by the pontiff. The writ was passed, and we contested it immediately. And we were not without our own influence. We, too, were heard, if not by the Pope himself, then at least by some of his most powerful cardinals. And the debate has lasted ever since, enabling the Church in Scotland to continue its mission."

"So pardon me, Master Nicholas, if I seem ignorant, but all this happened before I came to Scotland. On what grounds could you legitimately contest the Pope's verdict?"

Balmyle grunted again, almost smiling. "A good head for questions, Sir William. On grounds of morality and common law, first and foremost. There is theology involved, but most of it is cant, obscure and dense to common folk. We chose from the outset to take the common law as our defense. William?"

Lamberton was ready. "Intent and culpability in the death of Red John Comyn. Our defense of the King is built upon those elements and the doubts surrounding them. There is no doubt that the slaying took place. But there is ample room for doubt that King Robert did the slaying … You never knew John Comyn, did you?" Will shook his head. "I thought not. Had you but met him even once, there would be no need for me to tell you this. He was a … a difficult man, in all respects—difficult to like and hard to deal with. He was arrogant. Well, who among all these noblemen is not? But he was also obdurate and full of angry pride and self-esteem, greatly ambitious, with a firm belief that he himself should be the King of Scots. And, latterly, he had been proven treacherous, almost to the cost of Bruce's life at the hands of Edward of England. Bruce was forewarned by an English friend and barely escaped with his life from Lanercost Abbey, where Edward sought to hold him. He fled, barely ahead of his executioners, and crossed the border south of Dumfries, where he confronted John Comyn with the proof of his perfidy. You know the story?"

"No, I have not heard it."

"Aye, well, the two, as you know, were joint Guardians of the Realm at the time. And they had made a pact, in writing, to defend the realm against the claims of Edward. There were but two copies of that pact, one held by each of them and signed by the other. But when Bruce was called to Lanercost Abbey, he was warned that Edward had his signed copy of the pact. It could only have come from Comyn, with the intent of causing Bruce's death, for Comyn knew the temper of Plantagenet. Anyway, the guardians met in Dumfries, both of them angry and afraid of what had been done, and went together into the church to talk privately, alone ...

"We cannot truly know what transpired between them, for there were no witnesses, but tempers flared and blows were struck and Bruce came reeling from the church, distraught, to where his companions waited. From then on there are witnesses who swear he said that he feared he might have slain the Comyn. He *feared* he *might* have. At that point, one of the Bruce supporters shouted something like, 'Might have? Then let's make sure of it,' and ran inside the church with a drawn sword. And when the others followed him inside, they found him standing above the Comyn's corpse, his blade bloody."

The Archbishop fell silent again, his gaze focused elsewhere, then shook his head as though to clear it. "What happened then is well known. The Bruce was hurried away by his own men, and when he had gathered his wits sufficiently, he saw the die was cast. He seized the Castle of Dumfries, expelled the Comyns from the town, and claimed the kingship.

"Bishop Wishart and I were told of this soon after, and our duty, unpleasant as it was, was clear. It fell to us, as senior bishops of the Scottish see, to investigate the matter thoroughly, discerning what had truly happened, and it became very quickly obvious that there was room for reasonable doubt of the Earl of Carrick's guilt in the crime of murder. It was a time of chaos, with the fate of the realm itself in jeopardy, for Edward Plantagenet, we knew, would invade the moment that he heard of the affair, and would declare the crown of Scotland vacant and forfeit to his own overlordship. And it was then we decided that our only route, the only proper course of action, was to support the Earl of Carrick and ensure that he became our King, anointed with the blessings of Holy Church. It was barely done when the writ of excommunication was served, but by then we had already initiated our counterclaim, and the debate began."

"And now?"

"Aye, now ... In the past three months, our suit has enjoyed much support in Rome. Our own bishops there, among them your own uncle William Sinclair, Bishop of Dunkeld, have made wide inroads into the bog of claim and counterclaim, of outright lies and obscured truth surrounding this affair, and they are sanguine that we will have a favorable verdict within months."

"Then that is excellent," Will said, glancing sideways at the unreadable expression on Bishop Moray's face before turning back to Lamberton. "But what has it to do with me and my Templars?"

"Nothing, on the surface, but we have Templars of our own here in Scotland, and they have no knowledge of your presence here among us. Those Scots Templars themselves are become a problem."

"An embarrassment, you mean, akin to us."

"A potential embarrassment, because as you know Pope Clement has called for the arrest of Templars everywhere."

"That was expected."

"I know. But what was unexpected is King Robert's obdurate reluctance, his refusal to disown the Order here in Scotland. He is being stubborn over that, and though I can see why he takes the stance he has adopted, it increases our fears for the welfare of our cause with the Pope. Should Clement, and with him Philip of France, suspect recalcitrance on the King's part in this Templar matter, he will not feel inclined to be merciful in the matter of the writ."

"The King must surely see the danger in it."

"He does. But he has received loyal support from his Scots Templars, and few though they are—the fighting knights, at least— he has no wish to disown them. And the fact that the penalties for failing to take such action are being held as a threat over his head by people who know nothing of affairs in Scotland makes him the more stubborn. As we say in this land, he winna thole it."

"So … there it lies." Will stood up from the table and stretched backwards, loosening a kink at the base of his spine. "Forgive me. A saddle I can master, but a wooden chair is altogether different … Bishop Moray, you have not yet said a word."

Moray looked up at him and grinned. "I'll ha'e enough to say when you're a' done. Dinna forget I've known a' this for years.

My colleagues here are new to you and your thoughts, so I'm content to bide here and think my own thoughts."

"Aye, I have no doubt of that. And that brings us back to what you said, Archbishop—that this matter is of greater import now than it was at first. I see the why of that, but not the how. What would you have me do that is different now?"

The burnt-out logs in the huge grate behind Will collapsed into embers, releasing sparks and billowing smoke, and Lamberton turned his head to look at them.

"That," he said, pointing at the fireplace.

Will looked around to see what he was pointing at. "What?"

"When you came in, those logs were hard alder. Now they are glowing ashes." He smiled. "You did the same with your people on Arran."

Will looked from Lamberton to Balmyle. "Forgive me, my lord, but I still do not see your point."

"It is very simple, Will. We want your help in making the Scots Templars vanish, just as you did on Arran. It is something we ourselves cannot do, lacking the authority that you alone possess as Master here. That is the increased import of the convocation to be held. Originally it was to revive a sense of community among the Scots knights, to reassure them that they were not alone. But now the King's own fate, and the fate of this realm, may depend upon it."

"Hmm. I suppose all your Templars must wear the beards and tonsure."

"All of them. And they ride beneath their black and white baucents, defiantly, knowing they stand alone—or thinking that they do. They flaunt their Temple emblems—they call them jewels, do they not?—and the cross pattée. They no longer wear the red cross of the Holy Land campaigns, but they take pride in being seen for what they are."

"And that you cannot have. I see ..." He thought for a moment. "So then, tell me this. If we were able to accomplish what you wish here, what would become of these Scots knights?"

Now Lamberton frowned, his glance flicking towards his two companions. "Become of them? Nothing would become of them. They would continue as before, but simply unseen … at least unrecognized. No more than that."

"But people here already know them as Templars."

"Aye, and people forget readily. Within the year, once they have changed their outward show, no one will care or remember what they once were. They themselves will not talk of it, will they?"

Will smiled, grimly. "No, they will not. You may rest assured on that. They are Templars, doubly bound in secrecy and obedience."

"Then you will help us? It would increase your own community, perhaps substantially … And we would be greatly in your debt."

"I have no interest in incurring debts, nor have I need to add to our community." Will moved back to his chair and sank into it, deep in thought. The others waited, watching him closely, until he straightened up a little and raised a finger. "Although we may agree upon a *quid pro quo*."

"A *quid pro quo* on the matter of what?" It was Master Nicholas who asked the question, and Will answered him directly.

"Aid from you, in return for aid from me." Will could hardly believe that he was about to say what was in his mind, for the decision had come to him fully formed, based upon a sudden recollection of what Jessie Randolph had said about his obtaining help from Davie de Moray. "Do any of you have contacts in the area of Genoa?"

"I have a friend in Genoa," Lamberton said. "The Cardinal Archbishop there, Giacomo Bellini. We were in seminary in Rome together and have remained close, despite the distance separating us. He is one of our strongest allies in the Curia. What interest have you in Genoa?"

"They have the finest shipyards in the world, my lord, and until recently they built most of the ships in the Temple fleet. I have a need for ships now, but I know nothing about buying them. Therefore I need to find an agent there, to represent me—an honest agent, which might be hard to find from afar. It came to me that you, with all your connections throughout Christendom, might be able to assist me."

Lamberton pursed his lips, plainly not understanding. "You need Temple galleys?"

"No, not galleys. Trading ships. Stout, strong-hulled ships, the best I can find, and as soon as may be. It may be that the Genoans will have to build them for me, and that will require time, and I have none to waste. On the other hand, they may have ships already built, awaiting purchase by a Temple that no longer exists. I need to find that out." Will looked around the table, at each of the three men. "I will soon be leaving Arran with my people, taking them to safety, which should ease your minds on the matter of our being discovered here."

"Leaving Arran?" Lamberton sounded appalled. "But you are safe here, Sir William."

"I know that, my lord, but we pose a risk to you and to King Robert by being here. So we will go elsewhere."

"But there is no elsewhere … none that would be safe for you, not in all of Christendom."

"That is true. And yet I have a place in mind, my lord. A place where we will be safe and secure to live our lives with honor." He glanced at de Moray, who was staring at him, one eyebrow raised in surprise. "Bishop Moray knows whereof I speak. We have discussed it. But he cannot speak of it to you. He has sworn to hold it close."

The Archbishop rubbed his long, bony beak with a forefinger and then gazed at Will with narrowed eyes, his fingertip pressing idly on the end of his nose, flattening it slightly. "And if I were to swear the selfsame oath of confessional silence, would you entrust me with your confidence as you have Davie?"

Will nodded. "Gladly, and Master Nicholas, too, if he will swear the same."

"Then mine is gladly given, witnessed by my brothers here."

"As is mine," Master Nicholas added. "Though where your proposed sanctuary may be is beyond my grasp."

Will looked again from man to man, and then told them the story of Merica and how the admiral had gone in search of it. He held them rapt as he related the tales the mariners had brought back with them. When he was finished, no one spoke, each of them lost in his own thoughts, and as usual it was Lamberton who spoke first.

"You were wise to enjoin the seal of the confessional. This place of which you speak, this enormous land with such a lengthy coast and differing climes, might be a whole new world. If word of this were to escape, bloody wars would be fought to win it." He lapsed into silence again, then added, "But how do you intend to keep it secret once you are gone?"

Will's face creased in a gentle smile. "We will leave no one behind to talk of it. Our entire community will take the secret with us. Folk may wonder where we went, but no one will know, save you three."

"And what of the King?"

"The King has much to see to, settling this land and building a stable realm, without his knowing about this. Once we are gone, you may tell him, if you think it needful. By then, no one will be able to find us and we will be safe. But it will be a secret no less dire then than now. Knowledge of it might still set off a race to find it, with all the threats of war you spoke about."

"Hmm. Would you ever return, think you?"

Will nodded. "Almost certainly. Our people have already been there and returned, in search of aid. I have little doubt we will do so again in the future."

"And would you return here?"

"To Scotland? Most certainly." Will's smile grew wider. "Think you we might return to Philip's France, to spur his greed?" He shook his head. "We will come here, in search of information about our Order and its fate. By that time, if God smiles upon all of us, King Robert might be secure upon his throne, and therefore able to send new folk back with us, officially … Who can tell such things? But if it comes to pass, we will be well established in our new home by then."

"When will you go?"

This was the first time Bishop Moray had joined the conversation, and Will shrugged. "As soon as we have new ships. The few we have are too old and done for the voyage we will undertake. The returning ship barely survived the ocean's storms homeward bound. I want no such risks in our crossing."

Balmyle cleared his throat. "Have you the funds for these new ships?"

"We do. We have our own exchequer, brought from La Rochelle to keep it out of Philip's grasping clutch. We have enough." He decided to say nothing of Jessie Randolph's offer.

Lamberton sat musing, his head bobbing gently as he thought about what was involved. Finally he nodded decisively.

"I can send an envoy to Cardinal Bellini at once, but we will need to know how many ships you will require."

"Four at least—six if we can afford them. That is the sticking point right now. I have no slightest knowledge of the costs involved. Therefore the first thing I will need to know is the price of a new ship of the finest quality, and the choices available to us. Once we know that, then we simply divide our treasury among the ships."

"That could leave you penniless."

"It could." Again Will smiled, remembering what Jessie Randolph had called the place. "But in our wild new land we will have no need of money. The people there, I have been told, do not use it at all. They trade and barter what they have for what they need, but they have no use for either gold or silver. So penniless is how we will go."

"Could you not buy your ships here in Scotland? We have fine shipbuilders in Aberdeen, and they build large, fine ships."

"Aye, they do, Master Balmyle, but for local waters, the seas of Christendom. I need ships to go where only four have gone before. The Genoese have been building the kind of ships I need for more than a hundred years, since first the Temple went to sea as traders."

"So be it, then." Lamberton's tone was incisive. "I will write to Giacomo tonight and send the missive to him by fast ship from Leith. My messenger will await a reply and bring it directly back. It should be done within the coming month, and you will have your fundamental information." He nodded, dismissing that. "Now, back to our Scots Templars. What would you advise?"

"Much." Will sat thinking deeply, aware of all three men watching him and waiting. "There is much to be done, but none of it should be difficult. All it will take is time, and that time will begin with our convocation on Arran. In some ways we are fortunate. The brethren we will invite to Arran already know themselves outlawed and banned. They will not be expecting to find an established community of their own. Once they see the changes we have achieved—the disappearance of distinguishing beards and all other signs—they will all join us, out of obedience to my will as Master, if for no other reason. That does not concern me. Everything you require of them will be achieved as soon as we convene in chapter. From then on, the eventual vanishing of Templars from Scotland will be simple and ongoing …"

"But yet you sound concerned," Lamberton said. "Why?"

"Because I am concerned, and gravely so, about their future. When we leave Arran, these Scots knights will be bereft again. And yet I cannot take them with us. The numbers are too great. But so are the odds against their survival here, unless you will extend me your support in what I seek. First of all, why is King Robert so concerned about these brethren?"

"Because he feels an obligation to them, one that they have earned. They have supported him loyally and he has no wish to reward them by outlawing them, far less arresting them, at the demand of outsiders to the realm, irrespective of whether those be churchmen or otherwise."

"They are all Bruce supporters?"

"Aye, they are. Those who were of the Comyn camp retired to England with the other knights when the Temple here was closed. Those who remained were Bruce adherents, and the King is well aware of that."

Will nodded. "But what of afterwards, when these wars be settled, if they ever are? What will become of these men then? They are sworn to poverty, under the protection of their Order, but their Order is gone—and its protection with it—which leaves these men incapable of providing for themselves as knights and warriors."

Lamberton raised his hand. "They have managed until now. How should that change?"

"Because times change, my lord Archbishop. These men have armor, horses, and weapons, but all provided by the Temple. What will happen when the horses die, the armor rusts, and the weapons must be replaced? The commanderies that provided them are no more, and the cost will be too much for paupers. We in Arran can survive because we brought our Commandery's wealth with us from La Rochelle. These Scots Templars of yours will starve without renewed assistance. Can you understand my concern now?"

"Aye, when you put it like that, of course I can. What, then, do you propose?"

"A resolution, but as I said before, I would like your support. As Master in Scotland, I may release Scots Templars from their vows, both chastity *and* poverty, for good and ample reasons of necessity and moral need. But these men might not take easily to such a radical change, and I would therefore ask for your support in assuaging their minds and consciences."

Lamberton looked at Master Balmyle and then sat frowning. "I do not know if I can do that, Will," he said eventually. "I doubt I have the authority for such a thing. As you have observed yourself, the Templars are sworn to obey their Grand Master, and through him the Pope, not an arguably heretical Archbishop."

"Forgive me, my lord, but I disagree. You are Primate of Scotland and this is a Scots matter. The men involved are Scots, and your concern is to enable them to conceal themselves from the eyes of others who would use the knowledge of their freedom to cause further strife for the King's grace. You have already established your primacy, your authority and spiritual leadership, in this realm by your championship of King Robert's cause in the face of opposition from the Pope himself. Why then should you be impotent in this? Do you doubt the morality involved?"

The Archbishop had been gazing at Will levelly as he said this, and now he shook his head slowly. "No, Will, I do not. What would you require of me?"

"A letter, written from your viewpoint as Primate, or perhaps a delegate to speak on your behalf at our gathering, voicing your understanding and compassion in this matter of revoking vows. Your official recognition that, at certain times, drastic steps must be taken to address grave wrongs. That alone—the knowledge that they could provide for themselves thereafter—would make your Templar followers feel better about accepting the changes I decree. They would not talk of it afterwards—they are Templars, after all—so you need have no fears of being embarrassed later."

"A delegate, then, since I shall be back in England. Nicholas, would you do that on my behalf?"

"Happily, my lord Archbishop. The cause is just. And I will make it clear your approval is heartfelt."

"Thank you, old friend." He sat up even straighter. "So we are agreed. This will be done. When will the convocation take place?"

"As soon as it can be arranged," Will told him. "How long will you require to contact the King's people? Give me a list of those you wish me to approach and I will see to it as soon as I return to Arran." He turned to Moray. "Davie, have you made progress on any of that?"

"Aye, all of it. We can ha'e the whole thing done within the month from now, including your part. I have your list prepared—some twenty men. They'll bring their own sergeants. So will we call assembly for a month from this date?"

"A month from today, then. At Brodick Hall. So be it."

Lamberton clapped his hands together. "Excellent! We have done well here, my friends, and I look forward to better things ahead. Are we concluded, then? Poor Nicholas has far to travel ere he sleeps."

Moray intervened. "I ha'e a few questions I would ask o' Will, if we can take the time?"

"Ask away," Will said.

"Your friend de Berenger, the admiral. Is he still on Arran?"

"Most of the time, aye. He is in France now, in Aix-en-Provence, gathering information, but he should be back soon."

"Do you trust him?"

"Without reservation."

"And as an admiral, he kens his business, I suppose."

"Beyond dispute. None better. Why do you ask?"

"Bear with me. You have ships on Arran, too, do you not?"

"Sometimes. We have ships at sea, trading, and they come back from time to time. And we have galleys, as you know."

"I know, but I was thinking of ships. Archbishop Lamberton and you spoke of a letter to be sent to Cardinal Bellini, to await reply, and you said you have nae time to waste. It will take a month to receive the Cardinal's response, and then you'll ha'e to come and get it, and then arrange what to do next." He threw his hands wide. "Tak' the letter to Genoa yoursel'—in one o' your ain ships, with your admiral—and speak to the Cardinal in your ain voice. See for yoursel' what it will tak' to buy up your new fleet, then have de Berenger flesh out the purchase, as a seaman. You'll save months."

Will was twisted sideways in his chair, gaping at Moray, and now he laughed. "Davie, that is an inspiration! That is what we'll do. Of course it is." He turned back to Lamberton. "May we do that, my lord? Will you write your letter for me to carry in person?"

"Of course I will. I'll do it now, as soon as we adjourn here. You will have it in the morning. And now, I believe, we are done here, with much to do in consequence."

WILL SINCLAIR RETURNED to his hostelry to sleep and to warn his men to be ready to ride come daylight, when they would return to Nithsdale, to check on young Henry and take him back to Arran if he was yet well enough, and to tell Jessie Randolph of what had been resolved in the matter of buying his ships. And for the first time, he found himself looking forward to seeing her again.

That gave him pause, and his own awareness of the pleasure he was feeling was even slightly startling. He lay on his back for a long time. What was it that had changed? he asked himself. And the answer came immediately that it was the woman herself who had precipitated everything, by her very being and by her matter-of-fact assumption that he would be willing to take her with him to the new land. No thought of hazards or the risks of sailing into an unknown ocean, but merely the straightforward acceptance of the truth of things: that he would go, and that he would take her with him. That conversation in the byre, so startling at the time, had worked a spell on him thereafter, for he had never stopped thinking about it—even, he now admitted to himself, when he had been unaware of thinking of it.

Lying there in the darkness with no thought of sleep in his mind, he found himself smiling at the bald effrontery of her demand, until it came to him that there had been no effrontery involved. Now he acknowledged to himself, somewhat ruefully, that the "effrontery" had been but one more manifestation of the straightforward and uncompromising lack of guile that had fascinated him since first meeting this woman in La Rochelle years earlier.

He remembered, too, the guilt that had racked him then over his own simple awareness of womanliness—her beauty, he now acknowledged. He remembered inhaling the warm, disturbing scent of the subtle perfume she had worn that night, a wafting, heady aroma filled with the suggestions of body warmth and formless feminine intimacies, and he remembered gazing at, and trying not to focus upon, the way her clothes moved against her limbs and body. But only now could he admit to himself that the task of ignoring her presence had been akin to that of the legendary Danish King Cnut who had commanded the incoming tide to reverse itself and flow away at his royal behest.

But then, lying alone in the dark, the reason underlying the change in him broke over him like one of those same incoming waves, and the stark truth of it was so incontrovertible that it left him amazed that he should have failed to see it before, when it had been as plainly evident as an unsheathed sword in the hand of an angry man. The guilt that had left him hagridden from the outset with this woman had been false, ill founded. His guilt had all been Christian. But he had never been a Christian, he now realized, and he found himself wanting to laugh and whoop out loud. Though his outward affiliation was to the Order of the

Temple, his more profound allegiance was sworn to the Order of Sion. And the Order of Sion, founded mere decades after the deaths of Jesus and his brother James, was not, and had never been, a Christian order. It was Jewish at its roots, and its ancient rituals and lore, its teachings and its beliefs, were those of the Jewish sect to which both Jesus and his brother had belonged, the sect known sometimes as the Nazarene but known to all the Brotherhood of the Order of Sion as the Essenes, the Seekers of the Way to the knowledge and presence of God, the Way so often spoken of, but never explained, in the Christian gospels.

Will grunted suddenly and sat upright, blinking wide eyed into the blackness surrounding him, his mind whirling. He had sworn only two great oaths upon joining the Order of Sion: to own no goods in person but to share all things in common with his brethren, and to lead a life of obedience to his superiors within the Order. Those vows had essentially been the same as the Christian monastic oaths of poverty and obedience. The third monastic vow, the oath of chastity, he had sworn only on joining the Order of the Temple monk knights, and it had cost him not a thought at the time, for asceticism and celibacy had been entrenched in him by choice and dedication— regardless of the fact that the Order of Sion placed no expectation of chastity or celibacy upon its brotherhood.

He felt as if someone had lifted the weight of the earth from his shoulders. He was free to acknowledge, and to pursue, his attraction to Jessie Randolph—perhaps not without his customary awkwardness and difficulty, born of a lifetime of avoidance, but certainly without guilt. He knew now there was no impediment, moral or otherwise, to bar him from accepting the proposal she had made to him.

A COLLOQUY IN NITHSDALE

1

They rode back along the River Nith a few days later, and Will felt surprisingly carefree, considering all that he had to do in the weeks that lay ahead. The journey south from St. Andrews, far more leisurely and a full day longer than their outgoing drive, had been uneventful, which was no great surprise; five mounted, armored men, with the air of confidence these five projected, could expect to go unchallenged on the open road. Now, under a sunny, late-July afternoon sky with birds singing all around them, they rode easily along the riverbank, through grass as high as their horses' fetlocks, talking idly and glancing from time to time at the western edge of the great Forest of Ettrick that began on the other bank and stretched from there for scores of miles. The trees they could see from where they rode on the river's west bank were small, mainly alder and hawthorn and elm saplings, for the forest was still expanding and the mighty forest giants, most of them oak and elm, lay farther to the east. They followed a tight right-hand bend in the river, and the grass-covered hillside on their right rose abruptly, thrusting out a rocky fist directly ahead of them that pinched the steeply rising path into little more than a goat track, forcing them to ride in single file. Will rode at the head, alone and deep in his own thoughts, with Tam Sinclair and the two sergeants following him, and Mungo MacDowal bringing up the rear.

Minutes later, close to the summit of the path, Will twisted in his saddle to look back the way they had come. He remembered it well, because it was here, less than two miles from their starting point, as they reached the beginning of the long descent on their outward journey, that the first heavy drops of rain had fallen from the clouds that had blown in that morning. From then on, it had stormed incessantly, so that they had ridden drenched and chilled for four miserable days, their clothing sodden from the wind-driven rain, their armor and mail and even the padded tunics beneath them chafing miserably wherever their edges touched bare skin. It had been a form of Purgatory, and they had fallen asleep each night, numb, exhausted, and close to freezing, wherever they could find a spot that offered the slightest shelter.

Now, approaching the summit of the rise and aware that their destination was close, Will felt a tiny shiver of pleasure and kicked his horse to a canter, uncaring whether the men behind followed him or not. Beyond the crest of the hillside the land rose up again ahead of him, starting with a gentle dip before resuming its upward climb, though nothing like as steeply as before, for another mile towards a second crest, from which he knew he would be able to see the Randolph house of Nithsdale. He was careful not to allow himself to think of Jessie specifically, for the thought of what he would say to her made his chest flutter in panic, but the feelings of anticipation did not abate and he made no effort to rein in his horse, permitting it to start down into the dip immediately.

On his left, barely a yard from the path, the grassy hillside fell away steeply to where the River Nith now ran swiftly between deep-cut banks, some forty to fifty feet below. They reached the bottom of the dip and started climbing again, and he nudged the animal with his spurs, aware that he had opened a gap between himself and the others, but assuming that they would keep up with him. He became conscious of another strange feeling in his breast and recognized that it was something akin to gaiety and that he felt like shouting out loud to release the pressure of it.

The feeling was short lived, though, for as soon as his horse breasted the crest of the rise, he saw black smoke in the distance, where the Randolph house was, and he had been a soldier for long enough to know at a glance that what he was seeing had no peaceful source.

"Tam, to me!" He turned in the saddle in time to see Tam Sinclair's head snap up, and moments later the others arrived in a clatter of hooves.

Without another word being spoken, they launched themselves forward again, the path widening out ahead of them as it dropped down into the valley of the Nith. Will kept the lead, but now the others rode in a tight knot at his back, fanning out slightly as the road widened until they could ride down the hill at the full gallop, the distance between them and the Randolph house dwindling rapidly until they could see the activity around the house itself.

The fire seemed to be in one of the outhouses, and Will thought it would probably be the stables with their hayloft, but the frantic activity in front of the house had nothing to do with firefighting. Will saw the sun glint on a swung blade, or perhaps an axehead, and at the same moment he heard the first faint, distant shouts of angry men.

"The gates are still open. Straight in?" Tam was riding knee to knee with Will now, looking at his face for instructions, and Will nodded, raising his voice so that they could all hear him.

"Aye, straight in through the main gates! They haven't seen us yet, so we might be able to get in before they can shut the gates. How many d'you count?"

"Less than a score, as far as I can tell—three or four apiece."

"Then let's take them." He lifted his voice again. "Spread out as soon as we go through the gates! Mungo, go with Tam to the right. You others come with me, to my left. Don't be gentle with them. Sinclair!" The last shout was a battle cry as they thundered through the gates and found the enemy with their backs to them.

No one had seen them coming, and the closest of the raiders went down before anyone knew what was happening. The men attacking the house were all on foot, and from their rough and ragged appearance Will instantly assumed them to be bandits, but they were well armed and they showed no fear, despite being surprised. They were more numerous than Will's group, but Will's force was mounted, with weight and speed on their side.

Will rode down two men directly ahead of him, hacking one dead with a chop of his sword to the neck, then leaning forward to stab his point into the second man's mouth with the full momentum of his galloping horse behind the thrust. Then, with no one else within reach, he reined in his horse, taking stock. At the top of the stone steps to the iron-studded main door, several of the raiders were busily piling brush against the door itself, and already smoke was curling from the bottom of the pile as the flames took hold. There were three of them, and they were so intent on what they were about that the noise of the attack behind them was only now sinking home to them.

Will spurred his horse hard from a standing start, swung his left leg up and over the saddle horn and braced his right foot in the stirrup before launching himself onto the steps, landing among them before they could even snatch up their weapons. He pulled the first man off balance and kicked him hard behind the right knee, using the fellow's own falling weight to propel him sideways off the steps and crashing head first onto the cobblestones, where he landed almost beneath the hooves of Will's horse. He cut the second man down with a backhanded slash across the throat, and turned to stab the third, but the fellow jumped from the top stair, barely avoiding the lunge of the long blade, and scurried away to safety.

Will let him go, then sheathed his sword and set about hauling the burning brush pile away from the door, shouting for the defenders inside to open the door and let him in. He heard his name being called and looked over his shoulder to see Mungo waving urgently from the right corner of the building. He saw another of the attackers rushing on Mungo from behind, but before he could even start to shout a warning, the running man was hammered backwards to land sprawling on his backside, the white fletching of a crossbow bolt protruding like a sudden flowering from his breastbone.

Will knew the bolt could only have come from the roof, and so he jumped down from the steps and ran to where he could look up to the top of the small tower at the corner of the house. Jessie Randolph was there, with a cluster of four men, all armed with crossbows and sniping at the few remaining bandits in the yard, and even as Will looked up and saw them, he heard the clang of steel on stone as first one and then others of the attackers threw down their weapons. He turned away from the sight of Jessie and waved to Tam, who stood somewhere on his right, bidding him round up the surviving bandits, and then he looked back to the tower.

"Welcome, Sir William!" Jessie Randolph called down to him. "You could not have timed your arrival more perfectly."

"I am glad to see you well, my lady!" he shouted back. "Unharmed, I hope?"

"Aye, safe enough now, thanks to you."

"Is the rest of the house safe?"

"Aye. We saw them coming, thanks be to God, and got all the folk inside. They tried to force entry at the rear, but the door there is the equal of the one below." She looked beyond Will to where Tam and the others were herding the prisoners. "Tam! There's a byre at the back, with a stout door and a lock and chain. Put them in there for now. Sir William, come you inside. Hector should be there now."

As she shouted the words, Will saw the heavy front door swing open and the steward of the household stuck his head outside, sweeping his eyes about the yard and taking note of the scatter of bodies.

"Away you go in," Tam told Will. "I'll see to these creatures and make sure they move the bodies afore I lock them up, for *we're* no' carryin' them. Ye'll want them tied up?"

Will found it easy to grin now that the danger was past. "Just the living ones, Tam. The others will not go far, though. They'll have to be buried, so make sure you don't cripple the prisoners with tight bonds. They'll need to be able to dig."

He left the others to their work and removed his heavy helmet and mailed gloves, dropping the gloves into the upended helm and then carrying it in the crook of his elbow as he entered the house, addressing a word of greeting to Hector as he passed. He was just in time to meet Jessie Randolph as she swept into the hallway at the bottom of the stairs from the roof, and he noticed approvingly, almost absently, that apart from the high flush on her cheeks, she showed little sign of the excitement of the past hour. Notice it he did, however, and his heartbeat increased as she smiled at him and beckoned him to follow her into the main room.

The first thing he noticed was the absence of the cot bed that had been young Henry's. The space it had occupied against the wall by the big fireplace was empty, and the partitioning screens had been returned to their original position in the far corner of the long chamber. There was fresh kindling laid in the large grate and two piles of logs flanking the fireplace. Jessie, still without speaking, waved him towards one of the big upholstered chairs, and he hesitated before sitting, placing his gloves and helmet carefully on a side table before glancing back towards the empty fireplace wall.

"Where have you put the boy?" He had spoken in French, without thinking, but she answered him in the tongue of the Scots.

"Och, he is much better, so we moved him into one of the small sleeping chambers upstairs. He's comfortable there now. Still abed, but able to sit up and look about him. He is a fine young man."

"Young man?" The idea seemed strange to Will. "Aye, I suppose he is. Man enough."

"Aye, man enough, as you say … and fortunate. Brother Matthew thinks now that he will recover the full use of his arm and shoulder. Not today, mind you, and not tomorrow, but the wound is healing cleanly and as soon as it is closed and sound he will be able to start strengthening the muscles again."

Will was barely listening, gazing up at the high, narrow windows on the side wall, and now he dragged a high wooden chair under one so he could climb up onto it and look down into the courtyard below, where Mungo and another man he did not recognize were hauling a dead man away by the ankles.

"We have bodies to dispose of," he said over his shoulder. "Where would you have them buried?"

"Buried?" It was clear that she had not thought at all about that, but she was resolute nonetheless. "As far from the house as possible, I suppose, but I'll have to think on that. It's not something we are called upon to do every week."

"No, I suppose not. But these are not the first such, surely?"

"The first since I've been here, most certainly. But there might have been others. Before I came here, I mean. This road is much traveled by warlike men, I fear. But Hector will know where they should go, if they're not the first to be buried here. There must be such a place. I'll ask him."

He turned around and looked down at her, seeing the wide, white sweep of her shoulders above the scooped neckline of her gown and the way the light, from this angle, caught the high planes of her prominent cheekbones and emphasized the startling brightness of her eyes. Then, before she could notice him staring, he stepped off the chair and landed lightly on the balls of his feet.

"Who were they, these people? Do you know?"

"I have no idea. But they're no threat now, and we have no cause to mourn them or to grieve for them, for they brought their deaths upon themselves, threatening honest folk. So sit you down and be comfortable. I'll have the fire lit, if you like."

Will ignored the suggestion. "So they are not from these parts? You recognized none of them?"

"No, and I know every man for miles around here by sight by now. These ones are from beyond these vales, but from which direction, your guess would be as valid as mine. All I could tell, from the roof, was that they were hungry and desperate, and too many for us to fend off. They must have been spying on us, for they crept up on us. We saw nothing until one of them showed himself by accident and one of our people happened to see him. Otherwise they would have caught us unawares and taken us without any trouble … As it was, the alarm was raised and we had time to bring everyone inside the house and bar the doors, but there was little else we could do. And so we are all in your debt for our lives. Had you not come back when you did, you might have found nothing and no one here when you returned."

"Aye, well, we did come back, so thanks be to God. I am the grateful one. Will you not sit down?"

She cocked her head to one side, smiling at him. "I will sit if you will. But you have not even asked me if your treasure is safe."

Will smiled. "*Your* treasure, and there is no need. It must be safe, else you would not have told Tam to lodge the prisoners in the byre."

"They are not in *that* byre. There is another at the back."

"But still, the gold is safe enough, I'm sure. Your guests had not had time to break in here, let alone go prowling through the byres looking for hidden hoards, so your coffer will be where we left it." He lowered himself into the big, soft chair, and Jessie sat in the one opposite, tucking her legs up demurely beneath her although the voluminous skirts of her gown offered only the merest suggestion of what she had done. He gazed at the slight tautening of the fabric where her knees were, and then realized what he was doing and felt the color heightening in his cheeks as he raised his eyes to hers.

"So," she said, appearing not to have noticed, "was your journey worthwhile? I must admit I am curious, for Master Nicholas Balmyle is a man of great renown, and I suspect he summons few folk in person, save on the King's own business. Can you tell me anything about your visit?"

Will was mildly surprised to discover that he could, and without hesitation, where only a short time before he would have balked and felt resentment at having to admit anything about the Temple to Jessie Randolph or any other woman. Now he found himself answering without demur, and told her what he had learned at St. Andrews about the vacillations of the Pope in signing and then revoking his pardon, and about the loyalty of the Scots Templars.

"So what does Master Balmyle wish you to do?"

It was not Nicholas Balmyle's face Will saw in his mind but William Lamberton's, but he answered her directly, attributing the Archbishop's wishes to the former chancellor. "He wants me to strengthen and encourage the Scots brethren."

"And can you do that? I mean, I know you can, but how will you do it without breaking your own given word to keep your presence here a secret?"

Will explained then the plan to convene the Scots Templars in Arran, to release them from their vows of chastity and poverty, and to remove all outward evidence of their identity as Templars, as he had done with his own men.

"But what then?" Jessie asked. "When you and the others have gone to Merica … how will they be able to continue their rituals? Or will they not do that any longer?"

"They will return to the mainland and we will set up a new chapter for Scotland … perhaps more than one. I will know the answer to that riddle once I have discovered the makeup and distribution of the brotherhood. So, one chapter and one meeting lodge at first. More if required."

Her frown deepened. "But how will you do that without betraying their existence? Why change them outwardly, to be invisible, if you convene them openly as Temple knights?"

"And sergeants. Don't forget the sergeants. But I said nothing about openness. Ours is a closed and secretive Order. No one will ever know it is there, though it will operate almost in full sight. People see what they expect to see, my lady."

"Jessie. Please don't 'my lady' me."

"Jessie, then. If folk see men with forked beards and equal-armed crosses assembling, then they conclude that it is a Templar gathering. If they see farmers, they see a market gathering. In our case, they will see only knights and soldiers gathering openly for whatever purposes soldiers gather … and this country is at war, so no one will think further on that. And under that cloak of ordinariness, Scotland's new Templars will conduct their business, in secrecy as always, but free of the recognition as being Templars. It will work, believe me."

She sat silent for a while absorbing that, then nodded. "I do believe it. And if anyone can achieve what needs to be done to enable that, it is you. So you will hold this gathering within the month?"

"We will."

"And after that? Did you ask about finding an agent in Genoa?"

"I did, and received an unexpected answer." She frowned again and he smiled. "I was advised to take Admiral de Berenger and go to Genoa myself, to do my own negotiating and make my own purchases, with the benefit of Edward's profound knowledge."

Jessie's eyebrows shot up. "That is a wonderful idea. Balmyle advises that?"

"Well, Bishop Moray mentioned it first, and everybody agreed it was the most sensible thing to do. I will carry letters of introduction to Cardinal Archbishop Bellini in Genoa, who is a lifelong friend of Archbishop Lamberton and a firm supporter of Scotland's cause in the papal court, and his support should win me access to the best people for my purposes."

"When will you go?"

"As soon as I can. Immediately after the Arran gathering, I expect."

"And how long will you be gone?"

Will twisted his mouth down at the corners. "As long as I have to be, or am made to be, but I doubt it will be much more than a month … certainly not as long as two, unless something goes far wrong. We might find what we are looking for immediately, ready and waiting to be purchased, but that may well be wishful thinking. More likely we will have to commission a vessel—or more than one, depending upon what we can afford—to be built from the keel up. If that is the case, I'll leave de Berenger there to oversee the building and equipping of whatever we end up buying, while I return to Arran and dispatch more crewmen to handle the new craft on sailing trials. That way, they will be accustomed to the new ships before they reach home again. There is a multitude of details to be considered before ever we leave Arran, but thank God, most of those arrangements will fall into de Berenger's arena. I'll have much to do on my own behalf, too, of course."

"Of course." She was almost smiling. "So you will leave sometime during the month after next, and you will be gone for several months thereafter. Leaving in September, perhaps returning in November."

"Correct. Why are you so curious?"

"Because November is a sullen month and you will be crossing the North Sea, the stormiest in all of Christendom. You might not even be able to get back at all by then."

"I will, somehow. Believe me. But if it truly is impossible, why then I will remain in Genoa for the winter, to return in the spring. Young Henry would enjoy winter in Genoa, I think."

"Henry? Henry is not going with you."

Will cocked his head. "He is not? That surprises me—he is my squire, after all. Why, then, is he not coming with me?"

She flapped her hands at him as if he were a chicken pestering her peace. "Tut, man! Because he is not yet fit to travel—nowhere near fit enough. I will not hear of it."

"But … but I canna just leave him here with you, Jessie. That would be unseemly—"

"Un*seem*ly?" The look she threw him from beneath one arched eyebrow was filled with withering scorn. "Why should it be unseemly, Will Sinclair? You said yourself he is yet but a boy. I assume you mean he is not yet a rutting bull. Think you I might debauch him in your absence?"

"Jessie!"

She flung her head high, looking down her nose at him. "*Jessie!*" she mimicked. "What do you take me for, sir?"

Will, who had never flinched from an armed assailant, quailed at her scorn, and she immediately took pity on him, her voice sinking back into its husky gentleness.

"Will, the boy is too weak to travel, so he will stay here and there's an end of it. You have too much on your mind, too many other things to see to and arrange, for me to be encouraged to entrust you with his well-being atop all else. He will be safe enough. Today's attack was the first such we have known since I arrived here, and I will put out the word among the other folk in the dales, and we will be ready if the like occurs again. Believe me in that."

"I do believe you. What I cannot believe is that it will not happen again. The English at least will be back, and sooner now, rather than later. Their barons' greed will see to that, even had Edward Bruce not set a direct challenge for their King."

"What do you mean? I know nothing of any challenge to the English King, and Robert keeps his headstrong brother under tight rein."

"Not tight enough," Will growled. "I heard about it in Arbroath. It is the talk of the taverns there. The King set Edward to the siege of Stirling, months ago, thinking to keep him safely occupied in taking one of the only two Scots castles still in English hands. But instead of doing as he was bidden and tightening the siege, the gallant Earl of Carrick grew bored and played the headstrong, thoughtless fool, as usual. He chose the route of chivalry, ignoring the fact that his brother has fought a war of brigandage these past eight years, scorning English chivalry and chivalrous battles in favor of the savage and effective style of the late William Wallace."

"In God's name, what did he do?"

"He negotiated a truce with Moubray, the English governor of Stirling Castle, the terms of which will be an iron gauntlet flung in England's face. Robert is furious, but helpless. The damage is done."

"What were his terms, in God's name?"

"A year's truce, to be concluded by the surrender of the castle next Midsummer Day in the event it is not relieved."

"In the—? Dear God in Heaven! The man must be mad."

"Mad as a rabid stoat."

"He has given England a year to raise an army."

"Worse than that. He has given Edward of England a cause to rally his mutinous barons and end the civil war that has kept him useless. He has caused affront to the very honor of every Englishman who thinks himself superior to the Scots. Edward Bruce has guaranteed a new invasion, and this house of yours sits squarely on the only route to Scotland's west."

Jessie said nothing more for a long time, but as Will watched her, she squared her shoulders and finally tossed her head. "Aye, well, perhaps it does," she said defiantly. "But that's another perfectly sound reason for taking me with you when you sail away to your new land."

There was the merest hint of humor in her gaze, despite the gravity of threat he had outlined, but the unapologetic bluntness of her effrontery took his breath away again, making nonsense of his resolve to accept her forthrightness in future. He could only gape at her, aware his mouth was hanging open but unable to do anything about it, so that she snorted with inelegant laughter. "Your wits, Will

Sinclair! Gather them up, for I fear you're in danger of losing them.
That was a jest. I was but toying with you."

He swallowed hard. "A strange time to jest," he muttered. "And
a stranger topic on which to do it. Forgive me, my lady, I am ill
accustomed to women and their humor, as you know, so you have
me at a disadvantage … So much so, in fact, that I find myself
wondering how often you have toyed with me before, without my
knowledge or suspicion."

"So I am to be 'my lady' again, am I?" She shook her head, exasperated. "Och, Will, I wouldna toy with you unkindly, and sure, the
tidings here are dire, but sometimes we have to laugh at ourselves
and at the Fates or go mad altogether. Forgive me. It's simply that
you can be so … so predictable at times that I canna resist the urge
to make your eyes go wide like that." She rose to her feet and looked
towards the door. "I wonder if the house is settling back to normal
yet. If ye'll permit me a moment, I'll return directly."

He stood and pushed back his shoulders while she was gone, and
looked about the room, and he became aware all at once of how dark
it had grown and how cool the air was, even though the outside of
the house yet basked in warm, late-July afternoon sunshine.

Jessie came back into the room and returned to her chair, waving
Will down into his own as she did so. "Hector will send food in a
little while, but in the meantime you are still wearing your armor."
She smiled at him. "I know you are accustomed to wearing it at all
times, but it makes me feel confined merely to look at you."

Will frowned and glanced down at himself, then saw immediately
what she was talking about, acknowledging himself, uncharacteristi-
cally and perhaps for the first time ever, as being out of place in this
comfortably appointed, unmistakably feminine room. He was, in
fact, fully armored, save only for his helmet, and suddenly, unaccountably to him, he became aware of the odor of his own sweat
mixed with that of his hard-ridden horse, and the weight of his
heavily booted and armor-reinforced feet seemed leaden as he shifted
them uncomfortably. He wore a full suit of mail—a hooded coat of
heavy, burnished links that hung open to his heels and was fastened

in front with leather thongs and a stout leather sword belt worn over a full cuirass of steel, while at the back it hung divided from the waist down, to permit him to ride comfortably. Beneath the cuirass he wore a thick leather jerkin lined with padded fustian, and beneath that an undershirt of finely woven wool, his single concession to his own comfort, worn solely because he found the contact of the itchy fustian intolerable on his bare skin. He wore light Saxon-styled trews beneath his heavy mailed leggings, the ends of them stuffed into his high, thick leather boots. For the first time in his adult life, he felt clumsy and faintly ridiculous, grotesquely out of place.

Jessie was still smiling at him. "I hope you will not be offended, but knowing that you carry little in the way of clothing while traveling, I took the liberty of laying out some of my late husband's clothes on the cot in the chamber above this, next to the room you occupied when you were here previously. Etienne, God rest him, was of a size with you, I think—perhaps a little narrower across the chest and shoulders. You should find that they will fit you easily, and I promise you, you will find them far softer and warmer than that coat of mail." She waited for a reaction, and when none came she added, grinning in pure mischief, "I swear to you, you may walk about unarmored here with confidence. There is little likelihood of our being attacked again. Twice in one day would be inconsiderate and unacceptable."

Will was completely at a loss for words. He knew she was twitting him, but he was still too unsure of himself in this suddenly new relationship and incapable of forming an adequate response, fearing he might make a fool of himself by saying something inane, or yet again give the wrong impression by blurting out something that sounded curt and humorless. And yet the laughter dancing in her eyes was unmistakable, and he found himself aching to respond in kind. And so he forced himself to try to smile.

"You are toying with me again, I see, madam," he managed to say finally, keeping his voice gentle. "But I sense you mean no harm by it, and so in token of that, I will accept your kindness and make an attempt to fit into the clothes you have laid out for me. You say they are in the chamber next to the one I used before?"

"They are," she said, and now the raillery had vanished from her voice and eyes, replaced only with a warm smile. "And there are three sets from which to choose. Should I send one of your men up to assist you?"

He managed to raise one eyebrow in self-disparagement. "No, madam," he said formally. "In my years as both monk and knight, I have learned adequately well to robe and disrobe, and even to arm and disarm myself, without assistance. So if you will excuse me?"

"Wait, you will need a light. It will be dark up there. Take one of the candles there … And try the green pile. I think the color will suit you."

He bowed to her without another word and went to where a single, tall taper burned beside a box of candles on the table. He selected one and lit it, then sheltered it with a cupped palm as he made his way out of the room, conscious at every step of her eyes on him.

Great God in Heaven, Jessie thought as he went out. *Here is change indeed. Who would ever have believed it, and where did it spring from? To see the great William Sinclair blushing and gawking like a chastened altar boy. It is almost too much to be believed, but I thank Heaven it is so and pray God he does not have a change of heart and mood. Hurry back, Will Sinclair, hurry back.*

UPSTAIRS, WILL STRIPPED OFF his armor and his padded tunic and leggings until he was left wearing nothing but his white lambskin apron, and then he spent what seemed like an unseemly long time bending over the bed, peering closely by the light of his single candle at the three separate piles of clothing that lay there, and fingering the fabric of the various garments. They were fine and soft and sensually wondrous, and he finally decided in favor of the greens, simply because the hue seemed somehow brighter, even in the candle's light, and he felt an inchoate urge to wear something bright.

It was only as he lifted the delicate, square-necked undershirt of fine pale green wool, wondering if it would in fact fit him, that he noticed the washing bowl and the ewer of clean water on a narrow table or wash stand at the foot of the bed. He approached it cautiously and saw that it was flanked by a hanging towel of flocked material that he knew to be called Egyptian cotton, and a smaller, folded square of the same material, similar to one he had seen his sister Peggy use for washing her face, and a small bar of rich, wondrously scented soap that he knew had not been made in Scotland. He fingered the soap tentatively, marveling at its creamy texture, and on the spur of the moment decided to use it. He splashed water into the bowl, soaked the washing cloth, and then rubbed it with the soap, inhaling deeply as the scent of the moistened substance was released and threatened to set him reeling with the pleasure of it. Once committed, he wasted no time but washed his entire upper body, scrubbing the cloth beneath his armpits and reveling in the coldness of the water against his heated torso. He then dried himself with the rich toweling and splashed more water over his head, rubbing it into his scalp and then toweling his hair until it was almost dry, after which he combed it into some semblance of order with his clawed fingers. And afterwards, refreshed and invigorated almost beyond belief, he set about making sense of the clothing he must don.

He pulled on the softest pair of loose breeches he had ever worn, settling them almost comfortably over his lambskin apron, aware that even loose as they were, they stretched taut over his muscular thighs and calves. He tied them securely with the drawstring attached to the waist, after which he shrugged into the matching undershirt, feeling it hug him and then stretch easily across his chest. As he laced up the single fastening at the neck, he gazed down at the remaining garments on the bed beside him. There were hose, with knee ties, and he knew as soon as he looked at them that he should have put them on before pulling on the breeches, so he removed those and pulled on the pale green hose, stretching them over his bulging calves so that there was no need to tie them in place. He then donned the breeches again, snuggling them over the hose below his knees before retying them at the waist. Next he pulled on the softest pair of calf-high boots that he had ever handled. They were of supple dark green leather that he knew to be chamois, parchment thin and brushed to a silken softness, and they fitted him to perfection. Encouraged then by his success with the boots, he shrugged quickly into a loose shirt with a wide, deep vee in front, several shades darker than the square-necked undershirt that showed beneath it, and finished his transformation by donning the knee-length, open-fronted outer garment, like an open surcoat with sleeves, that he folded across his chest and tied with a long, woven belt of the same material. He had no means of seeing his reflection, but he felt more at ease and more unconfined than he could ever remember. He gathered up his clothing and armor carefully, slinging his buckled sword belt over one shoulder, and carried the heavy and ungainly pile awkwardly under one arm into the neighboring chamber, where he dropped it on the cot there, acutely aware all the while of how strangely shy and diffident he felt in his borrowed finery.

At the top of the stairs, he heard laughter from an open door nearby, at the far end of the passage, and he went and stuck his head into a well-lit chamber to find the boy Henry, propped up in bed and being spoon-fed from a bowl of soup held by one of Jessie's women, the one called Marie. Beside her, on a chair nearer the foot of the bed, the girl Marjorie sat chattering gaily, her eyes on the bright embroidery on which she appeared to be working industriously. As Will entered, she looked up at young Henry, her eyes dancing with mirth, and added some quip that made the boy laugh, even as he caught sight of his lord and mentor. The laughter vanished quickly and he sought to push himself up farther, wincing as his shoulder tensed, but Will stopped him with an upraised hand and told him to stay where he was. The sudden quiet in the room had a strange quality, as though all three occupants had been frozen in mid-motion, the woman Marie caught with the hand that held the spoon upraised, the girl Marjorie suspended in bewildered surprise, her smile fixed in place, and young Henry himself poised as though about to fall over on one side. Will nodded cordially and greeted each of the ladies in turn, then spoke briefly to the boy, asking him how he felt and embarrassing him by asking whether he was happy with the quality of attention being paid to him.

The boy was looking well, he thought; still pale and waxen looking, with deep purplish rings under his eyes, but the eyes themselves were bright and the lad's hair was clean and shone with health. Although he was still heavily bandaged, his injured shoulder appeared to be normally positioned, and his arms lay easily upon the bed's surface. Will spoke for a little longer, attempting to put them all at ease, though with little success, he felt, and then he took his leave, heading resolutely down the stairs with a profound sense of relief that his squire was thriving.

2

Seated in front of the fire that now roared in the open grate, Jessie Randolph kept her head lowered and pretended to be engrossed in mending the piece of fabric she held on her knees, but she had to fight against the impulse to look up eagerly when Will knocked and entered.

Now, come inside, Will Sinclair, and take your proper place without stopping to question every impulse that occurs to you. In God's name, play the man and not the monk, the champion but not the knight. Summon up that famous bravery of yours and let it strengthen you to see me as a woman and a friend and not as Threatening Woman. And when I do look up at you, God help me, let me see a change in the man to match the change in what he is wearing now.

Will stood silently just inside the threshold and stared at her, holding his breath and waiting for her to look up.

"Come and sit," she said quietly, without looking up. "If you will be patient with me, I will be no more than a few moments in finishing what I am doing."

He crossed silently to the chair opposite her, then stood there, feeling strangely shy and illogically awkward without the protection of his armor, but when she showed no reaction to his closeness he sat down slowly, watching her fingers at her needlework. Eventually he began to relax, lulled by her air of calm concentration, and he found himself enjoying the heat from the fire as it washed over him. She kept sewing, betraying no awareness of his presence. She was bareheaded, her hair parted straight down the middle of her bowed head and worked into two flawless plaits that were twisted into perfect spirals and pinned so that they covered her ears. In the stillness of the room, broken only by the fluttering of flames and shadows and the swift, deft movements of her busy fingers, he imagined that he could smell the scent of her, a wafting awareness of warmth and sweet-smelling cleanliness, and as he watched, moment by moment, he became aware that the stiffness and tension that had held him in suspense was bleeding out of him with each breath.

Jessie had to fight hard to keep her eyes on the sewing in her lap, but from the corner of one eye she could see his feet and ankles in their rich green boots and was aware when they crossed and uncrossed and finally rested comfortably, one flat on the floor, the other lolling sideways, resting easily on its heel. From that point onward, she could almost feel the strain easing in him, and as the awareness of that grew in her, the fiercely held joy in her burned brighter. Yet still she kept her head bent to her sewing, hoping he knew sufficiently little of needlecraft to be unaware that what she was doing there was nonsense.

Will, fortunately, knew nothing of sewing. But something strange was happening here, he knew, and he knew, too, that whatever it was, he was at ease with it, for reasons that he made no effort to define. As he gazed at Jessie's bowed head he was dimly aware of a tiny, tenuous stirring somewhere at the back of his mind that tugged at deep-seated ideas of loyalties and conflict, but he ignored it deliberately, content for the time being to trust his instincts as he always had before, to enjoy looking at what lay before his eyes and to believe that all was as it should be.

It was only when Jessie raised her head suddenly and smiled at him that he snapped to attention, startled that he had come close to dozing off, lulled by the fire's warmth and his feelings of well-being. He straightened guiltily, glancing about him and realizing for the first time that the two of them were alone in a comfortable firelit room, in a situation that could only be described as intimate. Embarrassed to be caught thus off-guard, and acutely ill at ease, he found himself almost glaring at his hostess.

"Where is everyone?"

Jessie merely blinked at him, her expression demure and slightly puzzled. "Everyone? Oh, you mean Tam. I told him to spend a night at leisure."

She stood up, her sewing still clutched in one hand, and moved towards a large side table that stood against the wall to one side of the fireplace, and as he saw the way in which her clothing shifted around her he was surprised to realize that, for all his sudden discomfort, he had been unaware of her body until that moment.

Jessie, unable to see his face, was still talking, speaking to him over her shoulder as she scanned the tabletop in front of her.

"That poor man has no life of his own at all, you know. He spends far too much time with you, waiting upon your every wish and whim. And so I set him free for the night, to thank him for rescuing us today. He is probably enjoying himself now with Mungo and the others, for I am sure Hector will have left them well supplied with drink and food, if he has not joined them himself."

Will cleared his throat, then blurted out what was in his mind. "I was not thinking of Tam, Lady Jessica. I was wondering about your ... companions, your ward and your two women. Should they not be with us?"

"And why should they be here, my women?" She turned to face him, holding up her sewing in both hands, and he could not read the expression on her face or in her eyes, though she gave him no time for either. "To ensure propriety? Are you concerned for your safety here, alone with me?"

"No, that is not what I meant at all." He threw up his hands, then let them fall to his sides and shook his head. "Of course I meant no such thing. But I have never known you be without them for so long.

The child Marjorie rarely leaves your side, and the two women are ever in the background, one of them or the other if not both."

"Things have changed here since the arrival of your young squire, and I have grown accustomed to being neglected, taking second place to his needs. He has bewitched my ward, you know. She has appointed herself his guardian, and she rules all of us like a tyrant in seeing to his every need. And so the women of this household wait upon Henry, and entertain Henry, and hover around Henry constantly—myself included, most of the time." The fondness in her eyes removed any possible sting from the words she uttered. "So that is where everyone is … seeing to Henry, while I have supposedly been seeing to you. But I have been neglecting you, I fear."

She turned away, set down her sewing, and removed the cloth that had covered the offerings laid out on the side table. "You must be hungry." She waved a hand over the items on display, and he felt the saliva welling in his mouth as she continued. "This is cold venison in a wondrous crust made by Hector, and the salmon here, baked and skinned for your pleasure, was also cooked by Hector, without whom I should starve in squalor. But if neither of those please you, this dish holds roasted piglet, still hot, and there beside it, its skin, intact and succulent, coated with flour and salt and broiled to a crisp perfection that I heard Hector say would make a dead man drool." She turned back the edges of a snowy white cloth that covered a trio of small clay serving vessels. "Cheese of our own making, sweet apples from our own trees, and fresh bread, crusty and warm from the oven. And to drink, we have the last of the shipment of wine delivered two years ago from Bordeaux, both the red and the gold."

Will stood up, blinking, dazzled by the variety of the offerings and completely disarmed by her pleasure in his presence. He nodded slowly, then went towards the display, where she stood holding out a wooden platter for him to use.

"The pig is wonderful. I tasted some of the crackling when Hector brought it in and you were upstairs." She was grinning, obviously greatly pleased with something, although he had no idea what it might be. He merely nodded and took the platter from her hand.

"Here. Let me cut some for you." She rapped the brittle crust of crackling sharply with a heavy-bladed knife, shattering it into several pieces, and lifted two of them onto his platter, then cut a thick slab off the bread and loaded it with twin finger-thick slices of succulent-looking meat before chopping a bright red apple into eight segments and piling half of them beside the crackling. Still slightly overwhelmed, he waved aside her offer of anything else, then stood looking around him.

"Sit at the table there. It is set for two, with knives and spoons and salt. Which kind of wine would you prefer?"

He opted for the golden color, then moved to take a seat while she poured and brought wine to him in a magnificent stemmed glass goblet. She returned then to help herself to a wedge of the cold venison pie and another of the salmon, onto which she spooned a generous portion of clotted, creamy golden sauce that she told him was another of Hector's secrets, made from eggs, cream, and herbs. She came and sat across from him at last and invoked a blessing on their meal before starting to eat with the appetite of a twelve-year-old boy. Watching her set about it, Will realized that he was ravenous, having eaten nothing all day other than the handful of dried oats and fruit with which he had broken his fast that morning. They ate in companionable silence, almost reverentially paying tribute to the excellence of Hector's cooking, until both their platters were bare and their goblets empty.

When Will sat back and pushed away his platter she cocked her head, smiling at him again, and it was a measure of how much his trust in her, and in himself, had grown that he merely looked at her with mild curiosity, one eyebrow rising in a wordless query.

"It pleases me that you chose the green," she said. "I was right, the color suits you well. And the clothes themselves might have been made for you."

He felt his face flush, but it was with pleasure, and he managed to respond gracefully. "I am in your debt—" He caught himself before the words "my lady" could spill out, wondering what to substitute and finding himself still uneasy with using her given name. But then, before she could interject, the words came to him and he smiled with relief. "You have introduced me here, this night, to the world of ordinary, well-contented men who live their daily lives unfettered by the constant demands of duty and a rigid Rule of conduct."

She dipped her head in a tiny gesture of acknowledgment. "Ordinary, well-contented men ... I wonder if such creatures truly exist in this world of ours. Ordinariness is less ordinary than it may at first appear, and you yourself are far from ordinary ... You have changed greatly, you know, since first we two met. A year ago, you would never have said such a thing, would never have thought of it. But to be truthful, I myself would not have believed, as recently as one month ago, that you and I could sit for so long together at ease like this. The grim Templar Sir William Sinclair would never have permitted it, lest he find pleasure in it." She grinned suddenly, her eyes alight with mischief. "I am glad my friend Will came here today in his place. Will is far more ... human ... far less predictable and humorless." Her grin faded as she sat straighter and glanced up at the windows high on the wall. "I have lost track of time, but I see blue sky up there, so the sun has not set, or if it has, the dusk is not yet full." She rose to her feet. "Come, then. If you have had your fill of eating, walk with me to the byre to check the safety of our treasure chest, for I confess I have not thought of it since your arrival, even to verify that it was undisturbed by our visitors. I will have someone clear away the food while we are gone."

"But not the wine."

She glanced at him in surprise, caught by the hint of levity. "No, not the wine. That we will keep. I will have the fire rebuilt, too."

3

They stood together in the gathering darkness of the byre, in front of the bundles of feed that covered the chest of gold coins, eyeing the undisturbed symmetry of the pile. Outside, in the gathering dusk, the returning cattle were clattering into the cobbled yard at the back of the cowshed. The mangers in the stalls on either side of where Will and Jessie stood were filled with fresh fodder for the coming night, but the hay on the shelf that held the treasure appeared untouched.

"Is it safe enough, think you, or should we unearth it to be sure?"

Will responded with the merest shake of his head, for his thoughts were elsewhere. He and Jessie had been seen by several people inside the house and on their way here, and although no one had seemed to take any special notice of them, the nagging notion had arisen in his mind that, in being seen abroad like this, they could be suspected of improper behavior. The thought of impropriety had stirred vague feelings in him of both disloyalty and dismay, since his hostess had given him no slightest cause for concern over propriety and it seemed to him the merest thought of such a thing was demeaning to both of them. He had tried to thrust it aside, but the harder he tried, the more stubbornly the notion held, so that now his mind was filled with wonderings about what Jessie's people might be thinking of her, spending so much time alone and unattended in the company of a man who was not related to her.

"What are you thinking about there, sir knight, with such a glowering frown upon your face?"

He pulled himself together with an effort and waved off her question, muttering something unintelligible in reply as he stepped forward to lay his hands on the undisturbed pile of fodder, but as he did, he became aware of his clean green boots and the building within which they stood. The central channel had been swept out long since and its surface was dry underfoot, but he saw the looming bulk of approaching beasts beyond the low doorway, and at once his nostrils seemed filled with the acrid, pungent stink of liquid dung mixed with urine. An image flashed into his mind of what the floor of this place would look like moments after its occupants returned, and he backed away quickly, lifting each foot with exaggerated care. By the time he turned back to face Jessie, however, he had regained his voice.

"Forgive me, Baroness, I was woolgathering. It's plain to see, even in the dark, that nothing here has been disturbed, save by our own presence, and now your tenants have come home. Shall we go on?"

The sky had faded to a dark, purplish hue, and the last lingering rays of the vanished sun were firing the low western clouds with brilliantly glowing, flaming tints of orange and gold and red. Jessie stopped walking and gazed up at the display.

"How can one look at that and not believe in God? It is different every night, never the same from day to day nor even from hour to hour, and it is never ugly. Even at its worst, the sky is always wondrously beautiful. But everything changes constantly, everywhere we look." She glanced sideways at him, standing quietly beside her as he, too, stared out at the panorama in the west. "I will admit, though, sir knight, that the changes I have seen in you these past few weeks have amazed me. I expect change, as a part of life, inevitable as night after day, but still you astound me."

"Astound you? How so, madam?"

"Let me see … you astound me in a host of ways, and I have to say that I would be hard put to name but one … But no, that is untrue. I have one. You have learned to listen."

His mouth widened slowly into a grin. "I assure you, Baroness—"

"*Jessie.*"

"Jessie, aye … I assure you, *Jessie*, that I have never had the slightest trouble with my hearing."

"Nor did I say you had. I said you have learned to *listen*, not to *hear*. Hearing is an ability, but listening is an accomplishment. I know few men who really listen to anyone or anything, let alone to women. Your friend Tam is one of them."

"Tam …? You will explain that to me, I hope."

It was Jessie's turn to grin, and he felt his spirits lift with the quick merriness of it.

"I will, and I'll do it slowly, for the sake of your masculine ears. But may we walk while I do so? It's growing cool."

She fell silent as they began to walk again, and before she could resume, Will turned his head towards the gates, attracted by the sound of voices.

"Did you not say you had given Tam the night to himself?"

She glanced up at him quickly and he laughed aloud and turned away again, failing to notice the look on her face as he crowed, "Well then, it would appear he didna listen to you. Tam! Sergeant Sinclair! Here, to me!"

A large group of men had just entered the enclosure, indistinct in the rapidly growing darkness, a mere block of black male shapes, some of them carrying long-handled shovels, but there was no mistaking Tam's upright form at their head or the massive bulk of Mungo MacDowal by his side. They stopped as one, and Will heard Tam say something to the others. He weaved slightly as he approached, but Tam Sinclair was a long way from being the worse for drink. When he was close enough to see them clearly he stopped short, his eyes widening and his jaw dropping as he looked at the spectacle of his kinsman dressed in the sumptuous garb of a French nobleman.

"Name o' God," he muttered, more to himself that anyone. "What in—?"

"Good evening, Tam." Jessie cut him short before he could blurt out anything else, and he turned to her, blinking owlishly.

"And a guid e'en to you, Baroness," he growled, his Scots burr thickened by drink. "A braw night." He swung his head back truculently to look again at Will, but Will was ready for him.

"What have you been doing out there, so late in the day?"

"Late in the day? We've been there a' day lang. What d' ye think we'd be doin'? We've been buryin' bodies. Ye may mind there wis a wheen o' them lyin' about the place."

"I do." Will looked towards where the last of the distant group was vanishing around the corner of the main house. "How many were you?"

"Six to dig—the prisoners—and eight o' us to guard them. The four o' us, and four o' Lady Jessie's men."

"And how many bodies?"

"Nine, and every one o' them a heavy whore to shift— Your pardon, Baroness."

Will nodded. "Well done. But the Baroness has just been telling me she set you free and at leisure today."

"So she did." Tam frowned. "Are you telling me I'm no'?"

"No, not at all. I merely wondered why you did not take her at her word."

"I did, and I thanked her for it. Did I no', Baroness? Aye. This night, I intend to get very drunk. We ha'e the drink in the bothy, and food to soak it up, thanks to the stewart, Hector McBean. So, 'gin ye'll let me, I'll—" He stopped again, scanning his kinsman slowly from head to foot, missing no slightest detail, and then turned to Jessie, pointing a thumb towards Will. "This is your work, I jalouse?" Jessie smiled, rather tenuously, but said nothing, and he shook his head. "I ha'e never seen the like. An' I wouldna ha'e believed it wi'out seein' it for mysel'." He looked Will up and down again, slowly. "Green boots! Green boots an' nae armor ... No' even a dirk." He glanced again at Jessie and then drew himself up to his full height, clearing his throat loudly. "Well, ye look grand, Will Sinclair. Grand and braw and ... no' just *different*, but ... *right*, ye ken? Ye should aey wear green." He grinned wickedly. "It suits ye." And with that he turned and walked away.

How long Will might have stood there speechless he would never know, but beside him he heard Jessie stifle a sudden shudder and saw her clasp her elbows, hugging her breast. "It's cold," she murmured. "I want to go back inside now."

They crossed the courtyard quickly this time, striding towards the house, and both of them were shivering as they entered the main room and moved directly to stand as close as possible to the roaring fire. They stood side by side, gazing into the flames, each of them lost in thought until Jessie broke the silence, giggling gently.

"You see? Tam approved my choice. Did that surprise you?"

"I've been speechless ever since."

They both turned to say something else, and suddenly they were face to face, no more than a hand's breadth between them. Neither said a word for some moments, until Jessie raised a hand wonderingly to her mouth.

"I had never heard you laugh before tonight. Did you know that?"

Will stepped away, lowering himself into one of the two large chairs that had been repositioned during their absence to face the fire, and Jessie sat down in the other. "Never? That is hard to believe," he said, resisting the urge to call her by name. "How long have we known each other now? You must have heard me laugh at one time or another."

"Six years since we first met, that night in La Rochelle. And you have never laughed. Not in my presence. Until tonight."

"That is ridiculous," he blustered. "You make me sound like … you make me sound as though … Bah!" He threw up his hands.

"I make you sound like a grim and intolerant knight I once knew, a Templar knight called Guillaume de St. Clair … a man who never smiled, as far as I could see, let alone laughed. Come now, be serious. When do you last remember laughing, really laughing so that it hurt your ribs? Can you recall?"

He sat still, thinking, his face growing sober as the moments stretched, and then his eyes lit up and he smacked the arm of his chair. "I can! It was the time when Tam fell in a river, fully armed, and couldn't climb out. I fell out of my saddle laughing, and the angrier he grew, the funnier it seemed." He laughed again, gently, recalling the scene. "It had been raining hard that day … straight down, relentless, and the riverbank was sodden. Tam slipped and dropped his sword in the mud—I can't recall why he had drawn it or why he was afoot—but he was angry at himself and went to wash it clean in the river. He stooped and stretched until his feet went out from under him and he landed on his backside. Then he spun around until he was looking up at me, his face wild with outrage … and he slid slowly backwards, scrabbling at the mud, his legs in the air, all the way down and off the bank, into the water. And once in, fully armored, he could not climb out." Will was really laughing now, pinching the bridge of his nose between finger and thumb and snorting with mirth, his eyes tearing over. "It wasn't deep, but it was slippery. I tell you, Jessie, he was howling, baying with anger, and it was the funniest thing I had ever seen." He pulled himself together then, shaking his head and blinking the tears from his eyes. "It took him a long time to forgive us, but he did, eventually. Sweet Jesus, that was funny."

Jessie was smiling with him, and as his laughter died away, she said, "I'm glad I asked you that. When did it happen? Was this on Arran?"

His face grew somber and his voice changed, becoming quieter. "No. It was in the Languedoc, close to the Pyrenees, on the way to Navarre to fight the Moors. It was … fifteen years ago."

Jessie sat stunned, for there was nothing she could say, she thought, that would not sound petty, but after a few moments she drew in a breath and spoke brightly. "Well! We may be glad it happened, for it has brought laughter back to you, for my pleasure, after all this time."

"Aye, mayhap, Jessie." His voice was barely audible. "But you were right. I doubt I have really laughed since that afternoon, for we lost more than half our number in the fighting that followed hard on that day. Fifteen years!"

A silence stretched after that, and she watched him. *Ah, Will Sinclair, you dear, dear man, how I wish I could show you what laughter does to your face, to all of you … It strips years away from you, years and years and years, and shows the boy in you …*

A log spat and cracked in the fireplace and the blaze subsided, throwing sparks and whirling smoke up into the canopied flue.

"What were you thinking there?"

The question caught her by surprise and she answered unthinkingly. "I was watching you, thinking you should laugh more often … all the time … and wishing I could show you how you change when you do …"

He sat gazing at her, and then a tiny smile tugged at his mouth. "That would be a clever—"

A shriek of female laughter rang out somewhere beyond the door and snapped them both out of the mood they had been sharing.

"Marjorie! That child is …" Jessie was on her feet, unaware of having moved, and now she stood glaring down at him as they listened to the clatter of running feet, her eyes sparkling with an emotion he could not define. "I swear, since that boy entered this household all sense of decorum has been tossed aside. And Marie and Janette are no better than my ward. Wait for me here, if you will. I have to go and assert some authority."

Wide eyed, Will watched her go, her skirts swirling about her, and he was still unsure whether the look in her eyes had been one of anger or of perplexed amusement. She left the door open as she went, and he heard her going up the stairs, her voice raised in exasperation until it dwindled beyond hearing. Only then, when he could hear nothing but stillness, did he settle back in his chair, gripping the arms and looking absently about him as he began to take stock of this unusual day. Unusual was not the word for it, he thought; this had been a day beyond imagining. This was her room, Jessie Randolph's room, despite whatever claims her nephew might hold to it. Her influence, the signs of her presence, her dominance of this household, were visible everywhere: they shone in the colors of the room, the banks of candles cunningly arranged, the shawls and cushions on the furnishings, and the jugs and pots of living flowers on practically every level surface. And in the middle of it all, he sat wondering what he was doing there … How had he come to this, and what was happening to him?

There was a time, he thought, when he might have believed the woman had bewitched him, and as the thought occurred to him, he acknowledged that she had, in fact, bewitched him, slowly and surely. But where years earlier he might have run in confusion to some priest, seeking absolution, he was now content to sit and await the next developments. He had become a different man today from the one he had been the previous year, or even the previous month, and he was well aware that the rigorous, unyielding Temple knight of a decade earlier was long since dead. But the process of that particular knightly death had been assiduously executed by men, by those same men to whom he had dedicated his life, swearing to serve, to honor, and to obey. No witchcraft there ... Exorcism, perhaps, in that the spirit that possessed him as a younger knight had been expelled, cast out forever. But that had happened through no fault or influence of Jessie Randolph's. All she had done was frighten him with unchaste thoughts and lustful dreams, phenomena that, in his single-minded dedication to doing his duty by and for the Temple, he had forgotten were harmless in the eyes of his true Order, the Brotherhood of Sion. And in the past few weeks, all that he had learned had combined with all he had decided in recent years to generate a new Sir William Sinclair, another man altogether; a man mature in years and battle-hardened, but owning all the terrors of an unworldly, virgin boy.

IN THE STILLNESS, THE LONG HOWL of a distant wolf came clearly through the unglazed window high above his head, followed by the sound of marching boots and a loud challenge that marked the changing of the night watch. The fire settled again, and he noticed that several of the banked candles on the table and sideboard were guttering, close to burning out. He had lost track of how long Jessie had been gone, but he felt utterly at ease as he pushed himself to his feet and went to snuff the dying candles, pinching them out between a moistened finger and thumb and smelling the odor of smoldering wick as he scratched congealed wax from his thumb afterwards. Only a few had burned out, and he left the others as he went to rebuild the fire, settling new logs in place and only remembering at the last moment not to push them down with his bright new spotless boots. He stood for a few moments gazing down into the fire and frowning slightly, and then he sat down again, plucking at his lower lip, and let his thoughts run free, aware only that he had never been indecisive, and that he needed to be constructively decisive now.

He was deep in thought when Jessie stepped back into the room and stopped near the door, observing him. But when she spoke he turned to her immediately, showing no sign of surprise.

"You are still here! I thought you would have tired of being alone and be abed."

"Not at all. I have been sitting here thinking, of many things—things to be done, decisions to be made. Are you for bed yourself?"

"No, not yet, unless you wish to be alone."

"No, I am content. Come and sit then, if you have a mind to share the fire." He watched her as she came to sit across from him again, and when she was settled, stretching out her hands towards the flames, he smiled. "You have quelled the mutiny up there?"

"Oh aye, long since. High spirits are a blessing from God, but they need to be curtailed from time to time. Now Marjorie and Henry are abed, lights out, and Marie and Janette are at their chores, preparing for the morrow, spinning yarn for the loom. Am I permitted to ask what you were thinking about?"

"In your own house you may ask anything you wish, Jessie ..." He hesitated, then plunged ahead. "I've been thinking about myself, in the main—about my life and what's to be done with it. I've never had to do that before, can you imagine that? Here I am, growing old already, and I have spent my life being told what to do and when to do it, so thinking about what I ought to do is a new concern for me ... very new ... and strange ... But you spoke of changes earlier tonight, and that set me off. My entire world has changed in the six years since I left Master de Molay in Paris. I still have duties, God knows—tasks to do and decisions to make that will influence far more lives than my own. But now I am thinking for myself, commanding others to obey my wishes and decisions."

He chewed on the inside of his cheek, frowning, and then he looked directly at her. "I have been thinking about you, too. About this wish of yours to sail with us when we leave. How did you come to that?"

She stared at him for a long moment. "Not with *us*, Will. With *you*."

He blinked. "You need to move away from here, I ha'e no doubt of that, but coming with us is nonsense. The place where we are heading is unknown, Jessie, it is—"

"What, dangerous? Savage? Wild? Filled with perils and uncertainty, with savage, brutal men on every hand looking to ravage, steal, despoil, kill, and destroy? It will be nothing at all like the douce and placid land we live in now, will it? Nothing like this civilized Scotland. Is that what you were going to say?"

"No, it wasna that—"

"Good then, for I would rather live in the uncertainty of your unknown Merica than live here in the sure and certain knowledge of being killed and in the foolish, hopeless hope that my death, when it does come, will be swift and painless." She inhaled sharply. "In God's name, Will Sinclair, where will I go if I leave here and do not go with you to your Merica?"

"To Arran. We have room for you there. You will be safe in Lochranza Castle, and all your people."

"Lochranza Castle." She almost spat the words. "And when you sail away, what then? The lord there is Menteith."

"Not now. He is disgraced."

"*He* may be, but the place is a Menteith fief and I will have no safety there. Take me with you, Will."

"I cannot."

"Why not, in God's name? Will you be taking priests with you?"

His eyes widened. "I hadna thought to. That will be no place for clerics. Even then, all our surviving clerics stand excommunicate, like the rest of us. But then again … a few good men, sound of wind and limb and trusted by the brethren. Aye, we'll take a few who once were priests."

"Good. Then one of them can marry us."

"*Marry* us? I—" He stared at her, then drew his hand down his face, pressing hard as though smoothing out the wrinkles.

She watched him tensely as he turned his face away from her, his eyes screwed shut, his wide shoulders stiffening as though in outrage. But then his shoulders slumped and he turned back to her.

"I was on the point of telling you I am a monk," he said calmly, "but that's another nonsense. I am not a monk, not now. They stole that from me when they took my life and spat on it. Now I am a man—no more, no less."

"You are a knight. No one can take that from you."

"True, lass, and I am well aware of it. But I remain a man. And a man, after all is said and done, with little to offer anyone, God knows. But as for being goodman, husband ..." He sucked in a great breath. "Would you ... Are you truly offering to wed me ... be my wife?"

He saw the flush rise in her face before she answered. "Wife, helpmeet, companion, concubine—whatever God sends us. Aye, Will Sinclair, and gladly." She held up one hand and grinned. "Even adviser, should the need for such arrive in your new land, and should you require a woman's common sense."

A solemn stillness settled as they sat back in their two chairs, gazing at each other in the glow of the embers that had flared and crackled such a short time before.

"Adviser ..." Will smiled more easily than she could ever recall. "Now there is a new idea. A woman advising a Templar knight, and through him a Templar community. Changes, indeed!"

"But only should you see such a need arise, in a new world."

"Of course ... But let me test you, as both woman and adviser. Give me some advice."

"Now? On what?"

"You said tonight I have learned to listen. Well, I am listening now, and I have sufficient respect for you that I have no doubt you hold opinions on some things that I should do. Therefore I am asking you, sincerely, for your advice."

Again they sat quiet, eyeing each other.

The man has just spoken to me openly of marriage. I would be a fool to risk that gain by saying something he might gauge as foolish for any of a score of reasons. And what could I tell him, anyway?

He was waiting patiently, and she noted that as another significant change in him. But when he raised a questioning eyebrow she spoke, surprising herself.

"The matter of Genoa. You intend to go, but do you need to?"

He pulled back his head and drew in his chin, and she was distracted for a moment by the columnar strength of his neck, and by the time she looked at his eyes he was already frowning.

"Do I need to go? Of course I do. I have business there, purchases to make."

"I know the purchases have to be made, but must you be the one to make them? Could not Sir Edward make them on his own? The Archbishop's letter of introduction could as easily be made for him as for you, could it not?"

"Aye, it could, but—"

"Tell me this, then. In the buying of these ships, however many there may be, will you make the decisions on design, size, and construction, or will you seek Sir Edward's advice?"

"I would seek his advice, of course."

"Of course you would, so let me ask you this. Would you trust this man with your life?"

"De Berenger? Wholeheartedly. I already have, with all our lives, your own included. He is my admiral."

"The guardian, keeper, shepherd, and captain of your fleet. Then why would you not entrust him with the mission to Genoa? You have overmuch to occupy you at home on Arran, and ships are Edward's life. He knows seagoing vessels and all their requirements the way you know and love the things you do that make you what you are— leading your squadrons of horse, training your men, administering your community, planning campaigns. And by your own admission, this journey to Genoa will take months, perhaps even half a year, depending on the weather. What will you do if Edward of England invades before you can finish what you hope to achieve on Arran?"

She fell silent, and he slouched sideways in his chair, one elbow on the arm in a position she had long since come to recognize as signaling consideration of a problem, his thumb hooked beneath his chin and the knuckle of his first finger pressed against his upper lip. His eyes were steadfast, drilling into her. She began to count silently, gazing back at him and schooling her face to be as unreadable as his own, but she lost her count in the second hundred, distracted by some random thought, and still he stared at her. She had never realized how big he was. He had always *seemed* enormous, bulked and bound in heavy metal that provided its own size, but now that he was unharnessed and wearing her late husband's clothes, she could see the depth and breadth of chest, the width of shoulders, and the thick column of his neck, with an errant wisp of hair curling at the neck of his shirt. She kept her eyes unwaveringly on his upper body, daring not to look at his thighs.

"I should have started listening to you years ago, Jess."

A rush of gooseflesh made her shudder when he used that name, and she felt her heart bound.

"You're right," he continued, more to himself than to her, she supposed. "It is foolish for me even to think about going to Genoa when de Berenger can do everything by himself. He has no need of me. My place is in Arran. No doubt of that. I must get back there, quickly. De Berenger knows what we need better than I do. And he may know better than either you or me the value of your hoard of gold." He looked straight at her now. "And that's another thing. That chest is too awkward for easy concealment. It's too conspicuous and far too heavy. It would draw other people's interest the way a rose draws bees, and that's the last thing we need. So tomorrow we will split the gold into smaller parts, easier to carry, easier to hide. Do you have leather bags?"

"Small ones, suitable for coins? No …" She shook her head, then brightened. "But we have three old leather tents, in one of the sheds. We used to use them to cover the threshing floor, and they are old and moldy, but they are sound enough to be cut up into pieces, to make strong drawstring bags. I can set someone to that task tomorrow."

"Someone you trust, and have them do it where no one can see. Be careful, Jessie. A sudden flurry of making leather bags—*small* leather bags—will draw attention, for there's naught you can do with such things but use them for holding coin."

"Hector will do it."

"You trust him that far?"

"And further. How do you think the chest ended up where it is? Hector helped me move it and conceal it there."

"Good. So be it." He stood up suddenly and began to pace the room, rubbing his hands together, then stopped and stood with his back to the fire, facing her. "About this marriage thing. Your mind is set?"

"Completely."

"Hmm." His lips quirked. "And if I were to ask you for advice on that, which I do not, you would advise me to proceed with it?"

She smiled. "I would."

"Aye, well, I will think on it, although I think you mad. But I will think on it. I have a condition, though, to be agreed to here and now. The boy cannot travel yet. We are agreed on that. But he was the sole reason for my returning here this day, to pick him up and take him back. How much longer, think you, before he can return to Arran?"

"A month at least, three at the most."

"Three is too long, too long and too dangerous. I will send for you in two months' time, in the third week of September—you, the boy, and your two women, and whomever else you wish to bring with you."

"What about Marjorie?"

He looked at her in surprise. "Your ward is the King's niece, Jessie."

"But she is illegitimate."

"Legitimate or no', her name is Bruce and she was sired by Robert's favorite brother. You canna simply whisk her off without the King's permission. That would be abduction. And a king's niece has no will of her own in such matters. She belongs to the kingdom, a chattel to be married off, if need be, for the good of the realm. That is beyond my ability or yours to influence."

Jessie wasted no time in protest. She knew he was right, and merely nodded. "Then I must seek out the King himself, between now and then, and obtain his blessing."

"To take the child away, perhaps to die, in some unknown land? He will never agree to such a thing."

"Perhaps not. But I must try."

"Fine. But you'll be ready to embark for Arran by September?"

"I will be ready, and more ready still to embark for Merica. Send out your traders to buy cloth."

"Cloth? What kind of cloth?"

"Any kind, and as much as they can buy. There will be no clothiers in Merica, but all who go there will need covering against the weather."

He stood blinking at her. "I will see to it. Is there anything else you can think of?"

"No, but I might as time goes by. Wait! Spinning wheels and looms. How many women will go with us?"

"I have no idea."

"Then you had best find out and let me know as soon as you can. We will need to plan for them, and if I know the numbers, I can be ready to start organizing them by the time I come to Arran."

"You are very sure I'll wed you, woman." His smile was small but ungrudging. "But I have not yet agreed."

She gazed at him and met him smile for smile. "You will. Now, when will you leave here?"

He shrugged. "The day after tomorrow. One of our galleys will be waiting off the Galloway coast. I have no time to waste."

"Then you had better get some sleep, for we have talked the day and half the night away. Go you upstairs, then, and get you to bed. I'll put out these candles and bank the fire before I go to mine."

"Aye ..." He stood for a moment, nibbling at his upper lip. "This has been a strange and wondrous day, Jessie, filled with things I could not have imagined when I left here last week to ride to Arbroath. We have achieved much, between the two of us ... Are you sure we are in agreement on it all?"

She stepped quickly towards him and lifted up her hand, laying her palm along his cheek, touching him openly for the first time, and he raised his own to hold it there, cradling it. "I am sure, Will, even if you are not."

He swayed towards her, his lips slightly parted, and she knew what would happen if he kissed her here, so she drew a deep, swift breath and patted him firmly on the cheek.

"Now go to bed," she told him softly. "You have much to do tomorrow."

4

He came awake slowly and with great reluctance, loath to quit the voluptuous enjoyment of the dream that had been enfolding him and the dream woman whose mouth had covered his own, drawing the soul from him with an agonizing pleasure. But when he opened his eyes at last and found the mouth still there, still kissing him, and raised a hand to touch bare, warm skin, he started awake, jerking upright, and would have shouted had not a hand clamped firmly over his mouth and a voice hissed sharply in his ear, "Shush, Will, shush! Be still. You'll wake the house and betray us both."

He froze, half raised on his elbows, blinking wildly in the pitch darkness and aware of the other body leaning over him on the narrow cot, and his skin rose up in superstitious terror, until he heard her giggle and felt her breath against his ear.

"It's me, it's me, and I didna mean to startle you. I only came to kiss you goodnight. Hutch you over and let me in."

Still befuddled, but beginning now to grasp something of what was happening, he pushed himself higher up. "Jessie? What is it? Is something wrong?"

She giggled again, quietly and close to his ear, bringing him out in renewed gooseflesh. "Of course there's something wrong, you great, dense lump. It's freezing cold and your bed's already warm. Lift up the clothes and let me in. Move! Move over!"

He did as he was bidden, shifting his weight onto one elbow and raising the covers, and he felt the smooth, warm rush of her climbing in beside him and then hugging him close, pulling him to her soft nakedness as her fingers twined in the hair at his nape and pulled his face down to her own. And for a long time after that, he lived in a maelstrom of taste and touch and smells the like of which he had never known, until he froze again, finding himself somehow leaning on straight arms and aware of the forked shape of her beneath him, her fingers clutching him.

"Do you not want me, Will Sinclair? Come, man, and be my husband."

The fingers tugged at him, insistent, guiding, and Will closed his eyes and sighed, shuddering, and entered his new world.

FROM DEATH INTO DEATH

1

It seemed to Jessie Randolph that all the world was coming to Arran that first week of May in the year of our Lord 1314. The northwestern harbor of Lochranza was crowded with so many galleys that the unthinkable had occurred and the harbor had been closed, incapable of accommodating a single vessel more. Four of the eight remaining Temple galleys were moored there, but they were invisible among the others, visiting craft from the isles and sea lochs to the north, many of which had borne the MacDonald blazon of the new Lordship of the Isles on their sails as they approached the anchorage beneath the cliff. There were more than MacDonald vessels down there, though; she had seen the emblems of Campbells, MacRuaries, and MacNeils as well, along with several others unknown to her that Will told her had come from the isles far to the north. They had filled the harbor, which had never seemed small before, occupying every foot of the wharves that lined the water, and in places so many of them were lashed together side by side that they appeared to form a series of floating bridges across the waters directly below where Jessie stood looking down from the castle walls.

She had been in Lochranza for nigh on a year and a half—the time had flown by almost without her awareness—and as chatelaine of the castle she had become accustomed to the always-busy harbor beneath the walls, with its constant procession of ships and galleys coming and going, but she had never seen anything like what was happening now. The narrow strip of land between the wharves and the castle itself was thick with men, all of them scurrying about like ants, but she knew that what she was seeing was nothing; beyond her sight, behind the curve of the walls to each side, the yards and buildings of the castle enclosure were even more crowded, and the mob of men spilled out beyond the postern gate to fill up the meadow at the rear.

She half smiled as the word *mob* came to her, for although the men below bore no resemblance to the kind of soldiers she had known most of her life in mainland Scotland, France, and England, to call them a mob was wrong. Although there was no uniformity of any kind among the Gaels, and none of the imposed restraints of chivalry, each man among them was a warrior, self-equipped and self-reliant, present upon his own decision to support his chief, and should the wishes of his own chief concur with the wishes of any other, each would decide for himself whether or not to continue to extend that support. She knew they were no mob, no mere disorderly rabble. She had heard enough from many sources to know that these fiercely independent men, so apparently undisciplined, were savage and unrelenting fighters who could tear down conventional military formations and overwhelm fortifications with ease, imposing their own form of discipline upon themselves when the need arose. Islesmen and Highlanders all, they lived by their own standards, beholden to no man.

Beneath her, two floors removed, their leaders were meeting with King Robert's representatives, Sir Robert Keith, the Marshal of Scotland, and Sir James Douglas, looking far older and more grim than he had when Jessie had first met him, a mere five years earlier. Two prominent members of the Scottish clergy completed the royal delegation: William Sinclair, the Bishop of Dunkeld and uncle to her own Will, and the formidable Bishop David Moray, dressed as always in the mail hauberk and steel cuirass of a fighting soldier and looking not one whit like a lord of Holy Church. Meeting with these four were Angus Og MacDonald, now the self-styled Prince of the Isles; Fergus MacNeil, the Lord of Barra; MacGregor of Glenorchy, chief of Clan Alpine; and a pair of taciturn chieftains from the islands of Lewis and Uist whose names she did not know, although she suspected that they were kinsmen to the MacNeil. They had been in discussions for three days now, taking over the main hall on the second floor of the castle and ousting its chatelaine for the duration, so that she spent most of her time now either in her own chambers with her women, including young Marjorie, or here on the battlements, overlooking the activities in the harbor below whenever the unpredictable spring weather permitted it.

Jessie, swathed now in a richly furred mantle of soft sealskin, was untroubled by the loss of her domain, content to let the visitors have the run of it. She understood the urgency of this gathering and so she simply left them to get on with their affairs, confident that the faithful Hector and his staff from Nithsdale would keep them well supplied with food and drink. She had other, more weighty matters to think about.

Will, her Will, whom she now gloried in calling her man, was deeply involved in convening another, completely different gathering at Brodick Castle. There, too, she knew, would be a great gathering of ships in the nearby bay of Lamlash, in the lee of the Holy Isle, Eilean Molaise, because in four days' time the last formal chapter of the assembled knights and sergeants of the Temple Order within the realm of Scotland was due to assemble there, and the brethren would already be arriving, openly or secretly, from all over King Robert's domain. And when it was concluded, the Arran community of Templars would disperse, some of them on the quest to the new land, others to serve King Robert as volunteers, based in a number of communal centers that had been set up on the mainland within the previous few months. These centers were few, but they were in place, widely distributed throughout the realm, and would be referred to henceforth as lodges; none would ever be called preceptory or commandery, but they would serve as rallying points and places of refuge for those who wished to retain their fraternal identities, and they would be tacitly acknowledged by the King's authority. The men based there, indistinguishable by now from ordinary men, would continue to function as Templars, but in a profound secrecy beyond anything they had known or needed in the past. They would observe their rituals and rites, nurturing and passing on the secrets and symbols of their once great Order to other, younger men in days to come.

Of course, the King's royal leave for the Scots Templars to attend the chapter gathering had not been given without conditions, and Will had discussed those conditions with Jessie, seeking her advice. The King knew of the resources Will had nurtured on Arran, and he was more than aware of the wealth of horseflesh, particularly the heavy horses, under Will's command. In all of Bruce's Scotland there were fewer than forty destriers, the enormous war horses that made the chivalry of England and France so powerful, and the worth of each one was incalculable. The small cavalry force that Scotland could field, seldom more than five hundred strong, was all light horse: scouts and skirmishers and mounted men-at-arms and bowmen, suitable enough for diversionary tactics and for nuisance raiding but utterly ineffectual against the fearsome, overwhelming bulk of massed English chivalry. Thus it was natural that King Robert coveted the Temple destriers, and knowing the King's needs and the dangers facing his realm, Will had had no difficulty in agreeing to provide them. After all, as he had said to Jessie, they could not take the beasts to Merica. They had more than seventy of the huge animals on Arran now, and they would have difficulty transporting them even across the narrow channel to the mainland, for the ships that brought them here from France had all long since been reconfigured for other cargo.

Jessie had agreed with everything that Will was saying, advising him to make an immediate start on reconfiguring the ships' holds yet again to accommodate heavy livestock. But then she had asked him about the knights' armor. King Robert would assign the destriers to his knights, she pointed out, but would those knights have armor sufficiently heavy and strong for the tasks they had to face aboard their new and massive mounts? Very few of them would, she suggested, since Scots knights, less wealthy than their English counterparts, had traditionally been unable to afford, or even to find, such enormous mounts, and consequently had no use for such bulky, reinforced armor. Their need had always been for lighter, stronger armor, mail that was more supple and less restrictive than the solid, unyielding plate worn by the English chivalry. Besides, she added, had he thought about how many of his own Templars would wish to volunteer their services as chivalry to Scotland?

That took Will aback, for he had not thought of it at all. His over-riding concern in recent months had been the composition of the group that would set out across the sea for the new land, ensuring that only the best, most versatile and resilient of his people would be included. De Berenger had crossed safely to Genoa late in the previous July, avoiding the English blockade of the North Sea coast, and had been able to buy two newly built ships, both commissioned and partly paid for by the Temple before its dissolution, along with two similar vessels that were unfinished when he arrived, their construction suspended in the absence of a purchaser. All four, he had reported back, were suitable for their expedition and in fact better than he had hoped to find. He had promised to have the four new ships back in Arran by mid-June, and all Will's efforts had been geared towards being ready to set out at that time.

Thus, in the hubbub of all the ongoing activities, Will had made a fundamental error in his calculations. For more than five years now, revolving shifts of armed and mounted men from their Arran community had been fighting with the Bruce armies, and Will had taken it for granted that they would continue to do so after their relocation to the mainland. But those riders—knights and sergeants alike—had all used smaller, lighter horses and mail armor, easier to transport across water. He had not considered the great destriers, or the fact that many of his men, the French knights most assuredly, would wish to rearm themselves with their own huge war horses and plate armor once that became possible. Now he had to plan to present King Robert not only with horses but with the armored knights to ride those horses. Chagrined initially at having overlooked such an apparently obvious development, he had nevertheless soon found the grace and humor to acknowledge, once again, his new-won spouse's value as an adviser. He had immediately issued orders to have all the Templars' heavy armor and weaponry brought out from storage and refurbished for use in the coming English invasion.

And so, as soon as the chapter meeting was adjourned, the business of transferring the horses, armor, and weapons to Scotland would begin, for they had no time to waste. She herself would have been in Brodick now, organizing the score and a half of women who would sail with the expedition to the new land, had Will not asked her to remain behind in Lochranza to act as chatelaine and hostess to the gathering there. That was a waste of her time, in Jessie's opinion—though she kept her silence—since she had contributed nothing but her presence, and that had been largely ignored, as she had known it would be.

A sudden upsurge in the noise from below attracted her attention. The apparently aimless seething of the crowd down there had altered since she had last looked, and now men were moving purposefully, pouring aboard the galleys, spilling from one to the other as they sought their own berths.

A discreet cough came from behind her, and she turned to find Hector standing at the turret door, holding it open for Sir James Douglas, who was stooped in the entryway, smiling at her.

"Sir James! Is something wrong? Do you need anything? I—"

Douglas doffed his feathered cap and bowed low in the gesture she had come to associate with him, but the smile remained in place on his dark-skinned, strangely attractive face. "No, Baroness, nothing is wrong. We are done our work and I need nothing ... except time—a few more months between now and the coming week, if you could arrange that?"

She laughed back at him. "Would that I could, Sir James. But are you leaving?"

"Aye, on the rising tide, 'gin we can board and clear the sea wall in time. It is gey tight down there." He stepped to her side and they stood together for a moment, watching the still-increasing activity below. "MacNeil, at the back there, will go first," Douglas told her, "and that will clear the harbor mouth. As soon as they have room to dip their oars, the others will follow. I would venture, though it seems impossible, looking at that, that your harbor will be empty again within the hour from now. These caterans know their business."

He looked at her again and stepped back a pace, inclining his head. "I have come to thank you, Baroness, from all of us who have gathered here these past few days, depriving you of house and home. Your hospitality and forbearance have been much appreciated, and we have achieved all that we hoped for. The Islesmen of the West will stand with His Grace when England comes chapping at our door, and those tidings will do much to soothe our noble Robert's cares. But I must now travel hard and fast to tell him, for he is on his way to Stirling to assemble our host, such as it may be. And so, 'gin you will grant me leave to go thus rudely, I must away forthwith. The others are waiting for me."

"Go then, and Godspeed, Sir James. Carry my blessings and good wishes to the King, and tell him I will keep his niece safe for him."

"I will. Adieu, then, Madame la Baronne." He bowed again, sweeping the ground with his bonnet's plume, and then he was gone, the sound of his booted feet dwindling rapidly down the narrow spiral staircase.

Jessie stood staring at the spot where he had vanished, her eyes narrowed in thought. She had been less than truthful with the King in the matter of his niece, for she had said nothing of taking the girl with her beyond the seas, and even now she was unsure what she would do when the time came to decide. It would all depend upon what happened in the weeks and months ahead; if she decided that Marjorie's life would be safer in the new land, then she would take the child without a moment's hesitation.

That Scotland would be invaded was a certainty. Edward Bruce had ensured that when he made his foolish truce with the English governor of Stirling the previous summer. England's King had used the ensuing year to settle his own internal wars with his barons and whip them into a frenzy of greed and offended chivalric honor, playing upon their lust for Scottish lands and wealth. The sole question remaining was the exact timing and strength of the incursion, and even that was finite. Midsummer Day, the date of settlement of the Stirling truce, was June twenty-fourth. England had until that date, now six weeks distant, to relieve Stirling or lose Scotland.

Edward of England had begun summoning his earls and barons months earlier, just before Christmas. Word had soon reached Bruce's ears, generating the urgency that had brought about this gathering of Scots and Gaels here in Lochranza, forging alliance between King Robert and the reluctant, independent Islesmen and Highlanders, for if King Robert's Scotland fell to the English, so, too, would the Western Isles and the Highlands.

A chorus of horns and shouts from below brought Jessie's attention back to the present, and she looked over the battlements to see, to her astonishment, that the harbor was indeed emptying rapidly, the sea beyond the entrance dotted with departing galleys, all of them using wind and oars to reach their various destinations as soon as possible. Another roar of approval reached her, and she looked straight down, recognizing Douglas and his three companions as they and their attendants moved quickly to board their own vessel, the massive galley lent to the King of Scots by his Arran Templars.

How long she stood gazing down at the King's galley as it was warped away from its berth and headed out to sea she could not have said afterwards, for her mind was filled with worries of another sort as she wondered what her own man would now do. He had told her that he would remain on Arran to complete his work; that the affairs of Scotland were Scotland's own; that he had made and would continue to make his contribution to King Robert's cause with men, horses, and weaponry; but that his overriding responsibility was to his own people and their journey to the new land. She had believed him at the time, but that had been a full month earlier, and now she was not so sure. Sir William Sinclair was not the kind of man who could turn his back upon his friends in time of need, and Robert Bruce and his closest supporters had become Will's friends. Knowing that, she knew too, in her heart of hearts, that as the threat of invasion drew nearer, her man must be undergoing torment from his divided loyalties.

He would do the right thing. She had no doubt of that. But the unease over what that might be, the decision he might finally make, had kept her awake every night since he had left for Brodick. She had waited far too long for him to come to her, and now that he had, she could barely tolerate the thought that she might lose him in the squalor of some muddy battlefield, slaughtered in the mire because his sense of honor and his conscience would not permit him to stand back and look to his own affairs.

She was still standing there, gazing sightlessly out to sea and hugging herself beneath her sealskin mantle, when she felt his hands close over her upper arms. She knew them instantly and whirled about, throwing himself into his embrace and kissing him wildly, feeling him stiffen at first at her unexpected ardor, and then enfold her, pulling her tightly against him as he returned her kiss.

Finally, after a time she thought was all too short, he broke from the embrace and turned her in his arms so that she leaned back into him, but in the turning, she had time to see the lines in his face and the deeply troubled look in his eyes, and she felt her heart fill up with apprehension, knowing that he should not be here.

"So, they are gone," he whispered into her ear, holding her steadily as he looked out at the last of the departing ships. "They reached an agreement?"

The question was rhetorical, but she answered it anyway. "Aye, they are gone. Sir James told me the men of the West will stand with the King when the time comes."

"I had no doubt they would. They have no option."

His voice was quiet, a mere murmur, but she twisted out of his grasp. "What is it, Will? Why are you here?"

His eyes examined the whole of her face, and then he shrugged and grunted softly, smiling sadly. "I am here to see you, Jess … to look at you and feel you in my arms, soft and warm against me … and to talk with you … to share some tidings."

"Ill tidings."

He hesitated, his eyes narrowing, then nodded. "Aye. As ill as might be."

"Come then, for this is no place to be sharing them."

She took his hand and led him from the roof, retaining her grip as she led him down the narrow, winding staircase to their bedchamber on the floor below. Young Marjorie was there, sitting before the fire with Marie and Janette, and all three of them glanced up in surprise as Jessie entered, still leading Will. She told them to leave, to go and help Hector and his staff in cleaning and readying the great hall below, and to stay away until she called for them again, and when they were gone, she turned again to Will, reaching up to touch his face, fingering the stubble on his cheek. "I want you, here and now, in that bed, but you have more need to talk than to make love. I can see it in your eyes."

She swung away, waving to the chair to the right of the large fireplace. "Sit then, and tell me, and when you have told me once, no matter how bad it may be, you can tell it to me again, in bed. I will listen closely both times, I promise you. And then I will tell you what I think."

He moved to sit obediently and she settled herself opposite him, her eyes on his, waiting until he had settled. "Now, tell me."

He nodded, complacently enough, but then sat silent, and she could see that his eyes were unfocused, his thoughts far away as he searched for words. She waited, and after a while he blinked as though awakening and dropped one hand to finger the hilt of the dagger at his waist.

"I have just received news from France," he said, his voice lifeless. "Jacques de Molay is dead, after seven years in jail. By now he would have been seventy-two, perhaps seventy-three. An old, done man, destroyed by seven years of abominations and abuse. They had sent cardinals to try him and his three remaining companions yet again, but he rejected their authority. He would speak only to Pope Clement, he said, and in person, in accordance with the oath he had sworn so long before. But Clement was in Avignon, at odds with Philip once again, and he would not go to Paris. And so, de Molay rescinded his confession once again. It had been drawn from him by torture, he proclaimed, and he now abjured it, denouncing Philip Capet for the greedy thief he is …" He blew out a long, shuddering breath.

"Capet was in Paris, and he reacted swiftly. They burned the old man at the stake that very night, on an island in the middle of the Seine, by the church of Notre Dame. The date was the eighteenth of

March. My old friend Antoine St. Omer was there among the hundreds that witnessed it. He said our Grand Master died well, cursing both Pope and King from the smoke and flames and calling upon God to witness that he and all his Order were innocent of the charges brought against them."

Jessie stood up and crossed to him, cradling his head against her breasts, and she said nothing. He sat with his face against her for several moments more, then pushed her gently away.

"So there we have it, Jess. The final betrayal of a grand old man and all he stood for, by the Pope he served faithfully and the King he would not serve.

"He did not die alone, though. The Preceptor of Normandy, Geoffrey of Charney, burned with him, close by. Nor did he die unheard, and the last call that he uttered was a summons to both Pope and King to meet him before God's throne within the year. St. Omer spoke of that, and he would not lie in such a thing."

"Oh, my dear Will, I am so sorry." He looked at her and twisted his mouth wryly, inclining his head in acknowledgment, and she asked, "How was the news received among the brethren in Brodick?"

"No one yet knows. These are ill tidings, my love, and their timing could not have been less opportune. And so I decided to hold them close until the time is right to divulge them ... although God Himself knows that time will never be."

"I see ... So, what will happen now?"

He expelled his breath slowly, wearily. "Now, Jess? Now I have to tell the brethren assembled at Brodick. Now I am Grand Master in fact, God help me, with nothing to be Master of. And now I must appoint a Master in Scotland, to guide the brethren who remain behind after we are gone. Does all of that sound as futile to you as it does to me?"

"Shush now. Come you."

She took his hand and led him to the bed.

AFTERWARDS, WHILE HE LAY SLEEPING by her side, she thought about what he might do, and arrived at a decision. It was a grave decision, and she refused to consider it at first, but she knew she had no choice but to accept it, though it might be the death of her.

She sat up and turned sideways to wake him up, and he looked sheepish as he realized that he had rolled off her onto his back, and there fallen straight to sleep, but she merely smiled at him and ran a barely touching fingertip down the line of soft hair that ran from his chest to his navel. Then she slapped his flat belly and told him to get up and dress.

When he was clothed again and sitting by the fire, she curled up in the chair across from him.

"Tell me now, what of the English? Have you heard anything new?"

"Aye, new and ever growing since Edward sent out his orders, calling eight earls and eighty-seven barons to assemble at Berwick with all their strength. The tenth of June was the assembly date he named, but more than two and a half thousand mounted knights, heavily armored and armed, were already there by March. And each of them brought two or three mounted men-at-arms to back him. By March, Jess, with two months in hand! The English crows are hungry for Scots flesh …

"That same month, word came from Lamberton, in a letter smuggled from where he is held in England, that Edward has increased his levy. He has called for an additional fifteen thousand infantry from the north and Midlands, and three thousand archers from Wales, and he has requisitioned more than two hundred heavy carts and wagons for his supply train. As I was leaving for Brodick four days ago, Douglas himself told me the latest numbers indicate that there are more than twenty thousand men at Berwick, all of them well equipped and slavering with thoughts of victory and plunder."

"Twenty *thousand*?"

"Aye, lass, that's what I said. Twenty thousand. And in all of Bruce's Scotland, even were he to raise every able-bodied man in the realm, there are less than half of that number, mayhap even less than a quarter of it, to withstand them."

Both of them stared into the sinking fire until Jessie asked, "Would you like to hear my advice?"

He almost smiled. "You would advise me even in this? Aye, I would. You have not failed me yet."

"Nor will I now, for I love you more than life itself, and because of that I will tell you what is in my mind." She looked down to where the fingers of her hand were pleating the fabric of her gown. "I thought about this long and hard, Will, and I believe I know what you should do—must do. So listen to me carefully, my love, and pay close attention, for I might change my mind later and try to tell you I was wrong. But right now, I know I am right."

2

The Great Hall at Brodick, the Chapter House as it was now known among the brethren, was full, with men packed shoulder to shoulder even on the alternating black and white squares of the ceremonial square painted in the center of the floor. Only two open aisles, edged by ropes and forming a cross, permitted access to the four rostra that held the chairs at the four cardinal points of the compass. The Eastern dais was the largest of these, holding the Master's Chair, and it formed the front of the assembly, the focus of all men's eyes.

The closed rites of the knightly brethren were complete, conducted according to the Rule, in the darkness of the night, and now with the coming of daylight, the sergeants had joined the knights for the less formal portion of the ceremonies. There was a profound, almost palpable air of solemnity about the occasion, for everyone knew that this would be the last such gathering—the last plenary assembly of the surviving members of the Order of the Temple in Arran, perhaps the last anywhere. Any gathering would hereafter be clandestine, private, of necessity—and that awareness lent an aching piquancy to the rumbling sound of the massed voices chanting the canons of the Rule.

Will stood high above the assembly, looking down from a curtained window in the carved wooden screen that concealed the suite of rooms at his back and waiting for the last of the canons to reach its end. He had planned this event carefully, bearing in mind everything that Jessie had said to him, and he was still astonished at the degree of insight she had shown into events about which she could have known nothing. She had divined the mood of this assembly, if not the content of it, and had considered aspects of this day that might never have occurred to him at all.

The chant reached the point he had been waiting for—he had heard it sung a thousand times and more over the years—and he turned and nodded to the men lined up on his right, then watched as they turned in unison and began to move in procession towards the door at the top of the wide stairs that led down along the east wall to the ceremonial floor. All four were dressed in bright white woolen robes over which each wore the emblems—the jewels—of his individual office. As they reached the door, each one in turn knocked loudly, and when the door was opened by the inner guard, the man who had knocked leaned forward and gave the password in a voice that only the guard could hear, then passed through, closing the door behind him.

Will watched them go, feeling love and admiration for each of them swelling in his breast. Richard de Montrichard, preceptor here since their arrival, went first. His was the Chair in the North, and none of the gathering below would dispute his right to hold it. De Montrichard had been a fine preceptor, and Will felt a familiar stirring of discomfort as he recalled his own doubts about the man's suitability when they first landed here. De Montrichard had blossomed at his post and had commanded from the outset with a sure and steady hand.

After him, the senior galley captain, de l'Armentière, knocked and was passed through. On the floor, he would occupy the Southern Chair, deputizing for Admiral de Berenger, who had not yet returned from Genoa. And behind him, bound for the Western Chair, the two remaining men sought entry in their turn. The first was Bishop Formadieu, the senior bishop of the Arran community and the rightful holder of the Western Chair. But Formadieu had recused himself from the Chair more than a year earlier, claiming to be unfit to represent the brotherhood because of his failure to influence the Church's decision to do what it had done to the Order. No one in the community had wanted him to give up the Chair, and no one believed that any portion of the fault was his, but the old man had been adamant, and Will had reluctantly acceded to his wishes, with the single but absolute proviso that Formadieu remain on the Western dais, behind, and at the shoulder of, the man selected to replace him. Of course, the selection of that successor had been Will's, and he had chosen to appoint Sir Reynald de Pairaud, now an old and wizened man, in recognition of the veteran knight's staunch but unexpected enthusiasm for what they had been able to achieve since landing on the island.

The sound of the door closing behind de Pairaud brought Will back to an awareness that it was now his turn to request entry to the proceedings below. He glanced down at himself and at the black leather bag in the crook of his arm, checking that all was as it should be, then walked forward and knocked on the door, which opened immediately. He whispered the password into the doorkeeper's ear, then stepped across the threshold to where the other four, already in order of precedence, waited for him on the narrow landing at the top of the steep wooden stairs. Below them, the last, sustained note of the deep chant faded to silence just as Will murmured to the white-robed brethren to start down. He himself was dressed from head to foot in black, in the cowled robe of a mendicant friar, save that the robe was of rich and heavy wool, unrelieved by any decoration and belted with a thickly plaited girdle of black-dyed, glossy linen fiber. He waited until the others began to move down the stairs, then hitched his leather bag higher and followed them, aware now of the silent faces that stared up at him and the expectant stillness that awaited his arrival.

He paused at the bottom of the last flight, then stepped directly to the Master's Chair on the Eastern dais, one pace to his left. His four companions waited for him to take his place, then moved on to the junction of the cruciform aisles, where de l'Armentière turned left and De Montrichard right, to the South and North respectively, leaving De Pairaud and Bishop Formadieu to make their way together to the dais in the West. When all four were in place, Will stood looking out at the assembled brethren, sensing the silence growing even deeper, as though everyone in the crowd was holding his breath.

He made himself count slowly to ten, dragging out the stillness, then lowered his bag to the table in front of him and unbuckled it before raising his head again and starting to speak, pitching his voice carefully so that it resonated in the crowded hall, and articulating his words slowly and clearly.

"Brethren, we are here together to mark a momentous occasion, one that none of us could ever have imagined when we left La Rochelle seven years ago. Since then, we have built a life for ourselves here on this little island, and we have struggled diligently to live by the Rule of our Order and to preserve our ways and our responsibilities against the day that every one of us once believed must surely come ... that day when we would be redeemed and would return to France, our names and that of our Order restored to honor, the spurious charges against us finally expunged. We have lived here in hope and in brotherhood, and within the past year, we have been joined and strengthened by our Scots brethren from the mainland.

"But within those same seven years, our hopes for justice and an honorable reinstatement of our Order have been crushed, dwindling steadily in the face of ever-increasing tidings of grief and disaster, treachery and malice emanating from France and from its King." He stopped there, giving his listeners time to accept what he was saying, and as soon as he saw heads beginning to nod in agreement, he resumed in the same voice.

"And so we have made changes—dire changes, indeed, but necessary in a swiftly changing world." He drew a deep, audible breath. "Now I have learned of one more such, one last, appalling change that has made exiles of us all, forever ..." The silence in the room was absolute, and he looked about him before he spoke again, making eye contact with as many of the assembled men as he could, and seeing the same tension of uncertainty and dread in every face.

"On the eighteenth day of March this year, the year of our Lord 1314, our beloved Master, Sir Jacques de Molay, was burned alive in Paris. The murder—for it was nothing less—was performed as a public spectacle by the direct order of Philip Capet. An obscene atrocity was treated as a festivity."

It was as though a silent gale had blown into the hall, its force rocking the packed crowd visibly, but before they could begin to react further, Will launched into the tale as he had heard it from St. Omer, omitting nothing and ending with the challenge—amounting to a curse—that de Molay had issued from the flames, summoning both King and Pope to join him before the throne of God Himself within the year. Then, when he had finished, he raised a hand into the profound silence.

"So there you have it. Our noble Order has ceased to exist beyond this realm of Scotland. It is finished, dead with the death of its noble Master and the simultaneous deaths of honor, justice, and nobility in our sad land. And with the passing of our Master, by his own written command, I am now become Grand Master of what remains." His eyes swept the crowd. "Master of what remains.

"And what is that? What *does* remain, what *can* remain, after such infamy and gross injustice?" What *remains*, brethren, is here with us now, within this Chapter Hall. It is our enduring spirit, our honor and our ideals, our clear understanding, unsullied by venality or envy, of our duties as knights and men, and our responsibility to ourselves and those who stand with us. We hold those tenets safe within us, untarnished and undiminished by the betrayals of Church and state and the horrors unleashed upon our innocent brothers by the Holy Inquisition.

"In the eyes of the world, then, our Order is dead, but we know, all of us, that that is not true. As long as one of us remains alive to nurture its memory and serve its purposes, our Order will continue to exist, and that becomes my greatest responsibility as Master now: to protect and nourish what remains. We must change, adapt, reform

ourselves completely. We *have* changed, greatly but not yet sufficiently. And now we are about to conceal ourselves completely from
the eyes and ken of ordinary men. We will become as ghosts and
phantoms. But we will continue to observe our rites and ceremonies,
to maintain our beliefs and to coexist in amity, as brothers, equal in
the all-seeing eye of God. Henceforth, we will pursue our goals and
dreams in utter secrecy, our existence veiled and hidden, our true
identities unknown. This is my oath to you: we will survive and
thrive, though hidden from the eyes of others, and the day will come
when this Order will arise again, from out of this realm of Scotland,
to honor the memory of the last, true Grand Master of the Temple,
who died on the island in the Seine last March. And thus I think it
would be fitting, as our last act in this, our last gathering, were we
to sing 'Dies Irae'—Days of Wrath—to mark the passing of a great
and noble man."

Across from Will, on the Western dais, Bishop Formadieu stepped
forward and began to sing the first line of the solemn, sonorous chant
of the requiem hymn, and by the end of his first phrase he had been
joined by the massed voices of the assembly, singing with a fervor and
solemnity that Will could not remember ever having heard. He stood
listening intently, feeling no urge to join in although the hairs stirred
on his neck as the waves of sound swelled and washed over him. He
had always preferred listening to music rather than marring it with his
own tuneless contribution, and now he pictured the dead man as he
had last seen him, grave, dignified, and deeply troubled by the seemingly preposterous warnings he had received. Remembering the
Master's reluctant decision to act upon those warnings, Will now realized how appropriate the words of this dirge were to that memory:
Day of wrath! O day of mourning! See fulfilled the prophets' warning,
Heaven and earth in ashes burning!

As the hymn ended, Will pulled the bag towards him. He laid
both hands on it.

"This would not have been a day of celebration, even without
these evil tidings, but it must not—will not—end in despair. Few of
you, I suspect, ever laid eyes on Master de Molay, for he lived most

of his life far from France, beyond the seas, working without pause for the good of our Order. But I know there is not a man among you who is unaware of the reverence, even the awe, with which he was regarded by all who knew him. He was a knight without peer, and it was, alas, his destiny to die in office, the last of an unbroken line of twenty-three Grand Masters of our Order, beginning with Hugh de Payens in 1118.

"Twenty-three men, Brethren, and one hundred and ninety-six years of rectitude and devotion to duty, all of it destroyed by one greedy, venal king. Philip Capet, known as *le Bel*—the Fair. Such *fairness* brings to mind the whited sepulcher of scripture ... But no more of him. He is not worthy of your time or of your thoughts. Think instead of Jacques de Molay for the remainder of this day, as you work at your appointed tasks.

"Before we stand adjourned, however, I have a few things— personal things—I want to say to you as Master here. I will not keep you long, for most of our work is done in preparation for this day." He looked around at their watching faces as he spoke, noticing, not for the first time, that few among them could be described as young looking.

"When we leave here today, we will begin the final stages of our preparations to quit this place for good. Horses, armor, weapons, and provisions, along with most of your personal possessions— those of you who have any—are all in place on the beaches by the wharf below, and the ships are waiting to take them on board. You all know what to do and you know we have no time to waste. I want to add a reminder, if you will.

"When we came here, we were exiles, homeless fugitives who still could not believe what had happened to our ordered world. We were confused and disbelieving, not knowing what to think and waiting, blind and deaf, for news to reach us telling us it had all been a mistake and that we must return home. But that word never came, and the world we had known fell into ruin.

"Yet we sat safe here, on this island, sheltered from the chaos by the goodwill of one man, Robert of Scotland, and his friends.

Of course, we were able to support him in return, from our own strength, limited though that was. And when we leave here today, most of you will continue to support him from your new homes in the lodges we have founded in Scotland, and your strength will hearten him in his time of need, as his understanding and goodwill heartened us in ours." He tapped his clenched right fist into the palm of his other hand. "But now the King of Scots faces the greatest challenge of his reign. England is set to destroy him utterly, and all who stand with him. I know you are all aware of that. It is not new. England has been determined to destroy the Scots for years now, yet the Scots remain unbroken. I know, too, that you are all aware of the new invasion now being prepared. I wonder, however, if you know the true extent of what is afoot this time.

"Edward of Caernarvon has assembled more than two and a half *thousand* heavy chivalry at Berwick. Two thousand and five hundred armored knights, each of them backed by mounted men-at-arms. He has raised four thousand longbows and fifteen thousand infantry troops. He has a supply train of hundreds of wagons, all of them poised and ready to move north at his word. And he has a fleet of ships already sailing up the coast towards the River Forth, where they will wait, with fresh provisions and supplies, until his armies reach them.

"Twenty thousand men, at modest count, poised to strike into Scotland. And King Robert will confront them close to Stirling, the narrowest point of their invasion route and perhaps the only spot where they might be stopped. The odds against the Bruce's army, including those of you who choose to stand with him, will be at least four to one, and perhaps greater."

He drew the black bag towards him, raising the flap with one hand while he reached inside with the other, and he drew out the great blazing jewel of red and white enameled metal depicting an all-seeing eye atop a pyramid that marked his rank as a member of the Governing Council of the Temple. He held it up for them to see, suspended from its heavy chain of silver links.

"I set this aside last night, in chapter, for the last time, laying down my role and rank as Knight Commander of the Temple Council. I will not wear it again because for now the Council has ceased to exist and I see no reason to replace it, since we are so few. And so I speak to you now as plain Sir William Sinclair, one of you—no more and no less. I have done my duty as prescribed, with the help of my own counselors, and all the arrangements are in place for our dispersal as a community, everything as planned, and for the good of all.

"But now I find that, as a man, I am far from happy and farther from content. I am, in fact, sick at heart. We have changed ourselves outwardly, disguising who we were. We have accepted what has been done to us, in silence and without open protest. We have been meek, and turned the other cheek, accepting undeserved shame and degradation from the hands of those we once were proud to serve. Well, I have had my fill of that!

"Pride is a sin, they tell us. But those very speakers, in their arrogance and pride and greed, have stripped us of everything that made us men and dutiful monks. So if pride be a sin, I am prepared to die in sin, rather than live in shame."

As he stooped to his bag again, he heard a growl of discussion arising among his listeners, shockingly loud in this chamber where silence was an inviolable rule, but he ignored it, pulling out a folded square of cloth, which he shook out and held up to their eyes.

"I doubt any of you will recognize this thing, so I will tell you what it is." He held it higher then, above his head, stretching it between both hands to show it clearly: a broad band of black forming the top half, against the lower half of purest white. "This was the first baucent to grace our banners, before we adopted the cross pattée. This was the Temple's standard in our earliest days. It represented the choices and the changes we had made in embracing the brotherhood of our Order: the black of former ignorance replaced by the white of enlightenment. This banner symbolizes everything we were and marks the progress that we made in assuming the responsibilities of brotherhood: from darkness to light, from ignorance to awareness, from despair to hope, from ignominy to honor. A simple standard, but containing more than we ourselves could ever voice."

He lowered his arms and stood a moment gazing at the banner, then raised it again, spreading it wide once more.

"I had this from the hand of Master de Molay himself, the last of its kind from the last of his kind. He gave it to me when we two last met, seven years ago, and bade me take good care of it and bear it with me everywhere. Look at it well, for you may never see it again. I am taking it to Stirling, to raise it in the cause of Robert Bruce. And I will go there as a Templar, fully armed and armored in my true colors—the white of knowledge and the black cross pattée of my Order's glory. I have had enough of hiding and dissembling! Enough of skulking with a lowered head! This King in Scotland intends to make one last, defiant stand, and I am going to stand with him, in defiance of Pope and Church and Kings of France!"

The roar of approval had begun before he finished speaking, drowning out his raised voice, and he waited, motionless, his arms still high, until it had subsided.

"Will you come with me?"

This time the noise was pandemonium and the crowd began to sway as men turned from side to side to pummel each other, roaring with enthusiasm. He stood smiling, waiting, and eventually they stilled themselves again, staring at him hungrily.

"So mote it be, then. But hear me! No red crosses, for this is no crusade." He lowered his arms, folding the baucent again with measured care, then draping it lengthwise over his left shoulder. "We will ride as Templars, knights and sergeants, in black and white, and for the last time. As who and what we are, in pride, and in defiance of all who have disowned and betrayed us. Knights to wear their white mantles, with black armor. Sergeants will wear black surcoats, with the white cross pattée. All shields, the same—white cross on black. And the same for horses' trappings. The two stone buildings at the rear of this house contain all of those, and there is paint, both black and white, to use as required." He eyed them now, seeing them straining like hounds at leash.

As he answered the few questions, Will was aware that the formal gathering had changed into an extended council of war, the planning of a campaign. He dealt rapidly with the timing of the matter—it was already the third week of May, the testing date of Midsummer Day mere weeks away. But everything had altered. Instead of riding piecemeal to support the Bruce as mounted individuals, they would now move as a powerful, unified force of heavy chivalry reinforced with disciplined light cavalry. Of the four weeks between now and Midsummer Day, therefore, two would be spent in renewed training on Arran, regaining their former battle skills as a single, cohesive entity. At the start of the second week of June, they would transport their various units, under the command of de l'Armentière as vice-admiral, from Arran to the mainland. Their two-day sailing route would take them up the estuary of Clyde to Dumbarton, where they would disembark and strike overland, eastward across the thirty miles to Stirling while avoiding being seen by any English forces that might be in that area. Two days at sea and four days on the march over the rough terrain between Dumbarton and Stirling: sufficient time to put them within easy reach of King Robert well before the English arrived.

He held up his hands.

"So, Brothers, it is decided, and so mote it be. We will ride as Templars once again, one final time in honor of our Order's ancient glory, and we will make our presence seen and known, in support of the one man, the single King, who has treated us with honor and compassion, Robert Bruce, the King of this Scots realm. And if we die in what we are to do, what matters that? Our Order is already dead, and so we will but ride from death, into death. Go, then, and make yourselves ready."

He had spoken in French, and as he fell silent one single voice, its owner unseen among the throng, took up what he had said, repeating it in measured cadence, "*From death, into death*," and as he shouted it others joined him, until all the men assembled there were shouting it. "*From death, into death!*"

"Go, then!" Will turned and crossed to the stairs against the rear wall without looking back, and as he went he heard the sounds of moving feet as the assembly broke up, the shouted chant finally dying to silence. He had no notion that he had just witnessed, indeed initiated, the birth of a legend that would be retold down the years, the tale of how a company of unknown knights, like a *deus ex machina* from some improbable Greek tragedy, had swept down, in the moment of Scotland's greatest need, to turn the tide of King Robert Bruce's greatest battle from defeat into a glorious victory. Instead, as he climbed the stairs to the gallery above, he was thinking about wearing his armor once again, and about sending Tam Sinclair to bring Jessie to him from Lochranza.

EPILOGUE

1

Stirling Castle sat solidly on its great stone crag, dominating the wide flatlands below, where the River Forth wound in great serpentine loops through the far-flung, treacherous bogs known as the Carse of Stirling. On a clear, moonlit night, the sentries on their high walkways might have been able, if they chose to look, to discern the black clump of the distant Tor Wood, knowing that beside and beyond it lay the still-churned ground along the Bannock Burn, and, if their imaginations stirred at all, they might have recalled the chaos and the slaughter that had occurred there mere months earlier, when King Robert had wreaked havoc on the overwhelming numbers of the invading English.

They had thought of it before, and talked of it in great detail—every man in Scotland had—rejoicing but unable to believe the miracle that had happened there on the banks of the Bannock on that Midsummer Day, when it seemed that the massed schiltroms of Scots spears would be incapable of halting the surging, implacable English advance; when King Robert himself, attacked and challenged to single combat between the armies, had come close to death, saving himself only by his own dauntless skills and the unerring sweep of a mighty thrust of the battle-axe that had been his only weapon.

And they had recalled the sudden, unforeseen appearance of a fresh Scots army, led from the west by heavy chivalry, an irresistible charge of heavily armored Temple knights—more Templars than had ever been seen in Scotland—that had tipped the balance of the day and thrown the densely packed masses of the English, chivalry and common soldiery, into fleeing, destructive panic, trampling and hampering themselves and their own, killing one another in their desperate attempt to find safety and solid footing in the slippery, murderous bogs between the Bannock Burn and the banks of Forth. They foundered there in the killing muck, drowning and dying in their thousands in the panic-stricken crush and leaving the Bruce and his men victorious …

But that had been in midsummer, months earlier, when the amazing victory was bright and fresh in the mind of every Scot and it seemed the golden light of joy would never fade. On this night, though, there was no hope of such a thing. Men had the reality of freezing winter to keep them mindless of such thoughts tonight. The cloud mass was so low that it boiled over and between the battlements as a swirling, icy, roiling fog, impervious to the wind and rain that lashed through it to flail at the castle's palisaded walls. The miserable sentries stood hunched in whatever shelter they could find on their walkways along the sheer drop of the giant crag's side, each man measuring the slow passage of time remaining until his relief, when he could shed his sodden cloak and escape from the brutality that howled across the flat and open miles from the Firth of Forth and the too-close, cold North Sea.

Within the stone walls of the central keep, however, no one knew or cared about the weather outside. The interior of Stirling Castle that late-autumn night was warmer and brighter, the atmosphere more joyous and carefree, than it had ever been in the memory of anyone who was there. Torches flared all along the interior walls, illuminating every entry, passageway, and stairwell, and within the enormous rooms on the main floor, the darkness was banished by massed banks of blazing candles, augmenting the flaming cressets on the walls and the giant fires that blazed in every fireplace. People thronged everywhere, all of them dressed in their finest clothes, with scarcely a piece of armor to be seen, and music swelled up from every direction, some of it fierce and warlike, some of it bright and brilliant, and all of it melding and blending distractingly in those places where differing sounds overlapped.

One such place was the wide flagstoned passageway that led from a suite of smaller anterooms to the massive, iron-studded oak doors of the King's Hall, the castle's largest and most ornately finished room. Will Sinclair had gone to collect Jessie from one of the anterooms set aside for ladies' use, and most particularly for those ladies' women and children, nursemaids and suckling infants. There had been a harpist playing there, soothing the babies' cries with gentle music, but as Will and Jessie moved away, bound now for the King's Hall, the sounds of the harp were quickly drowned in the skirl of wild, Gaelic music spilling from the narrow gap between the slightly open doors of the great chamber.

The two of them were alone in the passageway, walking easily, Will with one protective and possessive hand on Jessie's waist, when the great doors ahead of them swung open and the wailing music suddenly crashed through the widening space, engulfing the approaching pair. Will stopped abruptly, his eyes widening in surprise, and without thinking, he grasped Jessie's arm gently above the elbow and drew her aside to stand beside him with her back to the wall, watching what was happening.

A solid block of garishly colorful Gaels now filled the open doorway, five wide and occupying the entire space behind the towering figure of the saffron-and-scarlet-clad man in front, and all of them were blowing mightily on the wild bagpipes that were so much of their ancient, traditional way of life. Will could not see how dense the files of clansmen were behind the first rank, but he could see roiling smoke above and behind their heads from the fireplaces in the great hall at their back, and had the impression of masses of people swirling behind them, laughing and shouting in enjoyment and encouragement.

The man in the lead began to pace on the spot, raising his right knee high and beating time with one foot to set the tempo as the tune they were playing changed into another. Six times he brought his foot down on the floor, and then he began to march forward, his cheeks bulging with the effort of keeping his air bag full, frowning in concentration as his fingers flickered over the holes in the long pipe that produced the notes of the melody. As he passed in front of Will and Jessie, Will was astounded to hear that every man behind him was playing the same tune, keeping and sustaining the tempo perfectly. As they marched past him in a solemn phalanx, Will counted twenty men in the block behind the tall leader, and as the last rank passed him he turned to watch them go, aware that behind him the crowd was now spilling through the doorway, shouting and cheering and whistling.

When the sound of the pipes died away, Jessie smiled up at him.

"I never was able to make the French believe that the sound the pipes make is music," she said. "Who were those men? They have obviously practiced playing together like that. My guardsmen in France could never do that."

He grinned at her, lowering his voice to where only she could hear him. "Your guardsmen in France had other things to occupy them, my love. But you're right, nonetheless. I didn't know that could be done. Twenty men, all playing together and keeping the tune. I never thought to hear the like. But then, I've been told the Romans used the same kind of pipes, though smaller. Apparently they used them to keep their men inspired on long marches, so they must have known how to play in unison like that, now that I think about it." He straightened up and scanned the crowd around him, few of whom were known to him. "Anyway, they were all MacDonalds. The big fellow at their head was Calum MacDonald of Skye, and he's Angus Og's shadow, so that means Angus himself must be inside with the King." He reached down and took her hand in his, placing it on his arm. "So then, wife, shall we go in?"

Lady Jessica Sinclair saw no trace in her new husband of the grim and forbidding Templar knight she had encountered on that now distant day in La Rochelle. The William Sinclair who walked beside her now was another man altogether, tall and imposing as ever, but clad in a tunic and tight-fitting hose of the latest French style, in pale blue velvet from her own stores and made by her own hands. The yoke and padded shoulders made his width immense, and the tunic glittered, front and back, with silver studs, sewn onto lozenges of satin that was the mere hint of a shade darker than the tunic itself, while from his shoulders, sweeping down his back, was a magnificent cloak of light blue shimmering silk that she had bought years earlier from a merchant who had traveled widely in Asia and brought back the most wonderful fabrics she had ever seen. She knew that she matched Will in splendor, because she was still wearing the dress in which she had been wed earlier that day, a deep-bosomed gown of dark blue, its cuffs and bodice edged with French lace identical to the delicate lace that formed the now-raised veil on her high headdress.

Will, for his part, was highly conscious of Jessie's presence by his side, and of the still not-quite-accepted reality that she was now his spouse and consort, their marriage sanctified by the rites of the Church earlier that afternoon. He cupped his free hand more firmly over hers as they made their way to the door, and people parted to let them pass, many eyeing them with open curiosity. Will knew none of them, but he knew much of their curiosity must spring from the fact that they knew nothing of him, save that he had emerged somehow from obscurity as an established friend of King Robert, highly enough regarded by the monarch to have been wed in Stirling Castle, with the King himself in attendance to witness the event and share the celebrations.

Will and Jessie paused just inside the doors, scanning the vast, crowded room. An open aisle, roped on each side, stretched from where they stood to the far end of the hall, where it ended in a shallow flight of steps leading to a broad platform. Above their heads, the high, vaulted roof of soaring, hammered beams was barely visible, shrouded in darkness and flickering, hazy shadows reflected upwards into the drifting smoke clouds by the lights below. But it was the distant platform that captured their attention, for there, above the crowd, stood Robert I, by God's grace King of Scots, surrounded by, but distinct from, the small group of people attending him, and backed by a line of attentive heralds trumpeter.

Until that afternoon, when the King had attended his wedding, Will had not seen the man since the Bannock Burn fight, and even then, with a thousand details to attend to in the aftermath of his miraculous victory, the King had had time only for a firm handclasp, a smile of recognition, and a word or two of gratitude accompanied by a promise of meeting and talking later, at more leisure. Since then, four months and more had elapsed, and this great gathering here in Stirling, the first purely joyous event of the King's reign, was a landmark celebration to recognize the return of his Queen, Elizabeth, recently freed from the English prison in which she had been confined for eight years. Jessie had told him that the Queen had survived those years intact and unharmed solely because of who she was: her husband might have been a traitorous and rebellious dog in the eyes of her merciless captor, Edward Plantagenet, and that alone might have condemned her as it had Bruce's brothers, but her own father was Richard de Burgh, the Earl of Ulster, one of England's greatest nobles and King Edward's oldest and most loyal friend. Now Queen Elizabeth stood beside and slightly behind her husband, a tall and stately red-haired vision of regal dignity herself, dressed in a dark green gown that glittered, even from where Will stood, with gold wire and pearls.

The Primate of Scotland, Archbishop Lamberton of St. Andrews, stood on Bruce's left, and beside him ranged another cluster of well-known faces, among them David Moray and Angus Og MacDonald. Will scanned the crowded platform for Douglas, but neither he nor Sir Thomas Randolph was there.

Will hesitated, then grasped Jessie's fingers more tightly and began to make his way down the long aisle to the far end, but even as he started to move he saw the King look at him and raise a straight arm, fingers spread, to stop him.

Will halted in mid-step, almost off balance, and felt his own confusion matched in the sudden increased pressure of Jessie's grip on his arm as she stopped, too, beside him. Was the sudden frown on the King's face for them? He glanced quickly at her and found her looking back at him the same way, her brows wrinkling, and then both of them looked back towards the distant dais, where a flurry of movement had disrupted the group about the King. Two men had come forward, holding the King's tabard between them, the massive, ritualistic, and ornately rigid vestment that was the armorial symbol of the royal rank and presence.

Will could see that few of the revelers thronging the floor had even noticed as King Robert spread his arms and shrugged into the imposing tabard, with its crimson, gold-encrusted lion rampant on a field of purest yellow, embroidered so thickly, and in so many varying shades and hues of colored wire, that it seemed made entirely of metal. But they all took note, freezing into silence, when the royal heralds lining the rear wall stepped forward, raised their trumpets in unison, and blasted out the opening notes of a strident, brazen fanfare.

By the time the final tones died away and the heralds stepped smartly back to line the wall again, the stillness in the great hall was absolute, and every eye was trained upon the phalanx on the royal platform, where King Robert, in his formal surcoat, stood holding the hand of his Queen, gazing down at the assembled crowd and backed by a wedge of the most powerful magnates of his realm. He raised his right hand, holding his Queen's hand high.

"My friends," he began, filling the hall with his deep, sonorous voice, "hear me, and mark my words. Tonight is a joyous occasion for our realm, the first unthreatened celebration we have ever known since the moment I took up the reins of this sad land and set myself to ousting England from our bourns. But tonight, tonight our country is no longer sad … for we are *free!*" The crowd roared.

Bruce raised his hand again. "And we are here this day, this night, in peace and in unity, to give our thanks to God and to each other for the strength that we have found, the strength we have used so *puissantly*, to cleanse our land of the filth of invasion and foreign occupation."

Someone whistled loudly and started to applaud, but it was evident that the King had not finished and the sound died away quickly.

"That strength, the massed determination of the community of Scotland represented by all of you here, nobles, churchmen, burghers, and commonality combined, has made this gathering, this celebration, possible. Our Queen stands here tonight, gracing our festivities by God's grace, as does my beloved daughter Marjory, imprisoned in an

English convent these long years for her father's sins. And here are our greatly revered bishops, of St. Andrews and Glasgow, tried and loyal friends so newly released from England's prisons."

This time he made no attempt to stem the applause and approbation, and the Queen, Archbishop Lamberton, and several whose faces were unknown to Will acknowledged the plaudits, smiling and waving into the heart of the crowd. But as soon as the sustained roar began to lessen, the monarch raised both arms high, silencing them again, then spoke in a more measured, less formal tone.

"But there is something more to celebrate this night, an occasion already begun, but yet to be completed. Some of you already know we had a wedding here today. A bridal service months in the planning but meant to be held far from here, until I asked both celebrants, as close and trusted friends—which means, you all must know, close and trusted friends of this realm of Scotland—to delay their nuptials and join us here in Stirling for the happy and long-awaited occasion of their joining."

Will felt Jessie's hand tighten on his arm again. Their wedding earlier that day had been small and private, officiated by Archbishop Lamberton himself, assisted by Bishop William Sinclair of Dunkeld and the colorful Bishop David Moray, dressed for once in the episcopal robes of his office. But apart from the glittering assembly of celebrants, the service had been attended only by the bridal pair's closest kin and by the royal party, King Robert and Queen Elizabeth, and their most intimate friends and advisers, among them Sir James Douglas and Sir Thomas Randolph, the august Master Nicholas Balmyle, and Angus Og MacDonald, Lord of the Isles. He squeezed her hand back, feeling relief uncoiling in him as he began to discern the King's reason for stopping their approach when he had. Now he could see the people ahead of him beginning to look around at their neighbors, wondering what the King was talking about and who might possibly be involved. None turned to look at the far rear of the room.

"Years ago, when I was first crowned King and had to flee into the hills after the Methven fight, in what I now can see to be the bleakest, grimmest period of our struggle, a lady came to me from

France bearing great wealth from her own estates, to give it to me on behalf of Scotland. Wondrous and, at that moment, seemingly miraculous gifts. Chests of royal treasure when our coffers held none—coin and ingots, gold and silver that sustained me, sustained all of us, throughout those few dark years." He raised a solitary finger. "Few of you here assembled know her, but she is our bride today, and she deserves all our goodwill and our gratitude." He raised his hands commandingly to quell the rising murmur of comment and curiosity, and when he had their attention again he continued.

"Her goodman stands beside her in our esteem, blessed and joined to her in matrimony this very day by our good Archbishop here, and he is another unknown to most of you. But believe me when I tell you all that he is one of—and perhaps the foremost among—the true heroes of Bannock Burn, for it was he who led the unexpected charge that day, the charge of chivalry that breasted the Coxet Hill and threw the English into panic and confusion, thinking they had to face a second, new Scots army."

He waited for the buzz to die down, then spoke again, in a driving, rhythmic flow that held his listeners spellbound. "Had it not been for this man and his companions, for the perfect timing and surprise of their charge at the head of a new army that was no army at all, we might have lost the fight at the Bannock Burn. But come he did, and so we won the day, wreaking a storm upon the English that they will not soon forget and sending them home with their tails between their legs, lacking the flower of their vaunted chivalry and leaving us with prisoners for ransom sufficient to keep us in food and weapons—and in peace—for years to come.

"This man, too, is with us here tonight, from France, but a Scots knight, both namesake and nephew to our own beloved William Sinclair, Bishop of Dunkeld."

He paused dramatically, and beckoned to Will and Jessie to come forward, and then raised his voice almost to a shout. "Scotland! Join me in bidding welcome to our newest and fairest bridal couple. Sir William and Lady Jessica Sinclair of Roslin!"

The crowd erupted into a storm of applause, with more and more people turning around as it became clear that Will and Jessie were approaching from the rear, along the length of the central aisle. And as Will felt his wife's fingernails digging into the crook of his elbow, approaching the royal dais and the welcoming, applauding party there, his mind flashed back over all the years and grand occasions since his knighthood, and he could not remember ever having felt so proud or so grateful for his lot.

2

Later, hours later, after a long and wonderful evening of which he remembered very little other than his total enjoyment of being there and experiencing it as a married man, Will sat at ease in front of a roaring fire in a small, tapestry-hung room with the King of Scots and a few of his closest friends. None of them was drinking, for they were there ostensibly to discuss matters of state. The Queen and her ladies had all retired, and Jessie had left with them, after whispering to her husband, with sharp, warning nails on the inside of his wrist, that although she knew he had to spend time speaking with the King, he had better not forget that this was his wedding night, because she would be waiting hungrily for him.

Will smiled contentedly, aware that in the armchair next to his the King sat staring into the fire, his chin propped on one fist. On Will's other side, Douglas and Randolph were speaking quietly together, while beyond the King, Lamberton, Angus Og, and one of the other Gaelic chiefs—MacNeil, Will thought—seemed to be talking earnestly and with great solemnity about a possible new Bishopric of the Isles. Balmyle, an old man, had retired long since, and the two other bishops, Moray and Dunkeld, had gone about some business of the King's.

Will straightened his back, and as he did so the King spoke to him.

"I have been meaning all evening to ask you how you were able to time your arrival so perfectly that afternoon."

"To time it?" Will found it easy to smile and be himself with Robert Bruce, since first meeting him on Arran, masquerading as an ordinary knight. The man addressing him now might well be the fearsome and renowned King of Scots, his stature already approaching legendary size, but in person he remained the same soft-spoken, pleasant, but incisive man of that first meeting. "To time it ... Aye ..." His smile widened to a grin. "Well, Sire, it ill behooves me to—"

"*Sire?*" Bruce tilted his head to look at Will directly, one eyebrow raised. "You have not called me Sire save the once, when first you came to our land. Whence comes it now?"

Will hesitated, taken aback. "Well—it was ..." He snatched a deep breath. "Forgive me, Your Grace. I could not do so, in the past. Not as long as ... as long as I held true to my vows as a Templar. But the Temple is no more, and now I am free to lay my allegiance where I choose."

"Ask me not to forgive you, Will Sinclair. There's nothing to forgive. So now you offer your allegiance to me freely?"

"Aye, my lord, and willingly."

"Accepted, then, though I have never doubted it. It comes to me you would be a fine Baron of Roslin. What say you to that, Archbishop? Should not our faithful friend here be awarded the estates and title of a barony for his services?"

The Archbishop, interrupted, leaned forward and looked at Will, his lips curling up at one corner in a tiny smile. "Apparently not, I should say, judging by his reaction."

The King, who had not been looking at Will as the Archbishop spoke, now swung back to him. "What, man? You are ghost white. Have I offended you?"

Will managed to shake his head, raising his hand in a silent plea for patience and waiting for Bruce to grow angry, but the King showed only good humor, smiling in disbelief. "What is it, then?"

"Forgive— Pardon me, Sire, your offer took me unawares, but I have no wish to be a baron. That rank, should you bequeath it, should be held by my nephew, young Henry Sinclair."

The King laughed, slapping a knee in his delight. "You would turn down a barony and give it to someone else? Who is this paragon and why do I not know him?"

Will felt his face flushing. "You do, Your Grace. He is my squire."

"Your squire? The boy who was wounded? He's but a lad. I cannot dispose a barony upon a *squire*, Will."

"I know, Sire, but the barony of Roslin should be his, by right of birth. And he is due to undergo knighthood, and well deserving of it."

"Then I will knight him with my own hand, upon your word. Bring him to me tomorrow and we will make the arrangements. But he is yet far too young to be a baron."

"I know that, Sire. But he will grow quickly. The lad who leaves with me for our new land will return to you a man, and worthy of the honor."

"So … you yet intend to seek this new and fabled land?"

"Not fabled, Sire. We know now it is there. But yes, I do, with Your Grace's permission."

"You have that, though I could use you better here in Scotland. But how will you get there? Have you the ships?"

"We do, Sire. Four new ships, built in Genoa."

"And what of your new wife? Will you leave her behind?"

Will grinned. "Only in death, Your Grace. Jessie will come with me, as will two score and more of others, wives and mothers to my men."

"Hmm … And so, it seems, would my niece, young Marjorie. She came to me today and all but threw herself at my feet, begging my permission to accompany your wife on this venture of yours. What think you of that?"

The levity in Will's attitude was banished immediately, replaced by a frown. "Your pardon, Sire. I had no knowledge of that. I had already warned Lady Jessica on several occasions not to foster the girl's hopes. The two are close, more like mother and daughter than anything else, but I thought I had made it clear to Jess that the young woman is a Princess of the realm, with duties as such. I shall take it up with her again when I retire."

"You will do no such thing. I will not be the cause of strife between you two on your wedding night, so it is my strongly expressed wish that you will make no mention of it to your wife. Am I clear on that?"

"Aye, Sire."

"Good." The King looked about him and bent a little closer, then spoke in a lowered voice. "In the normal way of things, your thinking would be perfectly correct. But the times are not normal nowadays. Few things are as they were ten years ago. The child is not really a Princess of Scotland. She is the illegitimate daughter of my favorite brother, Nigel, dear to me, as was her father, but somewhat troubling, under present circumstances, in her presence here."

Will's face must have revealed his puzzlement, for the monarch leaned even closer and explained. "Scotland already has a Princess Marjory, Will—my own daughter—and she is beset wi' troubles enough to set the mind of a grown man reeling, let alone a slip of a girl. They held her in a convent for six years, shut away from all kindness and society, from the time when she was barely old enough to know what I had done. They punished her—an innocent—for being my daughter, and it breaks my heart to see how close they came to destroying her mind. She barely speaks— not a single word to me since she came home. But Elizabeth believes she will recover her wits, with time and patience and the forbearance of us all. Lamberton, on the other hand, while he agrees with the Queen, is strongly of the mind that the presence of another Marjory Bruce, of the same age but of a completely different temperament, light-hearted, laughing, and popular, might possibly—and I say only possibly—affect my daughter's recovery. Do you take my meaning?"

"Yes, Your Grace, I do …"

"Then tell me this. Do you know why I can speak thus to you?"

"Thus?" Will shook his head, his eyes widening as his failure to comprehend increased. "No, Sire."

"It is because you are the only man I know who wants nothing from me … not advancement, or reward or advantage, or patronage or favor. And atop all that, you never speak to me of politics or state affairs or my damned kingly duties. You want nothing from me, Sir William Sinclair, and that makes you unique in my eyes, and singularly trustworthy."

He sat back in his chair. "A new land, you seek. An unknown life in an unknown place. And you will take your wife with you. That is admirable, Will … and brave, to boot." He paused for the space of a few heartbeats. "You spoke earlier of your squire returning as a man. *Will* he return?"

Will nodded, wondering where this was leading. "Most certainly, Your Grace. We will send back envoys, and recruiters to swell our numbers from time to time if all goes as we wish."

"And you truly have no fears for your wife over there?"

The smile returned to Will's face. "No more than I would have for her here, Sire. Unknown shores may be dangerous places, but so may well-known ones. My Jess has lived in some truly perilous times and circumstances and has known her share of dangers. The life we will find where we are going might not be an easy one, but it will be a different and exciting one, and she and I will look out for each other there as well as anywhere, come what may. So be it we are together, that is all we could wish for."

"Tell me then, were you to take my niece with you, could you undertake to send her back someday?"

Will looked away into the fire, intensely aware of the monarch's eyes on him. They sat alone, surrounded by others, in what felt like an island of silence among the buzz of conversation around them. The question so simply posed had layers of complexity that swarmed and grew as he thought about it. Finally he grunted.

"That question has no simple answer, Your Grace."

"Forget my grace, then, and answer as my friend. Yes or no?"

"I know we would be happy to take her with us, Jess even more so than I, but no, I could not promise you to bring her back. In the first place, she is no longer a child, and by the time we settle there, long before we could dream of coming back, she will be a woman, with a woman's mind and will. I could say yes, and undertake to send her back someday, but by the time that day arrives, she might not wish to come. And we will be in a strange new world, with none of the rules and settled ways that govern people here."

"But you would take her, and care for her as your own daughter."

"Of course I would, and gladly. But that is all I can say with certainty. She might fall ill or—"

"Grow to be a woman. Aye. And when she does, what then? Will you have eligible men for her to wed, to suit her station?"

Will grinned again, in spite of the serious tenor of the conversation. "There may be no 'station' there, in the sense you mean, Sire. She will be as my own daughter, and thus will share whatever privilege we know, but more than that I cannot say. As for eligible men, there will be those. Jessie says young Henry would gladly lay down his life for the lass, as things stand now. It is but puppy love, all wide eyed and awe struck, but he will soon reach manhood, too, knighted by your own hand. And I could recommend the lad. He has everything required to make a fine and noble, honorable knight."

The King sat for a moment, pinching his lower lip between finger and thumb as he mulled Will's words, but then he nodded. "So be it, then. You have my trust, my confidence, and my friendship. I will tell young Marjorie she may go with you, and I will, if you are willing, give her guardianship to you and Lady Jessica." His voice rose slightly in volume then. "You were about to tell me how you arranged the timing of your charge at the Bannock Burn. Tell me now, and tell me why you smiled when I asked you that."

Slightly disconcerted at the abrupt change of topic, Will quickly sensed that someone was now standing close behind him. He glanced up to see that his uncle, Bishop Sinclair of Dunkeld, had joined them and was now inclining his head graciously as King Robert waved him to sit.

Will shrugged, deciding to be blunt. "I smiled at your choice of words, Sire. The timing of our arrival was perfect, as you say, but it was purely accidental—no strategic brilliance of mine at all, I fear."

The King's eyebrow rose again, and he glanced quizzically at Dunkeld. "Is that a fact? Tell me about the accidental part of it then, if you will."

Will shrugged again, aware that all the others were now listening. "We should have been there sooner ... were delayed ... and thus came later than we had thought to."

"What delayed you?"

"The English. We met a corps of them along the way, a body of infantry, perhaps six hundred, commanded by mounted knights. We breasted a hill and there they were, below us on the hillside."

"Had you no scouts out ahead of you?"

"We did, Sire, but they had seen nothing. The English were in a deep defile—a steep-sided gully—when our scouts rode that way, and were thus invisible to anyone not right above them."

"And so you fought, and evidently won. You had words with your scouts afterwards, I hope?"

"No, Sire, they were both killed in the fight that followed. We lost five men, and two of them were the scouts in question. But we destroyed the enemy infantry and harried the survivors, scattering them until they could not have regrouped."

"Hmm. What of the knights commanding them?"

"Five of them, Your Grace, all but one killed. The fifth one fled back the way they had come. The fight was straightforward, but it cost us nigh on half a day when all was said and done."

"And kept six hundred fresh Englishmen from striking at our flanks from the westward. How many were with you?"

"Sixty knights, Sire, and half as many again of lighter cavalry."

At the rear of the room a door creaked open, and everyone turned to see Bishop Moray entering, clutching a document. He nodded to the King and, with a muttered word of apology, held up the document to Archbishop Lamberton, beckoning with a finger. The Archbishop grunted an apology and rose to his feet, then followed Moray to a far corner of the room, where they stood close, murmuring quietly.

King Robert looked back at Will. "So, a hundred and fifty men against six hundred."

Will shook his head, his mouth quirking. "A hundred mounted Templars, Your Grace. Small odds."

"Hmm. True. But I was thinking more of the advance you led later. Whence came that army? I know who they were, but how did you conscript them?"

Will grinned again, broadly this time. "From your own camp, Sire. They were hostlers and wagoners, grooms, cooks and pot boys, even women—but brave, all of them. They thought us English when we first approached, and would have stood against us to protect your back, despite the certainty that they would all be killed against a force like ours. Then, when we had identified ourselves as Templars, there to fight alongside Your Grace, they told us the battle was already joined, beyond the hill that sheltered them, along the high road to Stirling and the vale of the Bannock Burn. And hearing that, one of my men, a kinsman of mine called Tam Sinclair, was inspired to say we should use them as they had first attempted to appear to us, as fighters. We quickly formed them up into ranks and blocks, pillaged some of your own banners from the wagon train, furbished them further with some of our own, and then had them march behind us as we advanced over the hill."

"Aye. We all noticed your arrival—have no doubt of that. Accidental the timing might have been, but it was fortuitous and Heaven sent. The sight of your advance up there, a mass of black and white chivalry, an army of Templars when no Templars could be there, was like ... what was it the Archbishop said? Like an oncoming host of avenging angels. And that's what it was—an intervention from Heaven. It gave new heart to our own men and kicked the guts out of the English. They were in dire straits already by that time, God knows, ploutering about in that killing bog, but the sight of a new army coming down on them panicked them completely, and they broke. When you bring your squire to me tomorrow, see you that you bring this kinsman, too, this Tam Sinclair. Scotland, it seems, owes much to his quick thinking. Would knighthood suit him, think you?"

"Suit him! Tam? My lord, he has been with me since I was a boy, and is an honorable and worthy knight in everything but name. But Tam is not of noble birth."

"That recks nothing nowadays. William Wallace was knighted on his merits, not on his birth. Why not this champion of yours? If it was his idea to conscript the camp followers, then he has all the initiative and insight required for knighthood. Will he, too, go with you to this new land of yours?"

Will's mind was agog as he thought of the effect this unexpected honor would have on his unassuming kinsman. "That he will, Your Grace," he said, knowing now that he was speaking to everyone there. "He and nigh on two hundred others. But if I may speak more on this, Sire, there is no uncertainty in any of our minds in this venture. We know the land is there. Admiral St. Valéry found it, God rest his soul, and sent word of it home to us. And this time, when we arrive there, we will have friends awaiting us, to welcome us. And we will make the most of what we find and send word of it back here to you. That will be when young Sir Henry Sinclair returns, triumphant, as my messenger to you, to take up his barony from your hands, and to make preparations for another, larger expedition."

The King placed his hands over his face and drew his fingers downwards until his fingertips came to rest against the end of his nose. He sat blinking into the space above the fire for a few moments, then nodded. "So be it. There is nothing I can do to persuade you to stay here. Your men are French, and free. When will you leave?"

"As soon as the winter storms die down, Your Grace. April, or early May."

"Can you be ready by then?"

"We are ready now, my lord."

"Hmm ... You should go there as a baron. There are people living there you say, aside from your own? If so, they will have kings."

"They have no kings, Your Grace. Or none that our people found."

Robert Bruce looked at Will wearily now, and twisted up his face. "You were a Templar, Will—you ought to know better than to say such things. Where men gather, there will always be kings, and others who want to be kings. It is human nature. Men *breed* kings, no matter what they name them. So be you careful in your new land … What is it called again?"

"Merica, Your Grace."

"Aye, Merica. A strange name, and it sounds ancient, not new at all." He pulled himself upright and flexed his shoulders. "A long day … and your wedding day. You should be abed by now, holding your wife, as I should mine. But you can go and do that now, whereas I still have work in hand here. A good night to you then, Sir William Sinclair, and may you prosper in all you undertake." He smiled and extended his hand. "This realm is in your debt, my friend, accident or no. So go now. We will speak tomorrow."

"Sire, if I may?" Archbishop Lamberton approached the fire again and held up one hand as if to detain Will. "I need to say one more thing about your charge, Sir William."

Will shook his head. "No, Master Lamberton, you do not, for I know what you would say. This charge of ours at the Bannock Burn was a final act of pride in what we once were, so I presume you are going to tell me that there will be a formal denial of any Templar involvement in the battle."

The Archbishop smiled. "No, Sir William, no. There will be no denials made. How could we deny it? Men saw what they saw, and there were many there that day. Thus, no denial, though we might, in time to come, omit your presence from our final records, stating that the appearance on the Hill of Coxet was, as you have told us, an army of camp followers. An omission, therefore, made in polity, but no denial. I merely thought to put your mind at rest and offer you some solace in the knowledge that the men you leave behind when you depart this realm will know no hardship or impediment when you are gone, for Scotland owes them much. They may continue as before, observing the rites and rituals they wish to preserve, in secrecy, within the boundaries of Scotland. That I can assure you, on my word as Primate of the realm." He paused. "You will be taking representatives of Holy Church with you, will you not?"

Will met the Archbishop's glance squarely, feeling a tension in his jaw as he nodded. "Aye my, lord. Our own bishops and clerical brethren sail with us, prepared to tend to our souls and bring the Word of God to the people we find living there."

He did not enjoy lying to the churchman, even obliquely, but he could give no hint that the Word of God his people would bring to the new land would be different from that preached by the Catholic Church. The bishops and clerics to whom he referred were all brothers of the Order of Sion, and in their new land the Truth that would be spread was the truth of the ancient fraternity: the Way to communion with God, as pursued by the man Jesus and his friends of the Jerusalem Assembly.

Archbishop Lamberton nodded, then glanced at the King and held up the document he had received from Bishop Moray, who now sat listening in one corner. "Your Grace, this dispatch contains tidings that I thought Sir William might wish to hear before he leaves this room."

Bruce nodded, solemnly, and the Archbishop returned the gesture, then looked down at the document in his hand and sighed deeply.

"Sir William," he said, "this confirms that your Grand Master, Jacques de Molay, died a hideous and inhuman death ..."

"I had heard of it," Will said.

"This document says that Master de Molay admonished his persecutors—some say he cursed them, but I prefer admonished—calling upon King Philip and Pope Clement to join him for judgment before the throne of God within the year. Were you aware of that, Sir William?"

Will nodded, scowling.

"Well then, know this now, in satisfaction of a kind for the pain it must have caused you. It appears that your Grand Master possessed more power in his admonition than his persecutors, combined, held in their desire to see him and his name destroyed." He took hold of the parchment with both hands and gazed down at it in silence while every man there hung on his next words. "I have tidings here informing me that Pope Clement is dead, at Avignon." There was a concerted gasp from his listeners. Lamberton spoke again into the shocked silence. "But that news, solemn as it is, is eclipsed by the later information that King Philip of France, too, is dead more recently … three weeks ago, in fact. Both of them gone, in obedience to your noble Grand Master's summons, within the year."

The words seared through Will's head as the Archbishop continued. "And so both your persecutors are gone, summoned to Judgment by the God in whose name they dared to sin egregiously." He raised the document so all could see it. "No man can say who will succeed either one of them, but this world we know is changed, and only time itself will expose what may come next. One more thing, though, is certain. With King Philip gone, it seems de Nogaret will not long survive in France … not when so many hate him." He held out his hand to offer the document to the King, but his eyes remained on Will's. "I thought you might enjoy taking those tidings with you when you leave here this night." He waited, and when Will did not respond, he nodded gently. "Go then in peace, Sir William, and with our blessing."

Will was aware, on some level, of the reaction of the others to the Archbishop's news, and he knew he behaved with propriety in bidding everyone there a proper goodnight. But as he walked along the halls towards his quarters, passing the motionless guards on every side, his mind was reeling with what he had been told, and what he would be able to tell his brethren afterwards: Capet and Clement burning in Hell; their own Grand Master vindicated thereby; and a new order dawning in the world.

He reached his room and found a solitary lamp burning low, its wick guttering smokily. He pinched it out and shed his clothes quickly, feeling the chill in the darkness as he fumbled to raise the covers and slip naked into the welcoming warmth provided by his wife's body as she turned sleepily to draw him close and embrace him; his new wife; a new life; and the promise of a bright new land.

FINIS

GLOSSARY

aey (aye)	always; ever
bailey	the defensive ditches surrounding a motte
bothy	a stone outbuilding, usually for cattle or herders
braw	fine; beautiful; admirable
cateran	a homeless vagabond; a Highland bandit
enow	enough; sufficient
fell	fierce; merciless; formidable
fleering	flagrant
forbye	as well; in addition; besides; notwithstanding
fower	four
garron	a small, sturdy workhorse
gey	very
'gin	given; assuming; on the understanding that
girning	whining, complaining, scowling, grimacing
gowping	gaping
guddling	a method of catching brook fish with bare hands
hinna	have not; have no
jalouse	to guess; to suspect; to deduce
kine	cattle; livestock
leal	loyal
mair	more
mind	remember; recall
motte	the mound, sometimes a rock, on which a castle's keep is built
moudiewort	hedgehog
ploutering	muddling, thrashing, wallowing
recks	matters, is important

schiltrom   a solid defensive formation of massed infantry with long spears

scone   (pronounced "skoon") the traditional coronation site for Scotland's kings

siccan   such

slaistering   floundering; making hard, muddy going of things

stirk   a bullock

syne   since

thole   to bear; to tolerate; to undergo; to put up with

toun   town

unkent   unknown

weel-kent   well-known

wheen   a number; a few

ACKNOWLEDGMENTS

The task of acknowledging the assistance and goodwill generated by contributors to any work of historical fiction is always a daunting one, raising fears of offending by omission, simply because the range of people who have contributed to the finished work, whether from their personal knowledge and research or by offering insights or encouragement, is always vast. I always start each book full of good intentions, resolved to make note of everyone to whom I should be grateful, but in the heat of writing the actual work, I invariably fall behind in doing so and end up wondering whom I've forgotten.

There are some people, however, whose contributions to what I do have been invaluable, and most of those are the writers and academics whose own works have inspired me and informed my efforts to grapple with the job of sorting fact from fancy and to extrapolate my own tale, with all its speculations, interpretations, and outright flights of authorial fancy. I have no doubt at all that much of the licenses I take in constructing my tales would pain some of the people who originally nudged my thoughts in the directions I have pursued, but the errors, transgressions, and omissions I commit herein are my own, and most emphatically not theirs. I have read widely in the years of preparing and completing this trilogy, and my sincere thanks go to several distinguished authors who have made me stop and think, compare events and opinions, and then proceed in the fictional directions they have indicated to me, mostly without their intent. Paramount among those have been Piers Paul Read (*The Templars*), Barbara W. Tuchman (*Bible and Sword*), and Malcolm Barber (*The New Knighthood*).

I also acknowledge, freely and with gratitude, the invaluable collaboration and assistance of my hands-on editors, Catherine Marjoribanks and Shaun Oakey, whose individual skills, after years of working with them, never fail to awe and impress me. To them, and to all the other Penguins at Penguin Group Canada, my sincere thanks.

Jack Whyte
Kelowna, British Columbia, Canada
January 2009

What's next?

Tell us the name of an author you love

| Jack Whyte | Go ▶ |

and we'll find your next great book.

www.bookarmy.com